F
KIR   Kirk, Margaret P.

The gypsy

$19.95   17976

DATE			
MR 19 '88	AG 12 '88	JE 29 '89	
MR 30 '88	AG 24 '88		
AP 9 '88	SE 22 '88		
AP 20 '88	DE 12 '88		
AP 27 '88	JA 12 '89		
MY 4 '88	JA 21 '89		
MY 12 '88	FE 8 '89		
JE 6 '88	FE 23 '89		
	AP 5 '89		
JY 14 '88	AP 29 '89		
AG 3 '88	MY 25 '89		

Gypsy

Books by Margaret P. Kirk

GYPSY   1987
ALWAYS A STRANGER   1985

MARGARET P. KIRK

Gypsy

NEW YORK *Atheneum* 1987

Library of Congress Cataloging-in-Publication Data

Kirk, Margaret P.
  Gypsy.
  I. Title.
PR6061.I69G9   1987   823′.914   86-47930
ISBN 0-689-11774-4

This is a work of fiction. Any references to historical events; to real people, living or dead; or to real locales are intended only to give the fiction a setting in historical reality. Other names, characters, and incidents either are the product of the author's imagination or are used fictitiously, and their resemblance, if any, to real-life counterparts is entirely coincidental.

Published simultaneously in Canada by Collier Macmillan Canada, Inc.
Composition by Westchester Book Composition, Inc.,
    Yorktown Heights, New York
Manufactured by Fairfield Graphics, Fairfield, Pennsylvania
First Edition

*To the class at Rogue, rogues with Class,
wherever they may wander...*

Gypsy

PROLOGUE

I T WAS 1945, the long war over. Victory fires dotted the English coast, flames and sparks carrying the golden message. Peace.

Inland, not every fire blazed in thanksgiving.

One, a careful heap of sticks in a clearing, smoldered in mourning, in shame, in a sadness so deep even its smoke rose in black crepe ribbons to hang from the trees.

The men of the *kumpania* sat quietly, thoughtfully, in the twilight of Deacon's Wood.

Their conflict was different, intensely personal and not yet resolved. It had nothing to do with soldiers or tanks or territories; everything to do with collective pride, laws and customs rooted so deep in the past that the outcome could not be in doubt. In less than an hour it would be over.

At the campfire a group of elders murmured into glasses of dark red wine. Cigarettes glowed, the last of the sun turned the wine to crimson, but the men's eyes were somber in the firelight.

This was their *kris*, their judge and jury. The verdict, when it came, would be absolute, no appeal possible, none considered.

They held court in a grove of ancient elms whose stark, late-budding limbs twisted upward to the darkening sky. In the grove's center an old-style caravan glowed bright with red and yellow paint, crisp curtains at its windows. A half dozen house trailers clustered around it as if on guard, some of them shiny and new, some dented and scratched with years. From every window but one, faces waited for the verdict of the *krisatora*.

At length their leader gave a low whistle and doors opened, paths of light spilling into the dust. From inside the one traditional caravan there was a brief glimpse of dollhouse perfection, of shelves agleam with china, of rich velvets and warm-shaded lamps, the silhouette of an old woman rocking a blanketed bundle in her arms.

The leader whistled again and called a name softly into the trees.

The shadow of a young man separated itself from the trunk of an elm and stumbled into the light.

From the elders a regretful, unanimous sigh. So he was drunk again, the young man; fear, gin, and remorse made for a potent brew. Despite the warm evening and the heat of the fire, every man among them felt the chill of the inevitable verdict, preordained before any of them were born. The *kumpania* was a man's life, his world, his only identity. Without it he had no more substance than smoke.

They turned their eyes to the fire, reluctant to look into the sullen young face. But it was time. It was the reason they were gathered.

The spokesman flicked a spent cigarette into the fire, splashed wine ceremonially upon the dust, and issued the verdict of the *kris*.

"We have kept you hidden as long as we dare. It is decided. You have done what cannot be undone. You have dishonored the Rom and brought the force of *gajo* law upon the families. This we cannot accept."

The leader stood, his arms described a slow, graceful arc that seemed to encompass and protect the assembled tribe. He looked directly into the young man's eyes and there was silence, broken at last as embers shifted in the fire, as sparks flew and died on the air. When the leader spoke again his voice was a hypnotic monotone, words that were not his own, words that had come down, generation on generation, through the long travels of his people.

"You are banished from the *kumpania*. You will shun all places where the Rom gather. From this day you are not of the people. You are no longer Rom. This we have decided."

The young man swayed, fear and defiance doing battle in his thin face.

Defiance won. His lip curled as his black eyes moved from one closed face to the next. He spat into the fire and the hiss of its burning cut the silence.

"That's it, then? That's all?"

The spokesman sighed and shook his head. "How can it be? In drunken rage you kill the mother of your children. She was your wife, my daughter. My only daughter." For the first time, blame and personal grief thickened and colored his voice. The purposeful line of his mouth sagged, became old, was weary of the long ordeal. "The children are still Rom. They must find their way."

As if on signal the old woman descended the caravan steps. The small bundle, now whimpering in its blankets, was held tightly to her breast. She avoided the eyes of her son-in-law and looked to her husband. "This Rose is too new to go. She needs a mother. One of our women has milk and will nurse her."

The leader nodded and beckoned into the dusk. Two small boys were led into the firelight. The taller, a child of perhaps seven, elbowed his brother aside and stepped forward.

The first smile the *kumpania* had seen for many days touched the old man's lips. "You know what has happened and what must happen now, Dui. You can stay with us—or go with your da."

The boy did not hesitate. He ran to his grandfather and took his hand. In passing, he threw his father a glance of pure contempt. "The *kumpania*," he said. "I want to stay with the *kumpania*."

The leader nodded and embraced the child. "So Dui stays." He turned then to the other, smaller boy, now alone in the circle of light.

"And you, Micah, what do *you* choose?"

Micah was not yet five. How could he choose, this small one with the quick dark eyes of his father and the soft-curving mouth of his mother—a mother who, one night of hitting, shouting, sobbing, screaming, had been taken away. When he saw her again she was in a box with big brass handles on the side. He hadn't seen her since, and understood now that he never would.

The crowd pressed in on him, waiting for him to speak.

He knew every face around him, liked many and loved a few.

There were his grandparents, head and heart of the tribe. How could there be a world without their voices in it, without their caravan ahead of him in the road, without the painted sunflower on its door? It was

Granddad who showed him how to groom the horses, told him where to touch them, what to say to them so they'd always come to him when he called. Now Granddad's eyes were closed and his lips were moving. Maybe he was praying. He did that, sometimes.

Next to him stood Grandmam, who now handed Rose to a younger woman. Sometimes Grandmam gave Micah hard mint candies and made him promise not to tell Dui. On winter days, when mud fouled the wagon wheels and the families could not travel, it was Grandmam who beckoned him through the sunflower door, made him wipe his feet on the mat, and let him unlock a leather satchel from its secret place under the floorboards. Then she spilled the family's wealth onto a blue velvet cloth and let him watch as she drizzled chains and bright necklaces through her knotty brown fingers. She made him repeat after her as she counted coins and stacked them into neat golden towers on the cloth. One day she rummaged to the bottom of the case for a twist of wrinkled paper, unfolded it slowly and touched something dark and smooth to his cheek, then turned it to catch the light so he could see fires burning inside it. It was a ruby, she said, polishing it on her skirt before twisting it back into its paper wrapper.

She was looking at him now, his grandmam. She didn't seem to notice that her apron was all scrunched up in her fist, that tears were running down the creases of her cheeks.

There was the baby. Rose. She was crying again. Yesterday she had clutched Micah's finger and tried to suck on it. Sometimes she waved her arms and sometimes she slept, but mostly she cried—Grandmam said it was because she was weakly, born too soon. He wasn't sure quite how he knew, but it was Rose's fault that Da got crazy drunk and hit Ma.

No, he didn't like Rose.

There was his second cousin Farah, just Micah's age but already she could charm any *gajo* out of a shilling or a chicken or whatever took her fancy. When you looked at her face it was a bit like looking into Grandmam's ruby. You wanted to keep on looking. Farah didn't sulk and cry to get her own way—she smiled or she bit, but she got what she wanted anyway. Grandmam said she was too bold for her own good, but he didn't care. He liked Farah and she liked him. When he grew up he was going to marry her; Da said he could, if she kept her place and didn't get above herself—and if they could pay her bride-price.

There was his brother, Dui, now clutching Granddad's hand and not looking at Da or Micah at all. Summer nights they slept together under a big feather *dunha* outdoors—but Dui wanted it all and Micah often woke up cold with no covers on him. When he threatened to tell Da, Dui thumped him—but Micah told anyway, and then it was Dui who got the thumping and it served him right.

Which brought him to Da. Micah couldn't ever remember seeing his father alone, but he was alone now, standing off to the side and not moving at all except for his eyes, which looked at Micah as if he wanted to ask him some favor. But no, Da never asked favors, not from anybody . . . "Only women beg, Micah." Da brought him a Shetland pony to ride once—"Just for the day, old cock. You can't keep him—he's kind of on loan." Then he winked, swung Micah onto its back and gave his big rollicking laugh as he whacked the pony's rump. Except for just lately (and sometimes when he was drunk), Da laughed all the time, draped Micah around his neck like a scarf and galloped him down the lanes, found where the fattest trout dozed under riverbanks and stroked them so they rolled over and you could pick them right out of the water with your bare hands. Da was clever, everybody said so. People liked him, liked to hear him laugh. Most of the time Micah wanted to be with his father more than anything.

And now Da was leaving too. Like Ma—only not quite like Ma. Dui said it last night, he kept on saying it even after Micah put his hands over his ears . . . "Just you wait, the Rom will send him off, they'll not keep him in the *kumpania* now."

Micah felt his chin start to quiver and he clamped his teeth shut to stop it. Something else men didn't do. They didn't beg and they didn't blubber. Da said so.

And now Da spoke. Just to him.

"What d'you say, laddo? Want to stay here with them"—a raking glance at the assembled elders—"or come with me?"

His father's eyes fastened into his like bright black hooks, and Micah didn't think at all after that. He nodded.

He nodded and tried not to see the quick flash of triumph in Da's eyes, to see Granddad and Dui move closer together. He tried not to hear the sounds coming out of Grandmam's throat, or Farah's quick gasp as she turned and ran through the doorway of her family's trailer.

The elders lowered their heads. The matter was closed.

The young man strode—no stumbling now—to the circle of the fire and gathered up his son. The old woman rubbed at her eyes with her apron and hurried up the steps of her clean caravan, reappearing with a bag of brown eggs.

"—for Micah, he's had nothing since—"

The young man spat again and swung his fist; egg yolks exploded and splattered the painted sunflower. Turning, he rumpled his son's black hair and swaggered to a battered trailer parked in the farthest corner of the grove.

A grinding of gears and the trailer roared out of camp, smoke from its exhaust drifting over the elders, mixing with smoke from the *kumpania* fire and the sudden keening of the women.

Book One

ONE

At CLOSING TIME they threw him out of the village pub and shot the bolt behind him.

Stumbling and cursing, he reeled into darkness, the cobbles sharp and cold to his feet. He blinked down at bare toes poking through the holes in his socks and wondered vaguely where he'd left his shoes. When had he taken them off? Disoriented, he paused under a streetlamp and squinted at his hand, which he could no longer feel. Lamplight touched black hair worn too long, too curly, too...different; it shone briefly on very white teeth in a thin, swarthy face and on the dirty red kerchief at his neck.

He clung to garden walls and fences as he plunged onward.

"I'll get me to the trailer, Micah'll look after me, he'll look after his da..." he mumbled. "I won't hit him tonight, honest I won't," he promised a passing oak when its branches rattled sullenly overhead.

Instinct took him down the lane toward his trailer. Instinct found a stranger's backyard where washing still hung on the line. Instinct and long

practice guided him to a pair of socks, then to a boy's shirt that should fit
Micah nicely in a couple of years. "See, laddo, your da thinks about his
boy." His voice thickened. "My poor little old lad," he whimpered, weak
tears tracking through the stubble on his cheeks.

He bumped into a fence and clung to it, catching his breath. That
numbness was in his arm again ... there'd been a lot of it lately and drink
didn't help like it used to, didn't help much of anything. Time was he
could flatten the world on a pint of gin, punch it and stomp it until it let
him alone and he could sleep sound. Now there was just Micah.... "Your
da's sorry, laddo, he told you that a lot of times, didn't he? We'll move on
tomorrow ... maybe up Appleby way for the horse fair, what d'you say?
You like the fair, don't you, me old cock?"

Micah didn't answer, of course he didn't, he was asleep in his bed ...
he'd better be, by God!

He shook his head to clear it and blundered to where he'd hidden the
trailer that morning, its patched bulk screened by a thicket of hawthorn
and alder. His feet, lurching across the meadow, sent up smells of bruised
grass and things growing unseen in the dark. Thoughts of the Rom and
Appleby came strong here, an enticing torture which deadened the unease in his belly and that new, tight heat in his chest. The horse fair ... oh,
they'd warned him, the *kris,* those stern Gypsy elders who, in their collective wisdom, could be as unbending as any magistrate when their private
laws were broken. And twice as final.

*You will shun all places where the Rom gather. From this day you are not of
the people. You are no longer Rom. This we have decided ...*

They had decided! Arrogant bastards. A lot *he* cared. He'd go to the
fair, him and Micah. They'd been before. What harm, if they camped
away from the *kumpania?* What harm just to lie low and look? What
could they do to him, the *kris?* Their authority was steeped in traditions,
not prisons; they wouldn't kill him—not a man among them would turn
him over to the coppers. It was not their way. So why not walk boldly
into their compound? But tradition bound him too, and he knew why,
he'd always known. The *kris* had spoken and the *kris* was law. There was
no other. To disobey was anathema, would bring down curses so powerful a man's entire line was forever damned, his children, his children's
children, a black river that had no end. The knowledge soured and saturated every cell in his body. He was dishonored among the wagons,
would not be welcome at the family fires ... such *warm* fires at Appleby.

He reached far back in his mind and found the River Eden running
clear and fast under a summer sun. Caravans and wagons of the Rom

lined its banks at horse fair time; women of the Rom gossiped and washed plates at water's edge, their long skirts swirling as they moved; children of the Rom, wild and sun-browned, splashed in the shallows; and the Rom themselves, thin men, quick as whips, bathed their horses in its deeper waters. They groomed them, caressed them, whispered to them, paced them down Gallows Hill with manes and tails aflying, all to tempt the wealthy buyers. At night guitars sobbed at *kumpania* fires, cigarettes like fireflies studded the dark as men of the Rom laughed with contempt, proud to know that every *gajo* door was double-locked against them, every barn and stable bolted and barricaded because the Gypsies were in town.

He laughed himself, forgetting he was no longer Rom, but as he stumbled through the trailer door the pain roared back into his chest. It was bad, the worst ever. He held his breath and waited for its ebb. God almighty, he wasn't going to snuff it, was he? He couldn't. They had to keep moving, him and the boy. It was the way of his people, it was *his* way.

Groping through the dark well of the trailer, his hand found the bed, moved over the pillow until it touched his son's face. Eyes closed as usual, pretending sleep—but Da was not deceived. Under his fingers a nerve in the child's eyelids twitched.

"Get up," Da tried to say, "I know you're awake," wanting Micah to find the bedroll and set it down outside for him—hell, the kid *knew* his da couldn't sleep inside four walls, *knew*, by Christ! "Come on, Micah, out of it!—" But his words, so hard to find this night, kept coming out wrong, coming out Romani. To mock him, dammit!

He reached for his belt as anger, the old enemy, galloped through him. But pain was in the saddle again, gripping at his chest, squeezing it, twisting it, and it was easier, at the end, to lie down and let it wrap around him.

Micah was ten when it happened, possibly nine. He'd never been to school, never had a cake with birthday candles on it, so how could he be sure?

A morning breeze stirred the frayed hem of the curtain when he woke up. Cautious to the bone, he listened. Crows bickered in the field, a hawthorn branch scratched at the roof, and in the distance a tractor stuttered and whined over the furrows.

Not a sound out of Da, not even snores. Micah knew better than to wake him. Bad enough when he woke naturally, groaning and holding his head as if left to itself it would roll off into the litter of spent matches and rusty rabbit traps on the trailer floor. He was best left alone when he'd been at the bottle.

Micah crept out of bed and around the huddle of blankets he'd thrown over Da last night after the muttering stopped. Picking his way to the corner that served as a kitchen, he almost tripped on Da's belt that lay, harmless enough now, by the quiet blankets. He hung it on a nail, grateful to have escaped its bite; remembering the click of its buckle in the dark, he knew it had been close.

There was a heel of bread left, and a few baked beans at the bottom of a tin. He bolted the food first, then boiled water for their coffee like Da had showed him. Before he set out he covered Da's feet, which were sticking out of the blanket, and set coffee on the warmer in case Da woke up before he got back. Not that he would. He slept long and heavy after a booze-up; when he came to, it would be all tears and pats on the head and I'm-sorry-laddo and what-can-I-do-to-make-up-for-it? And vows, too. May-God-strike-me-dead-if-I-ever-lay-a-hand-on-you-again. He meant every word he said, Micah knew he did.

Out in the meadow a couple of rabbits still twitched in Da's traps. Keeping a skinny doe for dinner, he sold the fat buck to a shop in the village for three shillings. On his way out he slipped a tin of lunch meat in his pocket. A good haul. Da would be pleased. Like as not he'd thump him on the shoulder and tell him how smart he was, and how a man was lucky to have a kid like him. Da still said that sometimes.

It was midmorning when he came back. The sky was high and very blue. A puff of cloud floated picture-pretty just below it and floated again on the pond behind the trailer, its reflection quivering under dragonfly wings, dimpling under the thready legs of water spiders. Micah sat on the bank and watched, the rabbit money a soothing jingle in his pocket. No reason to hurry, Da might sleep for hours yet. Micah hoped he would.

It had been different before the drinking got regular. They had adventures then, him and Da. Still did, sometimes, rolling along country lanes in the wood-sided van with the trailer rattling along behind. "A cigar box pulling a tin chicken," Da used to say, "but it's freedom, me ol' cock, freedom," flashing his quick grin as he let Micah honk the horn, laughing his big, rollicking laugh when real chickens clucked and scattered in front of them. If nobody was about Da would shift gear and hop out. A sweep of his arm, a flash of steel, and dinner was all but on the table. "Quicker than you can say 'knife,' Micah, that's the way it's done."

It was at such times that Da gave Micah the only lessons he'd ever had. "We tell the *gaje* nothing, then they can't blame us for nothing, see? 'Specially coppers—tell 'em anything but the truth, that's the way of the families. You know nothing. Not where you've been, where you're going, where you live, where your father lives, not even your name, savvy?" Micah savvied. It was an easy lesson, often repeated. He did not, to his knowledge, have anything to tell anybody. No address, no papers, no name but Micah. Officially, he and his father did not exist. When Da was challenged for his full name (as he often was) by police or farmers or other interested parties, he gave Johnson or Smith or Barnes or Wilkins, whatever came first to his lips. Once, to his own delight and Micah's bewilderment, he gave his name as John Romeo to the wife of a young vicar, and when he'd done nailing up a new trellis for the vicarage roses (at a good price, laddo, we don't work free), he gave Micah chocolate kisses and a bottle of pop to wait on the steps while his father went inside for his money and a cup of tea with the missus. Then and later, Micah waited a long time, with orders to whistle if the man of the house came home. Da shaved every day then, and he carried himself different; there was a swagger to his walk and little dark devils danced in his eyes. Lies flew off his tongue like drops of quicksilver, shiny little fibs they repeated and laughed over when they got back to the trailer.

Da was King of the World then, Micah his Crown Prince.

It was hardly ever like that now.

Micah sighed as he picked up the doe and the traps. They should be getting started if they were to make the next village before night.

He dawdled toward the trailer, his feet dragging through rough grass and bracken. In a patch of purple clover he found an argyle sock; a few yards more and there was its mate, caught on a tree stump. Closer to home he spotted the shirt and put it on, pleased Da had remembered him—although it must have been a very dark night or Da was drunker than usual, for the shirt was black and Da only liked bright colors, the brighter the better.

The sun was all the way up when he set the rabbit in a patch of shade and pushed open the trailer door. He was not surprised to see his father still wrapped in the blankets. Once Da had slept two whole days, and when he woke up, morose and begging for a drink, he offered no excuses, no reasons.

Despite the open window the air seemed thicker this morning, heavy with sweat and old urine and something else that sent out the first signals of panic, nailing Micah to the floor.

Branches still scraped at the roof. The distant farmer still plowed his furrow. In the meadow, wrens and sparrows had joined forces with the crows. Somewhere close a bluebottle was buzzing.

The one sound that should have been there, faint and rhythmic and familiar, was not.

"*Da!*" he shouted. "*Da, wake up!*"

But even before he slapped at the bluebottle and ripped away the blanket he knew Da wasn't listening. Without thinking, his hand brushed at his father's cheek. It was cold under the stubble, waxen under the tan. But it was the eyes, much too far open, much too much white, that sent him tearing out of the trailer, down the lane, past scattered lean-tos to the edge of the village, panic blocking any purpose but to escape the staring eyes, to get away, get away. . . .

When his lungs and his legs reached their limit he dropped down behind a hedge, the habit of concealment by now a reflex so ingrained he could not have denied it even had he wanted to.

His thin brown face against moist earth, he gulped in great lungfuls of air and closed his eyes. There were a million things he had never seen. The inside of a schoolroom, a doctor's office, a factory, a barbershop. But he'd seen death a thousand times. Rabbits they trapped or shot; chickens that kept on running long after their necks were twisted; trout they'd tickled on dark nights under the banks of the Eden. Death looked always the same. It was the eyes. His father's eyes. And his father's smell, as if all the gin he'd drunk in life were oozing out through his pores in death.

He began to cry into the grass, guilt and Da's voice coming at him over his sobs. *Stop your blubbering or I'll give you something to blubber for. Are you Rom or are you* gajo, *eh?* All his life Da had boxed his ears for crying, told him, *Shut your noise or I'll shut it for you,* so Micah half-expected a fist to come crashing out of the bushes. When one did not it was a hundred times more frightening than the worst beatings he remembered, and if another voice, a real one, had not come out of the bushes he might have wept there all day.

"Whatever's the matter, son? It can't be *that* bad!"

It was a woman, pinch-faced and carefully dressed, the leashes of two small white dogs twining about her ankles. As always when he was panicked, his mind closed up and Da's training took over:

"I've lost my bus fare, I don't know how to get home."

"Oh, that's too bad—why don't you run over to the police station, the constable will help—"

"I can't," he said quickly, "or I'll miss the bus, see? It's due any minute."

"Well..." She frowned and looked up the road, perhaps expecting a bus to appear on the horizon, but then one dog nipped the other dog's ear, and through a yelping tangle of straps she handed Micah sixpence and let herself be dragged away.

He pocketed the coin and tried to think. He couldn't stay here, he knew that. When she remembered this street had no bus stop she'd be back—maybe bring the police.

Police.

The word sent him plunging down a railway embankment and up the other side, his route leading him straight back to the trailer.

But he couldn't go in, could not bring himself to mount the steps and face the eyes again; their dull black fires already burned slow holes in his brain and he thought now that they'd likely smolder there forever. Why hadn't Da told him this might happen, why hadn't he told him what do do....

Because he could think of nothing else he went back to the pond to huddle against a willow, its trunk unexpectedly cold through the black shirt, the rabbit money hot and moist in the palm of his hand.

Three shillings. And the woman's sixpence.

Options scrabbled about in his head, but without Da to point out true north they led nowhere. If he just had a mother...he'd had one, he knew that. It was when he was little and they still traveled with the Rom. He'd had a brother and a baby sister and a granddad and grandmam. And he'd had Farah. Then Ma died. One night Da told him how, but he didn't want to think about that. Sometimes he couldn't help thinking about it, that's when he had nightmares and woke up with screams in his throat. After Ma died they were on their own. No mother, no *kumpania*, now no Da. No nothing.

He could neither read nor write, but he could count very well; he knew three shillings and sixpence wouldn't take him from here to next week. Unsure of his age, he knew himself far too young to get work on his own. Worse, just looking for it would call attention to him, the one thing he must not do.

Lie low, laddo, melt into the background, that's our way.

Last week they'd picked beans just south of Derby, so there'd be money in the marmalade jar under the sink—but not for a million pounds could he go back into the trailer.

Never for a second did he think to tell anyone his father lay dead inside it under a pile of dirty blankets. If he did they'd shove him into a "home" —which he knew to be another word for orphanage because that's what

Da said. Worse, they'd send him to school, "suck him into *gajo* ways." Da said it so often that Micah had come to picture school as an eager mouth waiting to inhale him the way his father had inhaled cigarettes.

School's not for our people, son. School is for slaves. . . .

So what do I do now, Da?

For want of an answer he peed into the pond and was surprised to see the arching spray turn to drops of pure gold. The sun was setting. Night not an hour away and him with nowhere to go.

When he finally turned his back on the sun and started walking, he carried with him a rabbit, a tin of lunch meat, and a deep resentment against Da, who'd given him a hundred rules to live by, but no road map to the future.

TWO

ONCE CLEAR OF THE VILLAGE he could breathe easier. No roads here, no houses, no people to hide from, just fields and dirt tracks and clumps of trees, dusk sweeping down in great streaks of rose and lavender and dove gray. Closer to hand the melancholy lowing of brown and white cows plodding home through lush grass to some farm he could not yet see.

Home.

Micah scrubbed a hand across his eyes and pressed northward, his stomach painfully empty. Just a bite of bread and a few beans since morning—was it only *this* morning?—but it seemed to him vital that he put distance between himself and the caravan. Soon Da would be found. They'd search the caravan. Then they'd look for the owner of the boy-sized clothes, the bag of marbles, the plastic sports car he'd taken (to Da's delight) from Woolworth's toy counter. *By God, but you're a light-fingered young bugger, you are!*

When dark came he was in the lane of a small farmhouse. The light in its window pulled him forward. It was a familiar scene, one which never lost its appeal. A father worked at a desk; a mother and assorted children were gathered at the hearth watching the telly and eating toffees from a painted tin.

Long before he was tall enough to see in, Da had lifted him to such windowsills to spy on the *gaje*.

Look at the poor sods, half dead and don't know it, trapped in their nothing jobs and their crummy little houses.

Micah wouldn't have dared admit it to Da, but many a cold night he'd longed to live in just such a crummy little house, surrounded by just such a family, eating toffees and watching a telly. They'd had a telly in the caravan once. Da nicked it from a parked truck while Micah tempted the driver with a cap full of free-range eggs "fresh off the farm, mister, honest." No lie. Like Da said, any fresher and they'd still be in the hens— he'd lifted them right off the coops not an hour before. With a telly installed in the caravan they'd sat glued to the flickering screen and the new world it opened up. Pretty people in pretty rooms that were always spic and span. Cartoons. Dramas so obscure they could have been in a foreign language. A kiddie show with a brave superdog who always saved the day. Quiz shows. The variety was endless, fascinating—especially when Da was at the pub and he had the caravan to himself. It couldn't last, of course. Nothing did. One midnight Da kicked its face in and that was that.

As Micah watched the family in the window, the smallest child reached out for another toffee, slowly unwrapped it, turned it this way and that before taking a long, lingering lick at nut-studded caramel. Saliva rushed to Micah's tongue. He smelled the rabbit still hanging from his shoulder. It must now be cooked; the lunch meat he would save for tomorrow.

Out back, another light showed him a kitchen, its door unlocked. *The daft buggers don't never lock a door till they go up to bed, Micah.*

He was in luck. The kitchen was empty, the next room loud with the rustle of toffee papers and television voices shouting news of famine in India, a train derailment in Camden, the death of a movie star in California, a trawler in trouble off the Cornish coast. All meaningless. What was important was matches on the stove and bundles of kindling by the coal scuttle.

He found a tree-screened hollow behind the barn; within an hour the rabbit was skinned, cooked, and eaten. In the dark barn he found a pail and an obliging cow. With his belly full of rabbit and frothy new milk, he huddled for warmth against the cow's square, rumbling side and settled himself for sleep, making a conscious effort to plan for the days to come rather than dwell on the day that was ending. *What's over's over, laddo, not worth thinking on.* Easier said than done. Even Da hadn't followed his own rule; life with the *kumpania* long since over, he'd seemed to brood on it all his days . . . in some vague way Micah sensed that Da's old life with the Rom, which he often claimed to hold in such contempt—*Who needs them, eh?*—was hopelessly tangled up with bottles of gin and all those marathon mutterings in the night. Some thread connected them, but just which one was never quite clear because he'd tried so hard no to listen. . . .

And now it didn't matter, did it? Because Da was gone.

He was alone.

And must be awake and gone before the farmer came in.

Echoes of Da's voice came often in the next weeks, warning him, guiding his steps along lonely paths, reminding him of little scams they'd pulled and ways to invent his own.

He was doing well. On the road a month and he still had his tin of lunch meat; the money he'd thought wouldn't last a week was almost intact. Grocery shops were laughably easy to pick off; nobody looked twice at a boy buying a penny candy, for who would expect he'd walk out with a tin of salmon in one pocket and a box of cream cheese in the other? Days were still warm, nights thick with stars and silence. Strawberry and cherry crops were done but now the orchards hung heavy with pears and apples. Fields were still full of tomatoes, lettuce, and carrots. Every farm kept hens, their eggs fresh for the taking if you knew how and when; thanks to his father, Micah knew. The same with milk and chickens, though he had to be careful with chickens—if he was slow with the twist they squawked.

Noise was dangerous.

So were dogs. They'd been the bane of Da's life and were now the terror of Micah's. *Face them before they bark, me old cock. Give 'em a quick one to learn 'em a lesson—don't mess with Dobermans, they're too bleeding quick. If they catch you, kick 'em in the balls and for God's sake don't miss.* So Micah was careful. He kept a chicken wing or a drumstick in his pocket and offered it at the first sign of hair lifting on a dog's back. A soft word, a rub at chest and muzzle, and an enemy became an ally whose alert ears told him far sooner than his own if the farmer was getting too close.

As Da's death became less of an aching wound he began to revel in his freedom. Abundant food, long warm days of summer, no bruises to body or spirit, all lulled him to believe he could wander the countryside forever.

But days began to shorten, the sky took on a milky, washed-out blue, clouds joined up into denser, dirtier clusters. In open fields the wind now carried the smell of rain on it and developed small cutting edges that found the worn spots in his clothes. Trees turned a darker green, grass grew a little thinner in the pastures, and straggles of starlings began to rise from woods and potato fields to push south.

He saw the changes, knew their meaning, but kept it coiled at the back of his mind, unwilling to face it.

He was not ready for it.

It was mid-September when his luck turned. It rushed at him with hot, angry breath, snarling and baring its fangs. Not a Doberman, not an Alsatian—of them he was afraid and therefore wary. It was not even the Lab who'd guarded the stable last night, its back hair ready to lift the instant he ceased his endearments, his rhythmic stroking of its deep black chest.

He wasn't even on private property when it happened.

It was early evening, the country road almost deserted, curtains already drawn in the scattered houses, lights coming on. At the curb a parked car, its windows rolled open and a man's wallet on the dash.

It was Lassie that did him in.

The collie sat straight as a duchess on the backseat. She did not snarl at Micah's approach. He didn't expect her to. She was aloof and unreal, groomed and golden in the last of the sun, her face as kind, as understanding as the Lassie he'd yearned for when they had the telly. She *was* Lassie. The breeze moved softly through her coat like wind over a cornfield. He held his breath, the wallet forgotten as he drew closer to her beautiful head.

She gave him her profile, pointed and elegant.

"Oh, but you're a beauty," he whispered, not moving. "Aren't you the super girl..."

His hand inched toward her, but slow, always where she could see it. *Never surprise an animal, Micah. That's when they snap.*

So there was no excuse, none at all.

And no warning. Her muzzle did not twitch. Her neck ruff did not lift. No hint of a growl from her throat.

One second a statue, the next a yellow blur shooting out at him, her neat, clean paws ramming his chest. Money spilled from his pockets and clinked to concrete. He felt himself falling back, heard his head thunk and bounce on the road. Arms over his face, he rolled, dropped into somewhere soft and dark. A ditch.

And now she had him, smothering him in golden fur, drowning him in saliva, her lips pulled back and back, long teeth clicking and clicking again. . . . His arms came up and she missed his face. He tried to punch out at her but the sides of the ditch pinned him tight. Outlines faded and with them his strength. He was turning, spinning . . . and still no sound, no snarl from her as she savaged him, even when her teeth closed on muscle.

Miles away a door slammed. A mouth whistled.

She hesitated, cocked her head, lifted her chin.

She *posed*.

Then she shook herself and trotted off.

He lay in the ditch an hour . . . a night . . . a day . . . he didn't know. A wisp of her fur drifted under his nose; it smelled of flowers, the same smell that hung over shampoo counters at the shops. Even her saliva, drying now on his chin, tasted sweet and clean. But then, she wasn't just a dog. She belonged in that rich world of the telly. And she'd tried to kill him.

Because he was Rom. It made her better than him.

They're all alike, toffs are. Fancy houses, bank accounts. They think it makes them better than us, see? So they treat us like dirt and always have. But we're free and they're not and they can't stand it. It eats at 'em, eats at 'em . . .

But I don't want to be free, he heard himself whimper. I want a house and a bed, dinner on a table and toffees in a tin . . . I want my arm to stop hurting and my head, I want . . .

After a while he began to want Da. He called for him, but he didn't come either. He thought perhaps he should move. He tried. The moon winked out. When it came back on there were pink smears on it and it wouldn't keep still.

Sometime in the night it rained and woke him up. Pulling out of the ditch he felt grass under his face and something thick and sticky between his fingers. The grass turned to stubble and hurt his hand. One hand. He couldn't put weight on the other so he dragged himself forward on his elbows until he was in a wood.

He was safe. He slept.

The next few days disappeared, he wasn't sure where. There was rain on his face, then sun, a lump on the back of his head and a moth walking on his hand . . . teeth nibbled him and he thought Lassie was back. He lifted his head and the moth turned to whiskers, rat's whiskers . . . he heard himself scream and it slunk off. He tried to keep awake then. One minute he was burning, shivering the next. His hand was big, hot all the time, the skin stretched tight and under the skin a drum thumped and pounded. . . . His tongue was dry, and Da was laughing at him. *One thing about England, laddo, nobody dies of thirst* . . . so he remembered and licked at the grass. And cried into it. Da, he wanted his da . . . Da looked after him when he was sick, didn't go to the pub, didn't hit him. He gave him milk instead, and hot soup from a tin, spooning it into his mouth. He stroked his hair, Da did. . . .

At first he thought the thunder was in his mind but then curtains of rain followed it, soaking him to the skin but refreshing him, waking him, clearing his head. But not his hand. His hand was bad. So pink and puffed up that every dirty little crease was clean from the rain. The gash started at his wrist and ended at his knuckles, a closed, tight wound with pain throbbing away inside it.

Lassie. The bitch, the beautiful rotten bitch.

Move, get food . . . no money in his pockets . . . maybe it was still in the road. . . . He staggered back to the road but he couldn't find his money and he got frantic, scrabbling his good hand in the ditch as a truck squealed its brakes and stopped.

"What the hell are you doing down there, mate?" The driver stuck his head out the window and blinked at the rain.

The old cockiness rushed back. *Never let 'em see you're scared, laddo.*

He didn't even have to lie. "I'm looking for my money, aren't I?"

The driver laughed. "You'll get none from me, you cheeky young bugger. Want a lift?"

The truck door swung open and he smelled the warm and the dry as swift-running ditch water filled his shoes. The truck was a trap and he knew it, but so was the pain in his hand—not even just his hand anymore, it throbbed all the way up his arm.

And the driver was eating a ham sandwich.

He climbed in, the heat and the scent of the ham almost as painful as his arm.

The driver changed gears. "How far d'you want to go then?"

"Just up the road a bit . . . to the next houses."

"Oh, aye." He pushed the packet of sandwiches across the bench seat. "Want one?"

He took one.

The driver shot him a quick glance as he lit a cigarette from the pack on the dash. "Going home, mate?"

"Yeah."

He switched headlights on. "D'you live far?"

"No." The bread was the best he'd ever tasted, and the ham.... Munching on it, lulled by warmth and the swish of wipers on darkening windshield, he wasn't ready when the driver said:

"Running away from home, are you?"

The last crumb of sandwich stuck in his throat. "'Course not—I live with my auntie." The invention gave him courage and he began to embroider it. "She'll have my dinner ready. Stew and dumplings—and chocolate cake."

Again a quick glance through cigarette smoke. "You don't want another sandwich, then, right?"

Even as his mouth formed "no" his hand reached out. The bad hand. He didn't care. With food so close he hardly noticed it.

The driver did. "You'd better get yourself to a doctor with that hand. It's festering."

"Nah!" he said. "That's how it always looks."

The driver was quiet then, intent on driving and the road ahead. The first building they saw was not a house but a tobacconist's. He swerved to a stop, the door already swinging open. "Wait here, kid, I have to get some cigs."

There were cigs on the dash, nearly a full pack. Trouble. Micah could smell it. Coppers. School. A "home" for boys who didn't have one. He watched the driver reach for change and duck into the lit telephone box on the corner.

The second his head bent to the mouthpiece Micah was out of the truck's off-side door and running through the rain, not looking back until he was clear of streetlamps and the brightly lit windows of shops.

He was shaken. He was soaking wet. Wind off the moors found every hole and thin spot in the black shirt. His teeth were chattering again. Every bit of his warmth was in his arm. He had no plan, no money, no place to sleep.

And he was lost. The beginnings of a town, it looked like. *Keep clear of towns, laddo, that's where the coppers are. Towns are trouble for our people.* Our people. "I'm not 'our people,'" he said aloud.

Whose are you, then? said Da....

A night like this, streets were deserted. Only the rain moved, long lines of it slanting under streetlamps, dimpling puddles, gurgling into gutters. The street he was on was half commercial—little shops, row houses, dark entryways.

ELDON'S PRODUCE: *Fresh Fruit and Veg —Fish on Fridays*
FELIX ABRAMSKY ELECTRIC: *Small Appliance Repairs*
ANNA ABRAMSKY STUDIO: *Ballet and Tap (no acrobatic)*

The studio was the only building lit. As he crept under the shelter of its eaves, music and voices seeped in thin threads through the window, a piano dominated by a woman's voice of piercing intensity. A cheap lace curtain hung at the window, so his first sight of the dancers was through a haze of pink gauze and runnels of rain. A dozen or so little girls in black leotards faced away from him toward the front of the room.

The music stopped. The voice, controlled but strong enough to crack glass, did not.

"I say the fifth, no? You are hearing Madame, are you not?"

A dozen neat heads nodded.

"Then give me the fifth, dammit! Fifth, fifth, fifth!"

The speaker moved to the front of the room, rapping her knuckles at a table as she said again, "Fifth. Fifth. Fifth."

Thus came his first sight of Madame.

Anna Abramsky.

She was tall. Teaching, she wore leotard and tights, ballet shoes, pilled leg warmers, and a shapeless black overblouse from which skeletal wrists shot out like bleached twigs. Pale, sparse hair was stretched up into a topknot and her eyebrows rose to follow it. In her hand a cane, with which she tapped an erring ankle here, a hunched shoulder there, a drooping chin.

As Micah watched she rapped on the piano behind her. "Begin. AND! *Grands battements à la barre. A la barre, Marcia!*—what are you doing on the floor?"

The woman advanced toward the window with such determined stride that Micah was sure she'd seen him. But no, she was headed for the unlucky Marcia, who was picking herself off the boards.

His eyes strayed to the man at the piano and the walking cane swinging like a metronome on the piano lid as he thumped the keys, his halo of silver-blond hair nodding to the same beat. Micah, trained to notice such things, saw mainly the cane. So maybe the man wasn't too fast on his pins. There'd be money in there somewhere, maybe food, maybe a corner to wait out the rain.... He wondered what time the dancers went home

—impossible they all lived here. He wondered if they carried purses that could be slipped quick as light into his pocket.

He wondered if his arm would ever stop throbbing.

But he began to take in, even now, the pattern of this life. A heap of coats, a row of rain boots, tote bags festooned with sweat towels, toe shoes, hair ribbons, camel's-hair sweaters. Rich kids. His lip curled, envy twisting to contempt.

Another bang on the piano, another break in the music. Profiles of the two middle-aged birds consulted, the teacher with fast, emphatic nods and shakes, the pianist with patient smiles and calm gestures of the hand.

A chicken hawk and a snow owl.

United, they again faced the class. They spoke. Together.

"From the beginning, ladies, if you please. AND!"

The pianist looked up before bending to the keys.

An overhead light shone full on him.

For a moment, seen through the window's rain-prismed glass and his own haze of pain, the pianist's fringe of silver-blond hair did indeed become a halo.

THREE

*H*E HAD TO RISK IT.

A covered entry ran down the side of the studio. Above it, what appeared to be a flat, with flowers and a pink-shaded lamp in the window. The flat was worth a try.

He waited in the entry, alternately sweating and shivering, listening to the piano and the woman's voice, wishing his arm would go away. Private houses were chancy even in the country . . . he didn't know about towns. Da would have known. Suppose there was somebody upstairs? Suppose he was caught and they called the police? Remembering the woman's voice he wanted to give up and try somewhere else, but then a duty cop pedaled slowly past the entry, his black waterproof cape gleaming like armor under the streetlamp.

The back door of the studio was unlocked, the downstairs hall empty. Somewhere he smelled soup simmering, a rich garlicky beef that made his head spin and his stomach cramp into a small, hard knot. Before the sandwiches, how many days hadn't he eaten? He didn't remember, had no idea how long he'd huddled in the ditch and then under hedges: he thought it had been a long time. But the flat was the objective, money or a quiet storeroom to hole up in—just until his hand got better.

He crept upstairs, sharply aware he was cutting off his escape route.

The landing at the top was draped with more lace curtains and a drying rack hung with odd-looking underwear and many pairs of the same knitted tubes the woman wore on her legs. They smelled of wet sheep. Wool, then. A pity they were wet, he could have used them to pull on under his trousers.

A living room came first, a crowded, padded granny of a room that pulled him to its bosomy warmth, stopped his teeth from chattering. Massive old couches, straight-backed chairs with velvet seats, thick curtains and plump cushions, all in brooding shades of wine and indigo, with white lace doilies on every chair arm, every headrest. Old sepia photographs of dancers lined the walls, figurines of more dancers stood on sideboard and mantel.

It was like nothing he'd seen or even imagined. Certainly he couldn't have imagined such heat. The room all but pulsed with it. Warmth enveloped him, rolled over him, swaddled him. It came from everywhere, a fire banked halfway up the chimney with glowing coals, a gas fire on the opposite wall throwing eerie blue patterns on the cracked ceiling. And the furniture itself, as if its upholstered overstuffed heart held storage tanks of heat it must discharge or burst.

He began to steam, to sweat, to reek. Nights huddled against assorted cattle rushed back to him on the sweltering air.

The temptation to sink into warm plush, to wallow in the staggering heat and his own animal aura, was a pain almost as intense as his arm, which now, in this atmosphere, throbbed faster, burned hotter, swelled thicker every minute.

Don't be sucked in to comfort, me old cock, that's the trap they set . . .

Yes, Da.

His quick glance swept the mantel, where a woman always kept her purse. It wasn't there.

He opened the bedroom door slowly, ready to run should some hidden silence speak. More carpets, more plush, many more photographs of dancers, all signed.

The bed rested dead center, a giant marshmallow covered in white eyelet. His hand sank down and down into the spread. A feather bed. He bit his lip and turned to the dresser. Hairpins, hair nets, strange curved combs with pearly tops.

But no money. He searched fast now, certain that any second the music would stop and the couple come up to bed.

As if his thought prompted it the music did stop, but only for a moment, then started up again louder than before, filling the bedroom with sound. He figured he had a minute or two, no more, until the song played itself out.

Nightstands and wardrobe yielded nothing. On top of the bureau was a tin box. In desperation he tried that. Yellowed theater tickets, a feather, a cork, a lump of amber oddly veined. An old brooch ... and the music was still playing.

Don't touch jewelry, laddo, the coppers can trace it.

A spasm of anger shook him. All very well for Da. Da wasn't hurting, he wasn't starving, he wasn't broke, he wasn't lost, he wasn't ten, and *he wasn't here!*

A sob rose in his chest at the same moment a hand clamped on his shoulder. A hard hand, a man's hand.

It was the piano player, his voice as soft as his grip was hard.

"What are you doing here, eh? Tell Felix, please."

The brooch rattled back into the box, an elderly pigeon returning to roost. "I'm looking for a button," he said, invention once again rushing all too quickly to his tongue. "I lost one off my trousers, see—" Show him the fly with the buttons all gone, show him the safety pins—

Felix Abramsky felt the boy's shoulder lunge as if to twist away, and he tightened his grip. The child's face turned up to his, instantly defensive, instantly sly. A narrow face, and filthy, with high cheekbones and a thin, tight mouth that was far too knowing for a child. The eyes were black, unnaturally bright against olive skin, eyes full of secrets and, for an instant, fear, but that was fading fast; a facile cunning slipped smoothly into place as he displayed the want of buttons on his trousers.

"I knocked at the door," he was saying now, glib as a parrot. "But I reckon you didn't hear with that din going on." A din which, at that moment, ceased. "I have to go, anyway, or I'll be late ..."

Felix's lips twitched. "You were maybe thinking to run off with Anna's bit of glitter from her grandmother in Kiev?"

The boy swallowed. His neck, besides being dirty, was unbelievably thin. And he kept one hand always in his pocket. Perhaps he'd already stolen something. . . .

"Well? Did you take something?"

"Nah!"

"It wouldn't help. Our things have no value but to us."

But the boy's confidence was back now. Again the shoulder, sharp under his hand—and unnaturally hot—gathered for action.

Felix tightened his grip.

In the studio below, little girls called good night to Madame, their clear young voices floating up the stairs like birdsong. The contrast between those clean, cared-for children and this one . . . Felix sighed. What to do with him?

Anna sailed in on a tide of indignant Russian, her usual release after the relentless ballet-French of class. She thumped the soup pot down and toweled her neck with never a pause in the tirade against her Tuesday beginners and their mothers. Marcia a hippo and Betsy a goose—and now Betsy's mother wanted her in toe shoes—

"Anna . . ."

"—a beginner *en pointe* yet! Not six months in class and already the mama thinks she's hatched a Fonteyn—"

"Anna . . ."

She stopped. One swift glance took in the open trinket box and the boy.

"So. They are in England, too."

"Who—"

"Gypsies—aren't they everywhere? Just look at him, barely out of the cradle and already a thief."

"But he took nothing . . ."

"He says."

"Anna, he's a child."

"A thief."

"He's wet to the skin."

"He's filthy, he stinks, he'll have lice, only the good God knows what's in the pockets—call the police."

"Anna!" Be it ever so gentle, he must reprove her. "*We* should report him to police, *we?*"

She looked away. Since the war they'd been refugees. They knew what it was to have no place to go.

"Perhaps he has family . . ." Even as she said it she was shaking her head.

So was he. What kind of family would claim this ragged child with steam rolling off him in malodorous clouds? He lifted the boy's chin and looked into his face, a puzzled face now. The Russian, no doubt. From

habit he excused himself. "Forgive us that we speak in our language...
Your family, where do they live?"

The face was guarded, then defiant. "Why?" he demanded.

Felix could almost hear wheels spinning behind the dirty forehead.
"Your family," he repeated, "where do they live?"

Wheels stopped spinning. Triumph flickered in dark eyes. A smile,
piercingly, angelically sweet under the dirt, curved the thin mouth into a
lyre.

"India," the boy said with certainty. "If you don't let me go now, I'll be
late and get a whipping."

Which would be Felix Abramsky's fault. He sighed. To seize an in-
spired lie, to impale guilt on its hook, to deliver it with aplomb... a child
of strange talents, this Gypsy—if such he was. Felix thought not. Gypsies
stuck together, that much he knew.

"India! You see?" Anna's Russian exploded over them all. "This is not a
good boy, Felix. It steals, it lies, it smells—either call the police or throw
him out. Is a civilized country, this England, they know what to do with
such as he, they find his people—and if he has none the government
takes care..."

He sighed again. Anna saw only black and white. "My angel, he is a
baby."

Her turn to look at him with reproach. Baby, whose memory brought
grief, was seldom mentioned between them, and only with love. Baby
was a toddling boy with full red lips and fine blond curls who'd been
staying with Anna's mother in the Paris apartment when the bullets came.
Baby was Sasha. The other one, the girl... she was a different story and
was never mentioned at all. Not by Anna. Not by him either, unless he
wanted trouble.

"This child, then," he said firmly. "He is here and must be dealt with."

"Then we deal with him. Look to his pocket—see how he keeps the
hand!"

She darted forward and snatched the wrist from its hiding place.

The boy fainted.

One moment a mass of heat and quivering nerves, the next a boneless
heap of wet rags.

Anna's flush turned gray. "My God, Felix, oh my God!"

My God indeed. From elbow to fingertips the arm was an angry, swollen red, the hand a mass of infection.

Easing him to the couch, Felix was again shocked. The weight seemed to be all rags. "I think he may also be starving," he said, as Anna forced brandy through the boy's lips and put her long, narrow hand to his forehead.

"He is burning... is not possible," she muttered, "in this country is not possible. The authorities—"

But if a child, a clever, slippery child such as this were to avoid the authorities?

The rags stirred and coughed, tried to rise. "I have to go, I'm late, see..."

"Is the doctor you have to see." It was Anna who spoke, her voice unsteady as she reached for the phone.

The boy, who had quietly fainted when Anna grasped the injured hand, now screamed. *"No! Don't call, don't call!"*—trying again to struggle off the couch.

"Anna, wait! Heat soup, eh?" He turned to the boy. "Look, your wound is serious, outside is pouring rain. Why cannot the doctor come here? Tell Felix, eh?"

For the first time a suspicion of tears glinted in the dark eyes. "They're all in it together, my da said so, doctors, coppers, teachers... they'll put me away, they'll lock me up—"

"But something must be done."

"They'll not catch me, I'll run away, I'll—"

Crouching beside him, seeing the stubborn set of the mouth, Felix believed him. "Your... da? Where is he?"

No mistake about the tears now. They spiked the long lashes, trickled down the dirty cheeks.

"Your mother?"

He shook his head.

"You have no one, no one at all?"

After many questions and much prodding, bits of story came limping out—seasoned, Felix was sure, by whatever little fictions came to mind.

He was Micah. Micah what? Micah nothing. The father died, oh, years since, the mother he didn't remember. An uncle lived in a big house and had a big car and barns full of cows and a dog called Lassie. Where did this uncle live? A hunt through the agile little brain produced "California" with the same speed and cunning it had earlier produced India. Why did Micah not live with his uncle? Because he had a belt, see, and when he was on the booze he hit Micah, hit him bad. So how did Micah live? Where sleep? How eat? A shrug. There was always a place to sleep, always food. . . . But where was it, this food? He found it, Micah said, just found it. He could look after himself, honest.

Felix stood and rubbed at his hip. "I think you will take soup, Mischa." Dimly he noted the subtle softening he had made of the child's name but did not pause to wonder—diminutives were a habit Anna constantly warned him against. It led them to take advantage, she insisted. "I shall speak some Russian with my Anna—she finds English . . . restricting. You see us, you see the telephone, you see we do not use it to call, yes? So you will relax."

They stood by the stove and listened to the boy drink soup.

"You are right, he starves," she said. "But Felix, the fever is high, a doctor must see him—"

"The doctor has to make a report—a child so young as he, so sick, with no family . . . they'll put him to a hospital or an orphanage. He will run away—perhaps before he is well."

In the end they compromised. If the boy agreed—and he was in no condition to make physical protest—they would tell the doctor he was their nephew who'd come to visit. He had been sick, this nephew, and was come for convalescence—

"Oh, but we would be shamed, Felix, he is so filthy, what would the doctor think of us, to have such a family?"

"The boy will take a bath first, he'll stay for a day or so until the arm is healed—and then we think what to do. . . ."

"Perhaps tomorrow it will not rain and he will run away from us also." Her expression was hard to read now, torn and oddly vulnerable. Then she shook her head, a characteristic clearing of disturbing thoughts. "You will give him the bath, Felix, use the scrubber, yes? and carbolic very thick on the hair. Take washcloth to the ears? Aha! Where can he sleep, this urchin? *Not* in our living room, no, never—"

"The cot under the stairs, it's big enough, and warm—"

Her nose twitched. "God, Felix, how he stinks! I'll have to Lysol the blankets when he's gone, the mattress . . ."

"Anna, my angel, are we buying a dog or giving a boy a place to lay his head, eh?"

"Until he heals, then," she conceded. "I call the doctor, you speak with the boy and start the bath. And be careful of the arm."

The man was explaining, pleading in his soft even voice as Micah tried to keep him in focus, but silver-white hair kept misting out to blur with light from the pink lamp.

"The doctor will make you better, Mischa. He will not take you away, this is our promise, you understand? If you are not treated soon—with antibiotics, I think—there can be gangrene and perhaps you could die ...just think, boy, only think—"

Micah tried but he couldn't seem to hold a thought. How could he die? You died when you were old...Da said he was thirty...but then sometimes little rabbits off the moor, too young to fetch a price, they died in the traps...

"First I shall help you take a bath so we do not shame Anna, for she has much pride."

A bath...he'd never had a bath, not in a proper tub, just the river sometimes in summer—or maybe he had, a long time ago when they'd lived with the *kumpania*...it seemed to him Ma soaped his neck, or maybe Grandmam—

The man was talking again, talking...

"But you will do me a small favor...when the doctor comes, let Felix talk, yes? Do not speak of India or California—"

Why not? They were real places, he'd heard them on the news somewhere...somewhere with toffees...

"Because it is not possible to walk there, not even to take a bus, not even if you were well. Look—"

He was holding a tin ball, mostly blue, with colored patches on it. A flick of the finger and the ball spun on its stand, making him dizzier than ever.

"Here is the world. Touch your finger here, England, there India and there California. The blue in between is all water, *much* water, so better not to lie if you can help it, please. She gets angry when you lie, my Anna."

Anna.

He said it like two words. An Na.

Micah let himself be led to the bath, weakly, eerily hopeful that this Felix would not let the doctor take him away. Therefore Felix, who talked so different, could not possibly be *gajo*. But he wasn't Rom either. He dimly remembered another word, *rai*—friend to the Rom. But he could hear the woman in another room. Her voice cut like knives, her eyes the same. . . .

An Na. In a dream Micah repeated her name, steam clouding over him as he looked down into soapy, swirling water, much hotter than river water, even a summer river. . . .

The water drained off what little strength was left, and he couldn't even help them dress him in clean clothes that were too big and the wrong shape, but very warm, as if they'd come from the oven. He smelled of camphor and carbolic and the same flower smell Lassie had on her.

Another man came. Micah didn't like him. He wore a gray suit and grumbled about the rain and clicked his tongue when he saw the arm, mumbling about infection and neglect and how he'd have to lance it. Tiny scissors glinted in his hand, a cloth was pushed at Micah's face . . . it smelled bad, he thought, but he couldn't remember much after that except that somebody stuck a needle in his behind and he heard himself shout. . . .

When he opened his eyes the gray suit wasn't there, just the man and the woman, the woman standing, looking down at him, the man in a chair, a funny smile on his face as if he couldn't decide whether to laugh or cry.

They gave him sweet hot milk, then the woman tucked blankets up around his neck and touched a hand to his cheek the way Da used to do. He heard her walk away, muttering. The man—Felix, was it?—spoke, calling him that name again. Mischa.

"You may sleep now, Mischa, and tomorrow you will feel better. You are safe here, no one will come."

Rain gurgled in the downspouts, cars whooshed by in the street, mice scratched in old walls. They'd put a flannel nightshirt over the bandages on his arm. There was still pain, but that ready-to-burst tightness was gone. So was the constant listening for enemies, the waiting for something to snarl at him or tap him on the shoulder. Maybe it was the pills they'd given him . . . he slept, floating off on the knowledge that never in his life had he been called Mischa, never had he been so clean, so warm, so safe. . . . Somewhere Da's face frowned, then Farah's and Grandmam's, but they were dim, misted over with honeyed milk and this new, unexpected kindness.

It was not just worry for the boy which kept Felix Abramsky awake. Anna, long and spectral in her white nightgown, lay beside him in the massive bed. Although he knew her every thought, he was not now sure if she slept.

He was troubled. Tonight she had neglected the small gestures of caring which usually filled her evenings, gestures unnecessary to him but vital to her. She had not warmed liniment for his hip, she had not turned down his side of the bed, and it was he, not she, who brought two glasses to the bedroom, poured tea, and added the small tot of rum to hers, to help ease her dance-stiffened joints for sleep.

A tart tongue was her defense; under sharp words and irrational angers lay a tumult too deep for words—but he'd seen the way she warmed clothes, warmed milk for this strange boy, touched her fingertips to his clean brown cheek.

Though her working life was spent with children, he had yet to see her help a child with shoe ribbons or give an approving pat to a little girl earnestly working *glissades*. What praise she offered was expressed only by a softening of the voice, for Anna kept her distance, shrank from touching flesh to flesh—or even using a child's given name, except to chide. For her this was necessary. The loss of Sasha had been grievous, in direct proportion to her love for him; the birth of the girl, whom some German stranger had name Gabriella, lacerated her pride.

Gabriella...about whom Anna would not or could not speak, except in anger. Would not even glance at the cool monthly letter from the child's paternal grandmother.

"Why should I care when the girl takes her first communion?" she demanded. "Her first swimming lesson? Did Sasha live to know such things? No! I have no wish to discuss it, Felix, none whatever. Nazi spawn! Haven't they done enough damage?" Once, only once, he'd caught her scanning the monthly letter, seen the terror in her eyes. It took him back to a time neither of them should have to relive.

After that he kept the letters, and the news they contained, to himself.

Anna's maternal instincts, twice thwarted, now found their only outlet in himself. Because he loved her he accepted the gift, burdensome as it often was. The balance was a delicate one, carefully structured over a decade—which sometimes felt like a century.

Perhaps now the balance would once again shift, but in what direction?

F O U R

*F*RAU VON REIKER'S HAND FELL cool and firm on the shoulder
of the little girl trying to flit unnoticed through the long windows leading to the garden and vineyards beyond.

The child heard the layered rub of dark, heavily starched cottons.
Under it, rhythmic as her grandmother's breathing, the creak of corsets
and the rattle of keys that Grossmutter wore always on her formidable
person. Overhead, the endless tick-tock of a carved oak clock that measured out their days.

"Your lessons are finished, Gabriella?"

"Yes, Grossmutter."

"No mistakes?"

"Some." The child stood firm on the parquet floor. "Miss Nolan says
my English will be good—and she should know."

Displeasure settled over lined, severe features. "You may tell the governess I shall see her in the library after dinner."

The library. Another "serious talk." Perhaps another governess. "If I went to regular school..." Where there were children, swings, even a seesaw...

"Out of the question—and you are giving me a headache."

Her grandmother turned to ascend the long staircase. On the fourth step she paused to press a handkerchief to her forehead.

"You were in the kitchens after lunch, I believe?"

"I was hungry."

"Yet you refused Lotte's excellent sauerbraten at lunch."

"I don't like sauerbraten."

A weighty sigh from on high. "I told you to avoid the backstairs—the staff does gossip. Now I must speak also to Lotte. In future ring the bell...Oh, my head is splitting, splitting. A difficult girl you are, Gabriella. If only your father—such a *good* child! You understand you make my position...delicate?"

Ellie's fingers fretted the blue apron that protected her Tuesday dress, but she said nothing. More and more it was impressed on her that she was an embarrassing complication in Grossmutter's life, that she was the cause of her grandmother's incessant headaches—and that she was not just different from Papa but, in some mysterious way, *less.*

Poor Miss Nolan. Poor Lotte, with her swollen ankles and her loutish, sniveling son. But Lotte wouldn't be sent away. She had been here too long and in any case was too fine a cook; Grossmutter had a delicate, if occasionally noisy, stomach.

The old woman swept now up the curving stairs, wafting back to Ellie a cloud of witch hazel and the special cologne made up by the village druggist and carefully cooled in the wine cellar before being sprinkled on the linen handkerchiefs of Frau von Reiker—who paused now on the balcony to remind Ellie once again of the message to the governess before quietly closing the door to her darkened room.

Ellie looked out on terraces of summer-yellow vineyards and the willowed banks of the Mosel below, but the desire to dabble her feet in its cool shallows had fled, chased away by what she knew would be her grandmother's displeasure. Only two childish pastimes were positively, invariably, approved; she could use the library at will or she could sit on the long oak settle in the hall and spin story webs around Papa's portrait that smiled down on her from the top of the stairs.

"He was a brave man," Grossmutter said often of her son. Ellie believed it. So handsome in his Oberleutnant's uniform, how could he have been anything *but* brave with that steel-blue gleam in his eyes and the reckless smile on his lips, the Iron Cross bright on his chest. "The artist had to come back later, Gabriella, make a special trip from Berlin to paint in the Cross"—here Grossmutter always flushed and dabbed at her eyes—"after the Russian front, of course." Ellie was treated then to rambling tales of Hans von Reiker, student and sportsman. "A clever boy, and powerful, such shoulders on him! He would have been on the Olympic rowing team after the war if..."

At such times Ellie sensed reluctant feelers reaching out to her, tentative, stiff with disuse—but the feelers never quite made contact and were withdrawn especially fast if Ellie were to ask, however obliquely, about her mother. "A dancer," she was told, "nothing but a dancer."

On Mondays, when her grandmother was driven to the shops in town, Ellie played records on the old phonograph in the attic and imagined her parents waltzing in a misty, romantic ballroom with pink velvet loveseats and rose-entwined pillars. Having no picture of her mother, imagination colored her beautiful, with porcelain skin and long, delicate throat, always smiling up at Papa. Ellie dressed her mother in pale chiffons or floating silks. Papa, of course, always wore uniform because he was brave.

Then one Monday Grossmutter had returned from Trier early with a headache. Still inside the music and the dream, Ellie hadn't heard the car or the heavy tread on the stair—but she couldn't fail to see the pain, quickly followed by anger, on the old lady's face. Ellie shut off the phonograph and waited to be punished, expected to be; only religious music was permitted in the house, and that very seldom. Grossmutter said nothing—but the next time Ellie slipped up to the attic the records had been taken away, and for several weeks Ellie's Monday dreams were pale creatures moving to hazily remembered music. And then the newest governess had arrived.

Ellie liked Miss Nolan, who brought with her a large record collection and encouraged Ellie to borrow at will. Not just waltzes, either. There was something Miss Nolan called boogie-woogie, which Ellie didn't like at all; the porcelain doll and the tin soldier simply would not move to its busy, rambunctious beat. But there were also foxtrots and quicksteps and languorous, slinky tangos which worked quite well if she gave her mother shorter hair and narrower, satiny skirts, if she penciled a thin dark mustache on the mental picture of her father. There was a whole new decor to invent too, different couples on the loveseats, orchid garlands growing up the white pillars.

Yes, Miss Nolan's records gave a new dimension to Mondays.

And now Grossmutter wanted to talk with Miss Nolan.

After dinner.

In the library.

The previous governess, in her haste to pack, had left a jar of hand cream in the bathroom; the one before that left a moth-eaten stole. Ellie couldn't remember what the one before that left behind her, but it must have been something.

Perhaps Miss Nolan would leave her records. . . .

FIVE

RAIN DRUMMED ON THE ABRAMSKY ROOF for many days after the boy's arrival. At first the doctor came morning and evening, then once a day. After that, Felix took Micah at intervals to the clinic, until at last the dressing was removed so that air could finish what care and penicillin had begun. He was left with a jagged scar that ran livid blue from knuckles to wrist, which Anna examined every morning in front of the window, remarking to Felix that it was fading, but slowly.

But still it rained. Every bedraggled dandelion brimmed, every bird bath overflowed; in Ryder Street not a cat ventured so much as a whisker outdoors. Rows of children's galoshes lined the studio entry, umbrellas puddled the linoleum, and the piano was hard put to compete with Madame's voice and the constant gurgle from gutters and downspouts. How to thrust a boy such as the dark one, undernourished and barely healed, into this miserable English autumn?

A problem, said Anna.

Unthinkable, said Felix.

Micah said as little as possible. With returning strength came confusion. These people gave him regular meals and shelter. Why? They demanded he keep warm and clean. Why? They woke him at the same time every morning and sent him to bed after supper whether he was ready to sleep or not. Why? With Da, he'd eaten when there was food, slept only when he was tired.

Strange ways the gaje *have, laddo.*

They rose at seven. Anna, in a robe the color of old bruises (she called it her violet tea gown), pummeled feather mattresses, smoothed white eyelet over them, stood back, hands on hips, and dared them to wrinkle. When every cushion and pillow had been punched into submission she ground the day's supply of coffee, her narrow feet splayed out in first position, her back baton-straight at the draining board as smells of coffee and oranges mingled, as she listened to the morning news and her own catalog of the day's lessons. Her every move was that of the disciplined dancer, wrist turned just so as she sectioned oranges for breakfast, head birdlike, slightly tilted on its column as she reminded Felix to warm the cups, and Micah to "make it your *toilette* before you come to table, boy."

Felix, his hip at its worst in the mornings, spoke in whispers and moved slowly as he built fires in the upstairs grates, coaxing reluctant coals with his breath until the blaze satisfied him, then limping down cellar steps to stoke the ancient boiler. Punctually at eight they sat down to fruit and croissants and cup after cup of steaming coffee.

Micah ate what Anna served, but with caution and some distrust. It was too regular, too carefully arranged, too different. No raviolis, no baked beans spooned up from a can, no shop pies or potato chips. No famines, no sudden feasts.

Breakfast never varied. Coffee with crisp rolls and honey. And fruit. Lunch could be a small slice of salmon with cucumbers, or a veal cutlet with salad, or eggs poached on spinach. And fruit. Dinner was also small, soup and a piece of chicken, or a single crab-stuffed crepe, maybe quiche, always vegetables. And fruit. "Don't gobble, boy. And eat it your apple! You want to grow up with pimples like the . . . nossinks?"—her word for the current crop of youths that nightly roamed the streets, Presley hairdos oiled, pustules freshly squeezed.

Thus, at Anna's lean table, Micah discovered food could be a lingering pleasure, could be more (and less) than a stolen can quickly opened, its contents devoured only to stave off hunger. It could be a ritual, with flowers on the table and a blue knitted cozy on the teapot; it could be a small ceremony which began with a murmured prayer in Russian and ended with another, more personal acknowledgment.

At the end of each meal Felix nodded gravely to his wife.

"Thank you, Anna, that was excellent," and looked at Micah as if waiting.

The boy felt something was expected of him but was not sure what. But as one awkward silence followed another, as Felix smiled encouragement, Micah eventually managed a mumbled "Thanks."

A day or two later it was "Thank you."

A few days more: "Thank you, Mrs. Abramsky."

The couple beamed.

"You may call me Anna," said Anna.

"Except in the studio," Felix warned. "There, it is always Madame. For respect, you understand?"

Micah didn't, but he nodded anyway.

"And I am always Felix—in my shop I have customers, adults. Anna has students. You see the difference?"

Again Micah nodded, trying to grasp the concept of respect as it applied to Anna and the pampered little girls who showed up daily for class, and the equally difficult concept of Felix's customers, for the cluttered repair shop next door seemed to do little business. There were electric kettles, irons, radios, a telly or two, all their insides spread out on a counter; the few items of new stock were dusted, arranged and rearranged by Felix every morning and evening—but when the rare customer asked a price Felix gave it in a subdued murmur and hurriedly advised that it was cheaper by far to fix the old than to buy the new.

"They can't afford it, you know—hand me the screwdriver, Mischa, please—this is not a rich neighborhood."

From time to time he rubbed at his hip. Rain aggravated the old injury, a sliver of shrapnel from the war which was still embedded in his hip joint. "No bigger than a *centime*, Mischa"—but it had ended whatever hopes he'd had for a career in dance. "Not that I had much—I hadn't Anna's flair, didn't want it enough, I suppose, so it was better I go into my father's shop, eh? Learn a different trade?"

When damp spots appeared in the ceilings, quickly followed by sudden plops of rain on the plush overstuffed chairs, Micah was sent running to the attic with saucepans, buckets, even an old chamber pot painted with vermilion plums. Used to such makeshift repairs (the trailer had leaked at every seam), he rummaged in the cellar, then climbed the steep roof with a tarpaulin stout enough to deflect the rain until the roofer arrived—"to make it the fix," Anna said. The drips stopped. After Felix chided him for the danger, the Abramskys agreed, in the privacy of the marshmallow bed, that neither of them could possibly have made the climb. And winter was coming, was it not, with snow to shovel and coal to haul upstairs? And the boy was responding to Felix's nightly reading aloud of the newspaper, was trying to pick out words himself. Such a pity if he left before he'd learned *something* . . . and where, in any case, could he go?

Week slipped into week, and for one reason or another the boy should stay a little longer. The smallest sniffle at breakfast and he must stay indoors where it was warm; lowering clouds in the chimney-masted sky brought on dire predictions of a vicious winter to come.

"Such a climate," Anna mourned, "who knows what to expect? In Paris we always knew..." She spoke often of Paris and sometimes of Russia, where neither she nor Felix had ever been. Though their fathers were born in Leningrad, both Anna and Felix had grown up entirely in the nostalgia-charged atmosphere of White Russian enclaves in Paris, spoke Russian as their first language, French second, and English a distant third.

"Paris weather reports you could believe," she grumbled, "but here is big secret—they don't want we should know."

When an early snowfall (predictably unpredicted) dusted the slate roofs of Ryder Street, Felix took Micah to town and bought him a winter coat and thick flannel shirts. He even helped him build a wardrobe cupboard in the niche under the stairs.

Then Micah knew he was safe. At least for the winter.

Safe, grateful, and happy—except for the nightly dialogues with Da, sometimes with Grandmam and Dui and Farah, for he had accepted, now, that the Abramskys were *gaje*. Not like the English *gaje* with their cool voices and milky tea, their crumpets and their ever-so-polite disdain. These Russians were different, but *gaje* just the same, so the comforts he now enjoyed were paid for in a hundred little guilts:

Grandmam: *Oh Micah, such shoes pinching your feet all day, it's not natural* . . .

Dui: *Think you've got a soft berth, don't you, little brother—but just wait* . . .

Farah: *They'd give you money if you asked them, Micah* . . .

Da: *Comfort! See how quick you're sucked in, laddo? Next thing you know it'll be school, a teacher telling you when to talk and when to shut your trap, when you can take a pee and when you have to hold it . . . one soft day after another, now't in front of you but the same again.*

In this, Da was wrong. Days might be all alike but they were far from soft. Life at the studio was not a free ride. He was expected to do his share. He cleaned windows, brought coal from the cellar, peeled potatoes, swept the endless dust of the studio floor. He even did the marketing, after Felix had taught him, in a brief, stern interview, that what he brought back must come in a shopping bag with a receipt, not fished out of his back pocket with a sly smile and a fruitless wait for approval.

"We are not rich, Mischa—but we are not so poor we must steal. You will go back and pay for the butter, yes?—for how else can we eat it? So perhaps the grocer did not see you take it—but his profits will be down and there will be a little less for his children."

Felix's argument carried less weight than a feather. Micah did not like the grocer's children. They only knew two things. They went to school and they played. He did not go to school; he had not played since the days of the *kumpania*. Now he didn't remember how. He didn't, in fact, like any of the kids in the street. After the first few weeks, in which he gathered in unwanted marbles and kites faster than he could find places to hide them, he gave up on kids completely. They were babies, too easily conned to be worth the effort.

But he did like Felix, and the look on his face when he made Micah return the butter was forbidding, reminding him that Felix was not Da, that Abramsky standards were different, were *gajo*, and that if he wanted to stay in this world, at least until better weather arrived, he would have to adapt—or appear to adapt—to its ways, puzzling as they often were.

He wanted to stay—where else could he go?—and so he did the best he could.

Except, perhaps, in Anna's dance class.

It was the single bone of contention, a torture to which Madame (in class it was *never* Anna) daily submitted bone and muscle. For the Abramskys a dance workout was as much a part of the day as eating, sleeping, brushing teeth. Even Felix, whose formal training had ended with the sliver of shrapnel, still made a daily, painful barre. Anna put herself through two.

Micah was expected to do the same.

"I'll not wear them things," he said bluntly when presented with tights and a pair of Felix's old ballet shoes. "What d'you think I am, a bleedin' fairy?"

"Posture," Felix insisted mildly. "A straight back is no disgrace. You see the photographs here? Of Anna? Of our old friends? Are they not a pleasure to look at?" A sweep of his arm took in walls covered with faded sepia prints of men and women in costume, limbs flung out in every direction, but always with grace, with style.

"Anna was one of *them?*" Micah said. "But they're young, they're fancy . . . they look—" It seemed to Felix that he hunted for a new word. Ethereal? Magical? No way to tell.

But Felix saw his awe, then his quick stocktaking of Anna, who was warming up in a shapeless old sweater and darned leotard, a ratty sweat towel draped around her shoulders and her hair stretched into a misshapen bun from which wisps already flew damp and untidy down her back. The veins in her neck were tight blue ropes, unbelievably delicate, terrifyingly strong in their effort to conquer time.

For a second he saw her through the boy's eyes.

He was shocked.

Where had it gone, all that life? that gaiety? Not a trace was left, everything bolted down under tight-held griefs and the stamp of a powerful personality. Each feature stood out separate, sharp. Strong nose and chin, the fierce flash of deep blue eyes as she forced herself through slow, tightly controlled *développés,* muscle overlying bone like illustrations in a medical text. The years had overtaken and darkened every soft plane of cheek and jaw, had thinned and faded her hair . . .

He closed his eyes and a picture, sharp as yesterday, sprang to mind. Anna in the Paris studio all those years ago, happy, flushed with her first success, a glittering review in the Paris *Soir* for her last-minute Odile of the previous night, a stand-in's triumph. Watching with Felix was the baby Sasha, his dimpled fists echoing the piano's beat, his blue eyes alight as he watched his mother dance.

Anna. Mercury and roses she was then, all quick smiles and confidence, steel in her step and hope in her eyes despite the new war that threatened her career and would ultimately lay siege to her sanity.

They'd been married just three years.

It was spring. A Parisian sun from the studio window shone full on her, turning her feet in satin toe shoes to pink and pointed fishes that leapt, darted, flashed in the sun—turned her light brown hair to bronze, the sweat of her forehead to gilded beads. Reflected in the mirrored walls there were four Annas, all dipped in gold, in happiness. She'd blazed with it then, moving with ease and innocence through the closing exercises of class.

The orchestra leader, White Russian like themselves, had just stopped by, bearing Beluga caviar and a bottle of genuine Crimean vodka to celebrate the day. There was talk of a party for her at some vague time after the tour. Filled with the future, she swept the conductor a deep curtsy, the arch of her neck a miracle of line, a magical mix of pride and humility.

Then her glance touched Felix and Sasha in the mirror, drew them inside her joy, warmed them with it. So much warmth then...

He sighed.

Was it a month later? a year? when a random bullet exploded Sasha's cherub face?

Later, but not much, when Hans von Reiker, proud young German of the occupation force, saw in Anna what Felix himself had seen, and fell foolishly, dangerously in love?

When Anna, whose grief and disgust could be neither controlled nor hidden, fought back at the Nazis who'd killed her baby? Fought them through the silly surrogate of the young soldier, insulted him, flung her contempt in his face, raved at him, riddled his pride with words no less explosive than the bomb that killed Sasha?

When she spat on his immaculate uniform, his incredulous patrician face?

And when Hans von Reiker, mad with lust and shame and rejection, took his revenge, took her body in rape and left his seed to grow in her belly?

Von Reiker's seed.

His hated Nazi seed.

Whom someone somewhere had named Gabriella. Whom Anna could not love, would not try to love, would not *see* through the grief that blinded her.

And now she was all flint, this Anna.

Beside him the strange boy stirred, reaching for electrician's tape and copper wire with quick Gypsy fingers.

"First you will dance," Felix said softly, *"then* you may help me in the shop." And once again he pressed tights and slippers on the child.

Soft black eyes hardened to jet. Young shoulders squared. "It's sissy. I wain't."

"Won't," he corrected gently. "You won't—but I think you *will*, Mischa. Each day you will dance a little for Anna, yes?"

So each day he danced a little—and not so little either, it seemed to him. At first his ankles wouldn't turn out, then his knees, then his hips. "It hurts," he complained, even before Anna tapped him smartly across the buttocks with her cane and instructed him to "Pull the hips *under,* boy, *under,* get the shoulders back and pick up the head. No-no-no-no-no! Why do you watching the feet? Will they run away? Look to the mirror. See the spine, see how you are taller, straighter—"

And he was! Da wouldn't have known him. He was clean, his hair had sheen, had health; his eyes sparkled and flashed; from rigorous brushing, his teeth, always even, dazzled him in the mirror—but the mirror was a cold imitation of Da, who'd thumped his shoulder, said *Whatcher, cockie, you're a right little smasher,* when he was pleased.

"My legs hurt—" he said to Anna.

"But of course! They will hurt tomorrow and next week also. Classical dance is unnatural, but beautiful, no? If Felix with his poor hip can do it, why not you, a healthy young boy? If it was easy *anybody* could do it— then what would be the point?"

She made him work in front of her at the barre, so no fault of posture could be hidden, no letdown in effort go unseen.

Not until muscles jumped and quivered like violin strings and they both dripped sweat onto the boards did she give the order for closing exercises—always with an air of triumph.

"Is not so sissy after all, eh?" she panted. "Tell, boy! Is it sissy? Or no?"

Maybe no, but he still didn't like it.

When she announced that he would not, perhaps, shame her, he was put in a class with her Beginning Boys, three young hopefuls older than Micah, and bigger.

He didn't like them either. These boys didn't play; they didn't do anything but dance. It was all they talked about. Who danced which role at the Wells last season, who had the best *cabrioles,* the best elevation, the best *tours en l'air.* Micah, on fire to be done with it, to get into the store with the man Felix who called him Mischa, who showed him electric stuff that *worked,* was bored blind by dancers' talk, but he absorbed it through every sweaty, wide-open pore and every twanging tendon, just as he absorbed fruit and furniture-polish smells from the upstairs flat and the clean, wool and shaving-cream smell of Felix when they worked together at the long bench in the shop.

As weeks became months he began to lose his fear of Anna, even sometimes to like her, but he did wonder why she never called him Micah or even Mischa, only "boy."

And why, since that first day when he was sick, she'd never touched him again; he was clean all the time now because she made him bathe morning and night, so it wasn't that.

Felix touched. "Careful, Mischa," he'd say sometimes in the shop, a companionable hand on Micah's shoulder. "If you connect this wire with that you can blow us into the next century."

"Where the 'ell's that?"

"Where the hell is that," came the careful correction. "But better don't say 'hell.' 'Century' is not a place, it is one hundred years."

He tried out "century," found it to his taste, and repeated it. When business was slow Felix showed Micah an invoice, stuck a pencil in his fist, guided it to copy words on scraps of wrapping paper. Iron, boy, delivery, wire, set, less 10% discount, screw, plug, driver, truck. From there a short step to connect: truck driver, screwdriver, delivery boy, fire irons. One day the quantum leap to "wireless set." Mistakes were corrected but never ridiculed. He was praised. Felix didn't tell him the street kids whom Micah so despised knew such words even before they began school because their parents had read to them endlessly, night after night from babyhood. What Felix did do was read adult novels aloud, a chapter each evening, as if it was a normal facet of family life. As a result Micah learned a lot more new words and how to write them down in the blue exercise book Felix gave him at Christmas. It was the first book he'd ever had and he put it under his pillow at night for safekeeping, wondering if they'd let him take it with him when he left. *When he left.* He wondered about that too, he wondered a lot about that. And worried. Da was right. Comfort did suck you in. The wind had soft edges on it now, rain came only in showers, and people were setting out pots of red tulips on their windowsills.

One blue and gold morning in May, Anna threw open every window in the flat to let the winter out, then saw Micah watching her and went around closing them all again, saying that it was perhaps not quite warm enough yet. In a day or so, maybe, but not quite yet.

Afraid, Micah kept out of their way until Felix ran him to earth in the broom closet.

"Anna missed you in class, Mischa. I missed you also in the shop. You like it here in the dark?"

He shrugged and closed his face up tight. "It's okay."

"You don't like the sunshine?"

"It's okay."

"Are you sulking?"

"No."

"Unhappy?"

"No."

"Well then." Felix sat down next to him on the floor. "We were talking, Anna and I. We are thinking you will want to leave us now the weather is better..."

Here it came. "Aye, well..." He pressed his back against the closet, felt the shelter of its four walls around him, four more walls in the corridor, and beyond that the four walls of the flat. Threads of Anna Abramsky's voice reached up to him from the studio where her Advanced Girls rehearsed a *pas de quatre* for next week's recital. His bed was downstairs too, fresh sheets on it every week, clean and safe, no lying awake listening for dogs or farmers or coppers, no worry about tomorrow's meals. And next to him this man who didn't get drunk, didn't hit him.

"I think you have been happy here?" Felix's voice had a catch in it, as if he too were holding his breath.

"It's okay," he said, turning away from the intensity in the man's face.

Just look at 'em, Micah, trapped in their nothing little lives and their crummy little houses—but their lives were *not* nothing and the flat wasn't crummy and he wanted to be trapped, wanted—

"Please look at Felix."

Something in the voice compelled, made him turn and look.

Felix reached out, his fingers white, almost frail against the brown of Micah's hand. "You have given us pleasure," he said simply. "Before you came we lived only in the past, Anna and I. We would be happy if you would stay as long as you wish."

See the trap, laddo? Remember the rabbits on the moor? They never saw the traps neither, but we had 'em for dinner just the same, right?

Downstairs, Anna Abramsky's voice berated her Advanced Girls. "No-no-no-no-no! Pick up the chin, present yourselves! What do you want? To look like ze *nossinks?*"

"Well, Mischa? You will stay?" Felix said quietly.

The four Advanced Girls were giving Madame their deep, fluid *révérences* when Felix slipped into the studio and caught Anna's eye. They exchanged brief nods, and to the astonishment of the girls Anna paused after making her answering *révérence,* set her cane aside, and smiled upon them:

"You were very fine today, ladies. Your recital will not, I think, bring shame on my studio."

To Felix she spoke Russian, saying simply, "Is good then, the boy stays. Now you will not again carry the coals and make the fires—"

Felix sighed. "Oh, Anna..."

"—and now we open the windows, let the winter go. Did you remind him, the boy, that he has not yet made barre today?"

"No..."

"Naturally not—you make him soft. Thank God you both have Anna."

"Yes, my angel—and perhaps, if you think about it, you might call him something besides 'boy'?"

But she was busy now with the sweat towel. There was the rosin pan to top up for the *pas de deux* class—"You'd think it was flour the way they throw it about."

At the door, Felix smiled at her. "Very well then. But *I* shall call him Mischa."

"You already do," she shot back.

He hummed as he climbed the stair. Anna. How unpredictable she thought herself. And how happy she'd made him. Now Mischa would stay, a lump of rough clay for him to shape, to teach, to make civilized. Already the boy began sometimes to speak as he and Anna spoke, to remember his manners, to wash without Anna's reminding him. Soon the people of Ryder Street would call Mischa what they now called the Abramskys. Foreigner. But such an exotic mix of foreigner, this Mischa!

SIX

*B*ORED, HUNGRY FOR DRAMA, Ellie was tempted briefly to see it as a biblical scene: *Outraged Populace Stones Transgressor*—but of course it was just Lotte's pimply son throwing a few rocks at her, which bruised her legs and her ego but stiffened her pride.

Until then her twelfth summer was as dull and interminable as the other eleven had been. Then suddenly, under a sizzling noon sun, evasions and doubts that had puzzled her for years took form, became questions easily answered by a single revelation.

By one brutal word.

The questions:

Why, despite obvious and growing declines in the von Reiker fortunes, could she not attend the local academy, which was surely less costly than a governess?

Why, when she defied Grossmutter's specific rules and became friends with the vicar's daughter, did the girl's mother withdraw her daughter's invitation to tea and make it clear that no more would be issued? And when Ellie, close to tears, hung up the phone, why did Grossmutter, who should have been angry with her, gather her into a cologne-and-camphor embrace—*and apologize?* "Ah, you poor child, how sorry I am . . ."

Why, now she was considered mature enough to take a hand in managing staff and vineyard, could she not go even so far as the village without a governess in tow?

Why, though von Reikers had clearly been prominent among local gentry, were they never asked out *anywhere?* (And why had the earthy Miss Nolan once said, for no apparent reason: "When the proud fall they fall with a wallop"?)

And why did the villagers, who deferred to Grossmutter as the local grande dame, show Ellie only casual courtesy and knowing smiles and barely concealed pity?

Why, on the lawyer's monthly visits, was Ellie included on vineyard matters and pointedly excluded later, sent outdoors on one trumped-up excuse after another?

Why were there no pictures of her mother in the house?

Ernst, Lotte's teenage son, answered these questions and more when he threw rocks at her and called her the *name.*

She'd never liked Ernst. He had thick lips and shifty eyes and the sullen anger of early teens; his interests seemed to be motorcycles, comic books, and girls. Whenever possible, Ellie avoided him.

It was a Monday and therefore free of Grossmutter, but by noon it was miserably hot, and Ellie escaped the closed heat of the house to watch field hands tend the vines.

The row nearest to her suddenly rustled and parted. Ernst.

"Want to play doctor?" he said, leering at her from a screen of grape leaves.

"You're disgusting," she said firmly. "Go away."

"The village girls talk to me."

"I am not one of them."

Echoes of her grandmother's tone were unmistakable in her own, and she was obliquely grateful. With such as Ernst it was the only way. She sauntered off, by design taking the path that would bring her toward old Heinz, the foreman.

Ernst followed close behind her.

"Too good for the likes of me, aren't you?"

She walked on.

"Think you're lady of the manor, don't you?"

And on.

"Cheap ale in a champagne bottle."

And on—but she was listening now. Ernst's words no longer sounded like his own. They were parrot talk, village talk.

"That's what they call you—and that's not all they call you, either."

She knew she should ignore him. *Never listen to servants' gossip, Gabriella.*

"If they're like *you* I don't care what they call me." But she did care, she did, her body walking calmly, proudly—but every nerve in it quivering and waiting.

"My folks were married proper," he said, his breath hot on the back of her neck. "Yours weren't!"

She stopped, felt the blood leave her face, felt herself begin to tremble as her palm aimed a ringing slap at his cheek. He backed off, his dirty paws scrabbling hastily at the dust.

The first rock caught her sharp and hard on the shoulder.

And now Ernst, his rage pumped up, was shouting.

"Just a bastard in fancy clothes!"

Rocks flicked her neck, her leg, her face—and with each rock the word.

Bastard.

Then the foreman was shouting too, but at Ernst, who fired one last "Bastard!" at her before the foreman kicked his behind and sent him running for cover.

"You're not hurt, miss?" It was Heinz, anxious beside her.

"Of course not," she said, frost in her voice, nothing in her mind but the word, the word...

"Maybe you should go to the house?"

She turned to go, the long rows of vines and the workers' faces a blur. She knew what the word meant, had looked it up with the same curiosity she'd looked up "sex" and "fornicate" and "male organs"—which, until the dictionary proved otherwise, she'd thought were baritone versions of what the minister's wife played at Sunday services. Years ago she'd seen the naked white behind of a field hand pumping on top of a woman they called Amy Anytime, who had no husband and four children. She told Grossmutter, who grew very red and puffed out her cheeks. "Outdoors? In daylight?" After a moment's reflection she added: "Peasants are not far removed from animals," and Ellie was left with the assumption that "better people" (like von Reikers) did something vaguely similar but behind locked doors and in the dark, always under special license from the clergy.

Growing older, reading more, she realized that it was the Grossmutters in their rural backwaters, living on inherited wealth and a dogmatic belief in their position of privilege, who were the anachronisms, the fossils doomed to die out. Cities, she believed, were different. Everybody there was equal—and across the Atlantic an entire nation grew and prospered under the very same premise. But she'd grown up under Grossmutter's heavy thumb—and the name Ernst called her jolted every precept that the parade of governesses had been hired to reinforce.

Ernst *couldn't* be right. She was a von Reiker.

But doubts, once entertained, swarmed over her. Papa was of course killed at the Russian front, that much was certain. Yellowed news clippings and Grossmutter's unbounded adoration for Hans von Reiker were genuine. The *implication*—which had never been denied—was that Mama was killed in the war...but if so, if all her carefully constructed scenarios were true, where were the wedding pictures? Surely Grossmutter, steeped in tradition, would have kept such things? So where were they?

Lotte. Lotte would know, she knew everything—

"You know what Ernst called me?" she demanded, the cook a bulky bastion that must somehow be stormed, but who was now scrubbing at an already clean kitchen table as if her job, her life, depended on it.

"I know. Heinz just called."

"Well?"

Lotte looked down, her beefy arms working. "My Ernst and his big mouth, if I've told him once I've told him a dozen—"

"But is it true?"

Lotte straightened, wrung out a dishcloth with trembling fists. "I only know what the old lady told me, and she told me only what I had to know. I nursed you."

Lotte, this fat, kindly woman—now a frightened one—had *nursed* her? "Then where was my mother?"

Lotte folded the dishcloth corner to corner before opening it up again to wring and wring and wring. It seemed a long time before she dropped into a kitchen chair and rocked back and forth, hugging herself with red, hardworking arms.

"Me and the boy, we're done for now. She'll send us packing for sure. They all heard what Ernst called you, *she'll* hear, the old witch...Fifteen years I've worked here, fifteen—"

"But my mother? Why didn't she nurse me herself?"

A spasm of remembered hate flushed the wide face. "She didn't have time, did she? Evening it was, a taxi roars up the drive and I think it's

Master Hans home on leave. But no, this young woman jumps out—crazy, she looked, frantic. I'd hardly opened the door before she pushed you at me. Pushed!—and you not two days old, with no clothes but what you had on your back and the midwife's bracelet still on your wrist. You were perfect, perfect . . . an ugly baby, deformed maybe, that I could have understood, but no . . . And even then, what kind of mother—"

"But Grossmutter—what did *she* say, what—"

"She was in her room, just sitting. I took you up, showed you to her. 'Look what a woman just left,' I says to her, 'look what—' She nods at me like she was expecting it. 'Yes,' she says, 'it's Master Hans's daughter.' I was flabbergasted. 'I didn't know he was married!' I says. 'Nevertheless, it's his daughter. She'll be staying here. There's a layette in the bureau drawer. Feed her, will you?' Just like that. 'Feed her, will you?' And me with Ernst hardly toddling, still at the breast . . ." And now Lotte began to cry, to dab at her round red face with the dishcloth. "It's been a good job, this, not many places let you bring a kid into service . . ."

"The midwife's bracelet." Ellie's voice seemed to be not quite her own. "What did it say?"

Lotte's eyes filled again with tears. "I can't read, can I? I can't do much of anything except cook."

Ellie knew she should comfort Lotte, but there was no time and she had nothing to give. There was a gaping hole in her pride which must be patched over quickly, quickly—A new picture of her mother, previously misted with ballrooms and soft music and orchid bowers, hazy with Grossmutter's patrician evasions, sprang suddenly to life. It was a picture she didn't want to look at, but then it was too late because the front door was opening and Grossmutter, packages dangling from her wrist, was in the hall, composed and corseted against this scorching afternoon.

"Take the shopping, Gabriella, there's more in the car—"

But Heinz was following her grandmother inside, his dull eyes unusually bright with interest.

"—how *dare* you use the front door? Go around to—"

But now Grossmutter was reading his eyes, too. "What's happened?"

"Not to trouble you, Frau von Reiker, but I'd like a word?"

When they emerged from the library—it would have to be the library, for this was a serious, if short, report—Grossmutter's handkerchief was pressed to her temples as she motioned Ellie to follow her upstairs, to draw the heavy bedroom curtains, to bring cologne, to close the door, to help her to the bed.

Outside, elms scratched summer-dry branches at the window.

"You know what it means, this word Ernst called you?"

"Yes."

"Then you know it all. I would have preferred you did not...I tried, I kept you away from people, from wagging tongues..."

"Yes, Grossmutter." She swallowed, all the time scrambling to patch over the holes Ernst's word had punched through her carefully woven tapestries, trying to form comforting new images based on novels she'd read, dreams she'd dreamed, music she'd heard from Miss Nolan's records. So perhaps she was a love child born of a tender passion—a young virgin meets a dashing officer, war exploding all around them, no time for marriage, then the Russian front..."Why didn't they marry?"

"She was married already."

Married? To someone not Papa..."But they loved each other, my father and mother?" Say yes, please say yes...don't even think of women like Amy Anytime...

Grossmutter's eyes closed as the lines around her mouth deepened. Her hands, white and well tended on the coverlet, tightened into fists. "She didn't want him, didn't want my son, that's why he went to the front, that's why...She didn't want you either, she dropped you off like a package..."

New, terrible facts, one after another, no way to fit them into any scenario she wanted to believe in. "But she must have said *something*, given some reason!"

Grossmutter's eyes flew open, fixed Ellie with an intense, burning fury before shifting, settling somewhere far into the past where Ellie could not follow. "I told you...she was a dancer, a performer. Such women say *anything*, make *any* excuse—"

She reached for Ellie's hand, her grip paper-dry and strong, her cologne heavy in the closed room.

"She's alive, my mother?"

Grossmutter's laugh, frightening in its brevity, cut the atmosphere. "Alive and prospering, living in England. Teaching dance, the lawyers tell me."

"She knows where I am?"

A suspicion of tears misted Grossmutter's eyes, and once again Ellie felt fragile filaments reaching out to her, trying...but they were too weak, too damaged by years of silence. "She knows. Now leave me, Gabriella, my head is bursting..."

As Ellie twisted the massive oak doorknob the old lady's voice stopped her. *"Your father was good—"*

But she couldn't finish, and for the first time Ellie felt something of what her birth must have done to the fiercely moral woman, the shame wreaked on this respected relic of an old and privileged family—who somehow must explain away a bastard because she would not place it in an orphanage or farm it out to a distant village where no one would know. She could easily have done that. Instead, for her son's sake, she'd made recluses of herself and of her grandchild.

Ellie had never loved her, seldom liked her, and at times hated her, but on impulse she moved to the bed and took the rigid woman in her arms —but then she too was inhibited, her words inadequate, not at all what she wanted to say. "I *wish* your head didn't ache..."

Across the hall Grossmutter slept. Ellie could not. Her room stifled her. The day's shock had gone and she waited for a shame like her grandmother's to fill up the space. None came—only anger against the dancer who'd rejected her like an unwanted role. Anger as hot and intense as the night.

Midnight already and no breeze yet off the river, the day's events drawing conclusions she could at last confront. Always she'd felt herself a prisoner, but she saw now that her jailer was more a prisoner than she, that the isolation had been for Ellie's benefit, not Grossmutter's, who'd sought only to make her a von Reiker, to give her pride to match the name. But she *had* pride, built-in and all her own—and Ernst's taunt, more painful than his stones, had released it.

All her life she'd obeyed, maintained von Reiker standards. Now she could make her own. She didn't have to be an Amy Anytime who had no standards at all—nor did she have to be like that distant mother, who apparently had none either.

She'd never before been to the secret little waterhole at night, only on sunlit afternoons, and then just to sit in willow shade and dabble her feet in deep olive-green waters.

Tonight, in her long nightgown of fine lawn, she slipped out quietly, the Mosel a cool and comforting magnet. The oldest willow offered the deepest shadow, privacy even from the moon. She ran her hands over cotton-covered hips and thighs, stretched herself tall, and slowly pulled at a ribbon the innocent pink of wild roses. The gown fell to her feet and she stepped out, for the first time in her life naked and alone *outdoors!*

The water welcomed her, cooled her, lapped at her knees and her waist and the new buds of breasts. She caught her breath and submerged, swam to the moon-silvered center of the pool, floated on her back and watched moonlight fan out her hair, glance off slender legs and lap at her shoulders, caress pale skin and long fingers, cool everything but the hard flame of anger that she thought now would burn until the day she died.

Back in her room she took out the journal with its little gold lock that Grossmutter had given her last Christmas: At one time, she'd said, young ladies of the gentry all had one, a place to record their private thoughts. Ellie had pushed it to the back of her desk then, thinking with scorn that *all* thoughts were private. But now she was no longer of the gentry. The bastard found a thought to record that the young lady could never have set down in writing:

Tonight I swam naked. I liked it.

SEVEN

ON RYDER STREET, ONE YEAR DRIFTED almost unnoticed into the next, and still the Gypsy stayed on with the Abramskys. There was no more talk of leaving; indeed, there was talk of what he'd do "when he grew up," a concept that gave him endless (but always concealed) amusement. Hadn't he always been grown-up? His world was filled now with the concerns of the Abramskys, which more and more became his own.

In the store he learned from Felix how to fix this and that, but mostly he learned how to sell. By recall, it seemed. With Da, the main aim in life had been to con the *gaje,* so selling them appliances they didn't know they needed was simply an extension of his early training. In no time at all the shop's first meager inventory was sold out. Now, after four years, new stocks were ordered monthly, a task that seemed to fall naturally to Mischa, once he'd learned how to read quickly, without moving his lips, without his finger leading the way across the page. Customers and suppliers all called him Michael. They said he had a way with him. If that way had undertones of flattery—well, they all needed a bit of that, didn't they?

Even Hamish Froggatt, who, it was said, had been a genius before the bottle got him. Hamish, when he was sober enough to drive his yellow van, sold Felix motor-driven novelties which he designed and manufactured in his father's old plant with a staff of two, which became one, which, as his fortunes declined, became Hamish alone. Sometimes the gadgets worked. Hamish had ginger hair, florid cheeks, and a boozy purple nose. Though Mischa wouldn't have admitted it to Felix and Anna (who still knew little about the *kumpania,* not much more about Da, and nothing at all about Da's belt), he despised and hated the elderly Scot. He hated his whiskey smell, his belligerence in drink, and his remorse after it.

"Sorry if I hurt your feelings yesterday, Michael. A drop too much and it makes a monkey of me every time. You'll keep it quiet, eh? I wouldn't want Felix Ab to know, he's a good wee customer, indeed he is—"

Mischa could have finished the sentence for him, but in accents somewhat to the south of Edinburgh. *I don't know what makes me do it, old cock, but I'll never do it again, your da's sorry, honest.* Tears rolled down Hamish's red-veined cheeks just as slowly, just as pitifully as they'd run down Da's.

But Hamish Froggatt didn't wear a belt and he had other uses besides, so Mischa always gave him his sweetest, most ingenuous smile before agreeing, almost in passing, that it would be bad all around if Felix knew Hamish had called him a bloody Russkie and himself, Mischa, a dago. With a smile marginally less sweet he handed over an invoice (for Felix's sake only lightly padded) for defective merchandise returned.

Hamish squinted at it, sighed whiskey breath across the counter, and wrote a refund check in his unsteady, sprawling hand. When the yellow van lurched off around the corner of Ryder Street Mischa watched it go with the old mix of triumph and contempt he'd felt when he and Da had pulled off an easy scam.

He said nothing about Hamish's name-calling. It was only charity on Felix's part that kept the Scot on the list of suppliers now; he would perhaps have welcomed the excuse to strike him off it.

"If the man were not such a sorry case...so foolish, so useless, his gadgets..." Felix sighed. "Tell me, what do people want with electric cocktail shakers, with teakettles that whistle 'Loch Lomond'?"

"They buy them," Mischa reminded him. "People want something different, something the neighbors don't have—even if it doesn't always work."

Again Felix shook his head in distress, the silver-blond hair more than ever a halo. "Poor Hamish, the education, the promise, the future that could have been his. It wasn't always kitchen gadgets with him, you know."

"He's a fool."

"We cannot judge, Mischa. Perhaps if his wife had not divorced him—"

—then he might have killed her.

The thought rushed at Mischa out of nowhere. Uncertain what prompted it, unwilling to lift the stone and remember the thing crawling under it, he pushed it firmly away.

"Hamish is a fool," he said again. "He's letting everything go, the business, that house..."

He still remembered his first sight of Greenlings. A good customer, more irked than most at a new mixer that wouldn't mix, had demanded instant replacement. Felix sent Mischa to get it. It had been a Saturday.

"If Hamish isn't at the factory, go to the house. You take the number eleven bus and tell them to put you off at Greenlings. Everybody knows where it is."

Hamish's factory looked as if no one had been there for a week. Windows boarded up, notes marked "Urgent" thumbtacked to the door, mail from several days poking out of the letterbox.

So it was the number eleven bus. Mischa didn't mind. He'd not been with the Abramskys very long then, and still harbored the notion that if he showed up late for Anna's evening class he could perhaps avoid it altogether.

The bus climbed windswept reaches above the town to hills that rolled out a soft, sunlit green quilt for as far as he could see. The bus set him down at massive iron gates which sagged open on broken, rusted hinges. A lopsided sign, also rusty, said: PRIVATE PROPERTY—NO ADMITTANCE. Mischa hesitated. He did not yet read well, but these were words he'd known all his life; he could pick out their shapes whether machine-stenciled on wood or hand-lettered on cardboard.

Private property.

The words were shadowed with Da's scowl, haunted by echoes of Da's voice, by the many times they'd been ordered to leave by farmers, police, gamekeepers, self-appointed busybodies...

"Off it, Gyppos! Get away home with you—you know you're not allowed on private land."

They'd always left meekly enough, Da flashing his smile and tipping his hat to the farmer but scoffing afterwards to Micah:

Private property! That's all a gajo *ever thinks about, laddo. His house and his land and his money.*

So private property was *gajo,* was forbidden almost before he knew what it was—maybe that's why he'd always wanted some of it. He'd wanted a lot of things then. Blankets, regular meals, toffees in a tin, maybe a bicycle. All of which he now had, thanks to the Abramskys. Except "private property." And how shocked he'd been to discover they had none, that every month they must pay rent for shop and studio.

"It's not yours?" he'd asked.

"Why Mischa, how could we ever buy all this?" Felix had spread his arms wide as though the tiny flat and its surroundings were vast holdings impossible for a person to own.

Yet a Hamish Froggatt, a drunk and a bigot, could call these rolling hills his own, this driveway that had no end, these walled grounds, these elms and beeches and chestnuts and larches grouped in protective, shadowed groves.

He'd followed a gently curving driveway for five full minutes before the house appeared in front of him, mellow and stately under a late sun. Many windows, leaded and deep-set, looked out from gray stone walls; fingers of ivy reached up over doorways and windowsills, every sharp corner softened by rampant, vigorous green.

Wisteria and honeysuckle battled for growing room over a white-painted gazebo to his right; behind it, willows hung cool green curtains over an overgrown lily pond. The driveway swept into a circle of the same gray stone as the house, gracious and welcoming for those who belonged, intimidating for those who did not.

Staring, he could almost feel himself shrink. This house diminished him, laughed at him, seemed to mock at whatever new pretensions had been forming.

Greenlings.

Hamish Froggatt's private property.

And Felix and Anna Abramsky, who'd given a sick and starving stranger the clothes off their backs and meat off their table, they lived in a little flat that until today had seemed a paradise of warmth and plenty. He thought of Felix limping from workbench to counter at the beck and call of every customer with cash to spend; of Anna, tired and dripping with sweat, molding a score of bored little nossinks into creatures with some claim to grace and beauty. Day after day, no end in sight, until they'd both be too old to serve, to cajole, to insist.

Too old to sweat.

Thinking of the two of them, he no longer felt small. He felt angry, shaken with a diffuse, unfocused rage at the injustice of it. He was almost pleased when a closer look at the house showed traces of neglect that had at first escaped him. Grime dulled the leaded windowpanes, spurge and dandelion clotted the driveway's gray stones, and the gazebo's white paint was peeling under the onslaught of weather and overgrown vines.

Hamish Froggatt had all this and was letting it rot. More than ever Mischa despised him, knew him for a fool.

He was sprawled on a bench in the vegetable garden, unshaven, unwashed, as unkempt as his property. Around him, empty bottles and the remains of a meal. He was more or less sober, rubbing his eyes and squinting at the sun.

"What d'you want?"

"Felix sent a note."

Groaning, Hamish read it. "A man can't even go on a decent bender ... You'll be a good lad and make a cup of tea to wake me up, eh? No woman around—treacherous buggers, women. Never there when you need 'em..."

Mischa was halfway to the kitchen when he remembered Da, recalled making his sober-up coffee in the mornings, his tea in the afternoons—and God help him if he forgot to stir raspberry jam in it the way Da liked it. He stopped, turned back to Hamish Froggatt. "I don't have time," he said. "Felix is waiting."

"You're a lying little sod!"

"Just fix the plug and I'll be on my way."

Grunts, grumbles, and whines, but the Scot heaved himself to his feet and lumbered into the house for a screwdriver. Mischa followed, finding the same disorder in every well-proportioned room. Brocade curtains tied back with bits of string, dirty cups and plates everywhere, overflowing ashtrays, every elegant piece of furniture fingermarked and cluttered. Lacing the dining-room ceiling, cobwebs radiated out from chandelier to walnut paneling, every fragile loop sagging with dust.

Behind him Hamish Froggatt rummaged through desk drawers and kitchen cupboards, chaos always in his wake. "You're thinking it's a mess, right? Can't find things—can't even find a woman to come in and work

... but when a wife takes off after thirty years, what's a man to do, eh?"

He could push a broom, move a duster, wash a cup maybe...

Before he left, Mischa paused in the driveway for a last intent look at Hamish Froggatt's private property.

The sun was almost down. In the center of the circular drive a single huge oak spread the dark green shade of summer's ending. Weeds and tall grass drooped parched and amber in its shadow. Thoughtfully, he reached down and uprooted a clump of dandelion.

Its pungent smell was still on his hands when he wrapped them around the barre in Anna's deserted, echoing studio.

"Hurry, boy, we do the barre quick before we go to center, yes? After, we eat."

"Yes, Madame."

"Very well then. *Pliés,* if you please. AND!"

He'd been back to Hamish Froggatt's house often since, and always the decline was deeper. In his mind he had repainted it a dozen times. In his mind the windows of Greenlings shone, its chandeliers blazed, its furniture gleamed under coat on coat of wax, its lawns rolled smooth and green down to iron gates that had been rehung and repainted and were always and forever locked. In his mind, the sign: PRIVATE PROPERTY— NO ADMITTANCE was new and forever fresh.

And each year imagination painted the sign just a little larger, a little more impressive.

The boy is a sponge, Felix thought, stacking books to return to the library, checking the titles against the list in Mischa's bold, oddly European handwriting.

In the four years since the Gypsy came to them there had been many such trips, many questions to Felix in the quiet evening hours after they'd closed the shop and studio.

He learned fast, disquietingly so, but to Felix it seemed that it was not a hunger for knowledge that drove this complex Mischa. There was aggression to his learning, urgency, as though he must quickly fill up a mysterious gap before it pulled him inside it. He grabbed up knowledge in indiscriminate chunks, assimilated it, and moved on to something else.

In the process, many passions had taken fire, consumed themselves, and eventually died of a surfeit of knowing.

Elephants had started it. That first summer Felix and Anna had taken him to the zoo.

"What's the 'ell's that?" Mischa demanded as the wrinkled mountain lifted its gray trunk, trumpeting rage and frustration into the hot afternoon.

"An elephant—but I thought you'd know," Felix said, not without a touch of malice as he accepted ice-cream cones from a passing vendor. "It's from India, certainly you remember India?"

Anna laughed, but the boy, characteristically, did not. Felix had never heard him laugh.

If they'd expected to shame him with the old lie about India they were wrong. The dark flush in his cheeks was excitement. He'd lied easiy and often then, and with great charm. His rare smile was never so soft, so piercingly angelic as when he spun lies for the gullible children of Ryder Street.

"I'll bet he's not ascared of now't, that elephant."

"Nothing, he's frightened of nothing," Felix corrected. "But you mean 'anything.'" His explanation of double negatives was absorbed as fast, as smoothly as the vanilla ice cream.

A week later, after a trip to the children's library (where a woman who smelled of mothballs took him in hand, guided his choice towards books that *almost,* but never quite, exceeded his grasp) and after much laborious picking out of words:

"They're in Africa, too. They've got bigger ears there."

After animals it was cars, but his enthusiasm was not that of the child. Racy lines and mph didn't impress him. What snagged his attention was size, solidity, permanence.

"It says here a woman's had the same Rolls-Royce for forty years. Why don't you get one instead of that little runabout?"

"Such cars are only for the very rich," Felix explained.

"You could be rich."

Felix laughed. "Few electricians are rich, Mischa. Dancers never."

"You could get rich in the shop if you wanted to."

"I don't think so—"

"You could sell more. People always want new stuff, you can tell the way they look at it."

"This is not a rich neighborhood, people cannot afford—"

But Felix thought now that Mischa had probably been right. He'd been right about many things to do with the shop. Now he was fourteen and customers (especially the women) obviously preferred to deal with the boy rather than Felix himself. They called him Michael and talked to him about everything from speakers and turntables to the manifold problems of adolescent sons; that Mischa was younger than their sons seemed not to matter.

"I wish he was like you, my Harry" (or my Jim or my Brian). "All he does is lollop about the house, bone idle, while you . . ."

While Mischa seemed never to have been adolescent, awkward, lazy, uncertain. His voice had not broken in sudden croaking descents, it had deepened gradually, naturally. He now shaved twice a day; when he did not, his dark shadow was the envy of every teenager in the neighborhood. No wonder they didn't like him; they aimed to go against the establishment in every way they could; Mischa's entire energies were devoted to joining it. He *did* work hard; Felix sometimes wondered how they'd managed before he arrived. He helped in the shop all day and taught Anna's less advanced classes in the evenings, and there too he was adored —by the mothers as much as the students, even on weekends when it was time to pay the piper. With Anna they were reluctant; with Mischa they were eager.

"We should put the rates up," he told her.

"Never! Already my best students cannot afford—"

"They can teach Beginners, pay their way and take the load off us. Then we could stay open all day, offer more classes—plenty of kids want them."

"Clods, yes, but I will not take their money. Anna Abramsky is *artiste!* To turn geese into swans is impossible!"

He shrugged, a graceful, almost arrogant gesture on him. "If they want to try, why *not* take their money? Somebody will."

Anna turned on him in fury. "Oh, you . . . Gypsy!"

That much he had by now admitted, except that he didn't say Gypsy, he said Rom. And he didn't say, "I'm Rom." He said, "We used to be Rom, before we left the *kumpania*." But always when Anna said "Gypsy" he seemed to withdraw, for he was still secretive, this otherwise confident young Mischa whom Anna still called "boy"—or, if others were present, "our nephew." Over the years he'd told them something of Da's death and the wandering life before it, the rabbit traps and fruit picking and odd jobs, even a little about the *kumpania*.

But he would never talk about why they'd left it, nor did he let drop a single name from the old life.

When he was pressed, the old furtive look slipped back into his face, and Felix knew if they pressed further he would lie.

"We ought to know," Anna said often. "You should make him tell."

"Then he will lie, which in the end will hurt him more. Let him alone, angel. He has pride, he has ambition . . . he is happy. Except when we force him to lie, he is honest with us, and I think loyal also. He needs us."

And you, my Anna, need Mischa—but this he could not say, for she too had pride, too much of it; witness her reaction to the monthly reports on Gabriella, which now came via the family's lawyer because Frau von Reiker was, it was reported, indisposed.

Which Felix translated as "Sick, the old woman is sick, Anna . . ."

"Not she! Such women live forever! You remember how she was. Granite."

Oh yes. They'd met only once, but how would he ever forget? Hans already at the Russian front; Anna gaunt, her eyes so deep in the sockets they seemed black, her reedy arms wrapped tight to conceal, to flatten, to deny the thing in her belly. Across the restaurant booth the two elder von Reikers. Not a word from the husband stooped in his seat, only a rhythmic, habitual sniff punctuated by the fish-blown pop of lips opening and closing on his pipe stem. In the other corner, stone-faced and erect, his wife waited her opportunity. From her, a pervading reek of cologne and the rhythmic grinding of teeth. It was she who made the proposal. Anna must immediately divorce Felix, marry Hans by proxy. (Such things can be arranged, we are not without resources, you understand?) Then the child—which their son inexplicably wanted—could be legitimate after all. For Anna's present husband they would be prepared, if necessary, to make some financial . . . adjustment. Thus with one wave of a cologne-drenched handkerchief she dismissed Felix—and forever alienated the already implacable Anna. Who for the first time in months had color, two livid splotches staining the pallor of her cheeks. Her long fingers were closing around a table knife when Felix, alarmed, led her outside.

Now he sighed. So many years ago, and still she forgave nothing, nothing.

She needed this Gypsy boy. They both needed him.

The boy was about fourteen when his relationship with Anna shifted to a new, unexpected plane. Mischa was upstairs making schedules for the extra classes Anna had finally agreed to offer. Then a determined rat-a-tat-tat on the studio door and Anna's voice, shrill and urgent, from the hall.

"Go away, go away, I say! We do not buy, you hear? We do not buy, no! Never! Go, I say—shoo! shoo!"

An answering voice, young, wheedling, husky, was already well into its spiel before Mischa, at the top of the stairs, looked down on the scene. Anna holding the door, trying to slam it, but too late. A foot was already inside, now a small brown hand waving a bunch of gaudy paper flowers.

"Flowers for the pretty lady, cheap they are, lovely, they'll bring you luck, money—"

"What for do I want paper trash? Be off with you—"

"Read your palm then, lovey? You've a lucky face—it's seen trouble, yes, you've known grief, but I see good things coming, lady, good days coming, never close your door on good days—"

The girl was well into her patter now. It ran like honey—flattery and mystery and warm, tantalizing hope, and only the hint of a threat, but Mischa heard no more of it. The foot and the paper flowers had been joined by a head, small and delicately poised on a long brown throat, black hair clouding about a pointed, high-cheeked face, bold dark eyes that missed nothing, that read Anna Abramsky like a map, a journey to be made for pleasure and profit.

Mischa felt the blood leave his face, then his legs, and he had to sit on the top stair and cling to the banister.

Farah.

He'd last seen her when he was almost five, she only a month or so younger. So she'd be fourteen now, and still the same wild face, the same fire burning in her eyes.

Like Grandmam's ruby.

It dazzled him, blinded him to leg warmers drying on a rack, to the banister, to sheet music for tonight's classes, to everything but that small, foreshortened figure waving her ridiculous flowers the way she'd once waved a stick.

The two barefoot children were sitting outside Grandmam's painted caravan, the sunflower door at their backs and the smoking campfire in front of them, Farah's mother dusting a chicken with paprika and stirring it into a pot with garlic and tomatoes. Somewhere close by, Grandmam smoked her clay pipe and Granddad groomed a horse for tomorrow's fair. In the background a river glittered and tumbled in the dusk. The Eden.

So it must have been Appleby. They were drawing pictures in the mud with sticks. The girl had the sharpest stick, so her pictures were the best. The little boy (Micah he'd been called then) said:

"I told Da. I said, 'Da,' I said, 'I like Farah and she likes me. When we get bigger we're going to get married, okay?' That's what I said."

She scratched another branch to the tree in her picture and drew a bird on it. "And what did *he* say?"

"He laughed, you know how he does, and gave me an apple."

"But what did he *say?*"

"That we were a bit young to be making plans."

"But what *else* did he say, Micah?" the little girl demanded, giving the bird a deep, round eye.

"He said it's okay with him, if we can meet your bride-price when the time comes."

Farah waved her stick at him, dusted off her skirt and smiled, her baby teeth small and even and very white. "It's fixed then, right? We'll have a trailer like my Uncle August's, a blue rug on the floor, velvet curtains and china cups—and we'll have cocoa every night and your grandmam will give me her ruby for a wedding present—"

"Grandmam says you're too bold for your own good—"

"—and you'll buy me a gold necklace, maybe two, and earrings like my Aunt Kodi's—"

Farah had her earrings now. They swung in the light as she reached for Anna's unwilling palm, but the dancer was too fast, too strong, her well-trained muscles steel against the Gypsy girl's silk.

"Go from here this minute or I call police, understand?"

A flash of teeth and Farah was out the door, mocking Anna with her eyes as she left on a whirl of scarlet skirts, a liquid laugh, and another flash of gold earrings as the door closed.

Some force very strong in Mischa made him want to stand, want to walk down the stairs and follow his second cousin Farah back to the families—but if Farah now had her earrings maybe she also had a husband. The Rom married their daughters off early (where had he heard that? Da). But Farah wouldn't be married—and what did he care if she was? He was done with Rom and everything connected with the Rom.

Salt stung his eyes and he stumbled instead to a window to look down into Ryder Street.

The women of the *kumpania* were working the neighborhood, invad-

ing it with baskets of clothespins and paper flowers, with hints and com-
pliments and subtle, smiling threats, fanning out past the grocer's and the
fishmonger's, ducking into alleys, wheedling a bag of something-or-other
from the butcher. An older, heavyset woman who could have been his
Aunt Olla waved her arms in a dispute with the owner of the hardware
shop; another, who looked like one of Farah's many cousins, turned a
brisk trade in clothespins at the bus stop. There was a girl of about ten
who could have been his baby sister Rose, but this girl wasn't crying so
how would he know? Surely the limping woman was old Delendi with
her half-sister Hela? A face that was etched somewhere very deep in his
memory was missing from the confusion below, a face he couldn't for the
moment put a name to. No sign of Dui either, nor any of the men, but
there wouldn't be. Reading palms, selling junk to the *gaje*—such was not
for men of the Rom.

He stood at the window for a long time, searching one bold face after
another until at last a cruising police car moved them on. With an impu-
dent smile at the car Farah disappeared around the corner on a flash of
scarlet skirt—

But no sign of that other face. Grandmam.

Who, with her towers of golden coins, had taught him to count, who'd
given him hard candy and the most succulent bits of chicken, who'd once
offered brown eggs for a boy she called Micah—and who had wept as
they splattered the clean steps of the caravan and the painted sunflower
on its door...

Maybe she was too old to forage with the others?

Maybe she'd died, his grandmam?

Overwhelming loss swept over him, a sense of bewilderment not felt
since Da's drunken death. Da... but it was Da who took him away from
the warm *kumpania* fires, sentenced them both to cold, poverty-stricken
years in the trailer for some terrible thing done to Ma a long time ago.

*And you, Micah, what do you choose? said Granddad. Micah, five, could
have been a fish the way Da's black eyes hooked him, glittered at him across the
family fire.*

A sound forced up through his throat, a sound so strange to him that
he did not at first know what it was.

Behind him, Anna Abramsky knew.

She saw the dark head droop, the sudden spasm in muscles of back and
shoulder, uncharacteristic vulnerability in the strong, dance-corded column of his neck. How thin it had been once, that neck, how dirty and
tousled the head, how agile the brain within. Was still agile.

And, despite all that had passed, was still Gypsy. Yet in so many things this boy was like her; struggle as he might, dodge and duck and deviate from the pattern, some part of him could not change, would be forever Gypsy. Watching him, seeing the ripple of hard-won muscles fight and lose the battle for self-control, the shell of her own long-frozen restraint began its slow, healing melt. For the first time in four years she stretched out her arms and held him.

"No, Mischa, oh no . . ."

Mischa.

From the doorway Felix Abramsky saw it all. He saw the unbending woman bend and the closed, secretive boy weep, and knew that some barrier of kinship had at last been crossed.

Anna had used the boy's name.

And she had touched him.

EIGHT

ᴮETWEEN MISSES NOLAN AND WARREN were two other governesses.

The first, a lady with good references but a disturbing passion for the parlormaid, lasted two months. The second, a squeaky little creature with dust-colored hair, absorbed herself with tracings of wild herbs on ecru linen later (she confided in her thin whisper) to be embroidered with threads of pale green and gray. She gathered up her meager salary with trembling, frightened fingers, as well she might—she could not have taught a mouse to steal cheese.

The best and last, Mary Beth Warren, was forthright, American, and fun; she was here only to teach and to improve her German. She was not a servant; additional functions—like weekly shopping trips to town—were optional. Her arrival coincided with a serious decline in the health of Grossmutter, whose self-control slipped a little every day; she now kept to her room and nursed her aching head; the special cologne had been abandoned as no longer efficacious. "I'm sure it never was," said Miss Warren crisply. "She needs a neurologist, not scent."

But Grossmutter scorned doctors, even her own, and only after a truly fierce siege, and Miss Warren's vigorous persuasion, did she agree to hospital tests in Bonn—an unexpected week of freedom for both governess and pupil.

The first day they shopped, toured old streets, browsed through the biggest library Ellie had ever seen and left with stacks and stacks of books, new and old, books that would never have been allowed in the library at home, books that carried her to cool Himalayan pinnacles, steamy shadows of Equatorial Africa, other-world vistas of the Grand Canyon. And (because Miss Warren turned an indulgent eye to some of her selections) she fell in love, briefly but totally, with Rhett Butler.

Which set her to dreaming, kept her glued to the mirror with greater interest than before. She was taller than Grossmutter, taller even than Miss Warren—and her legs were longer too. So was her hair, darkening now from flaxen to summer-streaked honey, now worn in a chignon on the advice of Miss Warren.

"It's really too old for you yet, but it gives you great dignity and it does show off your neck. At fourteen it should be in a ponytail of course, but the old lady would have kittens . . ." They both smiled at the idea of Frau von Reiker producing anything so weak and lovable as kittens. "And starting right now we'll do something every day she's away, Ellie. We'll begin with the art gallery, then lunch at a French restaurant, and in the afternoon a movie. I can't *believe* you've never even seen one. The life you lead here is simply Victorian! You might as well be in a nunnery! How I've stuck it out all these months I'll never know."

Ellie began to realize *why* Miss Warren had stuck it out as soon as they entered the art gallery. A young banker was waiting for them, clasping Miss Warren's hand in what Grossmutter would have said was a highly familiar manner. The banker had sparse pale hair and paler skin, full red lips, and moist light eyes that roved everywhere and into which Miss Warren gazed most of the time they were in the gallery and all through lunch, barely tasting her wine, picking idly at a superb *sole Sylvestre*— though it was far lighter than anything served at the house, where Cook's meals were heavy on starch and all too thin on flavor. When it was time to leave Miss Warren blushed, appearing slightly flustered as she drew Ellie aside.

"Look, there's a great movie at the Odeon, really romantic, I know you'll love it, but we saw it on my last day off. Why don't we pick you up when it's over?"

Movies were a new experience and should have been absorbing, but all through a newsreel and a cartoon about a canary, the one image Ellie couldn't dismiss was the soft shine in Miss Warren's eyes when the banker's pink hand had rested on her knee at lunch. Perhaps they thought she hadn't noticed? And what were they doing now, the banker and her pretty governess? Even as the question formed, an answering ache in her own body told her exactly what they were doing. She received a swift mental picture of them in bed, exciting at first, then almost immediately repugnant. The banker's lips were so thick, so wet . . . and Miss Warren was so very clean . . .

But then the main feature—about a bullfighter—began, and she forgot everything but the actor's image on the screen. Head up, he circled the ring of smooth sand, took his compelling stance, black eyes staring arrogantly, proudly, into the camera, into the heart of Gabriella von Reiker. His mouth was thin and curved and his dark hair curled to feathers in the slight breeze of the bullring; his brown hands held the cape lightly, with skill. And, aglitter in the sun, clinging tight to wide shoulders and flat stomach and taut, sculpted buttocks, the incredible suit of lights.

She thought of all the men she knew. The family doctor, the foreman and his shifty son, the milkman, the mailman, and today the slithery banker.

None of them compared with this. The bullfighter was the most splendid creature she'd ever seen—no, more than that, he spun dreams . . . There were other actors and a couple of pretty actresses, but Ellie hardly saw them, only the splendid figure in his tight, magnificent suit.

The ache she'd known with the knowledge of Miss Warren and the banker flowed back in a warm tide. His hands would be sliding up Miss Warren's calves, over her rounded hips to the pert American breasts. Except the hands were not banker's hands now, they were brown and sensitive, almost certainly tender—and the hips and calves were Ellie's, not Miss Warren's; the budding breasts were hers too, and the mouth waiting for a kiss that never quite came . . .

In the dark cavern of the theater she shivered.

They were waiting for her on the sidewalk, Miss Warren looking soft and vaguely disheveled, the banker jaunty and smiling. Then the governess left them briefly to buy a newspaper at the corner stand and the banker sidled up to Ellie, circling her wrist with damp fingers, looking her up and down, then deep into her eyes exactly the way he'd looked into Miss Warren's.

"You know you're a very pretty girl?" he whispered, one eye cocked to Miss Warren's smartly suited back. "I think you will be a beautiful, beautiful woman. You will have the body of a dancer, Fräulein, very slender, very—"

"Take your hands off me."

"But why? Mary Beth won't be upset—"

"It has nothing to do with Miss Warren—" But Miss Warren was coming back and there wasn't time to tell him that she didn't want to look like a dancer and when the time came for a man to touch her his hands would be dark and tapered and his mouth a long thin curve, the eyes dark and intense.

Next day there was a visit, unannounced and unprecedented, from Grossmutter's lawyer.

"But I thought you knew," Ellie said. "She'll be at the hospital until Saturday."

"Yes," he said, "that's why I'm here now. Perhaps we can talk in the library?"

So it was serious.

"I'd like it if Miss Warren..." she said, alarmed by his expression and his bulging briefcase.

He hesitated a fraction. "No, this is private."

He began immediately they were seated in the oppressive oak-paneled room. "The hospital has been in touch. No no, your grandmother is no worse," he said hurriedly, "but by all accounts she may not always be... quite herself..."

"I don't understand."

The lawyer frowned. "No, well... as you know, there is always business to be... transacted. There's the vineyard, the staff... The fact is, Gabriella (if I may call you that?), the fact is, your grandmother may not in the future be capable—" He held up his hand. "With your help she is managing, but eventually... What we're asking is that you keep your eyes open, check the bills she pays, the amounts... she may soon be in a vulnerable position; creditors can be unscrupulous." His smile was rueful, perhaps sad. "We understand she may be reluctant, at present, to allow it. You are very young and my client is... but there will be times when she will not remember things—"

"I see," Ellie said, not seeing at all. There was only the migraine—but there'd always been that...

"Just the day-to-day running of the estate. If you can help supervise... if you will watch her, that's all. You may call us if there are problems, but it would be better to avoid it. That way it will not be necessary to call a meeting of the trustees."

"She'll never let me—"

The lawyer studied his fingertips. "Eventually she will be glad of the help. Later still she may not be aware that anything needs to be done."

"But what's wrong with her?"

He frowned. "I can't tell you. The family trust is private and you are not a...legitimate...not a trustee..." His voice trailed off. "Which brings me to the other matter. As you no doubt know," he said rather more kindly, "Frau von Reiker has always maintained a certain...contact with your mother. Reports of your welfare and general progress..." He could not quite seem to look her in the face. "Lately, however, my client does not always remember to write. And we have a request from England—"

"From my mother?"

The lawyer coughed and again examined his fingernails. "In fact, the letter came from her husband, *Felix* Abramsky." Now he smiled as though to pull the sting. "I suppose you might almost call him your stepfather. He's very concerned about you. I have undertaken to keep them advised..."

"My mother hasn't asked?"

"Why no," the lawyer said, his voice as cool, as carefully flat as Ellie's. "Anna Abramsky runs a ballet studio—I expect she's a very busy woman."

"Anna Abramsky? That's her name?"

Surprised, the lawyer gave her a searching look. "Just how much do you know about your mother, Gabriella?" When she didn't, couldn't answer, he hesitated, then: "Your grandmother might take it amiss, but in the circumstances I think... Your mother, as I said, runs a studio and her husband an electrical business. They are comfortable enough, but they are not people of—shall we say—*means*. There are no children—except of course yourself."

Whom she does not want.

"I understand that a young man lives with them, helps them out. He's about sixteen. A Gypsy, or so I'm told."

She shivered. All she knew of Gypsies was what she'd seen from the estate, wandering bands who briefly marauded surrounding properties. But not *this* place, for Grossmutter kept everything under lock and key, especially when Gypsies were passing through. Scum, she called them, thieves. The servants and field hands echoed her; Ellie, instructed to keep close to the house when Gypsies roamed the district, had seen them only from some distance, clusters of trailers, groups of voluble women and children heading for the village, smoke from their fires spiraling into the sky for one night, at most two—for the local police were alert, quick to send them on their way.

But Anna Abramsky had taken one of them into her home. Which said a lot about Anna Abramsky.

"How do you know?" she demanded.

The lawyer smiled, again gently. "We have our ways."

So it was true. Such a busy woman, this mother. No time to ask if her daughter was dead or alive, but she could shelter a Gypsy behind her dancer's skirts.

Well, then the Gypsy was welcome to her.

"Is there anything else you wish to know?" the lawyer was saying.

"No."

Grossmutter returned from the hospital outraged and ill-tempered. For the first time in her life she'd had to obey orders; the experience left her shaken and unusually talkative.

"Sleep, wake up, eat this, drink that—from nurses hardly older than you, Gabriella. And the doctors! Such manners, such impertinence! They asked *highly* offensive questions, poking me here and prodding me there... It was a great mistake to go. I shall not go again. In future my own doctor will treat me. At the very least he knows his place."

"But what did they say? Can they help?"

"What I expected, one drug or another."

"But you seem to be in less pain, and you do look better..." She did—so what *had* the lawyer been talking about?

After some prodding Grossmutter admitted they'd "released some pressure" and that new drugs dulled the ache: "But they make me dizzy, Gabriella. I hardly trust myself on the stairs."

Only when Ellie was leaving the room did her grandmother show a flash of her old self. "Miss Warren tells me she took you to town, to the cinema. Without my permission."

"But you were not here."

"Nevertheless." Her eyes closed as fresh pain tightened her lips, as she pressed the back of her head into the pillow. "She has asked if she could install a television set in the library. Of course I refused."

"But everyone has them now!"

"Yes, even in the hospital. Trash, tasteless trash."

Ellie said nothing, afraid to upset what she knew now to be a delicate balance in her grandmother's mental state, but the blow was a real one. Without television Miss Warren might leave. Besides, with a set in the house they could maybe have seen the actor again, or someone like him, people who were different, exciting.

Grossmutter's eyes were open again and she was peering at her closely. "You look different, child. Older."

She blushed into the mirror. Did they show on her face, these new sensations in her body, sensations learned secondhand from Miss Warren and the banker and a nameless actor with compelling eyes?

"I think perhaps Miss Warren is not ... innocent, Gabriella. I am wondering if I should send her away."

No, surely she wouldn't—"Grossmutter, Miss Warren's my friend. If she left I should definitely want to go to school."

Mary Beth Warren had changed her life, brought laughter into it, an awareness that there was a whole world outside the estate, a world that moved and changed, filled with people who *felt* things, whose days were not dominated by the weather and next season's harvest, people who traveled and who had friends...

To distract her grandmother, perhaps to punish her for even thinking of firing Miss Warren, Ellie's voice was sharp when she said, "Are there pictures of my mother in the house? I should like to see what she looked like."

—because the banker said I looked like a dancer. But if she told Grossmutter *that,* Mary Beth's days would certainly be numbered. She waited for the chill that any mention of her mother always called forth.

Today it did not. The old woman's drugged, watery eyes panned from Ellie to her image in the mirror and back again.

"I have no picture," she said slowly. "I have never wanted one—and you, Gabriella, have no need of one."

"I *am* glad you came, Mary Beth," she said, several months later. "I never realized how lonely I'd been..."

"There are worse things than loneliness," Miss Warren said, her eyes strangely bleak.

She looked like that often now, and Ellie wondered if perhaps she'd reached the limit of her patience. Under the pendulum effects of one new drug after another, all of which Miss Warren had to bring from town, Grossmutter had been more than usually fractious.

"I know she's difficult," Ellie said, "but she doesn't mean—"

"It's not her," Miss Warren said, "it's—" She pulled herself up short. "Look, Ellie, you have to understand I'll not always be here. Eventually..."

Eventually came quickly. Miss Warren, on a surprise errand to town for a new prescription, had to wait for it to be made up. To kill time she dropped in at the banker's apartment.

She was weeping when she came back to the house, and she'd forgotten the prescription after all, intent only on slamming drawers and cupboards and at last the lid of her cabin trunk. "Men!" she sobbed. "The lousy—"

"Oh, don't go...please, Mary Beth—"

Over the top of the cabin trunk Miss Warren looked at her with envy. "You'll manage fine, Ellie," she said. "All your emotions nicely bolted down. I just wish to God mine were."

NINE

ISCHA HAD BEEN WITH THEM SEVEN YEARS when the Abramskys made it official and adopted him.

By the following year, signs over shop and studio indicated they were now the property of Abramsky & Son. And not only in Ryder Street. As post—World War II babies grew older and their families became larger, housing estates sprang up to accommodate them. When shopping centers followed, the new company was ready.

Mischa was persuasive.

"It makes sense, Felix. We lease the shops as showrooms, keep stock in a central warehouse and deliver from there."

"But we are only two persons, how is it possible to care for four stores?"

"Hire managers, pay them commission. That is how it's done, how it's always been done."

Felix had doubts. "Then we'd have to employ strangers . . . is that really our way?"

Mischa, busy scribbling figures onto a yellow pad, did not even look up.

"The numbers work. Mall shops come with upstairs storage right in the lease. With a central warehouse we can convert that storage space to dance studios—aha, something else! The malls have movie houses. We make a few commercials to show in the theaters, nothing fancy, appliances, stereos, televisions. Make a few for the studios too, little girls in class, keep it traditional, white tutus, *Swan Lake* in the background—"

"You *know* the tutu is not worn to class—" But as well to talk to the chair.

"—so people leave the theater and what's the first thing they see? Abramsky's. *Which they've just seen on a commercial!* They see what's in the window, compare it with the worn-out old stuff waiting for them at home. Maybe they've got kids with them—now you tell me, what's the secret dream of every little girl in the world? To be a ballerina, right?"

Anna, chopping spinach at the draining board, said: "And you tell me—how many have the body for it? Not one in ten. And the discipline? Ha! Not one in a thousand."

"But they don't *know* that. And if nothing else it gives them poise— you've said it yourself. We can't miss."

Such confidence. It made Felix uneasy. The boy looked mature, twenty-five at least—but he was eighteen. If he failed, what of the confidence then? "This warehouse," he said dryly. "You have a plan for that also?"

"Hamish Froggatt's factory. He has to close soon anyway, he owes taxes, utilities, everybody. We can buy him out, stock, patents, everything —and get him off the hook. The location's perfect." He pushed a map across the table, Hamish's factory circled in red, with lines radiating out to four neat squares.

Shops.

The elder Abramskys turned to him, alarmed. What they'd taken to be speculation was turning into detailed, concrete plans. "The money? What would we buy him out with?"

Mischa smiled his slow, indulgent smile. "That's what banks are for. I talked to the manager. It's feasible."

"But so much debt . . ." Felix fretted.

"Not so much. We take a loan. The deposit will come from Hamish. He owes us."

His voice was quiet, but in it was the silky flick of a whip, and Felix shivered in the overheated room, very glad he was Felix Abramsky and not Hamish Froggatt.

"How could he owe us? *We* buy from *him*."

"Junk. As a favor. And it falls apart. Did you know his last three checks for returned merchandise bounced? He's lucky we don't prosecute. Want to see the total?"

Not for the first time Felix felt twinges of guilt. Too many decisions were left to Mischa, far too many. Leaseholds, purchases, contracts—but unlike himself, Mischa enjoyed business, grasped it easily, instinctively. Let even the most resistant customer stroke the high shine of a stereo cabinet and a sale was as good as made. "Look, Felix," he said the first time, showing off a time-payment contract. "She signed, no outs." He'd been fourteen at the time. Useless for Felix to protest that the woman could barely afford groceries and that they should not tempt the poor into debt. "She *wants* it," the boy had insisted. "They all do. If we don't sell to them, someone else will."

Mischa had been right. Even then he'd known, deep in his genes, how to persuade, to sell. As Felix did not. Small repairs he understood. Thumping the piano for Anna's classes he understood. Business, as in planning for future profits, he did not. Nor did he care to. He had his Anna, and now this boy. What more could a man want? It was enough that basic needs be met. Enough for Anna also. But not for Mischa. It puzzled them, this craving for bulwarks, for walls of wealth around him.

Where did it come from, this drive? And this fixation with a harmless old soak like Hamish Froggatt?

"Without his business Hamish has nothing," Felix reminded him gently.

Anna sniffed, her contempt for the Scot as deep as Mischa's. "His whiskey stink, this he will have forever."

In the middle of the column of figures, Mischa stopped counting and stared ahead, brown fingers tight around the pencil:

"He has Greenlings."

Again that sibilance in his voice, and the cold black shine in his eyes.

And again anxiety stirred in Felix. An odd boy, this. Dearer to them with every year—but strange, complex. This business with Hamish . . . better not think, not speak of it.

"I thought you had a date?" he said instead, more and more alarmed as the pencil strokes resumed.

"No." Mischa turned his head and smiled.

As yet, no girl but his second cousin Farah had stirred in Mischa more than a physical interest, although his sex life—as shrouded and private as his thoughts—had begun much earlier and was more sustained than the Abramskys could possibly have imagined. In all the years at Ryder Street the subject had been raised only once, an embarrassed, ambiguous remark by Felix when Mischa was about sixteen:

"Teens are difficult years, Mischa. There are certain...needs..." His voice trailed off, uncertain of its direction. Then he brightened, satisfied he'd found a middle ground. "In the long run, my boy, friendship is better."

And even then Mischa had to hide a grin; he'd known since he was fourteen that Felix had it all wrong. These days the girls were young dancers with fine-tuned dancers' bodies—but that first woman had been married, a customer more than twice Mischa's age whose husband was gone a lot.

"On business," she said with a pout. She was lonely.

He'd thought many times since that he'd be grateful to her for as long as he lived. Not just for sex, not even for the superb instruction, but for her honesty.

His first good look at her came when she was sitting on the edge of her bed in a silk kimono and satin mules, slowly stroking her crossed ankles with jeweled, tantalizing fingers. Carefully made up, she smelled of wealth and languor and a French perfume with flowery top notes and dark, musky undertones. Her hair swung in a polished brown curtain and her eyes glittered hazel points at him as he worked on a new stereo installed in her bedroom just the week before—but he hadn't noticed her much then; her husband had been in the room.

With husband away she complained that the set hissed at her.

"Let's see," he said, turning the music on low.

"It's only when it gets warm..." she murmured, her lips moist and full, drawing out "warm" until the word almost moaned in the sumptuously feminine room.

Playing for time, he twiddled knobs and switches, already sensing more than Mantovani in the charged air between stereo and bed—and an unmistakable stirring under the flannel trousers Anna and Felix had given him last Christmas. "It sounds fine to me."

"That's because it's cold...you'll have to wait..."

Until it warmed up. That's when he knew for sure.

"How old are you, anyway?" she asked him.

"Twenty?" he said, aiming high.

"You young liar," she murmured, pleased.

He'd given her his sweetest caught-in-the-act smile, all charm and roguish apology. "How old d'you think?"

"Seventeen."

"Right first time," he lied.

"I can always tell," she said, running the tip of a pointed tongue over her lips as she looked him up and down, missing nothing. "Have you done it before?"

He was tempted to lie again, but a voice from the past, cocky and full of the devil, steadied him just in time. *Women believe whatever you tell 'em, Micah—until they catch you in the first lie. So if you're not sure, play safe.*

Right then he wasn't sure about anything much except what was happening under the gray flannel, every rock-hard muscle in his body pumping blood into one explosive rod.

"Well? Have you?" she persisted.

"I've read about it."

"I'll bet you have," she crooned, working red-tipped fingers expertly at shirt buttons and then the zipper on his pants. "It goes fast the first time, but practice makes perfect and we've all afternoon."

It *was* fast, no sooner started than done, but they practiced until the room filled up with dusk. She was a diligent teacher—and honest. She didn't sigh and say she loved him. Better yet, she didn't expect him to say he loved her.

What she did say, time and again, was: "My God, but you learn fast."

Then: "How d'you get a body like this at your age?" as she trailed her fingers across the muscular swell of his thigh.

"Dance," he said.

She nibbled delicately at his shoulder. "So you dance too—and I'd always thought they were queenies!"

After he'd proved once again, and for the last time that day, that he at least was not, she washed him and powdered him and did up his trousers.

"Well?" she said at the door. "Think you'll like it?"

"I know I will," he said in a dream, only mildly offended when her soft laughter followed him down the driveway.

Back at the studio Anna was tapping her cane, impatient to begin their evening exercises. "Late!" she said. "You expect to keep in shape if you are missing the barre?"

So there was nothing for it but to put himself through the grind of *pliés* and *grands jetés* and *port de bras* until ligaments screamed, sweat flew, and knee joints popped like firecrackers. And now the new, pleasurable ache in his groin.

Hardly a week went by that winter without the stereo unit needing some kind of service. He was more than happy to oblige.

Perhaps it took the merciless light of an April afternoon to spotlight impending saddlebags on the woman's thighs, the subtle dimpling of her hips, a distinct droop to her large breasts as she reached over him for the dish of chocolate creams on the bedside table. He looked away quickly, unwilling to admit the difference between her and the sleek, carefully honed dancers at the studio. He thought she hadn't noticed his glance, but the following week she was waiting for him downstairs, fully dressed, an odd little smile on her face.

"Time to move on before we both get bored, Michael. It's been fun, right?"

"Great, but—"

"But you need somebody closer to your own age, sweetie. So do I. You're wearing me out."

Generous to the last, she reached up and pinned a small gold arrow to his lapel.

"What's that for?" he said, halfheartedly reaching under her blouse for the bra hook.

"Graduation," she said, "with honors."

He was fourteen, gratitude and guilt so hopelessly mixed he didn't know where one left off and the other began. So perhaps this wasn't the first graduation present she'd pinned on, but who cared?

The couple had left the district soon afterwards, and Michael, with newly aroused hungers to be appeased, turned naturally to the dancers in Anna's senior class. In the beginning even they were older than he—but not a dimple or saddlebag among them. But for all their grace, their disciplined bodies, sex with them carried heavier baggage yet, wide-eyed invitations to meet their families, random-seeming pauses at the windows of jewelry shops, probing little questions about the future. He'd been learning ever since to see a hint before it trapped him, to deflect it, squash it, and move on.

And still, with each new girl he took to dinner and then to bed, images of his second cousin hovered over him, haunting his pleasure, taunting his choice of the moment. So compliant, these dancers, so willing. Farah would not have been compliant. She would have demanded. Adoration, a ring, a necklace, constant attention, at least as much love as she gave. And she'd have demanded he go back with the Rom. There were times, nuzzling a slender thigh, half listening to murmurs of love everlasting, that the picture of Farah came back so sharply he might still have been sitting on the stairs in Ryder Street, Farah harassing Anna in the hall below, bold dark eyes and quick Gypsy tongue confident and mocking. A brown hand (he remembered Farah's hands as always small, warm, and brown) reaching for Anna's obdurate palm. What *gaja* could compare with Farah, the childhood playmate that glowed in his memory like a ruby, a distant fire at which Micah knew he would never warm himself, for each year Michael Abramsky ran faster and faster from the ways of the Rom.

"No," he told Felix again, from a long way off. "No date."

Felix sighed. He must be patient. No explanations—such was Mischa's way. Dozens of affairs, none he'd discuss. He approached girls the way he had approached studies. Brief intense interest, then the move to someone new, always looking, never finding. Certainly there was no shortage of hopefuls. It wasn't just that he was handsome—if poise and good features were all, the world was full of handsome men. But the Gypsy had that one quality more compelling to women than looks. He had indifference. It was in the catlike ease of his shoulders, the flashing arrogance of his smile. There was passion in the curve of it, yes, and in the burning dark of his eyes, but it was passion for the experience, not the object.

The girls who flocked round him were dancers; not surprising—despite his skill in business, it was in the studio that his true nature emerged. When he danced, even barre exercises, the Gypsy blood flashed through, wild and exotic, eclipsing the urbane veneer he carefully cultivated for the outside world. In the studio he took fire, gave off an almost animal sensuality to which no girl was immune. But *such* girls, every one of them body-conscious. Like Mischa. Though he seldom taught class now (how could he have found time?), he still took barre with Anna, maintained a dancer's discipline of spartan diet and compulsive routine.

His one indulgence, Felix suspected, was these girls. Whom he would not discuss. Reticent still, his thoughts were as hidden and secret as they'd always been. And perhaps that, to women, was most intriguing of all. With Michael Abramsky they could never be sure. So they pursued him and he let himself be caught for just as long as they held his interest.

Felix, who'd known only Anna and wanted no other, saw Mischa as successful with women, with everyone. But there was something missing, one small elusive something this adopted son lacked. Felix hunted around his mind until he found it. Trust. He trusted no one but Anna and Felix himself. Who else, among all those Mischa knew—clients, neighbors, girl friends (no men friends, only friendly acquaintances)—could honestly claim they *knew* Michael Abramsky? Could claim to have his confidence?

Felix grieved. Though Anna insisted the boy was far too young, Felix had entertained hopes of an early marriage for Mischa, hopes of grandchildren that would perhaps fill Anna's emotional void, her need to experience again what she'd had with Sasha—and could have had with the little Gabriella. The bond between her and the boy was strong and warm, but she'd never known him as a helpless baby.

He felt the boy's eyes on him, amused and indulgent, the pencil still. "You're forgetting it's Friday," he was saying, smiling. "How could I have a date? We don't tend traps on Friday night."

Tend traps.

His one light, deprecating reference to the old life with Da, applied now to any routine task: bookkeeping, inventory, deliveries, orders. Had girls become simply another item on the list, rabbits to be caught, consumed, and forgotten?

But Friday it was. And so they must, at Anna's insistence, be civilized, wear jackets, ties, and "be tall in the chair, yes?" Television and radio were off limits, curtains drawn tight against trucks and buses and children's shouts, all the working-class noises of Ryder Street below them. The evening was set aside for them alone, to gather at the fireplace with pale dry sherry and tiny canapés.

They could have been a group of literati at tea. Anna's dress never varied. Full length and of vaguely distinguished cut, it hung on her gaunt frame in loose, whispery folds, a dolorous shade of plum that some dyer had perhaps mixed in a pensive moment, stirring blues and maroons and grays to arrive at the exact color of his melancholy. Ivory bracelets rattled at her wrists; her long dancer's feet—callused, misshapen, and a source of acute embarrassment to her—were crammed into pointed prewar shoes now fortuitously back in fashion.

Felix wore a three-piece suit with wide lapels and a silk hankie poking from the top pocket, black shoes that squeaked as he stood to pour small measures of sherry into Anna's best glasses.

"Rumanians," she said, "were always good with glass," twirling crystal stemware in the light of the pink-shaded lamp.

She talked of prewar days in Munich, Paris, or Amsterdam, pointing dramatically to pictures of old friends slowly fading to sepia on the living-room wall.

"That Nicolai, what a Petrouchka! what pathos, yes?—but poor technique, bad training, just like his cousin Piotr. Olga there, such a bird she was, wonderful arms, weak insteps. Ah, Mischa, if you had seen Tamara here, the presence—and such eyes for the stage, full of... Felix, what do we call it?"

Felix smiled. "Soul, my angel."

"Yes-yes-yes! Soul!—but then she married the cellist and made babies. Very stout she grew, this Tamara."

Anna frowned when speaking of Tamara. Physical disability was unavoidable. To grow stout was not.

Sometimes they played ballet music on the gramophone, sometimes Anna read, with sonorous expression, from the yellowed pages of old Russian novels, Felix translating under his breath for Mischa's benefit. They spoke of theater and art, and Mischa was given to understand very early that on Fridays business talk was unwelcome, that he was being exposed to cultivated society as the Abramskys thought they remembered it. They were doing their duty. Did they notice, he wondered, that these soirees bore not the least relevance to their everyday lives? that the rarefied tone of the evening floated miles above Ryder Street and the odd tomcat rummaging through a dustbin in the alley? If so, they gave no sign; the offering of another canapé, the ritualistic pouring of sherry were all:

"Sip, Mischa, sip! Is good wine, special. We don't guzzle it, like nossinks at their beer."

Day after day she hammered her nails until it was indelibly pounded into Mischa that fate could hold no worse than to become a nossink. Always he was aware that only Da's drunken passing had rescued him from that fate. Even now when it was no longer needed as a possible profession, his dancing was regarded as yet greater insurance against nossinkhood, and not only by Anna. Felix, in his gentle way, could be a snob also: "Each person should do something very well, something the riffraff cannot do."

"I can do business," he said.

"Business!" Anna said with scorn—but later, in private, she agreed when Felix said:

"Our boy has a head on him, Anna."

"But I wish...I do wish he could have liked the ballet...he has the fire for it, Felix, the *temperament*."

"But not the desire. It lacks the security he needs. And there is no dance company here, my love. He would have to go away to perform, to London, perhaps farther..."

Her sigh quivered between them on the still air. "Is okay with the shops then."

"Anna..." Felix hesitated, but it must be said, could not be forever avoided. "The letters from Germany...from the lawyer."

Her mouth settled into the familiar mulish line. "Of course from him, who else writes us from Germany, eh? He makes more fairy tales to bleed the heart?"

"No fairy tales ... each month ... Anna, the old woman *is* sick."

No denial tonight. Heavy-lidded eyes closed over her silence.

"We should plan," Felix urged, "decide what to do if—"

Her eyes flew open, fierce sparks blazing at him, an animal scenting a trap. "Not here! She does not come here, it is not to think about, is not possible, no!"

The blue eyes shone too bright, clouding over as she strode to the stove to stir her agitation into tomorrow's soup, to season it with seldom-shed tears.

Business was good to them that year. Hamish Froggatt, ever deeper into the amber treacheries of whiskey, brought his problems to Ryder Street. "Creditors, they're hounding me ..."

"If you could drink a little less, Hamish ... get back to the work you used to do ..." Felix suggested, wringing his hands at this waste of a man, sincerely wanting to help.

"I told you before," Michael said. His glance lingered on the Scot's red-veined cheeks before flicking to the desk and a small bundle of checks stamped INSUFFICIENT FUNDS, all bearing Hamish's shaky signature. "Any time you're ready to sell out—"

And this time Hamish was ready, eager to shake off the clamor of bill collectors daily pounding his door.

"We can take stock and patents off your hands if you like."

Hamish, fraying at the cuffs, assorted stains decorating his old school tie, was ready for that also.

"What for do we want his rubbish?" Anna demanded later when they told her. "It's worthless. Like him."

He shrugged. "Maybe we'll get into manufacturing ... If not, at least it gives Hamish a bit of capital to play with."

"To drink on, you mean."

"If he's fool enough ..." *He* was no fool. He began sifting the acquisitions—which he lacked the technical education to grasp. Finding Hamish at a local tavern, they spread blueprints on the bar. "What were you getting at here, Hamish? I don't understand."

"Of course not. You need years of university to understand the terms —and you'd still be no wiser."

"I don't have time for university."

Hamish laughed. "No, you're a young chap in a hurry, and now you've

bought yourself a pig in a poke. These patents . . . every one of 'em's riddled with bugs. A few came close—" He looked wistful. "I registered 'em
because I kept hoping young Petie'd crack it—"

"Preston? That kid used to work for you?"

"Aye—but I couldna keep paying him, and he needed the cash to get
through school, maybe he still does. *There's* the kid with the brain,
smarter than you'll ever be . . ."

"We've each got our own kind of smart." Michael rolled up his prints,
bought Hamish one last drink, and left.

He sought out Pete Preston, but not before he'd questioned his
teachers. Yes, Pete was a brilliant student in electronics with a reputation
for the unorthodox. Still studying, but at the end of his financial rope.
Inquiries, then a visit to the semidetached house where Pete and his widowed mother lived.

"Familiar?" Michael spread prints on well-polished oak.

"Flawed," Pete said. "Hamish had great ideas but . . ."

Okay. Suppose Pete were to sift through the mountain of dusty, musty
patents that Abramsky and Son had acquired, see if there was anything of
value?

"Maybe you'd better tell me what I'm looking for."

"A product we can promote as new, cheap to make, lends itself to more
sophisticated application down the line—"

"D'you want the sun and moon on a plate, too?"

But Pete had another year of school and no money to support his
mother. He agreed to "look through" the patents. "Likely a waste of
time, but maybe worth thinking about."

"So look," Michael said. "Take a year."

It was spring when Hamish Froggatt again showed up at the bulging
warehouse, shuffling toward the front of the desk that had once been his.
He was thin now, a broken-springed man who might have been tall had
he stood up straight.

Property taxes due on Greenlings . . . vultures at city hall bleeding him
. . . he'd lose the house if they didn't get off his back . . . maybe a small
loan? Michael knew how it was, right?

Michael did, and reached for a checkbook. Felix clicked his tongue and
drew Mischa aside.

"It's bad policy . . . give if you must, but do not lend . . ."

"We'll make him some kind of deal, keep him happy."

The arrangement, once made, had Felix's approval. "A loan against real property, yes. That way Hamish keeps his pride."

"Pride? He never had any," Anna countered.

Mischa thought she was wrong. The man who built Greenlings had been proud once. But so had Da.

We don't work free and we don't beg, Micah . . . only our women beg, from fools what don't know no better. Only women spin lies for daft gaje who think the future's writ on the palm of their hand. But us, we're clever, laddo, too clever to believe that stuff—we twist the gaje any way it suits us.

It was one of the bad days, a November morning, Felix forced to call for Michael's help. Last year he'd given up barre; too much strain on the hip, the doctors warned. Now they muttered of a walker for days like this when cold muscles cramped, pulled at already damaged joints. He was reluctant. Now a walker, how long before a wheelchair? Besides, would a walker get him downstairs? And today was the third of the month.

He sat on the edge of the feather mattress, his face pinched.

"I shall be fine once I'm dressed and the blood begins to move."

But even after Michael chafed the wasted hip and hauled Felix to his feet, maneuvered him into thermal underwear, still the hip would not bear Felix's weight.

"Stay under the electric blanket, have breakfast in bed."

"No time—no, I must go down, meet the postman—"

"That can wait—"

Felix took his hand, clasped it in a convulsive grip. "You don't understand . . . I never told you . . . but it's third of the month, the letter will come from the lawyer, Mischa . . . Anna should not see . . . it upsets her . . ."

"What lawyer? What are you talking about?"

Felix's eyelids closed, the skin violet, translucent, threaded with the thin pink of veins; his hair, as yet uncombed, stood up in white-blond wisps around an increasingly bald pate. In the harsh winter light he had the otherworldly look of a mystic, but there was nothing mystical in the grip of his fingers.

"I've told you of our Sasha, how we lost him—"

"Yes—but not now—"

"But you must know, Mischa, if something should happen to me you must know, someone must know of Anna's trouble, of the other—the girl Gabriella, she is Anna's secret and I should not tell, but the letter from Germany will come today and I cannot manage the stairs." He took a deep, shaking breath. "A long time ago, oh! how happy my Anna, dreams coming true. In six months they were gone, the dreams, hopes. Our son, home, families, my work in the theater—for a time Anna's sanity. She didn't *want* to go on that last tour, to leave Sasha, but it was our life, it was all we knew, yes? And Anna was to dance the lead."

His eyes opened wide, not to a rented room in Ryder Street but to a past Mischa had not shared.

"She was so excited, such a chance... opening night a triumph for her, curtain calls without end—then moments later a call from Paris... a bullet... mistake of course, but our Sasha, oh, my poor Anna!" As he talked his voice called up old angers, found strength as he relived the occupation, their dance company recruited to entertain conquerors. He told it as he remembered it, as Anna remembered it, as he thought von Reiker must have remembered it. And as he told it Mischa was forgotten in the reality of an old nightmare relived:

So often Felix had pleaded with his willful young wife, "Try, my Anna, only try. Don't let them see."

"Them!" A cotton ball flicked away the smudge of a bizarre *Firebird* eyebrow. Already she was swirling leg warmers in sudsy water, thrusting out her long foot for the ritual of powder, of lamb's-wool pads between opposing calluses. "After what they've done *I* should be careful? *I?*"

Oh, his reckless, splendid Anna with her anger, her pride, her grief that had no end. Anna who smoldered, flared, burned too bright. How often must he tell her that life could be worse, they could be sent to a camp? That pride was not hers alone, that the enemy treasured it above all? "Only be careful..."

"How," she pleaded, "can I hide what I feel?"

"Because you must, my angel. You want to make them crazy?"

"Perhaps they already..."

When she murmured in sleep beside him, Felix lay awake, searching through the darkness for an answer that never came. She could not change. She wore every emotion like a layer of shell, a costume from her theater trunk. She could no more conceal herself than he could shake off the weight on his shoulders.

There is nothing to fear, he told himself, there is nothing more they can do to her.

But fear was everywhere then, in the theater glossed over by marble columns and gilded chairs, muffled by carpeted halls and velvet drapes, blurred by colored lamps in the stage-door bar. At the Recreation Department's concerts fear was sweetened with music and dance, fine wines in crystal, all the trappings of prewar Paris mustered to divert officers on leave from the front.

The one reminder of the times was the Führer's picture in the lobby.

The dancers clamped their fear tight under stretched and painted smiles. Only Anna Abramsky danced with no smile, no fear. Her dress was pink and her hair was gold and her steps were crisper, sharper than the rest, pink satin scissors that cut the uniformed audience into contemptible little shreds; the hard, burning blue of her eyes showered scorn over the footlights even as her arms etched fluid poetry on the smoky air.

The officer in charge of the circuit was young, painfully romantic, distressingly naive. His one affair (he thought of it as that, though he'd been sixteen at the time) had been with Mama's parlormaid; she'd smelled of carbolic and her reddened knuckles had rasped Hans von Reiker's virgin skin.

Any wonder that this Anna, this pink and gold miracle of line, obsessed him? When he pictured her in his room at the barracks, in his home in the country, anywhere at all, he saw his limbs entwined with hers in ecstatic, endless embrace. So clear was the image that already he saw rapture in her eyes, smelled the lily scent of her hair on his cheek, heard the soft catch of her breath when he touched her, when he buried himself in a mist of pink chiffon and silken, yielding flesh.

The newly discovered effects of vodka sharpened the fantasy and he drank more and more as he watched her from the wings. Was that why his heart galloped and the blood pounded in his temples? Had it nothing to do with the gold snake's-eye gleam of her wedding ring mocking him from center stage, nothing to do with the faithful husband who appeared nightly under the theater clock to walk her home through war-dreary streets?

"Let me be your friend," he'd begged her once, reaching for her hand and not finding it. "Just let me be that, Anna. Let me look at you, talk to you sometimes."

Let me touch you, adore you, worship you, kiss you with my lips, my soul, my heart. Drown in you, die in you . . .

"Only let me talk to you," von Reiker had begged. Felix had known how he felt—hadn't he felt the same, once?

"And say what?" Anna turning away as she answered, the sight of the German uniform sickening her.

"Anna, Anna, don't treat me like a monster, a wild animal."

Ironic, when he'd never been so defenseless as now, out at last from the shelter of the family estate, open to the barbs and goads of soldiers who laughed at his safe commission bought and paid for with parental influence and his own shame. A booking agent in a fancy uniform—yet she thought him a brute. And even for that he loved her. Oh, the curve of her mouth, wondrous in its arrogance—but soft under his in midnight dreams, yielding, moist, parting for him, sighing.

"I am not a brute," he told her again and again.

"A killer. You murder babies, old women."

"Not me, I tell you I did not, could not—"

She wouldn't listen to him. Her baby and her mother dead—and Hans wore the uniform. To her they were all the same.

He heard the music change, the swish of satin slippers as the corps de ballet arranged itself into a pastel bouquet from which she would open like a rose for her solo. He stiffened, gulped again at a glass some unobtrusive barman had filled. How often? Five times? Six? And did it matter with the woman pliant as a willow not ten feet away, so close he felt the breeze of her skirt, smelled her clean-dancer sweat, filled himself with her warmth, her lightness, almost touched the ivory curve of her neck, delicate and birdlike as she rode the air. Now her music swelled to the finale and he felt himself swell with it, heavier, stronger with every pregnant note, the tympani coming at him louder, louder, throbbing drumbeats that quickened with his pulse as she made her final curtsy and the swift signal to curtain.

And now the barman gave him a knowing ferret's smile, nodded toward the stage where Anna Abramsky stood alone, impatiently taking bows, waiting for the curtain to descend.

"A spirited filly, that one"—he hesitated—"sir."

They all hesitated. They *knew*. In theory and practice one of the perks of the command was certain ... privileges dancers were assumed to provide.

But they all knew, fellow officers, orderlies, stagehands, waiters, that the one perk he wanted wouldn't give him the time of day.

Filly. See the barman smirk as he mouths the word, think what is implied.

"If you mean Madame Abramsky," he said stiffly, "I suggest you show respect." God, now he sounded like Mama. By tomorrow every bottlewasher from here to the barracks would be parroting his words, sniggering behind their hands. *I suggest you show respect* ... "*I* said 'respect,' did you hear me?"

"Yes." The barman nodded, smiling. "Sir."

Beside them the curtain rose again on a flurry of applause, shouts of "Bravo" and "Encore"—but she was already returning to the wings with that haughty dancer's strut.

"Please, Anna," he whispered as she swept past him with her head up, her eyes front, "please take your bows, thank them."

She paused. "I should thank them? For what?"

"You know . . . the appl—" But his tongue stumbled and tripped and he raised a hand to hold her there, make her listen, this porcelain figurine with dance sweat glistening like diamonds in the hollow of her throat. So for the first time he touched her, his palm closing on the blade of her shoulder, and even through the vodka haze a shock wave rolled over him, submerged him in want, in tenderness—the smooth warmth of her flesh, the fragile bone that could have been a swallow's wing trembling in his grasp—and now more, more, she was smiling at him, smiling wide. When the hard blue glitter of her eyes met his, flicking fast to his heavy fingers digging at her flesh, he was in heaven.

Her smile changed subtly. "So many brave soldier boys, how to thank them all?" Her voice was music murmured low, sweet as evening bells. "I guess you will have to do."

She seemed to lean towards him, her eyes larger, brighter as they gazed into his. Entranced, he saw nothing else, heard only rapid breathing, a whisper of chiffon, the hiss of a cornered cat as she spun away.

The long thread of her spit trickling down his cheek.

Her dressing-room door slamming shut.

A key rasping in the lock.

Silence all around him.

A roaring in his ears.

The barman offering him a towel and a small, sly smile.

Then rage blinding him, filling him. He was thrusting the man aside, gasping, lurching down the long, long corridor to the place she wove her spells—

Pigs! Vermin! They'd touched her. They'd smeared their filthy paws on her shoulder, her skin.

She was breathless, as if she'd run a long way—but she'd showed them, she'd showed them what she thought of them.

She'd showed them what they were and at last she was free.

Already the boiling thing in her chest was quieter, cooler, cool, cold . . . like Sasha's dimpled knees and waving baby fists were cold, like Maman's gentle liver-spotted hands were cold . . . no no, not to think . . . better to do, to get out, go home, run to Felix. Who will be angry with her, afraid for her, who will stroke her face. But first take down the hair,

dry off the sweat, untie the shoes, throw them at the wall, watch satin
ribbons catch on the light bulb, watch them swing... swing... watch
shadows swing with them, watch the door crack, burst its frame, see them
standing there, von Reiker and the multitude he has become, faceless
creatures who kill, who maim—

He does not stop, this cretinous giant, he lunges across the room,
breathes vodka at her, throws her to bare floorboards, whispers love as
his hands shout hate, as they pull at her costume, tear at it like birthday
gift wrap, hold fast to her arms as a mouth finds her breast, her thighs,
forces them open, and there are teeth and a man is panting as a woman
screams and a fist slams in her ribs and then darkness that comes and
goes, darkness and a heavy body pressing in on her, lips that slobber,
crawl down her stomach... down... down... oh no, oh no, no-no-no-
no-no-no-no-noooooo—

Now she is dreaming; there is an anvil and a hammer and there is
searing pain and explosive shouts and her thighs are wet and there are
whimpers, sobs that are not hers, there are tears scalding her neck, a voice
in the dark—

"... so sorry, I am so sorry, so sorry, so sorry—"

Still the hands fumble her but they are trembling and she pushes at
them, gets to her knees, her feet. She flies down the long corridor, pushes
through the curious theater crowd and out to the sidewalk in her tattered
chiffon—and there is Felix, her salvation, waiting under the clock...

Many weeks of hunting, searching out rumors of doctors and pseudo-
doctors and butchers in sleazy back alleys. Weeks of heads shaking. Sorry.
They cannot. Regulations...

In despair Felix went to von Reiker. Be calm, calm, he told himself, for
he can put you to a work camp and who will care for Anna then? This
officer's family has power, connections—

He began carefully. "She does not know I am here. Please understand, I do
not come from jealousy. If she had wanted you, if you had taken her with
love, then I—we—could accept. But you left her bleeding, my poor Anna
who has already lost everything and now also her pride, for she is pregnant
and no one will help us, and I thought perhaps you..."

He didn't know what to expect. Arrest? A bullet? Perhaps even an
apology—the boy was supposed to be a gentleman, though how a gentleman could do what he'd done—

But he was beaming, rubbing his eyes, blushing with pride. He looked dazed, humble, happy, unutterably young and foolish.

"Anna... she will have my child, mine—"

"You don't understand," Felix said gently. "She needs help and no doctor will touch her. You have influence—"

"Doctor? She is sick?" He leapt up, paced the floor between desk and window. "Our family doctor will see her, care for her until... No harm must come to her, to the child. I'll call my mother—"

No harm must come to her, no harm! Felix held tight to the edge of the desk. "She wants an abortion."

Von Reiker registered alarm, affront, disbelief, as if he'd heard a forbidden word. "She wants *that?*"

Felix sighed. To dancers the abortionist was as familiar, often as necessary, as the chiropodist—but perhaps to a von Reiker—

"She wants *that?*" he said again.

"But of course... she is my wife."

Pink lips began to quiver. He was a child being told he couldn't have the almond on the cake. "But I'd never agree to—it's my baby!" He stopped, suddenly suspicious. "How do I know? How can I be sure?"

Under different circumstances Felix could almost have smiled at his naiveté. "We are performers. A pregnant woman cannot dance. Her children are planned." Around the next role, next season, one sacrifice balanced against another. He remembered the discussions, the meetings, before they had Sasha, with Anna poised on the edge of her first solo. But they'd wanted him, how they'd wanted that child. Against all advice they'd shut their ears to the ballet mistress, the director, the dresser, even the pianist who played for class...

"Well then!" Confidence restored, von Reiker rubbed his hands, now the young family man with new burdens he was honored and proud to bear. "Then I shall see our lawyer—no, don't worry, there will be provision for you, then an annulment—"

It was Felix now who was dazed. Where had he lived, this man-child, that he could suppose...

"I think," he said softly, "that she will not agree."

Month followed month. They lived in apartments of friends where von Reiker could not find her, moving, always moving... Anna gaunt, curled into her silence, into the horror that grew daily inside her.

One midnight she was delivered of a tiny girl with Anna's long bones and a fuzz of pale hair. Felix prayed for a miracle, that its mother could reach down through the ice and find some morsel of love for it.

"Look at her little mouth, Anna. How perfect ... only look."

"Nazi bastard," she whispered, and turned away.

He laid it in her bed, in the crook of her sleeping arm, and kissed them, Anna's cheek cold, the child's warm and petal-soft under his lips.

He took to the streets to find milk. And he prayed.

When he came home the apartment was empty, and when she returned after dark she was alone.

She swayed at the door, her face gray and her eyes hooded, sunk too deep in their sockets. For Felix, the day's fears took sudden, terrifying shape. So many rivers, bridges, shadowed alleys.

"Where—"

"Where it belongs, with *them*. Where they live."

Like a sleepwalker she moved to the sink and washed her hands, kept on washing them long after Felix turned off the tap.

"Oh, my Anna," he whispered, gathering up her bones, rocking her in the chair. "What have they done to my Anna ..."

They waited out the war in Reims, where Felix's father had bought a small appliance-repair shop just before the war. Here they knew no one and no one knew them. Felix cared for Anna and worked in his father's shop. But for the unbreakable discipline of a daily barre the world of dance and their dream of success receded. Dancers of "promise" were young and dedicated. Now Anna was dedicated only to her misery. During a raid a sliver of shrapnel lodged in Felix's hip and punctured the last of their dream.

As soon as the war was over they took ship for England, where no memories lay waiting, a man with silver in his hair and a woman who could have been any age at all.

Nearing port the passengers crowded on deck, smiling at the smoked-orange glow of victory fires ablaze up and down the coast.

An old man, unmistakably British with his shabby bowler hat and tattered umbrella, began to sing in a thin, quavering voice. His song was from the wrong war, but the other passengers took up the tune, swaying in unison as they sang, as Felix swayed now, singing for Mischa:

> *"Keep the home fires burning*
> *While your hearts are yearning . . ."*

"Only look, my angel," Felix had said, taking her shoulders, making her face the land. "How happy they must be at their fires! It's over, everything is over."

She looked. For the first time in months, in years, the granite angles of her face crumbled; the line of her neck, still proud, turned and dipped as she rubbed her cheek into the tweed folds of his jacket. Her shoulders moved. Felix didn't know if they shook with sobs or bitter laughter.

Now, so many bitter years later, he still did not know as he told the story to this strange, dear young man who was also their son, their consolation. Who was now looking at him over the great bedspread with sudden doubt in his eyes. Mischa had listened, frozen first with compassion and then with horror. How could Felix, kindly—"But you, you let Anna give her child away?"

Felix's smile had bitter edges. "Mischa, life does not always give us choices, you understand?"

And when it does we can still make the wrong one. Mischa nodded. He understood.

"But it is better you know."

"Yes."

As Michael closed the door Felix spoke again, perhaps asking his forgiveness for Anna, for himself, when none was needed. "I think my Anna would have loved the girl if she could . . ."

So Michael's perceptions of the Abramskys changed yet again. He saw now why Felix let Anna cater to him shamelessly, bringing him a lap robe, tea, breaking off class to bring aspirin as he played the piano. It wasn't so much that he exaggerated his pain (on days like this it was obviously excruciating) but he *used* his pain because Felix (and he also) were surrogates for those Anna had lost and the one she had abandoned.

After that, in the stirred dust motes of the studio, with the thump of the piano thudding through him, Anna's strident voice urging him to *Present, Mischa! Make the back proud, pick up the head!* He never again saw her lean features as harsh. He saw a beautiful woman prematurely aged.

TEN

*E*LLIE WAS FIFTEEN when she knocked on the headmaster's door. She'd chosen the village school because it was free.

The headmaster raised his eyebrows. "A student? But you've had only the best in personal tuition—a couple more years and you'll be better qualified than I am. You can learn nothing here, only take up space. If your grandmother knew—"

"Certainly she knows." Oh, how she used Grossmutter's style—and how she lied!

"Well . . . we're open to all. We can't stop you."

Other students didn't see it that way. Everything about her was different. The staff treated her like fine china: von Reiker—Handle With Care. The students showed resentment. Her looks, speech, accent all set her apart. And alone. The headmaster was right.

"They won't even try to be civil!" she told him.

"Why should they? Mostly their parents are (or were) von Reiker employees. A lot of them are laid off. You're the girl from the big house—of course they're hostile, how can they see you any other way? Even my own grandmother was a washerwoman up at the house, so you see . . . You'd be more at home at the academy—though I'm not sure they'd teach you much."

The Academy for Young Ladies specialized in deportment and elocution. The academy spread no welcome mat either. It was a question of . . . status, of position. A few parents were insecure and perhaps some *were* overcautious—but in all good conscience the management . . . Gabriella understood how it was, of course?

"Yes. Your conscience is wonderfully selective. It lets you take fees from a woman whose child is hopelessly, incurably retarded; you teach country bumpkins to parrot bits of Goethe when they can barely comprehend 'Hansel and Gretel'—"

"Have you quite finished?"

"Almost. Perhaps you should teach your students to bathe daily. It's easier than Goethe—and still in fashion."

She wrote to Miss Warren in California, who answered:

> . . . *my, but you write well when you dander's up! You draw a wicked caricature, too—I'm proud. Forget the Academy. Deportment is as dead as the dodo. You're better off using the education and talents you already have—just how is up to you! Anyway, it's no use starting on anything new now. God knows I didn't like your grandmother, but I guess you do, so I imagine you'll be a full-time nurse pretty soon.*
>
> *Ellie dear, she won't get better. And even if you could afford it, nurses alone don't cut it because they don't care enough. I know. I'm at my father's home now, watching him die, helping, I hope. All I can do is hold his hand, give him comfort. It will be the same for you. Perhaps you'll plan a visit here when it's over?*
>
> Best,
> Mary Beth Warren

Miss Warren was right. Grossmutter's health went downhill faster with every month, and soon it was all Ellie could do to control her.

The seventeen birthday candles dipped and shivered in the slight breeze off the Mosel.

Hovering between the dining table and the door into the hall, an elderly housemaid cast nervous glances at the empty staircase as she assured

Ellie, alone at the table, that Frau von Reiker would be down any minute, any minute. Hadn't she poured the medicine with her own two hands and stood there while the old lady drank it? She was dressing, and the good Lord knew how long *that* took lately. Today is was to be the pink...

Ellie crumbled bread in her long fingers. "There's no hurry," she murmured. There wasn't. Except for the cake, which she did not in any case like, birthdays were the same as other days. Without the maid or the cook to mark the day, she wouldn't have noticed its passing. Grossmutter certainly wouldn't, just as she didn't notice when Heinz complained of broken fences and blight on the vines, or the cook of mice in the pantry. Now it was Ellie, not Grossmutter, who ordered plant sprays and new fenceposts, who called the pet shop for a kitchen cat.

Grossmutter noticed little now beyond the time of day; her medicine was given every four hours, and the delay of a second or two set bells clanging all through the house.

If the portrait hung a fraction of an inch askew she noticed that. Her dead son filled her days, the strands of his memory hopelessly entangled with those of his father and the twin threads of pain and senility, all twisted now into bizarre new patterns through which she saw little else.

The candles were burned halfway down before the maid gave an agitated little sigh and Grossmutter appeared at the top of the stairs, twirling and simpering under her son's portrait like a lovestruck girl. She was indeed in pink, all faded chiffon and lace, her thin white hair pulled into corkscrew curls around a gray, melted face. Until lately she hadn't used makeup at all, but these days she smeared it on hurriedly and inexpertly in the hiatus between one slab of pain and the next, kewpie-doll circles on her cheeks, red slashes on vanished lips, thick white powder on chin and stringy neck. Today she'd forgotten her shoes and stockings, and the elastic edges of brown interlock bloomers peeped out under pink chiffon.

She pouted up at her son, who was still twenty-one, still stern and handsome and brave in his painted uniform, the Iron Cross bright as a new Deutschemark on his breast.

"Well, Hans? What do you say? Am I still your pretty girl? You always liked me in pink, remember?"

She cocked her head as if listening, gave a gay little laugh and twirled again before taking the stairs, step by lurching step, to her granddaughter's birthday tea.

She surveyed the table and Ellie with vague, unfocused eyes. "Gabriella? And what have we here then?"

The candles hooked her gaze. She swayed, mesmerized as they flickered and flared in the breeze.

Ellie waited, as did the maid. Between the drug and the pain there was perhaps a half hour when it was possible to hold normal conversation with Grossmutter, but that time was not yet.

"You'll have cake, Grossmutter, and coffee? Aniela is holding your chair... if you'll sit down I'll pour—"

But Grossmutter was drifting off, her corseted dignity only slightly marred as she tripped over a footstool, steadied herself and stumbled on, pausing now at the sideboard to examine her reflection in a silver tray, now at the buffet to run pale, liver-spotted hands over the ruddy gleam of mahogany, now at the casement, where she ignored the long terraces of vines outside and instead rubbed gauzy window panels between paper-dry fingers. It seemed almost an afterthought when she reached back, plucked a candle from Ellie's cake, and set fire to the curtains.

Stepping back, she watched as pungent smoke eddied and curled in the breeze, as hot candlewax dripped to the parquet floor.

"*Ach,* Frau von Reiker!" The maid darted forward, easing the old woman aside to drag down the panel and crush the flames with her hands, her stout oxfords beating out a tattoo on the remains.

"*Mein Gott, Frau, oh mein Gott!*"

Ellie took in a deep breath, pushed Grossmutter into a chair, aimed the fire extinguisher at the drapes, and sent the maid to the kitchens to plunge her blistered hands into ice water. Then she blew out her birthday candles and called the doctor.

"But Fräulein, I told you last week the medication cannot be reduced. It should, in fact, be increased."

"First come and attend to the maid, then we'll discuss my grand-mother."

Who was now frowning, drumming fingertips on the damask table-cloth. Her eyes, for the moment, were clear. "Gabriella, have you no control over the staff? The ceiling over the window is filthy and someone has definitely been smoking in here. What *are* the maids thinking of—"

"Maid, Grossmutter. We have only one now, remember? Aniela—who has just burned her hands."

Her grandmother's glance shifted uncomfortably from Ellie to her own wax-smeared fingers and back again. For an instant she had the furtive look of a child caught in some mischief, but then old habits asserted themselves. "So careless..."

"Grossmutter, the doctor's on his way—*please* talk to him about a hospital," Ellie said urgently. Her grandmother's lucid periods were briefer every day and there was so much to say—and never a solution. "Last week it was the bathroom mirror. You could have cut yourself badly."

Before that it had been an art collector wanting to buy Papa's portrait —but the less said about him and Grossmutter's sewing scissors the better. If the foreman hadn't been around, if the collector hadn't been heavyset and powerful, if the old woman had been steadier on her feet...

If the doctor would take a stand perhaps she would be convinced—but he was an easygoing procrastinator who'd served von Reikers all of his life; before him his father and his grandfather had ministered potions to all the ancestors whose portraits lined the upstairs hall. For him to go against a von Reiker...it was unthinkable.

"Please, Grossmutter..."

Frau von Reiker hesitated, visibly pulling together the tattered, glacial shreds of her dignity before she answered:

"I have lived in this house since the day I was married. Hans was born in it, and I shall die in it. These accidents wouldn't happen if you controlled the nurse, if you wouldn't let her gallivant off whenever she fancies a day in town—"

"She walked out a month ago—in any case, nurses need holidays, they must sleep..." And this old woman could not be trusted alone for a moment.

"Then get another nurse."

Ellie sighed. "With what?" The household accounts were a disaster, letters from creditors flooding every mail, grocers, bottlers... There had been a time (how naive she must have been) when she'd thought they were rich, that the vineyard supported this massive house and grounds. And how bitterly Grossmutter had laughed—she'd been in better health then.

"The vineyard? Why, that's the biggest drain of the lot—only my personal income keeps it going. The principal stays with the trust—you'll get nothing, of course; the cousins in Stuttgart will see to that! Every penny of capital reverts back to them. What you'll do when I'm gone... the house is von Reiker, so I might be able to salvage that—the lawyers are looking into it—but what you'll run it on...if my poor Hans had only known...if your mother had just been a reasonable woman, oh, if only you'd been legitimate, Gabriella..."

How much more she could have loved me, Ellie thought now, staring into her grandmother's small, dogmatic eyes.

"The situation's impossible," she said quietly. "We can't go on." She had one card to play, one bluff; it was far from a trump and was perhaps cruel. "Since you won't go to the hospital perhaps I should go away—"

The fires of an old anger burned in Grossmutter, rocking her briefly into some semblance of sanity. "Your mother won't have you—she made *that* plain enough from the start—"

"My mother's the last person I'd go to, you know that—"

"Hasn't got the time of day for her own flesh and blood, oh no, but she'll take in some thieving tramp, give *him* a home."

Ellie sighed. She was no longer interested in poking over old bones. Anything her mother chose to do had long since ceased to hurt. Childhood pain had crusted into bewilderment and then to a distant, cool hatred. It was many years since she'd indulged herself in romantic dreams of a dancing mother endlessly waltzing with a brave, handsome soldier who was her father—and the son of this cold, bitter woman.

"I was thinking I might go to Bonn, perhaps get secretarial work in... oh, maybe a publishing house. When I've got a foot in the door I could try my hand at a children's book, but in the meantime I'd be earning... it would help."

The sly, self-preserving smile of the old and infirm touched her grandmother's sunken, painted lips. Hard on its heels came the first frown of returning pain, but she was a determined woman, this, and her fingers bit hard into the edge of the table.

"Then who would look after the house and the field hands?—they'll none of them work if they're not watched. And who's to look after me? Secretarial work indeed! You're far too well educated for that! You know how to conduct yourself, you have excellent manners. When I'm gone you can get work as a governess anywhere in the world."

Never. Whatever she did, she wouldn't be at somebody's beck and call. Even now that she had a modicum of freedom to go to town, she couldn't leave. She was tied to this house, to the alarm clock which woke her throughout the night because Grossmutter must be supervised. Only once, desperate for relief, she'd left her in the care of a housemaid and taken the train to town, bringing back an armload of books and vague feelings of guilt—all too quickly confirmed when she found the maid sipping wine in the kitchen and the invalid locked in her upstairs bed, out of sight, out of mind, out of hearing. Grossmutter, the most fastidious of women, had wet her bed. And she was weeping.

"So ashamed, Gabriella. I rang and I rang and I thumped on the floor, but no one came to unlock the door—and the bathroom not three yards down the hall!"

After that Ellie depended on no one but herself—at least her services came free. A small enough return. Von Reiker money had kept her in comfort (if not in happiness) all her life. Now it was time to repay by constant, endless care. No, not endless. Some days it just seemed that way. Mary Beth was right about that, too. As long as the need was there an obligation remained. To hold the hand until the end, to *be* there...

"How soon to my medicine?" Grossmutter was asking now. "It must be due—and I want to go to bed. Where's the doctor?"

"He'll come up when he's done Aniela's hands."

Again the flash of guilt, then a quickly drawn breath. Ellie could almost see the next tentacle of pain reach behind the eyes. This fiction of a migraine, so long believed by both of them, was wearing thin. Grossmutter was not a stupid woman. Surely she suspected that this thing pressing on her brain grew a little larger, a little stronger every day?

The untouched birthday cake forgotten, Ellie helped the shaken old woman to her feet and steered her towards the staircase and the massive painting hanging above it.

But even now, with new pain pulling at every line of her face, Grossmutter paused to look up into the face of her son. "Hans, how much easier if you were here...what a comfort you would have been..." Petulant, she turned on Ellie. "When you are angry you look very much like her, you know."

The doctor was brisk, rubbing his hands over a glass of excellent Mosel, the customary von Reiker hospitality.

"Superficial burns, Ellie, nothing more. A couple of days and she'll be fine."

Aniela, yes. "And my grandmother?"

He shrugged. "I've had to increase the dosage."

"She belongs in a hospital," Ellie said sharply. "She's dangerous."

"A woman in her position, a fixture in the community, how could I commit her without her consent?"

"Which you know she'll never give."

"She may, one day she may." He topped up his glass.

"Do you think she knows?"

"Perhaps, perhaps...She said you spoke of leaving. Of course you wouldn't...?"

"Of course not, how can I?" How stupid this man was—perhaps they all were, and how would she ever know? What men did she meet but the doctor, the foreman, and assorted field hands?

"Good." Another swallow, another reach for the bottle. "It wasn't easy for her, you know, taking you in. This house was the center of social life around here—and she was the hub." A thumb pointed upstairs.

"I'm grateful—I don't need to be reminded, thank you."

"Oops! Sorry! What are your plans when she's gone? Have you thought?"

My God, had she thought! "Maybe I'll get into publishing, perhaps there'll be enough money for some useful training...oh, I don't know, I know there's nothing for me here. I want to get out just as soon as I can."

He nodded. "In the city somewhere, very wise."

Where nobody knows or cares. "How long do you think it will be?" she asked. And how cold *that* sounded—but she needed to know, to have some idea—

He turned the glass against the sun, admiring its sparkling prisms before taking the next long, reflective drink.

"There's no telling with a case like this. It can arrest itself—then again ...It could be a month, a year, maybe two...Wonderful stuff this, Ellie, wonderful—"

She obeyed the hint and gave him a bottle for the road before showing him out, then she climbed the stairs to her room and sat on the edge of the bed, her palms pressed tight together, but not in prayer. Badly as she wanted out, she couldn't bring herself to pray for it.

She didn't allow herself to weep either—Grossmutter had taught her that. But she did wonder as she listened to the old woman in the next room toss and mumble in her drugged, beatific sleep, sometimes snoring, sometimes mumbling about a pink dress and a brave boy, his portrait and his Iron Cross.

She wondered how heavy it had been, that cross.

And why had she never actually seen it? Only its painted, forever shining image.

ELEVEN

*W*HEN HAMISH FROGGATT began to complain of ants oozing through the buttery cracks in his breakfast muffin, the Abramskys took action.

It was Felix who contacted Hamish's nephew in Edinburgh, writing partly from concern, partly from a vague but lingering unease about Michael's relationship with the Scot. Yet it was from Michael that the suggestion to help Hamish had come—which irritated Anna but seemed to please Felix.

"This is a kind thought, Mischa," Felix said, surprised. "I have sometimes thought you were perhaps a little . . . unfeeling with poor Hamish."

"What for do we bother?" Anna demanded. "Is not enough he stinks up my house with whiskey? With cigarettes? Staggers through my studio? Watches the legs of my teachers? Why do you worry on this foolish man?"

Michael worried. As Hamish had come to spend more and more time at the warehouse or the flat in Ryder Street, he worried a lot. Far better than Felix and Anna, he knew what to expect, knew that someone would eventually find Hamish the way he had found Da, eyes open, a fly buzzing the funeral dirge close by. The fear lurked always in that dark place between wakefulness and sleep, shadowing his days, haunting his nights, ready to drop him again into a world of no walls, no shelter, no family he could call his own, a world he'd thought permanently sealed off by success. Yes, he wanted Hamish gone. Then he wouldn't be forced to think of Da, to make the treacherous connection.

Much better that Hamish leave.

The nephew arrived at Ryder Street all business, rubbing his hands, eager to be off, his glance never far from his briefcase on the dining table and his overcoat on the chairback.

"He'd best come away home with me where he can be watched."

He spoke to Michael and Felix but not to his Uncle Hamish, who slumped in Anna's favorite easy chair and fixed a sardonic smile on his only living relative. The syrupy strains of "Sugar Plum Fairy" reached thinly though worn floorboards below them, through Anna's voice instructing her class to hold it the *demiseconde* longer, dammit, longer—a bizarre counterpoint to the business at hand.

The nephew seemed not to notice. "I'll drop Hamish off at my house and be back within the week," he said briskly, "get his affairs in order, the property fixed up to sell. Pointless to hang on to it."

"Hamish needs care," Felix said mildly, a trace of reproach in his voice. "Perhaps a sanitarium? One reads about them in the papers . . . he's been ill a long time, your uncle."

Watching the tableau that would set him free, Michael held himself very still. Hamish Froggatt was not ill. D.t.'s were a symptom of weakness, not poor health. The man was weak, lacking even Da's excuse.

. . . and what was that, young Micah? A place called Deacon's Wood, maybe? A dimly remembered thing called a kris?

You have dishonored the Rom . . . you will shun places where the Rom gather . . . you are no longer Rom. And Da's bitterness all the long years after. His braggadocio: *Who needs 'em, me old cockie? Them and their bleedin' laws—I can look after my little lad fine, you'll always have your da, laddo.* Yes, Da. Sure, Da. But Hamish was pathetic—as Da, even at his worst, had never been.

Oh, but the swagger of Da then—as long as they were in the south. Headed north, he grew more morose with every mile they covered, skulked down narrow lanes when they could have taken the main road over Shap in half the time. Though he never mentioned it by name he took Micah every June to the horse fair at Appleby, parking the trailer outside town, close enough to hear the Eden tumble and gurgle over boulders, but well away from Romany bands on Fair Hill. *Gallows Hill as used to be, Micah.* Da spied on them through the trees, his face hard to read as he muttered under his breath. Young Micah saw the flicker of campfires, their reflection in his father's eyes, and at first he wondered, but as the pattern emerged he waited only for June to finish. For the pear harvest, and safety, to begin.

They'd loiter around Appleby two days, sometimes three, before Da shrugged, scowled, and pointed the trailer south again. In the weeks that followed Da couldn't seem to pass up a single pub, propping up bar after saloon bar, lingering until he was ejected at closing time with an extra bottle in his pocket, weaving his way back to the trailer maudlin drunk, muttering and cursing, falling over the step, kicking the door in, loosening his belt... Micah, who saw the pattern when he was too young to understand it, asked once why they went to Appleby at all—but Da was full of gin that day, so Micah took a beating he remembered for a very long time. He never asked again.

Da had hankered after the Rom. God alone knew why, but that, such as it was, was Da's excuse. Hamish Froggatt had no excuse. He lolled in weakness, indolence, total lack of ambition—and who could sympathize with that? Not Michael Abramsky.

Felix, yes.

The nephew, brusque, impatient, was trying to avoid Felix's farewell handshake. Felix sighed, feeling that Hamish's wasted life, as well as a troubling chapter in his own, was about to close. And why was Mischa so silent, so watchful?

"We'll be off, then," the nephew said. "I'll see you again next week. I'll have to hire painters and gardeners before we can even think of finding a buyer for the house. As if I didn't have enough to do—to tell you the truth the whole bloody trip's a bother."

Hamish might not have been there.

And now Michael, not looking at Felix, was speaking in that careful, deliberate voice he used for business. Quiet, with much authority. "I think we can save you a journey."

The nephew brightened. "You know of a good man to handle it? All that work—any help you can give me. Greenlings is—"

"Entailed."

The word dropped like a small pebble between them. The nephew blinked, flushed, stepped back. "Entailed? It can't be!" For the first time he turned to his uncle. "Uncle Hamish owns it free and clear—"

"Did," Michael said softly, distinctly. "Hamish did own it. It is a very large house—upkeep is expensive. Hamish has had reverses. There have been loans."

"Oh, loans..." The nephew waved his hand, dismissing them. "Small loans, obviously I'll pay them off. Who holds the paper?"

"Abramo, our company, carries the paper—and the loans are not small. Hamish's equity will barely cover selling costs. I'm sorry."

The news was absorbed in silence. Felix shivered. Michael was so assured, so smooth, with just that silky hiss in his voice, always there when Greenlings was the subject. There were times, and this was one of them, when Felix was afraid for him, for this ambition that had no end. Everything he touched turned to gold, yes, but if one day it did not...

And here was poor Hamish, rousing himself now, lighting a cigarette (in Anna's chair!), and shooting his nephew a death's-head grin over the smoke of it:

"You should have come sooner. You left me to rot. The Abs at least took my pulse now and then, checked I was still breathing. Russkie"—he pointed at Felix—"that sly sod even locked my bottles up when he got the chance. And when I was short a wee shilling or two for taxes and such...well, it was the swarthy bugger there who came through, wasn't it?"

"But you're an educated man! Your degrees, your—"

"Not worth a tuppenny cuss if a man's thirsty." Coughing, he laughed through smoke and his thin, fleeting triumph. "As for the house, it's been a boulder on my neck for years. There's nothing left worth scrapping about."

"But your work...all the patents..."

Hamish waved his cigarette at Michael. "Sold 'em to the boy wonder, didn't I? Legal as legal."

"Oh, Mischa," Felix said, his hands fluttering, when the Froggatts had left for Edinburgh. "The nephew, what he must have expected, a blood relative—"

"Where was the relative when we had to lock Hamish in the attic?

When he cursed and thumped at the door night after night and Anna without a wink of sleep? When the police picked him up for disturbing the peace, did the nephew bail him out?"

He closed his eyes to block the memory and the shudder that came with it. So many years, and still he could neither say nor think the word "police" without flinching. Da's legacy.

Blood relatives. They were due nothing they hadn't worked for. Real relatives were those who cared, like Felix, like Anna.

"Greenlings needs work, Felix. The nephew's lucky we didn't hand him a bill."

Felix walked around the familiar room, ran his hands over patches where last winter's rain had seeped through. After some prodding the landlord had plastered them over, but not soon enough for Anna's sepia photos, marred now by green mildew and yellowing runnels of damp. But still he was uncertain, afraid of a step more grandiose than any he'd envisioned.

"The house, Mischa... it's so big. Are you sure we want to live there?"

Michael had no doubts at all. In his mind the grounds were already freshly landscaped, every room furnished with solid, enduring pieces. There was central heating, no more fires for Felix to build and feed. The butler's pantry off the main hall would become a small elevator and Felix would never again have to climb stairs. He'd get a housekeeper for Anna and have one of the upstairs rooms converted to her personal studio. There was nothing they could not do, nothing!

"Naturally we want to live there, Felix. It's our property. We've bought it."

Up through the floor, Anna dismissing her students just as the office phone shrilled. She sounded tired.

"Something else," Michael said. "People feel free to bother her any time they fancy a workout. It has to stop. At Greenlings, Anna won't be teaching at all."

Felix smiled. "Of course you are right, Mischa. Always, always you are right. In you, we are so very lucky."

The contractor curled his lip at gates sagging on rusted hinges, at yellowed grass and broken walls, and estimated that the transformation would take a year. All the remodeling, was Michael *sure* he wanted a complete restoration? All this rubbish to cart away, empty bottles and milk cartons, old fenders. Dumped by that old sot Froggatt? By passing villagers?

Michael neither knew nor cared. To get rid of it was what mattered. Quickly. They'd waited too long already for this house, this one house among millions, the one he'd set his heart on with that first errand on the number eleven bus.

"We expect to move in by spring," he told the contractor.

"Three months? You expect the bloody moon, mate."

"We're paying for it. See that we get it."

They could afford it. A small network of shops crisscrossed the country. Electronics was the wave of the future and Abramo rode its crest, would eventually be in a position to compete with the biggest in the field when Pete—who'd started out as "that brilliant student" and now headed up Research and Development—had confidence to match his knowledge. It would be soon. Already it was in his walk, his air of barely suppressed tension.

Even the studio franchises, started simply to utilize space over the shops, had paid off, giving the lie to Felix and Anna, who maintained there was no money to be made in dance. Scarcely a major city now lacked its mirrored rooms, its bright-eyed children diligently learning the Abramsky Method, their doting mothers lining the benches with knitting or crewelwork in hand.

Yes. They could well afford this estate that would soon be the Greenlings of his imagination.

When it was done Michael made the inspection alone. Felix's runabout was in the shop for repairs, and Anna, as always, flatly refused to climb into the black Mercedes:

"A German car? No, never!"

"German, not Nazi," Felix gently reminded her.

"Same thing."

"Not the same," Michael and Felix said together, exchanging glances over her head as she furiously "sewed her shoes," that unending dancer's ritual of stitching ribbons, darning worn-out toes. Felix shrugged. "So I stay with my Anna, keep company..."

Michael nodded. Everything must be perfect before they saw it.

It was. Lawns lush and green, the driveway regraveled, fresh paint everywhere, shrubs in bloom, the lily pond cleaned and stocked, sturdy gates hung and fastened, every wall built up. Even the new sign.

The trees had thrived, arching the curved driveway into a cool green

tunnel through which his car scattered new gravel and the tired remains
of old fears. He parked by the big double doors and approached the
house alone, first peering through leaded windows at gracious, high-
ceilinged rooms, at sunlight dancing from chandelier to amber wall
sconce to sparkling glassware in tall, glazed cabinets.

Inside, Anna's kitchen gleamed with stainless steel and copper and
enamel; already in the small elevator an easy chair waited on Felix
Abramsky's pleasure; the living and dining rooms were warm with deep
red carpet and heavy velvet drapery.

Up the gracefully curving staircase, in a room lined with mirrors and
filled with light, stood a piano and Anna's barre. The main bedroom
struck a single discordant note. Adamantly rejecting the suggestion of
new furniture, Anna had clung to her massive feather bed and her brooding, plum-colored overstuffed chairs. Michael approved. More than any
of them, Anna needed familiar things about her. Even her prints, of the
Nicolais and Olgas and Tamaras and Piotrs—all were restored and re-
framed, integrated into the decor. Michael's own rooms were spartan by
comparison; pale woods and light carpets, a few modern prints on stark
white walls, a single bed with a bone-white spread. Separating the two
suites, a wide hallway dotted with brocaded chairs and small antique
tables.

Outside again under a pale spring sun, the door locked carefully, cere-
moniously, behind him, he breathed deep, relieved there were no eyes,
not even the benevolent gaze of Anna and Felix, to see him wrap his arms
around the huge oak that centered the drive, its bark rough and cool to
his hands and then to his cheek as he closed his eyes and let tears of
triumph soak dark and round into the rich earth of Greenlings.

Ten years from a battered trailer filled with Da's guilt and remorse, ten
years from terror, the bewildered uncertainty of that sly, scruffy Micah
who was more and more a stranger to Michael Abramsky.

Ten years of Felix and Anna Abramsky.

And security.

And now this. A solid house that would not blow away, high walls
around it and iron gates that locked.

And the sign. PRIVATE PROPERTY—NO ADMITTANCE.

For days Anna flitted from kitchen to cellar to attic, her mauve tea
gown a delighted wraith fluttering though the halls. "Oh Felix, is a
dream, this house! A fantasy! Whoever could imagine—" A brief pirou-

ette at the mirror in her studio, then a few notes on the piano. "The work, the planning, and all for us—" A flick of her duster over spotless sepia prints on the bedroom wall. "Is big pleasure, no, to wake up in this room, to look out—" A sweep of her arm took in flower beds bright with tulip and daffodil, the driveway a sweep of rhododendron in riotous pink bloom. "Is miracle, Felix!"

Felix took her bony shoulders in his hands, looked down into a face glowing with pleasure. How many years since he'd seen her so? Many, many...

"You will be content here, my angel?"

"Content! For me is new life, Felix. Not the luxury, no—but is nice, yes, to have things rich?—but no, it is not only the having. I feel—I feel I can move here...be free."

Be her old self, before Sasha, before the girl Gabriella. Already it was in her face, this freedom, in her exercises at the barre. Once again she performed them with joy, not the grueling tedium of work for work's sake. There were no bitter memories here. Once he'd thought Ryder Street would hold none, but she carried them with her from France, draped them like gray wraiths about her through the years. But here "was new life," and so for him also. A new life built by Mischa. With love.

Anna *was* happy. Did not darling Felix look fine, walking strong and straight with a cane over velvet grass? examining each new plant? nodding gravely with the gardener just as if he understood the talk of mulch and moss and hybrids? In this place she no longer thought even of the girl Gabriella—well, maybe sometimes—but who in any case was almost eighteen, nearly grown up, responsible for herself; a little while more and it would not be necessary to think of her ever again. Memories of Sasha had lost their bite, their sharp edges worn smooth with years and the tender solicitude of Felix and Mischa. How could she ever have thought him strange, the dark one? so distant to all but herself and Felix? And now he'd found a new girl again—fine dancer though not good enough for him of course, who was?—and perhaps he was not too distant with her? If not, was it possible he would marry and bring babies to these rooms? And if not that girl, then another... No matter. He was happy. With light step he walked the grounds every morning. He took barre with Anna before driving Felix to the office, and each evening he personally locked the gates and hung the key on the hat stand before consulting them on possible new plans for the gazebo, maybe a swimming pool in the future, perhaps a trip to London for Anna to see the Royal Ballet. Ah, what a boy, this Mischa...

Their few neighbors were some distance down the road, a small disappointment to Felix—he would have liked a neighbor or two such as
they'd had in Ryder Street, other lives he could unlock with the key of his
unending concern. The lack of company suited Anna and Michael very
well, however. Both knew what Felix seemed unwilling to face. They
were resented. To the locals they were known by the name Hamish had
called them. The Abs. Foreigners who'd bought out Froggatt's business
and then elbowed their way into the finest property in the district. Worse,
they were successful foreigners, only look what they'd made of Greenlings! Which made them pushy—though how Felix could be perceived as
pushy was beyond Michael. Anna, well, she was sometimes abrasive,
scornful of local shopkeepers; Michael himself had neither time nor any
desire for friendships that did not involve business, but Felix . . . Felix
minded.

"It makes me guilty driving into the corner gas station, Mischa," he
said, looking doubtfully at his new Bentley (in which Anna would ride
because it was demonstrably *not* German). "If we'd kept the old runabout
they'd feel less . . . threatened. To them we must look like . . . opportunists,
perhaps?"

"Would they like us better if we were a blight on the area? Greenlings a
crumbling ruin in their backyard? They're jealous. The opportunity was
there, wasn't it? We took it, that's all."

You took it, Mischa, Felix thought. You take and work where others
are too timid.

Michael was driving through the open gates late one afternoon when
he saw the stranger. The man stood under a pigeon-gray sky that threatened to storm, his back to Michael as he contemplated the long driveway
and the house beyond.

From his stance he was not a young man. Heavyset, a little stooped, his
pants bagging at spindly knees, an unseasonably sharp wind off the moor
inflating his dirty blue shirt. On his feet, torn rubber boots tied on with
bits of frayed rope. But he had much hair, this stranger, dark and wild—
and he leaned on the gates, one hand in his pocket, the other shielding a
cigarette from the wind.

A tramp. Michael stopped the car in a shower of gravel and climbed
out.

"What do you want?"

The man turned sharp black eyes on Michael, looked him up and down slowly, calculating. A sudden weakness at Michael's knees, a prickling at the back of his neck that made him want to leap back into the car and run the man down.

But he was reasonable enough, the stranger, his voice conciliatory, low-pitched. "Just a camp for the night." He waved his cigarette toward the road, where a small truck was parked maybe a hundred yards away. It was piled high with bundles of bedding and pots and pans; two young men perched on its hood and a woman's head poked out the cab window. "Same time every year he lets us pitch a tent under them trees. The ginger feller."

"He doesn't live here anymore."

"We wouldn't harm now't—what's a few tent pegs in all this grass?" he wheedled. "We'll be away by morning."

Tent pegs and piles of trash, burnt circles in the lawn from their fire. Michael pointed to the sign, its red paint livid in the prestorm light.

"Can't you read?" he said, knowing now what the man was, knowing he could not read.

What do we want readin' and writin' for, Micah? That's only for gaje, *isn't it?*

But for sure the man understood the sign. *He* always had, since the day he was born.

"You're on private property. Please leave."

But the man stood his ground, shifted to a more comfortable position against the gate. "Ah now, what difference does it make, one night, two—"

Michael felt keys dig sharply into his palm. "Off!"

The man smiled, almost laughed at him. "You'd chase us off? *Tacho rat* like you?"

For a second Michael couldn't see him, gray of sky and green of trees running together, turning red, red as the words the man slid at him. *Tacho rat.* True blood. To quiet their echo, Anna Abramsky's words flew quick to his tongue, were shouted into the dirty mocking face of the Gypsy:

"I said go, be off! We don't want your litter, your lies, your thieving—"

The man's expression changed in a flash, from lazy ridicule to injured pride. *"Tshorav?* From you? We don't never take from our own, you know that!"

Don't argue. Get rid of him. "D'you want me to call the police?"

The face changed again, closed up. Shrugging, he walked out through the gates, his stride easy, oddly graceful—and not in the least intimidated. In the middle of the road he turned, touched a quick hand to his forehead in farewell.

"*Kushti bok!*"

Michael could not have stopped his answering good night if his next breath depended on it. "*Kushti bok!*"

He heard the truck rumble and shake, watched it disappear into the dusk before he locked the iron gates and looked up at the lowering sky and the sign in which he'd taken so much pride, then at the gleaming black paint of his car, another symbol of security. On its hood a small length of ash from the Gypsy's cigarette. Any other time he'd have reached inside for a soft dustcloth, but tonight he shrugged, a gesture much like that of the stranger, and bent to flick it away—just as a new blast off the moors picked up gray ashes and blew them back into his face.

He climbed into the car and tore over gravel towards the house, which this night loomed slightly less substantial than last, the glow from its lighted windows not quite so warm through the gathering dusk.

We always know our own, laddo.

Yes, Da.

TWELVE

*G*ROSSMUTTER HAD ACCOMPLISHED THE IMPOSSIBLE. She had outlived the family doctor. In alert moments, she relished the triumph.

"Imagine, only fifty-nine and self-indulgence finished him off. Drink and rich food, I told him they were no good."

"His replacement will be here soon," Ellie said. "He's young, Heinz says, and very good—he's already helped that lame little girl in the village."

"Young, old, they're all alike, know all and nothing—"

Her eyes opened very wide, the unfailing signal for piercing screams to follow. Deftly—she'd now had much practice—Ellie forced a washcloth between Grossmutter's teeth. The medication that had been so troublesome last year had been withdrawn. Pain from the tumor, previously an unrelenting buzz, now came less often but with greater force. Like an ice pick, Grossmutter had told her once. A drug strong enough to kill it would kill the patient too. Constant small doses of analgesic were all she got now—and Ellie's hand to grasp until the siege was over. Always the washcloth so that she did not bite her tongue. The old doctor had even suggested extracting her teeth as a precaution, but Grossmutter would have none of it.

"I have excellent teeth—and you forget my delicate stomach. I won't take infant slop. Headaches I have. Senile I am not."

Ellie hoped the new man would bring new remedies. She'd long since given up the dream of nursing care for Grossmutter and freedom for herself. No hired nurse would give this difficult old woman love, and that Ellie could offer—and admiration. Who could ignore the will that kept old fingers in a bruising grasp on her own for minutes on end, and when it was over the small triumphant smile (showing the renowned teeth) as she said: "And now, Gabriella, it is time for our tea. You will please ring."

This doctor was a different generation. He arrived on a motor scooter, curly blond hair blowing in the wind as he ran lightly up the front steps and greeted Ellie at the open door. His face was wide, freckled, and smiling.

"Peter Heinrich," he said, "and you must be Ellie."

She led him up the stairs, where he paused under Papa's portrait. "And this must be the famous Hans—"

"How do you—"

"I worked with the old doctor for almost a year—not a day went by without some worshipful reference to von Reikers past and present. I know this family's history better than my own."

So he undoubtedly knew *her* history—but looking at his cheerful mouth, his big, comfortable frame, she felt for the first time that with this man it would not matter.

He spent a long time with Grossmutter, and when he came out the smile had an underlayer of gravity.

"The tumor will not kill her—it seems to be shrinking—but the pain from it almost certainly will. I've given cortisone—she should have had it before to reduce intracranial pressure and relieve some of the pain. But her heart is weak. I think perhaps you should prepare yourself—if you have not already."

"Yes." Hadn't she had years to prepare herself? But he spoke to the point, as the other doctor had never done, and she felt she could trust him. She reached for the tray that was always prepared in advance for the doctor's visit.

"Wine?"

And now he laughed, perhaps the first laugh to be heard in this waiting household for many months. "I have other calls—how would it look, wine on the new doctor's breath so early in the day?" He hesitated only a moment. "But I think *you* need a change. Perhaps later we can have a drink together in town? Away from here, from the old lady's bell? You're far too young and pretty to be kept like a princess in a tower."

"I'd like that," she said. Her first date—she wasn't sure how to accept or even if she should. "But I'm not sure I dare leave Grossmutter."

"The new maid can watch her. I'll check on her when I pick you up and when I bring you home. Now *that's* service you won't get in the city. Okay?"

"Okay," she said. "I'll enjoy it."

She did, much more than she expected. Riding pillion on the back of the scooter, his breezy comments flying by her, only half heard on the wind, she clung to his waist with some reserve at first, but as their speed increased on the straightaway she hung on for dear life, exhilarated by the speed and his comfortable, booming laugh. This young doctor seemed to belong to a new breed. Grossmutter's acquaintances were all old, staid, but this Peter Heinrich swept formality aside, called her Ellie and not Fräulein, tightened the safety strap at her belt with never a suggestion of shyness. Stopping at a roadside dairy for glasses of milk, he picked a cornflower from the field and wove it into her tangled chignon.

"Sorry," he said, "I should have warned you to wear a scarf. What beautiful hair!—and why do you wear it like a librarian?" Again the generous laugh. "It's attractive, yes, but you're too young to let an old woman make you old—even a grandmother."

"It's a compromise..." She found herself telling him about Miss Warren whom she'd adored and the banker whom she had not. Peter Heinrich was so easy to talk to she could have told him anything at all—except about the bullfighter. She'd never told anyone about that and never would. Especially not after...

When Miss Warren left there was only Ellie to do the shopping. For weeks she combed the stands for movie magazines, and eventually found a cover with his picture looking straight into the camera, body in profile, the suit of lights stretched tight over hard buttocks and lean, muscular thighs. That night she cut out the picture, pasted it on cardboard, and propped it on her dresser. His eyes touching her, she undressed slowly, seductively, in front of him, brushing out the long fall of her hair before she turned off the lamp. For the first time in her life she climbed naked into bed, only firelight between the sudden silk of her skin and the probing black of his eyes.

"Now," she whispered to his picture, "we are alone..."

She didn't hear the door open.

It was only after someone snapped on the light, Grossmutter's black wool robe—full length and buttoned all the way to the neck—drifting between the actor's image and the bed, that Ellie scrambled to cover herself, sharply conscious of nipples hard and hot against the cool of the sheet, dark upthrusting circles illustrating all too well the guilt washing over her. Not since she was three or perhaps four and could bathe without Lotte's supervision had anyone seen Gabriella von Reiker naked. Even on the hottest days of summer, when girls from the village leapt shrieking into the Mosel wearing swimsuits or daring bikinis—even then she was made to wear modest shorts and a high-necked blouse.

Now, to be caught naked...

Grossmutter, her face in shadow, turned this way and that as the scene slowly penetrated.

"Do you need something, Grossmutter? A drink? A snack?" Anything to stop her noticing, remembering.

But the gray head still swung, still harbored the briefly glimpsed scene that crawled haltingly from retina to brain.

"You are not ashamed to lie naked on your bed, Gabriella?"

So she'd seen—and understood.

"My room is...a little warm."

Grossmutter's eyes hardened, suddenly shrewd. "In winter?" Holding tight to the brass rails of the bed, she reached out for the photograph on the dresser. "And this...this...what is this? Spaniard? Italian?"

"It's a clipping...from a movie magazine..."

The patrician lip curled. "And you have him to your room."

"It's just a photograph!" Ellie's words came out hot, angry. Guilty as charged.

"A cheap entertainer. You, of all people, you *know* what such people are..."

"It's just a picture, Grossmutter..."

"But you *wish* for such a man, oh yes, you wish!" Small old eyes roved the sheet and incriminating nipples beneath it. "Today a picture...and what tomorrow! *What?*"

The cardboard image went spinning into the fire. Smoke. A vivid scarlet blaze. Black flakes crumbling in little heaps to the hearth.

Then Grossmutter, whose creed never permitted a voice raised in anger, shouted.

"Slut! Tramp! Nothing but a vulgar—"

"Grossmutter, don't! Your head, please don't—"

"Lusting after a black-haired lout—*you're no better than that wanton—it's in the blood!*" She lurched for the door with hands to her head, chairs toppling in her wake.

Oh God, she'd fall downstairs—was there no end to guilt, to recrimination?

Forgetting she was naked, she scrambled off the bed. "Be careful—let me help you—"

But Grossmutter turned, ice in her eyes and the vindictive set of her mouth, from which saliva now ran in shiny little dribbles.

"*Cover yourself.* The maid will take care of me."

Ellie pulled on a nightgown no less frumpish than her grandmother's, swept the hearth clean of black flakes, and crept into bed. It was a long time before she slept.

The incident had not been mentioned again, and Grossmutter's mind was now so clouded it was unlikely she even remembered it. Ellie remembered. How could she forget the rage and the shame? the accusation that she was no better than the dancer? the feeling of total dependence, of no privacy?—and how foolish she'd felt reading later that the fifty-year-old actor had just divorced his fourth wife to marry a teenager.

No, she could not tell Peter Heinrich of the shame that burned in her through the long winter of her sixteenth year—but she felt, hugging his broad back as the scooter rounded a corner, that he would not have condemned that youthful, foolish passion.

As Grossmutter's life inched daily towards its close, Ellie's began unexpectedly to open. Her friendship with the young doctor bloomed, grew to be something more. Until Peter, her dealings with men had been remote. Civil, yes; some, like the lawyer, had shown kindness—but none had brought life to this gloomy house, none had breezed through the front door humming with youth and vigor, none had swung tennis rackets in summer and ice skates in winter, none had ruffled her hair or thrown a casual arm around her shoulders as he talked. And no one, ever, had folded her in an impulsive hug just because a patient had rallied, or because her hair smelled good, or because it was April. Her grandmother (had she not been past caring) would have seen Peter Heinrich's affection as overly familiar or—worse—insolent.

Ellie liked it. She liked tweedy arms to lean into, the honest bulk of him, the feel of warm friendly fingers under her chin—above all the knowledge that she was not alone. After one of Grossmutter's midnight crises, which he'd rushed over to treat, he wrapped Ellie in a blanket and carried her to her room.

"Nothing to be afraid of now," he said. "She's sleeping."

"But the screams, Peter—"

"I know..."

"Don't go," she begged. "Stay until we're sure it's over."

She clung to his neck and he set her gently on her bed, took off her heavy winter robe and kissed her forehead and then, for the first time, her lips—which opened under his and clung, because without him she was alone and so very cold. Oh, the comfort of his big warm body, this shield against the night, against a dying old woman, against this bleak room and a bleaker future. But flesh touched flesh and she warmed, pulsed, flowered under his weight, discovered that the books had been all wrong, had not come even close to the pleasures that one experienced and considerate man could disclose to a young woman too sheltered for her years. In one night, with deliberation and caution, he answered every question, solved every mystery. No stranger to the responses of the body, he stripped away her fears as tenderly as he removed and folded her robe and nightgown, her doubts and inhibitions.

It was dawn when he left Ellie to a brand-new world filled with knowledge, not speculation; warmth, not endless chill.

Just as he opened her body to sensations she'd only imagined, so too he opened up her life—but even in the beginning she never thought of it as romance such as she'd read about. The blond doctor was not to yearn over, to weave dreams around. He was too hearty for that, too cheerful, too kind. Peter Heinrich was to lean on, and that winter she needed to lean, needed the support of his arms waiting for her after all the hours' watching Grossmutter's slow decline. And just when the nursing seemed to be too much Peter would appear with tickets for shows in town, button up her coat collar against the rushing cold of the scooter, rub color into her cheeks with brisk fingers, and carry her off for a few hours' respite in town.

They went to movies and musicals and sometimes a concert. One morning he arrived with tickets for a ballet.

"Oh Peter, I don't know...I don't like ballet—"

"You've never seen one!"

"No, but—"

"Get your coat."

The curtains opened on a pair of dancers—the girl weightless as cobwebs as she drifted among papier-mâché trees, the man tall and virile in the uniform of a hussar—and Ellie could have been five again, sitting on the oak settle in the hall looking up at Papa's portrait, spinning little-girl stories of a pretty mother and a brave father revolving endlessly, gracefully, through the years. Then Peter handed her his opera glasses. Focusing on the girl, Ellie saw a face hard with concentration, leg tendons stretched and taut, a brittle gash of a smile and the harsh artifice of painted eyes. Surgical tape supported bony ankles, and on each thin arm a large bruise where the partner gripped her into a lift. The sight of the bruises gave Ellie an obscure pleasure—and shamed her at the same time. In the blessed darkness of the theater she shivered.

"Are you cold?" Peter said, at once solicitous.

She didn't know what she felt except that she did not want to be here, to see this. "No."

"You're not enjoying it?" His hand, large and heavy, kneaded her skirted thigh.

"I'd rather be with you," she whispered.

"In that case . . ."

On his narrow bachelor's bed she pushed away his stroking fingers and thrust him into her quickly, deeply, eager for the pulsing warmth and size of him to fill her, to push back bitter old yearnings for a dancing mother and a brooding dark lover. When it was over for both of them it still was not enough and she pulled him to her breast and held him there a very long time, comforted by the rhythmic pressure of his mouth.

"Ellie, when . . . we don't have to wait for your grandmother . . . we could marry, be like this all the time."

"Later, Peter, maybe later," guiding him again to her breast.

Grossmutter died in her own room. It was spring and very late into the night, a scent of narcissus heavy from the open window. Peter was there to disconnect oxygen, close the old eyes, and pull Ellie into his lap. When daylight crept through the curtains he laid his lips against her cheek.

"This may not be the best time, but . . . well, there's no reason to wait, you don't want to live here alone."

Stirring in his arms, she roused herself from a relieved sleep. Stay in this house? Why would she want to stay in a place where her only real happiness had been two years of Miss Warren and the times spent with Peter. Considerate Peter—who deserved better than affection and gratitude. Did she want to marry him, be a doctor's wife? It was tempting, an escape from no profession, nothing to offer but a small knowledge of literature and music, the running of a large house—and the patience to nurse to the grave a sick old woman. Whom, in a confused way, she had loved, and who, equally confused, had loved her, the source of their confusion an aging dancer who'd garnered no reviews, no applause, no headlines.

Marriage to Peter meant safety—but in the obscurity of this house and the vineyard she'd been safe all of her eighteen years. It had not brought her happiness. And Peter was exactly what he appeared to be. Modern man, country doctor, content in his job. With all his kindness, Peter would not grow. He'd be the same at fifty as he was now. He was not deep, had no burning ambition to cure all the world's ills, not because he didn't care but because he knew it to be impossible. In a detached way she admired him more than any man she'd met—but how many was that? Peter's life would stand still. Hers had stood still too long; now she wanted it to move, to change.

"I'm sorry," she said, quite certain now. "I'm not sure what I want— except to get away from here. I don't think I want to marry, not yet."

"But the house, what will you do with that?"

She sighed. "It's mine, Grossmutter saw to that—but I can't keep it up. The vineyard's too small to be really productive. I may sell it, or lease it out, see what I can get in the way of a job . . ."

"If you change your mind . . ."

"Yes. And Peter, thank you for asking, for caring."

In all the months of their loving friendship the word love had not been mentioned between them. Nor was it now.

Grossmutter, the last legitimate von Reiker, was buried next to her husband in the village churchyard. Most of the villagers, as well as field hands and what was left of the household staff, were there, traditional in their mourning, wearing deep black, touching white handkerchiefs to their eyes. Did they weep for Grossmutter? Ellie wondered. Or the passing of an era? Or a secure livelihood that would now almost certainly disappear? Heinz the foreman, in his sixties—who would employ him now? And his sons? All they knew was tending grapes, and soon there would be none to tend. Whoever bought the estate must break it up for housing.

And Ellie, when they said words and lowered the heavy box into the earth, felt tears in her own eyes. They were not tears of grief. Regret perhaps, for a relationship that could have been warm, affectionate—and had been instead cool and distant to the last. Because she was illegitimate —as if anyone cared anymore, now that Grossmutter was gone.

Only Papa waited for her in the empty house, his painted smile ever young. His mother dead. Soon this house as he'd known it, the vineyard paths he'd run as a boy, would be dead also.

"I'm all that's left of you," she whispered to Hans von Reiker's portrait. "And I never knew you."

The lawyer showed up next morning to offer condolences and to remind her, as if she needed it, that Grossmutter's income from the trust had ceased from the hour of her death.

"I have, of course, advised your mother and her husband of the situation—"

"You had no right! I am eighteen—"

"I promised them I would let them know, Gabriella, and I have. My secretary sent a telegram this morning."

THIRTEEN

A SECLUDED TABLE IN A DISCREET HOTEL. Michael Abramsky at dinner with the latest girl, a redhead with pale, elongated hands and transparent skin. He smiled as he poured the wine, anticipating a languorous evening in an upstairs room, the girl's green eyes moist with wanting, her superbly trained limbs intertwined with his.

She pouted prettily over a glass of *Blanc de blanc* and licked melted butter from an asparagus spear before nibbling it slowly, delicately, with small, even teeth, then running the tip of a pink tongue over coral-painted lips. She was considering, she said, a contract with the Royal. Too bad it would mean leaving the studio and living in London... but if the audition went well— A practiced shrug from shoulders that could have used a little more flesh.

A long pause, Michael's cue. Beg me not to leave, her eyes said. Beg me to stay here. With you.

He suppressed a flash of irritation. She had no audition, no thought of leaving. They were such feeble liars, the *gaje*. Why did they bother? Why shame themselves?

They think lyin's a bleedin' sin, Micah! Not us—it'd be a poor Rom that couldn't fool the gaje *any old day.*

Himself, Dui, especially Farah—they'd learned to lie as they learned to speak, rapidly, fluently, aggressive one moment and conciliatory the next, always ready to switch gears, to sow confusion—it was a skill much prized at the fires, a game whose challenge never dimmed, played with a zest incomprehensible to such as the *gaje*.

"You didn't call me for a whole week," the dancer was saying, too edgy to wait him out.

"No."

A toss of carefully casual red hair. "I wouldn't have been home anyway . . . other people *do* ask me out, you know."

He smiled. "You're very pretty," his brown fingers brushing the curve of her jaw—which hardened for just an instant.

"You arrogant bastard, Abramsky! You're damn lucky I didn't hang up on you. I should have."

"Maybe." They never did. These were just the opening moves, predictable as the mating dance of peacocks, the outcome as inevitable.

"Only because . . ."

"Because what?" The pale arch of her throat pulsed under his hand.

"I keep hoping—I don't see why we can't—" Her words came in little gusts, breathless, a child who'd rehearsed a speech many times over. "I mean, why does it always have to be a *hotel*? Why not the house? Lord knows it's big enough—I've seen it when I've driven by—oh, only through the trees and from the road, but who could miss it? I mean, you can't deny it's huge, you've even got your own suite!"

He lifted an eyebrow. "You could see all that from the gate?"

Pink crept into her cheeks. "I ran into Felix at the studio, didn't I, and he just happened to mention . . ."

Not without prodding, Michael was sure.

"Greenlings is our home," he said simply.

"And you don't take in stray cats, is that it?" She gulped quickly at her wine and a few drops fell unnoticed, darkening the front of her chiffon blouse. "But you expect me to go upstairs with you *here*, right?" When he didn't answer, her flush deepened.

For a moment he was sorry for her. She'd prepared her little script as carefully as her hair, her nails, her perfumed skin soft to the touch, her eyes wide with yearning and a perfect makeup job. If only she could resist playing the game—but none of them could. They all worked toward the same end. The big diamond, the commitment, until death—or a better offer—did them part; they hinted at "open" marriage, freedom for both and security for none—perhaps they thought that's what he wanted. If so, they were wrong. When he married it wouldn't be any of these. He'd seen two marriages up close. One came to him only in nightmares, a younger, handsomer Da, his kerchief askew and his face flushed with gin, reeling through the trailer door with his fist and his voice raised in anger as a woman cringed and a new baby woke and whimpered.

The other was Felix and Anna, two halves of a whole, impossible to separate. Felix and Anna. That was a marriage.

"Well?" he prompted, his thumb tracing the curve of the dancer's cheek ever so softly.

She sighed. "Oh Michael...let's go up now," she whispered, her eyelids heavy with promise.

Upstairs, his mouth had just begun to explore the small white breasts when the phone rang. Pete was calling from the lab, exultant, out of character, babbling of triodes, crystals, semiconductors, solid state amplifiers—all Felix's department, not his. Besides, he was busy.

"I'll get back to you."

"You don't understand, man! We've cracked it, what we've been working on for months! That canny old Hamish had it after all—can't you come over?"

He weighed the triumph in Pete's voice against the softness of the dancer's eyes, the pull of business against the erotic tension of well-disciplined muscles. He could be at the lab in minutes. "Give me an hour," he said, hanging up.

Already she was pouting again. "Business always comes first with you."

"Not entirely," he said, his face dark against the sculpted white plane of her stomach.

The engineer's desk, usually neat, was a snowstorm of crumpled paper and rolled blueprints; his mouse-brown hair, normally slicked down and dark with oil, stood on end. Pete Preston was lanky, with a rather precious mouth which looked as if it said "appreciate" very often. And very likely it did, Michael thought. Pete appreciated Bach, Beethoven, and Reed's butter cookies; he appreciated his widowed mother, who'd given him everything but confidence; he appreciated the Abramskys because they let him alone to do his job and because they were different. (After a single glass of champagne last Christmas he'd confided owlishly that meeting them was like finding three white unicorns browsing in the local park.) But most of all Pete Preston appreciated the electron, source of constant, gratifying accomplishment. Silicon chips. Wires on boards. Schematic layouts. They made more sense to him than the most simple, easy-to-read girl...

Shy Pete, at the moment anything but shy. He beamed with triumph, waved his arms, grinned, and blinked behind his specs.

"Hamish's junk. I thought we were scraping the bottom of the barrel but we've found a couple of pearls. His calculations were a bit off, but reworked and combined, they're dynamite! You take this, marry it with this"—he drew another blueprint towards him—"bingo! In time it will add, subtract, divide, multiply—in ten years it'll do everything but print money. It'll change everything!"

An adding machine? For this he'd left a soft bed and a satin girl? "You called me out of a hotel for a calculator? What's new about it? And why didn't you call Felix? R and D's his department."

Pete swallowed his prominent Adam's apple. Michael gave orders softly, politely, but with the clear expectation that he'd be obeyed; disturbing him at a hotel was an unspoken but implicit taboo. "Sorry, Michael, I couldn't reach him and I couldn't wait. Look, we'll need a real research team, blitz effort, but if I'm right we could make a gizmo this thin and this big." He drew a tiny rectangle. "And for this price." His neat hand wrote a figure impossibly low. "That's what's new. Hamish started fine but transistors were too new then, he missed the connection."

Michael's mind was making connections of its own. Abramo sold many such devices, larger and clumsier—produced by other manufacturers under license from the originators. Which all added to Abramo's cost. Done right, this thing could be within reach of every pocket. *In* every pocket. Maybe just for offices now, but eventually for schoolkids, housewives, anybody who wanted to add two and two. His mind raced ahead. Peter was right, this thing *would* change the world—hell, it would revolutionize it! Right now a handy gadget, a bit of a toy. How long before it evolved into an actual computer, mass-produced and in every home, right along with stereos and television sets? And Hamish's patent was solid, registered a long time ago, now the property of Abramo.

Which meant they'd cut out the middlemen.

"What d'you think?" Pete said, reverting to his usual diffident manner now his news was spilled. "Is it a 'go'?"

Michael paused. "The right marketing...hell, if we can swing financing, beef up R and D, if you're right, we could hit the market this year or next. In those ten years you're talking about we can be right up there with the big fish." He leaned forward, not a trace of annoyance left, his voice low and urgent as he spoke of the future. He'd forgotten about the girl.

Sitting back, Pete felt tension drain out of him. Always a chancy business, disturbing Michael when he was with a girl. Chancier still that he might not grasp what they had, the potential of it. Pete had been thinking a few years down the road, but here was Michael characteristically grasping the whole shot, not just future prospects but present certainties, naming the device Abramo One and already mapping out a promotion campaign, which he said he'd direct himself. Pete could see it already, Michael lean and compelling in light gray suit and white-on-white shirt, his thin brown face and sincere flash of smile as persuasive as a ten-year warranty. Pete felt relief and envy at the same time. He'd have given anything in the world to be more like Michael Abramsky and less like Pete Preston.

Turning into Greenlings, Michael hardly noticed the gates, the grounds, the rolling acres around him. These years of alternately smoothing and goading Pete Preston's fragile ego—they'd pay off handsomely now. Abramo One. No limits. In two years they'd be multinational, giving the giants a run for their money. Wait until he told Felix and Anna—

One look at them and he knew why Pete couldn't reach Felix, why this was not the time to talk of Abramo One. Seated on Anna's blue plush sofa, the two of them took up barely a fourth of its length as they huddled into a corner, Anna almost out of sight in Felix's arms, her voice muffled somewhere in his brown wool cardigan as he rocked her back and forth, back and forth, his eyes making frantic signals to Michael over her head.

"...is yours, Anna," Felix was saying sternly.

"Never! Sasha yes, even Mischa—"

"But look, my angel, now you must hush." Felix made the polite automatic switch from Russian to English. "Mischa is here and we must make reasonable talk."

"Reasonable? Reasonable?" Anna's voice rose as she struggled to free herself, to throw her arms in the air. "We have the new home here, the new life! Is reasonable to turn it upside over? You are soft, Felix, soft! I nothing more say, not a word!" She flung off Felix's sheltering arms, her face an arena of raging emotions. Anger flushed her cheeks, fear stiffened every muscle, but it was panic that glazed her eyes and sent her storming to their bedroom. The door slammed behind her, then the rattle of a seldom-used bolt shooting home.

Felix fluttered his hands, empty with no Anna to shield. "Ah Mischa, what to do, what to do? I knew it, all the time I knew it and now—"

Michael knew it too, even before he read the telegram. So it was over, Anna's waiting.

"...and now the girl is alone, no family, nobody in the world but us..." Felix said it like a chant he knew by heart—as no doubt he did. Hadn't he had years to practice?

"She's old enough to take care of herself," Michael said coldly.

"But she is a child..."

At eighteen? By then he'd lived two lifetimes, wandered the backroads of England scheming and thieving to stay alive; he'd learned a Romani-English jargon that passed for a language; he'd learned Felix's courtly English and submitted to Anna's ballet classes and the French that went with them; he'd even acquired, by osmosis, a smattering of Russian. He'd started businesses, bought a house, and sampled every girl he'd ever fancied. And he'd put the past firmly behind him. My God, eighteen was Methuselah—

"For you it was different," Felix said gently. "Gabriella has been sheltered. I think, Mischa, that we must bring her here—"

"But this is our home!" And when had he last said that?—not an hour ago to a young dancer too ambitious for her own good. But to bring Anna's torment here? To this house where she was happy? "The girl would drive Anna mad."

"She would not be here long," Felix pleaded. "Soon she'll marry and leave us, then our obligations are discharged."

Wrong. Once accepted, obligations never ended, and theirs were only to Anna—but how could he tell this to Felix, of all people? But poor Anna, his—no, not his mother, more than a mother. After the uncertain years with Da it was Anna's brusque hands that bathed his fever with cold lemon-scented towels and uncharacteristic tenderness, turned his pillow to cool it. Why, in her middle years, should she be burdened with the pain of old wounds reopened? No, this girl must not come. Anna was right when she called Felix soft. Much as he loved them both—perhaps

Felix most because he was easier to love—it was Anna who compelled his admiration. The spine of fine-tempered steel, the stubborn will to stick by her course no matter what. Not easy to lock up the past and build afresh —and who knew that better than Micah-Mischa-Michael? Certainly not Felix, who'd never had to make a choice he must forever reexamine, end-lessly reconvince himself it had been the right, the inevitable choice. And when conviction was hard to find (as sometimes it was), then doubts must be stomped on, hammered flat, killed at birth—because to let them flourish was to question the choice itself.

"You are wrong, Felix," he said softly, not to hurt, for didn't he care about Felix, too?

In the distance another door slammed, quickly followed by a blast of Tchaikovsky.

Anna was at her barre.

Michael, who still took a morning exercise, had not joined her in the evening for many months. He did so now, changing hurriedly from busi-ness suit to practice clothes and making his entrance from his own suite, since the other door was securely locked.

She was in a *penché*, foolishly high after the brief warm-up.

"Anna!" No, not Anna in the studio. "Madame—" And that wouldn't do either, not today—and in any case she couldn't hear him. He turned the tape player down and took her hands from the barre. "Look, your legs are not warmed up yet—"

The muscles of her face were rigid; only her eyes flashed sparks. "Who decides if Madame is warmed up?"

"You do, of course, but—"

"You came to make barre? Or no?"

"To make."

"Then begin. AND!"

A grueling, furious hour. From *pliés* to *tendus* to *rondes de jambes* and on through the entire routine of class until they both glistened with sweat, until muscles burned and tendons quivered, until fatigue had blunted the sharpest edge of her anger.

Michael made his *révérence*, the closing bow from pupil to teacher, traditional thanks for instruction received. Tonight he made it extra deep, then put into words as much as he dared.

"I think, Anna, that you are right."

A small tremble in the hard line of her mouth, quickly controlled—she would never break in front of him, he knew that. Instead she tossed him a sweat towel and applied one to herself, scrubbing at her face so it was impossible to know if the flush came from friction, anger, or incipient tears.

"That Felix!" she said. "Soft as summer butter!"

"He means well—"

Her long, elegant nose sniffed contempt for such weakness. "Go take your shower before you catch cold."

"Anna—"

"Go."

When the door closed behind him she took in a ragged breath and put her hands to her ears. It was no good. The voice was still there, Hans von Reiker's drunken voice, his hot hands ripping at tutu gauze and the flesh of a young dancer, his shout of triumph as he entered her—but of course, was he not the invader? No, the girl must not come here, never, for how could she live with such a reminder in this house, this beautiful house that Mischa had created for them. No-no-no, it was not to think about, the shame of that wailing foreign infant digging seashell fingernails into her breast, draining at her sanity... and they'd be stronger now, those fingernails, daily picking holes in carefully woven fabric.

Hungry for escape her mind darted everywhere—should she clean her grandmother's silver candlesticks that had lain in a drawer for years? Boil beets for tomorrow's borsch? Too late, too late—the daily woman did them this morning. The studio scrapbook then?—but that was to be quiet, to sit still, to let nightmares invade the quiet body just as the Nazi had—

Hunting, her eye pounced on a drift of fluff by the door. Yes! She would vacuum and polish if it took all night...

When Felix tapped softly at the door she called out: "Please to leave alone, do you mind? A little peace—is it too much to ask?"

Breakfast was an awkward silence broken now and then by obligatory pleasantries through which Michael deftly slipped the solution.

"Eat the fruit, Mischa," Anna said, although he already had.

Folding a napkin across his empty plate, Felix's gratitude was subdued. "Thank you, Anna. Excellent as usual."

She frowned. "The croissants were not fresh—I shall complain to the baker."

"I hear his little daughter is not well." Felix said it with just a trace of reproach. Perhaps he too had been waiting for an opening; he could be devious when he chose.

Michael let the word "daughter" hover just long enough. "About the telegram," he said smoothly. "We could send her an allowance through the lawyer, let her stay in Germany. She's at home there...among friends..."

Anna did not look up. Her tapered fingers shredded orange peel into ever diminishing slivers, adding the scent of citrus to an atmosphere already sharp with coffee and tension.

Felix studied the top of his wife's head before turning to Michael in despair. "This stubborn woman, all night she did not come to bed. What are we to do with her, Mischa?"

A strip of orange peel shot across the table. "We do what Mischa says we do. Send money!" Her long upper lip twitched. "Is foolish to talk more—and past time you went to work."

A long look passed between husband and wife. Felix was first to turn away. "It is possible she might be...happier in Germany."

But he had not entirely surrendered. He was quiet driving to the plant, but as Michael parked the car in the Abramo lot Felix touched his arm.

"We should not, I think, arrange it through the lawyer. Too cold, impersonal. I should go there myself..."

And Felix was, as Anna said, soft as a feather duster; would not be able to tell the girl she was unwelcome, would return with her in his back pocket, everything more complicated than now.

So he gave him Pete Preston's news of the day before. "You're needed here, Felix, production has to be stepped up."

"But we can't leave Gabriella to lawyers," he protested. "Such cold people...kinder if she hears it from family..."

Michael didn't hesitate. "I'll go." And why not? By now he *was* family, far more than Gabriella von Reiker would ever be. "First I'll map out the preliminary promotion—"

"No, first the girl, Mischa," Felix pleaded. "Promotion, it's too soon, it will take time, can be later, Mischa, later—"

"Now. This whole industry is volatile as hell. If we're not quick we can be pipped at the post. We've been in business five years now. When I come back we'll roll."

* * *

It wasn't that simple. Was anything, ever? Anna and Felix had instructions for Michael which they each delivered in private. Felix gave his with sighs and much wringing of hands.

"You will be kindly with her, Mischa? See to it she is comfortable, knows we are here and that she would be welcome if she chose to come?"

By Felix, perhaps. Not by Michael.

Nor by Anna, who cornered him in the studio and whispered fiercely: "No, Mischa, never!"

FOURTEEN

ONLY ELLIE'S ROOM WAS UNCHANGED. In the rest of the house furniture stood dusty and neglected in auctioneers' lots. Grossmutter's desk, from which she'd directed a house, a vineyard, and a rigid, unfulfilled life, had been dragged from the library and now stood next to anonymous wardrobes from the servants' quarters; schoolroom benches rubbed elbows with leather armchairs and a wooden horse on which generations of young von Reikers had rocked themselves through childhood; baskets of kitchenware shared a corner with carefully boxed Steuben and Orrefors glass. Numbered red tags dangled from handles, mirrors, chair legs, fire irons, and lamp switches. In the distance an auctioneer's patter and the constant fall of his hammer.

Up in her room Ellie ripped a red tag to shreds and hid the roll of canvas behind the dresser. Lot Number 85 indeed! They were welcome to everything else, but Papa's portrait would *not* hang, a hedge against inflation, in some stranger's gallery.

"It's listed," Peter Heinrich had reminded her. "Valuable—Hella's in vogue now. They'll want it."

"They won't get it."

But they'd try. They were on Lot 42 now, so it would be some time. She wished, almost, for it to be over, the house and everything in it already sold so she could pack her clothes and the portrait and leave... avoid a meeting she had not asked for, did not want. That he'd had the gall, Felix Abramsky, to send condolences!... *and of course Anna joins me.* Not "your mother" but "Anna"—who hadn't even bothered to sign the letter: *We hope you will allow us to help; soon our dearest Mischa will come to you—do not hesitate to tell him your wishes.*

My wishes, Mr. Felix Almost-Stepfather Abramsky, are to be left alone. Not to be the responsibility of a stranger, a charity case—as Grossmutter must often have thought, as Felix Abramsky no doubt thought. And who was "our dearest Mischa"? From his name obviously Russian, lawyer or accountant, some minion paid to cover the dancer's indiscretions. And what did he bring? An offer to be taken in like a poor relation? Or, after all these years, a message of motherly love and remorse? Blood money to keep out of Anna Abramsky's life? They could keep their help—

An impatient thump at the door. It couldn't be Peter—he was downstairs playing host to villagers avid at last to touch von Reiker treasures and possibly pick up a bargain that would eventually become an heirloom. Theirs, not hers. Another thump at the door, which abruptly opened.

It was the bailiff, red in the face and sweating, a list in his beefy fist. He wore a green felt hat that he didn't trouble to remove.

"Lot 85, portrait by Hella. It's gone."

"I have it." She nodded toward the empty frame propped against the wall.

He scowled, obviously prepared. "It's part of the estate, Fräulein. We must remember the debts."

"And I must remember my father."

"The artist's an investment—"

"I said no."

"The frame alone—"

"Take the frame, leave the picture."

"Look, I'm a busy man—"

From the hall someone shouted his name and he left, wagging a fat finger as he went. "I'll be back—and there's a man asking for you down in the garden."

She sighed. Another tradesman from the village bearing an inflated bill? Hesitant to dun Grossmutter, they crawled out of the woodwork every other day now, afraid to be left in the cold when the bailiffs were done. They wouldn't be. There was enough to cover everything and leave just enough for a small house in Bonn. Or somewhere. Somewhere away from here, from these small minds and smaller horizons.

Halfway down the stairs she spotted the bailiff's green hat and ran back to her room for the portrait, determined they would not have it.

In the overgrown garden Michael Abramsky looked around him with mounting scorn. What fools the von Reikers must have been to let this splendid estate run to seed, its vineyards even now crosshatched with surveyor's tape, productive acres scheduled to be chopped up into row on row of gimcrack gingerbread houses.

To let it all slip away, this security, these thick walls, the massive locks on these iron gates!

He touched warm brown fingers to cold metal and wondered... were they up for auction, the gates? But no, Anna would want nothing from the von Reikers at Greenlings, no connection, however tenuous, with the past. He remembered her face yesterday morning as she saw him off from the hall, fussing with tickets and packing, busying herself with a dozen irrelevant details because Felix persisted in hanging about within earshot.

"You will eat civilized food, Mischa, and bring your shirts home for me to wash. Laundries are vandals the world over—when I think what they did to your cream silk shirt in London...you have vitamins? a book for the plane? You will be sure and take barre, stay in condition, yes? In Paris it's easy, so many studios by the Opéra. You may even meet with some of the old ones—I hear Piotr still gives class." For an instant she looked almost wistful, an expression totally foreign to her face, then she laughed sharply. "Take his class but pay no attention to him—bad dancer must be bad teacher, yes?"

Felix sighed. "Anna my darling, Mischa goes to Germany, he will only fly over France—"

She rounded on Felix. "Always there is time for class—*if* he does not miss the plane. Are you driving him to airport or no? Then where are your shoes?—or will you drive Mischa in your stocking feet and shame us all? Go, hurry!"

With Felix dismissed she touched Michael's hand, looked hard into his face. "It's good that you go and not Felix."

"Don't worry, Anna—"

"I don't. You are strong man, Mischa, like I am strong. Only my Felix is soft—"

Then Felix limped downstairs, shoes in place, so she reached up and kissed Michael's cheek with lips that were too warm, and not quite steady. "You will come back quick and then everything is finished, yes?" she whispered.

Yes, everything would be finished. And no, Anna would want nothing from the von Reiker place, not even these gates whose every iron stanchion gave out the same authoritative message. PRIVATE PROPERTY.

He heard the front door open and a burst of auctioneer patter. A moment later he looked up—and heard nothing else.

A young woman watched him from the top of the stairs. She wore a suit the color of old roses; her eyes and the curve of her neck were vaguely familiar, yet achingly, surprisingly different. She had the long bones and the imperious tilt of head—but her hair was orderly, controlled, the pink stain of anger in her cheeks involuntary. Her eyes were as deeply blue but cooler, calmer. Only the hands were truly Anna's, narrow and tapered—and even these were young and soft, clasped about a rolled canvas. For a moment every word of his carefully prepared message was forgotten, drowned out by the memory of Felix Abramsky's wistful lament:

Ah, you should have seen Anna then, Mischa. Magnificent she was, all roses and mercury...

Ellie paused on the step. So it was not, as she'd expected, a creditor from the village come to hound her with another bill. The man waiting for her in the garden was a stranger. He stood easy. Arrogantly, even contemptuously masculine in the dappled shade of laburnums by the gate, his shoulders relaxed, catlike under a light, casual suit. His hair, worn longer than was usual, lay in black curls thick upon his head—a head now bowed to examine massive old gates no one had bothered to lock for—oh, years, not since Grossmutter used to secure them against—

But now he looked up in surprise, his eyes burning into her, intense black hooks that seemed to be drawing her down the steps. She felt herself resisting the pull as a dozen impressions rushed in, pinning her to the iron railing, hushing the murmur of bidders in the house, rooks in the trees, quieting even the Mosel, full this season and surging fast between its banks. How many years since she'd thought of the bullfighter... but she thought of him now, remembered the way his cardboard picture had once turned her to water, had infiltrated every small defense she'd built to shield her against Grossmutter's coldness and Anna Abramsky's long silence.

But the actor's face had been bland, superficially handsome, no character discernible under its makeup.

This face was *all* character, intense and brooding. Dark fires smoldered in eyes that searched everywhere, missing nothing; only a hint of curve to the thin, sardonic mouth.

A buyer? If so, he already knew the price of everything.

Then he smiled, unexpectedly sweet, a brief flash of white in the smooth olive of his face, and she forgot Papa's portrait in her hands, forgot her anger with the bailiff, everything but the stranger. She knew now who he must be, *had* to be.

This was Anna Abramsky's Gypsy.

But then where was the lawyerly figure she'd expected? That pallid creature of a dozen nightmares? Where was his briefcase and rolled umbrella? the steely glance with which he would offer her a paper to sign, an ironclad contract that would forever release Anna Abramsky from whatever guilts she harbored?

"The keys are lost," she said clearly. "And the gates go with the property. They are not for sale," knowing as she spoke that he was not here to buy, this Mischa of whom Felix Abramsky had written so warmly. *Our dearest Mischa...*

He surprised her with a small bow, faintly old-world, but full of pride, of presence. He did not extend his hand, and when he raised his head the features were again guarded.

"Fräulein von Reiker?" he asked quietly. "Michael Abramsky. Felix wrote you I was coming, I think?" The accent was precise and subtly foreign, nothing like the English governesses, not even like actors in British movies Peter took her to see. It was almost as if he'd learned his English abroad somewhere...

"Yes, Mr. Abramsky wrote me."

He was speaking again but she had difficulty concentrating, all her preconceived ideas of Gypsies turned upside down by this urbane stranger, the dark power in his eyes, the voice pitched just low enough that you had to be still to hear—and it was hard to hear anything in the spotlight of his eyes.

". . . and my parents send their condolences. I am to make sure you will be comfortable—"

His parents? And he'd called himself Michael Abramsky. Mischa. Michael. Same thing. So Anna, the reluctant mother, had adopted him.

"—but they feel you might be happier in Germany, where you feel at home."

She made a conscious effort to meet his eyes, to keep her voice steady. "This house was my home, Mr. Abramsky. Soon it will be someone else's. But you may tell my . . . tell them I'm not a welfare case. I'm sure they'll be relieved."

"Why don't you call me Michael?"

She turned away—directly into an angry glare and an overpowering blast from the bailiff's cigar. His meaty paws were already clutched tight around the roll of canvas. "Give it here, Fräulein. Lot 85's coming up—"

"No."

"Under the terms of the contract—"

"—which I have not signed."

Beside her a gray suited arm moved. Quick brown fingers closed on the bailiff's wrist as Michael Abramsky's voice, quieter even than before, cut between them.

"Drop it."

The bailiff inched back a fraction, not yet ready to give up. "It belongs to—"

But the Gypsy was again questioning Ellie with his eyes. "This is yours? *Your property?*"

The emphasis, silky smooth but unmistakable, brought her up sharply, and she felt the bailiff jerk to attention beside her.

"In my opinion, yes," she said steadily.

Almost without seeming to move, Michael Abramsky edged her aside and turned his attention to her tormentor.

"Any further questions, take it up with our attorney. In the meantime you may be damaging a valuable work of art. For which you could be sued."

The bailiff's fist relaxed and opened as Michael Abramsky loomed over him.

"Just doing my job, sir," he stammered.

"Do it somewhere else. You are menacing your client."

It seemed to Ellie, looking from one to the other, that it was the Gypsy who menaced. The bailiff backed off, his blue eyes watery and unfocused. Then they blinked and slid away. The green hat came off in a belated— and uncertain—gesture of respect and he shambled away, scratching at his head.

"I'm not his client," Ellie said.

"So? The picture's important to you?"

"Oh yes! As long as I can remember I've..."

A shrug, and again the smile, all the sweeter for its brevity. "You have it, so keep it. Possession is nine-tenths of the law anyway. Surely you've heard that?"

She hadn't, but she found herself laughing in spite of herself, in spite of her resentment that Anna Abramsky had sent a Gypsy to...but the audacity of him! Ownership of the portrait *was* questionable; a court would probably decide against her. Possession nine-tenths of the law, indeed!

Through the library window Peter's beaming smile shone out at her over a tray of coffee he was handing to the ladies. She knew what *he'd* say about the portrait. "A picture of a man you never knew? Forget it, it's not worth the trouble."

This stranger was not Peter Heinrich, he was nothing like anybody she'd ever known. But when had she ever known a Gypsy, even seen one? Echoes came back, Grossmutter's voice heavy with scorn as she ordered gates locked, doors bolted, windows barred:

The scum of the earth. Liars...thieves...a shiftless lot, Gabriella...

And now one of Grossmutter's old friends tottered up reeking of mothballs and tugging at her elbow, demanding to know when-when-when the Venetian glass would be offered. "You know my legs, child. I can't stand about all day. Those goblets were my wedding gift to your grandmother—haven't I wanted them back for years? And would she sell them to me? No! This morning they told me to wait for Lot 19, then 91. Naturally they are in neither!"

"I'll show you," she murmured, reluctant to leave but glad of the time to think, to assess this disturbing young man.

Who was again giving her that oddly formal bow. "You're busy. We'll talk later when you're free. In the meantime I'll hang onto this for you."

Before she could remind him there was nothing to discuss he'd taken the roll of canvas and moved off to mingle with the crowd—but she couldn't help noticing, as she shepherded the old lady among baskets of glassware, that Michael Abramsky didn't really mingle at all. Even standing perfectly still at the back of a restless crowd his every muscle seemed ready, every movement around him observed and cataloged, filed some-where behind the watchful eyes. He didn't mingle and he didn't blend.

There was nothing shiftless about him, either.

A thief? She *hoped* not, with Papa's portrait in his grasp—but from the way he dressed, the easy assurance, he didn't look like a man who needed to steal.

Which left "liar." No doubt, and a smooth one at that. He'd had no trouble confusing the bailiff, convincing him that his rights to the por-trait, not her own, were on shaky ground. She felt a laugh bubbling up even as the old lady complained yet again that the auctioneers were less than efficient. Yes, Michael Abramsky could probably bend the truth to whatever shape suited him, and it didn't seem to matter in the least. She reminded herself that he was merely Anna's messenger, come to do a distasteful job the dancer wouldn't do for herself, but that didn't seem to matter either. Anger refused to rise to its usual pitch. The acid of old resentments no longer had the corrosive bite of yesterday, last month, last year...

And her pride, where was that? Was it such a fragile thing that one burning glance from a swarthy charmer could sweep away the humilia-tion of years? Of course not—but all that endless afternoon, no matter where she moved—speaking to neighbors, ex–field hands, the postmas-ter, the vicar, sundry creditors—she felt his dark glance touching her, warming her.

Peter Heinrich saw the stranger too, was more than curious as he watched dark eyes return again and again to Ellie. Seldom jealous, he still couldn't avoid a feeling of...disquiet. Must be the eyes. Some kind of foreigner, maybe Gypsy—he looked like one, like the teenager whose broken arm he'd treated last summer; he remembered her vividly. She seemed watchful like this man, quick, sharply intelligent—even after he discovered she was illiterate. Above all she'd been thin...but not all his pressure could persuade her family to give her into foster care, even for a few months. He sighed. Too bad the whole world couldn't be taught to read and write, couldn't be given four squares a day—though certainly this dark young man looked anything but poor—and should be wel-comed.

Elbowing through the crowd he greeted Michael, steered him deftly toward a caterer's table by the window. "Ellie's swamped today, poor dear"—offering plates of sandwiches already curling in the heat. "Have some—I don't think I caught your name? I'm the village doctor, family friend, official hand holder, meeter and greeter—and you? Your name again?"

"Abramsky—and no, I'm not hungry."

Peter felt the chill but chose to ignore it, again thrusting forward food and a tray of ale. "Hard work, bargain hunting, a man needs sustenance; you must be starving."

"Thank you no, I'm here to see Fräulein von Reiker."

Michael gave him a thin, closed smile and knew he was being deliberately churlish—but he'd heard the warmth in this doctor's voice when he spoke of "Ellie"; already it enraged him, as did the tweed jacket, the warm, easy, indulgent, overfed smile. Benevolent. Concerned. About as intuitive as a mutton chop. The kind of man everyone liked—why not? He threatened no one. So why did Michael feel so suddenly threatened? Some word he'd used? Yes—no doubt at random, but lifting rocks that should never be disturbed, releasing things best hidden. And other words Michael couldn't quite nail down but were there, afloat in some dark recess he'd thought walled off with routine, self-discipline, the hatred of excess that Anna had instilled in him over a dozen years. God, the power they had, words, to reach out and catch him, terrorize him even here, in a foreign country on a warm day, drag him back, too far to go alone, oh, much too far...

It was near Christmas and they were on the move. In the uplands a frieze of snow and mist draped the bare shoulders of fells; on the lower moors dusk was filling up the valleys, snow flurries thick upon its back. Bleak, deserted, the way Da wanted it, not a living thing in sight but black-faced sheep huddled in any small shelter they could find, in folds of hills, under hedgerows and wind-flattened shrubs, in coomb and hollow and crevice. Up here cold was a tangible thing, ice a lacy border on the windshield, Micah's hands numb, no feeling at all in his feet as the wind found every crack and gouge in the battered truck body.

They were lean, him and Da. Neither food nor heat in the trailer behind them, the truck guzzling what little petrol was left, not a penny in the marmalade jar—and Da fierce with a thirst gone unslaked for a week or more. And somewhere in this harsh northern landscape they must quit the road and find a place to park. Soon.

A village slipped by, its pub drawing a lingering backward glance from Da, but still they went on. Then a lane end and a sign. Da grunted and hit the brakes. They were at Hobbs Farm, NO TRESPASSERS ALLOWED—

which didn't worry Da near as much as another, more cryptic, message scratched into the gate, one that only Da could read, his face a study in pride and shame as he told Micah:

"A *patteran*. That's a signal what the Rom leaves behind 'em. It says folks round here don't much cotton to travelers. Likely the farmer has a gun handy, so we take it quiet, okay?"

Not so easy in the old truck, but snowbanks muffled its wheezy ascent up a rutted farm track into the fells, just high enough so they couldn't be spotted from the valley. They parked under the only tree in sight, a dead oak, and lit the paraffin lamp in the trailer. In its dim glow and the cloud of their mingled breath, father and son stared at each other across the empty table.

Micah, maybe seven at the time, clasped his arms tight over his stomach. "My belly hurts, Da. It hurts bad."

"No worse than mine. Get in bed and forget it."

Micah couldn't forget, couldn't seem to leave the table, as if just sitting at it could fill the aching hole in his gut. Wrapped in threadbare blankets that smelled of rusty metal and his father's sweat, his small dirty hands splayed out to the warmth of the lamp, it seemed to Micah he waited hours before Da's thin face lifted and sharpened. He was sorting sounds. Branches scraped the roof; wind howled under the tin door; the regular pop-pop of the oil lamp; intermittent rumbles from two empty bellies.

"Sssh!"

Then Micah heard it too, the plaintive bleat of a sheep in distress.

Between boy and man a single thought:

Food.

Quick on its heels, another:

Caution.

The calculating glitter of his father's eyes across the table. A warning scratched on a gate. The knowledge that a spot of bad luck could bring a farmer with a gun. Who'd bring cops, blue-suited busybodies eager to stamp CLOSED on a thousand petty larcenies and an old capital crime.

Da stood and stretched, his shadow elongated, oddly graceful in flickering lamp shadows. Then his laugh, big, rollicking, reckless, bounced off walls and ceiling, filling the trailer with vitality as he reached for twine and knife.

"Fuck the farmer," he said. "Go make us a campfire, laddo."

A match box skittered across the table and Da opened the door to twilight and snowflakes gusting in on a biting wind, Micah close behind him with old newspapers, dry sticks, and a tarp to shield the blaze.

The sheep was alone, floundering belly-deep in frozen reeds as it strug-gled to clear the lip of the gully and rejoin the flock. Seeing two humans, it bawled louder than ever.

Da looked down into its gentle, foolish face and shook his head. "You poor old sod," he murmured, dragging the mass of wooly misery over the rim.

A breath of sympathy in his father's voice. Micah, hearing it, felt acid gurgle up through the void in his belly. The first meal in days—surely Da wouldn't let it trot up the fell to freedom? "No Da, oh no . . ." he whim-pered.

"Not to worry, old cock, he's too weak to run, ain't he? He's no young-ster, neither. Likely he'll be a tough bugger."

His left hand twisted brown and deep into the thick cream of winter wool; his right whipped out the knife.

Micah shut his eyes and turned away, busying himself with a tarp shelter under the tree, tenting sticks over paraffin-soaked rags, striking a match and watching, warmer already, as orange flames feathered first over sticks and then over the dented bottom of a skillet. His belly hurt and his tongue floated in saliva, but it didn't matter now because it wouldn't be for long. Wonderful quick with a knife was Da.

In seconds it was over. A grunt, a flash of reflected fire on Da's knife, a single cry, hapless, hopeless, helpless—then new snow bloomed crimson as pulsing life met winter air and his father's sharp grin.

Da worked fast. In minutes the sheep was skinned, cleaned, and jointed. The pelt, branded and still steaming, he tossed to Micah. "Burn it—what they can't find they can't prove, right?"

Oh, he was a clever one was Micah's da, whistling through his teeth as lamb chops flew like kindling, as roasts (quickly trimmed and knotted with twine) stacked up, his dark face flushed with triumph, eyes glittering like black rubies in the firelight.

"Enough for a week, this lot, and the price is right on the button. What d'you fancy tonight then? a cut off the leg? a slice of liver? a good thick chop off the loin? They don't come no fresher than this, Micah."

Lamb chops cooked quickest.

And stomach juices churned, roiled . . . oh God . . .

Father and son threw chops in the pan, capered like a pair of devils as forks and fingernails jabbed, mouths shrieked in ecstasy as grease sizzled and spat in their dark, frost-bitten faces, as meaty smoke drifted through dead tree branches to a dark, crystal-sharp sky.

The first bite and Micah thought he was in heaven. Warm juice dribbled pink off his chin. Fat burned his tongue. Crusty mutton jarred every tooth in his mouth—but what did he care? He was eating. One chop, two, three, then more and more, Da tossing them into the pan with reckless abandon and a sprinkle of salt, urging him on: "Eat up, Micah, we share and share alike. Get your fill, plenty more where them come from."

With Da insisting on one for one, Micah kept at it long after he was full, cramming in mutton as fast as he could chew until his distended stomach groaned for mercy.

"No more, Da. I'm full, honest I am."

His father scowled, belched, and loosened his belt. "There's no pleasing you, is there? Sit there, then, and watch. Maybe *this'll* make you happy."

Micah's stomach lurched as he watched his father string meat high into the tree where dogs and foxes couldn't reach, each new bundle dripping blood puddles in the snow. He could feel Da waiting for praise, for pride, for amazement at his ingenuity, but all Micah could see were red splotches quickly freezing over, and later, as it grew colder, snotty-looking drips hanging in pink icicles from the branches. His belly churned and rolled over, a turmoil of long denial and sudden abundance. He turned away, gagging.

"Hey," Da said, resentment creeping into his voice, "how many kids gets a Christmas tree the likes of this, eh? Do I look after my kid or don't I?"

Still Micah said nothing. He didn't know any kids and he'd never had a Christmas tree, but he'd seen plenty in people's windows and they didn't look like this. Christmas trees were green, with lights and shiny balls, chocolate soldiers and candy pigs, all propped up with boxes wrapped in fancy paper.

"*Do* you like it or don't you?" Da's voice had a whine in it now, one that Micah should have recognized, for God knew it came often enough. "Well, *is* it Christmas or ain't it?"

But Micah's stomach hurt and he staggered into the trailer without answering. He couldn't have answered in any case. What did he know from calendars? The weather was their calendar. And what did it matter? All he wanted was to crawl under his blanket and pull his knees up against the knotted pains in his belly. He drew the blanket over his head and cringed, waiting for the expected whistle of Da's belt.

But instead there was a martyred sigh and the abrupt slam of the trailer door.

Micah waited a full half hour before he dared sneak outside, scrape a hole in the snow, and empty his distended stomach.

The pain ebbed then, and he slept, dimly aware that Da blundered in very late, to toss and turn and eventually to snore.

As always, Micah woke first, the window full of harsh white light. Sometime in the night there'd been a heavy new fall—what if they were snowed in? He thought for a moment of waking Da, but it was too early yet and his stomach felt like an empty kettle. With the first pang of hunger came the reminder of all the meat in the tree. No revulsion now, just a ravenous need to eat. His mind, way ahead of his nose, already smelled the breakfast Da would cook. He'd have got food from somewhere, brought bread and spuds and bacon from the village. They'd have that with the liver, then coffee the way they liked it, strong and creamy sweet with condensed milk from a can. Yes, that's what they'd have. Being Christmas, maybe Da thought to bring strawberry jam for the bread... yes, oh yes.

It was way too early, but just the same he edged aside the curtain to peek, only to peek...

Still bleak, the hills were dazzling crystal under their new coat of snow, the tree gnarled and twisted against a clean morning sky, its thin branches stark and empty—

Empty. He shook his head to clear it, and looked again.

Snow on every dead branch. No meat. None. No paw prints round the bole either, just deep untrodden snow.

Disappointment converted hunger to panic. On silent feet he searched the trailer, but in no corner could he find bread, bacon, jam, or milk. There was only that smell, all too familiar—and it told him everything he needed to know, that there was no point in looking further, that his father had sold the meat in the village and spent the profits at the pub.

Da was still snoring, a gin bottle cradled in his arms, another at his feet. On his face a three-day growth of beard and the vacant innocence of sleep. Something in Micah's spirit shifted, ripped in two, one part yearning to touch his father's sleeping face, the other raging to stomp it till it woke up screaming. But he was seven and frightened, so he did neither.

Outside, he swung his arms to keep warm, paced round and round the trailer until he'd packed a narrow path in the snow. On each circuit he stared at the tarp shelter of last night's campfire, mounded now with six inches of snow. Under it the dented skillet, which neither of them had washed.

Micah was on his knees in front of it, his tongue licking up frozen pan drippings and congealed fat, when the farmer's voice hit him like a sledge-hammer.

"What d'you think you're up to?"

Micah froze, his black eyes hunting for the gun. It was there, silver-gray barrel and polished wood stock carried easily under the farmer's arm. A big man, weathered country face, wind-whipped red cheeks and a Christmas scarf to match. At his heels a spaniel, trembling to jump but holding. By his side a chubby little girl in fur-lined parka and snow boots, a new doll clutched in one mitten and a toffee apple in the other—which she was trying to lick, except her father held her wrist several inches from her moist little mouth.

"Well?" the man prompted. "What are you doing on my land?"

Licking fat from a pan is what he was doing, any fool could see that. "We're lost," he gabbled, "me and my da's lost, see? It's this bleedin' weather, right? Couldn't see hand in front of us last night, so we end up here..."

The man's blue eyes moved from his daughter's plump little face to Micah's—now up to its gaunt cheekbones in skillet grease and smoky streaks. From there to a zigzag trail up the hill. Which was how the farmer had found them. Da had made it easy, had left his meandering footprints so deep in the snow that a blind man could have followed them.

Micah sighed his seven-year-old's sigh. Sober, Da was wily as a ferret, could have sneaked back some way and nobody the wiser. But last night he wasn't sober, was he? Micah's perceptions of his father took an earth-shattering shift. One moment an idol who mocked the universe, a curly-haired god who could charm a woman, steal a pipe wrench or a penny candle as quick as he could wring a chicken's neck, who could hear trout dreaming under a riverbank, who could talk to a horse and know exactly what the horse said back to him. The idol's feet, now swaddled in dirty blankets, turned to dust, a dust Micah could taste in his mouth, his empty gut, his soul. His clever da was a fool, snoring off a binge in the trailer while a *gajo* farmer had them both in his sights. And now the man would wake him, prod him with the gun, take him to a cop... and what about Micah then? Micah, whose chin was starting to quiver under the farmer's hard blue stare.

"Poor little sod," the man said at last. "You poor, unlucky little sod."

He tugged at his daughter's arm and called for the dog to follow him up the rise. At the top he paused and looked down on Micah. "Tell your father to be off my land by noon or I'll have the coppers on him, okay?"

"Okay-okay-okay," he said, relieved but canny enough not to show it, still defensive until he looked again at the farmer—and turned away.

What he'd seen in the man's eyes shamed Da, shamed himself, shrank their pride to a thing no bigger than nothin'. Hatred and contempt he'd seen often, always overlaid with fear of the shadowy secretive Rom. He'd seen it on *gajo* faces all of his life, had come to expect it, even take pride in it.

He'd never seen pity before (who pities the Rom?), but that day he learned the look and sound and feel of it, and knew it for what it was.

"You poor little sod"—the same kind words Da gave the sheep before he slit its throat.

So it could reach out, the past, catch him even in a foreign country on a warm day. It could drag him back and back, no handhold to grasp, no firm anchor to stop its impetus.

What was it he'd said, this bluff German doctor who seemed so very much at home around the von Reiker place? "You must be starving?" *Starving*. What did *he* know about starving, handing around pastries with his comfortable smile, pressing them on him, Mischa, with an earnest "They're the village baker's specialty"—nibbling a small macaroon perhaps to convince Mischa it was okay to eat, really it was.

No, Michael wasn't impressed with Peter Heinrich, who now said: "Can't we tempt you with *anything*? You've been here hours, man, you *must* be hungry."

A figure of speech no doubt, but Michael stepped back, a momentary flash of anger tightening the Anna-trained muscles of his shoulders and neck.

"Hunger is universal," he said coldly. "Greed is not."

A Gypsy knew the difference even if a doctor didn't.

Leaving Peter with bewilderment in his eyes, Michael Abramsky walked away, his shoulders as easy, as relaxed as before—but he knew he'd overreacted, that Peter's eyes followed him with speculation. The hell. He dismissed Peter Heinrich from his mind and looked again for the only thing here he wanted to see.

Anna Abramsky's daughter. When he found her, the soft pink of her suit lending grace to these austere rooms, he couldn't seem to look away, couldn't pull his eyes from that provocative tilt of chin, from hair smooth as poured honey, from delicate breasts and fluid waist, the smooth line from hip to thigh to calf to ankle and back again to that face, coolly patrician and smiling as she moved through the crowd, nodding here, shaking a hand there, conferring with an auctioneer, a caterer, a local *grande dame*. Eighteen and already the perfect hostess, even in these circumstances. What had Felix said of young love? *When you find the right girl you will want to conquer the world.* For the first time Mischa knew what he meant.

For this girl he could harness the sun, ride it like a chariot to the edge of the earth and beyond. She was that enigma, a girl-woman, innocence and knowledge in one package, naiveté and sophistication—and some iron imperative that would not be overridden, was intensely private. He remembered the way she'd held on to a roll of canvas because it was for some reason vital to her, even as every descent of the auctioneer's hammer shattered her past into smaller and smaller fragments. But look at her now, scanning a bill, diminishing with a glance the man who presented it. She murmured and the man reached for a pencil, deleting several items before handing it back with a subservient bob of his head. No fool, this girl. Untried, charming, captivating—but no fool. She had self-possession. Perhaps from the grandmother's training? Or inherited from the von Reikers? No, not if her father's passion . . . but her father had been in love, and surely this girl wasn't, not with that earnest doctor playing host, trying to protect a girl who could clearly take care of herself.

As Mischa watched she nodded to a local matron, deftly relieving her of an empty cup and plate, steering her to a chair, moving away with that gracious, noncommittal smile. He closed his eyes and this room, loud with the chatter of burghers and their wives, vanished.

Behind his closed lids the solid bulk of Greenlings rose up, warm and protective in the dusk, its many windows laying paths of gold on well-tended lawns. Gabriella appeared, standing in the hall, light from the chandelier touching her hair as she greeted Abramo clients arriving for dinner. She wore something soft and flowing; it was sea-green, vaguely Grecian and understated, but with that special stamp of quality that was never for sale. Its wearer either had it or she didn't—and this girl had it. A dozen times he'd tried to put the succession of dancers into just that picture and they'd never quite fit: they wore too much makeup or not enough; their voices were too shrill or too timid; under pressure, they either gushed or they froze. But what could he expect? They were entertainers, trained to play a part they could never in a million years learn to live.

For Greenlings they were simply not right.

And this Gabriella von Reiker met every criterion but one.

She was Anna's daughter, living evidence of a woman's murdered child and two shattered careers.

Greenlings was Anna's home. Was it possible these two women could share it? Even as the thought came to him he tried to discount it, succeeded for all of five seconds—until Gabriella von Reiker once again moved close to him, her light fragrance drawing him closer. To a believer, everything was possible. That's what Felix always said, and when had he ever been wrong?

Never, said Michael Abramsky.

Often, said Micah.

FIFTEEN

*H*E HAD GABRIELLA TO HIMSELF under the softest of lights in a restaurant of his own choosing, the evening an enticing prospect still to be explored. But behind the anticipation doubts ominous as bats filled every small silence, dark wings of unease that swooped and nibbled at the edge of his too busy mind, disconnected little forays he could not shut out.

Who did he think he was, to appear on her horizon and expect (expect?—he intended!) to dominate her entire landscape? The Abramskys —how could he face them after this, especially Anna? The girl herself, perhaps there was an understanding with the young doctor?

For years he'd worn confidence like an armor—why now did he feel out of his depth, vulnerable, of no more substance than when he'd first swum the Eden, Dui already in deeper waters, Micah and Farah tiny then, splashing in shallows, Farah teasing, pretending to swim but daring Micah to go farther, deeper, until his feet couldn't find bottom anymore and Da had to haul him out, coughing and spluttering, wrap him in the big man's shirt still warm from Da's body, still smelling of sweat and smoke and horses and safety, laughing as he did up the buttons. *You're a daft young tuppence, our Micah, getting in out of your depth*...

Now he was treading water again, the girl a new experience he was not sure how to approach; she was gracious, well educated in spite of her sheltered existence—but she lacked the brittle sophistication of dancers he'd known; there'd be no verbal games with her because she wouldn't know how to play and would scorn to play them even if she knew how. This girl would speak truth and expect it, be contemptuous of anything less. And already he knew himself wanting, for the first time, to give that truth, his own truth, his past, everything about him; wanting hers in return. Already he knew he wanted to see her again, to build her a new world far wider than village life.

Seeing her, you wanted to conquer the world, Mischa... Yes, Felix, you did.

But Anna's spirit intruded, too dogmatic to be silenced, Anna waiting at Greenlings (surely with impatience) to hear that *everything is over, Mischa, yes? What's past is done*. Just when everything seemed to be beginning. Abramo. The house they all loved. Until now she'd wanted the same things for him that he'd wanted for himself. And if now her "everything" were to change, Felix caught in the middle wringing pale, placating hands?

But then Gabriella touched a slender finger to the stem of a water glass, and all thoughts of Greenlings, of Anna, were lost in the girl's delicate perfume reaching him across the table.

"You like it here, Gabriella?" he asked softly.

"Ellie, my friends call me Ellie," she insisted, knowing as she spoke that she had no friends except Peter Heinrich, his concern already melting to mist in the warm restaurant lights and the fire in this Gypsy's eyes.

Peter was upset about the portrait, afraid she'd be in legal trouble; he'd advised her to give it back, said if she *must* keep it she should at least talk to a lawyer herself. He frowned when she told him it was out of her hands, that Michael Abramsky had it now, and wasn't it marvelous, he was taking her to Luxembourg for dinner? "Across the border, Peter, isn't it exciting?"

"If you'd said something I'd have taken you, any time."

"I know, oh I know, Peter..."

But he *waited* for her to say something; Michael Abramsky seemed to know before she knew herself. She and Peter were provincial, thinking of

Luxembourg as foreign—and of course she was excited. She'd never before left Germany and the prospect overwhelmed her with its symbolism. The vineyard chapter was at last closed. Auctioneers gone, the house nothing now but empty echoes. No Grossmutter, no staff, no bills, no worries. Even the library, scene of so many "serious talks"—even that was now four musty old walls covered in faded wallpaper.

But here, under the dark glance of the stranger, she felt reborn, pampered and beautiful in her one sophisticated dress, a black silk sheath bought hurriedly for Grossmutter's funeral and enhanced now with an orchid and Michael Abramsky's oblique remark as he gave it to her: "Pearls would suit you better," his face cool and oddly calculating in the harsh light of the empty hall—but the hand that lightly brushed against hers was warm and his words were forgotten in the rare effervescence of an evening *out,* away from the past and all the people in it.

Out.

Free.

The start of everything new.

And, intentional or not, it was the Gypsy who'd found the perfect way to mark the transition. With Peter it would have been lager and sauerbraten at a roadside café and perhaps polkas on the radio as background to his rich laughter. Darling Peter, and how guilty she felt, enjoying herself without him.

The restaurant Michael Abramsky chose was a converted hunting lodge, hidden and exclusive, redolent of cut flowers and cigars and exotic hor d'oeuvres that would have been a mystery to Lotte and the succession of cooks who followed her. Here were truffles, pâtés of hare and of lark, caviars from Murmansk and Tehran mounded on artfully carved citrus, escargots, in a dozen fragrant sauces; wines of awesome repute even within the trade; lovingly curled petals of pink ham from Paris, Milan, and Warsaw; oysters both smoked and marinated (or perhaps Madame would prefer them *au naturel?*). Madame didn't know, but she was definitely impressed.

Ellie was used to solid fare served with indifference by lumpish girls from the village who needed reminding daily that cabbage need not swim in bacon drippings, that thumbs should not rest in soup, that tureens must not be thumped down, with the inevitable splash, on serviceable, neatly darned linens—for even when Grossmutter's fortune was intact, the Brussels lace and fine Irish linens remained prudently in the attic with the Steuben and the Limoges: *Fine things are for entertaining cultivated people, Gabriella, and as you know, my position is . . . delicate.* Because she couldn't bring herself to trot out an illegitimate grandchild. As a result, they hadn't "mixed" at all—and if they had it wouldn't have been with people such as these diners who chatted in every language she knew and some she did not, all with that assured air of never having stepped into a butcher's shop or a fishmonger's—only *couturière* houses and discreet tailoring establishments. These people twirled crystal stemware in manicured fingers and their lightest gesture called up soft-footed waiters, faceless men who murmured and served and bowed but did not intrude.

Somewhere an orchestra played old operettas and a woman's voice, husky and distant, throbbed with the hope that one day her prince would come—and surely if a prince belonged anywhere it was here.

For Ellie, the evening was dream stuff spun years before by a little girl sitting in the hall gazing up at her father's portrait—which Michael Abramsky, with a word to the management, had magically whisked into the restaurant's strongroom.

Perhaps Michael Abramsky *was* magic—at the very least, resourceful.

His first day in Germany, most of it spent at the house, yet he'd found a restaurant she hadn't known existed. How he'd done it was as much a mystery as where he'd got the car, a vintage Daimler whose burgundy seats had enveloped her in luxury and the smell of soft leather as it purred through the night, Michael silent beside her.

Now, without consulting her, he ordered their salad, watching carefully as yet another waiter mixed dressing with ceremonial flair and much consultation, Michael answering in fluent French that ran between them like a Gaelic river. It could have been his native tongue—but of course, it was Anna Abramsky's. With the reminder, bitterness rushed back, dimming the flickering ambience of candles and this unexpected, baffling man.

"Where did you learn French?" she said.

"It's the language of dance," he said quietly. "I learned from Anna and Felix."

"I see." It was in his voice again, always that softness when he spoke their names.

Ignoring the waiter, he touched warm brown fingers briefly to her wrist, and for the first time doubt shadowed his face. "You don't see. I owe them everything. It would be hard for you to understand and this is not the time . . . tonight is to be a pleasure for you, an experience. Not to talk of future things . . ."

"But isn't that why you came? Why they sent you?"

"To Germany, yes, but I came here"— his gesture took in the room, the softly lit table with its centerpiece of gardenias—"for other reasons. One,

I wanted to see you here—and tomorrow is soon enough for business—maybe even the day after."

He talked in riddles. Business?—was that all she was? But now he smiled at her, a flash of white subtly alien even to this cosmopolitan setting, and again she felt bitterness crumble to curiosity, then to intrigue. She shivered, wishing suddenly that he would touch her again and wondering how that thin smile would feel over her mouth... She reminded herself firmly that he was a Gypsy. Worse, he was Anna's Gypsy.

Who now raised his fork. "Please? Our friend here has made a great effort."

Despite the interest he'd shown in its preparation he ate sparingly of each course, nodding his appreciation to the waiter even as he gestured for his plate to be taken away.

"You don't like it?" she said, horrified at the waste. In Grossmutter's house even eggshells were pounded back into the chickenfeed.

Again the flick of a smile, the sudden warmth in his voice. "It's very good indeed, but gourmets are often stout—or so Anna tells me. Excess offends her."

A selfish, pleasure-seeking woman could say *that*? The contradiction hung for a moment, balanced against the ingrained litany of years. But of course. Dancers, performers... naturally their first duty was to the almighty body, for which they'd sacrifice anything. Anything at all.

"She also told me to find a class—which I must take care of tomorrow."

"Because she told you to?"

He shrugged. "Because it's inevitable. That's the trouble with dance training, once you start you can't stop. It becomes a necessity, like sleep and food."

"You've never wanted to... go your own way?"

"But I do," he said, surprised. "Anna would have had me a performer, but I couldn't see it. There's no security in it—an unlucky fall, one accident, your career's down the drain and what do you have?"

"What *do* you do, then?"

"I sell. Electronics, appliances..."

It called up an incongruous picture, this face of hollows and secrets and swift changes of mood meekly persuading housewives to buy electric mixers. "That doesn't seem to fit you at all."

"That's how it began, anyway—then we started Abramo a few years ago and it took off like a rocket."

"Felix is a businessman then?"

"Hardly," he said, again with that loving smile. "Felix doesn't quite approve of profit. Fortunately, I do."

And so she heard about the shop in Ryder Street and all its successors, the dance studios, even Hamish Froggatt's little wonder, soon to become Abramo One.

Last of all he told her about Greenlings, its high walls and acres of green, the long drive which shielded them from the street. "I wanted it for years, that house, planned every room before we had even a dog's chance of owning it, but now it's ours and it's beautiful, better even than I expected."

Telling her, his face shone with pride, his voice almost reverential. She pictured Anna Abramsky living in it and wanted to ask sharply if she loved it too, if it was her substitute for a family—but she couldn't say that, not to the worldly man opposite, who clearly loved the woman. What conversation *could* she make? He was worldly, this man, would expect civilized talk over dinner—but what to say to him, when every subject led back to his life with the Abramskys? Trying again, she reached, perhaps unwisely, for the mystery that truly intrigued her.

"Grossmutter told me you were a Gypsy... I've never met any, of course, but I didn't expect... I mean... well, you seem—"

A chill seemed to touch him, leaving him colder, the curve of his lips thinner, more enigmatic than ever.

"My grandparents were Rom."

"And your parents?"

"My mother, yes. My father too, for a time. He left the Rom when I was very young. I went with him." The chill set and hardened, and a vein beat livid blue in the strongly corded neck. "We never went back."

"Did you want to?"

He seemed to look beyond her and was a long time answering. "I suppose I was too young to care, and my father..." Fingering the neck of the wine bottle, he flushed to a burnished tan. "I think he wanted very much to go back."

"Why didn't he?"

"They banished him. That's how they punish."

Banished. A word nobody used, years since she'd even seen it written —and how archaic it sounded.

"The Rom are an archaic people," he said. "They've wandered every country in the world for a very long time. They've developed their own laws."

"But what had he done?" she insisted. "Why—"

"Because—" He stopped, his mouth thin as a chisel, and she knew she'd pushed too far. He hesitated a long time before he spoke again in a bleak, flat voice with not a shred of emotion in it. "Da drank," he said. "And he laughed too much."

Sudden cold lifted the fine hair on her forearms, and she spread butter carefully on a croissant she did not want. So the father, too, was off limits. But not, perhaps, the Gypsies, although he seemed to avoid the word. "You were with them once, the...Rom—of course I've never known any but I've seen them pass through...the way they travel's so... romantic, spontaneous, one day they're camped in the village, a couple of days later they've disappeared, nobody knows where..." Why was she talking so fast? He'd be thinking her gauche, young, silly—but she hurried on. "At the house everything was predictable, each day like the last. Breakfast at eight sharp, lessons, bookwork for the winery; afternoons we sewed and shopped. My grandmother said our lives were 'orderly,' but compared to traveling with the Gypsies...well!"

He grasped her wrist and spoke carefully, with intensity, as if each word must be weighed for feeling, measured for depth, as if every syllable was pulled from a great distance:

"From what I remember it was good with the Rom. Different, but good. Vital. Not glamorous, not at all, but very...secure. The Romani needs that, his family around him, *all* his family, aunts, uncles, brothers, half-brothers, cousins, sisters, parents. He's never alone, he's not meant to be, can't live that way. That's why...when we left them, we didn't have that, my father and I. We kept moving because we couldn't stop... nothing was certain but the winters..."

He made a visible effort to bring himself back to the table, to Ellie, relaxing his grip until his thumb found the pulse in her wrist, which she knew to be pounding. "Perhaps your life seems dull because it's all you've known, stability, a settled home." He smiled. "You can't imagine how I wanted them, once."

"And now?"

"I have them. I have Anna and Felix."

Later they danced under dim amber lights and frescoes of gilded nymphs, and Michael was reminded again that this girl was nothing like his usual date. He was used to professionally trained partners, their performance so polished as to clear the floor of other couples until to all intents and purposes they danced a *pas de deux*. Ellie was light and pliant, willing to be led, but she moved like the amateur she was. She did not "perform." Clearly, she danced seldom, and it was unlikely she'd ever had a lesson.

After the first shock he found it endearing. It made them a couple, like the others, moving to music because it gave them pleasure; nothing to prove, no skill to demonstrate. He began to notice things he'd never been aware of in more accomplished partners. The feel of her hand in his, soft, almost boneless, the fragrant drift of her hair under his chin, the feathery touch of her breath on his neck, warm and sweet and innocent. Virgin? Maybe...but the doctor back at the village, his manner had seemed familiar...possessive.

"I'm sorry," she whispered, stumbling slightly on a turn. "I don't dance often—Miss Warren, one of the governesses, tried to teach me, but after she left..."

"*One* of them...there were so many?"

She nodded. "Grossmutter was—well, demanding. Some only stayed a few weeks...I can't even remember their names."

So her life hadn't been as secure as he'd imagined. "You liked your grandmother?"

He felt a sigh start at her waist and end in a breathless little flutter on his cheek. "She did the best she could. It wasn't as if she was my mother."

Dangerous ground, daring him, perhaps, to discuss Anna? Clearly there was resentment here, but it was too soon to probe, to scare this trembling girl into flight. Already she was stiffening in his arms, looking at her watch:

"Perhaps we should go," she murmured, sorry already that she'd spoiled it by alluding to Anna with that edge to her voice. "It's been a long evening." And it had begun so well.

For her a magic evening and not long enough, but this Gypsy was too close, too disturbing, danced too well, made her feel gauche, naive, vulnerable, afraid—less of him than of herself. "And we have to stop at the manager's office for the portrait."

"You can forget it," he said easily. "It's a hundred miles away by now."

Every word smooth as a pebble.

"Away?" She stopped dead still in the middle of the dance floor. Oh, she should have *known*, she should have *known*. Thieves, liars—

Now that smile again as he tilted her chin, made her look into his eyes. "Relax," he said softly. "Your property's safe. I haven't stolen anything for years."

"I didn't say you'd—"

"It's what you thought."

"But...I mean, how will I get it back, what—" Be calm, don't make a scene, keep your voice down, tomorrow you'll call Peter, call Grossmutter's lawyer...

"Abramo has a deposit box in Switzerland. I had the manager send it by special messenger. Want to check?"

"Yes."

He motioned a waiter to bring the manager, who confirmed that a roll of canvas had been dispatched within the hour.

Suspicion began to fade slightly, but why Switzerland? Why not here, where could she touch it, feel the comfort of her father's image, the pride in his courage? And how would she get it back? "It's important to me—"

"And to your grandmother's family. Now they can't get their hands on it. Your nest egg's safe, Ellie. Trust me."

Well, maybe—and she'd know where to track him down if...But: "Nest egg? Have you *seen* the portrait?"

"I didn't have to. If it's a Hella, that's enough. Von Reikers were your flesh and blood and they left you nothing." A contemptuous snap of finger and thumb. "In ten years Hellas will be worth a mint. D'you think they don't know that?"

Now a new rush of anger. He wouldn't understand, no one would. "That 'mint' you're talking about is my father. Not a tax shelter, not some murky little scheme for getting rich and staying rich. *My father,* all I've ever had of him! And you, of all people, know exactly what I had of my mother!"

It was as if she'd slapped him. The vibrant darkness of his face turned to a thin sallow triangle with black holes for eyes, which he closed, shutting out ballroom, lights, the fierce blue blaze of a girl's anger.

So the Hella was of Hans. Anna's rapist. And for this he'd rushed a roll of canvas across one border, sent it winging over another to be transplanted in the security of Abramo's strongbox.

Behind closed lids he saw reality and fantasy, security and risk, pleasure for himself and intolerable pain for Anna and Felix. There was the girl again in the hall at Greenlings. The perfect girl, the perfect hostess, classic green gown floating like sea spray about her. Arriving guests impressed by her poise, charmed by her youth. But instead of the chandelier he saw the face of von Reiker smiling down on them.

On Gabriella. And on Felix and Anna Abramsky.

He was quiet on the drive to the house, and when Ellie asked him in he surprised and disappointed her by refusing.

"Tomorrow," he said vaguely. "There's a lot to arrange. I'll have a receipt for the Hella by morning."

"Tomorrow then," she said, trying to flatten the eagerness in her voice. She wanted a second chance, though at what she wasn't yet sure, except she knew she must trust him, especially about the portrait, and was mortified now that she hadn't—and had let it show. "I'm sorry I thought... you know..."

His grin flashed white in the dark entryway. "It's a common misconception."

"Stealing to live—how awful it must have been."

"It was exciting, a challenge! We *lived* to steal! I'll never forget, never." That first time he was three, his heart a hammer as he stuffed a can under his little shirt; running down a lane, showing Grandmam, her hands petting him, praising him as she dumped half the can of paprika in the stew; a shopkeeper showing up, Grandmam denying absolutely that there were boys in camp, Micah cowering with fright behind her skirts. Later laughing, accepting everyone's pride—

"Better than stealing an account from a competitor." Then he did kiss her, but on the cheek, and was gone before she knew it. "Tomorrow," he whispered. "Receipt in hand."

The Daimler's taillights winked out through the gate and Ellie entered the empty, echoing house, except now the echo she heard was her own soft humming as she climbed the stairs, and in the dresser mirror she saw a smile to match it.

Tomorrow.

SIXTEEN

ELIX WASN'T SURE if he should be relieved or afraid. He knew he was confused, had been since the arrival of that ambiguous telegram—an ominous sign in itself because the telephone sat in mulish silence on the hall table. Anna should have shouted, erupted, exploded, rampaged through the house with vacuum and duster, scrub brush and pail—maybe she should even have wept.

Instead she withdrew, spoke in subdued tones, drifted from room to room like a mauve shadow in her tea gown, scarcely bothering with breakfast, seldom dressing before noon, then rousing herself briefly to give him a hastily made sandwich and soup from a can. A can. Anna serving him soup from a can. And nothing at all for herself, claiming vaguely that she'd already eaten and could stand to lose an ounce or two, though he couldn't see from where. She was skimping on her barre work, too, for her an unheard-of indolence. Oh, she retired to the studio, played her music for the requisite hour, but when she emerged her face lacked the sheen of sweat, the coils of her hair were still unruffled.

He tried to make her talk but she would have none of it. "An oversight, my angel. Has Mischa ever worried you without cause?"

She shrugged. "Who's worried? The young, they think only of themselves. He'll come back when he's ready"—her face flat, her eyes dead.

"I hope soon—he's needed at the plant for this new gadget. Preston's hopeless on the administrative end—all he can think of is the One's potential, not a thought about how to sell what we've got now."

"Why tell me? Tell to Mischa, he'll come running back soon enough if business calls to him. In any case, is time you go again to office."

When he'd gone she shut herself in the studio and stared long and hard into the mirror. She saw a woman in her forties who looked sixty, an old sixty. Worn, no color to her. Gray spirit, gray hair, gray skin—yet under that skin a red, relentless tide pounded in her temples, galloped up and down the blue veins of her arms and the steel-roped muscles of her legs, thundered through the chambers of her heart until she had to gasp for air and lie down on the studio floor, closing her eyes, searching, as she'd searched too many times these last days, for a peace that was neither within nor without.

No point to talk with Felix. Felix was torn also, but too kind, would say not a word against the enemy, even if that enemy were to rip up their lives like used train tickets. The girl was as much the enemy as Hans had been, as the grandmother. Felix saw the same signs she saw, but would be hoping, as always, that somehow things would work out.

They would not. With people such as the von Reikers it was not possible to work out, only to give in. But Mischa, no, surely he would not give in.

No!

Not Mischa, her Mischa. He was strong, like her, with will, with purpose. Yet the telegram lay there on the desk, evidence enough that anything was possible.

DELAYED. GABRIELLA CHARMING. LETTER FOLLOWS.

A week ago, and no letter had followed. No phone call, of course not, he wouldn't dare talk to them, not after he promised. "Everything will be finished," he'd said—all of it finished. And instead a new horror starting, she felt it in every overworked tendon of her body, in her tortured bones, in her head, in the quiet rooms of this house she had loved. All very fine for Felix to say she must be calm, to wait and see, to try to relax. Who could relax with this thing in the air, this threat hanging over them, closer now than ever? Over and over she counted the von Reiker sins on the abacus of her memory. Sasha they'd taken. Maman. Felix's career. Because of their war her own career too, in ruins even before that soldier's—violation. Now they wanted Mischa, she knew it. They wouldn't rest until they had taken everything.

In the well-heated practice room she shivered, pulling her woolen robe closer. Once, all of life had been warm, had pulsed with love. And now again she was cold, cold as she'd been in the war, and even at the house on Ryder Street until Mischa...

Now again, in the nights, the feather bed and the blankets she heaped upon herself gave out no warmth, only pressed down on her spirit, suffocating her, cold, always cold. She'd been the same when Sasha was murdered, no anger to sustain her, just this depressing, humiliating dread. Other wounds, however deep, had been buttressed by her own fury hurtling her through the most tragic of landscapes, smudging the image, blurring the pain...but fury wouldn't come this time and the events of her life slowed into a long cortege, every detail in sharp perspective.

Maman walking her down the rue Cujas in pursuit of the dream, for the young Anna (with a new pair of dance shoes, soft as doeskin, and a few subtle hints from Maman) was to have her first lesson. A few years and much work later (it hardly seemed like work because she still had the dream), the first big audition for France's most famous school of dance and the almost certain reward, a place later on with its company. She was accepted. Anna, so mother and daughter were told, had the body type, the temperament, the perfect arch to the feet and was therefore a natural. With many more years of work and considerable correction... "You think she could be prima ballerina?" breathed Maman (who still mourned Mother Russia, Papa's military career knocked into a cocked hat by the Bolsheviks, her own youth in St. Petersburg before they took over). Poor Maman beamed, pink with pride. "A prima ballerina, my little girl. Anna, you will thank the *messieurs* and promise to work very hard." Young Anna, all of twelve, promised, standing center stage, breathing in the smell of dust, talc, liniment, sweat, coffee, and ambition that would soon become her world. Then she curtsied to the ballet master and the *régisseur* as she announced: "But not just a prima ballerina" (as if they were so many pebbles on the beach) "I shall be *ballerina assoluta*." Amused glances passed over her head, and the ballet master said, "Better don't aim so high, child. Pride is the great spur, but it can make the great fall."

So many falls. At the rue Cujas school she'd been the best; at the new school she was the worst. But she still had the dream and so she worked until she was not bad, then better, finally good but not yet the best, still many ahead of her; then she was promoted to the corps, after that a few feature roles and the occasional minor solo—but then she met Felix, whose adoring heart gave her love and adoration and the second dream, marriage, which led to the third, the best dream of all. Baby Sasha cost her a year of training and frowns from the management, but he was worth all the other dreams combined, a miracle of pink and blond, of gurgles and dimpled fists that gripped her heart as well as her fingers.

War. Chaos to Europe, uncertainty to the ballet world—but she would have settled then for two dreams out of three. Then from nowhere came the big chance, the *major* solo. Maman kept Sasha in Paris as Felix swept the new star north to meet her future. *And she was a success!* Fifteen years' work and rivers of sweat watered the fruit of that one glorious night—a storm of applause bathed her young limbs in warmth, in love, and from the wings there was Felix's proud smile. So what matter if her toes bled and her insteps screamed? If ever she earned every decibel of applause it was that night, even the girls of the corps beating their palms with fervor, and from the wings a parade of roses (a few of them company props, as was the custom, to be presented night after night until they wilted—but there were many from the audience and of course from Felix). Yes, that night she was a success. So smile through the curtain calls, hurry to Felix, then to a backstage phone to make the triumphant call to Maman and Sasha—whom they would take to the coast when the tour was done, forget this stupid, inconvenient war, splash his baby's body in the waves, build him castles in the sand, watch him turn from pink to golden peach in the sunshine. But some nameless face intervened—carpenter? scene shifter? it no longer mattered—except the face was gray with shock, sobbing noisily behind the fire curtain. She hadn't wept, not even when he told her the news from Paris. She couldn't weep, hadn't for months, her face stiff with horror, that frozen picture behind it, Sasha's chubby face exploded with a single Nazi bullet. Random, she was assured later, but there was nothing random about the little casket in the little hole in the cold churchyard.

After that von Reiker's face, all worship and adoration, was an irritant, one more thing not to think about. Until she made the mistake. Such a small mistake, to reject an officer—well, so maybe she spat at him too— she thought she had, told Felix she had, and she never lied to Felix—but still a *small* mistake. For that she should pay every day of her life?

Until today this girl, spawn of a Nazi, had been an aberration, the residue of a shameful memory.

Now she was with Mischa, their Mischa who had not telephoned, not written home for over a week. Felix said it was an oversight because that's what he wanted to believe. She wanted to believe too but could not. It was starting again, Mischa threatened now like the rest, the best, of her life.

And Felix, what would he have left if he should lose Mischa, his unlikely consolation prize, a scruffy, thieving little Gypsy who'd become a son to take pride in? She shivered again, a skin of old bones huddled in the studio Mischa had designed for her. With love.

God, she was so cold.

SEVENTEEN

*H*E'D COME TO THE HOUSE the morning after the auction, arriving before she was dressed or had even thought about breakfast—which was perhaps a blessing, because the larder, like every room in the house except her own, was bare of everything but cobwebs. She should have thought of that, of many things, but her mind was filled with yesterday, with Michael Abramsky and the anticipation of today, with wondering when he'd come back or if he'd come at all. She'd still been wondering, still sleepless, at four in the morning, and when she slept it was with the reminder of his light kiss on her cheek and the lingering subtlety of his nearness, the touch of fine suiting against her arm as they'd danced, the whisper of his silk shirt, of warm brown fingers firm on her pulse.

Not expecting him early, she was wearing a lavender robe, faded from two summers and many trips to the village laundry, and she'd just washed her hair. Loose, it hung to her waist and took forever to dry, but it was already warm outdoors and she was brushing it dry in the sun, the scattered shade of laburnum leaves etching purple shadows on the back of her robe. She heard no car in the drive. One second she was alone, the next he was there, watching her from the gate, nodding at the rhythmic sweep of the hairbrush. On his lips a smile, in his hand an official-looking paper.

"Just so we start off on the right foot," he said. "Receipt for one Hella issued to Miss Gabriella von Reiker, owner. Can be redeemed at any time by the bearer. That will be you."

The warmth of his hand was still on it, and she thrust it deeply into her pocket, felt the comforting crackle of the paper and the relief that came with it. Her father was not lost to her. And now she could trust Michael Abramsky. "But so early—how did you get it?"

"I drove."

"To Switzerland? You must have driven all night!"

"Why not? It was good weather and I wanted you to have it quickly. Besides, I didn't feel like sleep."

Neither had she. "You'll be hungry, and there's nothing—"

"I can wait." He touched her hair lightly, draping a strand of it over his hand as if it were a length of fine fabric. "The color of heather honey," he said, lifting it so sunlight shafted through, its shadow darkening the change in his face, one moment urbane, confident, the next exotic, wild, subtly distant. "We used to find it on the moors sometimes, and my father always said there was nothing to match it for flavor. It was the devil of a job to get though; we had to smoke out the bees first, so it always tasted of woodsmoke."

"You didn't get stung?"

Again that dazzling flash of smile that transformed him. "With Da around? Never—he was too fast. 'Micah,' he'd say, 'when you've made your mind up get at it.' Very quick with his hands, my father."

If they were like yours, she thought, they must have been beautiful, watching the play of sun on bronze fingers as they touched the lighter filaments of her hair, wanting his arms around her but not to lean into, as she had leaned into Peter's. "I'll dress," she said quickly, "and we'll find some breakfast in the village and—" And what then? Will you go away, back to that house you love, those people . . .

"—and then I should find a studio and afterwards a place to sleep . . ."

"There are no studios near here, not even a hotel, and the house, as you know . . ." But if only he wouldn't leave, not yet, not before she knew him.

He looked hard into her face and she felt herself disappearing into the black depths of his eyes, strange eyes that seemed so bright but which reflected nothing, not even her face, just warm darkness drawing her inside. It seemed natural, inevitable when he put his arms around her and drew her to his chest, which felt very lean and hard, all bones and smooth muscle that turned her own muscles to moving water, treacherously weak. She felt her mouth softening, her lips parting, waiting for a kiss that did not come. Instead he hesitated, smoothing her cheek with the back of his hand.

"There's something I have to ask, Ellie, but you may not want..." No, not about Anna, not yet, she didn't want to think about her mother, only the two of them here, breathlessly close. "And it may shock you. You've been sheltered here, I think—"

Sheltered! Her jaw set but she was reluctant to move away from him. "I had books," she said tightly, "newspapers. Until the auction there was radio, even television, because without it no nurse would come out for Grossmutter, not even a maid come in by the day. Just because I'm not traveled doesn't mean I'm a child, that I'm naive. I do know—" About caring for a bitter, pain-ridden woman and a depressing old house whose twelve never-used bedrooms were crammed with bric-a-brac to be dusted, rugs to be cleaned. She knew what it was to be treated like the lady of the manor by some and like a shameful secret by others. She knew about vines and crop failures, bills and payrolls; she'd known rejection and bitterness, acceptance and comfort; she knew about men and women together, what they did and what they felt; Peter and herself, Miss Warren and her banker; Anna Abramsky and the brave officer and the baby she made and didn't want. Oh no, she wasn't naive.

"I'm not talking about newspapers or television, Ellie. I ask because... Look, I've lived in the dance world half my life, and it's very physical— how could it be anything else?—so some subjects are bandied about pretty openly." He paused. "You don't have to tell me unless you want, but—"

"Yes?" she said, tense.

"Are you a virgin?"

Relief swept over her, broke into giggles, then to laughter. She'd been so sure he wanted to talk about her "welfare" and "allowances" and spoil everything. She didn't even bother to ask why her virtue should be any concern of his. She'd known since she saw him standing by the gate at the auction that everything about her could be his concern if he wanted it to be.

"No, I'm not."

"The doctor?"

She nodded. How had he known?

"Good," he said softly. "You don't lie, play games—I like that. It means we start even."

"Start?" She looked up at him, but she wasn't playing games. The only question was when.

"I think with breakfast. Your hair is dry, the car's here—so let's go, let's drive and find a place."

"But I have to dress, to put up my hair—"

"Dress yes, but perhaps today you would leave your hair free?" His long hands again fingered a gleaming strand.

"It blows all over the place—"

"Not in the car—and it would please me." As she turned toward the house he said quietly: "If you pack a small bag we can go anywhere at all."

"Overnight? Oh, but I have things to ... I'm responsible for the house and—"

No she wasn't, not anymore. It came as a shock each time she was reminded. No Grossmutter, no maid, no vineyard staff. She was responsible for nothing now but herself. She was free. "Yes yes, I'll do that!"

He watched her fly up the wide front steps, that magnificent hair a banner streaming behind her, but made no attempt to follow. The house was oppressive to him, every polished floorboard overlaid with an atmosphere that spoke of meticulous care but of no joy in the caring; such a place was no setting for this girl who was already too serious for her years, and he did not want to see her in it. He wanted ... he wanted to see her by a lake, perhaps Como if they got as far as Italy. Or maybe strolling through a Paris boutique, choosing a dress or shoes or some elegant hat for her hair? He wanted ... but he knew where he really wanted to see her and it was a long way from here, why was he backing away from it? But Anna ... how could she take it? How would she accept? And how easily you go from "could" to "would," Mischa Abramsky, as if anything about this triangle is going to be easy. He'd felt the girl tremble when his words even approached the subject of Anna. He'd seen her face when she thought she'd lost her father's portrait. Clearly she admired him, loved his memory, must be ignorant of the circumstances of her conception. Ellie's pride equaled Anna's, so how could her bitterness be less?

He turned his back on the house and approached the Mosel as if an answer lurked in its waters. Nothing there but the ripple of an occasional fish and the reminder of Da's morose stare into the clear olive-green sparkle of the Eden:

Some folks can get used to anything life throws at 'em, Micah. The gaje *are good at it, same way as cattle. But the Rom, he's different, see . . .*

No he wasn't—*gaje* and Rom alike clung to hate far more tenaciously than to love. Even his feelings for Da, love and contempt woven so tight they were inseparable—his mind hung on even to these poor remnants, lied to him when it said they were dead. Waiting, they lurked just under the surface, bobbing up more and more often, especially since he'd met this girl.

Why? He'd told few people of his beginnings, though not because he was ashamed—he enjoyed a certain pride in being "different," foreign; the dawning fear and respect he saw in strangers' eyes only added layer on extra layer to his confidence. So why now?—but he knew, didn't he? Because a girl had waited in his mind, a girl who was all his mind had prepared him for, who didn't have to pour pity over everything to give off warmth. Inherently respectable, she had no need for society's confirmation of it. Her past was no less shadowed than his own and he was tired to death of lies and evasions. He needed to open shutters and let light in, be honest with someone, and with her it came naturally. Her judgment would be of him, not his connection with Da or the Rom or Anna and Felix. Strange how it lightened him, to talk to her of the past . . .

But could he talk of Felix and Anna the same way? Not for some time, he thought—and time was short.

What did he have? A day, a week to smooth the path? A few days more and Anna would begin to rage, to fear; already Felix would be wringing agitated hands as he attempted to calm his wife and keep the factory wheels humming on schedule. The wire sent from the Swiss bank wouldn't fool the Abramskys for a minute. Development of Abramo One churned on regardless. Soon it must be revealed to the industry with suitable flourish—no, more than suitable. A new product, even the best of them, had to be *unveiled,* blazoned, trumpeted from the rooftops. Lacking that, it would sink without trace, all its successors with it—and some other company would grab the ball, score the goal, win the game. Stifling all his plans for expansion. He'd have failed himself and the two dear eccentrics waiting for him at Greenlings. Who, since the day he showed up at Ryder Street with holes in his shoes, terror in his heart, infection in his blood, and lice in his hair, had never once failed Micah-Mischa-Michael.

From the corner of his eye a flutter of ivory skirt. It was Ellie in sandals and a simple sheath which on her looked like a Paris original, the long, wild-honey spill of her hair caught in a bronze ribbon, the sun in her eyes and a small suitcase in hand. "Ready...?" she was saying, tremulous but sure.

They stopped in Trier for milk and a bag of peaches—*eat it your fruit, Mischa. You want to be a nossink?*—and crossed into Luxembourg, then France, swept through miles of rich wine country, a score of tiny hamlets in Alsace-Lorraine and Champagne, all lying hot and sleepy on this blue and gold afternoon, Ellie wide-eyed beside him. Somewhere down a shadowed tunnel of trees they passed a schoolyard filled with squealing children on seesaws and roundabouts, a young teacher laughing with small boys as she gently pushed first one swing, then another.

"I'd have loved to go to a real school," she said. "The one time I was ever on a swing was when Miss Warren took me to the village park. She even swung herself, and when we got home Grossmutter was livid."

His quiet comment, that both school and play were overrated and a great waste of time, was forgotten in the new wonder, mile on mile of vines sweeping by them and Michael should *look* at the strength in the rows! Could he *imagine* the staff it must take to—but oh! do slow down, there's a château—and he mustn't miss that flotilla of nuns sweeping down a side street, habits and white headpieces in full sail...and the valley down there, surely that was a—

"You've never been here before?" He sounded surprised.

"I've never been anywhere except in books, and it's not the same thing. I don't know how you're finding your way..."

"I can always find my way."

"Oh? Yes, I suppose you could..."

He laughed, tossing a peach pit out the window. "Romani blood, Ellie, a built-in compass," he teased.

"Yes?" In her eagerness to know she looked fifteen and touchingly innocent.

"Besides, I checked the map in the glove compartment. Will you see how much farther to Reims?"

"There's supposed to be a great cathedral—"

"I was thinking more of a dance studio and a good hotel, but you can do the cathedral while I take class."

"I..." She looked at him sideways through a curtain of windblown hair. Would he mind? "If it's not an intrusion I'd rather come to the studio and watch. I've never seen one."

"You're in for a shock then. There's nothing romantic about mirrors and bare boards, and studios are always kept hot for the muscles, so dancers sweat a lot, grunt too, drown out the music—and their language is not always choice."

"Why?"

"They hurt. They all hurt somewhere, all the time."

A flash of that long-ago ballet came back to her, the man virile and athletic, the woman skeletal and bruised, and her own puzzling reaction afterwards with Peter. But still she wanted to go, to see Michael in his own setting—or one of them. He seemed to have so many. The house he spoke of. The world of electronics she couldn't begin to imagine and didn't try. That was "business." Deep in her head a niggling little voice said: And perhaps you are business too, and soon he'll propose that bribe designed to lay Anna Abramsky's guilt—but she pushed the voice aside.

She found the studio in Reims intensely romantic, though no doubt Michael would have disagreed. At home in his own sphere, he made inquiries, found an advanced class about to begin, and she was astonished how fast he could whip a suitcase from the trunk, rush her up three flights of stairs to a crowded room which did indeed reek. Of embrocations, powders and colognes, stifling heat and, just as he'd said, sweat.

Then he was in tights and a white tanktop, lined up at the barre with a dozen others. She sat among mothers and fathers, dancers sewing shoes as they waited for the next class. And she tried to be like them, to watch all of the dancers, not just Michael. To a point, she succeeded. There were boys and girls, men and women, but all were polished, fluid. They frowned as they concentrated on what was clearly work, not the pleasurable exercise she'd supposed. All through the barre work the dancers seemed identical: each toe point took the same direction, each leg bent at the same angle or extended to the same height; every neck reached and stretched, regal and serene, especially the younger girls, their free arms curved now like lyres, now lifted to wings she was sure could float them to the ceiling were there no barre firmly holding them down. Watching the girls, some her own age, Ellie knew a swift stab of jealousy. Michael had known such girls for half his life. Who was she, born of Grossmutter's stolid line, to imagine he could be interested in her? True, her grandmother had accused her, with disdain, of being just like "that dancer," but she knew she was nothing like these girls. They were magic creatures, not earthbound, living in a world where all was grace and beauty and resilient strength—but then the ballet master gave a command she didn't understand and shouted for them all to "HOLD! HOLD!"

And slowly everything changed as they fought to maintain position. Muscles began to tremble, to quiver, to jerk as if from an electric prod; eyes glazed; teeth at first clenched, then opened, lips rounding to small, agonized O's. An occasional whimper or groan as twinkles, then beads, then great drops of sweat erupted on foreheads and chins, soon covered every face, polishing all the proud young throats to a high shine. Not until they seemed about to collapse with tension was the order given to relax. A few more stretches and bends and they were ordered to what Ellie learned later was "center"—where the music and real dancing began.

A piano thumped in the background as precise positions of foot and arm changed to "attitudes," then to steps, to jumps, to leaps, and with each new move Michael's difference was more striking, more emphatic in this drab room that now suddenly began to pulse with motion, with life.

And now all she could see was a stranger, not the businessman of the auction nor the worldly urbanite of the restaurant. He was the Gypsy, the Micah his father had called him, and he flashed and shone and glittered like mica itself, gave off an aura of healthy animal flesh taking its exercise. So too he must have appeared to the other dancers, for they missed beats, registered surprise and sudden interest at the visitor in their midst, granting him space.

Then to *tours en l'aire,* turns in the air. Such turns, such dynamic air.

The girls, angels, seemed to drift upwards rather than jump.

The men, princes, leaped with classic, imperious grace.

But then it was Michael's turn, and she sat transfixed to the hardwood bench, gave up all pretense of watching the others. So, for that matter, did the ballet master and the spectators.

Airborne, the Gypsy compelled the eye, his skin slick and burnished to bronze, his curls a tight black cap, eyes glittering jet chips above flaring nostrils and arrogant, thin-stretched mouth. He was not a dancer. He was a blood stallion on the rampage in a deer park. He neither leapt nor jumped. He sprang, wild and exuberant, eyes flashing, arms reaching, body stretched, extended, shooting up like a spear, arching to a taut bow that must surely explode or break. At the apex of trajectory he seemed to pause, to ride the air for a single breath-stopping moment before touching down, only to fly again and then again, thrusting against the air, turning as he flew, head whipping, eyes glazing, sweat beads like diamonds flying with him.

Ellie felt a small hot splash on her wrist, and in a dream touched it to her tongue, anticipating him, tasting him, salt and man and sensuality, all of life in a single gleaming drop.

In the same dream she waited until he showered, reappearing as Michael Abramsky, cool and efficient, to drive her to a hotel.

"You're quiet," he said. "Sorry you missed the cathedral?"

She shook her head. She'd seen him dance, and he glorified creation better than any edifice cut from stone. "How far to the hotel?" she said, making words. "You drove all night, you'll need to sleep."

He didn't sleep, not right away. As always, class restored him, cleared his vision, cleansed his blood, set it to racing. And Gabriella von Reiker was gazing at him through the dresser mirror as she brushed tangles from dark blond hair. She was waiting, wide-eyed and pliant, indefinably innocent—yet knowledge smoldered in the blue depths of her eyes, knowledge that held him quite still as slowly, deliberately, quietly, she set down the hairbrush and reached upwards. Her long pale fingers went to the neck of her dress, opened button after slow button, her eyes compelling his, their pupils contracted to points of midnight blue. With a silken hiss her dress and slip fell to the floor in a pool of ivory the exact color of her skin. And still she watched him, watched him, until she stood, slender, naked, beautiful, stepping out of the pool of cream and opening her arms to him.

"You're sure?" he said softly—but he didn't need to ask. It was in her moist, softly parted lips, her transfixed eyes, the pulse beating fast and faintly violet in the hollow of her throat, her cool fingers tracing the pattern of his cheekbones, his jaw, his shoulders.

"Yes."

Her mouth tasted of milk and peaches, her body of health, clean cologne, and a vibrant young passion that as yet had only been awakened, never brought to full flower, never slaked. Exploring, her tongue touched his with warmth, with wanting. Firm breasts brushed his chest, smooth, electric to his skin, and he knew, as he stroked the taut satin of her belly and guided her to the bed, parted the slender thighs, that the commitment was made, had been since he looked up from the iron gates and saw Anna Abramsky's daughter on the steps of the great house.

And he knew nothing could stop it.

* * *

It was much later when he said: "You belong at Greenlings, Ellie, not some secretarial school in Bonn," her body languorous next to his, a long strand of her hair circling his neck. His monotone pictured the house, the stand of elms, the great oak at its entry, each perfectly proportioned room, french windows opening to sloping lawns, to no neighbors. His words built up the great stone walls, the heavy gate, the locks, the sign... "You belong there, where I can be with you every day. I've seen you there already, my wife, living with me in my home—"

She held her breath and didn't move, yet he sensed her flesh shrinking, drawing away ever so slightly, from his.

"You already have people living with you, Michael. So tell me, whose home is it, yours or theirs?"

No, she wasn't playing some coy, avaricious game. If only she had been. Her question finally gave voice to the barrier that had been there from the first.

"It belongs to all of us," he said. "I told you, we're a family. You're Anna's daughter, part of the family. By right."

Now she edged away, no part of her touching him, pulling the sheet over that long, narrow body. "You came here, I think, to—"

"Yes I know, I'm supposed to get you settled, make sure you want for nothing, that you're in a 'respectable' neighborhood (that's Felix talking) ... but everything's changed now."

She shook her head. "Michael, I can see what the house means to you, but nothing's changed. She wouldn't want me there."

"I'll talk to her, reason with her. She's a proud woman, but she's fair, she'll see it's not right to punish us because of your father." At the mention of her father her eyes showered him with blue sparks and he hurried on. "She loves me, Ellie. I'll persuade her." You too, he thought, I'll persuade you.

She took in a long, ragged breath, but her voice was steady. "You don't understand, Michael. *I* wouldn't want *her* there either. Why should I? For eighteen years she ignored me and I hate her for it. She threw me away like a bad review because I was in the way of her career—"

He took her chin, firm and so much like Anna's, in his palm, forced her to turn to him. "They lied to you, Ellie."

"No," she said, very definite. "My grandmother had her faults, but lying wasn't one of them. Anna Abramsky dropped me off at the house when I was one day old. *One day old.*"

"You've only heard one side—"

"The cook was my wet nurse. I got the story from her, not my grandmother until I made her tell me. What kind of woman would do that—leave a new baby with a sick, crabbed old woman who raised me as the skeleton in the family closet? the bastard? When I was little I had this fantasy she'd appear one day, all scented and glamorous like the ballerina I'd pictured, gather me up and take me home with her. Fantasies die hard. It took a long time...and for all these years she's known exactly where to find me, and never a letter, an apology...So you tell me, Michael, what kind of woman you think she is."

He forced her to look at him, and her eyes were too blue, too bright, would soon brim with angry tears he knew he had no power to stop. "Perhaps a woman whose baby son was shot? whose mother was blown up, husband injured, his career ruined—"

"It was wartime, such things happened to families on both sides."

He hesitated, cupped her face in his hands. "Perhaps," he said gently, "a woman whose newest baby—you—was the product of rape?"

A second to penetrate. Then fury struck. She flung his hand away, an Ellie he hadn't seen before, was off the bed in an instant, throwing on clothes, gasping as she thrust feet into sandals.

"My father would never—" She stepped into the dress. "He was a brave man, they gave him the Iron Cross—" Fingers flying, doing up buttons. "He was a gentleman, he'd never—"

"If Anna says so, he did."

"Anna-Anna-Anna, that's all you can say! How dare you judge my father? You never knew him!"

"Did you?" he asked quietly.

"I knew where he grew up, I knew his picture—which is a lot more than I knew of her!" She was at the dresser, raking a comb through love-tangled hair. Ice crystals in her voice and her eyes now, she picked up her suitcase and reached for the doorknob.

Which turned but wouldn't give.

"I have the key, Ellie."

Her breath escaped in a soft whoosh. "Open it, before I call—"

"When you listen to reason," he said, grateful for the practiced smoothness of his voice. "Look Ellie, the word is overworked so I'm not going to use it, but I've been looking for you all my life, for stability, for permanence, respect—"

"You think I haven't?"

"I know, that's why we belong together. I need a wife, a mistress for my home—no, homes—it won't be just Greenlings. One year, two, we'll need a base in San Francisco, then Tokyo, so we'd travel, be away a lot. Felix and Anna, they've been my..." The word embarrassed him, but it was the right word, the true word. "They've been my saviors, Ellie. How can I toss them aside now? You of all people know—"

"Yes." Her shoulders and the proud tilt of her drooped. "I know—and I've looked for you, but it's too much..."

No, too soon was all. She'd see, he'd make her see. Or Anna see. If one gave in, so would the other. But one had to make the first concession.

As a child he'd begged often and with vigor, but now for the first time in his life he pleaded. "A few days to ourselves, Ellie. Please?"

They drove to Paris, where he dressed her in a blue linen suit from Chanel, then on to Vienna, where she scorned the canals as "not very clean, Michael"—but she adored the gondoliers. Then to Italy and Lake Como, its azure depths a perfect match for the new blue linen; Como, where she nibbled on prosciutto under the lascivious eye of a maître d'—then back to Germany, to Trier, to Grossmutter's house which she must soon relinquish to the new owners, and where Michael gave her his ring.

"Why would we have to live with them?" she asked. "We could live somewhere else"—her lips against the facets of the stone.

He tried the light reference that always seemed to soften her: "It's the Rom way, young couples always live with the parents. It's expected."

It didn't work. "I'm sorry, I won't live in that house with her."

"Ellie, it's home, the only one I want... I'll talk to Anna."

"You'll ask them to leave?"

"I said I'd talk to her."

He knew the phone wouldn't be right, not for this, but he tried, Ellie well out of earshot—lucky, because Anna answered.

Much too quiet, much too polite. Yes, of course she understood. He was young, time to be married, no? And he shouldn't worry about them, she and Felix would leave, no problem, Ryder Street was still for rent, they'd move back there—

"Anna, you'll move nowhere, I'm coming home, we'll work it all out."

So he must go back, make peace with them—but no, only with Anna, for Felix *was* peace; he must also attend to the One, cornerstone on which all their futures would rest; he must do this, do that...bring all the elements together.

He could, yes he could, talking to himself as he talked to others, smooth and convincing. You started from nothing, no name to call your own; from nothing you built a business, a home, laid foundations for an empire; surely you can bend two obstinate women to your will?

EIGHTEEN

*I*T ARRIVED, the eruption Felix had waited for.

Mischa brought it with him—not the girl, thank God, not yet, just a new softness in his eyes—but a set to his mouth Felix knew all too well. It said there were problems, and one way or another Mischa would solve them.

He came direct from airport to office, cleared off pending items from the previous week in two decisive hours, approved publicity for Abramo One, rejected a few proposals with an emphatic NO over his bold signature; he held a terse conversation with the company accountant, followed by phone calls to bank manager and architect—his office door closed then even to Felix. When it was over they drove home together to face the storm that was Anna, waiting for them at Greenlings.

"Is not so good with her, Mischa," Felix warned.

"I know, I talked to her—but I'll try again."

"Better you go in alone, I'll lock up here."

Felix spent a long time lining up the car exactly in its spot, making his labored arthritic walk to the gates, listening disconsolately to the smooth turn of the key in the great lock. After he'd checked for the third time that the gate was well and truly fastened he made his slow way up the walk again, reluctant to enter, to hear, even to think what must be passing in the house. The past week had been a hell he was in no hurry to return to, Anna misery itself stalking the rooms. It would be harder than Mischa could possibly imagine. Perhaps not possible at all.

Even before he touched the doorknob her voice reached him, piercing in its pain, typically focused on the inconsequential because she could not bring herself to speak from a heart nourished for too long on buried things.

"Absolute no! Definite no! I not share kitchen, never!"

"Except with the daily woman, who is a stranger." Mischa's voice low, controlled. "Ellie doesn't want your kitchen, Anna. I don't even know if she cooks. She doesn't have to—neither do you."

"Is still my kitchen."

"And Ellie will be my wife, a daughter to be proud—"

"His! His! Not mine—"

The thump of a fist—Anna's, of course, never Mischa's—then a pause.

Felix shivered, already feeling the chill, the clash of wills. They'd be glaring at each other across the table now, Anna flushed, arms defensively crossed; Mischa's eyes hooded and flat, black with waiting, with watching for some small weakness he could turn to his purpose.

Heat and ice, those two.

"She's not exactly panting to share a house with you either, Anna—"

"Then what's to talk?" From her tone, haughty, arrogant, Felix could see the melodramatic overdone shrug, the theatrical spread of long hands, the long nose high with disdain. "We go, like I say. Felix and me. Two weeks, one. Already I start, I pack china, linens, all my shoes—"

"Try to listen. We can add another wing, angle it around the oak tree ... the architect says it's feasible, and so does the bank. Still Greenlings, but like two separate houses."

"I told you! Don't be worry about houses. Ryder Street did not blow away—"

"You are not leaving." Finality in his tone.

"Tomorrow we are gone if that's what you want."

"You know I don't."

"I know nossink, nossink!"

"If one of you could be reasonable—"

"Reasonable! Favorite word from Felix, now you!"

Felix waited for the slam of interior doors before turning the knob. Downstairs all was quiet, empty now.

From Mischa's suite a calming drift of Debussy; Felix imagined him lying fully dressed on that hard monk's bed, brown arms folded behind his head, eyes closed, every muscle still, only the agile mind moving, hunting, sifting solutions, weighing them for shape, for feasibility.

From their own room the thump of closet doors, rattles of hangers, a rumble of heavy drawers opening and closing. He sighed. Anna wasn't packing at all, simply going through the motions, keeping herself busy, underlining her agitation—he refused, absolutely, to see her furious activity as a touch of feminine blackmail, but why could she not see the inevitable, bow to it—but when had this stubborn wife of his ever bowed to anything? She was unlikely to start now, not over something touching her as closely as this.

These past few days his feelings for her had been tried as never before. For the first time in their long marriage he'd threatened to let her go off alone if that's what she wanted. He'd told her unequivocally that he was staying here. Definitely. But she knew a bluff when she heard it, wouldn't give an inch.

So for how long could Mischa's patience hold out when his own was pulling at the seams?

Mischa didn't know and Debussy was no help. He was full to bursting with an emotion he seldom allowed to overtake him. Anger was dangerous, nonproductive, a waste of time and energy, but it rode him now and he was powerless to shake it off. He'd often resented Anna, hour upon hour perfecting a step, a turn, when he could have been at his desk spinning money; as a teenager he'd been impatient with her rigid strictures of what must be eaten and what was forbidden, had yearned for sticky cream buns that other children wolfed by the bagful on street corners, despising his own single, perfect apple; cold Sunday mornings, all of Ryder Street lying in warm beds with tea and the weekend scandal sheets, only the Abramsky household up at first light, kindling fires, squeezing oranges, making the barre—but later he'd come to appreciate and admire her, for in time he saw the difference between themselves and others, saw the logic of her iron rules, could see the health in his own body and the languor of the slack, pimply youths around him.

But this thing between her and Ellie had no ultimate logic; it was born of fear, and who could admire that?

The record ended on a plaintive note, and he paced the floor on silent feet, the enclosing walls of Greenlings no comfort. Through the window June twilight turned from blue-gray to moonlit darkness and still he lay quiet on his bed. The rest of the house was silent now, so Felix must have given Anna her tea with rum. Pacifier, he thought with scorn, shrugging into a light jacket and slipping noiselessly out the back door to walk the grounds of this house he'd schemed for, worked for, a fortress for them all—yes, for his wife and his children too. If he had to, could he leave it? For Ellie? He didn't know, didn't want to face the thought. You live day and night with a plan, a dream, can you toss it aside like a peach pit?

Under his feet the gravel of the front walk scrunched, the great oak's shadow as black, as impenetrable, as his mood. As Felix had done earlier he walked to the gates, double-checked the lock, then took the long way back to the house, beyond the driveway that had seemed, once, to have no ending; he walked past wisteria in the last throes of bloom, its flowers nothing now but a purple slick underfoot, its scent a random echo that pursued him up the long grassy slope of beeches toward the back of the house.

He'd almost reached them when he began to sense it. Something waited for him. Not just apprehension for emotions he must confront, arguments from Anna, pleas from Felix, the inevitable ultimatum from Ellie.

Something else, some long-buried instinct stirring, warning.

There was something here. Now. Close to that patch of seedlings under the wall.

He stopped, listening.

Under the young beeches a shadow darker, denser, more solid than branches. A shadow which moved, shouldered itself free, stepped openly, casually, into a patch of moonlight.

A young man, thickset and confident in his stance. On his face a mustache, luxuriant and drooping—and under it a barely remembered grin that cajoled and reproached and placated all at once. At his neck a kerchief the color of old blood.

"Micah!"

The word a caress, a question, a conspiracy, an accusation.

Dui.

Michael froze, his mouth too dry to speak as he battled anger, shock, the clamor of confused and warring elements that roared between his temples. They approached him *here,* within the bounds of the sign. What did they want? Protective covering a dozen years in the making peeled off by a word. His name, spoken by his brother.

Above all, an ache strangely compounded of fear and grief and nostalgia—and in the silence a suddenly remembered babble of tongues, excited, mournful, happy at the fires; a late sun shining on Granddad's old wagon with a sunflower painted on its door, Grandmam stretching dough for honey-sesame cakes, telling Micah and Dui they'd have to wait, to wait...

And now brother Dui, his grin unmistakable, his arms stretched in welcome as if he were the host, Michael the intruder.

Michael found his voice. It was hoarse.

"How did you get in?"—knowing the question to be foolish, they could get in anywhere.

Dui shrugged, began to answer in Romani, but Michael stopped him. "Stick to English. How did you find me?"

"How could we *lose* you, Micah? We've kept track, don't we always? Watching out for family, right? You've done well, little brother, you've done the families proud." He stretched his arms wide to encompass rolled lawns and well-tended shrubbery, then tapped his pockets ostentatiously. "What d'you know, I forgot cigarettes again. Got one for your big brother?"

"I don't smoke."

The moon glittered on strong teeth and smiling mouth. "You did once, remember? We *choored* one from Da's pack and smoked it behind the wagons...you threw up."

"So did you."

"Yes, well..." His hand slipped back into the pocket and of course came up with a cigarette. He was still laughing as the match flared. "Them were good days, weren't they? 'Course, things are changed now —but you won't want to hear about our troubles..." He drew deeply on the cigarette and waved the glowing tip in a wide arc. "Like I was saying, you've done us proud. All the shops, the studios, this mansion—who'd have thought our little Micah—"

"Exactly what do you want?"

Now the hands spread again, this time with injured pride. "After all these years, my own brother asking what I *want?* To see you, what else? And here's me thinking I'd be welcome, that you'd want to catch up on things, hear about the *kumpania*...they're all up at Appleby now for the horse fair, coinin' money hand over fist. Too bad Da scarpered like he done, I'll bet you miss all that, eh Micah? It's been a long time..."

"I've forgotten it, I live a different life now," he said coolly, wanting to shout that he missed nothing, nothing, but he knew it wasn't true and in any case the voice went crooning on, hypnotic in its power.

"Granddad died last year, Grandmam's getting on, aches and pains, the usual...Delendi's youngest married a *gajo* but it didn't work out, what could they expect, Rom for the Rom, *gaje* for the *gaje*, eh? Bilbo's in jail for poaching, due out next month...Farah (you always fancied her, remember?) she married a Kalderash from the States, last we heard she was out California way. There's talk of us all joining up with 'em, but Grandmam can't see it—" He shook his head at the incomprehensible whims of the old, and Michael wanted to hit him.

"—but I'll be Rom Baro when she dies...yeah, it'll be me calls the tune then, and we'll have changes, you see if we don't. We'll stick with the towns, that's where the money is, no more country roads for us. It'll take some doing, mind, moving'll cost us a bundle...two dozen in the *kumpania* now and more on the way." A sigh, heavy with the burdens of future power as he flicked the spent cigarette into the trees and cast a speculative glance around moonlit acres. "But then, you wouldn't know about that, right?"

Michael relaxed, turmoil subsiding as it all came back, the jockeying for whatever pitiful position would soon open up among the group of families they called the *kumpania*. Nothing had changed. Dui was the same, playing him like a fish, alternating charm and flattery and reproach, now and then touching on old guilts long suppressed, and still not finished.

"We gave Granddad an old-fashioned send-off, the best *pomana* the families have seen in years...folks rolled in from Scotland, London, even Belgium and France, we poured brandy on his grave, burned his old bowtop and everything, it went up like a rocket—"

"You burned the wagon?" In his nostrils the acrid stink of a painted sunflower put to the torch, behind his eyes an old woman rocking herself in the smoke...

"It's the old way. Too bad you didn't burn Da's trailer for him, the least you could have done, better than *gajo* police poking about in it like they did. It would have been no more than fittin'—Da was Rom, like us, you and me." Dui's three-fingered gesture snapped like a whip, raised welts of kinship that stung and bled, that forced Michael to deny, to defy, to answer the way little brother Micah would have answered:

"Da wasn't Rom and he didn't scarper. They kicked him out, remember? And I went with him, so I'm not Rom neither—" He heard himself and stopped.

Dui let the silence linger just long enough.

"*What are you then, Micah?*" So soft, sympathetic, barely a hint of threat.

What was he? Da had asked him that once, and now Dui, Da's echo. No, don't let him lead you, don't fall in the trap . . . remember the rabbits-rabbits-rabbits-rabbits—

"I'm Michael Abramsky." Businessman on the move, adopted son of Anna and Felix, fiancé of Ellie von Reiker. "What d'you want, Dui? Get to the point. I don't have all night."

Dui nodded, understanding. "All them shops keep you busy, eh?" Then empathy shifted smooth as silk to reproach. "You've not asked about Rose. Remember Rose, your baby sister?"

Yes, he remembered Rose. Born too soon, cried too much, made Da crazy, made him— "What about her?"

"A sick girl, Micah. Tubercular, see? Well, I've looked after her till now, right?—but the *gajo* doctors keep on about some clinic in Switzerland, it'll take a year at least, that's what they're saying, see?"

Michael saw. Dui's finger and thumb were rubbing together in the age-old gesture, and Michael felt a net closing over him, stifling, familiar, clinging, as reproach turned to supplication.

"So we thought . . . you know, now you're . . ." Another long look down the slope towards a fine house nestled in lush lawns.

"Where are they, these doctors?" Michael demanded.

"There's one right in Appleby, she saw him yesterday—"

"Then I'll see him tomorrow, hear what he has to say. And I'll see Rose."

He expected Dui to backpedal now but he came closer. "Great! I'll drive up with you in your big black car, leave my truck in that locked shed back of your—"

God, was there nothing they didn't know? And he'd give Dui no chance to worm his way back here. "We have no space. I'll see you in Appleby—I have to leave word, pick up a warmer jacket—"

"You mean you don't want to travel with me, Micah?" Wounded, desolate.

"No."

Dui wasn't quite done. He touched Michael's shirt. "Nice, nice—wish I had one like it. Remember when I used to lend you mine, when they all came out of the same hamper?"

"And both of us wore smaller shirts?"

Michael flicked off the wheedling fingers like crumbs, and was rewarded at last by a glint of honest dislike in his brother's eyes.

A quick word with Felix—who looked worn, Michael thought, but there was no time now to soothe. A fire had been lit in Appleby and must be doused before it could take hold, before it scorched his future. He'd see the doctor, see Rose, and if she was as Dui said, needing help, then he'd give it, no choice. How else could he keep piling up success with a specter like that crouched in the cupboard? If she was okay he could kiss off the past for good. And tell them so.

"I have to go, Felix, emergency in the family...shouldn't take long. When I come back we'll get Anna sorted out—"

Felix's eyes widened. "Family? *Gypsy* family? Oh Mischa, oh Mischa—"

"I know, I know, I'll explain later—"

Jacket, keys, checkbook, credit cards. As an afterthought he emptied his wallet, taking just enough for food and gas. Guilt brushed him as he slipped surplus cash into his desk drawer—*we never steal from our own*—but he shrugged it off. Maybe they didn't, but Michael Abramsky was no longer "their own."

Dui had already shown him what he was. A rabbit prime for skinning.

NINETEEN

*T*HIS EARLY IN THE MORNING the road north lay empty before
him. The car smoothly rolling up the miles, Michael kept a
steady pace, hands deliberately loose at the wheel. Looking ahead
wouldn't help and he tried resolutely not to look back. With Leeds behind him and nothing but open country beyond, he kept his eye on the
road, seldom letting it stray to side tracks that had been all too familiar
once. He'd forgotten the names of hamlets. He only knew he was on the
old Great North Road, the lie of the land on either side of it. Nothing
had changed; stone walls still snaked up bleak fells, sheep still dotted the
lower slopes, every tree and bush still bore the distortions of winter's
raging winds—but it was June now, and dawn came up on clear pink
skies, draping scarves of mist over every valley. The land was fresh and
fair, surely a good sign. He laughed, kicking the car into second for a hill.
You didn't depend on signs, you rolled your own.

He parked once, walked to stretch his legs, sat on a stone wall and
looked far, far down at a blue thread in the surrounding green.

The Eden.

Seeing it, his first thoughts were not, as he'd expected, filled with dread and memories. Instead he ached suddenly for Ellie at his side, seeing it with him, showing her all the rills and hidden places where trout swam sleek and fat, but then he realized he no longer knew where to find them; so no matter, they'd find them together when he brought her here. Which would be soon, because this was the top of the world and standing on it he was king, so there was no doubt at all that soon he'd have a wife, that the future he'd planned would happen, two families made one, all Abramskys in the shelter of Greenlings' walls, united, a thriving business binding them together. He was free to make it happen, to create his own Eden anywhere he wanted.

Just before Appleby he paused for breakfast, telling himself he was hungry, that he was postponing nothing. But eventually he must approach the valley, feel the wheel tighten under his fingers, swallow a bitter knot in his throat that tasted of dread and anticipation mixed, a knot that pulled him forward, pressed his foot harder on the pedal, quickened his breath. When he edged into a parking slot in the square it seemed that a stranger switched off the ignition, patted his pockets, adjusted his tie, smoothed his shirt, checked his reflection yet again in a shop window. He was reassured; he looked exactly what he was, a businessman far removed from anything called a *kumpania*.

Early as it was, horse buyers clotted Appleby's main street; already gangs of dark-haired children harassed the *gaje* to buy wooden clothespins and paper flowers, pulling at sleeves, at skirts, parroting a hundred little lies; their mothers were gathered at the Romani woman's Mecca, a china shop whose owner turned a brisker trade with the Rom in fair week than all the rest of the year with the tourists. Michael could smile now at Da's bitter comment:

Give a Rom his horse, a set of Royal Doulton for the wife, he thinks he's died and gone to heaven.

But the men wouldn't be here. This time of day they'd be at the river washing their horses, polishing them to a high shine. They'd have fed them salt for weeks to put on flesh, taught them when to lift their heads, to curve their necks just so. Dui would be there with the others, men of the Rom smoking, planning their little scams, laughing as they plotted.

Michael turned uphill instead, to the encampment where the women were, where Rose would be if she was sick. Where Grandmam would be. The knot in his throat spread to his chest. Of all of them he'd loved his grandmam. Not Ma—his only memory of her was a casket with brass handles—but he well remembered an old woman with gray braids stacking golden coins on a blue velvet cloth, touching a ruby to his cheek...

His first view of the encampment was a surprise. Rom life was not timeless after all. More than five hundred house trailers crowded the heath now, polished homes with wheels and windows sparkling under a cobalt sky, doors open to show compact but sumptuous furnishings, all so clean—but then, living quarters had always been clean despite the *gaje*'s contemptuous imaginings. No more than a handful of the old wooden wagons now, the caravans of legend—but their painted sides and high wheels lent grace notes of the past. They held charm, tradition.

As he walked among the trailers a pack of lurchers set up a furious barking, bringing suspicious faces to peer darkly from the clean windows, to look him over, to let him pass.

We always know our own. Yes.

Inquiring, he found Dui's *kumpania* off to the side (so their stock must be falling), was admitted to Dui's trailer by a nephew who said he was Tomo, a tousle-haired kid of maybe three years, with a quick tongue and eyes to match. Yes, Aunt Rose was here, his da had said Uncle Micah would be coming, that he should let him in, look after him proper. A flash of liquid eyes, an engaging smile, a butterfly touch on Michael's silk handkerchief.

So what could he do but offer it? "Here," he said. "At your age, it's just big enough for a *diklo*."

The smile he got in return—the child tying his first kerchief with quick fingers and a popinjay's glance at the mirror—was a triumph of innocence and greed, and Michael could well imagine how Dui had prepared the ground. When he comes, your *rich* Uncle Micah, treat him nice, huh?

Rose lay on a daybed in the corner. The trailer's curtains were drawn against the sun and he heard her before he saw her, long rattling breaths, dry coughs, brief silences between. She'd be fifteen now, he calculated, time for marriage among the Rom, but looking at Rose he knew it would be a desperate Rom indeed who'd offer bride-price for such as her. Impossible to tell if she had been or could ever be pretty. In the gloom of the trailer her features were smudged as a charcoal drawing; as she coughed her hand came to her mouth, and he saw that the curled dark bud of her baby fist had become the starveling claw of the chronic invalid. So Dui had not lied.

"Rose?"

She turned huge dark eyes on him. "Our Micah?"

He nodded, took the burning claw into his hand, where she let it lie, weightless as a sparrow.

"Dui tells me you're sick."

"I'm not goin' in no hospital. I keep tellin' 'em but do they listen to me? Oh no, nobody listens to Rose"—resentment spurting thin drops of venom through her apathy.

Behind her, Tomo stopped fingering the new kerchief just long enough to point to Rose and tap an eloquent finger to his temple.

"Want tea?" he said hopefully. "Beer?"

"Show me Grandmam's trailer, okay?"

It was parked behind the rest, and at once he saw why. It was scratched and dented, the curtains threadbare—but its door was open, waiting for him. She was sitting motionless at the table, still in the long skirts of the old-time Gypsy woman. Hesitating, his long shadow crossed the steps. She stood to face him. She had not changed. More wrinkled than he remembered, yes, smaller, braids a lighter gray, mouth stitched tighter with age, but her eyes were the same, wary black buttons, perhaps a little dimmer, but warm, still warm.

She was slow to speak. Instead she rubbed the fine tweed of his jacket with callused fingers, gauging its quality, its richness.

"A *gajo*," she mourned, "my grandson a *gajo*."

She moved away, and as in the past he did not follow. Nobody badgered Grandmam. But *gajo!* The term should have pleased him—wasn't that what he'd wanted to be, striven to be?—but from her it stung. He looked around, saw clean shelves that were mostly empty, no proud Crown Derby plates displayed on stands now, just cheap white cups (white!) and linens that had rubbed too many wash stones in too many rivers.

Now she set the kettle to a bottled-gas stove, burrowed deep into a clothes hamper, came up with a single cup and saucer of eggshell china, its outside deepest red, roses twining up its inner surface.

"Gone," she was saying, "the good stuff's gone, not much left now. That Dui's stupid, all talk, nothing do," her tone flat, but when had she ever showed emotion? Only once that he remembered, and how deep he'd buried that keening cry when Da splattered her sunflower door with egg yolks and carried off her grandson. "Dui! Didn't I tell him, 'Leave our Micah be'? Didn't I tell him and tell him? But no . . . the easy way for Dui." As she talked she rinsed the cup in a special bowl kept for dishes, never for washing the flesh, not even hands. No, some things hadn't changed. "Now it's a new notion," she said. "California." Again the rub of finger to thumb, but on her the gesture did not speak of avarice. "Has he asked you for money?"

"Just for Rose, for the clinic."

She nodded, pouring an amber stream of tea upon red roses, adding milk, setting it in front of him with the old flourish. "Rose, she's been in and out of clinics for years, did he tell you that? A week she stays, two, then she's back with the families, can't keep away from the fires."

"Maybe this time . . ."

She closed her eyes, and he thought she was indeed failing, was nodding off—but she returned to her theme: "That Dui squanders everything he gets his hands on. In Granddad's time we had wealth, but you'll remember . . . Worst thing we ever done, to let your da take you. You'd be top Rom when I'm gone, they'd vote you in, you're not thick like Dui with his big ideas." She chuckled and her face lit briefly with a long-anticipated triumph. "But he'll not get everything . . . you were always my favorite, you know that. Have you got a girl, Micah?"

So he told about Ellie and the Abramskys, everything that had happened to them. "But she'll come, Grandmam, things will work out—"

She rocked herself on the hard chair, nodding her wisdom, her old suspicions confirmed again. "Strange people, the *gaje,* and cold to give up their children. I've always said so. And rape? They done worse than that to our people, Micah, remember after the war when it all come out? On the wireless, it was. No, you'd be too young. They locked us up, gassed us in them places with walls and guards and ovens. Thousands of us, Micah! The *gaje* on this side made out they didn't know till after, but *we* knew, we knew all the time . . ."

Her eyes glazed, seeing the past, then closed again, and Michael left her as he found her, sitting at her table.

She appeared again at the family fire that night, to serve Michael stew that tasted of his childhood, rich and earthy, sharp with spices, and he felt the muscles of his face begin to relax, to soften. A few of the family he remembered, Delendi and old Hela's branch, but Aunt Olla was long gone and Farah, as he was told over and over, was in California. It seemed to be a magic name to them, California, no doubt instilled by Dui, who sat at his right, endlessly pushing wine at him, making toast after toast. It would have been worse than bad manners to refuse, so Michael drank too, more and more as smoke drifted up to a starry sky, horses nickered in the distance, as lean greyhound shapes of lurchers prowled the shadows, muzzles lifted, canines gleaming as they waited for scraps.

"Drink, Micah, drink! How long since we've seen our little brother, eh?" Hands touching his, voices wrapping him in the past, in warmth. Greenlings and two unyielding women lived in another world, another culture that receded more with every hour.

Rose was not at the fires, Dui bragging that he'd threatened what he'd do if she got out of bed just once.

"Night air's no good for her."

"It's not the air," Grandmam shot back, "it's the smoke."

Dui spread his hands. "Whatever, she's sick, she'll have to go to the clinic," giving Michael a swift glance. So Michael, the horse-and-sweat smell of Dui all over him, said of course he'd help, glad to, feeling he was paying a debt that all his industry, his work, his house, his security had somehow incurred. But no matter what its base, his offer was the signal for handclapping, thanks, more wine passed from hand to brown hand, some splashed ceremonially upon the dust. Elaborate toasts to Rose's recovery were offered. Michael, amazed, heard himself respond in Romani:

"*Bater.*" May it be so. As if he'd never been away, had grown up Rom. Whether it was wine or smoke or nostalgia, he was slipping back as smooth as a hand into a well-worn glove, reminding himself that life with the Rom was not what it had been with Da, that—

But Dui was speaking again, his arm around Michael's shoulder. "Tomorrow you'll see me sell a roan, Micah. Nothing when I got him, skin and bone and no wind to speak of, but wait till you see him, he'll bring in a tidy bit of brass—"

Michael's hands curled in his pockets. He didn't look at Grandmam. "Tomorrow I'll be gone. I'm leaving when I've seen Rose's doctor." Perhaps he'd be sober by then.

"No! Oh no!" Beside him Dui was astonished, wounded, bleeding, dying. He was also offended, calling on all present to witness this stab in the back. "A big man like you, can't spare a few days for his own people?"

The waiting faces around him echoed Dui's hurt, and he felt the rasping jaws of an old trap beginning to close.

Grandmam spoke up. "Tonight he sleeps in my *vardo*. Tomorrow we tend to business. Then he goes home—if he wants to."

But when she threw a quilt over him later in her trailer she applied her own brand of pressure; in the beginning she had a lighter touch than

Dui, humming some elusive tune as she lit a candle under a picture of Granddad and a young woman, brewed herb tea, again serving it in the red cup.

"No thanks, Grandmam—"

"Drink—if I only get one day of my grandson (I don't count Dui), better he has a clear mind for it. For what'll ail you when you wake up there's nothin' like peppermint tea."

"Who told you that?" His head, light and fuzzy with wine, with doubt, sank deep into her down pillow.

"My grandmam was the herb woman, she knew everything, told me bits of this and that, so of course I know. Now it's all aspirin and that penicillin rubbish—nothing but mold if you asks me, but I still picks me own herbs—"

"It won't work."

Silence for a moment, then it came:

Deft, quick, easy as a knife through butter. "It always worked for your da."

The first time he'd been mentioned, and it had to be Grandmam. But who else really cared? Michael's mother was the one child she'd had, and Da had killed her; who could blame her for brooding on it? For poking her little guilt-dipped pins through the buzz in his head, and all the time the candle melting its waxen tears.

"I'm not Da, Grandmam."

She turned away, and he was already half asleep when she returned to stand over him, rocking herself, rolling her apron, smiling down on him.

"The Russian woman. Have you thought...maybe you'd do her some good if you's gone a while, set her to thinking..."

"You're forgetting the business, and Ellie. I have to call her."

"Her you can call from anywhere, but what will you tell her?" She closed her eyes. "Folks plan and they plan, but sometimes, *chala*, it pays to wait, to see what comes. Me, I plan nothing, but things still happen."

In the candlelight the sockets of her eyes sunk to huge black pits and he seemed to be falling, falling...

She watched him for a long time, and when his breathing steadied she sighed and snuffed out the candle.

Whatever it was she'd brewed in the red cup worked like a charm. It was late when he woke next morning, but he was fresh and clearheaded to drive Grandmam to the doctor's office where they were kept waiting long after the appointed time, until Michael asked tartly whether patients were welcome here or not. The receptionist's glance flickered from the old woman's gray braids and dusty skirts to Michael's London-tailored jacket, to the car standing at the curb. In seconds they were facing the doctor across a desk, being shown deference along with X-rays of Rose's lungs and pictures of mountain chalets with wide verandas, swimming pools, young patients with tennis rackets—at which Grandmam laughed.

"Our Rose with a bat and ball? She'd burn 'em and sit at the fire!" But she spoke in Romani and the doctor let it pass, put on a grave face as he warned of months spent on the open road and the threat of pneumonia.

Michael was convinced. He signed agreements, wrote checks, promised Grandmam he'd stop in to say his good-byes later, and dropped her at the trailer. Then he drove to the quieter reaches of the river, the siren he knew now that he must stare down.

On this hot afternoon her song was sweet; her waters ran clear and swift over mossed boulders, darted through bushes and fallen trees; at a waterfall she caught her breath before tumbling over it with a flash of sequined skirt more enticing, for the moment, than any woman's. Gulls swooped and dipped to her in homage, reeds bowed at her passing; her green banks were shadowed, quiet, well out of range of the fair and its frantic bargaining.

It was peace, and thoughts of Da and the Rom came not at all until his shoe touched the body of a trout. Stooping, turning it over with a stick, he at first thought it was dead. The gills did not move, nor the open mouth—but its fish eyes, pearly in the shade, flickered slightly. Still alive, then. It didn't breathe but it lived. Like the spirit of the Rom in him, it lingered somewhere. Heart, brain, genes, he didn't know where it lived, but it clung like a barnacle, scabrous and furred.

The fish at his feet gave a convulsive twitch. Startled, he picked it up and smashed it against a rock before cleaning his hands in the pure waters of the Eden.

Felix didn't put on the light, the moon was enough. He looked down at Anna, frighteningly narrow in the center of the huge bed, arms and long misshapen feet crossed, her nightgown silvered with moonlight. It came to him that she looked like a spear . . . but she was pointed at herself —oh, this foolish woman . . . almost asleep. Thank God he'd given her so much with the tea—enough lemon and sugar and she could never tell how much rum.

"What is it?" she said foggily. "Was that the front door?"

"Mischa leaving. A brother came for him—some sickness in the family."

The words slowly sank in, to emerge slurred and bewildered. "Brother? Family? Ah, family...somebody say it, Tolstoy, yes, he say it...happy families all the same, only unhappy families are diff..." Her main thread lost somewhere in Russian literature, she unraveled the thought slowly to find it again. "Sickness in Mischa's family? *We* are Mischa's family, and no sickness...What nonsense you are talking now?"

"The Gypsies. He's gone to them..."

"Oh..." She seemed to be reaching but her hand wouldn't quite leave the counterpane, and he wondered dully how many hours since she'd eaten? How many days? He should have thought of that when he poured the rum..."Mischa...he goes where?"

"North. Westmorland, he said."

She nodded, sinking deeper yet into the bed, heavy lids closing. "Not far...will be back tomorrow." The pink-shaded lamp gleamed on a small dribble of saliva at the corner of her mouth.

He was turning away when rage, a stranger to him all his life, flicked a whip, grabbed up the woolen collar of his cardigan and thrust him forward, made him shake the long white figure until he felt her bones must surely rattle under his hands.

"Anna-Anna-Anna!" he shouted. "It's been eighteen years! If you can stand it I cannot! Is time to let go, let go!" Her eyes flew open, shocked awake by the ungentle grasp of his fingers, the desperation in his voice. "Eighteen-eighteen-eighteen—"

She stiffened, rolled her head from side to side. "Eighteen or eighty the same to me. At my grave I'll see that Hans-face in my head, robbing me, slobbering—"

Firm in the grip of this new, strangely exalting rage, Felix snapped on the light, pushed a hand mirror into her face, wasn't sure if he thought or spoke until he heard the biting edge in his voice. "This poor Anna, never so robbed as she robs herself. Look at her, just look, my beautiful girl! This anger, this hatred, it's all grotesque, ugly."

She sat up, swung away from the mirror. "If I'm ugly I'm ugly, what's the difference?"

Heedless of his hip, his love, the tenderness grown to worship over the years, he dragged her to her feet. "Your will, your wonderful strength... so proud of them, aren't you? I too, I was proud also. But what if I tell you now they are nothing but self-pity, that you lie to yourself? That they

have cost you a career, a homeland, your peace of mind and mine? That
we are not today a happy family, that we can none of us be happy again if
you force him to choose between us and the girl..."

Gasping, his brief fury burned off, he left her clinging to the bedpost to
steady herself. His shoulders drooped, his hip again an infirmity, an old
man ponderous in his moves, he backed away from this avenging rage
and the woman who'd kindled it. But not from disillusion, he couldn't
back off from that.

"Anna, if he decides our world is too unhappy to live in, if this thing
—whatever you call it—costs us our Mischa..."

She pulled herself tall, straightened that long narrow back of which she
was so proud. "Cost? How cost us? So he makes quick visit to the Gypsies—they are nothing to him now—"

"Are we sure? Has he ever said so? And if he does not come back?" Silence
between them, uncertainty stretching out the seconds, the minutes. When
he spoke again it was the voice of an old man, high-pitched and trembling.

"That, my angel, I could not forgive."

He watched her already pale face turn to gray as pride fought and lost,
melted to pain, to fear, to panic, at last to realization before she turned
away from him.

"So okay, okay." Her voice low, hoarse. "You send the telegram, but—"

"No telegram. The phone. And you, Anna, you will make the call, tell
her where Mischa has gone, tell her she is welcome here, if not as your
daughter then as our daughter-in-law."

When Ellie's plane landed, Heathrow was all confusion, a diplomatic
delegation to her left, a group of missionaries to her right, but nowhere
was the confusion greater than in herself. Perhaps she shouldn't have
come, the woman's voice had sounded anything but welcoming, but
where was Michael, why had he gone to the Gyp...Romanies, after
everything he'd said, all his talk of security, high walls, a solid home that
didn't move?

Then a man with white hair and a cane was touching her hand, her
face, her cheek as if to soak up the feel of her skin.

"Gabriella...Gabriella...of course I know you..."

In a dream she followed him, this elderly shepherd who kept up a
constant murmur as he picked up her small case and her coat, led her
through a bedlam of bustling corridors. "...so I know how you must

feel, yes, so reluctant," he was saying, "sometimes I find it hard to forgive her myself—but then I've never quite been able to forgive your father either..." Waiting for the elevator, he fumbled in his pocket, at last finding his glasses, polishing them on a red and blue silk scarf, still talking "...but I guess that worn-out old saying is true after all. What we can't forgive we must try to forget..."

With glasses firmly on his nose he leaned in on her, peering at her eyes, her hair, her mouth, turning her hands palms up and bringing them to his lips as he closed his eyes. When he opened them they were awash with tears.

"Are you ill?" she said, alarmed.

"No, no." Again the glasses came off so he could scrub at his eyes. "It's just...your smile is so like hers, the way I remember it."

Book Two

TWENTY

*S*HE SEWED, ONE STITCH ON ANOTHER, pulled needle and pink
thread mechanically through a shaft of late sun. Worried school-
children chewed pencils; anxious wives plumped cushions; dancers sewed
shoes.

Turned against the light from the window she could not look for the
sweep of headlights, Mischa's car already two days late . . . oh, why had he
gone back to them, her cautious Mischa? Suppose they didn't give him
soap and water, the rough towels he liked? And where was he sleeping?
Not the floor? Would they know, this "family," that he required clean
shirts and socks every day, sometimes twice?

How, in so short a time, could her whole world have turned upside
over?

Left alone, the thing with the girl would have faded away, but no, Felix
must bring her . . . trouble, only trouble—was it any wonder she sewed
shoes? Better than watching the window—for soon Felix's car also must
creep up the driveway.

With the girl in it. Who had wasted no time. Well, maybe a second, that screaming silence flapping like vulture's wings over her when she'd called to Germany because Felix kept on and on, grabbing the phone, talking, thrusting it back at her: "Speak kindly to Gabriella!" Then a girl's disembodied voice, cool and confident, such perfect English:

"Is this an emergency, Mrs. Abramsky?"

Mrs. Abramsky. Well, what had she expected? Mama? Anna? Mother? But it surprised her into gabbling: "I don't know ... Felix makes me call because our Mischa left with those people and is not home, he has not phoned. Maybe he called to you?"

"No."

And again Felix reached for the phone to talk, to persuade.

So of course the girl took the next flight, couldn't wait, Mischa a prize anybody in her right mind—but to think that he, who could have anyone ... but no, it had to be this one, who would seize on a tepid invitation ... and Felix so gullible, bubbling like a *bébé* when he called from Heathrow:

"Your girl is lovely as a flower, Anna. Such taste she has, such manners—" Di-da-di-da-di-da-di-da. Anna bit off a thread. Felix was not done. Maybe Anna, his angel, should fix something special for dinner? Maybe even wear a dress, not an old tea gown?

Well, she'd told *him!* No false feathers, thank you very much. Bad enough she must open her house to strangers, to trouble.

After he hung up she closed her eyes. When that door opened what in God's name was she supposed to say? "Welcome"?

Dusk gathered and lights were already glowing at the house when Felix approached with Gabriella, whose hands curled only a little too tight in her lap. He rounded the last curve and slowed to a crawl within the gates. Where was Anna? Locked in her studio, buffing up her pride with a frantic barre? Maybe gone from the house because she couldn't face the girl?—but where would she go? Perhaps, against all odds, she'd dressed in her best to wait on the steps for the arrival of her daughter.

She was not on the steps, nor at the open door.

She sat by the window in an easy chair, but she did not sit easy and her face was turned resolutely away.

"I'll put away the car and bring in your valise, but please wait," Felix cautioned. "I'll take you in."

Ellie didn't wait. She nodded to the kind man even as she opened one door and then another, finding at last the place where a lamp shone on a woman who scowled as she sewed—a plain woman, the antithesis of everything Ellie had ever imagined.

She'd expected an aging beauty coarsened by time, selfish lines etched in pampered flesh, well-tended nails and hair, artful makeup and the latest fashions—but here was an angular bundle of bones under some kind of faded wrapper; wild gray hair sadly in need of shaping; vivid blue eyes that shot hostile little jabs at her but wouldn't take a really searching look; a mouth as straight and tight-closed as the shell of a razor clam.

A mouth not about to launch into any kind of welcoming speech—but it had been obvious anyway that the husband had forced the invitation and made it stick.

Now, standing before this unbending woman, eighteen years of suppressed anger rolled over her and she wanted to shout, to shake the tousled gray head, to knock needle and thread and dancing slipper from that long thin hand. But then blue eyes were pinning her to the rug, eyes too much like her own, and Ellie felt no bigger than a child. She forced herself to stand up very straight.

"Michael is not back?" she said at last, because one of them must fire the first shot.

Sparks from electric blue eyes, the only real color this woman seemed to have. "Mischa. His name is Mischa."

"To me he calls himself Michael."

"But within the family..."

Ellie's right hand brushed, not accidentally, at the diamond on her ring finger, and she asked again: "He is not back?"

"No." Anna wound pink ribbon rapidly around the instep of the slipper, a gesture as final as the turn of a key, but Ellie persisted.

"He hasn't called?"

"No."

"But you know where he is?"

Under the shabby wrap Anna's shoulder twitched. "North."

Felix appeared, blinking anxiously from one to the other, a magician whose conjuring trick is over and he is uncertain, now, what to do for an encore. Both women declined the drink he offered. "I think," he suggested carefully, "that tomorrow I might drive to Mischa's people, see if I can find him, talk with him. He should be told that Ellie is here, in his house."

Now Anna stood to speak to him, and Ellie was surprised she was so tall—taller than Ellie.

"Where is your pride, Felix? *We* are his people—and we do not hunt our son among the Gypsies. If he wants us he comes back, if not—" Her long hands spread. "He makes his choice." She jabbed the needle firmly into the spool of thread, gathered up her sewing, and swept from the room.

"You will forgive my Anna," Felix pleaded. "She is not an ungracious woman, she would have had a meal prepared—but she worries so about Mischa."

And I don't? Ellie thought, for the moment resenting even Felix, who tried so hard. "Your wife's manners don't concern me, I'm not her guest. I came only to see Michael, to find out where I stand."

"Where . . . but I am sure . . . why, when you marry—"

"*If* we marry. Unless he comes back soon . . ."

"But you love him?"

"I know the man I met in Germany. I don't know the Gypsy, nor anyone called Mischa."

"That's just our name for him, nothing more—"

"Your wife thinks it very important."

"My wife." He spread his arms and sighed, led her to a chair and patted her hand. "Sit, child. My wife . . . also your mother, yes, so we must try . . . once she was a gentle thing, as I think you too are gentle. But she turned bitter, my Anna—oh, not your fault, Gabriella, never, no—but if Mischa does not come back then of course her world is again finished." He spoke as if the point he'd made should be obvious to all. "But I know Mischa. He will come back, and then she will have a son and a daughter and she will learn to love you—"

Ellie felt herself drowning in his sweetness and made a conscious attempt to resist him.

"Mr. Abramsky, I have no quarrel with you. Michael says you are a saint and I'm sure he's right—but you must understand. This woman you call my mother neither looked at me nor offered me her hand. If she had I wouldn't have taken it. We are strangers. I have already told Michael I won't live with her."

"But Mischa, he thinks, child! How he is clever! Already he has the solution, arranged with the architect. The house will be made into two, so we can be separate families until . . . well, until we are comfortable with each other."

On impulse she took the hand of this troubled man. It was thin, papery, surprisingly cold. "Two families, Mr. Abra—"

"Felix, call me Felix—"

"Felix then—but you must understand. *We'll always be two families.* I'm sorry. Now I think I'd like to sleep—"

"Yes, yes, I'll show you your room, quiet and warm, you will like it, the electric blanket is on."

"Thank you—but I'll use Michael's room."

In Michael's room she took a long deep breath, tried to feel his presence among these spartan furnishings, so unlike the rest of the house— but there was no sense of the man she knew here; everything was cold, neutral, almost colorless but for a dark green couch and two starkly modern paintings on the wall. No snapshots of family (which didn't surprise her) and none of friends (which did). One wall was given over to encyclopedias, electronic texts, many books on marketing and the psychology of selling; there were books on stock markets, banking, taxation, a sprinkling of history and a half dozen well-thumbed classics. Not a single book devoted purely to pleasure, escape.

In the large walk-in wardrobe the same feeling, that it belonged to a stranger. Conservative business suits and starched white shirts—but then she found a sports jacket that looked familiar, a tie she'd given him in Venice, a sweater he'd worn in Reims with the faint odor of his talc still on it. Relief swept over her and for a second she was with him again, happy, laughing for no reason except that they'd just made love and soon would again, that the sun shone on them and always would. He existed, the man who'd taken over her mind and her senses, edged out Peter and Bonn and all the optimistic dreams of an independent future.

This was the room of Michael Abramsky.

Then where was *he* and what had sent him there? Illness in the Gypsy family, as Felix had said—or panic that he must choose between her and the implacable harridan downstairs?

She sat on the edge of the narrow bed, the wool of his sweater soft to her fingers. England was small. Easy enough to rent a car, head north, and find him; there couldn't be too many places the Rom gathered en masse. But if she found him, would it help, would she know any better who he was? How could the man who'd opened his past to her, confided in her, simply have walked out on his life as Felix said he had?

One week with him, one week—and in spite of everything, even Anna Abramsky, she'd agreed to marry him.

God, that woman! Ugly, domineering, pathetic in her helpless rage, hamstrung by her own pride—she of all women, who had so little to be proud of. How silly they seemed now, all the dreams she'd spun around her mother, gauzy things, all melody and rose petals and butterfly wings —when all the time there was nothing but a hornet ready to sting.

The next days she walked to escape the house and the silent Anna who brooded in it, the vigilant Felix who hovered in her shadow. In the village as an anonymous stranger, Ellie heard what she could never have learned under Greenlings' roof: that Mrs. Ab was a trial to the local merchants and that she had a tongue on her like a viper when she was crossed; that she had no women friends and didn't seem disposed to make any. The mister was a decent soul, never a bad word for anybody. But of course it was the Gyppo who ruled the roost—independent young sod he was, went his own way and the hell with everybody. When he refurnished Greenlings he bypassed local tradesmen and took his custom to London —made for bad blood, that.

One day Felix took her to Abramo, and she saw the extent of what she had imagined to be a small business. Full warehouses, men in white coats scurrying around with clipboards, Abramo trucks being loaded with boxed appliances, washers, mixers, toasters, televisions.

"And when everyone has such things?" she asked. "What will you sell then?"

Felix laughed. "Mischa says demand never stops, that people just keep on wanting more and better."

He showed her the lab and told her that here was where Mischa would make his fortune. "He is ambitious, our Mischa," Felix said. "I think he will not rest until he has more money than he can count—and he counts faster than anyone I know."

"You make him sound perfect," she said. "He must have *some* vices."

Felix sighed. "But I told you! He has ambition. Between that and greed is a very thin line, Gabriella."

Michael was gone four days.

He came back at dusk, the smell of the fires still on him, distance in his eyes, great distance, as if he'd traveled far beyond the narrow confines of northern England. His walk was different, easier, a subtle shift from its customary arrogance. The car he always kept immaculate was gray now with a dust he seemed not to notice, and when he emerged from the garage he left the door swinging on its hinge.

His hair tumbled to the collar of the same shirt he'd worn when he left—which was unironed and unstarched, washed hurriedly last night by

Grandmam and dried on a branch of hawthorn. The shoulder was ripped and every button was undone.

They'd heard the car, and from their various windows Felix, Ellie, and Anna watched him approach the door of Greenlings, saw him shake his head as he touched brown fingers to the knotted trunk of the oak tree, saw the flash of smile as he ran lightly up the steps and turned the door-handle.

Without Ellie in the house, Anna would have rushed to the hall and embraced him and called to Felix to come quick, come quick! Without Anna and Felix there, Ellie would have run into his arms. As it was they waited quietly in their places, unwilling to share him.

To the two women he looked like a stranger, and only Felix made a connection between the grown man and that scruffy little liar he'd taken into his home so long ago. For a moment, a long, disquieting moment at Greenlings' elegant casement, Felix saw what the boy Micah, amongst his own people, would have grown up to be. Secretive, alien, even hostile.

He sighed and slipped into the studio, where Anna, paler than usual, pretended to warm up. His whisper was soothing, hypnotic: "... so we must be easy with him, my angel, leave him alone to be with Ellie, listen carefully when he speaks, for remember what I am telling you now. We can still lose him. If not to the girl then perhaps to *them*—for I think he was not unhappy at their campground." He gestured north before smoothing Anna's hair and sitting at the piano to play her through a barre.

Michael knew a great surge of relief—but no surprise—at finding Ellie silhouetted against the white walls of his room. Hadn't Grandmam predicted it? "With you gone they'll worry. Sometimes it's best just to leave, Micah, give everybody time to think." So no, Ellie's presence didn't surprise him, only her anger, well hidden until he kissed her, but then there was that quiver to her lips, the sharp "No!" as his mouth found her throat, the force of her hand holding him away.

"You knew I'd be waiting for you, didn't you? That Felix would call me, that I'd be frantic."

"I thought he might call, yes, but there was no reason to worry—"

"Felix seemed to think so."

"Felix can be a sly old bugger on occasion. He saw a chance to get you under this roof—where we both want you to be."

"But not Anna."

"You didn't expect it."

"I did expect you to call. You could have."

"Yes."

"It didn't matter that I listened every second for the door, the phone?"

He sighed. "Ellie, listen to me. Close up, Anna and Felix between them tend to overpower. I had to think. Then back with the Rom . . . at first I found myself *liking* it, wondering what I'd missed by leaving them . . . but then there was you and the Abs and this place, and I couldn't let all that go."

He forced her to lie beside him on the narrow bed and listen as he told her about the Rom, the things he neither understood nor sympathized with, things that irritated and confused him, their lack of any ambition beyond next week, next month. It was insidious, a trap all too easy to fall into. He told her of Dui and Dui's boy, of Rose and Grandmam, of the horse trading and the fair. As he talked his thumb stroked her chin, felt it relax and soften until he could tilt it, look into her eyes before setting his mouth gently, firmly on hers.

"I need to shower," he said softly.

"Yes."

"You could help."

"Yes."

After, when they lay on the bed, clean and satisfied and close again, he asked about Anna, what kind of reception had she —

"Cold."

"But civil?"

"Barely."

"You should have said something."

She looked hard into his eyes and he felt she was thinking now as much about the two of them as about Anna Abramsky. "Arguments never get anywhere. Actions get you what you want."

"And what *do* you want?"

"To be your whole world."

"You already are."

Below them an oven door slammed in the kitchen and a murmur of Russian floated up the stairwell.

Anna tossed carrots and turnips into the pot-au-feu on the stove. "What can be keeping them all this time in his room?" she hissed at Felix, jabbing at beef with a fork, sniffing critically at fragrant vapors rising from the kettle.

"What do you expect is keeping them, angel?" Felix teased. "They are in love. Patience. They will be downstairs soon—he has missed your good table, I'm sure, so we shall be very nice and quiet and let them eat in peace. And then maybe we will all begin to discuss the future like civilized people, yes?"

An hour later they were all at dinner. Ellie was quiet, a glow about her the Abramskys had not seen before. Anna watched Mischa taste the meat, then set down his fork.

"Is not good?" she demanded. "I made it like always."

"As usual it's delicious—perhaps just a little flat."

A week ago she would have declared with spirit that only peasants larded everything with spices, but now she whisked his plate away, ran to the kitchen for tins of paprika and garlic powder, shook them generously into the pot before offering up a new serving. "Try now," she insisted, "perhaps is better."

Michael turned away, unable to mask the pity he knew to be in his face. Anna Abramsky, afraid of nothing but the past and what it might bring, ruler of what she saw to be her house and her men, now had a new, completely unfounded fear.

That her Mischa might, at any moment, return to the Rom.

TWENTY-ONE

*I*N THE WEEKS FOLLOWING MICHAEL'S RETURN, each dawn found the house swarming with workers. Power saws buzzed, hammers rang, cement mixers rumbled, bricklayers shouted back and forth as they brewed billycans of tea. The new wing for Felix and Anna must exactly match the house, as if it had been built at the same time by the same builder from identical materials. Only the massive old oak was a constant; previously the landscape's centerpiece, it was now to form the inner cornerstone of a great ell. Shrubs were dug up in their hundreds and encased in burlap, only to be moved a few feet right or left to accommodate the new design. From the wide central sweep of driveway each wing was to have its own walkway separated by an avenue of young cypress which, when mature, would form an effective screen.

Already the locals were calling the addition Gypsy Folly; privately, many of the contractors would have agreed. The project was costing well beyond what could be recovered by resale in the foreseeable future.

"It will never be for sale," Michael said flatly, but only he and Felix and their banker knew just how close they sailed to the wind that year, how carefully sales and profit curves were monitored, how hard he rode Pete Preston on Abramo One, the success of which was now vital.

"Safer to find a separate little house for Anna and me," Felix offered, but in the thunder of hammers Michael heard the affirmation of his dream, both families under one roof until they themselves became one. When he speculated on the future he saw Ellie and himself with their children, who, if not actually eating toffees from a tin, at least had available the finest fruits to be found; the parents of these children hovered over them; adoring grandparents were no farther away than a child's cry.

"We're free, Micah, not like them in the kumpania," *Da used to say when Micah was little. "Now we've no in-laws minding our business." But he always said it on his way out the trailer door to the pubs, right after he told Micah to get in bed and stay there, and not to be messing with no matches.*

When he remembered these things Michael sometimes thought: Am I building my *kumpania* because Da took me away from my own? But then he'd laugh; only a fool would equate the grandeur of Greenlings with a cluster of trailers always on the move.

It was to be a September wedding, the reception on the long slope of lawn leading down to the beech grove.

Nothing could have underscored the bizarre mix of family and acquaintances so much as the guest list; small as it was, it included such hopelessly diverse groups that even Felix despaired of pleasing everyone. Abramo executives and their wives must be invited, but they were few and would balance the handful of dancers who ran the studios. The best man would be Pete Preston. Ellie's only bridesmaid was to be Mary Beth Warren, presently teaching in London and the one guest who could honestly be called a friend. Sundry shopkeepers from Ryder Street completed the *gajo* side—but it was Michael's Gypsy family that raised doubts, turned every tradition into a question mark. Naturally Grandmam wanted to be there; Rose refused to be left out and was flying in from Switzerland. Which left Dui.

"It's going to be a small affair," Michael said firmly when Dui stopped by to negotiate terms. "Just close family."

Dui was at a loss, devastated, heartbroken. "I'm not close family? My wife? Little Tomo, the only nephew you've got?"

Michael hesitated, a mistake—for Dui immediately began lobbying for a full scale "do" to include the entire *kumpania:*

"You're not poor, Micah, we should do like in the old days. 'May wine flow like water and whiskey flow like wine, may the families rejoice, may—'"

"No!" He tried to picture Ellie confronted by old rituals; to see Anna queening it as mother of the bride (that alone brought his imagination shuddering to a stop) as she proudly waved a bloodstained sheet from the marriage bed to prove the innocence of a beloved daughter whose virginity was now lost, sold for an appropriate figure after much haggling.

"No," he repeated. "That stuff's died out and you know it. Even if it hadn't, Ellie and I are not Rom."

Dui let it go. He had other arguments to advance and could do justice to only one at once. "You've got all that room, we could get twenty trailers easy on that south field there—"

"It's a *lawn*." Michael pictured its immaculate greenness gouged with trailer wheels, pocked with charred remnants (perhaps a week's worth?) of fires. "Come if you want, Dui, but come alone and just for the afternoon. You won't need a trailer."

"Mischa is right," Felix said in fear, thinking of bottles and cans on his lovely lawn. How would he ever apologize to the gardener when it was over?

Ellie said nothing, but when she shut herself in Michael's suite she couldn't help laughing. The Abramskys—even Michael—thought themselves so worldly, would have laughed at Grossmutter's pretensions—but when the subject was Gypsies they all thought alike. She didn't like Dui and didn't want the tribe at her wedding any more than the others did, but oh how she'd love to see Anna's face with Gypsy children wiping ice cream on the Irish linen, swarming through the rose arbor, leaping like brown frogs into the lily pool.

And if it should rain, if the affair must be held in the house? A fear Anna was already examining in some panic:

"What then, Felix, what then? Gypsies in this house? *Inside?* So I should hide all the silver, put away the crystal, send my jewelry to the bank?" She spread her arms, desolate at the prospect.

"Your jewelry is precious only to you, Anna. How can you think that Mischa's grandmother would steal from us?" Felix said firmly.

But he too had his doubts, concerned more with family clashes than with stealing. He did not tell Anna, who must be kept calm these final weeks of the remodeling. A fragile peace reigned in the house now—a peace dependent on the knowledge that soon it would be over, if only they could find restraint enough to get them there. When Anna filled the house with music for her barre and waited for Mischa to join her, Ellie walked the grounds. While Ellie and Mischa debated upholstery swatches and color charts in his suite, Anna rearranged her scrapbook, mourning the frailty of yellowed notices and faded photographs. All of which took care of evenings and weekends. How the two women occupied themselves on weekdays he did not know ... if he inquired, Anna said, "Only a man could ask this question; a woman never has the time." He only knew that each evening when he returned to the house he was uneasy until he'd seen both versions of the face he loved.

Ellie could have told him if he'd asked her. She and Anna spent their days avoiding one another, a difficult task within the same four walls. When Michael was home and in view, the two women were hawks, distant and wary, perpetually circling disputed territory. When he was away there was no territorial imperative to dispute; they could quietly and openly despise one another, play tit-fot-tats that shamed them both—but the childish little games were safety valves and both recognized them as such.

From the beginning Ellie had intended returning to Germany until the wedding—but then Anna made a caustic remark about the morals of today's young women, and Ellie, in retaliation, called the storage company with orders to forward all her things to Greenlings; under Anna's disapproving eye she arranged underwear and scarves alongside Michael's socks and sweaters, and enjoyed the triumph. Ellie, an indifferent cook, grew tired of Anna's pointed little asides to the tradesmen: "No fat on the roast—you will recall Mischa does not like it!" "Brown eggs for Mischa, Mr. Yates." "Yellow apples today, please. Mischa prefers." On and on until Ellie could have screamed—but she did not because it would have suited Anna much too well.

Instead she announced one day that she would make dinner herself, ordered a superb roast, and spent half the day in its preparation; Anna, after an enigmatic glance at the kitchen table, remained in her studio until dinnertime, to emerge all dressed up in maroon silk, her hair freshly done, even a dash of plum-colored shadow on her hooded eyelids.

"Is great occasion," she told Michael when he noticed. "Gabriella has cooked dinner for you," folding her hands and waiting for the inevitable.

The rack of lamb looked magnificent; she was proud of its rich brown gloss, the paper frills she'd cut with such care, the sauce in its china boat. She expected praise; there was only a long embarrassed silence as she passed Michael the platter for carving. When pink juices oozed out under the prod of the carving fork his olive skin turned the murky green of a neglected pond; with a napkin pressed to his mouth he asked Felix to carve. Then he ran, very quickly, upstairs to his suite.

Felix sighed. "Poor Mischa cannot eat lamb, never could, even the smell of it upsets him . . . but never mind, Ellie, we shall have it and enjoy. See how juicy—Anna, pass your plate—"

"Thank you, no. Like Mischa, I don't care for—"

"Anna, you will love it! Please, your plate."

Felix could serve it but could hardly make her eat it, so there was just Felix and Ellie and this mountain of lamb.

"She knew all the time," Ellie raged later, "the bitch—"

Michael looped a strand of her hair over his finger. "I guess she forgot. It's old history now, anyway."

He told her about a Christmas tree with lamb ornaments; as she listened Ellie felt herself brimming over with compassion for the boy he had been, forgetting all about Anna, as he'd no doubt intended she should. But she remembered later, and reminded him.

"I *hate* her, Michael. She's bitter and crabbed and self-centered and . . . oh, how *can* you love someone like that?"

"Because," he said softly, "she was there for me when no one else was. Except for Felix—and it was easier for him."

Another oblique reference to Anna's supposed tragedy, a subject they skirted because it created instant distance between them. Even before she met Anna she hadn't believed her father capable of rape; once she'd seen Anna Abramsky she was sure. What man would want that unyielding bundle of bones enough to take it by force? Certainly not the painted hero of her little-girl fantasies.

But she resolved that when they were married and in their own quarters, Papa's portrait would hang in the hall. Anna Abramsky had been catered to quite long enough.

September, hot and yellow. Smells of cut grass and leaves burning. In the deepest shade of the great oak the honeymoon car waited, already stripped of ribbons and flowers, loaded now with luggage for the airport. The couple were to fly to Kyoto, where the groom's itinerary, between old temples and strolls down the Ginza, included plans to tour a couple of transistor factories and a precision welding shop.

Wedding guests had sorted themselves into predictable groups. At one end of the lawn Abramo men made wedding jokes and laughed a lot; those with paunches sucked them in when they were introduced to the dance teachers. Abramo wives smiled pleasantly and correctly, eyes raking husbands, dancers, the groom they'd heard so much about (not all of it flattering)—and the bride's dress, a soft sea green instead of the expected white. All of them, husbands, wives and dancers, tried not to stare at the head table with its motley assortment of guests, but from time to time curiosity won out. Then the toasts began and they could relax, gape in comfort at these strange birds who would be good for months of gossip.

For Mary Beth Warren, seated between Michael's two families (diplomacy on someone's part?), the scene would linger in her mind, its moods and colors all trapped under an amber bowl of sky, all its faces set—faces which, even years later, would frame love and hate in a single moment. Everywhere were smooth surfaces; under them resentments so strong they quivered on the air. Fresh from Maine, London, and civilized parts between, she had never seen variety such as was gathered at the nuptial table of her pupil and friend Gabriella Abramsky, née von Reiker.

Except for the best man, pale as a moth and typically Anglo-Saxon, each face reflected a different exotic aspect of the human race. Ellie's letters had prepared her for Anna and Felix; she had them almost right— though Mary Beth thought she'd been too kind to Felix and overharsh to Anna. Oh, Felix was angelic—no doubt about that. Goodness shone out of him like a beacon—but with age he could well become petty, old-womanish. Anna . . . here Ellie seemed to have lost all objectivity. Where she perceived arrogance Mary Beth saw strength, a will far beyond anything the frail husband could harness; he only thought he was in control, had never understood that such women are harnessed only when they wish it. But even the Abramskys, vivid, crackling with tensions, were overshadowed here, set pieces frozen into whatever roles they had choreographed for themselves a quarter century ago. It was the others, the Gypsies, who drew every eye.

Not all of Ellie's whispered phone calls between Greenlings and London could have prepared Mary Beth for these Gypsies:

There was the true crone, gray braids and long skirts, quick black eyes that missed nothing and scorned everything; she sniffed each dish, sampled few, scowled her suspicions with every bite; between courses her knotted brown fingers filled and tamped an old clay pipe; she lit it, puffed it, and fanned it live, blew clouds of pungent smoke over the table. The toasts and the wine she ignored completely, but she watched the bridegroom as if she would drink him with her eyes.

The girl next to her, thin and peevish, ate nothing either. She busied herself squirreling ham slices and salmon puffs deep into the capacious

pockets of her dress. Ellie, the embarrassed but tactful hostess, murmured: "I'm *so* glad you like them, Rose, we'll send some home with
you." Rose's answer came straight from the gutter, a triumph of spite and
self-pity: "Rose isn't going home, is she? She has to have bread and milk
and afternoon naps at that bleedin' clinic," shooting ferocious black
glances at the heavyset man on her other side.

The bridegroom's brother Dui, whom no one seemed to like. Neither
did Mary Beth. She'd been present earlier when he borrowed a tie from
the groom, silk, with pale gray fleurs-de-lis on a ground of deep maroon.
Already the tie was smeared with pâté and dotted with tomato seeds from
the salad. Already the wearer was noisily and offensively drunk as he
touched sweaty hands to Ellie's wrist.

"What a poor bit of a wedding after all, eh? Just think—Ellie, is it?—
just think, you could have had a week of feasting, music, danced till your
feet fell off... But he's tight with a shillin', our Micah."

He stopped when Michael's thin hand closed on his wrist. "I think
you've had enough to drink."

Dui laughed and reached for the wine carafe. "I can hold me liquor,
ain't that right, Grandmam?"

"About as good as you hold your tongue."

The look that passed between Dui and his grandmother would have
soured cream. The old woman turned to Ellie. "You're lucky. Micah
knows when he's had enough. This Dui's just the way his da was. He
don't know how far he's gone till he's too far gone to know."

Dui was on his feet, gripping the table, stumbling over words that
Mary Beth, with all her education, didn't understand.

The grandmother's lips closed tight around the pipestem. Taking in a
great gout of smoke, she let it trickle out slowly for the breeze to take up
and float like a banner over Dui's head. Her answer, when it came, was in
the same language—probably Romani—spoken with a hypnotic dignity,
almost like a spell.

Mary Beth felt the hair on the back of her neck lift ever so slightly. Was
this to be the Gypsy "incident" the Abramskys seemed to fear?

Now Michael was speaking, his voice low but in English, for the whole
table to hear. "Da is in the past. Leave him there." A rapid gesture, two
fingers to his lips, a sign sketched hastily in the air; it carried authority
and silenced them all.

So inevitably Mary Beth's eyes were drawn to the last Gypsy, strongest
personality at the table, the star, the enigma. Michael Abramsky. Or Mischa. Or Micah. Depending on who was speaking. An unsettling man, she

thought. The kind you would never quite get to know. That odd stillness about him, as if the September air paused and quieted itself before passing over him. The contradictions in his face. Long, passionate mouth. Eyes so dark they should have been soft, but they shone with a hard, all-seeing glitter. So many faces he seemed to have, none of them false yet none of them wholly true. Dimly she sensed that he was the center of the storm; the others all swirled around him, particles drawn into the core.

The way he looked upon Anna and Felix, fond and uncritical, so indulgent that love and gratitude were inseparable.

His brother, Dui, to whom he showed little but contempt. No resemblance there.

To his sister, Rose, the obligatory pity one offers a wounded animal. He spoke to her, yes, but he seldom looked at her.

He looked at the grandmother. With respect and awe, perhaps even love for the embattled old bones—but again pity clouded the mix.

Then the way he looked at Ellie, showed her off like a newly crowned queen, all pride and admiration instead of the simplehearted adoration one might have expected from so young a man. That he loved Ellie, Mary Beth had no doubt. But because she didn't yet know him, had not yet felt the force of any specific facet of him, she could still see the whole man and she sensed the hunger there. It was too deep for Ellie to fill, too deep for money to fill, also. He needed more, but what? To find it would take patience, infinite knowledge... but oh Ellie, my friend, somewhere in this world there *is* infinite knowledge... and you with your one affair are so innocent.

How did he see *himself*, this man caught at the crossroads of too many cultures? Perhaps he was a searcher who would never find because he did not know what to look for.

"He used to be Gypsy," Ellie had said in the beginning, "but now he's just like everybody else."

Mary Beth Warren shook her head. If that's what Ellie truly believed, then God help her. Somebody would have to.

Just as surely as if she'd told him, Michael knew what Grandmam would do, had known from the moment she'd said the words to Dui. Stupid Dui, to taunt her with his drinking, bringing life to the past, the bitterness that would never die.

Da killed Grandmam's daughter, stole her grandson. In such stark terms she saw her life.

"Forgive and forget," Dui had said—handing Grandmam the whip to beat him with.

"When stones float on water I forgive."

That's what she'd said. With the saying came the decision. Michael saw it form, and so was not surprised when Grandmam got to her feet, raised a brown fist very high, waiting in patient dignity for silence. Which came.

Turning slowly, she placed herself directly behind the bride and groom and took their joined hands to her lips, whispering into the pink and brown shell, squeezing it until Michael heard Ellie's muffled gasp of pain.

She faced the finely dressed guests, this old woman in long skirts only slightly less dusty than those she wore every day of her life. Her shoes, down at heel, lay discarded under the table; the toes she dug into Greenlings' fine lawn were long, bare, and not altogether clean. A front tooth was missing and when she smiled—as she did now— there was a gleam of gold from inside her mouth.

"Today I see my grandson's house. For people who like houses perhaps it is a good house. All of you have given Micah and his wife many presents for this house. I have a present also. Small, not fancy-wrapped, and not for the house. But it comes from my heart, so I think they will take it."

It was perhaps the longest speech she had made to strangers in all her life and she seemed dazed by the flurry of polite applause. Then there was silence, expectation, everyone waiting to see the gift handed over. They were too late. It lay already in Ellie's palm, a twist of paper, perhaps an old wrapper from a candy mint. Uncertainty in Ellie's eyes. For all her social graces she had no idea into what taboos she might blunder.

"Open it," Michael said, wishing she didn't have to, wishing it could be given back, but it "came from the heart" so of course they must take it. "Open it, darling. It's something for you."

Paper rustled and fell as Ellie, then everyone at the table, gasped at what lay in her palm. Dui, suddenly sober, was first to speak.

"The ruby! All these years you made out it was lost."

The triumph in Grandmam's little smile! "Now it's found."

Ellie folded Grandmam in a graceful, grateful embrace, and Michael looked over their heads at Dui, who was watching him, hating him, hating *him* even as he spilled angry Romani over Grandmam. "You've no right! It belongs in the family."

And in Romani she answered. "Micah *is* the family."

Then Ellie was pressing the ruby into his hand, her whisper for him alone. "I'm afraid to lose it—oh Michael, how kind of her, when she has so little—"

It was cold, a shock to his palm—and not given out of kindness at all. For Grandmam it represented yesterday's *kumpania*. In depriving Dui of its worth she thought to dam up the future with a pebble. And now his brother and sister—yes, even Rose—would hate him for it as long as they lived.

They'd been in the air many hours, Michael almost asleep, Ellie dozing restlessly beside him, when something deep in his memory stirred, triggered perhaps by the day's talk of brides. Your bride. The bride's table. The bridal bouquet. Bride.

The word lay there, a magnet to attract a ruby . . . which glowed now, and when he held it to the light there was fire in its heart and a little girl's voice, husky and determined:

"So what did your da say, Micah?" Her pointed stick gave a deep round eye to a bird she'd drawn in the dust.

". . . if we can meet your bride-price, and if . . ."

The engines changed pitch and Ellie murmured beside him. He stroked her hair, pale honey in the polar dawn. How vulnerable she is in sleep, he thought. How precious. And how secure, how happy he would make her.

TWENTY·TWO

*I*T WAS SPRING in the first year of their marriage, that heady time of discovery, of wonder, when concessions are freely given and gratefully received. When paths to the future are strewn with roses and lined with love. When outsiders, however dear, are misty strangers who could never for a moment understand the miracle. When each day begins and ends in each other's eyes.

She wore a pale yellow peignoir and she smiled against a lace-edged pillow the color of heavy cream; primroses nodded in a window box and on the polished oak of the dresser pools of sunlight held out a fey promise of summer to come. A tranquil, unremarkable morning, yet small events of the day were fingers pointing (unheeded because their import was unknown) toward the future.

Secure and private, they still woke at dawn in their own half of Greenlings, reluctant to lose one moment together before Michael took barre with Anna, before he departed with Felix for Abramo. Lately he'd taken to making morning coffee himself and serving Ellie's in bed with the newspaper. Often a flower, a note, perhaps a small trinket would be hidden under the headlines of the *Telegraph*.

Waiting for her to discover it, he'd sit on the edge of the bed and drink in the picture she made. Hair a dark gold tangle on the pillow, skin rosy from sleep, mouth still a soft curve from last night's loving, the whole of her enhanced now by that special aura.

Perhaps she felt his glance touch her, linger on the almost undetectable swell under the wisp of gown, for she blushed and smoothed the blanket over her. He smiled fondly. As if he cared. He'd be glad when the world knew. First child, first of many, many... such lives he'd give them, his children, such warmth he'd wrap them in... always a family to lean on, always food in the larder. And this house, solid, impervious to snow and rain, walls a foot thick, no cracks for winds to sweep in, fires in every room, locks so the world couldn't reach in, the Rom... no, he hadn't thought that, pretend he hadn't thought it—he didn't mean Grandmam, who'd looked smaller, darker, at Christmas. *Not Grandmam!* his thought loud, imperative on this too perfect morning, lest some avenging fate misunderstand, be tempted to punish. Punish! Superstitious rubbish! If he didn't watch it he'd be as stupid as Dui—worse, because he knew better.

He eased his shoulders, slipped back smoothly, quickly, into the urbane skin of Michael Abramsky, who had everything in the world to be thankful for:

"They'll have to be told, darling," he said, pride and the hint of a plea in his voice. He *ached* to tell Anna and Felix, to see their faces, to draw them inside the shining circle. Why must they hold the knowledge between them, a secret until the last possible moment? "They'll see soon, anyway."

"I know," she said lazily, smiling. "But then it'll belong to everybody. But you're right. Felix gave me that look again yesterday when we walked to the village. We took the shortcut over the heath and he made a point of helping me over the stile—with *his* hip, d'you believe!" She hesitated. Then: "Maybe it's time we asked them to dinner..."

The fresh pink of her cheeks deepened, and he wondered if perhaps she was softening, if pregnancy was forming some bond. As yet he'd seen no sign of a thaw between Ellie and Anna; they were as cool to each other as the day he returned from Appleby—cooler, for now they'd learned where to place the barbs, where the sore spots lay under the other's armor of silks and powders and frosted little smiles. He'd come to believe there would never be anything closer than this guarded truce. Sometimes he wished for an explosion, that honest air might reach the wounds—but he was afraid of that, too, and daily congratulated himself on dividing the house. Not to have done so would by now have split the families in two, the businesses—and with them his loyalties.

But Ellie, giving in? "Sure it's not too much for you?"

"*A dinner?*" She laughed, but there was an unfamiliar edge to it that puzzled him. "Michael, don't think I'm complaining, I love Greenlings and I've loved decorating it with you, but it's done, isn't it? When you're here it's perfect—but you *are* away a lot, Geneva, San Francisco—and if I don't go with you I've nothing to do. Oh, I cook a little, I garden, I shop, I tell Mrs. Finn which floor to scrub, which windows to clean... the exact same things I did at Grossmutter's house!"

"But this is your own place—"

"Look, I'm not blaming *you*—" But she saw she'd hurt him. He was so proud he could give her this leisured life—but for her the leisure was idleness. Soon it would be boredom. Abramo One was close now; as he worked more evenings at the plant the days stretched empty before her and she knew she'd have to change things if she was to continue happy here, if it was to be truly a home and not just a setting. Jewels had settings, and perhaps that's how Michael saw her—but she was a person and needed a purpose. Maybe that's why she'd agreed to announce the baby to Felix and Anna. One small concession in exchange for another.

"In a few months you'll have plenty to do," he said now.

"No I won't, you've already talked about a nurse—"

"I'll be traveling, selling the concept, I'll need you with me a lot of the time—"

"And I'll be there—but I'd like something of my own, too. The years I nursed Grossmutter were a prison, all I could think about was getting out, working, achieving something—and now that I *am* out I'm right back in the country, running a house again!"

He drew slightly away. "For a girl who's not blaming me, not complaining, you're doing a good job. Just what do you want? Some kind of shop like every bored housewife the world over—"

"Michael, I love you. I don't want to fight, I'm not bored, and I don't want a shop." She'd had no idea *what* she wanted until she mulled it over with Mary Beth last month. Since then she'd thought of little else.

"Don't be modest," her friend told her. "You had that played-out old vineyard ticking over like a metronome. If the old girl threw in some capital you'd even have made a profit. You have the knack of smoothing edges, softening corners. You *handle people,* create order. You could throw a garden party in the middle of the Calgary Stampede and not even chip the Spode. You're an organizer." Ellie muttered that it was hardly a glamorous quality, and Mary Beth laughed. "Honey, efficiency equals economy equals *profit*—the sweetest, most glamorous word a businessman knows. Talk to one—maybe Michael?"

So today she looked beyond him to the garden, to her army of purple crocus massed on the sloping lawn, daffodils flaunting golden shields to the east, tulips even now thrusting spears of apple green through Greenlings' well-tended earth—all just as she'd planned last autumn.

It was time to talk to a businessman, one she could help, one whom she loved and who worked too hard. But he was turning away, a dark silhouette against the morning window.

"Not Abramo, I don't want you there—"

"It's grown too fast, it *needs* organizing, you've got people duplicating people in some jobs, while in others—"

"I know that. It's Felix's department and he's soft. He hires out of charity and can't bring himself to fire..." He sighed. "When the time's right I'll bring in an office manager, but I have to do it without hurting his feelings..."

His face was in shadow—deliberately, she thought. "Why not hire me? Now. Part-time." She sounded bolder than she felt.

"That would hurt him more than if I hired a stranger."

"I don't agree. He likes me—"

"He loves you... but that's not the point."

"Then tell me what is." Because it certainly wasn't Felix.

After a long time he leaned down and smoothed her hair, let his lips linger in the hollow of her throat. "Abramo is mine," he whispered. "Felix is there because it would kill him to be idle, treated like a charity case—but Abramo is mine the way this house is mine—built for you and for our children and for *their* children. I'm going to make it succeed and I want to know I did it. On my own and for us. Understand?"

Yes, but understanding would not fill her days, would not stop her wondering if she could have accomplished something. "So then I'm to be what?" she asked quietly. "An ornament to show off on special occasions? A baby machine to fill your house? A brood mare such as Dui might—"

He sprang away, stung. "Don't ever compare me with him. If you insist on work, go ahead—but it won't be at Abramo and the children mustn't be affected."

"Child. Right now there's just one, not yet born. And I *shall* go ahead, look for something..."

"Not hard work—"

"Then there'd be no point in working at all." She marveled at herself, her words so crisp, confident. She marveled even more at him when she heard what he proposed. She'd never held down a job, never applied for one—yet now here was Michael suddenly offering her one, clearing his throat, contrite—pulling it out of the air like a rabbit from a hat, exactly the kind of thing she had in mind. And now she was hesitating.

Why? Was he humoring her because she was pregnant? Did he think she'd tire of it and give up? What he was suggesting was too easy. How would she know she'd succeeded? *If* she succeeded.

"Simple," he said. "Studio income is way down, any profit will be a plus. Felix doesn't care and Anna never approved of the student-teacher setup, has no idea how to manage it. She gives the best jobs to the super dancers, but it's often the average dancers who'd make the real administrators—they've still got something to prove."

Like me, she thought—and maybe Michael was thinking the same thing, that once she'd proved herself she'd be content . . .

She took a deep breath. "Full management then? And shall we say twenty-five percent of the net?"

He laughed. "No, we'll say ten. Of the profit."

On the promise that the money would be paid into a new account, entirely hers (She: I've never bought so much as a lipstick with money I made myself. He: You've *got* your own account! She: Which you keep topping up!), a bargain was struck, sealed in intimate, unbusinesslike fashion. Then, in the reluctant separation of their flesh, his warm cheek against the new fullness of her milk-white breasts, his brown finger tracing the delicate blue web of veins, she remembered.

"What will Anna say? The studios are her baby."

"Tonight we're to announce her grandbaby—she'll be too delighted to care about a few dusty old dance studios then."

Ellie knew better, but she knew when to keep silent, too. She'd scored a victory and could afford to be generous. So, apparently, could Michael.

"If you're through playing big business maybe you should look under the morning paper."

A green foil box tied with a gilded cord. Her elation drained away. She knew what must be in it, knew she didn't want to wear it, ever. She was right. Grandmam's ruby, now hung from a small gold claw threaded on an intricate golden chain.

"It's pretty, Michael. Thank you . . ."

He smiled and slipped it to the back of the bedroom safe. "It's not your style but it's hers. When we see her again she'll expect you to be wearing it—"

"And she'll expect Dui to be hating me for it—"

"He will. For her that's the beauty of it."

She didn't wear it that evening, and Michael was obscurely grateful. That ruby and the setting he'd chosen belonged on a brown neck with pendant earrings gleaming above it; there should be firelight to reflect the blood-red heart of the stone, the gold of the earrings, and the warm gleam of dark eyes. Grandmam meant well, but Ellie was matched pearls and stud earrings. When she was older, diamonds. She would never be rubies.

By Michael's reckoning the atmosphere over dinner, while not cordial, was a beginning. The elder Abramskys arrived late and entered through the back door via the kitchen—though Anna was all dressed up in one of her prewar silks, a pigeon-gray memento with padded shoulders, a thing she called a peplum accentuating her tiny waist, hiding the skeletal hips and thighs over which she never ceased to labor. As Felix proudly said, Anna could still achieve every ballet position in the book.

Tonight he was in splendid humor, rubbing his hip and his halo simultaneously as he babbled on that of course he'd known about the baby, oh he'd known, yes, hadn't he said so to Anna? Anna very properly allowed that she was pleased—and how clever of Mischa to have this perfect house ready, the country air so clean, the grounds so private, idyllic for a child...

"I found childhood in the country rather...dull," Ellie said smoothly, "but of course my circumstances were different."

Michael intervened to refresh their wine, but Anna touched a finger to her glass, murmured that it was a little acid on her stomach, and swept out the back door to fetch club soda from her own quarters. When Michael reminded her there was bottled water here if she needed it, Felix put a finger to his lips.

"She only wants to use the toilet."

"Why not use ours?"

"What? Walk through the hall? Under the portrait of Hans?"

"She doesn't know it's there. This is the first time she's been over since the wedding."

"But when you're both away she stands on the planter and peeks through the window. A naughty old child, my Anna, yes?"

Both men laughed indulgently, but Ellie resolved to draw the curtains in future. Michael outlined to Felix the plan to put Ellie in charge of the studios. "Do you think Anna will mind?"

Felix considered, then nodded over a spear of asparagus. "She grumbles about the paperwork, neglects it, loathes it—but she'll *say* she minds. At first."

Naturally her objections were routed through the conduit of "darling Mischa." "What? Do I not make paperwork on time? File employment records, injury reports, the stupid insurance forms—"

"Not always," he said gravely. "We understand. Routine must be intolerable for someone with your creative gifts. We're lucky Ellie is experienced with routine—it will free you to—"

"But she knows nossink! nossink about the dance!"

"She knows organization. She can drive herself from one studio to another—you always said trains were a chore. Of course she'll get a percentage," Michael said, as if the matter were already closed. "To give her incentive."

Anna sniffed and poked her long nose into a glass of wine that not five minutes earlier had been too acid. "This whole year I kept the books alone, no one to help me—I had no need to travel, and not one penny of profit did I take!"

No one pointed out there'd *been* no profit. Her daughter might have, but Anna's tone was so clearly that of the vanquished martyr that Ellie knew she'd won—and in any case the toe of Michael's shoe lay lightly, casually, across her own.

As her pregnancy progressed, Ellie's marriage was inevitably a concentration on Michael, an endless yearning for him that even the most intimate depths of their passion never quite slaked; every newly discovered imperfection fascinated her, was explored and analyzed when he was away, compounded by new facets when they were together. He was an enigma, a mass of contradictions, an impervious ego who believed utterly in his own ability. Cruelly contemptuous of idlers, of schemers such as Dui, Michael was nevertheless quick to grasp at opportunities himself.

"Why not?" he said once after a particularly rapacious deal with an overextended competitor needing help, which Michael gave—at a considerable profit to Abramo. "The same pit was there for both of us. Is it my fault he fell in it?"

Impatient with incompetents and dreamers, he could find endless compassion for Felix and Anna, never for a moment letting them glimpse their limitations—which were more and more apparent every day.

Ellie's work at the studios went well. The basic structure was sound and only Anna's contempt for record keeping had left them open to loss. As her pregnancy advanced into the final months, trips to the more distant studios were, at Michael's insistence, curtailed, but thanks to well-chosen staff the profit curve kept its steady rise.

Inevitably she grew fond of Felix. Through the worst days of winter his hip troubled him more and more, sometimes too much to go to Abramo with Michael, and on those days he'd be waiting in Ellie's kitchen, her afternoon tea ready for pouring when she arrived home from the studio office.

"So cold for you, this English winter," he'd say, rubbing her hands (always cool) between his (always warm). Over tea he drew fanciful sketches of sandboxes and playgrounds. "I think under the apple tree should be good for the swing, perhaps a seesaw here, so that if he should fall he (maybe she) will land soft into grass and not the cinder path. Why, I wonder, did we choose cinder? Perhaps after all we should have grass instead, babies fall and fall—our Sasha, so strong, he fell all the time, every night my Anna bathed his skinned knees, the same time I make the salt soak for her poor feet. Oh, such a hospital our bedroom in those days!"

Between Anna and Ellie the mood was still cool if the men were around. If not, the women ignored each other—though Ellie felt the probe of Anna's stare each morning when she crossed the cobbled yard, the scene of their first open clash.

In May an unseasonable snowfall blocked the garage door. Already late, Ellie began to clear it. She'd barely begun when Anna dashed up the walk in nightie and slippers, arms waving, wisps of thin gray hair flying like cobwebs as she grabbed the shovel from Ellie's hands, tossing great heaps of snow aside and shouting: "Are you out of your mind? What do you try to do, lose Mischa's baby for him, you wicked, willful girl—I tell him when he comes home! Maybe I even call to him at the office!"

Two women, one old, lightly dressed, hot with anger; the other young and warmly clothed, astonished, late, impatient to be gone; between them, endless streamers of snow, one soft missile after another punctuating their frustrations.

"It's you who's crazy," Ellie said quietly. "Outdoors in your nightie at your age!"

"Provincial!" Anna hissed, fresh snow flying farther, faster.

"Crazy!" Ellie hissed back, rattling car keys in her mother's face.

The path cleared, she threw open the garage door and Anna, the shovel in mid-swing, had to jump out of the way to stand gaping as Ellie snapped on the ignition, shot the car in gear, whipped out of the garage and skidded around the oak tree.

All down the driveway and into town she trembled, furious at her mother for being an old bat, unhappy with herself for reacting like a child, and feeling vaguely that although she'd had the last word she had not won the encounter, had not, in fact, come out of it with any more credit than Anna.

She did not mention it to Michael—and neither, apparently, did Anna.

"Two?" Michael said. "We're having twins?" He sat down on the bed with a thump and said he didn't believe it, simply didn't believe it.

"You'll admit I'm pretty big...and the doctor hears two hearts, so unless it's one very unusual child—"

"Two hearts...two hearts." Already he was on the house phone, giving the quick three-buzz signal for Felix. "Twins!" he shouted. "It's going to be twins!" Then to Ellie: "When? Felix says when?"

TWENTY-THREE

THE TWINS WERE BORN A MONTH EARLY into unexpected chaos. Labor began easily but seemed to make no progress, then suddenly a single agonizing scream from Ellie. Even Mrs. Finn who'd had six of her own (but one at a time) knew something was not right.

The weather, a sultry, brooding heat wave, didn't help; the electric storm which followed it knocked out half the phones in the village including that of the old doctor, who in any case would have been hopeless for this kind of emergency. The live-in nurse engaged to be on hand before, during, and after the birth was, when called, indisposed—her agency said strep or flu or shingles or maybe tonsillitis...Michael could barely hear over the roar behind his eyes.

"No replacement? What kind of agency—"

"We're trying, but it *is* after midnight, sir—"

"What about my wife?"

"The hospital in town...excellent reputation, excellent—"

He hung up on the woman's murmured regret, too sweet, too soothing. Meaningless. Terrifying.

A hospital was not in the script, had never been considered! His children were to be born at Greenlings, within these walls, behind the gate and the sign and the property that was his and would be theirs. But now Ellie lay on the bed, her eyes glazed, her face pale, washed with sweat, pain, and desperate self-control. She made no sound, but her fists convulsed around a wadded sheet and her eyelids squeezed tight against this new world of pain.

Habit guided him to dial Felix's three-buzz signal, but after a moment's incoherence between them it was Anna who took the phone, who moments later appeared beside him, clucking like an old hen. She took car keys out of his grasp, called an ambulance, gave the address and astonishingly lucid directions:

"... I turn on all house lights and open gate. No, I do not drive and the men here are helpless, helpless, so you will come fast. No questions. I hang up."

But first: "I watch clock. I wait!"

They all waited. For the ambulance. Later, at the hospital, for the anonymous doctor to emerge from the delivery room. Later still for a surgeon hurriedly flown in from Manchester. He was to perform Ellie's hysterectomy and Michael, under intolerable pressure, must agree in writing.

"But then she can have no more..."

"You're lucky, a wife and two healthy babies—could have been the devil of a lot worse, the first one arriving breach like that... of course the hospital might have anticipated it if she'd been here at the start. Maybe a cesarean early enough..."

So he was doubly guilty, and now must wait again, watch as Ellie returned to here-and-now, the flutter of long honey-colored lashes opening on relief. On blue, vaguely focused eyes.

"Have you seen them..."

"No...oh, Ellie, I'm sorry, I should have known—"

"The doctor should have known."

"But I could have lost you...lost you"—his arms around the cocoon of sheets that was his wife. "All because I wanted them born at Greenlings..."

She smiled through a tranquilized haze. "I wanted it too. I assumed it was a Gypsy tradition, that they be born at home."

"No." How to tell her it was the opposite, that among the Rom a pregnant woman was unclean, unfit even to touch food; men of the blood avoided contact; what better solution than a *gajo* hospital to shelter the new mother and child when the *kumpania*, by custom, could not? Just one more of the *gaje*'s many uses.

No way to explain this to a *gaja* like Ellie, for whom a newborn was the essence of innocence. He didn't try, for behind the immediate worry and regret something dark and primitive was trying to break through. It was all he could do to hold it off, to fill up his thoughts, say them louder and louder in his head so there was no room, no corner for the thing to gain entry. He was afraid to speak, to drop his guard, but "No," he said, "I can't blame the Rom, this was my own conceit. I thought I could build a tradition in one generation. I wanted a thriving business and I got it. I wanted a house—hell, I wanted a mansion!—and I got that. I wanted a wife to be proud of, who loved me. I got her too—and I nearly killed her…"

He'd nearly killed her.

There.

He'd left an opening and it slipped through sly and easy as a shadow. He groaned. The past, would he never be free of it? He'd buried it in work, money, ambition, but it never died, just waited its chance—and when had Da ever missed a chance? His voice was maudlin tonight, but clearer than Micah had heard it in years, smoke and gin in its echoes, drifting up the trailer steps on summer evenings where young Micah lay on his bunk, blankets over his head to shut out what he couldn't bear to hear, Da not drunk enough yet to fall down, not sober enough to stifle the whine, the tears of remorse tracking a well-traveled path through his stubble in a fruitless search for absolution.

…I never meant to hit her, honest I didn't, I wouldn't have killed her on purpose, only wanted to keep her quiet, that's all, her and the kid, but that Rose screaming night and day and your ma nagging for a new copper kettle like what your grandmam had…a man can only take so much, I just gave her a swipe to shut her up, Micah—I mean, a man's got his limits, how could I know she'd snuff it, eh? How can we see into the future, eh?

Dui had seen. A dozen times he'd told Micah: "One of these nights he'll do her in. I heard Granddad at Da, warned him, he did. 'If I was a young man I'd thump the daylights out of you. One time you'll go too far. There'll be more than black eyes to answer for then.'" The frequent fights terrified Micah the way thunderstorms had. They were noisy, destructive (Ma bruised like a boxer for days after), but a fact of life, unpredictable, soon done. But even before it happened he'd known that last fight to be different, Da scowling days on end before it, Rose mewling nonstop, Ma not letting up on the copper kettle, specially when Da brought home a fat wad of money, tossing Micah in the air in triumph, shooting a look of pure bravado at Ma who was murmuring about the kettle with new hope in her voice. Da left then, swaggering in after midnight, the door slamming behind him, waking Rose right after Ma had her quietened for the night.

"Now listen to what you've done," she said, gathering up the screaming bundle. "I reckon you spent it, I reckon you—"

She never did get to say what else she reckoned. She barely had time to set Rose into her crib before the fist crashed into her and she screamed. So did Micah. He knew the sound of blows well, but not this bone-breaking thud he'd remember all his life. Man's calloused fist on woman's delicate cheekbone. Then another and another, shouting, screaming, more thumps, ominously soft now, lights from a dozen trailers streaming in the window, Granddad gathering up Dui and Rose, Grandmam reaching for Micah, pushing them outside... *How could I know she'd snuff it, eh?*

How indeed. His own bit of harmless conceit... one touch of snobbery and it had almost killed Ellie.

When he spoke to her again his words were slurred, thick with inexplicable tears.

"I'll make it up to you, Ellie, we'll go away, have a holiday when you're better—"

But she was smiling at him, her long cool hands pulling his face down to hers. "Go see our babies."

Babies. He didn't even know what they were, hadn't asked.

"One of each," the head nurse said proudly, as if she'd produced them herself. "Jennifer and Simon. Fine names. Your wife tells me you picked them."

"Yes... yes." He'd forgotten that, too.

He lowered himself onto a couch and she laid them in his arms, a blue bundle and a pink, and again tears sprang to his eyes. He waved her away and he wept, he who hadn't wept since he wrapped his arms around Greenlings' oak tree and spilled his tears on its bark. Where did they spring from, all these tears? Why now? Why the hurt under his ribs as if his heart were swelling beyond its limits to include these new manifestations of Micah/Mischa/Michael? For the first time in his life he felt love stir in him for something that didn't, as yet couldn't, love back—but they *would,* soon he'd be their world, himself and Ellie and the Abs. He'd give them everything because they were his, pink and white and a misty, unfocused blue...

Oh, his golden, golden children, both with the promise of Ellie's honey hair and cool, classic features. In an agony of delight he examined seashell fingernails and satin toes, palms like crumpled tissue and a soft, pulsing place on each skull so vulnerable that he wept afresh, tears rolling unchecked down his cheek to splash on the translucent eyelid of his son—who whimpered and joined his own tears to Michael's, who next pressed trembling lips to the girl's fragile wrist. She opened her eyes, gave him a brief glimpse of blue before closing them again on an infant's inscrutable secrets, refolded her bud of a mouth, and sighed back to sleep. Jennifer and Simon.

Leaving his car at the hospital for Felix and Anna, he walked home alone through the dawn. A scimitar moon still hung, swinging with his mood, a stage prop of silver foil in a sky of mauve-lemon streaks. Already Greenlings was awake. A gardener tossed withered asters into a wheelbarrow; beyond the gazebo the musical splash of a fountain; from an upstairs window Mrs. Finn shook the life out of a duster and yelled her congratulations and an offer of coffee. He smiled, shook his head, and ran whistling upstairs, to disappear into Anna's studio.

For years now he'd danced for exercise and discipline, but today was different. Today was joy, energy, power, a muscular celebration, a shout of triumph, a renewal of ambition—perhaps a touch of fear and superstition—all of it seeking release in explosive movement and crashing, reverberating chords.

Afterwards, spent and showered, he stood for a long time in the rooms of Felix and Anna. He stroked the silk pink-shaded lamp and ran a hesitant finger across the yellowing faces of the Olgas and Tamaras and Nicolais, remembering the first time he'd seen these things, the boy he had been then, crawling with lice, burning with fever, the bath they'd given him, the smell of the soup and the unbelievable luxury of clean sheets and a warm bed.

He saw how far he had come and how far he could go. No limits. A picture flashed to mind, Dui's boy Tomo laughing as he dug his bare brown heels into the flanks of a winded old nag at Appleby. Michael smiled. None of that for Jennifer and Simon, thank God. They'd have the best.

Looking out on smooth grass and olive shaded walks, he felt gratitude spill out of him like water from the fountain.

To Ellie, for herself and now for his children...but first to the Abs because all the rest was balanced, an upside-down pyramid, on their singular act of kindness to a stranger.

Now that she was recovering the days flew by, too bright to hold. She longed to be home but it was enough, for now, that she was free of pain, that these twin miracles were hers, available to her whenever she asked. She asked often, always to feed them, to watch their every blink and breath as she held them. Michael's anguish, that there could be no more children after these, was incomprehensible to her. Weren't they enough? Their gurgles; their sighs; the newborn fluff on their shoulders—inescapably like the down of a chick; their wobbly heads and sturdy feet that pushed against her palms; genitalia touchingly innocent; the honest, instinctive greed of blind mouths fastening on a feeding bottle, a knuckle, the corner of a blanket.

"They're always hungry," she said to the nurse in awe.

"Preemies...they have to catch up."

It wouldn't take Jennifer long. She applied herself, allowing nothing, even Ellie stroking the wisps of blond fuzz, to divert her. Replete, she'd sigh and gently burp, laughably genteel, then primly fold her mouth for sleep. The nurses adored her. "Such a *good* baby." After her bath she flailed her arms and kicked her legs as vigorously as she was supposed to; exercises over, swaddled again in blankets, she obligingly went to sleep. Already she seemed to sense that what was done to her was done for her own good.

Simon, a larger baby, was much less consistent. Some days he drank ravenously, his mouth fastened like a small suckerfish to the bottle or whoever's thumb got in the way; when the bottle was empty he waved furious red fists and screamed until a nurse came running with a second bottle, which he polished off as fast as the first. Perhaps the next day he'd choose not to take nourishment at all. The small mouth clamped shut, implacable as a bulldog's; when an adult finger wiggled through and deftly inserted a nipple he refused to suck, milk running maddeningly off his chin. When the nurses gave up and he was put back in his crib he vented piercing screams on staff, patients, and visitors; the administrator was heard to remark that Simon Abramsky caused more commotion than all the other infants combined. Ellie, hearing it via hospital telegraph, made a point then of gathering him up, holding him, rocking him, humming old German lullabies to him that she hadn't known she remembered—or from whom. Lotte, probably. Not Grossmutter, who wouldn't have rocked any baby, even her own, certainly not the bastard daughter of a dancer. But then, how could she herself have been this endearing?

"He'll be easy to spoil, that Simon," the nurses murmured. "They always are, the awkward ones."

Awkward? He was perfect! Both children were. She wouldn't hear them criticized, couldn't bear to hear them cry. And who could let them suffer? neglect them? abandon them? It seemed impossible—but it wasn't, because Anna Abramsky had done it; Ellie, with Simon and Jennifer in her arms, was farther away than ever from understanding how.

As yet Anna had not favored Ellie with a visit but, according to the staff, she'd been to the nursery several times, arriving by cab in the middle of the day (so Felix and Michael wouldn't know?), standing at the visitors' window, staring down into the cribs by the hour, from time to time stroking the glass as if it were a baby's cheek, but mainly:

"... just standin', ma'am, like she wasn't really seeing 'em, know what I mean?"

No, Ellie didn't know, didn't want to think about it. There was no need. Michael and Felix came daily, Pete Preston brought chocolates and a potted plant, Mrs. Finn stopped in twice to pass on the latest bits of news from the village, and several times Mary Beth Warren called from London for the usual frank, if not always agreeable, exchange.

"I'll be up for the christening."

"I hope so—you promised to be godmother, remember."

Mary Beth laughed. "I will, I will, but from what I've seen of Anna I'll be as much use as a bump on a log."

"She couldn't mother a radish!" Ellie said.

There was that small silence, Mary Beth having something to say but hunting for a diplomatic way to say it.

"You'll admit she did a pretty good job with Michael."

"Felix! She farms them out if they're a nuisance."

"—said good old Grossmutter—"

"—who took me in, who had *some* moral standards."

"Mmmm. A pity she was in love with her own son..."

Ellie sighed. "Let's not talk about it, Mary Beth." How childish she must sound...she *did* like Mary Beth, felt closer to her than to any woman she knew...if she just wouldn't cut so close to the bone. "Besides, I've some real news. Guess where Michael's opening his next office? Los Angeles—*and* he's talking about New York too if the One makes a splash—"

"You make it sound like a performer. The One! The Only!"

Ellie laughed softly. "To hear Michael talk it *has* to perform—or this time next year I might be selling paper flowers."

"Really? He said that? *To you?*"

"Joking, you know how he is—the only money he risks belongs to the bank—but dividing the house did cost a mint, and worth every penny. Anyway, *if* he gets that base in the States he says we'll need a home there, and if you're back home by then . . ."

Now Mary Beth laughed. "And in time the babies will need a governess . . . look, don't let's count chickens."

But Ellie had every reason to. Since Michael diversified, concentrating more heavily on manufacturing and opening up the retail end to franchises, buyers were waiting in line; for every new location he opened up there were half a dozen takers. He couldn't find new premises fast enough.

All it took was time, time and capital . . . on which publicity for the One was a heavy drain. In the interim the studios brought in revenue as steadily, as monotonously as the beat of their pianos. Even now, the warmest time of year, when families fled the cities for holidays by the sea, even now the children, skinnies, solid little porkers, the round-shouldered and the buck-toothed—all lined up at the studio barre, the mecca, for would not the Abramsky Method give them that one quality parents apparently could not? Poise? Perhaps.

A nurse darted in to shut the window—another storm due, she said— and Ellie lay back, drowsy in the cloud-darkened room, in that pleasant limbo just before sleep; she barely registered the silence, then the footsteps in the corridor. Even when a narrow shadow fell across the bed she assumed it was a nurse with yet another pill.

It was Anna.

Her hooded eyes blinked as she stood in the doorway, gaunt and solemn in a navy blue silk coat of no discernible shape but, like everything she wore, it had that air of faded, impoverished distinction. Perhaps it was her thinness. It certainly wasn't her hair, which as always looked like the inside of a knitting basket—but instinctively Ellie ran a smoothing hand over her own hair and adjusted the lacy collar of her bed jacket.

They looked directly into the other's eyes; their meetings were battles neither could afford to lose. Now they nodded cautiously and Anna advanced into the room, lowering herself to the extreme edge of the guest's chair.

"Is my first visit to you," she announced, as if, left to herself, Ellie might not have noticed. "You are better."

It was not a question, but Ellie nodded. "Thank you." She knew she should also thank her for taking over in a crisis, that any two women, however hostile, could share a patronizing smile at the expense of men's ineptitude in an emergency—but every word between Anna and herself was set about with traps, counted, measured out in points won and lost. Why was she here? Felix must have sent her. Ellie could imagine the exchange:

"Anna my angel, how can you be so hard? Ellie has been very sick, surely you can visit her one time."

"And say what?"

"Does it matter? Only go, show her you care!"

Then Anna would have laughed, her long lip curling, fingers raking the bird's nest of her hair. "I am many bad things but hypocrite is not one of them."

That's how the conversation would have gone.

"I understand you've seen the children several times," Ellie murmured now, not by way of reproach. Quite.

"Naturally."

"Yes."

"The feet are well arched, especially the girl's."

"Very important," Ellie said dryly.

"If she will want to dance the instep is imperative!"

"At ten days old, I hardly think—"

"Neither of them looks like Mischa, a pity, but the boy can be much handsome. Very much."

"I think they both can. Are."

"They look like you."

"And you."

They began to laugh but quickly stopped, embarrassed, the gulf too wide now to span with laughter. Then Anna's hard blue glance slid away, to settle somewhere over the bed. She licked her lips and fretted with the baroque beading on a scarf clearly made to match the coat.

"There are two kinds of children," she said slowly and very carefully, as if she'd rehearsed the words many times. "Some are conceived in love..." She paused, as if speaking of a rare and beautiful thing. "Even for me there was once such a child..."

This austere woman looked out the darkening window to travel back in time. From her expression, unwillingly far. Was this to be it, then, twenty years late? The dancer's confession?

Ellie held her breath. Her past and her future waited, both balanced in the scale of Anna Abramsky's guilt. Now there would be an apology, one Ellie knew she subconsciously longed for and could perhaps accept—and then life could settle down to a semblance of normality. So they might never be close; they could at least be civil.

Her mother's words came, hissed, almost spat into the quiet room. They felt believable. The moment she heard them, Ellie knew they were the only spontaneous words her mother had uttered from the moment she entered the room:

"Some, as I say, are born from love. *Others—like you—come from hate.* I am sorry."

She was sorry.

And now she stood, buttoned a threadbare button, picked up her beaded bag, and left.

It was some time before Ellie could identify the hollow inside her. It was sorrow, a lingering, unfocused regret...and disappointment. Today something had stirred and could have been fanned to life, a willingness to examine the possibility that her father might have been something less than Grossmutter's loving imagination had painted him. Anna's simple "I am sorry" was honest and perhaps reluctant, but it carried the unmistakable ring of finality.

The twins and Ellie came back home and life fell into a routine. Much of the studio work she could do from the house; when she had to leave, which was seldom, Mrs. Finn "kept an eye out for the babies"—an unfortunate expression in her case, as her left eye already drifted nervously and permanently towards the outer corner.

On the pretext of washing them, Lily Finn spent most of her days at Greenlings' windows, so it was inevitable she be first to witness the ragtag procession as it assembled at the great gates of Greenlings.

She was a Felix protégée—he would not have them called lame ducks. Laid off from the factory, Lily Finn had wheedled her way into housekeeping at Greenlings "for a week or so until something permanent turns up." Nothing did, and at Felix's suggestion she now divided her time between the two Abramsky wives, both of whom would have been delighted to see the back of her but, as Felix said with undeniable logic: "Who else would give the poor woman a job?" Who indeed? She was garrulous, overly dramatic, and an incurably avid gossip, but of all her faults, by far the worst was her singing. It was pervasive, constant, and piercingly soprano. She sang of pale moons arising, pipes acalling, larks ascending, red suns declining—and she drove the two women mad.

The night the trailers came she'd already served dinner to the younger Abramskys. Ellie planned a walk through the grounds as soon as she'd finished coffee; Michael was peeling an apple and frowning as he added this month's expense overruns to what he already owed the bank; outdoors in the arbor Felix watched the twins kick and wave and bubble in their prams.

Upstairs, Lily's raucous song still rang from glen to glen and down the mountainside. She was cleaning an attic window, the one place in the house from which the massive front gates could be seen, when her song stopped abruptly in mid-scream.

A moment's silence before she skittered down two flights of stairs to stand breathless in the dining room doorway.

"It's them," she gasped, "there's trailers at the gate!"

Ellie sighed, uncomfortable as usual under Lily's antic eye, but Michael was already on his feet. "God almighty! How many?"

"Four house trailers," Lily said, pleased with the reaction she'd provoked. "And two police cars behind 'em."

TWENTY-FOUR

*A*FTERWARDS HE NEVER REMEMBERED STARTING DOWN that long curve of driveway. He remembered small signs of ownership, improvements he'd made. Gravel underfoot; the last of the roses scenting the walk; red petals dripping to immaculate grass. He remembered quiet, and birds rustling as they settled for the night, the pond a sheet of sunset copper ruffled by nothing more than a waterspider closing in on a careless gnat.

Anger propelled him past them all, perhaps too fast because Felix, even with Simon's pram for support, had to limp heavily to keep up.

"Why bring him?" Michael demanded. "I don't want the Rom near my children, I've told you."

"He was fretting." But the baby was sitting up, quiet now and wide-eyed, diverted by the pram's unusual speed, and there was reproach, however faint, in Felix's tone. "You told your brother not to come to your house, Mischa?"

"Yes."

Especially not with trailers. Now he'd brought four, with God only knew how many families in them. The thin end of the wedge? It was disturbingly late for them to be on the road; they should be camped now, dogs watered, fires lit, women cooking. Horses, if any, put out to grass. But not *his* grass, by God, not these lawns! He tried to block out the memory of Dui at the wedding, who'd called them fine fields...

"Tsk, just look at the red sky, Mischa. In the old country was a sign of hard winter."

Michael lengthened his stride. Typical of Felix to worry about winter when summer wasn't over. There was enough trouble here and now with the families on his neck again. Perfect timing. The Abramo One all set to launch next month, all his concentration needed for the push to get it *out,* shipped, selling, bringing back money, beginning to justify its crippling investment.

But now he could see the road, four battered trailers pointed snout-first at the gates, patrol cars to their rear blocking any retreat but through the gates.

His gates.

No, oh no...

More than a dozen adults. Dui's wife and three others in varying stages of pregnancy; men old and young hanging about, mustached and kerchiefed, cigarettes drooping from lazy smiles, Dui himself the center of attention and loving it, spreading his arms to prove he had nothing to hide, smiling to show he wasn't insulted at being asked—which could change in an instant. All had that hapless, helpless air of being tossed about on political winds beyond their ken or intelligence.

Dusty dark-eyed children swarmed everywhere, pranced on trailer roofs, swung from doorknobs, laughed, waved, catcalled, insulted the coppers in Romani, enjoying every second of the drama. God, what infants they all were, even the men and women! But no, he knew better. This children of nature routine was cultivated with care. Even as he watched, a mother-to-be, at the approach of a policewoman, began furiously to scratch herself, raking at legs, hair, armpits, anywhere she could reach. Right on cue the policewoman backed off, her clean fingernails making reflexive, surreptitious scratching motions of their own. So the trick still worked, had for thousands of years; would it ever fail to keep the gullible *gaje* at a distance?

"Mr. Abramsky!" The officer in charge had seen him, was approaching the gates. "A spot of bother here. They seem to think you can help..." His glance shifted from the ragamuffin children now bunched like grapes at their mothers' skirts to baby Simon, pink and blond in his coach-built perambulator, immune and privileged on the respectable side of the gates and the sign.

Speaking to the police, he realized too late that his first words were the typical *gajo* cliché. "What seems to be the trouble, officer?"

The trouble was Dui, suspected of stealing from a nearby poultry farm. "Like Da showed us, Micah, a chicken or two, where's the harm?" he said in rapid Romani.

Michael smelled him through the bars, sweat and horses and slippery little lies. *But Da had been a good liar,* not like this. "How many?"

"Three."

"Three crates," his wife said with pride. "Ninety birds."

Dui shrugged. "So? A treat for the *kumpania,* big farm, big haul, what's wrong with that?"

What was wrong with that? Michael's answer came straight from Da's trailer, maybe from Da's mouth. In Romani: "You got caught, you stupid bugger, that's what! I was nicking birds before I was five and they never caught me. Da either. So what's *your* problem?" He leaned forward as Dui recoiled. "Greed! Tonight you've eighteen or twenty mouths to feed, right? So you take ninety birds? For what? It's summer. You've no freezer, you cretin!" God, why was he arguing, spouting the same old Rom rhetoric he'd learned at the fires before he could walk. He had to stop, stop, he wasn't *with* these people, *of* them...

He turned to Felix. "Take Simon home, okay?"

Dui, suddenly bereft, chose that moment to play high drama. He pointed to heaven, to the golden cherub in the pram, to his own family huddled at the trailer door, to little Tomo impossibly innocent at his side. In English he called on all present to witness that the police were depriving him of a first sight of his beloved nephew for which purpose—the *only* purpose—he'd come to this district at all! To prove kinship his hand shot through the bars of the gate to stroke Simon's head.

The sight of his scruffy brown fingers smeared with chickens' blood resting on his son's silver-blond hair brought a rush of anger to Michael's head and an intense, frightening calm. "Touch him again," he said in Romani, "and I'll kill you."

So quietly, smoothly was the threat made that the policeman assumed it was a cordiality. "If we'd known they were family, naturally..." He took out his notebook. "But there's still—"

Michael got the farmer's name. "A friend—I'll see to it."

That settled, the policeman coughed discreetly and murmured of a more delicate matter...vagrancy laws...traveling people...one night only in the borough and not on a main thoroughfare..."you do understand, sir?" You should, the eyes said, you're a Gyppo like them. The officers all nodded agreement, and Michael felt every glance jab a little more at his self-esteem.

Then he caught the drift of Ellie's light cologne. Her voice, cool as iced limes, cut through the tension-packed group. When he heard the words he didn't know whether to admire her spirit or explode with frustration.

"The law you quote doesn't apply here. These people are family, guests on our private property. *In our care.*" Her stress on the last words was subtle but unmistakable.

She turned away with an apparent afterthought: "It *is* a warm evening, officer. If your people care for lemonade I'm sure the kitchen staff...if you'll just go around to the back door."

The spokesman looked from his shining shoes to the locked gate, and then to Michael Abramsky's wife who had somehow snubbed the entire county police force with her kind offer.

"Thank you," he said stiffly. "Perhaps another time..."

On the pretext that the gate key (in his pocket) was at the house, Michael drew Ellie away, saying nothing, not a word, until they were out of earshot of the Gypsies milling outside the gate like excited children waiting to be let in the palace. Then:

"Guests? In our care? Have you gone mad?"

"The police were insulting them and us."

"Dui's been stealing."

"Oh? Are you so moral now your stealing days are done?"

"Very clever. Now we have to let them in. You've given them Open Sesame to Greenlings whenever they're in the neighborhood."

"You exaggerate—and how can we leave them in the road? The police will pick them up again, you know that."

Yes. Already patrol cars would be parked at both ends of the road. If he didn't let them in the Gypsies would get tired, finally, of waiting. When they tried to leave the cops would have them. "Why should we be responsible?"

She sighed. "I'm sure the children haven't eaten since morning. Rose was there, Dui's wife is close to term. Imagine if it were Simon and Jennifer or me—" She gasped as his fingers bit into the flesh of her upper arm.

"*No way, never!* That's what all this"—he pointed to the house—"was *for.* Now it's jeopardized—"

"They'll stay the night, park the trailers under the beeches, by morning they'll be gone."

"Where will they cook? Over fires on the lawn?"

"We have two kitchens, surely they can—"

"Not inside the house," he said, suddenly tired. "I can't." He searched her eyes, the same clear blue she'd given the twins. "Ellie, do you understand what you've done? No, how can you, you don't know the Rom."

She lifted his hands to her cheek. "I know you. Always so cool, controlled . . . now look at you."

The scent of her skin reached him, soft to his senses, her youth at odds with that tremor, that excitement . . .

All this. Ellie, the children, how hard he'd worked for it, to earn it, keep it, expand it. Harder yet to escape a past that still dogged his steps. "Not in my house, Ellie. No."

Inevitably Dui came, first for aspirin for Tomo, who had a bit of a head on him; later to borrow brandy for the wife—her stomach got queasy at night. He stuck the bottle under his arm and helped himself to lager from the fridge. A silver bottle-opener slid into his pocket. Michael took it back.

"Keep your fingers clean in my house, okay?"

A grin. "Habit—"

"Okay, you've got your brandy and beer. Now let's have it. What are you really here for?"

Dui sighed, scratched his belly, sat heavily to the kitchen table and began his weary catalog. In less than ten minutes Michael knew the *kumpania*'s recent history and its prospects:

It was the rain, see? Cherries hadn't made nothin', same with strawberries. Beans had looked good but some fool knackered his trailer so how could they get to the fields? Mento's daughter died in Scotland; she lived with the *kumpania* before she got married so naturally they all had to go pay their respects—that ate up three weeks, then back too late for apricots and too early for apples; there's always lettuce but picking 'em didn't pay. Farmers were that tight a man couldn't save a shillin'!

And what exactly was Dui saving for?

Well, didn't he keep saying it? California's where folks went now. Sun, money, and welfare, who could beat it? Four families wanted to go, but with kids and elders they were talking maybe two dozen people, a lot of tickets! And their stuff!

Why should Dui worry about the others? Michael probed. *His* family was small enough, just the wife, Tomo, and the new baby... one crop-picking season should do it.

Stunned silence, Dui genuinely horrified.

Leave the *kumpania*? And him the Rom Baro? Head man to 'em all, like a father? How could any man leave his *kumpania*?

Da left... they made him... and the going finished him off.

Times change, Michael said aloud to Da's other son.

Well, there were other reasons besides... Dui's glance skidded off Micah as he resumed:

Around apple-pickin' time they had a bit of trouble wiv a horse, not cleared up yet... if they were still in the country at the next assizes the families all had to give evidence...

In Michael's gut a sick feeling he'd learned, to his cost, to trust. "Want to tell me about it? The truth?"

A promising racehorse was ailing; its owner-trainer gave up on New-market vets and called in Dui, who had some reputation as a healer when conventional methods had failed. Dui saw it was hopeless but didn't say so; instead he milked gratifying fees from an owner who had reason to believe Dui's methods a success. Was not the horse more sprightly on workouts? Were its times not improved? Its appearance? When it dropped dead in mid-gallop the owner filed suit, charging malice, false pretenses, extortion, practicing without a license, and administering stimulants.

"And the money he paid you...?"

Dui spread stubby fingers and Michael almost saw silver, bright as tomorrow, trickle through the cracks. Listening to the excuses, a single disconnected thought snagged his memory. Rose. Ellie had mentioned her. And where was Grandmam?

"Grandmam's camped at Burbage. Rose, hell, she's with the wife and Tomo in my trailer, still coughing blood. Problems... you're young, Micah, you know nothin' yet—"

Young? He was twenty-two going on Methuselah. "I paid Rose's bill at the clinic to the end of the year."

"But she can't stand it, Micah, so what can I do?" Again the spread of hands. And this helpless lump called himself a Rom Baro!

"I'll fix it tomorrow," he said quietly. "That's when you'll all leave."

* * *

Outside was bedlam. Secure for once behind locked gates and a land-owner's protection, the families let rip. Radios played full blast; under the beeches a black-and-white telly flickered eerily among the leaves; smells of chicken and garlic permeated the night; children squealed, women chatted, men argued about nothing. Mrs. Finn, unasked, elected to stay until morning and help out, ensuring enough tidbits of gossip to feed the village for months to come.

Inside, Michael weighed the choices. Family conferences were not an Abramsky tradition. He made the major decisions and none had ever been questioned. But this was different, a problem that wasn't theirs—or really his—but one that would deeply affect them, that could not have been foreseen. A solution must be found and quickly, just when his own judgment was clouded, when it was impossible for him to say, with certainty, that yes, this thing should be done. That they, as a family and a business, could sustain it. Thus the conference.

The twins were asleep. Michael and Ellie waited in the sitting room for the older Abramskys to appear. Since Anna had chosen to "dress," the wait was long, but not without incident. Although the green velvet curtains were drawn, Ellie and Michael were kept relentlessly updated on what the Gypsies were up to. Every few seconds Lily Finn's head poked around the door, her free-floating eye fairly leaping with excitement.

They were lighting fires outside, was it okay? Draping wet wash on the rhododendrons, was it okay? They'd chucked empty tins and milk bottles in the lily pond and stripped the raspberry bushes right down to the canes, was it okay? A little lad was peeing (and God knew what else) behind the garage; when she shouted at him to stop he told her to fuck off.

"The F word!" she said, "and he doesn't look a day over three!"

"If you stay indoors," Ellie suggested, "you won't have to listen," laughing when Lily bustled off again, F word be damned, to keep an eye out for the intruders.

"Not funny," Michael said. "Monkey see, monkey do. Do you want Simon saying that? To anybody?"

"It's not the same thing at all, he'll go to good schools—"

The door flew open and Anna sailed in, a mauve silk stole drooping from her shoulders like bruised and tattered wings. Felix followed with a bottle of their special sherry and best Rumanian glasses. As if, Michael thought painfully, this were a celebration.

At a sales meeting he'd have called it a presentation. Here he called it a crisis, but ticked off the points on his finger in precisely the same way: The Gypsies now enjoying Greenlings were his flesh and blood, in trouble with the law and always would be. They were nothing if not resourceful; now they had discovered a bolt hole, this visit would be repeated at will; four trailers was only a small sample. Short of turning them over to the law his hands were tied. Greenlings, all its peace and quiet, its privacy, would be at risk, forever under siege. More important were the twins. He refused to expose them to the influences of the *kumpania*.

"I have," he said simply, "tried too hard, come too far."

He could carry the tribe on his neck like a yoke forever or give them what they wanted, one-way tickets to California.

"Is blood money!" Anna cried. "Bring in the police and have done. Such people are not family, they are accident of birth! *Family is growing up together, is taking care—*"

"Anna!" Felix looked quickly at Ellie, whose complexion had flushed to an angry rose.

"No, Felix, Anna is correct. 'Accident of birth' is not true family, is it?" Ellie said, folding her lips in the same stubborn curve as her mother's; already Michael had noticed the same characteristic in young Jennifer.

Enough. "I propose sending them where they want to go."

Felix voiced doubts. "But passports, visas, where would such people get them?"

"Documents are no problem." Law-abiding to a fault, Felix would have been aghast at the number and assortment of passports Gypsies owned. Grandmam alone kept five in an old fuller's earth tin under the bed. There wasn't a border in the world they couldn't cross within forty-eight hours if need be.

And if they had the money.

"Then you must send them," Felix said, running his hands through his halo. "You need no permission from us."

Michael sighed, poured them sherry after all, and continued. To finance remodeling and then Abramo One, Greenlings had, as they all knew, been remortgaged. Heavily. It would be at least a year before the calculator began to return its investment. If ever. Nothing was certain. Now this problem with the Gypsies. "There is no way to borrow more without putting Greenlings at risk," he said bluntly. "Which I refuse to do."

Watching him, his long brown fingers tight around the stem of the glass, his eyes glazed with worry and uncertainty, Ellie wanted to tell him it didn't matter, Greenlings was only a house. There were others as good, with walls as thick, fences as high, but she knew that for him this would never be true. Greenlings was security, a dream that had grown to an obsession; having won it, lived in it, loved it—to lose it would sour him, tarnish all that bright, brash assurance that *was* Michael. Already it was under siege, his mouth tense, not quite firm. In his eyes there was guilt for bringing this on them, anger that the Rom could still dictate policy and threaten his future, fury at his own impotence where their demands were at issue.

"There's the ruby," Ellie offered.

He shook his head. "It's the *kumpania*'s. Grandmam gave it to us so Dui wouldn't waste it, a kind of trust. We have to keep it for her lifetime. It wouldn't be enough to help anyway."

Anna examined her impeccable instep. "Perhaps," she said, "the studios could . . . how you are saying? put on the benefit."

To their credit, no one laughed.

Oh, Mother, Ellie thought, to be so stupid! To think unknown dancers, mere students at that, could raise this kind of money, any kind of money!

Mother . . . Mother . . . Mother.

The word echoed and reechoed in her head.

So. Out of pity and surprise she had finally thought of this eccentric woman as Mother. A foolish mother. Not cruel or bitchy or self-centered. Only naive, pathetic. Unaccountable tears thickened her throat and something in her chest tightened as she opened the door into the hall.

There was one thing to do, what she should have done at the start, except she knew it would please Anna Abramsky immensely, so how could she consider it? Now, having seen this small frailty in her, she could.

She reappeared with the portrait, which she propped against Michael's chair. In the softly lit room it smiled as benignly as the day it was painted.

"Have this," she said, her voice deliberately light. "Mary Beth says Hellas are bringing top dollar at the auctions."

Michael made an odd, involuntary sound, whether a sob of relief or a groan of anguish it was impossible to tell. "You mean it? You'd let me sell it? For Greenlings?"

"No, for you."

He pulled her hand to his mouth and set his lips against her cool palm. "I love you," he whispered. The others might not have been there. "I won't sell, I'll use it for collateral, take a short-term loan against it—but look, the bank may want to keep it for a while . . ."

Over Michael's head Anna and her daughter looked directly into each other's eyes. In her mother's, Ellie saw overwhelming relief that she would not again encounter the face of Hans von Reiker in the hall of this house; in the hard bright blue there was for an instant something else too, a softness remarkably like gratitude—gone as quickly as it came.

And Anna, Anna had to turn away from the glow in Ellie's eyes when Michael said he loved her—it was too much, it was like looking into a mirror of the past, but oh, had her own hair ever had quite that sheen of beaten gold, had her skin been so fine-textured, so fresh? How could she be so lovely, this girl conceived in hate, despised every moment Anna carried her under her ribs like a cancer that spread and spread? And how could she, Anna, have become so old and crabbed? It was not fair, not fair. If the girl had been ugly, as vile as her beginnings, then Mischa would never have wanted her, loved her—because yes, now she must admit what she saw with her own eyes, that Mischa loved her, this Gabriella who had just given up that terrible picture.

Strange, strange . . .

Early next morning Ellie drove Rose, who was sulking, to the airport for yet another flight to Geneva. Michael and Felix watched at the gates as four trailers pulled onto the highway, delighted smiles at every open window for Micah, the man Dui had just announced was to send them to America.

Beside him Felix echoed Michael's thought of yesterday: "Only look, Mischa," he said as he waved his good-byes, "what innocent, happy children they all are."

Only wait until you've seen the disemboweled mattress on the south lawn and a shredded blue raincoat hanging from the tallest poplar. Not to mention several dozen chickens and their swarm of blowflies. But they were leaving, thank God. With luck they'd never see Greenlings again— but what was this? Dui's trailer making a U-turn at top speed, its horn, its driver's rollicking laugh shattering the morning as he pointed to something over Michael's shoulder.

Tomo, five years old and grinning like a monkey, swung himself back and forth on the PRIVATE PROPERTY sign in Greenlings' imposing entry.

Michael seldom allowed himself to show anger but it grabbed him now as hard as he grabbed his nephew.

"Can't you *read*, dammit! Don't *ever*—oh, get off my land, get off my land."

The boy leaped into the trailer. Dui, still laughing as he tousled the boy's hair, was already away up the road in a cloud of exhaust smoke.

"Mischa, the child is your nephew," Felix said, shocked.

"He's nothing to me, none of them are."

Except Grandmam.

Before Dui and the rest could spread the word, he drove out to Burbage that morning, the twins asleep in their car cribs on the backseat. Grandmam's trailer was alone and empty, nothing around it but moorland and a fast autumn sky pushing westward in packed gray masses.

He found her kneeling on a bank gathering ground ivy and stuffing the leaves into an herb bag, her long skirts blowing in a wind that soon would turn bitter on these bleak, lonely reaches.

"Micah!" She looked up, thinner than she'd been.

"I brought my babies to show you."

She nodded, pressed their limbs with knotty fingers, lifted eyelids, cupped her hands around each small head as if they were crystal balls she could read through her fingertips. "Healthy," she pronounced. "They don't look like our people, but you never can tell, maybe they'll be better Rom than Dui's bunch—"

"I don't want that for them—"

"Only because you was with your da. With the families you'd have been as happy as Neddy's Nag."

He smiled, set the twins back in their car cribs, and walked with her to the trailer. "I came to tell you before you heard it from Dui. Four of the families are going to California."

"Aye. Where the sun shines." It was as if he'd said they were going to the next village for a bottle of olive oil. She made tea for Micah and infused some of the fresh-picked leaves for herself. "Wonderful soft on the stomach, this."

"You're not sick, Grandmam?"

She smiled. "Just old! Some can't tell the difference. I can." She seemed to snooze, then: "Where's the cash coming from? Be a handy roll of scratch and Dui's got now't saved."

"I'm lending it. To hear Dui, it rains gold sovereigns in California. He says he'll pay me back next year."

They laughed together at the very idea. "You'll be lucky. But have you thought? If he owes you big he can't come knocking no more or you can bring the *kris* on his neck." She sighed. "If they go maybe you'll never see your old *kumpania* no more."

"Yes." He should be happy. Why did he feel like a traitor?

"It's worth that much to you, to get rid of us?"

He told her the truth.

"The others, yes." Would Dui take care of her? he wondered.

"I wish you were staying," he said, not sure if he meant it.

"Good, because I am. I've been to Yugoslavia (that's where my great-great-great-grandmam come from), then Spain, France, Hungary, even Poland and Czechoslovakia when I were a tiddler. At my time of life I want my own fields, the same lanes what me and your granddad worked, Appleby in June and mint picking in Brierly Woods...your ma were born there, you know..." She sighed, brought herself to the present. "So tell me, Micah. That sun in California what shines every day, how they goin' to notice it's ashinin' after they gets used to it? Me, I'll not cross the water no more."

"You won't be on the roads alone? There'll be families left to keep you company, right?"

She laughed, her gold chains glittering in the light. "Not on your life! As soon as they know you're paying the piper they'll *all* be off, you won't see 'em for dust. Dui told you two dozen? Fifty will be more like it!"

The clouds thrusting westward looked bleaker than when he arrived. "It looks as if we're in for a rough year."

TWENTY-FIVE

*I*T TOOK THREE YEARS. White-knuckle, cutthroat, tightrope years—but heady, crackling with new hope, new energy, new demands, turbulent not just for Abramo but for the world. Change bred excitement. Envy spawned anarchy.

Danger and opportunity ran neck and neck, especially in the United States, to which Michael, with sales offices in San Francisco and Los Angeles, was increasingly, inevitably drawn. Here new industries were spawned and new horizons glimpsed. The sky was no longer the limit. Beyond it was space.

An old Bolshevik with blunt features (*peasant!* sniffed Anna Abramsky) saw his first cancan on a Hollywood set and was not amused; a charismatic young president smiled upon Dallas and his widow took home blood and roses to their children in Washington, D.C.; in a Bay Area suburb a thirteen-year-old science student built a parallel digital computer, lighting a fuse that would galvanize old industries and spin off a host of new ones.

Abramo was positioned exactly right.

Some established companies floundered, held under by business-school dogma, weighted with deadwood and that inertia which grips and eventually strangles management-by-committee.

Abramo, unhampered by tradition, contemptuous of orthodox business practice, fought its own fight and prospered. There were no executive washrooms with keys to covet, no sun-and-sea conferences, no company cars; no two-hour martini breaks at noon; in the early years no annual bonus, what was left over was plowed back and back again—but nonunion workers could and did opt for stock in lieu. Chief engineer Pete Preston's bank account was no fatter now than it had been that first year, but his mother's thin porridge and runny poached eggs were ambrosia with stock market pages propped against the coffeepot.

Greenlings was little changed. There were ponies in the stables now and plans for a hothouse behind the garage. Though not yet among the superwealthy, the family was no longer at risk. The year after the Gypsies moved to California was, thank God, behind them. Grandmam had been right. When word spread that Michael was to underwrite the move Dui's entire flock chose to go, plus several strangers who married suddenly, fortuitously, into the *kumpania*. Only Grandmam remained. As predicted, the cost had been monumental, but for Michael worth every sacrifice they'd made. Each time he noticed the empty wall on the stairs he was reminded of *Ellie's* sacrifice—yet the portrait, once again hers, was still propped at the back of the wardrobe. When he asked if she intended to rehang it she looked at it thoughtfully and shook her head.

"It doesn't go with the decor," she lied, firmly closing the door and the subject.

Perhaps she no longer cared with the old intensity? With two small children to watch, studios to run, the occasional trip with him to London or San Francisco, it might be that present happiness had eclipsed old hatreds, wiped the slate clean? She didn't say, and no amount of watching could tell him. He sensed a slight thaw but no warmth in her relationship with Anna; there was still more dividing the two households than a red-brick path and the stiff spikes of a cypress hedge.

All he knew for sure was that she was happy, that the day he saw her on the steps of her grandmother's house was the luckiest in his life. He'd thought that she was everything he'd ever wanted, but he'd been wrong, incredibly, wonderfully wrong. She'd been only a promise then of what she was now. That self-confidence which had so devastated him in the eighteen-year-old girl was based on far firmer ground in the young woman. It stood on success she herself had achieved and could measure.

The difference showed even in her body and the way she carried it. She still moved smoothly, not a trace of that look-at-me swing of haunch and hip, no outthrust of the small bosom—but there were subtle differences perhaps only he noticed. Breasts once tiny and almost virginal had some fullness now, an individuality he would have recognized blindfold, firm ivory curves with their blue tracery of veins, texture silken and cool, nipples small and pink and innocent—but aggressively, shockingly thrusting when aroused.

So many nights they lay in their bed, sated, satisfied, quietly happy, senses filled to overflowing with each other, almost touching sleep when he'd feel her turn to him again, take his hands to brush their brown palms over her burning nipples, already darker and harder, their color a yearning rose-beige, pointed and hot to the touch.

He'd pull her to him, bend her in an arc until her thigh touched his, hip touched hip, mouth lay on mouth and her nipples electrified his own, burning them with her fire. He marveled then that she was his, this woman whose body welcomed him openly, traveled with him to endless, pulsating heights, and hovered with him on achingly breathless plateaus.

Yet there was a core of reserve even he couldn't penetrate, an air of being able to shut out the world if she so desired, of wanting him but not necessarily *needing* him. She was an intensely private woman. It would never have occurred to her to change a bra or pull on pantyhose with her dressing-room door open; to show him a letter from Mary Beth, no matter how innocuous the contents; to leave underwear hanging around the bathroom. She left each room as spotless as she found it, and on intimate matters there was a delicacy amounting almost to reticence. All through adolescence Michael had been accustomed to the casual atmosphere of dance studios, where bodily functions were as natural a subject as weather or the latest movie. Not Ellie. Even a headache was private, to be treated with aspirin behind a closed bathroom door. Once, during her pregnancy, he'd caught her swallowing prescription medicine for morning sickness.

"Why?" he'd asked. "I know you're not feeling well, so—"

"So why should I bother you with it? I already know the dosage, why do I need help?"

Pleasure she shared, but sorrows, if she harbored any, were hugged to herself—perhaps because until her marriage there'd been no one she could share them with. A stranger, seeing its manifestations, could mistake this reticence for coldness, but Michael knew better. It was inherent, as much a part of her as the honey shade of her hair when an October sun touched it, or the quiet efficiency with which she could plan a dinner party for twenty, write and send the invitations without the faintest indecision as to whom to ask, where to seat them, what to serve—a talent becoming more and more necessary as business improved.

At the start, Abramo One had not been quite the rocket they'd hoped. The trade press was hostile, ridicule the weapon of choice—much of it based on envy but some on plain bigotry. Abramskys were Buttinskys, Johnny-come-latelies, foreigners, and a mixed boiling of them at that! Huns, Russkies, and Gyppos, what a bouillabaisse that must be! It took a few very fancy dinner parties indeed, limousine service to Greenlings, Dunhill lighters for the men and bottles of Joy perfume for the ladies— and the gracious smile (why, she's really *quite* lovely!) of Gabriella Abramsky, before the industry press gave the product its blessing, forgave Abramo for succeeding, and incidentally slipped Ellie into the society columns.

For Abramo, acceptance came not a moment too soon.

"Too lavish, such entertaining is poor taste, ostentatious!" Felix still wailed. "We could have been penniless, Mischa."

"Without it we'd have been bankrupt."

When the last limousine had gone Michael silently gave thanks that the Gypsies and thus the bankers were finally off his back. Suppose they'd showed up at an affair like this?

Grandmam lived alone now and he kept a careful eye on her, took the twins to see her, offered her money she wouldn't accept. She refused to come to the house, walls and fences made her nervous, but in good weather Michael often left Simon to "camp out with Gran" for the night, a treat beyond any other for the truculent, difficult little boy.

Who adored her. The first word he said clearly was Grandmam as he bubbled and chortled and reached for the smoke trickling up from her pipe. A year later he was asking to go see Grandmam all the time, to roam the moorlands with her, to crawl in her lap and be rocked to sleep, to stay all night long in her trailer under the hill. From the moment Michael picked him up, untidy and unwashed, gleefully spouting words Ellie didn't understand, he pestered to go back.

Ellie didn't like it.

"She's old, Michael, and he's a baby. It's lonely up there. Suppose something happens?"

"Less than an hour's drive away? What could happen?"

"If she fell, got sick..."

"She's the old breed, good for years yet. And he's no baby, this year he'll be four, for God's sake!"

"A baby. You said you didn't want them growing up Gypsy—"

"Look, we're all she has left and she's his grandmother."

"—and he's learning these sly little tricks."

"What tricks?"

"Oh, childish things, like I rinsed a glass in his bathroom the other day and when I turned away he deliberately broke it, said it slipped out of his hand. I know it hadn't, Michael, I *know* he was lying. The glass wasn't valuable and he knew it, so why lie? I just don't like what he's learning."

He sighed. "Just an old Rom custom he must have picked up from her. They don't wash dishes in the same vessel they wash themselves, that's all. No mystery, nothing evil about it—"

"Then why lie?"

"He probably knew you wouldn't understand, and you don't! If he gives Grandmam pleasure, where's the harm? They'll be in school next year. The lying's a phase, I was the same—"

"But you were a Gypsy!"

"All children lie."

"You'd never let him go off with Dui like this!"

"Of course not, Dui's sly and he's not Grandmam. Why not let her enjoy him? How long can she have left, for heaven's sake?"

"A minute ago she was going to last forever. You're not being consistent."

He knew he wasn't, but with Grandmam he couldn't seem to help it. She was the line holding him to the Rom, a line that wore weaker every day but always some part of him felt its pull because he was the fish under the bank, hooked but wily, too strong to reel in but too weak to snap the line. Weak—or just guilty? And why guilty, in some way indebted, as if he'd robbed her? *You did rob her, you had your choice and you picked Da.* He was a small boy caught in the hooks of his father's eyes and the drama of a *kris romani*—could she count that a sin? So what did he owe Grandmam, what, what, what?

Oh, he knew. He could squirm and dart or lie belly up and float dead, but he knew. In choosing Da he'd robbed her of a Rom Baro wise enough to follow Granddad, powerful enough to hold the *kumpania* together as it had once been. Rich, proud, respected among the wagons.

Now they were respected nowhere.

Dui couldn't write but sometimes he'd call, much noise in the background; he'd be in a tavern or maybe a cockfight held in somebody's backyard, but anyway half drunk and bragging about the bird that was going to make him a millionaire next time out. Then he'd come over for a visit, pay Micah back, see Grandmam, show them all a good time. Sure, Dui, sure. He even called from a house once; he needed money.

"A few hundred dolla', Micah, peanuts to you, right? just enough to see me through a spot of bother. You don't believe me? Would I lie to you, my own brother? Wait, here's my social worker, she'll tell you true!"

Here's my social worker. (Here's my chef—if you need a banquet cooked, feel free.) Oh, Dui.

But Dui was seven thousand miles west, couldn't pull into Greenlings with a dozen house trailers now, so Michael said, "No, sorry," and hung up. After that there was silence for some months, then a collect call which Michael refused.

The families were off the road at the moment on a project near Sacramento. Once Michael received an address carefully typed on Department of Social Services paper—a sympathetic social worker, no doubt—but in all his business trips to San Francisco he was never once tempted to make that short drive east, nor had he called the social worker who had kindly given her go-between number. Such a contact would have ruined this new country for him, and that he would not risk.

Michael and the United States were made for each other. After slightly-behind-the-times-and-proud-of-it England he saw this new land with the eyes of a child at the circus for the first time.

Brash, bold, daring, not shy at tooting its own horn, a minirecession just over and the next one not yet on the horizon, the entire country was an entrepreneur's dream. An Englishman faced with a purchase thought twice and twice again, counted his money, and conferred with his wife; maybe they'd buy, maybe go home empty-handed anyway. An American barely needed selling; money burned holes in his pockets and he couldn't wait to get rid of it, to give his family every modern appliance; when it broke he went right out for a new one.

The charge account.

The Englishman still regarded it as a temptation to be resisted at all costs; the American embraced it as a long-lost buddy. As Michael Abramsky embraced the United States. Here (at least to his knowledge) nobody called him Gyppo, nobody looked at him aslant. Here there were far darker skins than his own.

So far, he knew only the coastal strip between northern and southern California, but already it was the promised land, all challenge and precipi-

tous bluffs, the Pacific a wrinkled blue impossibly far below, white surf
spuming, exploding, endlessly hurling itself at a yellow glare of sand.
Here loomed boulders bigger than English hills; in these mountains rac-
coon and rattlesnake and coyote prospered. Above him in the high wide
sky hawks spun lethal circles black on blue, their predator heads down,
peering, peering until they dropped with a scream of triumph. This land.
It exhilarated even as it intimidated, and he could never get enough of
looking.

Ellie liked it, but from the car. It was beautiful, yes, but vast, threatening, as if it would outlast the human race.

"It will." He laughed.

Anna and Felix refused to come. "To go so far at our time of life is
madness!" Anna declared. "And who would look after everything here if
we were away?" Felix wondered.

Michael forbore to mention the plant manager and Lily Finn. "We
could get people in, a woman already takes care of the San Francisco
apartment for us."

"To buy another place... are you sure it is wise?"

"Essential. Soon it'll be worth double, I think maybe we should diver-
sify, get a little land, hold it for a few years..."

His U.S. accountant had told him about Orange County to the south.
"Milk farms now, Michael, but building's started..." In the end he
bought a modest thirty acres of cow country and leased it back to the
farmer. Three years later the freeway rushed through on its way to San
Diego and Michael found himself with a hundred and fifty prime city lots
and developers camped out in the lobby of his San Francisco apartment.
He sent them home. He wanted to think about it. Maybe for a year.

"Sell!" begged Felix when better and better offers came to Greenlings
by wire.

"No." And they hadn't, but when in California he often made that
short extra flight south to look down on the shrinking areas of vacant
land in the middle of a burgeoning, beautifully planned city of homes and
banks and theaters and malls; each time he saw it he smiled to himself on
that long polar flight to Greenlings.

Ellie at the office, Felix at the zoo with Simon, Mischa in London.
Anna and Jennifer in the studio, Anna in her element.

"Pretty hands, Jennifer! Make pretty hands for Madame!"

The old woman demonstrated in front of the mirror. The granddaughter, already in tiny leotard and leg warmers because she wanted to be like Anna, obediently lifted dimpled arms above her head.

"When can I get toe shoes, Anna? Will Father Christmas—"

Anna mimed ultimate horror, hand over mouth, blue eyes wide. "Toe shoes? Oh, my poppet, to spoil such feet, such exquisite feet?" In a frenzy of love for this tractable, adorable, and adoring child, Anna smothered the tiny feet with kisses. "Only look, my darling, see how perfect, how high the arch?"

"Yeth—but Anna," the child insisted, "if I learn to twirl I can show Daddy when he gets home—" She spun until the mirror spun with her and she fell on her neat little bottom.

"See? And this not called 'twirl,' angel. In any case is too soon for my little ballerina to learn." Anna beamed. Such a student she will be, this one; she tried and tried and tried again. In her very bones (so strong, so well formed!) she already knew there was no discipline like self-discipline, that practice would indeed make perfect. If only Ellie could see.

She showed her years ago, oh yes, but a stubborn woman, Mischa's wife. Opinioned, that was the word. "Look," Anna had said before Jennifer could walk. "See the spine, is it not straight? the neck—is it not long? the instep, how high? A ballerina would give the world for such an arch!"

"A strange value system," Ellie murmured.

"All I say," Anna pleaded (oh yes, she, Anna, had pleaded!), "is that she could perhaps...if everything should go right...if the bones grow straight like mine—and yours," she added generously, "then she could have a future, this small one."

"She already has. Later she'll decide what it's to be."

"But is wrong, wrong, oh, why does nobody understand?" The words were wrung from her, wrung! When she thought of the waste, perfectly formed children—she forced herself to speak with dignity, with calm, to make that pounding in her head, such a nuisance lately, a metronome at double time, slow down. "Look, if parents wait for the child to decide, then it is already much, much too late!" She paused to fling out her arms, to breathe, to dramatize her plea. "The dancer, the violinist, the athlete, the grrreat—" (how she had rolled that *r*!) "composer, they could not exist, never come to full flower. Learning for such artistes must begin young, young—"

"Surely not before toilet training." Ellie had scooped up the child and whisked her to the nursery for a change of diaper; Anna stormed later to Felix that the woman was a barbarian. "But what did you expect, my angel?" he said sweetly. "You let her be raised by von Reikers, and you've always said—"

That Felix! Even he could spit venom when it suited him!

Now she checked her watch and sighed. Almost time. She'd told the nurse to take an hour off, put up her feet—they must be aching—and she, Anna, would entertain the little Jennifer. Both Anna and nurse knew Ellie's rule, that Jennifer could go to the studio only to watch, and only if she wanted. (Even that had been forbidden until Mischa put his foot down!) So Jennifer just watched—if she happened to wave her arms to the mirror and the music, point her perfect little toes, was that also a crime?

The new car made good time heading north, and Michael forced himself to slow down, to look. Spring. Catkins dangling yellow tassels over the ditches, sticky red buds on the chestnuts, tender new green on the beeches. Easy. No rush, the business in London had gone well; next month it would be neatly tied up; when the lawyers were done he'd have sold the Orange County acres and bought a few hundred more up behind San Diego, where progress had to go next. Everything perfect. So where's the fire, as they said in the States? So nowhere. Ease off. Ellie wasn't due home yet, Felix either. Anna would be enjoying her lonely little session with Jennifer, and although Ellie disapproved he didn't. Kids had to learn discipline, why not from what they enjoyed?

Time to stop for lunch . . . but it was no fun alone and he hungered suddenly for Ellie next to him. She could have been here, dammit! But no, a general meeting of studio heads or some fool thing, and she was right. Security, as he reminded himself yet again, was like money, *was* money, which did not make itself. Maybe it was time to look for a tutor or something for young Simon? And what brought *that* on? God, he was tired, but he'd promised to look in on Grandmam on the way home.

He was crossing a humpbacked country bridge when he felt it, faint at first, no heavier than a cobweb brushing against a bare shoulder. Some small tension, naggingly familiar, was draining away, letting go. It wasn't business, God knew. Enough tension there to stretch a tightrope across the Atlantic. So what, what? Maybe hunger.

He shrugged, pulling into a pub for a snack. But by the time lunch arrived he was gone, gone, miles flowing under the tires, an odd compulsion driving him to hurry for that turn he knew from before, a ruttted cart track he'd traveled last week with Simon whining from the backseat to hurry-Daddy-hurry-Daddy-hurry! This lane, this bank of elderberry, these rabbit burrows dotting it like holes in a strip of film, and at the end behind a screen of hawthorn—God, in full bloom and less than a week since he'd seen it!—there was Grandmam's trailer, empty but the door swinging open, so she wasn't far. Inside spick-and-span and poor, as usual, her herb bag missing from behind the door. So she was clipping herbs.

Outdoors you could almost hear them grow. Weeds sprouted from winter's mud. New couch grass pushed through a path of flat stones leading to the stream; meadowsweet spread a milky haze over a fallen log; from the hills, a spring runoff had turned a murmuring stream into a miniature torrent. In its own little pool a clump of watercress flourished and he made a mental note to show Grandmam—as if she'd miss that! He'd take a bunch home for Anna, too. Cress butter was one of her pleasures.

He climbed down to the stream carefully, mindful that its muddy banks would do no good at all to the Italian shoes and silk tie he'd got in London. Hanging onto a tree limb, he was about to make the long reach for the watercress when a patch of brown caught his eye—brown wool where there should have been only the strident green of new ferns.

Brown wool.

Grandmam's skirt.

Grandmam's brown wool skirt very still, its hem almost black where clear waters lapped it, her bare feet shockingly white and old under the ferns. She clutched her old clay pipe in gnarled fingers; it was full of baccy, a wet box of matches beside it. She'd been settling for a smoke and left it too late, time running out on her last little luxury.

She was on her back in the shadows and it was a long time before he could bring himself to look at her face. He was ten again with a few shillings in his pocket and two rabbits on his shoulder and frightened to death because this *was* death and maybe her eyes would be open like Da's, he didn't think he could stand it if her eyes were open, if he ran away again . . .

They were closed, peaceful. As if death hadn't surprised her in the least. A small green beetle labored up the bony ridge of her jaw and began the long traverse of her cheek. He nerved himself to bend and pick it off just as a shaft of sun struck its shell and flashed him an iridescent emerald wink.

He jumped back, his heart hammering as he almost lost his balance on a mossed-over rock. That beetle.

It was as if Grandmam had laughed at him, mocked him gently, triumphantly, the way she had when the *kumpania* was hell-bent for California, when he'd said "... but I wish you weren't going," and not sure if he meant it. Now she'd gone away anyway, and he found too late that he'd meant it. Her quick bright eyes, this wise-walnut mouth and the cockeyed bits of wisdom that came out of it, they'd served their time. Her face hadn't always been clean and he'd been ashamed of that, defensive—as if Grandmam ever needed defending! She had a wide face once, he remembered. Wide and weeping when she handed Da a bag of brown eggs and he smashed them on her painted sunflower door.

In death her face had the fleshless skinned-down look of a woman who'd spent a lifetime facing into a bitter wind. And beating it.

He knew then what it was, that cobweb tension that left him all those miles back. Grandmam dying, letting go the line.

"Of course they must be told." Felix was on edge, they all were, Michael stalking through the house like a mad bull, blaming them. "Buff paper, Department of Social Services and a phone number on it—God, is it too much to ask that you empty the pockets before suits go to the cleaners?"

Lily Finn's eye wandered off the charts. Even Anna spoke in a conciliatory whisper. "Is possibly in your briefcase, Mischa?"

"You think I didn't look?"

"Only on top," Ellie reminded him. "Let me ..."

She found it, which didn't improve Michael's mood. Bad enough to lose Grandmam—*how* to tell Simon?—now he must call Dui, renew that damn contact. For the last time. Grandmam was gone now, the line cut. They had no more power over him.

He went through the typical elaborate system of numbers. Trust the Rom to be cautious.

Was Dui there?

No, but somebody knew where, who's callin'? His brother? Oh, get a pencil. Finally Dui telling a noisy crowd behind him to quiet down, that his brother the big businessman was on the line. From his mansion in England.

"So! Micah! What can I do for my brother?"

"Grandmam's dead."

A long silence. "In her trailer?"

"No. Outside."

Was that a sigh of relief he heard? That the trailer need not now be burned to appease tradition? The trailer registered in Dui's name? Yes, relief—but what, now, was this?

"Grandmam? My old grandmam dead? No...no...no...no—"

"I thought we'd bury her in Appleby...Dui? Are you there?"

Crash! Thump! Dui dropping the phone.

Michael shouted, whistled, rattled the hook, but who could hear over the sobs and shrieks that now came to him from the dubious charms of a welfare project near Sacramento? God, how could he have forgotten the extravagant display so vital to the Gypsy's grief?

At last a calm voice, warm and husky, unexpectedly familiar:

"Micah?"

"Yes—"

"Dui can't come to the phone, you know how it is—" A hint of amusement, an irony that almost added "—how they have to make a production." It was as if the speaker knew Micah, drew him into her patronizing silence, her affectionate contempt for the weeping group around her. Aloud, she said: "I suppose Dui'll call you tomorrow about arrangements...It sounds like he'll want to come over."

"I expect so..." He'd expected no such thing, but—

"I'm sorry about your grandmam, Micah."

"Yes."

"'Bye then—"

"Wait! Who *is* this?"

A pause, a sigh.

"Farah," she said softly.

TWENTY-SIX

*W*ITHOUT REGARD FOR THE TIME DIFFERENCE, Dui called Michael at four A.M. Collect. Okay, put him on...

Dui'd been thinking...no time to call before...too busy bein' Rom Baro, seeing as arrangements were his job...family plot over by Matlock, on the Eden it was...Ma and Granddad in it, Da too...a good spot, dry, big field back of the cemetery for the feast after the burial, farmer a nice chap, no trouble...lots of Rom coming from the States...leaving tomorrow...he'd gather 'em all up...Micah's the tycoon, too busy piling up money to bother with details like that...if Micah would just call these few numbers Dui'd be ever so pleased...Micah handle Micah's side of the water, Dui would do the rest...hadn't had a wink of sleep since Micah called yesterday but not to worry...

Michael, eyes still closed, tried to shut him out.

He didn't want Grandmam's funeral made a circus.

He didn't want the hordes descending again.

He didn't want to know where they'd put Da.

But he wanted everything done with.

Dui was running down like a penny-arcade watch when his words began to click in Michael's head. "Dui, wait. Back up. What do you mean, 'handle things my side of the water'?"

"Just call, let 'em know. Ready?" He reeled off numbers and names, key Rom families of England, Scotland, and Wales. He was approaching France and Spain when Michael stopped him, appalled by the transportation bill for this army—which he would unquestionably be expected to pay. The Rom did not travel cheap. And our Micah was the big tycoon from whom all blessings flowed. He sighed.

"I'm not Midas. Half these families didn't even know Grandmam."

"Oh Micah-Micah-Micaaaaah! Everybody knew her, loved her, met her at the fairs, didn't they? Thought the world an' all of our grandmother."

She'd been a quiet woman, Michael protested. Surely her funeral should be a simple affair, just the family?

A windy, long-suffering pause then Dui explaining as if to a child the history of the family: "One way or another them people's *all* family. Back before we was born we had Lees, Ayers, Boswells, Herons, Locks, Greys, oh I've no head for names—but all the good old families married in with us and us in with them. You don't know about your own people, Micah, that's your trouble."

And do not want to. "Look, I don't have time for this—"

Oh, blasphemy of blasphemies! "Time? Time? How many times can a Grandmam die? Thank God she can't hear you, our Micah, she'd be too shamed to hold up her head—if there's one thing she had was honor, when she had nuthin' else she had that."

Honor—an odd word coming from Dui. Honored among wagons. Familiar...a poet, Welsh, Michael thought. Honor. He remembered campfire talk after a funeral, elders drinking, one then another gratefully reciting names of families who'd showed up, the pride in big numbers, shame in small; right or wrong, the esteem in which a Gypsy was held was measured by how many came to pay respects. Dui wasn't typical. There *was* honor among the wagons. Among his family, too, before Da disgraced it, before Dui took hold. Dui, whose labored breathing and histrionic sighs came to him clearer now, across an ocean and a continent, than Ellie's gentle breathing beside him. How many of the *kumpania,* Michael wondered, were this minute packing for the trip? For Grandmam *had* been well liked, the Rom *did* grieve for their own. Often loudly but sincerely, with full hearts. Could he say the same?

Oh, this Dui, who had now turned to flattery, to wheedling: "Our people are so proud of you, *she* was so proud. Her favorite grandson—just see what he made of himself! Now how would it look, Micah, what would the Kalderash think, you the big tycoon and us pinching pennies on the old lady's *pomana?* Make the calls, Micah."

"I think—but Felix tells me I have no head for figures"—Anna paused to drop sugar lumps into her tea and into Michael's. "What I think is"—another pause as wafers of lemon were added—"of course I'm no expert—"

Ellie added milk to her tea, pretending to watch as amber clouded to beige. Ridiculous woman! How she built up her silly little dramas! If the men would just not indulge her! Look at them now, heads cocked and eager, waiting for that pearl of wit or wisdom (spontaneous of course) that she'd no doubt spent all night rehearsing.

Well. *She,* Ellie, had things to do if they did not. Before she left she must tell the twins about Grandmam in terms they could accept. Michael, with the best intentions, would become the moody, all too literal, Gypsy, and frighten them...and Simon was an odd, prickly little chap where Grandmam was concerned. But dear God, how much more talk, this one disguised as breakfast, to discuss the funeral? To which she was determined the children would not go. Gypsies, Gypsies, Gypsies. Oh, she was so tired of them, their demands, their influence, the way they disturbed Michael.

"I think," Anna said tartly, ready at last to let fall her pearl, "it must be easier to charter a Concorde and ship Grandmam to California, hang crepe in the cabin—than to bring the Gypsies to this country, feed them—"

"Anna, sssh!" Felix turned to Michael. "Try to excuse her, Mischa. Sometimes her jokes are not—"

"I not *try* to make joke, I angry! It is ridiculous these people have always the hand in Mischa's pocket and time!"

"Kinder at the moment," Felix told her, "to worry less about his pocket and time than what is in his heart."

"Well! If my opinion is not welcome!" She got up, pausing just long enough at the door to say: "Today Mischa will not forget barre? Again?" —the door snapping shut behind her.

Ellie let out a sharp breath and stood up also. "Really, Michael, *must* she talk to you like a child?"

So Michael was alone with Felix, to whom he could talk. "I am the knot in a piece of string, Anna pulling one end, Ellie the other."

Felix sighed. "So much time and still they do not like each other... and I think you feel another string also? It is hard, this Gypsy family pulling at you, and us? We pull also."

"You gave me the chance to pull myself, to be something."

"You were always something, Mischa. For us you have been everything. Anna can be sharp—she finds it difficult to speak from the heart—but she means only sympathy; we know how it is to lose family, to hear the dominoes begin to fall."

The breakfast room was sunny, all yellow light and a pitcher of daffodils painting the room with spring. Jenny at the window seat reciting her multiplication table in a dazzle of sunshine. "Two times two is four, three times two is six..."

Ellie let her finish, a tenderness almost unbearable in its sweetness washing over her. The first brush with death for this trusting child, this frighteningly *good* child. Jenny, pick up your toys, please? Yes, Mummy. Jenny, wash your hands. Yes, Mummy. Jenny, learn your numbers. Not yet in school but already she heard that internal clock telling her to do, obey, learn, not to waste time, for it was a commodity too soon spent.

How to begin, how to broach death? How had Ellie von Reiker learned? Bedpans and dirty sheets, night screams and hungering flights to Peter Heinrich because somewhere there must be arms to hold her, want her. No, not for this child. For Jennifer, as far as Ellie could ensure it, life would be as sunny as the room in which she was teaching herself to multiply.

Ellie pulled her close, pressed her lips to a rosy young cheek, firm and tender... warm, fragrant, pliant...

Rose-pink lips puckered softly, returning Ellie's kiss. "Did you hear my tables, Mummy? Except for nine-times (I forget that) I went all through. I don't think numbers are silly at all, Simon says they're stupid—"

"Where is Simon?"

"The stables—why didn't you and Daddy eat with us?"

"We were talking about Grandmam. You know she was very old?"

"Like Anna and Felix?"

"Oh, much older—and when people get that old... remember how she always took little naps because she was tired? Now she's extra tired and she's gone away for a long nap."

"Will she be there long?"

"Yes. We won't see her again, darling. I'm sorry."

A puzzled frown shadowed the innocent blue of Jenny's eyes, and Ellie was afraid for a moment that she'd ask exactly where Grandmam had gone, but:

"Did they let her take her pipe?"

"Of course they did." And why was this child born with concepts of "let," "allow," "may I" apparently built in? Concepts she seemed disinclined to test. Unlike her twin she lived her days entirely by rules and permissions. Ironic that except for the occasional nightmare she was much the happier child. "It *was* her own pipe."

"It smelled funny . . . when she smoked it *she* smelled funny too," Jenny stage-whispered into Ellie's ear.

"Some people liked it."

"It made me cough. Heh-heh-heh!" The cough was theatrically genteel, fingertips touchings lips. Ellie wondered where in the world she learned such things—

But now here was her twin, hay in his hair, barefoot, mud on knees and elbows, his face tight with hostility.

"Simon! Where were you?"

"In my room."

Ellie sighed. "There's no mud in your room. Why lie to me?"

"*You* lie!" He thrust out his lower lip. "You told Jenny that Grandmam went to sleep."

"I know—"

"She's dead! You know she is!" His eyes were dangerously bright and his lower lip quivered, but when Ellie reached out to hold him he stuck his flat palms in front of him like a shield. "Simon—" Sobbing, he squirmed away, arms flailing as he rushed to the door, tugging sharply at Jenny's immaculate ponytail in passing. "That's for telling on me!"

"I didn't either—"

"You did, you said I was in the stables."

"Because Mummy asked me," Jenny wailed. Too late, he was running out the door—full tilt into his father's arms.

Over his head Michael exchanged a quick glance with Ellie, who nodded, murmuring, "*And* pulled Jenny's hair."

Michael, with Simon firmly by the collar, made for the stables. "Now. Why did you pull Jenny's hair?"

"She ratted on me—and she said Grandmam smelled."

"So she did. She smelled like a Gypsy herb-woman and a grandmam. And Jenny's entitled to her opinion."

"No she's not—Jenny didn't like her." Simon turned away, his cheek against the Welsh pony's gleaming neck. "If you'd told her not to die she wouldn't have."

"She was old, son. Tired."

The boy was quiet a long time; Michael felt himself being watched from behind long blond lashes when the next question came. Calculated. "Is it finished now, for the families?"

"No," Michael began carefully, uncertain just what Grandmam had told him. "We're the family, all of us at Greenlings, Mummy and me and you and Jenny, and Anna and Felix—"

"Not us, I mean *real* family, Gypsies like she told me about. She said we had family in Over-the-Water . . ." For the first time he looked lost, uncertain, an unhappy little boy whose voice began to tremble. "But I don't know where it is."

"They're Gypsies. You're not. You're an Abramsky like me."

"And the family in Over-the-Water?"

"I have a brother in California. That's over the water, a lot of water." California, where Micah once invented an uncle who had a belt and hit him real bad when he was on the booze—then a kindly man who seemed old at the time had shown him the world. Given it to him, spun it for him. "We have business in California. When you're older I'll take you. It's beautiful. Mountains and lakes—"

"Will I see the Gypsies again?"

"—in California oranges and lemons grow right on the trees."

Simon was not to be distracted. "What will they do with her now she's dead?"

"Bury her."

"In the ground . . ." He thought about it and nodded. "She'll like that, leaves and grass on her. She's not scared of spidery things the way Jenny and Mummy are."

"No.'

A wise child despite his truculence. Grandmam lived off and from the earth, dug into it for saffron roots, plucked its foxgloves and coltsfoot flowers, violet leaves and honeysuckle berries; was there any growing thing she had not used in her ointments and powders and the healing teas she sold? Oh, she peddled clothespins door to door, but she cut and dried the hazel branches herself, whittled them to shape with nothing more than a blade and her hard brown hands. No doubt at all that Grandmam and nature had an understanding.

From somewhere far back in the past a funeral chant flashed its Romani semaphore:

> *May the earth rest light upon thee.*
> *Oh, Grandmam.*

"When?" Simon asked. "When do they put her in the ground?"

"A few days . . ."

"May I go? I want to see."

He hesitated a long time. They'd agreed, he and Ellie, that the twins were too young, that it was an unnecessary trauma—and why involve them with the Rom at all, even for a day? But Simon wasn't asking out of morbid curiosity. He really wanted to see, to say good-bye. "Okay. You can go."

"Oh, Michael, how could you!" Ellie cried when he told her what he'd done. "We agreed!"

"I know."

"Then why?"

"It seemed like one last thing we could do, take the children. Simon loved her—"

"There'll be crowds of them with their Rom talk and their ways . . . and Simon drinking it all in. They'll *be* there!"

"They'll expect us to be there too."

"You mean Dui expects."

"So? She's our grandmother, the twins' great-grandmother. Did outsiders tell you how to bury yours?" His mouth was a thin hard line and his voice cut like a whip. Outsider.

Quick tears stung her eyes as she watched him walk away, his shoulders still easy, arrogant, no matter what the pressure. Oh, sometimes it would be easy to hate that cool hard center of him that admitted no one, not even her. In so many ways they were one now, each knowing the other's thoughts, needs—but about the Rom he was as closed to her as ever.

Five years, and in that one way as much a mystery as when he'd stood by those great gates of Grossmutter's. But outsider! How could he even think that when he worked so hard for her and the children, built their security as if the world depended on it. So many times he'd said he *loathed* the Gypsies, their hand-to-mouth lives—and of course he must, why else would he struggle so hard to be opposite? So why was he upset if she didn't like them much either? Oh, Grandmam had been all right, but strange, unknowable, really interested only in Michael and Simon.

If Michael had asked, Ellie might have admitted to being (just like Jenny) a tiny bit scared of Grandmam with her potions and her ointments and her hard, crabbed hands.

Of course he'd never asked.

And now he was in the garage, waiting for her in her car, taking the keys away and tilting up her face, stroking her cheek with his warm brown hand.

"I don't know what to say. Sorry doesn't cover it, but I am. I don't know why I said it, I didn't mean it, I've never once thought you an outsider."

"Then where did it come from?"

"I don't know...oh Ellie, I am torn so many ways and I'll be so *damned* glad when it's all over and we can be Abramskys again."

"We've never been anything else."

"I know, but sometimes I am so torn...Can you forgive me?"

Michael Abramsky begging. What could she do but nod, offer up her lips which parted under his, help him when his fingers fumbled with buttons and hooks and straps.

One of them locked the garage door, it didn't seem to matter who, and they were together in the warm leathery darkness of the car.

A bright day, too bright for a funeral. The Abramskys all attended. Both cars were waxed to a fare-thee-well and all six mourners, including the twins, were dressed far more carefully than usual. In their various ways they felt there were standards to be maintained in face of...what? They did not know.

Anna and Felix were in one car, Felix in his eternally squeaky shoes and old-fashioned black suit, his white hair the usual silver in the spring sun. Anna told him fondly that he looked like an angel the casting office had sent over. She herself wore a tiny gray hat that sat precariously atop the gray bird's-nest hairdo and a lilac cape that smelled strongly of sachet and camphor balls.

"Mischa says the coffin will be open," Felix warned. "Gypsies like to see the body...so if you do not care to look—"

She sniffed. "Of course I don't care to look. Am I such a barbarian to be curious about a corpse? Such low instincts these people have... when I die you may cremate me and mix my ashes into the rosin tin."

"Tsk! Anna... I hope, my angel, you will be careful what you say. They are strange, Mischa's people, with strange customs. We do not wish to offend."

"In the first place *we* are Mischa's people. Second, is it my fault if their customs are not those of civilized peoples?"

Oh yes, Anna was in high fettle today, Felix decided. He was pleased. Lately she'd been quiet, and he'd worried.

In the other car Ellie looked almost dowdy in a black suit of severe cut and a wide-brimmed matching hat hiding all but a glimpse of her bright hair. Unrelieved black drained her, she knew, but by the time Michael told her it was unnecessary at a Gypsy funeral it was too late to change; besides, accustomed to the conservative funerals of Grossmutter's set, she would have felt disrespectful in anything else.

Michael looked the handsomest she'd ever seen him and she knew, if she were meeting him for the first time, that she'd be even more helpless now than she'd been then. His eyes were grave, clouded with an unreadable mix of emotions, his shirt almost too white against the corded brown of his neck. He wore a dark gray suit and tie and he moved, as usual, with that catlike elegance she'd seen on no one else. He seemed deep in thought and spoke not a word from leaving the house to arriving at the cemetery.

As he parked, Ellie gave her lipstick a last quick touch-up, tilting the mirror to see the twins in back. Jennifer was a composed little doll waiting only to get home again so she could have her dancing lesson with Anna. It was supposed to be a secret from Ellie, but she'd known for months, would have stopped it if she thought she had the slightest chance of succeeding—but Michael was as keen on the idea as Anna, so Ellie wisely closed her eyes to the inevitable. And she had to agree that for a disciplined, bookish child like Jenny, ballet was probably the perfect exercise.

Beside Jenny, Simon scowled straight ahead, as silent as his father. Ellie reminded herself that in a few hours the Gypsies would be out of their lives forever; despite everything Michael had said she had the feeling he would miss them...

Under protest he'd made all the calls Dui asked, but even he was astonished by the group at the cemetery. He'd expected a couple of dozen at the most, but over five hundred people crowded the church steps. Dui, as

Rom Baro of Grandmam's *kumpania,* made the most of center stage, rushing down the steps to clasp Michael in open arms, whispering excitedly through his tears that the crowd on the left were all from Canada...imagine, all that way! and *every one* of the Melrose lot from North Wales had turned up, could you beat that? His own little band from California were here, them as could manage, a grand *pomana,* Micah, they'll be talkin' about it at the fires for years to come. Roman-itchal, Lowara, Kalderash, all come together to bury Grandmam, oh it were fine, fine...

In spite of himself Michael felt pride too, that so many had come so far to say good-bye to this simple brown woman whose sole estate was a china cup and saucer, all she had to show for a lifetime's toil. He wondered if they knew or cared, this crowd? Both, if he knew the Rom. She had been rich once. It did not reflect well on Dui, as Rom Baro, that on her death she had nothing left. But then, what did reflect well on Dui? And after today, why should he care?

The crowd was mixed. Flashy suits mingled with unpressed castoffs, their wearers all speaking with that hushed, bereft air of having suffered loss. As a mark of the times many of the men wore a formal tie instead of the kerchief. Jewelry was everywhere, its jingle a constant background for the murmurs.

Women of all ages, the graceful and the bent, were laden with it. A scrawny throat bore a necklace so solid with gold coins you wondered how the old bones tolerated the weight; for the wild black hair of a Gypsy child someone had woven white moonpennies into a circlet—the result, though hardly funereal, was charming; a young woman with her back to Michael wore a black lace head square with the haughty aplomb of a mantilla. There was much red among them, from somber maroon to the brightest crimson; and always a glitter of gold as the sun touched ears and necks and quick brown fingers—but tears shone, too, and Michael was glad he'd made the calls, glad for once he'd listened to Dui and not to his own cringing distaste.

As he studied them they stared back at him frankly, in their eyes an odd mix of envy and pity. So this was the young rebel with the *gajo* family and the businesses and the money. And what good did it do him now? He'd still lost his grandmam, this poor devil that left the families for four confining walls and a locked gate.

He took Ellie's arm and Jenny's hand, told Simon to follow him close, and they entered the church with Anna and Felix.

The service was decorous, almost without incident, until they were invited to view the body, then sobs and wails waxed shatteringly loud as Dui and his wife made their pass of the open coffin, little Tomo following until all three stood immovable, tearing at hair and clothes, raking at flesh, howling to prove their anguish. Alarmed, Michael looked for Jenny; as he expected, her face was buried in her mother's lap. She was terrified, would certainly have nightmares for weeks. Ellie shot him a furious, betrayed look that said all too plainly, "Why didn't you *say* it would be like this? Why did they have to be exposed to this?"

The worst was not over. When he moved to slip a comforting arm around Simon it was too late. He'd wriggled free, raced down the aisle to stand on tiptoe, lean over the coffin, peer into the wizened brown face on the satin pillow.

As he stood, at once defiant and vulnerable, colored lights from a stained-glass window turned the tears on his cheeks to sapphires, emeralds, rubies; Michael had a premonition, so strong it was almost a physical blow, that the boy would remember this moment all of his life, exactly what he saw, where he stood, just whose arms were around his thin shoulders.

Simon was standing between Dui and Tomo, his tears matching theirs, his sudden screams even more piercing than their wails in the quiet church.

Ellie pulled Jenny into the aisle, glancing once more at her son, almost unrecognizable in his extravagant grief, before turning her blazing glance on Michael.

"Are you satisfied?"

"Ellie—"

"Jenny and I are going home. I'm sure the Abs are ready, too. When you've had enough of this...performance perhaps you'll bring young Hamlet home. If you can tear him away." She indicated Simon, still sobbing, still enfolded in the sympathetic arms of his Uncle Dui.

TWENTY-SEVEN

*A*S IF ON CUE AN AFTERNOON BREEZE ROSE UP with the laments of the mourners; it moved smoothly down the opposite hill, barely bending the grasses where a hundred or more trailers were massed in a field; in the river valley it ruffled up a few whitecaps on the Eden's soft-flowing blue surface, picked up extra bite on a limestone wall; thus strengthened, it swept up the long slope of the cemetery to sharpen its edges on row after flinty row of stone markers. No trouble at all finding the source of warmth, the gathering of Gypsies who swayed in shared grief to a chant that recited in hypnotic catalog the many virtues of the old woman, devoted wife, mother of one, grandmother of three, great-grandmother of four, herbwoman of thousands...

Did she not give health? Ayee...ayee...

Did she not keep the laws of the people? Ayee...ayee...

Did she not love her daughter, her daughter's children, *their* children? Ayee...ayee...

Sympathy from hundreds of eyes poured over Simon and Michael on one side of the grave, Dui and Tomo on the other; the keening grew louder. Did not all present suffer and share their loss? Were not the families gathered to pour balm on that loss? Ayee, ayee. She had brought honor to the fires, to those travelers who were blessed to be of the Rom, ayee . . .

Michael closed his eyes. Thank God Ellie had taken Jenny and the Abs away! If the histrionics in church were enough to send them running, whatever would they have made of this primitive chanting? Even he, who knew what to expect, was embarrassed.

Young Simon, apparently, was not. His eyes were glued to his uncle. The boy was moonstruck, looked almost drunk as he watched Dui and young Tomo, both now firmly in the grip of self-induced hysteria, open their arms to God and to heaven, beat their breasts and demand why, why, why this prize among women had been ripped from their midst—as if, Michael thought, they'd been here with her all the time, as if Grandmam had been a young woman in her prime, her death an unexpected tragedy.

The next moment they were sobbing, throwing themselves to the ground, tearing up great clods of turf as they peered into the hole, imploring her to rise up, rise up, not to leave them. At one point Dui seemed ready to throw himself in, but was held back by more prudent members of his *kumpania*.

From the beginning Dui had insisted that everything be done according to the customs of the families, forgetting that each *kumpania* had its own customs, different from his. Typically, he was trying to follow them all. Maybe conscious that he could have done more for Grandmam in her lifetime, he chose this method to deny his neglect? Maybe he wanted to restore his *kumpania*'s image before it fell apart, as it eventually must under weak leadership, only to reform in another place with a new Rom Baro? Or had he heard the old rumor, that the chief of a revered Romanitchal family routinely had to be dragged protesting out of the grave when a relative died?

Whatever devil drove him, Dui wasn't about to miss a trick that would render Grandmam's funeral a talking point among the Rom for the next fifty years. He even maintained (and who among them would deny it) that his people had not broken fast since the news of Grandmam's death. Three days, much travel, and no food or strong drink. So of course a gargantuan meal must follow; already that breeze from the opposite hill brought the rhythmic squeak of a turning spit, the crackle and sizzle of fat as ten plump young pigs slowly browned for tonight's feast.

To his annoyance Michael began to feel almost sorry for Dui, whose values were so meager he must adopt those of everyone else.

The first clod of earth thudded on the coffin lid. Rich soil and pebbles scattered, signal for a new outburst of tears from the crowd and a disturbing echo in Michael's mind. Looking down the grave's sheer sides, hearing earth fall and pebbles rattle on polished oak, an odd lightness took hold of his spirit. It was as if he were at his own funeral, mourning himself.

But I am, he thought, surprised. That's exactly what he was doing. Burying and mourning a boy called Micah. In this fancy box that Grandmam would have scorned and mocked there lay more than her shrunken old bones. Who else but she truly remembered the little boy he'd been, learning to count by building towers with her shining golden coins? Not Dui, who saw only a blood tie he could tap at will, just as he was milking every drop of drama from this day. No, the real Micah was gone; the knowledge should have made him happy—surely he'd been running from that boy long enough? But he was not sure now whether to weep for Micah the way the others wept for Grandmam—or to walk away smiling with the certainty that Michael Abramsky was more in every way than that scruffy child Micah could ever have become.

As he watched there was a stir on the edge of the crowd. Rose, provisionally released from the clinic but dark and crabbed as ever and in her element on this day of sadness, was thrusting forward the child with moonpenny daisies in her hair—a tiny girl who tried to shrug Rose off, looking quickly around and clutching at a skirt of garnet velvet, then at a woman's small brown hand hidden in its folds.

The hand belonged, Michael saw, to the woman who could wear a wisp of black lace as if it were a mantilla. Her back still to him she stooped, whispered to the child (who could have been little more than three), cajoled and flattered her, laughed quietly and musically at the child's answer. Then she stepped back and the child again held center stage, tilting up a flower face, a perfect oval, darker and sweeter than any moonpenny, each feature smoothly, perfectly innocent.

Gravely she removed the circlet, picked out the largest, freshest flower, and sent it fluttering down the deep grave to Grandmam's oaken box.

A charming gesture, Michael thought, the only one yet that was not overdone—but oh God, what was it in this child's face that moved him so, that carried him back? Its every feature seemed strange to him, the chin soft, no rebellion there, the forehead narrower—yet he wanted to stroke the hair from it, tuck soft blankets around the tan velvet cheek the way he did around Jenny's face—but surely it should have been Jenny, paler, simpler, somehow more biddable, who wore the moonpenny daisies? (At a funeral? he could hear Ellie say. At Grandmam's funeral, yes! he would have answered.

This dark child was hibiscus, bougainvillaea, frangipani—

The mischievous curve of her lips, baby teeth small and white and very sharp. A stranger's child, unknown to him until now, yet there was something—surely the eyes? their outer corners? that delicate upward slant which came, yes, straight from her mother.

Farah.

Her mother Farah who was smiling at her, whispering again, so the child took two more flowers from her circlet and offered them to Tomo and Simon. Tomo at eight knew good drama when he saw it and sent his flower to follow the first. The mourners sighed and dabbed their eyes.

Simon stood perplexed, looking from his flower to the girl and back again. When uncertainty turned his cheeks to crimson he crammed the daisy into his pocket. Someone laughed indulgently and Grandmam's burial service was effectively over.

Surely the next minutes moved in slow, slow motion, crowds breaking up, joining others, chatting, talking, whispering, all the time people drifting away down the cemetery hill, the men to linger by the river to light cigarettes and boast a little, exchange news of this and that, the women pressing uphill to the trailers—was there not food to prepare?—hordes of children as hungry as young animals clustering around their skirts, Simon with Tomo and the moonpenny girl, his platinum head as easy to spot among the dark ones as a bead of quicksilver.

Now only Michael and Farah were left, their dark glances locked across the grave, a few feet of earth and almost twenty years of not knowing and not seeing except for Michael's brief foreshortened view from the upstairs hall at Ryder Street.

Farah had matured well. There was a delicacy about her; the boldness was tempered now, only a hint still smoldered under the surface. (Wasn't it Grandmam who'd said she was too bold for her own good?) The promise of a determined cleft in the chin had been fulfilled, but the entire image was buffed to a high up-market shine. Even the clothes—undeniably Gypsy on this so-Gypsy occasion, long skirt, demure jacket, a froth of embroidered lace at the throat—all had a quiet, subdued glow which subtly converted the old aggression to assurance.

Farah, a smile deep in her eyes, came towards him, hand outstretched. Something in the shoulders, the carriage of her head, that slight backward lean as she advanced said it clearly as any label. Dancer. But Gypsy girls didn't go to dance class, any kind of class if they could help it.

Then her hand touched his and all he could think was: Were her hands always so warm? Yes, memory answered. *Yes!*

"Micah!" Her voice was low and husky, just this side of sultry. "I was behind you in church—I guess the rabble shocked your lady-wife just a tad, huh?"

For a second Farah's image disappeared from his retina and he had a swift rerun of Ellie's restrained anger when she'd left Simon and Michael to enjoy the performance without her. He shrugged. "Of course," he said,. "She's a *gaja*."

The smile deepened. *"Ame Rom sam . . ."*

And we are Rom. She was flirting with him.

"Not me," he said. "I gave up the life a long time ago."

"So I heard." She slipped her arm in his and began to steer them slowly downhill. "We've kept up over the years, Dui never stops. It's Micah this, Micah that, Micah the millionaire—"

"He's not, you know . . ."

"—our Micah the great dancer—"

"He's not that either—but what made *you* take it up?"

"How d'you know I did?"

"It takes one to know one?"

She shrugged again—and such a shrug, casual, easy, but somehow desperate, vital.

"It was *who*, not *what*. Momma made me take it up, you saw her in church, hell, how could you miss her, all the necklaces? That fortune clinking around her neck is my virginity, for God's sake! The *gaje* haven't cornered the market on stage mothers, you know. Remember when we were kids how your da kept on about my bride-price?"

"Vaguely." Definitely. Also a little girl pestering until he in turn pestered Da, who thought the whole thing very funny.

"That was because *Momma* kept on about it. She knew where she was headed, did Momma." A rushing, headlong bitterness sharpened her voice, quickened her step.

"She looked ahead," Farah went on. "She planned. By the time she'd done with me your family couldn't have forked over my bride-price in a million years." A sigh now that should have come from a woman far older than the one beside him. "Anyway, these cousins fifth-removed, *gitanos* doing flamenco in Vegas, New York, Monte Carlo, Paris, Rome, you name it—Momma made sure *the man* spotted me when I was twelve.

They were about thirty-five and doing *well!* The wife still performed, but she had cancer—flamenco does that to a woman if you don't watch it, no joke—that stomping's tough on the insides. Trust Momma to see the writing on the wall. Next thing I know I'm living with 'em and the woman's teaching me. Nice woman, she was. He used to hit her. When she died I was fifteen, primed to step into her shoes and Vittorio's bed. Big wedding. Momma picked up her necklaces and headed out for California. She did well out of me. Trained dancer, young virgin, beautiful—I *am* beautiful, Micah."

But she knew that; she just wanted to make him acknowledge it. He wasn't about to, but couldn't quite stop the swift glance at her body, dressing it in sinuous taffeta, hearing in it the swish of ruffles and the quick indrawn breath, the jingle of bracelets as her uplifted hands must weave *filigrano* patterns on the air, pulses of men beating just a little faster... Stop it, he wanted to say—to her and to himself. I'm happily married, I've got everything I ever wanted. You are wasting your time. Instead he said:

"She did a fine job."

"Because *I'm* fine. The world puts the same value on you that you put on yourself—you understand that, Micah, right?"

"Michael," he corrected. "Right." And of course she *was* right. They were two of a kind. "And..."

"It took me years to gnaw myself out of the trap she'd cornered me into. I ran off damn near every week, but Rom are like Mafia, once you're in, you're in. He'd call Momma, she'd track me down, drag me back. Then all of a sudden I'm eighteen and pregnant! No need to run and hide. I go to court instead! Oh Micah, the to-do, the fuss! Momma begging me to go back, begging me on her *knees!* Because surprise! surprise! my husband was turning into a vindictive bastard—he hauled her up before the *kris,* tried to get his money back! You saw my daughter Feya, with the daisies? He even tried to get her back!"

"Obviously he didn't succeed."

"Are you kidding?" she said, genuinely proud of the woman she'd been railing against with such bitterness. "Didn't I tell you Momma was smarter than the rest?"

"Yes." Something else he'd forgotten, the ambivalence, the impartial admiration of a prized Gypsy trait—in this case unswerving resolve— even when one had been its victim.

"I'm... surprised you came over here."

"I told you, I liked your grandmam. I've a Paris booking starts tomorrow, then two weeks in Copenhagen . . ."

"What I meant . . . I'm surprised you're still with the Rom."

She threw back her head, the slender throat vibrating as she laughed. "I take them or leave them alone. I'm gone weeks on end sometimes, can you figure better baby-sitters than women in the *kumpania?* Nobody messes with Gypsy kids. No, when I'm working Feya's safe. I do what suits me. I've seen too many backstage brats. They see things, hear things —don't I know? wasn't I one myself, once? That's not for Feya."

"And when you're not on the road?"

"Summers I don't work. We jump in the trailer and take off, me and Feya. I'm Gyp when it suits me, that's all. Between bookings I don't stick around."

"But you're still too much Rom for a house?"

She stopped, throwing out her arms as if she'd embrace the whole wide sky, darkening now and streaked with rose; for a moment the repertoire of flamenco mannerisms, the great cities of the world she reeled off with such aplomb, the twenty years since they'd talked, all of it fell away and they were children again drawing pictures in the dust.

"Houses! I'd suffocate in the walls! Oh Micah, how can you stand it in the summer of the year?"

"You just said it. You do what suits you. So do I."

They must cross the Eden now, its waters dark dark blue in the dusk, a cream cow plodding slowly along its banks to the milking shed. He remembered how it used to be, would still have been if his da hadn't . . . if her momma hadn't . . .

Even as tots they always got away with it, two kids ducking into some farmer's early-morning barn, picking out an obliging cow, giggling as they hugged her great square bulk and squirted her milk into a pail.

Farah licked her lips. He felt a sudden thirst. For a millisecond it was daybreak and she was laughing at him through a milk mustache and sharp baby teeth.

"We were a good team, Micah," she said now, giving him an over-the-shoulder look of tentative yet lingering guilt for promises made too long ago and many years in the breaking—then she shrugged . . . nobody's fault . . . but her shrug honed itself on broken vows as sharp and cutting as shards of fine china.

The little girl in white waited at the bridge, was about to clasp her arms around Farah's knees until, with that swift appraisal second nature to

Gypsy children, she reached for Michael's hand. "Oh, you'll be the travelin' man," she parroted, "I can see you've had your troubles, sir—"

"Knock it off, Feya! This is my second cousin Micah. He's Rom."

To Michael, Farah said: "Sorry. It's your pants. They've still got creases. She thinks you're a *gajo.*"

"I am," he said. "I am."

"Okay, don't shout! I got you first time."

The hillside above them was blooming with campfires now; at the main fire Dui waved a carving knife, presiding over the pigs.

"Look at it," Farah said with contempt. "Dreams of glory with barbecue sauce on its sleeve."

Dui, one-man band, beckoned and sliced and guzzled from a bottle, offered passersby great hunks of pork from his dirty bare hands. "Farah! Micah! Perfect timing! Biggest feast the families have ever seen . . . "

Farah immediately veered off in the opposite direction, pulling Michael with her. "Some dreams," she said. "His Rom Baro days are numbered, always have been. Everybody wanted Grandmam to take over but she wouldn't. It took the ginger right out of her when . . . well, what happened with your ma and da and all . . . God, that's the first *kris* I remember."

"How about you?" he said. "What are your dreams of glory? If flamenco's as hazardous as you say . . . "

"Three more years and I quit. Then I plan to be Rom Baro instead of Dui."

"You? Isn't that a contradiction in terms?"

"Oh, but you're la-di-da since you turned *gajo!* Lots of women run *kumpanias,* always have. They don't call themselves Big Man or Gypsy king (Dui introduces himself to *gaje* like that, did you know?)— but they've more power, some of those women, than . . . " She turned to him, flames from the fires leaping into her eyes. "You s.o.b., Micah! You've kept me talking all this time and not said dicky-bird about yourself! How's business? the marriage? has she genteeled you to death yet? how's—"

He held up his hand. "Everything's great. Marriage, house, business, Jenny and Simon—speaking of which . . . "

He took Farah's hand in both of his and for a moment she let it lie there, a small brown animal; when she withdrew it he felt he'd lost something warm and vibrant, quivering with life. "You've done well, Farah. I'd hate to think of you . . . unhappy."

A long, long pause—perhaps she had not expected a good-bye so soon? "Unhappy? Me?" Now the dancer spoke again, haughty, distant. "I've been around, nobody'll give Farah trouble. I know what I want."

She'd fight for it till she dropped . . . so *much* fight in this girl. "You're lucky," he said. "Not many know what they want."

"We do," she whispered. "We always did, me and you."

"I like Tomo, Daddy." Simon squirmed deep into the plush front seat. "If he didn't live in 'merica I could play with him every day."

"Mmm." He passed tissues from the glove compartment. "Here, clean yourself up before Mummy sees you. Where's your watch?"

"Tomo liked it. I gave it to him."

"Why . . ." Careful, Michael. "Did Tomo ask you for it?"

"'Course not! I told you, I like him."

"Look, the watch doesn't matter. Just think, son. *Did he ask you for it?*"

"No!"

"Hint?"

"No!"

"Uncle Dui?"

"No, he just said to Aunt Rose that Tomo never had a watch, that's all."

"And you happened to be there."

"Yes. Does it matter?"

"It's . . . not good to set patterns, they're hard to break." The boy was frowning, puzzled, and Michael knew he should say more but didn't know where or how to begin—how do you tell a small child that certain relatives could become rocks that grew heavier with the years? and why trouble Simon? Tomorrow the Rom would be gone and the boy himself again. Then they'd find a primary school or get Mary Beth to come out, Ellie could call—

He half-expected her to be waiting in the hall but instead there was Anna wagging a finger in his face. "I wait, Mischa, I telling true! How often do I agree with Gabriella? Never! But today she is right . . . Jennifer is upset, this excess is bad for children, is breeding morbid ideas—"

But her voice was too mild, he knew there had to be something else— and that he must wait for it to surface. "I saw plenty of Gypsy funerals," he said, "they didn't affect me."

"You were born to it, they are not—"

"But the twins were born to *me,* it's my business—"

"Anna is speaking, do not interrupt. There is something else." Ha-ha, now she was coming to it. "A long time ago a girl pushed her way into Ryder Street. Today I see that girl in the church. Brazen, her eyes are everywhere. Today she watches you, looks—"

"Can't she look at me, a second cousin?"

"Related?" For a moment she was mollified, but having worked herself to top pitch she was not about to withdraw with no shot fired. "So is Dui, so is Rose related! If this new one hangs on to you like they—"

The comparison alone made him laugh. "Farah hang on? Anna, between you and my second cousin, I think you have the world market on pride all sewn up."

Ellie, hating the clinging black and the way it made her feel, had changed into a negligee Michael had not yet seen, pale mint green with floating side panels, chic but nicely understated. If only she'd been more subtle in church. She could have pleaded a headache for herself or Jenny, she need not have made her contempt so obvious.

"I'm sorry, darling," she said, the moment he came into their room.

"So am I."

It was impossible to read him. He was sorry the children had been exposed to the funeral? Or sorry she'd objected? "That howling, I've just never . . . and Dui . . . it was a little *much* . . ."

"Yes."

"Mmm . . . well, I thought—you haven't said a word about the robe, don't you like it?"

He looked her quickly up and down; he was usually interested in her clothes, yet tonight she could have sworn he hadn't even noticed.

He smiled. "It looks . . . tasty, like an after-dinner mint."

"That bad? But I did look all right at the church?"

"Of course. You looked—genteel."

She threw the negligee onto the bed and touched the green satin bodice of her nightgown. "Come," she whispered, opening her arms, softening her voice with invitation and anticipation. "It's ages since we've been alone . . . and I really *am* sorry."

"I know." He sighed deeply and she felt the warmth of his breath on her throat. "I've been an unfeeling bastard but after today . . . oh Ellie . . ." He murmured apologies, regrets, found refuge in her elegant flesh, looked deep into her eyes as he loved her. "You have," he said later, "so much more patience than I have a right to expect . . ."

Usually they talked afterwards, small events of the day, intimate things.

Tonight he said he was tired, it had been a long day, and simply kissed her palm and closed his eyes. Some time later, when she closed her book and reached for the light, she saw he was not sleeping. He was very still, but his mouth was firm and a dark pulse beat quickly at the base of his throat.

Sleep did come to him, but in confusing drifts, in odd, disconnected bursts of taste and sound and color. There were suggestions of mints a little cool to his palate and from somewhere the sharp tang of paprika; there were wails and well-bred protests and under them all the rapid rhythms of flamenco. Before tonight he never remembered dreaming in color, but now there were tumbled clothes on a bed, something green and cool to his skin that darkened, turning to smooth-flowing blood. There was the touch of flesh, a woman's palm, again cool and controlled —which turned warm and quick and very small, then suddenly the telltale callus from a castanet under his lips.

Why? he thought, drifting in and out of sleep.

Why is Ellie's hand always so cool?

And Farah's so warm?

TWENTY-EIGHT

*F*OR A LONG TIME Simon dreamed of the funeral. Not nightmares such as Jenny had, babyish screaming fits during which
everyone spoke to her in whispers. Oh no. Simon's night dreams were
like his daydreams; he found refuge in them long after contact with the
Rom seemed to have stopped.

He knew it had not. A few times he heard Daddy talking that language
on the phone; they flew to California, Daddy often and Mummy sometimes, either to San Francisco or the house in L.A.—but for one reason
or another the twins couldn't go yet: Jenny was just getting over measles;
Simon had a cold; right after that he failed beginners' composition and a
tutor came every day for a month so they couldn't go then, now could
they? Jenny had to rehearse her stupid little part in a ballet recital. Simon
fell out of a tree and broke his wrist. And sometimes they were just plain
too young for "abroad"—though they'd been to Paris and New York and
even, last Christmas, to Tokyo.

Never to California.

Then Miss Warren came and sat on him for a year until he learned to read and write properly.

One night he found old phone bills in Daddy's study, but when he tried to call a California number that must be, had to be, Tomo's, something always seemed to go wrong. Maybe Lily Finn or Felix or Mummy came in as he was dialing. Once it was worse—that nosy parker Anna, all wrinkly corners one minute, turkey-red and panting the next, pulled him by the ear just when a phone began to ring at the other side of the world. Her long fingers grabbed the receiver and thumped it down. She shouted that he was naughty, how dare he use the phone in the middle of the night without his father's permission? Anna didn't like him, he knew that; he wouldn't stand at that stupid barre grinning into a mirror and tying his legs in knots, that's why.

The few times he got through, Tomo wasn't home, which made him wonder where they really lived, where they went, how they ate, what it would be like to sleep somewhere different every night, wake up to a new town every morning? He'd like that, he thought. He'd like that a lot.

He wanted to know how they talked, too, but Miss Warren said it wasn't a real language because it wasn't written down so how could he learn it? That's what she said. She was lying, they all lied, Miss Warren said anything Daddy told her to. One of these days they'd send him away to boarding school, *then* he'd find out, *then* he'd learn it.

Grandmam's funeral was two years ago, then three, then four, yet in his memory it still burned like a hot coal, loss and grief and warmth, Uncle Dui hugging him, talking man-to-man about traveling and horses and fairs—picking out the cracklingest bits of pork just for him, scraps that wouldn't even be let in the kitchen *here*—too fatty, Simon, such grease! But he liked it like that; he liked it when Tomo strutted between feast tables in his California cream suit and let old women pet him for a moment before he shrugged and moved on; he liked the way Tomo did whatever he wanted; nobody yelled at Tomo for climbing trees, getting dirty, watching the telly, sipping a grown-up's wine; when a woman shook her fist because Tomo kicked dust on her fire he simply kicked again; even though Simon hadn't understood it he hungered again and again for the stream of Romani that Tomo let fly at her like a gob of spit, translating to English straightaway so Simon didn't miss a word. He liked being treated grown-up for a change—he liked everything about the Rom that he remembered, and he'd forgotten nothing. The next chance he got he'd call again and keep trying. One day he'd get an answer.

* * *

Jennifer loved everyone, even Lily Finn, and everyone loved Jennifer. Anna devised lesson structures as carefully as if her one pupil were Anna Pavlova. Felix, overseeing piano practice, tapped his cane and closed his eyes, every scale a concerto under the pounding of small dimpled hands on yellowed keys. Even the mailman waited for her smile each morning and felt the poorer if he missed it. Yes, Jennifer was Daddy's little angel and Mummy's darlingest treasure. She was also Miss Warren's dream student.

"The best I've had, Ellie," Mary Beth said reluctantly. "She likes learning. If she were less lovable she'd be an insufferable prig." And perhaps that's why she secretly preferred Simon.

"Mmmm...Mary Beth, I think Michael's really worried about Simon —men always seem to want the boy to have the brain and—"

"*If* they're chauvinists, which Michael is," she said crisply. "But he needn't worry about Simon's brain—the boy has a fine one, quicker than Jenny's if he'd just—"

"—apply himself, I know. It doesn't seem fair. Michael works and schemes and buys and sells just so the twins will have their future handed them on a plate, so they can be whatever they want to be—and Simon doesn't show the slightest interest in being anything at all."

Poor Ellie, who didn't understand her son any more than his father did. "You can't tell yet," Mary Beth lied. "He's still young." *But had he ever been a child?*

"I don't know what more we can do." Ellie picked up a thread from the couch and wound it absently around her finger. "Michael could have just got horses and turned Simon over to an instructor, but no, he even took lessons himself so they'd have something to share, and then Simon won't even *try*, won't *go* to formal classes—so who does Michael ride with? Whose self-image doesn't need a boost? Who brings home the ribbons and trophies? Jenny! While Simon rides off bareback on his own! Swimming the same, that beautiful pool, yet he'd rather swim in a polluted ditch everybody's pleased to call a river. Now Michael thinks if we get a telescope Simon might develop an interest in astronomy—"

"And he might not," Mary Beth said sharply. "You do too much already. Every child isn't born to conform. And don't worry about his self-image—right now he thinks the whole world is out of step but Simon."

Yet on occasion, even to Mary Beth, he could be intensely, almost unbearably loving, would dash up and for no reason at all hug and hug until you had to beg for mercy—but she had never seen him kiss Michael beyond the obligatory good-night peck—and even that had to be prompted. The more his father did for him, the more the boy seemed to doubt him...

On only one point did Mary Beth's opinion match that of Ellie and Michael: Simon was not the happy, easygoing child his sister was. But if his parents underestimated Simon, Mary Beth did not. The boy was ingenious at finding excuses to duck out of schoolwork or chores, but he was not lazy, merely unwilling to follow instructions. If he decided to tidy the grounds, he raked up every leaf and twig—but she once made the mistake of praising him for "a job well done" and in a fury he kicked at the pile until every leaf was scattered to the winds. "I don't do 'jobs,'" he said clearly. "I do what I want."

Another day he refused lunch (not unusual, he ate only when hungry), then devoted the next hour to separating the gardener's apprentice from a meager fish-paste sandwich. Utterly charming, he smiled and cajoled and wheedled until the young man handed it over—then Simon took it around to the kitchen quarters and fed it to Lily Finn's black and white terrier.

"Why?" Mary Beth pressed. "He'd worked hard, the sandwich was all he'll get until supper. If you didn't want it—"

"You know I hate fish paste."

"Then why take it?"

"He didn't have to give it..." That shrug, so much like his father's... "The dog was hungry, Lily doesn't feed it enough."

Small things, one after another, month after month, but in a cockeyed way they began to add up, she wasn't yet sure to what. He didn't lie a lot, but he used truth so creatively, wove fact and fiction so skillfully that it was often hard to find the seams. At an age when most children couldn't keep a secret if you paid them, Simon Abramsky guarded his like treasures—but because he was still young, ignorant of many things, it was inevitable that some treasures would come to light.

Had he not been fighting on so many fronts at the time, Michael might have seen it coming and perhaps subconsciously had, because when it finally blew up in his face he was not so much surprised as bombarded by anger, wave after hot red wave of it as Ellie opened the mail across the breakfast table.

Usually on such mornings he counted his blessings, had to hide his satisfied smile behind the *Times*.

Ellie lovelier and more steadfast every year, a success as wife, mother, administrator for her own business and hostess for his. A wife who loved him. Beside her his golden children, healthy, well loved, wanted, living proof that care counted for more than heritage. Who, looking at them, could say their father once stole bread to stay alive?

The Abs aging but secure, happy in their grandchildren, Felix's hip deteriorating more slowly now thanks to a Swiss therapist and the indoor pool they'd had installed, Anna in splendid shape except for that elevated blood pressure she'd been warned about and took medicine for.

Mornings like this, sun and snow filling all the hollows outdoors, mounding tree and bush and cypress hedge with pristine glitter, splashing sunshine onto polished parquet and copper urns filled with huge red mums—it hardly seemed to matter that Ellie and Anna, who met every day of their lives, were still polite strangers; that Dui's fishing expeditions sometimes caught a mackerel—or at least enough to keep him off Michael's back for a month or two; that Rose (almost out of spite, it seemed) acquired every new disease as soon as it was discovered. Farah...oh, Farah, how to forget the warm brown hands callused with the marks of her trade, her quick, assessing glance, the angle of her chin, at once graceful and haughty—but he'd quelled every impulse to seek her out, beaten down every desire to hear that husky voice say:

"We know what we want, we've always known, Micah."

Micah, always, Micah.

But *Michael* always knew too. He knew he had it all, this young businessman with the *gaja* wife, everything he ever wanted, all gathered under the stout roof of Greenlings.

They were all there this morning, even ghosts of Abramo One and Two immortalized in lithographs on the wall; in his briefcase Abramo Three's space-age curve was sketched into the mock-up of an ad campaign; also the prospectus for a real estate development in Southern California—but this time Abramo was the developer.

Abramo was now like the Greenlings oak, several vigorous branches—but none of them vital except the main, the permanent trunk.

The Abramsky family.

The household was larger now by Mary Beth and assorted help; Lily Finn lived in and her daughter Darlene (who had inherited her mother's unfortunate love of singing) came in mornings to help serve breakfast, the one meal at which they were all, invariably, together.

The twins were still home, no question of sending Jenny to school —Ellie couldn't bear to see her go, not even to get her out of Anna's benevolent clutches...later would be soon enough, they rationalized; she did love the dancing so, and simply adored Anna. But surely it was time they cut Simon from Mary Beth's apron strings, sent him to a boys' school with real discipline? Several times Michael wrote for brochures, but they lay on his desk, eventually found their way into a drawer, then a wastebasket...the boy was small yet, thank God he *could* stay home. At his age Michael had been a little old man who bartered a day's work for an old blanket, who stole eggs and sold them, who...

Today one school sent a reminder, which Ellie handed over without a word before shuffling her own stack of mail, separating household from personal. Household was the bigger, so she started with that, grumbling mildly that Greenlings must cost as much to run as Buckingham Palace.

"I'd like to live there," Jenny said, watching the way Anna sectioned an orange, copying every move. "Maybe Princess Anne would let me play with her toys and—"

"See how beautifully Jennifer peels the orange, Mischa—"

"You're silly, Jenny," Simon said to his sister, as if Anna hadn't spoken. "Princess Anne's too old for toys."

"Now, children..." Ellie didn't bother to finish; like everything else it was part of the morning ritual. Simon ignored the fruit, piled his plate with bacon and eggs, which he peppered heavily. Felix shook his head at Anna's use of butter on her toast. Anna checked that Mischa ate his fruit (though surely all danger of nossinkhood was past?). Mischa looked at his watch—less than an hour to a downtown meeting, Felix not dressed yet, Ellie only half done with the mail—

Then her gasp of disbelief.

Anger.

"I...Michael...this bill...it's...I don't believe it!"

He smiled. Ellie the Efficient, frugal housekeeper, shades of Grossmutter—for whom, he reminded himself, he should be grateful. Waste not want not.

Then from the corner of his eye he saw Simon—then Mary Beth Warren—stiffen. Why?

"A call to a Sacramento suburb," Ellie said steadily. "We have no office there—"

He shrugged. "Just Dui playing games, calling collect, maybe Lily accepted by mistake."

"And chatted?" In one smooth motion Ellie threw down the bill, the envelope, and the gauntlet. *"For four hours?"*

If this elegant a creature could be said to breathe fire then Michael could swear he saw flames lick out from his wife's patrician nostrils. "The billing office makes mistakes..."

Ellie folded an immaculate napkin. "They haven't before. I'm sorry," she said, shooting Mary Beth an apologetic glance, "maybe I'm being plebeian—but this one call is more than we pay the gardener *and his son* for an entire week's work."

"So," Anna said, safe in her own small corner, not unhappy to see Ellie's feathers ruffled. "Who can talk so long? Not Felix, not me, sorry. We are not traveled, our friends are in Europe only—"

"Anna!" Felix shut her up, telling her by signals developed over three decades that this was not their quarrel.

"Who?" Michael said, but he was going through the motions. Deep in his gut he knew. "Show me the number."

Of course he was right, Dui's old social worker pal, but he couldn't, didn't want to believe that a boy Simon's age could be that devious, secretive. But it all fit. Wasn't it about a month ago that he'd seemed happy, uncharacteristically cheery, even cooperative? When he wandered around in a dream, whistling all day, smiling for no apparent reason? And all the time, under that smile—

And Micah, wasn't he secretive, creeping from barn to barn, stealing from this farmer or that, doing whatever Da told him. When there was no more Da he did what he'd been taught all along, or what his genes taught him, to beat the gaje *no matter what.*

But that other boy had no choice. Simon had.

"I haven't spoken to Dui in months," he said steadily. "Which means somebody else has. Simon? Did you call your uncle?"

"No." Not a second's hesitation. Blue eyes innocent. "But I don't see why—"

"Stop it!" Michael didn't realize just how furious he was until he saw his hand shaking. "Let me put it another way. Did you call this number?" He threw the bill, with the offending number now circled in red, across the table. "Yes or no?"

A sullen shrug. "Jenny calls *her* friends, so does Mummy and Mary Beth, I don't see why I can't talk to Tomo—"

"Oh Simon!" Ellie could not keep quiet. "You know your numbers, can add and multiply, you surely know the difference, the enormous cost—"

"Cost is not the point," Michael said.

"It most certainly is!" Ellie said hotly.

"Simon, wait for me in the study, please?"

The boy heaved a sigh and slouched out the door. Michael waited for it to slam behind him before speaking to Ellie.

"I'll handle this myself."

"Are you going to let him get away with—"

"My point," Michael said, trying to hold his voice steady, "is that the cost of one call is nothing compared to—"

"Four hours and seven thousand miles is nothing?"

He stood up, tired before the day had even begun, and crossed to the door. "It's not how long he talked. *It's who to!*"

Simon lay sprawled on the study couch. When Michael walked in he looked up, scowling, but made no effort to stand.

"Please get up. I want to talk with you."

"I can hear from here."

Michael looked down at him, his well-dressed, well-loved son. Even through his anger it came to him he was being tested. The twitch in Simon's neck was a pathetic betrayal of all that languid unconcern; under it, he was watchful as a cat. This deliberate rudeness, like the studied refusal to sit up, wasn't Simon. He was trying to goad him to—to do what? No, he would not let himself be driven to that, ever.

"I have never believed," he said quietly, "that a grown man should hit a child. So far I have not touched you. It does not mean I won't. I asked you to stand. Now I'm telling you."

Blue eyes looked up, tried to look into brown—but the blue dropped first, and slowly the boy came to his feet.

"Thank you. Now we can talk. Why didn't you ask if you could call Tomo, instead of grubbing through old phone bills for the number—"

"Who says I did that? They lie, they lie!"

"You must have. Your uncle's number is unlisted." *Watch it, old cock, never spread your lies where they can trip you up! Yes, Da.* "And I no longer keep it in the book here."

"That's because you knew I'd call! Why don't you want me to call?"

"Let me ask the questions. You should have got permission."

"Would you have given it?"

Michael felt he was arguing with an equal, not a child. He even recognized the pattern, attack before you are attacked, keep the questioner off balance, answer questions with questions. Very well, he'd give it to him straight.

"I don't want you to associate with Gypsies. Ever. At all. Is that clear?"

"Why? You're Rom."

The *R* hard, rolled, breathed on just right, lovingly practiced. Tomo had not been idle. You're Rom.

Michael felt lost, outmaneuvered. "It's a way of life I didn't want. I've traveled the roads. It's not adventure, it's a hard life, hand-to-mouth. It rains and snows out there, a cold world with no walls to keep the wind out. I thought my family deserved something better. I even thought they might appreciate it." He couldn't believe himself. He was whining, asking for thanks, torn between wanting to thrash some sense into an eight-year-old and the desire to rock him, hold him, to tell him that each generation doesn't *have* to make its own mistakes, that it *can* profit from secondhand experience—but a little smile played around Simon's lips. In this mood and this atmosphere . . .

"I like the Rom," he was saying. "Just because you don't . . . because you think you can buy your way out—"

Michael's patience snapped. These were not Simon's words he was hearing. They were Dui's to Tomo, Tomo's to Simon, all acquired during four intensive hours. At *his*, Michael Abramsky's, expense. Ellie was right, dammit, cost *did* matter! It added insult to what God knew had been injury enough, Da's belt, his morose mutterings, young Micah's terror. And now the grown man was frozen with a foreboding that had no shape, no name, his voice all the quieter for it.

"There's no more to say, Simon. I'm going to put locks on the phones. We'll decide on a school for you."

"I don't want to go—"

"I've put it off too long already."

"Tomo doesn't go to school. He knows stuff."

"I'm sure he does. How old is he now? Twelve? If you wrote him a letter *could he read it?*"

And now his fury turned on himself. In his bitterness he had shown Simon another door to the Rom. If Tomo couldn't read, a social worker could. Gypsies in the States had plenty of those and cultivated them like prize artichokes. "They're miracles," Dui had told him. "If you play dumb they think you've got a screw loose! They apply for these 'benefits,' fill out the forms and everything, all you got to do is put a cross at the bottom and checks roll in like clockwork. Illiterate and unemployable, that's what they're for. You didn't know I knew words like them, didja? I don't let on to *them* I know 'em, neither!"

So proud Dui was—and why not? He'd discovered another wrinkle to the same old game.

Beat *gaje*.

Within a week Michael did all he said he would do and one thing more. He called Dui. Who was at home and receiving.

"What can I do for my brother? Just tell me, anything—"

"One thing. If my son calls, hang up. The same goes for Tomo."

"Oh Micaaah! My own nephew! Last time he called, Tomo was pleased as punch."

"I wasn't. I got the bill."

Agonized silence marred only by uncontrollable coughing as Dui lit a cigarette. When he could talk: "That's the trouble when you have money, too much is never enough. What's it for but to spend, eh? And what good is it when we've Rose on the oxygen—"

"Again?"

"She were fine till she went east for a *pomana*—is it my fault she won't miss a good *pomana* to save her life?"

"How far east?"

"Pittsburgh."

"In January? In a trailer?"

"Aye, well, the heater don't work too good neither, the walls sweats something fierce, but it's all she's got, in't it?"

"I sent you money to get her a decent trailer, no leaks."

"Hell, I've got me own troubles right now, what with—"

Michael tuned him out, uninterested in the catalog of Dui's perpetual problems with the families, until:

"—Farah not out of the flamenco lark three weeks and she's moving in on my territory, bringing in Kalderash boyos to team up with my asphalters. Hell, we had the driveway scam sewed up tight as a tick. Well, I soon told *her* where to go, you know what she's up to, don't you, wants to get her hands on everything . . . 'Course, if I had a bit of money to fight her with, splash it about a bit, throw a feast or two, give the families a treat . . ."

When Michael hung up he laid his head on his arms in the empty office and he wept. No more did he ask: Is there an end? He knew now there was none, that Dui would never let go. But then he thought some more and he laughed. He thought of his melodramatic brother smoking and scratching his belly in some poky trailer park over there in Sacramento.

"Dui, my brother, you better watch your lazy ass. Farah's been around, she knows just what she wants. And nobody, but *nobody,* gives Farah trouble."

TWENTY-NINE

$\mathscr{U}$NDER A LEADEN SKY Ellie's car swept from village to early-morning village, tunneled through arching black limbs of winter trees, sped past churches, pubs, privet hedges rimed with frost.

Simon scrunched down in the seat beside her, his uniform of maroon cap and gray blazer suit painfully new. The suitcase, which he refused to let out of his grasp, stood between them on the front seat. A screen. Didn't he know that on this sunless day the windshield was as good as a mirror, showing her the excited curve of his mouth, the shine in his eyes, his busy fingers twirling the yellow address tag until she could have screamed. He was looking forward, why couldn't she?

"You'll break the cord," she said sharply.

He stopped and checked. Yes, the label still swung from its hanger, Mary Beth's firm script reversed in the windshield's reflection: Simon Abramsky, c/o Brimley Boys' School.

It shouldn't have been like this, just the two of them speeding farther and farther away from Greenlings. Surely if Michael were here she wouldn't feel quite so much as if she were driving her son into exile?

"You do understand, darling?" she said, not for the first time. "If you'd been willing to wait one more week until Daddy came back... a pity he had to leave like that, he really wanted to take you himself, see you settled in, make sure you liked it—"

"I will."

"He couldn't just ignore the telegram." Did she sound as resentful as she felt? What was more important, a sister who might or might not be sick (and with Rose who could tell?) or a son leaving home for the first time, needing that extra paternal support? And this time not even a phone call pulling Michael away, just the old emotional blackmail with a twist in the tail: ROSE SICK. SWITZERLAND OR GREENLINGS? No signature—but who could it be but Dui? When called, the tame social worker's phone, from which Michael had avoided calls for so long, was "not in service."

But oh, the explosion when Ellie suggested, tactfully she thought, that maybe somebody in the California office could go out and take a look—

"Look *where?*" he'd shouted. Michael shouting! "You think the Rom have addresses like normal people? that you thump on the door, 'Knock, knock, is Michael's brother Dui home?' 'Dui who?' 'Dui I-Don't-Know-What-He-Calls-Himself-This-Week but he's got a wife and two kids and a sick sister Rose?'"

"It was just an idea—"

He swept a hand through black hair and for an instant she saw a prize bull trapped in a pen. "And after our man found Dui, how much respect would I get in the boardroom? Dui? The boss's brother?"

She'd tried to tell him that respect didn't enter into it, that Americans were not snobs, that Abramo was his company, not Dui's, but he stormed out and slammed the door behind him, unable to admit even to her that he was ashamed of being Rom. As if she didn't know. And now this little scrap of a boy was off to boarding school without his father because Rose must again be found, arrangements made.

"I 'spect he'll send her back to the clinic."

"If she's really sick, what else can he do..."

"She couldn't live at Greenlings anyway." He spoke with absolute authority, amazed at his mother's ignorance. "Aunt Rose is true Rom, not like Daddy..."

She paused, biting her lip. "Simon, Grandmam's funeral was a long time ago. I don't really think you remember Aunt Rose."

"Tomo told me *everything* about the family!"

Oh, why did she get into it, why not talk about *our* family—"Next Saturday we'll go to the airport to get Daddy, just the two of us and Jenny, he said for sure he'd be back then. Would you like that? Watch the planes come in?"

He shrugged. "I guess."

The signpost for Brimley loomed up, beyond it a red-brick wall and playing fields, boys in shorts chasing a soccer ball among patches of snow. "Look," she said, tears thickening her voice, "we're almost there ... Just remember you're a weekly boarder, that you'll spend every weekend at home, that we love you, and if you really don't like it all you have to do is call us? That we'll come and get you?"

"Mmm ... you're sure they go on hikes like Daddy said?"

"Sure."

"And we go camping at the river—"

"Later in the year when it gets warm. Remember, you'll call me if you want to come home?"

Why did she keep saying it? Practically inviting him to run home at the first breath of homesickness. Because she meant it, that's why. Because he was so small. It was true what Felix said at dinner last night. "A barbarism, the boarding school. Only the English upper classes send their children away at such a tender age. Perhaps they do not like them ..."

But I, she thought in sudden panic as she drove through the gates, I am not English, Michael is not upper class, so why are we doing this? Because Michael says so. But Simon's *my* son too, why don't I refuse, take him home, give him hot chocolate and cookies and hug him until he falls asleep? Because if I do, and Simon fails to become the gentleman his father wants, expects, works for and plans for, then I'll be blamed.

Also because it was painfully obvious that Simon *wanted* to be here. He bounced up and down on the seat, blond head popping up over the suitcase as he pointed to this, implored Ellie not to miss that, oh look, Mummy! do look at the swings, the lake, see, they've even pitched a tent! He knew almost nothing about this place, but he wanted to be here. Anywhere but Greenlings.

No sooner had she braked at the steps than a starched apron sailed out to meet them, under it a pouter-pigeon woman who cooed that she was Matron and would handle everything from here. In one practiced move she whisked Simon out of the car and turned to Ellie, pumping her hand as she assured her that the little chap would be fine, fine ... best keep these partings short and sweet...not to worry about a touch of homesickness...keep 'em busy was her motto...always the answer...they got over it—

Ellie almost had to knock her down to open the car door and struggle out just as Simon called: "Don't worry, Mummy, I won't get homesick," giving Ellie that piercingly sweet smile that ripped her heart in two.

"No kiss for Mummy?"

Ignoring Matron's exasperated sigh, Ellie opened her arms and Simon ran back to be kissed. Willingly? She couldn't tell until he suddenly threw his arms around her, smothering her in little boy smells of wool jersey and clean hair and the faint tang of pepper sauce in which he swamped his breakfast sausages.

"I'll like it, Mummy, really I will," he whispered.

"I know." But I want you to *miss* us too, her heart cried, why don't you say you'll miss us, miss home... "I'll be here for you on Friday."

But Matron was right. It didn't do...and Simon was running up the steps, turning, giving her a wave and a last wide smile as he disappeared, a tiny figure maneuvering the big suitcase through tall polished doors.

She turned the car toward the long hundred miles home.

Greenlings drowsed in midmorning quiet, Mary Beth at a museum with Jenny, Felix at the office, Lily Finn grocery shopping in town, Michael hunting Rom dragons in the seedier suburbs of Sacramento.

Would she have married him if she'd known, she asked herself over and over as she ground coffee beans and brewed, pretending to herself that she enjoyed the aroma when all the time she listened to the terrible silence from upstairs, from that empty room with carousel wallpaper and a green wing chair full of teddy bears, pretending she was giving herself a small break before climbing the stairs and making his bed.

Would she have married Michael if she'd known the depth of his hatred for the Rom, his fear of their hold on him? This unswerving resolve to build, shore up, hold all against the tide, somehow to escape his past by rooting his present (and theirs) in Greenlings, into stereotypes of landed gentry. Not that he cared about the gentry part except for the children, but land yes. He cared very much about that. Property. Normal enough, surely. She'd wanted it for herself once, when Grossmutter owned everything she touched and wore, when she was beholden for every crumb she ate, for the comb that smoothed her hair and the water that washed her body. Had that been obsession? To own? She thought not. Was Michael's?—or was it just honest ambition that his children should have the good, the easy life he'd been denied?

Whatever it was, would it have made a difference if she'd known before? How could it? How much resistance did a woman have when she wanted a man, one specific man?

Just thinking about it she wanted him again, that sharp swift melting at the memory of his hands on her. Oh, the treachery of sex, throwing love dust in your eyes, blinding you with shooting stars and spinning planets and symphonies—no wonder you didn't hear the slave bracelet click into place. Then the dust clears and what's under it but real love after all because by that time it's too late. There is still the wanting, but now there's caring too. *One* must be happy before the *other* could be happy, round and round it went, a perpetual catherine wheel, no end in sight. So the answer, of course, was yes, she'd have married him if he'd been Attila the Hun. But she loved him now because he was Michael.

But he wasn't here and she could no longer avoid climbing the stairs . . .
Simon's room.
Dim.
Green velvet curtains still drawn.

Unlike Jenny, Ellie liked to come here, though she usually entered with caution; until yesterday's determined clean-out of perishables, there'd always been life here, unexpected life. Minnows in a jar on the windowsill, tadpoles sprouting legs in the washbowl, a moth at some mysterious stage of metamorphosis. Sometimes unwelcome life, a mouse in a chocolate box, a beetle in an aspirin bottle, once a huge yellow toad in a shoebox. All gone now, nothing waiting for her but this empty room and a nagging guilt that he was too young to leave it, much too young . . .

This room was his refuge from Mary Beth's lessons, Michael's dogged attempts to get him to ride or walk with him; more than any other, this had been Simon's place; it couldn't ever be again, not in the same way. No more creatures, welcome or no.

She paused at the door like a sleepwalker, feeling somehow the presence of green-tinted ghosts—then telling herself not to be silly, he'd only be away weekdays. Her shoe touched small slippers hurriedly kicked off; in the corner of the bed his blue pajamas with red trains tugged at her heart.

Tonight his place would be a narrow cot in a row of other cots, one small corner of a dormitory. Next to him maybe bigger boys, boys who'd snigger if he cried a bit under the covers this first night away. She touched the pillow, cold now but still hollowed from his head; she held his pajamas to her cheek for a moment, smelling talc and all his squirmy little-boyness before she wadded them up, tossed them hurriedly into the laundry hamper for Lily Finn.

Then she froze.

Disbelief.

Anger pouring over her in a scalding tide.

How *dare* she?

Anna Abramsky sat in the green wing chair by the window, her back to the light.

She'd been watching. All this time Ellie thought she'd been alone Anna was spying on her...

How dare she come here?

Despite free access between both sides of the house, by custom neither family entered the other's wing uninvited. A rule even the children observed.

"Already you miss *bébé,* yes?"

Ellie barely heard. She felt exposed, naked... imagine, to be caught standing here touching the pillow, pressing his pajamas to her face, and all the time this... *creature*... watching, storing it all up, laughing to herself, would laugh all over again as she worked at that idiotic barre.

"I too," Anna went on. "The boy does not like me, does not like discipline, but I also will miss Mischa's son." She didn't *sound* amused, not yet. "It is hard to lose *bébé,* very hard."

She wanted to answer, with dignity, that she had not given hers away—but wasn't that exactly what she had done, if only by the week? To a starched apron and a cheerless dormitory? And there was that treacherous lump filling her throat so the words couldn't get past anyway.

The shadowed head nodded, its features all enigma. "This morning I remember Sasha. You only think of that other *bébé,* yes? The girl. I do not think of her, I did not know her—but I never forget my Sasha. When he died, he died very bad. For years I see his poor smashed face under my eyelids like he is printed there... but then Mischa came, took his place, so maybe life balances the scale, yes? And you still have Jennifer."

Dimly she saw that Anna was trying to comfort her and as usual overdramatizing. "Simon's only away at school, he'll be home every Friday."

"Yes." Anna went on, relentless, "You have Jenny, she will give you no trouble... but poor Simon, pulled so many ways. Like Mischa—when he came to us he was not the Mischa you married, oh no, Gabriella! You remember Tomo?"

Who could forget? And Ellie didn't remind her that she'd married Michael, not Mischa. It seemed petty even to think it.

Anna gave her short, sharp laugh. "This Tomo is a saint compared with the small Mischa. But you see? From me discipline, from Felix love—and *voilà!* Now he is perfect—"

Ellie laughed in spite of herself. "I am not complaining—but Michael is hardly perfect."

Between them a long silence, broken only by a rhythmic plop of icicles melting in the sun, slow diamonds dropping one after another from black winter branches to a green cypress hedge, absorbed then into the rich brown loam beneath, gratefully gathered up by roots and weeds and next season's flowers.

The silhouette in the chair stirred, stood, turned to the greenish winter light, and Ellie saw an unaccustomed curve to the straight mouth, a trace of dried tears on the cheeks.

"The perfect child has never been born," she said, "but Mischa was good for me." A long pause as Sasha's mother battled Mischa's inside the gray head. Ellie's mother seemed not to be in there at all, but then, had she ever? But the concession came at last; from Anna it was a remarkably generous one: "I shall tell you, Gabriella. You are making good wife for Mischa. You understand him. The ballet girls did not, I never knew why. Many things Anna does not know..."

Now she would go. The point of this extraordinary visit, as yet incomprehensible to Ellie, had somehow satisfied Anna. She drifted to the door with angular grace, to pause theatrically on the threshold as she issued some suitable curtain line.

Before she could deliver it the front door slammed. Lily Finn's cuban heels skittered across the hall. Grocery sacks rustled and thumped. A voice like a laser cut through solid stone walls and several thicknesses of Axminster carpet:

It's a long way to Tipperareeeee, it's a long way to go.

Anna's tapered hands flew to her ears. "Not far enough, not far enough!" She swept down the hall to her studio; soon the crashing chords of Beethoven's Fifth locked horns with Lily Finn's tortured soprano.

Ellie flung open the curtains and gathered up the laundry. Greenlings was back to normal. And Simon would be home Friday.

* * *

When Anna and Jenny disappeared into the studio for the evening barre and Mary Beth took off on a date, Ellie was not surprised that Felix came to join her in a cocktail. Anna had of course reported her morning visit, and any conversation held with her daughter seemed inevitably to require a translation from Felix.

"She is trying, Ellie," he said. "She knew you would be saddened today, leaving Simon—"

"He's at school. We haven't abandoned him."

He let it pass. "But you are sad? Uneasy for him?"

She nodded, wondering if he slept yet, or did he lie awake crying quietly into unfamiliar blankets because his own were a hundred miles away?

Felix sighed. "Ah, children . . . we expect so much happiness from them, they bring so much pain."

"Pain? Jenny's no trouble, never was!"

His white hands fluttered, Jenny's perfection accepted—with reservations. "One never knows."

Perhaps. A little girl's eager smile, the desire to please, the willing offer of a rose velvet cheek to kiss—didn't every submissive trait carry within it the seed of the born drudge? Ellie imagined her with a tyrannical teacher, later a demanding husband. Yes I will. Only if you say I can. Yes, darling. I've warmed your slippers, dearest. No, one never knew.

Felix filled her glass, kept up his soft patter. "Simon is different as Mischa was different. But enjoy him. You worry, you do not enjoy enough, such a good boy." He sipped slowly at his drink. "I hope Anna said nothing to hurt? Sometimes she is wanting in tact."

"She waylaid me in Simon's room, performed another variation on the insignificance of her daughter Gabriella—of whom we both speak as if she is not present—then a hymn to the wonders of Mischa and the terrible tragedy of Sasha." She closed her eyes. Sasha had been Felix's child, too. *Now* who was "wanting in tact"? "I'm sorry, Felix. Anna's many losses grow a little old, a little more . . . orchestrated in the telling."

"But of course. The calluses grow thicker, protecting a wound she doesn't know is healed. What do you want from her?"

Ellie stared into the fire. Abramskys. Except that they'd given her Michael she often grew weary of them, even Felix. What *did* she want from Anna? "A show of remorse might help."

"You will not get it, my dear. You lived and Sasha died."

"She could have had me. Instead she hates—"

"She is sick, she hurts." He tapped his temple. "A river must find a course. If your father had lived her hate would have flowed to him. Instead it found you. Once I thought she was all courage and pride—I know, I know, I speak of this before, but how could you know..."

He stopped, seemed to look beyond her. "Now she is all fear, my Anna, afraid to love. Suppose she gives it again and one day the child is blown away? You cannot relive her years, Ellie. How can you judge her pain? Now she lives through little Jenny and is terrified every moment that she will lose her."

"We are not at war, Felix. She spends her *life* with Jenny!"

"A privilege you can withdraw at any moment." He took a reflective sip and rubbed his hip. "Jenny is her whole life; you can take it away with a word. If tomorrow you say 'no more ballet for Jenny,' then Anna is finished. So again she lives from day to day, again von Reikers punish her."

The thread of his logic escaped her, but did it matter? Unwittingly he'd given her a weapon against Anna, one she would have used without hesitation years ago. Now her nerves jumped and quivered with immediate worries. Simon at school. Michael hunting Rose in California. Was Felix pointing out that even hate loses its heat if left unfueled? Who knew? He talked in circles and tonight even *his* words carried a sting.

"Punish? I was von Reiker, I don't punish her—neither do I believe my father did what she says." If they just wouldn't brood on old hurts. "I didn't know him, Felix. You did. But you have never told me about him—the real man, not the monster in Anna's head."

"But you have not asked," he said gently. "He was not even a man, he was boy, an innocent boy with old-fashioned ideas of honor—why else offer money for Anna to divorce me, marry him, make you legitimate? He was the conqueror—he had only to give the word, I would have been dead in a moment. His parents had influence, no need for him to go to the front. Guilt sent him to Russia and guilt shot him."

"An old-fashioned man wouldn't rape."

"Can you be sure? Think. A world such as ours, all sequins and sweat, we grew up so fast, then the war comes, everything is faster still. In comes young Hans. He is raw, without a shell. He sees Anna—she was a sun then, Ellie, and he is blinded by the light. Still hurting from Sasha, luminous with grief, with anger, she must hurt back. He wears the uniform. Even her scorn is a challenge, it beckons and tantalizes. One night he drinks too much. A moment—poof!—and all our lives are changed. But you must not believe, as Anna believes, that you sprang from hatred. Hans von Reiker loved his ballerina."

Perhaps.

But Felix was bending over her, lifting her hand to his lips. "I have wished many times that you were my child, but I'm sorry, you are his. I think he would be very proud."

Oh this dear, this good man—too good for Anna. Who could believe her theatrics—but who could doubt Felix? He never lied, even when his truths cut deep into cherished beliefs.

THIRTY

ICHAEL HEADED OFF HIGHWAY 101 and pointed the car's nose at 80, at Sacramento, at trouble he couldn't wait to settle.

Once clear of the Bay Area he floored the pedal and shot through traffic, grimly determined to find the *kumpania*, sound a wake-up call to Dui's dim wits, give Rose an ultimatum she'd remember beyond the next *pomana*, then maybe, just maybe, he could do some business this trip. There was a mall partnership to consider in Santa Clara and an appealing corner of river property in Oregon that harbored possibilities more lucrative than pine trees.

Abramo Three was doing less well than they'd hoped despite a prestigious award for design, enthusiasm within the trade, and enough advertising to sell snowplows in the Sahara. He'd called a sales meeting in San Francisco for tomorrow to try to pump up the force, but prospects were dim. A steady influx of competitors into the high-tech market already posed a threat to all but the giants; he congratulated himself for having foreseen it, investing in California land as well as in the Silicon Valley plant. He didn't plan on hanging on to the plant much longer either, despite pie-in-sky analysts predicting it could only go up-up-up. The Three might very well be last in the series. Abramo Investment had done better in one year than Abramo Electric had since its inception. "But!" Felix reminded him daily, "without the small capital from the shops, what would we have to invest?" True enough.

The Lincoln cruised smoothly forward and he tried to sit easy, enjoy the ride. At Greenlings this car would have been pretentious; here it was perfect. It matched the country. Big, new, brash. Rich and not apologizing for it, a great black cat purring through acre on acre of rice, green beans, lettuce, and tomatoes. Miles of fruit orchards in bloom, nut trees —it should have been an Anna Abramsky paradise but for some reason she, alone among the family, disliked the country intensely. She'd finally been once and vowed never to return, proclaiming her opinion like the holy writ and sticking to it. "The only country in the world where eating and shopping are prime entertainments. Television is to kill time, nobody buys books, and the young are too fat. *They have superb dancers and pay them like scrubwomen!*" The final indictment. For Anna, it closed the case. Silly old bird, Michael thought indulgently. All bones and prejudice, no logic at all. But endearing. If only Dui and his brood were half as independent, one-tenth as industrious.

Damn, but would he ever get Dui out of his hair? This latest stunt was the limit, no address, no phone number, all that Sacramento sprawl to hunt through. Where to begin? For sure the location would be low-rent and fairly close to the old place, whose phone prefix he remembered. He'd start in the approximate area; after that it was a matter of reading the scenery for signs of the Rom.

There'd be late-model cars, somewhat beat-up—Welfare didn't encourage its clients to buy new; they were not supposed to have the money.

There'd be trailer parks lined with luxury trailers, the insides of which would be immaculate. Outside, not a flower or blade of grass in sight— the Rom weren't much for gardening; they grew transmissions and old batteries instead, a few dented car bodies, hub caps, rusted pickups.

Near each trailer park's entrance a couple of men loafing, lazy as a summer Sunday, chain-smoking as they talked, cigarettes drooping, black eyes squinting through smoke; trailer curtains twitching at a strange car's arrival; a few lurchers prowling the shadows, lean and gray and ready to growl. What was that in the Bible about a rich man's chance of entering the Kingdom of Heaven? Like trying to thread a camel through the eye of a needle? Close enough. A *gajo* stranger had about the same chance of slipping undetected into a Gypsy compound.

You were on trial before you opened a car door, questions hitting you from both sides as you rolled down windows.

Who do you want to see?

On what business?

Who told you he'd be here?

A crowd begins to form, spectators more or less, but dark faces seem to close in on you. Who are you looking for again? Oh, him! And *your* name again? Shoulders twitch, shrug. Oh, too bad, the man you're asking for went to Vancouver—or was it San Diego or Portland?—a few weeks back. The spokesman turns to the crowd. Isn't that so? They nod and smile but press in tighter until you can smell the oil on their clothes and the garlic-and-pepper sweat of their bodies.

By then all the males are there. Maybe Michael will be recognized, maybe not—*kumpanias* are elastic, people come and go for many reasons, usually to do with the law. Eventually somebody remembers him; maybe Grandmam's opulent *pomana*. Aha! Michael the Generous! Transformation! Arms spread; tight brown faces open into wide white smiles. Somehow, locked car doors spring open and in a second the car is filled with laughing Gypsies wanting to touch, to embrace the brother of their Rom Baro. Outside, a crowd of children gather, small hands stroke hood ornament and headlights, dark eyes look with envy at leather seats and the phone in the dash. Somebody goes to dig Dui out of a bar; as they wait a bottle appears, toasts are offered...

That's almost how it was, right up to the time he was recognized and officially welcomed. Then one man shuffled his feet in the dust, another shook his head.

Sorry, Micah. Dui had a spot of trouble. You'd best see his wife, she'll tell you...

She could hardly wait.

Dui had been in jail for a month, since right after Micah called him about...you know, Simon talking to Tomo? Another month more before they'd let him out...drunk driving and they couldn't come up with bail money this time. Of course Dui called Greenlings, only wanted a hundred or so, but that Lily Finn wouldn't even take the call, said she wasn't allowed to take no collect calls no more.

Her tone put Michael on trial, prosecuted him and convicted him for Dui's predicament—but then she caught herself up, clearly remembering that all might not be lost. "Anyway, now you're here you'll maybe go talk

to the family's social worker, you'll know what to say, put in a good word
for Dui—"

"I have to leave tonight, sorry."

Another sigh. "So I'll make tea anyway, that's still cheap enough, thank
God."

Tomo was out working. His mother didn't say at what. Their daughter
was there, younger than Simon but looking older, peeling potatoes at the
sink.

As she talked, Dui's wife cut out paper flowers, arranged them in a box.
"Nobody wants 'em no more but it gets you talking, if you push you gets
in the houses, then maybe you can *dukker* if you find a mark. Can't set up
storefronts no more, the cops are on you like lightning. Don't want you
making an honest living—"

Oh, what the hell did it matter to him, the ups and downs of fortune-
telling as a living, honest or not?—though he was well aware that a
Gypsy woman's bride-price was determined in large part by her skill at
manipulating the chosen mark.

"Where's Rose?" he interrupted.

She frowned, gave a green wire stem a vicious twist before jamming it
onto orange Day Glo paper. "Nursing home a few blocks over, Great
Western somethin', who knows—I got plenty to see to here, scratchin' a
living for us." The next baby already bulged her apron; all about her the
smell of seldom-washed linens and dying hopes nourished by poisoned,
idle dreams.

"Then who sent the telegram?"

"Not me, where'd I get the money?" Dui's wife (surely she'd been the
mildest of women?) shot him a look dripping with the acid of a brand-
new hatred. "If it asked for money for Rose's hospital bill the new Rom
Baro must have sent it."

"Then Dui's not..."

"Dui's not nothing no more. Who wants a Rom Baro that's in and out
of the pen every few weeks? The families had a meetin', said what the hell,
let somebody else have a go at it, but what I want to know is, how'm I
going to feed my little 'uns with no man bringing in? *My* family look after
their own, not like you lot. Dui never even got his grandmam's ruby like
he should've."

Michael didn't answer and he didn't say he'd help. It was in any case
the Gypsy *woman* who earned food for the table. A Rom bought a wife,
she fed him forever. A *gajo* chose one and worked for her until the day he

died. If Dui's wife was bound and determined to stay Rom she'd have to live the part. And she had Tomo; at twelve he was surely old enough to turn a dishonest dollar.

"Where's the new Rom Baro's trailer?"

"Big cream job in the corner, but they'll not be back before midnight."

Her farewell smile harbored the bitterness of the born shrew and he turned away, happier than ever that he was not Dui, not Rom, and that Ellie, clean and cool and elegant, waited at Greenlings.

But gratitude brought guilt which stuck with him like a wad of old gum under his shoe. Was not Dui Grandmam's kin too, Ma's firstborn? But you don't even remember Ma, he reminded himself. You owe them nothing. Except for Rose, even if Ellie didn't insist—and she did. "The rest of them, no," she'd murmured, "but somebody has to be responsible for Rose, never a home to call her own... imagine growing up with nobody *wanting* her!" Because of her own childhood Ellie imagined she understood Rose very well indeed, but Ellie had never liked Grandmam, never believed that if there'd been a single redeemable facet in Rose, then Grandmam would have found it and polished it.

No, this was definitely the bail-out. All he had to do was find Rose and get back to San Francisco for tomorrow's meeting.

The new Rom Baro's trailer was indeed shuttered and quiet, but it demonstrated in perfect proportion the power and wealth the leader of a *kumpania* enjoyed, compared to the rank and file. Occupying three times the space of the others, it was surrounded by a portable picket fence on all sides. Inside the fence a Saluki posed in silky silence at the door of an immaculate doghouse. Flower borders of blue larkspur and red poppies rioted (but neatly, in serried regiments of ten) with Shasta daisies and yellow tulips. The Saluki was real, the flowers plastic—in the world of the Rom everything must be instantly portable.

The trailer was the richest in the compound, cream enamel polished to a high gloss; tinted windows draped in peacock blue velvet shut out the blazing Sacramento noon. Gleaming aluminum steps climbed to a door whose honeycomb bronze knob formed the center of a painted sunflower. And yes, Dui's wife was right. Nobody was home.

Michael, who'd tracked Rose down to several such places, could have described the Great Western Convalescent Home blindfold. Sometimes he got there before she escaped, sometimes not. With this one he needn't have worried. It was run like a penitentiary. There were three escape routes: a lonely, lingering death; a journey to a state-approved facility for the insane or indigent; a solvent relative to settle the bill.

Paint flakes as dry as old skin peeled onto a cracked and littered sidewalk. The lobby reeked of stale smoke and urine, and from the kitchen a powerful combination of boiled cod, onion, and institution hash penetrated down a long hall to where a receptionist kept one eye on the door and another on "Days of Our Lives."

Michael pressed on, the routine familiar.

Down the hall to Admissions.

A woman with laser eyes set aside the *Enquirer* to appraise Michael's clothes, car, perhaps the label in his suit. Middle-aged, middle-weight, trying desperately to be middle class, *some* class as she looked up the name of Rose's next of kin. Who but Michael Abramsky? Another man, name of Dui?—he'd admitted the patient weeks before—emergency basis, of course—and promised on his honor to come back with a social worker to take care of paperwork. They'd never seen him since. Some people!

Her voice dropped, one of the cognoscenti to another: Michael *did* know these people were Gypsies? Couldn't read or write? Her thin lips curled, lips from which magenta lip gloss radiated. Bills piling up so what could they do but call somebody higher up in the . . . what was it? *Tribe?*

He nodded, neck muscles tightening under a designer label even she would recognize. *You* despise the Rom, lady? You? They don't learn to read because they don't need to, they can read you and your kind quicker than you can read SEX SECRETS OF THE STARS! on page one of the *Enquirer.* You've never owned the roof you live under, perhaps not even the bed you sleep on, in ten years never *quite* paid off your Visa, never seen Madrid, Rome, Athens, never dreamed of such places, never watched the sun plunge into the South China Sea—yet even *you* feel superior to the Rom. He wanted to smash in her simpering, powdered face and shout that she was not, was not—but then there was Dui and Tomo and Da, so perhaps she was superior to some of them after all . . .

Oh, why bother, get Rose's condition, pay her bill, and get the hell out.

Her doctor was at lunch, would be for an hour. Michael said tightly that he wanted to see the director, who could maybe explain diagnosis, prognosis, and what seemed to be a discrepancy in the records? She paled slightly under sunglow blush, whispered into the phone, and led him into a small room in which a tiny old woman sat behind a large, battered desk.

"I'm looking for the director," he said, acidly patient.

"You've found her."

"My sister." He threw the records across the desk. "What's her condition?"

She marked off symptoms on her fingers. "Ah, Rose. In 202. Emphysema, malnutrition, depression, cultural deprivation. And she's incurably, terminally bored. That enough for openers?"

"I'm trying to help her."

"Some conditions are helpless. Sorry." She wheeled herself beyond him and for the first time he saw she was paraplegic. At the door she paused. "If you want to discharge her, Payables is on the right as you go; if she's to stay it's in the same place—we're not a charity; if you'd just as soon duck the whole thing the back door's in back, where else? Which means Rose will leave through the front door. By ambulance. To County. Tomorrow. After that...sorry." She threw up her hands, gave him a savage monkey grin, and rolled herself out on silent rubber legs.

Room 202 was an oven, Rose a scrawny brown hen steaming on a sill whose window was barred and braced; outside, a meshed screen was equally fortified. Both locked. They took no chances here.

A small bed and table ostensibly furnished the room, but dense smoke from Rose's cigarette and the ominous rattle of her breathing filled it to the rafters, impossible to ignore, weary bellows pumping recycled air through an overburdened system.

"Well, if it isn't our Micah come to put the family skeleton back in its closet! Switzerland again?"

"No, I've had enough."

"You better get me outa this place before I go round the bleedin' bend."

"That's up to you. Are you supposed to be smoking?"

"Who cares? Two months I've been in this rotten prison—"

"Dui's in a real prison. He can't help you now, can't even take care of his own."

"His own? What am *I*, then?"

Lord, if she'd just ease up on the self-pity, make *some* effort. Twenty-four years old and more helpless than Jenny—

"You start by getting rid of this." He mashed her cigarette into a chipped saucer serving as ashtray. "Then you'll listen to what I have to say because I came seven thousand miles to say it. First: I've got you a trailer. Again. Nothing fancy. Sturdy, weatherproof—and the last you'll get from me; it's in my name so neither you nor anybody else can sell it; a maintenance contract comes with it."

He paused. Perhaps she might want to thank him? Apparently not. She glared sullenly at her wasted cigarette.

"The director tells me you came here undernourished. I've sent Dui a monthly check for your food for six years, Rose. In future it goes straight into this account. I opened it an hour ago. It's yours. The bank knows about you, they'll give you grocery money every week. What you do with it is your business. When it's gone it's gone."

"I'm not goin' in no bleedin' bank! I can't write my name!"

"If you want money you'll learn. You're not stupid like Dui. You're bright but you're lazy. You have health insurance but you wait until you're at death's door before going to a doctor. In future you'll see the one near the trailer park. Twice a month, no excuses. He'll report directly to me."

"I don't want no doctors tellin' me what to do, there's a free clinic—"

"You need care, not the welfare variety. It's your last chance. If you mess up again I'll put you back here or take you home with me, board you out with Lily Finn in the village—"

"The screamer? Not fuckin' likely, I'm not livin' in no house with *her*—"

"Then you'll do as you're told. I'll take care of the bill, you pack your stuff. Be ready when I get back—"

"I don't got no 'stuff.'"

"Just as well, we'll go shopping this morning, get your hair done, find some new clothes—"

"Ashamed to be seen with me, are you?"

"Don't be silly." But she was right. He didn't even want her in his car. And what man would want to walk the city with this scowling bundle of rags? With Grandmam he hadn't cared; she was a Gypsy, she looked like one, and he loved her. Rose looked and smelled like a skid-row bum. How long since she'd combed her hair? "Don't be silly," he said again.

"You sound just like *her*."

"Like who?"

For the first time Rose smiled.

Furtive. With an underlayer of triumph.

"The new Rom Baro what sent the telegram. She said it'd bring you running."

"*She?*"

Rose, showing the first sign of youth he'd seen since he arrived, giggled behind her hand, the gesture typical of a consumptive child told repeatedly to cover her mouth, not to breathe on people. The giggle became a throat-clearing, then a full-fledged hacking cough through which she couldn't speak at all for several minutes. When she could, Michael asked again:

"She?"

"You got it, our Micah! *She!* Surprised, huh?"

Shaking his head, weary of denials that meant nothing, that wouldn't have fooled young Micah let alone Michael Abramsky, he closed his eyes and turned away, such excitement rising in him that he felt, for a moment, as if hot dark blood pumped out of his veins and shot across this seedy room. No, our Micah wasn't surprised. He wished to God he had been.

Subconsciously, under layers of *gajo* conditioning, worries of Simon, Ellie's continued contempt for a mother not deserving of it, the foreboding of Anna's dizzy spells, regrets at missing Jenny's recital, his anger with Rose and disgust for Dui, concern over the Three's lackluster sales—under all the niggling doubts in his life, one certainty had lain, warm and secret, gloated over in half-sleep, set aside as too dangerous to examine in daylight. At some deep and tingling level just below knowing he'd felt it, anticipated it, ached for it long before he read the telegram and stepped on the plane.

And he'd come anyway.

"You might find her at her nightclub," Rose said, sly with knowledge. "She calls it the Filigrano."

She would. Flamenco. That grace of raised and rounded arms, knowing hands that twisted and stroked the air, the spirit, the past, hands that warmed the flesh and stirred the blood, evoked memories and a future from which there was no escape.

Oh Ellie, my beautiful innocent Ellie whom I love, whom I must protect from every blow, even those I deliver myself...

Gypsy music throbbed, spilled to the sidewalk, beckoning, enticing, a timeless stream of joy and despair, a respite from countless journeys that knew no end.

Inside, fires smoked and barefoot girls swayed between tables with trays aloft, their bracelets a soft gold jingle under the throb of guitars and the strident jangle of coins and rustle of paper money changing hands quickly, smoothly, in the light of red and amber candles. Mustachioed men in cummerbunds and kerchiefs smiled and nodded and tended bar, some hovering close by the door to watch, to listen. Bouncers. Open-handed tourists already drunk guzzled happily at watered drinks which arrived in rapid, bewildering succession; sober newcomers like Michael who lacked the innocent stamp of "sucker" were made to wait for service a long time in the semidark as closing time approached.

Finally his fingers grasped a passing wrist.

"There's a floor show?"

"Last one starts any minute."

He ordered wine and settled himself to wait.

A nightclub. Why would she start a business so alien to the Gypsy life-style? Auto body work, driveways, roofing for the men; for the Gypsy woman, begging and fortune-telling, her stock-in-trade a convincing patter, a card table, a glass ball, a pack of cards—all easily portable if the cops should patrol out front. But a nightclub? A Gypsy going legit?

Drumroll.

Houselights down.

First a juggler in tight pants and frilly sleeves, one earring and an uncertain routine; after him a fan dancer fanned, a knife thrower threw, a baton twirler twirled, tumblers tumbled, each act better than its predecessor. The tumblers, Zandar's Hungarian Flyers—who called each other Debbie and Linda and Ken and Dwayne in accents far removed from Budapest—turned out to be excellent gymnasts who more than earned their encore. Then houselights came up briefly for a garbled announcement: . . . straight from . . . Barcelona . . . Madrid . . .

La Rubi!

She was there.

Her glance flicked over him once, no more.

Flame-colored silk tight to the knee, exploding then into swirls and flounces shading to crimson, scarlet, burgundy . . . shiny black shoes and silver buckles twinkling in the ratatatat of *zapateado* and light from a hundred candles. Blue-black hair pulled into the classic coil. Her eyes were caverns of despair, darkness, then ablaze with reflected light and a hint of anger barely controlled; hands weaving and twisting, body swaying, now a sapling, now a cobra. And such a body. Perfect for the dance.

Farah.

Farah giving a bravura performance—a magnificent rip-off for an audience on its feet cheering, too ignorant to know it had been taken. She'd given them the main components of a classic, revered art. The highly arched back, the pride and line and passion of flamenco in all its variations. Its essential mood, subterranean rivers restless underground, volcanoes that glow and smolder, craters slowly turning red. She knew the art and she'd given them that. Missing were the exhausting steps of the *far-*

ruca and the sustained, kidney-bruising stomp that could drive a Spanish audience to ecstacy and the artiste to the grave.

There was no encore from Farah.

The audience shouted, thumped tables, whistled, but when the lights dimmed again it was not for her, but for a magician in black with white doves sitting on his shoulder.

At Michael's elbow a waiter whispered, ushered him to a dark red booth lit by an amber candle.

"Wait."

Then she was there, flame silk and the scent of honeysuckle intolerably close as she leaned across him to pinch out the candle. Before the light died he saw that her performance hadn't even worked up a sweat.

"Micah."

Her voice was warm and husky, then peremptory as she snapped fingers for a waiter. "A bottle from my office, not this slop from under the bar." She settled back and regarded him through the gloom. "So the lady-wife let you off the leash."

When he didn't answer she smiled, her teeth very white against dark stage makeup and darker hair. "How's Rose? Did you spring her?"

"You didn't give me much choice. New trailer, wardrobe, hairdo—it should hold her for a bit."

Her glance shifted to the door, then back again to Michael. "Our Micah, the easy mark."

He ignored it, she knew better. "I hear you're Rom Baro."

"Sure—didn't I say I would be, at Grandmam's funeral?"

"Then you have to take care of the families. Rose is your own *vista,* your first responsibility. She has insurance, you could have got her out or else called me—"

"But then you wouldn't have come... Besides, just suppose your wife answered? I thought you wouldn't like that."

Her fingers brushed lightly, warmly at the back of his hand and he tried to pull away but his hand didn't want to move. "So you got Dui's title. What are you going to do with it?"

"Get the families out of the system." She withdrew her hand and poured wine before going on, nodding to herself as she spoke.

Years ago, when they'd fed off the *gaje,* used them like milch cows for sustenance, the Rom had prospered, thousands of years they'd prospered —just studying the *gajo* until they knew his every thought, could predict his every move; the *gajo* knowing nothing about Gypsies except myths he spawned himself. In fear. A good balance. It kept the Rom sharp, the *gajo* in his place. But now there were leaders like Dui taking the easy way, living off the *gajo* system instead of off the *gaje*—and what a system gives it can take away. Welfare, social security, pension, aid to dependents—tags made no difference, it was the Rom who were dependent now. The system kept records. If they knew all your names and where to find you, they'd got you. In the *kumpania* one woman collected benefits in each of five names in three different counties. She thought herself brilliant. She sat home watching television all day, getting fat and forgetting her trade.

"Which is?" he said. "They can't *all* do flamenco, even that penny-ante version you passed off tonight."

She nodded. "I figured you'd notice. I'll stop altogether when I get this club off the ground, get clients regular so our women can get back to what they know. Fortune-telling's pretty much illegal here, which Dui should have found out before he brought everybody over. You need a front to make a living at it. Noticed people wandering out back? They have 'appointments.' Consultations. To be told exactly what they want to hear. For a frustrated woman, a tall dark stranger is on the horizon; for the poor, an unexpected legacy; for the vindictive, bad luck to their enemies. They listen, love every word, and pay . . . Why not? It keeps 'em going . . . what could be fairer than that?" She sat very straight, certain in her convictions.

Then why did she constantly glance at the door? "Who are you watching for?" he said lightly. "Cops?" Sharply aware of his own tension. Maybe she waited for her own tall stranger.

She sighed. "My mother. To you I'm a grown woman, know my way around the world, right? To the *kumpania* I'm Rom Baro. To Feya I'm Mom. But to my mother I'm fourteen and still a virgin. She lives in the next trailer, shops for me, looks after Feya, my interests, things like that." She suddenly grinned, and she wasn't even fourteen, she was five again, cocky, a finger on every pulse. "She called me this morning not five minutes after you left camp, told me what you'd come for, what you said to Dui's wife, what Dui's wife said to you, when you were leaving town and where you were going. So there! Can the CIA do better? After work she comes to get me—because wolf packs prowl the streets just slavering after her daughter's lovely damaged little bod." She laughed. "It's not so bad. She travels. Weddings—she's off to Alberta tomorrow—funerals, feasts, so I get my breaks. My mother's all right."

He didn't ask why she put up with it. She was Gypsy. Family was all. But what else had she said at Grandmam's funeral?

"You told me you could live with the families or not, that you stayed only when it suited you."

"Things change," she said steadily. "Like I said then, who'd watch over Feya better than my mother? Besides, I can't pound myself to mincemeat on stage anymore—"

Fear had him by the collar, shook him. "It's not—"

"Not—but it was iffy. My mother saw the signs so she's not what she seems, she got me off the road in time." She brushed her hands together, shaking off a career and a near miss with the darkest stranger of all. "No more kids, even if I wanted to get married again, which I don't. Marriage is the pits."

"Not with the right person."

"And her?" she whispered. "Is *she* the right person?"

He hesitated only a millisecond.

"Yes."

Their eyes met in the dim light of the booth. He licked suddenly dry lips and noticed that she was doing the same, her tongue sharp and pointed and infinitely threatening. Her voice wasn't quite steady when she said:

"So if I asked you, next time you're coming, to maybe call your second cousin...spend time with her like you used to, like your da promised when we were little—"

It seemed to Michael that the air between them quivered, melted away, and there were only dark eyes and hands touching his, warmly familiar. When she spoke again he could feel her breath soft on his cheek, bringing back bluebell woods and spring mornings in the north, summer cherry picking in the south, ripe red fruits she hung over her ears, laughing at him. "See my new earrings what the Gypsy king gave me?" They always laughed about the Gypsy king, knowing he didn't exist. Unlike the *gaje*, who believed whatever you told 'em. But Farah and Micah were better than them, they were Rom, they were *chosen*.

"*Would you come if I asked?*" she whispered.

THIRTY-ONE

"My LOVE, WE MUST TALK."

They lay in the great feather bed with their rum and tea and nightly confidences to share. It was easier, Felix had found, to speak of difficult subjects in that brief time after she'd had her tea, worked through the last of her exercises, and said her perfunctory prayers. A lifelong agnostic, she nevertheless went through the motions of faith much as she'd made *révérences* to the ballet mistress in all her years of training.

"I listen..." One yawn, then another.

Drowsy already, so at least she had taken her medicine; it was perhaps safe to speak. "The young Jenny."

"Yes?" The voice sharpened slightly.

"We know, my darling, that soon she must change..."

"No! She is baby still, much too soon to work *en pointe!*"

"You know that's not it. She is too long with one teacher. It is bad. How will she find her own style until she sees many—"

She sighed, almost moaned. "I know, I know, I think and I think, but oh Felix, I hate to give her so young to a stranger. First I thought that Harriet here in town, but no, she produces girls fit only for the chorus ...then I hear Malowa up in Leeds is a good technician—but I find out her real name is Twitchett! I ask you, a name like that, how good—"

"My darling, names have nothing—"

"So I decide. Jenny is still too young for the Wells school, but if I take her once a week to Romanovna in London—remember Eugenia from Paris?—she will listen to me, she will not touch the arms, I will not have the arms changed, Jenny has the best—"

Felix stroked her cheek. "Due to you, my angel. Be calm. No one will change the arms. I shall speak to Ellie."

"Why not wait until Mischa is back? In his own home is he nothing, is he—"

"Calm, calm, Anna, remember what the doctor is telling you."

He shook a warning finger in her face, pulled the blanket over her shoulders and shut off the light. When soft snores reverberated between them he slipped on a robe, mixed two whiskey sours, and took them to Ellie, at work on a studio balance sheet in the library.

Driving from studio to studio all day, running this household, reading to the children (now only to Jenny) every night—yet how peaceful she looked, the lamplight turning her hair to gold, the soft welcome in her eyes, the air of tranquillity she wore like a cloak. Impossible to imagine her shouting...perhaps it came from growing up with an old invalid who needed quiet, but it was an attractive trait, like entering a cool church on a hot afternoon. There was a lovely word if he could...oh this English! He had it! Balm...balm to the soul...Michael was a lucky man.

"Anna agrees," he said. "With reservations, but she too had settled on Romanovna and speaks of taking Jenny to London herself—you know it would break her heart not to watch the lessons."

Ellie set down pencil and reading glasses and tipped her head as she smiled—just to let him know she saw through him. "She'll interfere abominably...no self-respecting teacher will work with Jenny under those conditions. Anna herself would not."

"No...but if we could find some way...I would like it if she could not be hurt."

Ellie touched his hand across the desk and he felt, as he often did, that she was a daughter touching him, smoothing the way—not so much for Anna as to spare him worry.

"I thought we'd try this," she said carefully. "London is a long trip,

Anna can't drive, Jenny gets trainsick, and it seems a pity she should lose a whole day of school a week—but with Mary Beth along she could do lessons between dance classes—perhaps Anna may even restrain herself, might not try to dominate a class that Mary Beth is watching?"

Gratitude welled up in him. "I think Mischa married a genius." However, he could not resist adding: "Mary Beth will be good with Anna, she has always liked her." He said it with some reproach. It was a source of real pain to him that Ellie had no more sympathy for Anna now than she'd had in the beginning. True, she showed less hatred, for familiarity had indeed bred contempt—but did not ridicule hurt as much as hatred, or more?

They'd finished their drinks and were poring over London train schedules when Pete Preston brought Mary Beth home. For the second time in a month they'd been to a concert together; both times Michael had been away and Pete brought three tickets, inviting Ellie to go along; both times Felix saw her invent flimsy excuses to stay home; both times he saw Pete Preston's long intelligent face settle into disappointed folds.

Felix saw him nod at what Mary Beth was saying, but his eyes never quite lost track of Ellie as she plumped cushions, put out drinks and coasters, served a tray of tiny sandwiches perfect for an after-theater snack. When she leaned toward him to offer the tray he seemed to tense, his big gangling hands all thumbs...and now he dropped his napkin, blushing to the roots of his pale hair as he fumbled to pick it up—why, he was in love with her! Pete Preston in love with Ellie! Not Mary Beth as they'd suspected and wholeheartedly approved, but Ellie. Oh, the poor man, as if he stood a dog's chance with Mischa around—even if she hadn't been married. And wasn't it the same for Mischa, who'd never looked at another woman since he found Ellie?

A burst of laughter—Mary Beth's—as they discussed the coming summer in L.A. Mischa had promised they were all to go, Mary Beth and the children included—Pete and Mischa would be in San Francisco, close enough to commute by the week.

"The house is *so* easy to run and the beach superb, we'll get splendid tans," Ellie said. Pete looked away, no doubt imagining her in a swimsuit. A thirty-year-old adolescent. "You *must* come and stay with us, Pete, Mary Beth will be there, and the children, and Felix of course..."

So gracious, but *must* she always ignore Anna?

"I think Anna will not go," he heard himself say, "therefore I shall not." Then he spoiled it (he knew he had) by adding, "But I do like the racetrack at Hollywood Park!" The older and frailer he became the more he enjoyed the sight of healthy young bodies in motion. Jenny in an exquisite arabesque, Simon's young limbs shinnying the great oak, glossy brown horses prancing on a green pasture. What he'd give, in old age, for the animal power of a Nureyev, a Villella, the blond calm of a Peter Martins! And what foolish things he thought and said. Hollywood Park indeed!

Worse when Ellie answered with a twinkle in her eye: "You *can't* miss the races, Felix. Anna can stay here and supervise Lily Finn, they'll have a lovely lively summer together."

The others laughed. Oh Ellie, you never miss a chance . . . The one flaw in a truly remarkable woman. But then Pete Preston was leaving, his heart in his eyes, and Felix must show him out. Imagine, this innocent genius in love with Anna's daughter! What a pity, what a great, great pity . . .

Mary Beth said much the same later, but to Ellie, who knew in any case, who'd watched it grow for a year, helpless to stop it and determined not to discuss it. She was sorry about it, but it was Pete's business; if he chose to tell her, then she'd discourage him, but until he did she wouldn't presume—

"*Presume?* Oh, for God's sake, Ellie, the poor soul's dying for you to presume, to say *something* if only to put him out of his misery."

They were in what used to be the nursery, talking over the day just ending, planning the one to come. For Ellie, a restful time. Mary Beth could be trusted absolutely. She gave advice when asked, did not ram it down your throat and jump in after it, she was a friend as well as an employee, and it occurred to Ellie now that Mary Beth was still her only *real* woman friend. All these years, and she had no other friends but Felix and Michael, Pete in a pinch—but that would soon be impossible.

She felt uneasy, restless, many more things on her mind than Pete Preston, who'd no doubt drifted through adolescence and young manhood without so much as touching a girl's hand. He was sweet and likeable and she was sorry his late-blooming attentions had settled on the unreachable, but she turned to Mary Beth.

"I've been gone all day, you're *quite* sure he hasn't called?"

Mary Beth laughed. "He? Now who would that be? With all the men in your life . . . okay—okay—if you mean Simon, why should he call? You may hope he yearns for home and hearth and good old Mum—but he may be happy as Paddy's pig at good old Brimley. You'll get him back tomorrow for the weekend anyway. Sweetie, I think you're hitting the empty-nest syndrome a tad early—"

"Oh, I *am* worried about him, but I meant Michael, he's always called before—"

"Oh great heavens, he left six whole days ago and you're getting *him* back this weekend, too! He's always gone, what's so different this time? Why should he call?"

"I don't know, except he usually does..." Not quite true, sometimes he called the office and had his secretary relay a message, but this time nothing at all, just when she'd thought he'd at least be anxious about Simon's first weeks at school.

"There's something else," Mary Beth said quietly. "Under all that serenity you give off like soft lights and Muzak you've seemed a bit down in the mouth lately. There's nothing wrong between you and Michael?"

Ellie sighed. "Not a thing. But you said it earlier. 'He's always gone.' In the last six months he's spent less than three here at Greenlings."

"You're faulting a man for taking care of his sister?"

"This time it just happened to be Rose and no, I don't mind. But mostly it's business-business-business. He's way beyond his original plans of electronics and nothing else. Now he's into real estate investments, running all over the place to see them, to buy, to oversee, to sell. I thought I'd married a man who wanted three things, a successful business, a home and children—and me!"

"Why put yourself last?"

"Because that's where I seem to *be*."

"He worships you."

"I know that."

"You could go with him, he asks you often enough."

"Yes, but he expects me to be here with the children, too. I can't be in two places at once. And what about the studios?"

"So what about them? He's always bragging about the way you manage them."

"If I went with him often I couldn't manage them at all."

"You're not indispensable. Hell, I could run them! I'm not tied to governessing forever. Jenny can start some kind of school next year, I'd still be here when she got home."

"But I don't *want* to give them up. I've *built* that system. It's mine. Each year's balance sheet tells me I've accomplished something, that I'm not just *kept*, like a jewel in a box."

Mary Beth laughed ruefully. "Do you know how many women would like to be on the horns of your particular dilemma? Me, for instance."

"I know I'm lucky, but sometimes I feel as if I'm losing control of things. Look at Jenny. The last thing I wanted her to be was a dancer—but with Anna egging her on..."

"Jenny *loves* ballet and I think she's going to be damned good. Anna's doing one heck of a job on her, you know."

"I think it's called sublimation," she said dryly.

"Ellie, you're the least bitchy woman I know, but when it comes to Anna you have a blind spot as big as Crater Lake!"

"Oh no you don't! I've had that from Felix already today! And that's something else. I'm tired of having to be civil to her just so's not to hurt Felix—when I'd just as soon never see the woman again. Then there's Simon...oh Mary Beth, I really do think it's dreadful to send him away so young, but he doesn't seem to care about home..."

"He just doesn't show it like Jenny, and you really *are* never satisfied. You have: a great husband; great kids; a friend and factotum who'd just about lay down her life (notice I said 'just about'); even a lovesick swain —and to top it off you're going to be disgustingly, bloatedly rich. Think back twelve years—then tell me you're not the luckiest woman alive."

What could she do but laugh? Of course Mary Beth was right. Twelve years ago her life had been governed by Grossmutter's bell and her screams, by the whispering contempt of the villagers and the precarious state of the bank balance. "Mary Beth wins again! I suppose that means *you're* indispensable even if I'm not."

She felt better when she went to bed, but there was still that niggling little worry that wouldn't be satisfied until all four of them were together again on Saturday.

Simon seemed no worse for his first week at school; since she'd picked him up yesterday he'd talked of little else but the other students, of whom he spoke with an odd mix of awe and arrogance. The Williams boy had given him a new bag of marbles; Bertie Phelps let him wear a gold tiepin that had a diamond in it—imagine lending a *real* diamond!—and next week James Porter said he'd share a box of marzipans that his gramps promised to send from Fortnum's. "First he said I could have one, but after a bit he said I could have half the box!"

Now he was running about the airport checking departures, *look* at that plane go, Mummy, it's off to Moscow—when can I go there? That one's for Pakistan, I do wish I could go there, oh look at that! Hong Kong, that's where I *really* want to go!

Was there anywhere in the world he didn't want to go, she wondered? "We came to see the planes *arrive*, Daddy's should land on that runway..." Too late. He was already following the diminishing speck of a Boeing pointed at Turkey.

Jenny, prim in a blue plaid dress, navy blue tights, and black patent shoes, every golden hair in place despite the breeze—she watched arrivals. Not her father's plane yet, it wouldn't land for some time, but she checked out passengers arriving from all corners of the globe; when four Indian women in saris with gold studs in their ears came through the turnstile she was ecstatic.

"Please look how they walk, Mummy," she whispered—Jenny was very polite—"what pretty carriage!"

This month carriage was her thing, last month charisma. She still played with dolls, couldn't sleep without her teddy bear on the pillow and an old baby blanket under her cheek—yet she noticed how Indian women held their heads! Again that sensation for Ellie of things drifting, getting away.

But what *pretty* children hers were, even Simon with his hair in silk knots and a speck of mustard on his cheek. Invariably strangers stared and said to Ellie: "Twins, how charming!"

Then Michael's plane touching down, a scrub at Simon's cheek with a tissue, a dab of powder on her nose, a film of lipstick—

That deep, secret fluttering when she saw him, always there after an absence—and when he emerged from a crowd, ah...Even from a distance there was none of that straining to pick him out. Not just his coloring but, as Jenny would have said this month, his carriage. Others shuffled down the steps, allowed themselves to be herded like laden pack animals through customs. Not Michael. Without a hint of pushing or shoving he managed to reach the turnstile first, unencumbered as he hugged his children, one in each arm, handing them each the inevitable gift.

Jenny, already the performer emphasizing every tiny move, widened her eyes that little extra at a yellow T-shirt with "San Francisco Ballet Company" stenciled on it in black.

"Oh Daddy, it's just exactly...thank you a whole..."

In contrast Simon looked almost surly when Michael handed him a soft leather pouch drawn together with a thong, telling him that Indian braves used them on the warpath.

"When they were tracking deer and stuff too? When they were just going someplace on their ponies?"

"Sure, I'll bet they never let them out of their sight."

"*Okay!* I'll keep my marbles in it."

Then, although he still held the children, he concentrated on Ellie.

He simply looked, as always—but such a look! It started at her eyes, smiling into them, lingering on her mouth, her throat, traveling slowly, pausing at breast and hip and calf—then the same slow journey back to her eyes, the smile widening as it moved. He hadn't even touched her and already that sweet warm melting.

"Why don't I ever get more than a look and a touch of hands in public?" she'd asked him once. "Other people kiss and hug."

"Not Abramskys," he'd said with pride. "Felix loves his wife as much as any man I know, but he'd no more kiss or hold hands in public than he'd brush his teeth in the village fountain!"

Remembering how she'd welcomed Peter Heinrich's easy familiarity, she hadn't understood Michael until, mimicking Felix's precise accent, he explained:

"One night we saw a couple kissing in a doorway. I was early teens, probably I stared. Felix gave me a lecture I've never forgotten: 'Love is a private emotion, Mischa. To display in public is poor taste, bad manners. People see it who have never in their lives been loved, never been touched in affection—imagine how alone they must feel! No, hand-in-hand is for small children skipping to school—or the hoi polloi who know no better. On mature persons it shows lack of dignity, they try to forget old age and wrinkles and slip back to childhood. Pathetic, no?' I thought he was an insufferable old snob then—but I've decided he's probably right. He usually is."

How exactly like Felix—and perhaps he was right. Over the years she'd come to savor this moment of *looking*, an hors d'oeuvre holding out the promise of a superb meal to come.

Tonight was slightly different; as always when he came from the Rom she sensed differences, that he needed transition time to change his mindset, make that subtle shift in the volume and patterns of his speech, even his taste buds. And tonight there was an expression in his eyes she'd seen only once, just before they were married, when he'd come home from Appleby to find her waiting at Greenlings. This time he wasn't disheveled, no smell of smoke on him, but those same shadows were in his eyes, that pursued look she knew she could not easily dispel.

He held her briefly, said he'd missed her . . . but she eased him gently away, turned down the stereo, and made light unwinding conversation. Business okay? So-so, sales down but they'd pick up. Rose? As usual, now she'd got her fix of attention... Dui was in jail, drunk driving—

"His wife... can she manage? Two children—"

"Nearly three—and she'll have to manage. Little brother Micah declared his independence. Again."

"Oh dear... and Sacramento, what's it like?"

"Hot and sprawling. Nothing like L.A. or the Bay Area."

"Did you go to the *kumpania?*"

"Mmm, your accent's almost perfect, we'll make you a Gypsy girl yet." His lips found her throat, but she thought his voice had sharpened. "The families are fine. Now they've a new Rom Baro they might even be solvent one fine day."

"Dui's lost his title?"

"He deserved to."

"You think the new man will be better than Dui?"

"Who could be worse? The new man's a woman, my second cousin as a matter of fact... Did I mention I'd seen a piece of real estate out there, run-down, has possibilities? I'm looking into it—and did I tell you Tomo's working? Roofing, I think."

"What? But he's a child!"

"He's Rom. I told you, they grow up fast."

"I'd hate for Simon to be working that young."

"No way. He seemed to like the school all right? There were no complaints?"

"Who from?"

"Him... them... I don't know, I just wondered, that's all."

"They love him at Brimley—"

"—his mother said primly."

"If you're going to make puny little rhymes—"

Finally he was laughing instead of pretending to. "And if you'll be patient I have something for Simon's prim mother—"

"A bit early for that, isn't it?"

"Never too early—but it's not what I meant, unless you insist—but first close your eyes."

She felt their weight, cool and satin smooth on her neck, and she was drenched in an acid tide of guilt, left weak in its aftermath. So hard he worked and planned for her—yet still she resented Abramo, the Rom, Anna, even—and this was truly a sin—she sometimes resented Felix for every moment they took him away from her. "Oh Michael . . . pearls . . . but why? Not my birthday—"

"I had dinner all alone at that place in Chinatown with the bouncy waiter, but he fell kind of flat with no Ellie across the table. Outside, the shops are open until all hours, so—" His lips followed the pearls, leaving warmth wherever they touched.

"Michael, I *would* have gone with you. Next time I will."

"Don't make rash promises—next time I might be giving pep talks to a new sales force or scouting a tacky income property someplace. You're busy too. Children, studios, house, pretty soon you'll have to keep an eye on Abramo's finances here when I'm away. Felix tries, but it's a losing battle. He's never been really interested in money and it begins to show."

"Can't Pete Preston—"

"Hell no, he's a genius. They're hopeless with money. He couldn't read a balance sheet any more than Jenny could—and in a few years she'll be able to do it standing on her head. The profit motive, it's so simple an ant could grasp it. Most people can. Pete can't."

She wasn't sure just what stung her in his words, the implied contempt perhaps, but she *was* stung—and then he was unbuttoning her dress, slipping bra straps down, unfastening hooks. "Oh, but I missed you this trip, Ellie, I was lonely—"

She laughed softly, already anticipating. "With all those close relatives around?"

She felt him freeze, hold his breath. Looking at his eyes, she had to force herself not to recoil. It was gone in a moment, but there was no doubt at all what she'd seen deep in the black eyes. A blaze of hostility so naked, so powerful, she could have been an adversary instead of a wife to whom he was preparing to make love. "Anything wrong, darling?" But what *had* she said? Something about his relatives . . . he'd thought she was disparaging them! Oh, what a bundle of contradictions he was . . .

"Of course not!"—pushing her back onto the bed, undressing her until she wore only the pearls and his cloak of kisses that rained down, covering her from head to foot. His mouth and his hands were gentle, practiced—but even as he kissed her his eyes were wide open, still hostile. Did he know that? she wondered.

He entered her quickly, with what sounded very much like a sob, and their lovemaking was soon over, leaving her physically satisfied but somehow empty, alone, none of that lingering oneness so special to her. But he was tired, such a *long* trip . . .

A good-night kiss, a brief touch at the pearls, a murmur. "Sleep in them, just tonight? The first time I saw you I thought you deserved pearls. I like to think of you in them."

THIRTY-TWO

*T*HE REST OF THAT WINTER it seemed to Michael he marked time, waiting for some nebulous event that would somehow free him from an inevitable but equally hazy future. From time to time he fingered the business card of the Sacramento realtor, but his hand trembled like that of a timid child clutching the money for his first roller-coaster ride, and he never quite got around to calling the man.

He felt an urgency, almost manic in its intensity, to pile security so high around them they couldn't see over the top of it and could not *be* seen, or touched, or hurt.

When he was not working for them he was with them. He showed Ellie off at theaters and industry balls. He entertained heavily at home where he made sure she was the center of attention.

Some weekends he and Simon fished or stalked the woods for imaginary deer, taking aim at likely-looking bushes with any one of a thousand marbles slung in Simon's Indian leather bag—but when Simon begged to be taught how to tickle trout instead of standing on the bank with a

fishing pole he refused. "Illegal," he said firmly. "D'you want to end up in
Borstal?"

"Where's that?"

"Where they lock up bad boys."

Occasionally he gave Mary Beth a day off and drove Jenny to London
for her class with Romanovna, shared Anna's gratification at this fragile-
looking child who seemed to gain in confidence with each new step mas-
tered. Also with Jenny he sometimes rode to hounds, self-conscious in
impeccably tailored hunt coat but unbearably proud of a daughter who
was reputed to have the best seat of any rider in the county for her age
and class. Anna was incensed: "What use to have perfect arms for ballet if
the neck is broken flying over a fence?" Even when Michael took Anna
along, wrapped her in plaid rugs, and let her watch from the car, she
didn't quite believe that the pony class walked their mounts sedately
through gates. "Someday," she warned darkly, "will be the knock on the
door, they will be holding her, poor little broken Jenny..."

"Anna, I'm careful, I promise I am," Jenny said, near tears, torn between pleasing Anna and enjoying this sport in which she excelled and
made real friends who liked her, who called her on the phone, invited her
to their birthday parties.

"They're the right kind of people," Michael said. "If Simon would
cultivate people like that..."

Ellie teased him, said he was a bigger snob than Felix, but he didn't
care. He was determined to put all the space he could between his children and the Rom; the hunting—shooting—country-club set were about
as far as you could get and still live on the same planet. If only Simon...
almost a full term at school and still a loner. He brought no friends home
and none ever called him.

The principal, however, called Michael. It was a few weeks before end
of term and Parents' Day was coming up. He understood the whole
family was coming for the day? It would be helpful then if Michael could
stop by his office for a private word? could he pencil him in for four
o'clock?...best not mention it to Simon, right? Right, Michael said.

An incredible spring afternoon, the sky a flat blue sheet, a cricket field
too tender a green to bear, still jeweled from this morning's shower, little
boys in white togs taking their turn at crease while the games master sent
down googlies and spinners, terms as alien to Michael as the sport itself.

Afterwards a garden party. Ellie, in cream shantung dress and wide
straw hat with pink ribbon streamers, more than held her own among

local notables, a few of whom very nearly eclipsed Anna and Felix for eccentricity. Anna stalked the lawns in something vaguely maroon that did not enhance the increasingly high color in her cheeks. Felix wore a new suit indistinguishable from all his others. Jenny, her hair long and spun gold in the sun, looked so exactly like Alice in Wonderland that more than one parent begged her "not to *touch* the grow mushrooms" in case they made her shoot up like Alice. Jenny was perfect just as she was, no improvement possible.

Any other day Michael would have swaggered with pride, but the principal's message had nagged at him for a week.

"What can he possibly want with you?" Ellie whispered as Michael found a table for them under the marquee before hurrying off to the principal's office. No other parents were headed there, he noticed. Ellie was optimistic. "Maybe they want to advance him to the upper form, he's very bright for his age. Mary Beth says Simon's a top-class brain if he'd—"

"And you really think he has? Applied himself?"

"I don't see why not!" Instantly defensive.

"I'd like him to do well too, you know."

"You'd like him to. I expect him to," Ellie said firmly.

He tried to carry her optimism with him, but the look on Mr. Brimley's face was not encouraging, and he was suddenly glad Ellie had not been asked to the conference.

"There are times," the principal said slowly, "I'd rather be digging ditches than doing what I do. I'm afraid this is one of those times."

Michael's back teeth clamped shut. "Simon's not working?"

"Hardly. When he came to us he could read and write and add. Since then we haven't seen the slightest improvement—"

"Perhaps your staff is less than . . . competent?" Why was he defending Simon when he'd known, he'd *known!*

He defended him so that later he could assure Ellie that he'd done his best. If she were here she'd be crisp and dignified—and she'd defend Simon to the limit. Proud of her loyalty, he had a deep foreboding that in this case it was misplaced, that the battle was lost. It was not the staff, it was the child.

"Not just schoolwork . . ." Mr. Brimley steepled his fingers and looked anywhere but at Michael. "The fact is, Mr. Abramsky, he's an accomplished liar."

"All children lie!"

"Children fib," Mr. Brimley corrected regretfully. "To keep out of trouble. To avoid tasks they despise. A dozen reasons, all fairly innocent. Simon, I'm afraid, lies for pleasure, to see how much the other boys will believe. They're young, innocent."

"And Simon is not?" Michael tried to still the roar in his temples. "You're accusing him of having an imagination?"

"It goes farther than that. The fact is there's been an incident—several actually, but this was the latest. You perhaps know that he keeps marbles in a leather pouch? Yes... well, a few weeks ago he'd been playing about in class, typical boy nonsense but disruptive—anyway, the bag was confiscated for the rest of the term, put in a trunk of such items we keep in the masters' common room. Off limits to the boys, of course."

A tight feeling started at the pit of Michael's stomach. He knew exactly what was coming, would have shut the man's mouth if he could.

"The next day the pouch wasn't there."

Correct. At this moment it swung from a hook in the garage at Greenlings. "Are you saying a seven-year-old picked a lock—"

"Eight, he's eight years old, and the trunk wasn't locked, we trust our boys. Simon said he took it because—"

"—because it's his! I brought it from California for him—"

"But this is a school. We have rules."

"That I understand, but you're accusing him of stealing his own property!"

The principal sighed and checked his watch. "There have been other incidents, rather more serious, to which he has not admitted, so I will not go into—"

"Oh yes you will, Mr. Brimley. In detail. You'll go into them now."

Once again Da had been right. Schools were traps, rules hedged in with rules hedged in with rules.

"I hardly think—"

"I do. If he's suspected of other things I have a right to know what they are."

But no desire to hear them—and Ellie, oh God, all that dignity, that pride...

"Very well. Bertie Phelps, a truthful if somewhat stodgy child, says that months ago he lent Simon a tiepin with a small diamond in it—of no great value and I agree it's idiotic to give children such things but..." He spread his hands at the foolish indulgences of parents. "I understand Simon was to wear it for a week and give it back. Which he refused to do. Each week a different excuse—he'd left it at home, it was on his other tie ... finally he insisted Phelps had given it him. To keep. In any event, it's disappeared."

"Oh hell, Simon's always been a scatterbrain, he probably borrowed it, lost it, daren't admit it!"

The principal checked his watch and stood, clearly relieved that the interview was almost over. "I think you'll find there's precious little that Simon dare not admit to."

"I'll have a talk with him, of course, but—"

"I am sorry ... but under the circumstances there won't be a place for him at Brimley next term. If I might suggest a military type of establishment? With discipline rather more ... stringent?"

He walked to the door as if on rubber rollers, standing in bright sunlight holding the door while Michael, stunned, not yet fully understanding, walked through it into the warmth. As Brimley waited he turned noncommittal smiles on parents strolling the grounds. *Gajo* parents. Then smoothly, easily, he took Michael's arm, running lightly down the steps with him, best of friends, affable now the dirty work was done; for the benefit of whoever might be watching he smiled directly into Michael's face as he babbled on.

"In spite of everything that's happened I must admit, Abramsky, Simon's an *engaging* youngster, remarkable imagination—he even spread word all over the school that he was a Gypsy! *And* had the boys believing him! Can you imagine? With blue eyes, that light hair and—"

"He's half Gypsy. With your splendid education you surely know that Gypsies are not all dark." Michael shook off the patronizingly offensive arm. "I am dark—and I am Gypsy." He looked around picture-pretty grounds, well-tended shrubbery, rosy-cheeked boys and gung-ho masters. "I never had all this. My father told me I was lucky to have missed it, and I didn't believe him. I see now that he may have been right."

"Oh, my dear man, no offense—"

... there won't be a place for him ... there won't be ... ?

Michael clutched his elbow, Simon and even Ellie forgotten, gone, nothing left but that pounding in his chest. "What did you say about not having a place for him?"

"Next term, naturally ... better he stays here the balance of this one ... for the sake of appearances."

Yes, appearances must be served. The roaring in his head stopped. Everything stopped, was still. He thought for a moment that perhaps his heart had stopped. "You're saying that as of next term he's expelled."

"Oh, he's young, let's avoid *that* word, so archaic anyway—"

Perhaps "banished" instead? Or was that more achaic yet? But even these days boys were still expelled from school, grown men still banished from their *kumpanias*.

Sent away.

Discarded.

Of no further use.

In biblical terms, cast out.

You have done what cannot be undone ... *You are banished from the* kumpania ... *From this day you are not of the people*.

His father shunned by the Rom.

Now his son unwanted by the *gaje*.

In the distance he caught sight of them, a perfect family group surrounded by other perfect family groups as they sat at this polite gathering sipping cool drinks and nibbling cucumber sandwiches not much thicker than a credit card. Comparing Simon (despite the thunder in his ears Michael thought he saw them all objectively) with schoolmates aged seven to twelve, he perceived Simon as *better* than they were, more aware, his eyes sharper, quicker, wide open; his hair a nimbus in the sun; none of the furtiveness of the others, no suggestion of smutty little ambitions entertained but not yet experienced.

Talking to Ellie was a florid man in country tweeds. Michael knew him to have started as a bookie's runner; he now headed a large London corporation of turf accountants; for R & R he kept a yacht bobbing at anchor off Cowes and a very fancy woman indeed in his Fifth Avenue flat in New York. On Ellie's other side the lady magistrate of a nearby jurisdiction sipped tea; had Da lived it was more than likely this forbidding woman would eventually have convicted Gypsy Micah and his father for vagrancy—in these rural parts "no fixed abode" carried a stigma not much above murder; now the lady chatted to Michael's wife and no doubt felt privileged to do so. A local drama critic was holding forth at Anna and Felix, whom he had virtually boxed in at the bar. The games master flirted mildly with Mary Beth; a retired barrister gravely admired the blue satin ribbon in Jennifer's hair.

Only Simon stood alone.

Glowering.

Sullen.

Hands in pockets.

Even if Brimley hadn't kicked him out Michael would have withdrawn him now anyway. The boy had no friends here. Three months in this place, at an age when children make and discard friendships as easily as gym shoes, and Michael had yet to see fellow students speak to Simon or him to them.

He looked vulnerable. Hopelessly alone.

Watching him, an odd wave of tenderness and irritation washed over Michael. His work—the money he'd made, the contacts, travel, the right address, the right clubs—all to make sure that doors would be opened for his children, that they could sail through them unchallenged. Yet his boy seemed bent on nothing so much as kicking them shut as fast as Michael could pry them open.

In one respect Simon was lucky. When the Rom banished they meant it. The *gajo* world was more forgiving. In time they forgot. There would be other doors for Simon, but oh Christ, seven years old (sorry, Mr. Brimley, eight), but at eight he'd already managed to get himself banished from the enclaves of the law-abiding, respectable *gaje*.

But every world had its corners. Maybe in time Simon could find one to suit him.

For the first time Michael ached with pity for this troubled son, an ache stronger than the approving affection he lavished on his daughter. He wanted to hold him, tell him it didn't matter, he didn't have to go to school if he didn't want to—but how can a boy become a man in this world without the right schools, the contacts, the old-boys' clubs?

You did it! Micah became Mischa became Michael. Ah, but I attended a harder school than this boy will ever, ever know.

Then Simon looked up, his scowl deepening.

"How much longer to summer?" he said.

"You know how long. Two months. Why?"

He gouged holes in immaculate turf with his heel. "I'm waiting for California."

"If we go."

He thought he'd loaded his voice with threat, passing a hint that pleasures such as California summers had to be earned with good behavior at school—but of course, the boy didn't know yet that he'd been expelled. And would he care?

No.

But his mother . . . she'd care. Oh yes.

She came over just then and took their arms. Michael felt a drenching wave of tenderness break over him; if only she didn't have to know. "The drama teacher tells me they're doing a version of Hiawatha next term," she was saying. "Why don't you try out for it, all about American Indians . . ."

"I think," Michael said quietly, "we'll postpone any plans for next term."

"Why? What—"

"Later. When we get home..."

How *dare* they? It was unfair, inhuman—if Michael had only told her before they came home...

They'd left Simon there for the sake of appearances? By now he'd be lying awake in that cheerless dormitory—no, she'd forgotten, he didn't know yet. But tomorrow morning she'd drive the hundred miles and bring him home. Felix was right. The system *was* barbaric. He was repeating it now; amazing how everyone agreed—even Michael, who'd sent him away in the first place.

But you agreed too, Ellie, you were the one who took him, left him there when you knew it wasn't his kind of place.

But what is? The question ran, a desolate echoing thread through her every jumbled thought. Why couldn't he be like Jenny? Everyone loved her and she loved everyone, needed everyone, didn't hesitate to show it. Simon could hardly bear to accept affection, and showed it only when it suited him. *Like Michael,* came the treacherous unbidden thought, quickly suppressed.

What on earth did the boy need? What, in this perfect world Michael had made for them, would make this defiant child happy? He'd loved Grandmam, yes, but after that a void. Simon, my baby, her heart cried, am I nothing that you can't even love *me*? Your father, step-grandfather, sister—they love me, I know because they show me, tell me! So why not *you*?

"All along I have believed," Felix was saying to the room at large—to Anna, Michael, Mary Beth, herself, even Pete, who had once again dropped in and was sipping an unheard-of Scotch and water—"I believe them too young to leave home. Everyone agrees Jenny should stay home —but they agree because she is a girl and so *agreeable!* It is Simon who needs the attention, he is the more complex child, he needs...oh, how you say—"

"The velvet glove," Anna whipped in, "in which he will put to bed a frog or a hamster. You say he needs pampering, I don't."

"Hush. No, Simon needs...that someone should *know* him, and this is very hard. I try to know him myself and I do not succeed. Since the day they could speak I knew what Jenny was thinking, at that moment! But Simon—I am sorry, if he were my child I don't know what I would do."

"If he were mine," Anna said, biting into raw cucumber, "I would put him to the ballet, there is no stronger discipline—"

"He thinks it's sissy—" Michael said.

"You thought so too, but you learned to care for the body, pride in yourself. If you were not so good at making money you would today be a principal dancer."

"Maybe. And for as long as my knees or back or ankles lasted I might have made a bare living. Why should he take chances when there'll be a sound business for him to step into?"

Mary Beth spoke up. "Has anybody thought Simon might have his own ideas what he wants to be? When he's much, much older? Maybe he'll get religion and be a priest—"

"Hah!" Anna snorted.

"—or painter, dentist, plumber, poet, blackjack dealer, a bum if he likes! It's *his* future you're plotting, not yours!"

"He's our son," Michael said with deceptive quiet.

Oh, Mary Beth, she meant well but...Ellie shifted in her chair, planned her escape from this suddenly explosive room. The shock was over, they'd all accepted—*accepted!*—what had happened; now Mary Beth chose to interject her education-major platitudes. No children of her own, how easy to see what should be done for the children of others. You didn't tell a man like Michael, who planned his life around home and family, that his son could be a bum if he so desired. She'd sing a different song if it were her son who'd been unfairly expelled from his first school.

Ellie reached for the tray, gathering cups and saucers as Pete Preston rose to help her, following her to the kitchen.

"It's really upset you, this business with Simon?"

"It's upset both of us," she said carefully.

He lay his hand, gentle with concern, over hers. "But not the same way. Michael's pride is bruised, a son of his being kicked out of school, putting a crimp in his plans. You're hurt because you're afraid Simon will be hurt."

She sighed and disengaged her hand. "I keep wondering how he'll feel when we tell him he can't go back. And why."

"Want to know what I think?"

She nodded.

"He'll be delighted. I doubt he had one happy day there."

"Oh Pete . . . now I feel worse for taking him in the first place—"

Emboldened by the Scotch, he said: "I expect Michael didn't give you a choice," looking utterly, deeply miserable, all his feelings in his eyes. A child could have read them.

"Why d'you say that?" she said sharply.

"He expects his own way. That's why he so often gets it. He uses people—he does it with me, mainly for my own good, yes, but I don't like to see *you* manipulated . . . I know him like the back of my hand. Everything he does is planned, well planned. I've never seen him do an impulsive thing. Don't misunderstand, Ellie, I admire him, I'm grateful to him and I wish to God I were like him. I'm not complaining but—"

"Who's not complaining?"

It was Michael at the door, smiling at some secret joke just as Mary Beth's voice sang out for Pete to come catch something on television.

Ellie was alone with Michael for the first time since they'd returned from Brimley. He shut the door.

"I'm surprised," he said. "Who'd have guessed it, Pete Preston—and I thought he was after Mary Beth."

"You heard what he said about you?"

"Some."

"You're not angry?"

He shrugged. "Why should I be? It's the truth—in business you use people to do what has to be done. How else are you going to accomplish anything? What I don't understand is how I missed the way he feels about *you*. How long has it been going on and why didn't I notice?"

"Because you're hardly ever home?"

He trapped her against him from behind, thumbs stroking cream shantung and the underside of her breasts, circling the treacherously tightening nipples until she had to make a conscious effort to slow her breath. He wasn't fooled for a moment. Seeking, his hands slid into the short wide sleeves of her dress, pigeons coming home to roost, warm dark wings folding over alabaster breasts.

If his actions were romantic his voice was not.

"Poor Pete, what an innocent. All the women in the world, he falls for the only one in his orbit who is positively, without a shadow of a doubt, uninterested and unattainable."

He thought it was pathetic, funny! "I don't see why you're amused— most men might be at least a little jealous, might wonder if—you know."

His lips traveled the hairline at the nape of her neck as his fingertips traced smaller and smaller circles around her nipples, which obediently hardened, yearned for his mouth. "Why should I be jealous," he murmured. "If Pete touched you like this would you want him?"

"No."

"But you want me."

"Who says I do..." Her body said it, ached for it, oh God, he was doing just what Pete said. Manipulating. Using a physical want to obscure an emotional one. And dammit, it worked!

He chuckled, pulled her back against his hips so she could feel the rise of him through the thin silk of the dress, telling her she was not alone in this seemingly endless need.

Before they slipped upstairs he made one small concession. "I'll take the day off tomorrow, we'll drive out early and get Simon. Why leave him there till end of term?"

Pete had been right. When they told Simon he was going home he was overjoyed, had his things rammed into a suitcase with time left over to jiggle on the car seat while Michael went for a final word with Mr. Brimley.

"Don't rock the car, darling," Ellie protested. "When Daddy comes out he won't be *that* pleased as it is."

"Why?"

"Because of *why* you're leaving. It's not from choice, you know. First there was your work, then—"

"Two, four, six, eight, ten...and again, two, four..."

He fingered marbles into lines of ten, arranging them carefully down the quilted hollows of the car seat. He didn't hear a word she said.

Michael arrived frowning, slammed the door, threw the car in gear with a lurch that scattered thousands of glass balls into the deep plush of the rug.

"Daddeee..."

"I'll speak to you when we get home. Until then, be quiet."

Another incredible spring day and for Ellie an agonizing journey home. A hundred times she wanted to say, "Oh, do slow down, you missed a splendid cock pheasant in that lane...Look, Michael, they've painted that lovely old pub pink, how hideous...Simon, you mustn't miss—"

Ten miles from Brimley she gave up, blanked her thoughts until Greenlings' gravel crunched underfoot. "Now we'll all have a cup of—"

"Now Simon and I will talk. In my dressing room. Go up and wait for me." He spoke so sharply that Simon almost ran for the stairs in his rush to obey.

"Don't be too hard on him," Ellie breathed, afraid of the darkness in Michael's eyes.

Then it was Michael who looked as if he'd been slapped. "Hard? Have I ever been?"

Michael took the stairs slowly, pausing to listen to *Coppélia* and Anna's voice through the studio door: "Land soft, Jenny, soft, softer...I don't want to hear you, my angel...ah, that is good, better, much much better, how clever is my girl!"

He closed his eyes. Anna and Felix. Had he ever given them trouble such as Simon seemed destined to create? Worse, surely. Yet they had persevered, and he was not even theirs. Not their flesh and blood. Mr. Brimley's words from this morning still stung. "Had you said you were a Gypsy to begin with, I'd have had some reservations about admitting Simon at all, Mr. Abramsky."

"It's against the rules to be a Gypsy too?" Michael had said.

"This is a democracy and I run a private school. We make our own rules. Trying to combine incompatible cultures doesn't work."

So much for democracy.

He opened his dressing room door quietly, wondering, much as he would plot strategy with a valued but difficult employee, just how to approach his son. He expected to find a chastened small boy sitting on the edge of the great leather chair looking—dare he expect it?—afraid and repentant, and phrased his opening sentence accordingly.

"Maybe Brimley was a poor school anyway—"

The leather chair was empty. Simon postured before the great cheval glass, his fingers nonchalantly flicking Michael's best silk tie he'd knotted kerchief-fashion round his neck, a candy cigarette drooping from the corner of his mouth, eyes screwed up against imaginary smoke.

Time shuddered and stopped.

Ran back to Appleby.

That first visit to see Rose and Grandmam, three-year-old Tomo strutting like a peacock with Michael's handkerchief knotted round his neck, the smile of an angel, as if manhood were somehow conferred by a rag around the neck. Now Simon.

"What d'you think you're doing?"

He whispered, but some silken menace in his voice must have warned Simon, who licked his lips.

"Playing..."

"At?"

"They had these candy cigs at the tuck shop—"

—as far as he got before Michael's thin flat hand connected with his son's peach-velvet cheek, whipped the blond head quickly from side to side. Michael froze. He couldn't believe he'd done it, expecting Ellie to come in accusing him. Or Felix. Expecting Simon to let out a scream. The slap had not been soft.

Nothing.

Simon's face turned white except for livid fingermarks on his left cheek. His chin quivered but held firm. Only his eyes moved, alive with a blazing triumphant blue.

"You're lucky I don't wear a belt," Michael said softly. "Get out of the room, go to your mother."

When he'd gone, stiff-necked, his lips still holding firm, Michael locked the door behind him and threw himself onto the daybed, trusting to *Coppélia* to muffle his sobs.

THIRTY-THREE

 SNIFFLE.

A child's mortified eyes.

The everlasting squeak of the nursery rocker. It needed oil. She hadn't rocked the children since they'd been babies but she rocked her son now, pressed her cool palm to his burning cheek and tried not to think ahead beyond ten minutes.

"He didn't mean it, Simon, I know he didn't."

"Yes he did."

The child was right. Of course Michael meant it—whatever "meant it" meant. He'd *done* it, left angry red fingermarks on the child's face and a permanent memory of violence in his mind. A man's hand, long and brown, graceful, confident, sensitive—and oh so gentle and *knowing* on her body last night—this same hand could do this, could slam into this tender flesh.

"What *were* you doing—"

He swallowed and scrubbed at his eyes. "Nothing! I put his tie on, that's all. When he came in I was sucking on a piece of candy—Brimley's tuck shop sells white candy cigarettes with a dab on the end. You know?"

She nodded. "That's *all* you did, not . . . not insolent?"

"No, he just asked me what I was doing and hit me . . ."

Hit me . . . hit me . . . hit me . . .

A good—no, a perfect marriage for close on ten years. Ecstatic. Even his faults you love. If sometimes he seems like a stranger you love the stranger too—but how do you love a man who hits out at a child for no reason? How can you let him touch you again with love . . . There was a reason, must be . . .

"Simon, you weren't . . . cheeky? Sometimes you are."

"Oh, you're on his side, everybody always is!"

He wriggled to get down but she held him firm. "Families don't have 'sides.' Wars and battlegrounds have sides. We have each other and a home."

"It's a rotten home, lonely, big . . . I hate it."

How could he? "Look," she said. "If you'd only look."

Nothing but beauty, even from this nursery window at the back of the house. A kitchen garden rampant with cicely and rosemary, thyme and peppermint. Beyond its brick wall flapped Lily Finn's airings—today red velvet cushion covers—fluttering like exotic windsocks in the breeze. Behind them in the paddock the children's Welsh ponies and Michael's hunter frisked and bucked, sunlight chasing them across daisy-starred grass, rippling off heaving chestnut sides, glancing off tossed manes and lifted, whinnying lips.

Everything bursting with life, hope—like the ride to Brimley this morning, their errand not the happiest, but they were getting Simon home, home! Surely cause for celebration?

Then a blow from a dark hand and everything falls to dust.

"He didn't mean it, Simon . . ." Why did she keep saying it as if constant repetition would make it so? And he wasn't listening anyway, he was watching the hands of the clock creep towards noon and lunch. At which he'd have to see Michael again.

And so would she.

What would she say? What *could* she say, the family and Mary Beth there, Lily Finn screeching and clanging in the kitchen. These ugly, ugly welts on Simon's face?

"I'll bring your lunch up here."

"I'd rather eat in the dining room. With *him*."

Him.

His father, his enemy. He wanted it *known* his father had hit him.

Oh Michael, the welts, they'll all see them. Felix will mourn you, smother you *and* Simon in sweetness, in feathers of dusty old doves, of gratitudes, platitudes, seraphic homilies. Then there'll be Mary Beth, my dear friend, my oldest, my *real* friend, armed to the hilt with the latest psychological insights; one look at Simon's face and she'll come out fighting. And Anna, she'd hunt up some justification for Michael; she'd rummage deep in that sad Russian soul, come up with a bit of Dostoevski and convince herself Simon must have committed some grievous crime to merit such punishment.

And we mustn't forget Lily Finn, who skitters, running and humming and clutching her purse, carrying her tales to the village pub, paying for her Saturday gin-and-tonics with gossipy tidbits about the Gypsy owner of Greenlings. Oh yes, Lily would do very well off one angry father striking one recalcitrant boy. Coin of the realm in these parts.

And Jenny.

How to tell her? She'd ask her brother straight out. "Who hurt your face, Simon?"

Simon, angry and sorry for himself and looking for an ally besides, would say: *"Him! Daddy!* Who'd you think?"

Need she know it was her father, her God, in whom she'd always had absolute faith? Who could do anything, fix anything?

Daddy-I-hurted-my-finger-will-you-kiss-it-better?

Later, after a few rigorous years of Anna and ballet, it was: Daddy-do-look-at-my-*développé*-I-think-it's-low.

Just yesterday: I-think-there's-a-pebble-in-Jellyroll's-hoof-would-you-look-at-it-Daddy?

She forced herself to think of children everywhere, in Trier and San Francisco and Milan and Los Angeles—probably Caracas and Paris and Istanbul and Bombay, anywhere there were parents, kids, disappointments, and hot tempers; common sense told her most children were occasionally slapped by most parents, often without just cause. But *her* children had been touched with love or not at all, and there lay the difference.

Simon.

Michael.

I love you both.

What are you starting and how can I bear it? Already I know I cannot stop it.

"I'm sorry, Simon," she said crisply. "You'll have lunch up here today. Better wash up, okay?"

He gave her an impulsive hug all the sweeter for its rarity, pressed his lips roughly to her cheek, and scrambled away.

She tapped lightly on the door of Michael's dressing room, then tried the knob. Locked.

"Please, Michael."

She heard him get up—surely he hadn't slept?—and stagger to the door. His eyes looked swollen, his mouth puffy.

"What d'you want?"

"To know what happened."

"You do know. I hit him."

"But I don't know why. He says he had your tie on and was eating a piece of candy."

"Then you do know why."

"You hit him for that?"

"Yes."

"But—"

"But he was playing the game, wasn't he? Pretending. That tie of mine around his neck was a kerchief, that piece of candy was a cigarette hanging out of his mouth. It's the same damned game he's been obsessed with ever since he met Tomo."

"Are you sure it's not you who're obsessed, making something of nothing?"

He loomed at her, his fingertips digging into her shoulders. In a minute he'd be shaking her!

"Stay out of what you don't know. He's my son and I know what I want for him."

"He's mine too—"

"He will not be Rom!"

"How could he be, he lives in the lap of luxury—and don't shout at me, please. You're getting paranoid, Michael—"

"And you've been dipping into Mary Beth's *Psychology Today* again. He gets six months to shape up and start some decent schoolwork with Mary Beth. If not, it's military school. They don't play games there."

"He's eight years old! What d'you want? A tycoon?"

"No, I want a normal *gajo* son who kicks a football about and rides a bike and makes friends with kids like Peck's boy and Martinson's boy. Normal boys."

She didn't remind him that Peck and Martinson were *gajo* fathers and she did manage to hang on to her temper. "It's almost lunch. Do you want to come down for it? Simon's having his in the schoolroom—I didn't want Jenny asking about his face."

He squeezed his eyes shut, raked his hands through his hair, reached out to her. "Oh God, Ellie, she'll be terrified of me, how could I have done that, what can I do to—"

"You could tell him you're sorry..."

"No..." He groaned. "Not Simon—he'd use it and use it—"

"You can't know that!"

"Yes I can. At his age I *was* Simon. I know him very well."

And you don't like him, she thought—hardly even surprised when Michael echoed the thought:

"I love him," he said, "I want to see him happy, I want to give him the world—but I don't like him."

She walked downstairs stiffly, her back much too straight, aware that she would never forget what he'd just said and might not be able to forgive him for it.

Michael didn't come down for lunch and no one seemed to ask why. Afterwards she drove down to the studio offices, hoping that when she came back father and son would be reconciled. They were not. Michael was out riding with Jenny and Simon was writing a letter in his room, his tongue poking out the corner of his mouth as he laboriously cross *t*'s and dotted *i*'s.

When they came in from riding Jenny ran to hug her mother and Michael followed suit, but Ellie found herself pulling away from him, his words of this morning rustling like shrouds at the back of her mind.

I don't like him.

How could a man not like his son?

Later, in their room, when he reached towards her with a clear plea for reconciliation in his eyes, she turned away. He wouldn't say he was sorry, she knew that—and in any case how could he? Hurtful as it was, he'd spoken the truth. Suppose he said it to Simon sometime? What would happen then? From somewhere deep within her a small voice answered before she had a chance to block it out. What would happen then?

Nothing—because Simon doesn't like his father any more than his father likes him.

"Are you going to hold it against me forever, that I hit him?" Michael said, untying his shoes. "Most fathers hit their kids when they deserve it."

"But he didn't."

"By your standards he never does."

"He's so small . . ."

"It's too late when they're big."

"Why can't you just admit that you're human, that you lost your temper? Everyone does."

"You don't."

She shrugged. "Some people throw things, I'm more likely to cry, that's all."

"Ellie . . . please?"

As far as apologies went she knew it was the best he could do. Tonight it wasn't enough. Not yet.

They undressed in silence, then instead of reading she turned out the light on her side of the bed. He did the same, leaving the room splashed in moonlight, oppressive with this new atmosphere of hostility.

After half an hour of it, each of them struggling to simulate the steady, regular breathing of sleep, hugging to their own extreme edge of the mattress so as not to touch inadvertently, he got up. She heard him fumbling for practice clothes, then the studio door opening and very faintly the throbbing, sobbing, wild and plaintive *Slavonic Dances* pulsating in disconnected threads through the heavy walls of Greenlings.

Though she stayed awake a long time waiting for the music to finish, pictured him working out, sweat flying, great salty drops splashing the mirror, the angry power of his leaps, he did not come back to their bed.

After a long time she heard sounds in his dressing room, the cautious turn of a key in a seldom used lock, then the final hiss of the studio shower.

Exhaustion pulled at every muscle. Emotionally, physically, he was as drained as if he'd worked two barres with Anna—and all he'd done was sit cross-legged on the wooden floor and think, stare at his hand, think some more, let the music wash over him.

One slap to one child. That he'd hit him didn't matter—unlike Ellie he saw nothing wrong in reminding a child that he lived in an adult world and the sooner he conformed to it the more comfortable he and everyone around him would be. But there was a fine line between chastising the child and gratifying the frustrated parent. And he knew in his heart that he'd crossed that line, crossed it by a mile. If he'd walked into the room and found Simon parading about in his evening jacket or his riding boots he'd have been amused, charmed, laughed with him, joined in the charade.

So it wasn't the blow, it was what it was *for.* That's what stung, nagged at him, raised welts of guilt on his conscience far more livid than anything he could raise on Simon's face.

He remembered Greenlings as Hamish had left it, weeds, trash, a thornbush thrusting through the driveway near the great oak, obscuring the best view of the front of the house from drawing room and library and living room, ruining the aspect of gracefully proportioned walks and beckoning vistas. He'd ordered it dug up with the rest and put it out of his mind. Months later a whiplike thread pushed through new gravel. Again he called the contractors. "This time do it right," he told them curtly, stood over them while they dug first a hole, then a crater, then an abyss. Three times contractors and landscape gardeners met, scratched their heads, took samples, leaned on shovels and conferred before they came up with a plan of attack that would kill the upstart thornbush but *might* not jeopardize the great oak nearby. They injected a pint of poison into the seedling whose root seemed to have no end. Within days, magic happened. New leaves turned brown, spindly branches drooped; two years ago the whole thing lay down and died. Last week he stubbed his toe on a new shoot as vigorous as its predecessors, ready to burst into spring leaf not an inch from where the last one perished.

That was the Rom.

Soon to be thirty, where had all his work got him? Not an inch from where he'd stood at five, hot with the drama of a *kris romani*. Yes, he had money and position—but hardy new branches of the same Rom family still depended on our Micah because our Micah was there, convenient, available, saturated with a guilt that could be milked and milked and milked. Guilty because he'd succeeded *without* them, dammit!

And because he'd left them.

Now this new enigma of a son with no greater concept of his advantages than a young hawk, a boy as hard to read as he was difficult to hold. A squirmy, wriggly child, one minute you had him, the next he was gone. Quicksilver. A child who could be milked just as readily as our Micah because wasn't he our Micah's son? Blood calls to blood—and by God if it doesn't call loud enough let's make it scream, amplify it . . . oh Christ—

Simon's sweet sister, just looking at her he knew he had to build fences around Jenny, barriers to keep out bitter winds, that harsh world outside the gates of Greenlings.

Then the Abs. He loved them, he loved them, yes!—but they aged fast, dependents now just as the children were; the children would grow out of their dependency; the Abs could only grow farther in.

Responsibilities like barnacles fastened on him—how in the world could a penniless orphan have gathered so many?

Ellie, who managed to look as if the most demanding part of her day was doing her nails, was the one member of his extended family who was truly independent—who could, without a breath of doubt, succeed on her own—and at the moment she wanted nothing to do with him.

A sound escaped his chest—a laugh or a sob, he was too tired to know which . . . Where was it written that wealth was the key to idleness and freedom? Maybe he'd imagined it, he was tired, very tired . . . as much the slave now as when he crept around the trailer brewing coffee for Da, keep him happy and maybe he wouldn't lash out with his belt . . . Micah could use some of that coffee now, wake him up . . . he needed to think, think . . . how could a man think half asleep . . . why should he . . . It seemed, peering through the studio window, that the sky over the larches grew gray, the day's first tender light when mist off the river softened every tree, every leaf, Grandmam's best time for picking the good herbs before "that damblasted sun drained 'em dry."

Clear as if she'd been there—or perhaps he dreamed her—he saw Farah opposite him over an open grave. "Do like I do, Micah," she'd said, chin up with the same pride as when she danced her cautious flamenco. "I can take 'em or leave 'em alone." She meant it. When it suited her to take them she'd done it, she'd *really* done it, taken Dui clear out of a job that was the last bit of pride he had left . . . And now Ellie floated into the picture, superimposed her patrician face on Farah's bold features—Ellie aloof, saying nothing—but receding, blurring, rejecting his approach just as surely as if her hands pushed him away.

The first time. No woman had turned him down before, even Ellie was eager for him whenever he wanted her. Until now—as if what was between Michael and Simon had anything to do with what was between *them!* Well, he'd be damned if he'd beg, she must know he'd never . . . never . . .

Perhaps he slept a little in Anna's familiar studio. He wasn't sure, but at some point he smelled bacon and coffee, at another he took a shower; at another his brain told his hand to reach for his jacket, to finger a dog-eared business card.

At last more or less awake, he walked into his office and called a realtor in Sacramento.

That investment property he'd looked at a few months back? Run-down? Well located? Still on the market by any chance?

Funny Michael should ask. It sold a couple of months back, but damned if it didn't fall out of escrow—buyers these days don't have enough up front. The price was down some, wouldn't likely go no lower ... Did Michael want to make a firm offer? Not yet—well then, did he want to stop in and take another look? Where was he located again? The Bay Area?

Michael didn't contradict, said he'd see him in a couple of days, and hung up.

Again at breakfast Simon did not appear. Jenny was excited about a trip to the zoo with Mary Beth, Ellie was hurrying to her office, markedly cool as she handed Michael his mail. Felix and Anna were indulging in a small spat of their own—it seemed he'd cast joking aspersions on her choice of new brocade for a bedspread. They'd had words and were now having silence.

Michael brought up the trip casually. "That property in Sac looks as if it might be a buy, Felix—remember my telling you about it, eyesore old shops, half of 'em empty, smack in the middle of suburbia and not a mile off the freeway? I talked to the realtor, we'd make out if we could get the price down, level it, develop it."

"But Mischa!" Felix's eyebrows shot up. "We're *all* going to California in couple weeks, even my Anna agrees—so why not wait? And why property in Sacramento? Already we have so much, why not put into the shops—"

"Because land can't skip town, go bankrupt, burn down. Besides, it might be gone ... I'll be back in a few days, help us all pack."

Ellie studied her toast with some care. Sacramento. Where the *kum-pania* was at the moment. *Them* again!

"Perhaps," she said quietly, "you might take Simon with you, leave him until we get there—I'm sure he'd love it."

Sarcasm didn't suit her, she didn't do it well, but it hit home. "He's better off at a desk with Mary Beth, unless he wants to see inside that military school everybody thinks will knock some sense into him."

*   *   *

In silence Ellie helped him pack, and as usual walked down to the gates to wave him off—but for the first time since their marriage she was glad to see him go.

As the gates clanged behind him the tension gripping her for the last two days loosed its terrible hold. Foolish of her to let one tiny incident, surely commonplace in every family but this, assume such monstrous proportions.

Close by the oak she stopped. How lovely Greenlings was in the mornings. Her house. Her home. Every lintel, chimney, stone block, and studded door as dear, as warm and familiar as she'd willed it to be on those days when Grossmutter's house seemed it would press her into the ground with its relentless gravity.

She continued, her spirit eased by the house's grace, hardly noticing a whippy little weed pushing through the drive until she felt it under her shoe.

From habit she bent to uproot it. Of course it broke, she knew better than to use bare hands on greedy little shoots like this which, unless checked, would sap the old oak's strength.

Tomorrow she'd tell the gardener, he'd know what to do.

Book Three

THIRTY-FOUR

HE HAD THE DISCRETION, barely, to show up at Rose's trailer space first. It was empty, thank God!

Her neighbor poked her head around a door to say Rose was gone these two weeks, there was no holding her since she got that new trailer; he should check with *her*, *she'd* know where Rose was, she knew everything, that one.

As he opened the gate in the picket fence he thought he saw the lace curtain twitch, but it was a moment, no more. The saluki remained in its kennel, which today had a blue and white sunshade on the roof. It gave Michael a perfunctory growl through almost palpable waves of afternoon heat but made no move to leave the shade to challenge him. He rang a bell hidden in the door's sunflower center and waited in the blistering heat for it to swing open, the humming throb of an air conditioner overriding any sound from inside.

The door opened a cautious inch.

A thread of honeysuckle reached out, drew him forward.

Inside was mysterious, dark, a wonderful coolness beckoning him through the small crack which widened slowly. Through the gloom a little girl slightly younger than Jenny smiled up at him with the gap-toothed grin of the grade-schooler—except he knew that this child would never see inside a school if the families could avoid it. Michael did not at once recognize her, but then he noticed the eyes, that slight upward tilt at the corners.

"You don't remember me, Feya?" he said—but how could she? A baby with moonpennies in her hair. "Is your mother home?"

From the cool interior that languid husky voice: "Let Uncle Micah in, then go see your gran for ten minutes, *chavi*—leave the door open when you go."

A hundred and two in the shade, air conditioner going like thunder, but leave the door open. Of course. Propriety. A Gypsy woman might have many faults, but promiscuity was seldom one of them; she was too well protected by custom, by the fear of gossip, by a static culture that conferred monetary value on her virginity, a price her own quick brain could increase. And, except with her husband, by her own innate reticence in things sexual. A Gypsy man would tell off-color jokes to women of the *gaje*, never to a Gypsy woman.

One appraising glance from liquid black eyes and the child slipped by him, running to a tan trailer at the other end of the park. As Michael watched her he saw another curtain twitch, then another and another. Was he being watched from every window in the compound?

"Micah..."

Disoriented by the sudden gloom, he stepped inside, his mouth dry, a pounding in his chest that had nothing to do with romance, attraction, compulsion. Instead a sense of destiny fulfilled.

A man is chased all of his life, and all of his life the man outruns his pursuers. Just when he's established unassailable distance between himself and what follows him, when he's so close to victory he no longer even has to run—that's when he stops, turns, opens his arms to his tormentors.

"You finally came," she whispered.

"You knew I would."

His eyes were adjusting and he could see her now. Pointed little face, cloud of black hair, long brown throat. She sat at a card table she'd draped in—yes, a square of velvet the exact blue of the one in which Grandmam had kept her hoard. Gleaming against the rich blue of the cloth stood dozens of towers of gold coins ranked like soldiers to guard a cut-crystal bowl in the center—a bowl large enough to serve punch to a regiment but filled now with golden hoops and chains, some plain, sturdy as electric cable, some finely carved and twisted into ropes—but in that whole bowlful of gold not a chain was thinner than twine; each one as long as the reach of a woman's sinuous brown arm.

"Looks like you don't need this," he said, tossing a jeweler's red satin box into the pot. "But you always had your demands and I figured you'd remember these."

Her laugh was rich and throaty as she lifted that delicately poised head in triumph. "Let me guess. Two gold necklaces and maybe earrings like my—"

"—Aunt Kodi's."

She shook her head and pushed the box aside unopened. "Not in camp. Here I'm the leader, Feya's mom, and somebody's daughter. And you've been too long inside these walls already."

"Seven thousand miles! I've been in here five minutes!"

"Go. People watch. I call the tune now. I want to keep on calling it. For that I need their respect. How long do you think I'd have it if they thought I had a *gajo* on the string—a married *gajo* at that." Her mouth tightened. "You *are* still . . . ?"

"Both. I'm going to keep it that way."

"Then why are you here?"

"I couldn't stay away," he said simply.

"From what?"

Over the steady hum of the air conditioner the sound of waiting, of nothing moving, of the world standing still.

"You. I want you, Farah."

Her smile was secret, triumphant—possibly calculating as she busied herself with an arrangement of chains, perhaps taking a moment to gather her wits.

"I waited for you more than twenty years, Micah. You can wait a day or so for me—deals to make, Feya to settle . . . my mother to get out of the way, she'll have a stopwatch on you this minute. How long are you here for?"

What could he say? I came because I want you and I'm leaving when I've had you? When I'm satisfied you're nothing more than the tattered thread of a childhood friendship? How long was he here for? Her black eyes pinned him down, implacable.

"Well?"

He sighed. "As long as you want me."

She stretched, arched her back. "My trailer. We'll have a couple of days at Sea Ranch. Know it?"

He shook his head.

"You take One north from Sausalito. Pass Stewarts Point and a yellow barn. Take the next left. It's a track, brings you to a place the woods grow down to the sea. It's . . . quiet."

The way she whispered "quiet" was more intimate than a kiss.

"I've an apartment in the Bay Area," he suggested.

"I know. And a house just out of Malibu. I've seen them, but they're *her* places. I want you in mine."

And she called the tune.

"When?" he said hoarsely.

"I'll phone your apartment."

As he was leaving she pointed to the satin box. "Bring it to Sea Ranch, okay?"

At no time had she touched him, or even the box, but he felt its heat like coals in his pocket as he ran down the steps into a scorching Sacramento afternoon. He ached as if he had fever, felt his knees unsteady as he crossed to his car.

All the way to San Francisco to wait for her call he tried to recreate her in her setting until he realized he'd noticed nothing but the woman, the velvet cloth, a dozen golden towers, and honeysuckle soft on the air around her.

She made him wait a week, a week in which Felix called and called and called.

"Have you decided on the Sacramento property, Mischa?"

Decided? He hadn't even looked at it. "Not yet, it's a big investment, there's a zoning problem, we don't want to be hasty, I'm seeing people, I can't be sure."

"Anna and Ellie are—"

"They're okay? The children?"

"Fine, but I think they expect a call. In two more weeks we come to L.A. We don't even know if you will be back in time or if you will meet us there. You know how it is . . ."

I know how it is and I know I can't talk to them now, that what is in me is also in my voice, that Ellie will pick it up, perhaps Anna also. He'd learned, over the years, that women did indeed have intuition, or at least heightened suspicion. Men were easier to lie to.

"I've had no time and no reason to call. If I'm not back I'll meet you all in L.A. You have this number, if something were wrong I'd be called, right? If not—"

For a moment neither of them spoke. Transatlantic static crackled between them.

"If not," Felix prompted gently.

"If not I am very busy and these overseas calls are a waste. Nobody is more frugal than Ellie . . ."

"Oh Mischa, Mischa . . ."

Could anyone, just by saying your name, reproach like Felix? He had a patent on guilt, its brand name Mischa-Mischa, and who but Felix could deliver it in that sorrowing I'm-not-complaining-but-how-you've-let-us-down tone?

"Later, I'll call later," he said, hanging up, wanting the line kept clear for Farah's call.

It came early Monday, brief and anonymous, breathless with an undercurrent of excitement. "I'm leaving in half an hour. See you about noon."

The farther north he drove the more staggering the view, colors so bright their intensity caught in his throat, made him want to live forever, for who could bear to leave paradise? Far below him to his left the sea was a deeper, brighter blue than even Farah's velvet cloth, shifting with depth and sun to turquoise and cobalt and ultramarine; green pines clung tight to white and orange cliffs; where the road dipped close to sea level, white spume flung itself against yellow sand and gray rocks that were there before Micah and Farah and Gabriella von Reiker were born and would be there long after they were gone.

The thought gave added urgency, pressed his foot harder on the gas. This close to the sea the car remained cool and fresh but his palms were clammy and from time to time he dried them on a towel and wondered what was the matter with him. He was thirty years old, for God's sake, not a twelve-year-old kid on his first date. A dozen times he checked the hamper beside him, champagne and caviar in the ice chest, small coral-colored roses in an antique china bowl, nectarines of unbelievable perfection. And of course the red satin box.

The trailer stood locked and isolated under a coastal pine. As he switched off his car he heard her call to him.

"Micaaah! Micaaah!" over the pounding surf. "You wore a jacket to the shore!"

She was running barefoot in the surf, laughing at him, at her freedom and the waves splashing her cotton skirt, the sea wind whipping her hair into a long black scarf behind her.

In a second she had his jacket off, threw it into the car, sent his shoes after it, grabbed his hand and ran again into the waves. The air was cold, the water colder—but her hand was warm, always warm, and when she stopped for breath he pressed it against his lips but she shook him off, pulled his mouth down to hers, opened her lips on small even teeth and a bright tongue that flickered in his mouth like a hummingbird's, licked salt and sand off his lips—"Oh Micah, Micah," nibbling little barracuda bites at his neck, then running and running again, sobbing, laughing—and she didn't even have to tell him at what.

They were children, knew each other's every thought. She laughed, they both did, at themselves for childish eagerness contained in mature and knowing bodies. She sobbed, they both did, for time and chances lost. They ran and they stopped, they kissed and they touched, his shirt was open, a pale blue kite flapping between them and around them, then it was lost, taken up by the wind, blown who knew where—and they laughed at that too.

"Oh, that lovely silk, all the way home to Italy—"

"How did you know?"

"I can read labels, I always do—bet you didn't know I could read, huh?"

"I know nothing about you, nothing—" But his mouth was on hers again and they couldn't breathe. Already they were one and only their mouths had joined.

He groaned. "Here, Farah, now! now!"

"*No!* The first time in *my* trailer, in *my* place, I want you in *my* place, Micah, oh Micah . . ."

She breathed the words into his mouth, shuddered at them, licked his palate and his teeth as they stumbled through the sand, as they lugged the basket from the warming car into the cool of the trailer, poured champagne as they held each other, splashed it on her dress and his pants which they took off and then there was nothing, nothing else in the world but Farah and Micah and warm brown flesh and hard muscles honed with years and years of dance.

"Christ—"

"Wait, wait . . ." With warm greedy little hands she tore open the satin box, slipped giant gold hoops in her ears, hung his two great chains at her neck, where they glistened between small, pointed breasts.

"God, Farah..."

"Wait!"

She rummaged in a trunk and spread the blue velvet cloth on the rug until all her treasure lay spilled out around him, chains and hoops and coins, the trailer a corner of a Midas cave as they plunged their fingers into one gleaming pile after another, threw more ropes of gold round their necks as she pulled him down with her into a pool of gold and watched him drizzle a fine chain over her nipple, now as hard and dark as a blueberry.

It seemed to him that he couldn't wait another second—then he knew he could wait as long as she, that a thirst twenty-five years in the making should not be slaked in a moment, and that they were in any case in limbo, had slipped back to a childhood where only their bodies were grown; their dreams were those of children, innocent, pure. The rules of the universe did not apply. This was magic land.

Their land.

She bent over him, busy as a little girl playing tea party, setting her table with chains of gold, saving her finest bangles and hoops to arrange around the centerpiece that was Micah, opening his arms so he was crucified on the cross of her fantasy.

"There," she whispered, "you're my prisoner, in my power, and I'm never, never, never going to let you go."

He took her by the long rope of her hair and pulled her down to him, just close enough to touch his tongue to her lips, her eyes, her ears, the long thin throat and the hollow between her breasts, close enough to hear the catch of her breath, smell the faint honeysuckle of her scent and the sharp smell peculiar to the Rom, paprika and rosemary and dill, then to spread her on top of him, take the full bird-weight of her, press her into him so wherever they touched they were one body, not two, the same one-body that had huddled for warmth under feather quilts when they were three years old, the same one-body that gloated over cherries and strawberries in the picking fields, that hid where the foreman couldn't find them and stuffed themselves with loganberries until the one-body had two purple tongues which they showed with pride to other children at the fires.

Even as he entered her and she moaned his name over and over they were still children playing a game that would never end, her mouth all over him, voracious little fish kisses that nipped and sucked and bit until he gasped and she laughed and they began again and again and again until at last they could wait no longer, could not again draw away, go back to the beginning, but must plunge forward until they could see and hear and feel nothing but each other's eyes and sobs and fevered skin, until they were oblivious to golden skeins digging at their flesh, tangling their hair, catching sunbeams and showering their frenzy in a golden light.

"Micah," she breathed into his open mouth when they lay exhausted. "You'll stay with me some, you won't go back today." It was not a question. Farah called the tune.

"I'll stay..."

When he opened his eyes again the sun was beginning to go down but he could look around now, see the trailer where before he had seen only Farah. Opulent. Cut-glass mirrors on closet doors, brocades of amber and rose, carpet the pale pale green of a good Mosel. Mosel.

The reminder was a slap in the face. Ellie. Whom he loved. Would always love. But this... thirst for Farah that was thirst for the Rom, would he always want that, too? Farah curled beside him, draped over him? As he moved cautiously she woke, stroked his belly and kissed it. "Oh... if I'd known it could be like that. Before you it was only Vittorio."

He believed her. He knew the Rom. A beautiful woman, a talented dancer, until now she'd slept with only one man. Her husband, because her mother sold her to him for chains of gold; virginity and eternal fidelity were part of the deal.

She stretched, arched, flexed her legs, and he noticed the gleam of a very fine chain indeed, no thicker than a human hair, on her ankle. He touched it lightly. So much thinner than the rest, it suited her fragility if not her taste. "Sentimental value?"

Her laugh was short, quick, harsh. "Slave chain from my ex. A reminder. I never take it off, never forget it."

"Were you his slave?"

Again that laugh. "I was frightened to death of him. At sixteen I weighed seventy-four pounds. He was built like a bouncer. His wife was sick for two years before she died, then he married me. Figure it out. He was an erector set."

"Christ." He held her glass as she sipped the red wine she preferred to his champagne.

"Vittorio was a finishing school. I learned to make my own way. If he'd been decent, a pushover for a pretty face, I'd be just another wife now instead of a Rom Baro making other people's decisions and money that's my own, mine, mine, mine."

"It matters to you that much? Money?"

"Yes." Not a moment's hesitation. "I want all I can get, just like you do—and don't tell me I'm wrong."

"You're not wrong."

She peered through the burgundy into a lowering sun. "What happened to Grandmam's ruby?"

"It's my wife's. Grandmam gave it to her."

She grinned at him through a wine-red mustache. "I know, I wanted to see what you'd say."

"Why did you call yourself La Rubi?"

She shrugged. "For the *kumpania,* what else? Sort of like a charm, the only thing Dui didn't spend. Remember Grandmam showing it at the fires at night, oh such a warm glow it had, remember—"

"No, and you don't either. It was hers, not common property. You knew about it because I told you, you greedy little minx."

She pouted slightly. "I always wanted that ruby—"

"I'll buy you one."

"Wouldn't be the same, and anyway Dui thinks it belongs to the *kumpania.*"

"Dui doesn't have a whole lot to think with."

She licked her lips, the Farah of old whose moods could switch from tough to playful to earnest in the flick of an eye. "So okay, you want to make love with me again, Micah?" The same voice as when she was five, saying, "Wanna pick mushrooms with me, Micah?"

"I thought a swim first—"

"No, we'll shower now—when it's dark we'll go in the sea—then we can do it in the surf with the waves crashing over us." She giggled, touched him lightly with that warm palm and hung a heavy gold rope around the resulting erection.

They spent four days at the beach, days of chasing and splashing and yelling themselves hoarse in Romani over the thunder of the surf; days of drinking from the same glass at the same time and licking the drops from each other's lips; days of eating from the same fruit, juices of nectarine and Micah and small Farah and the great blue Pacific mixing, fizzing, transmuting into a potent alchemy of dreams made real, the future blinded by surf and windspray and sun in their eyes; days of screaming gulls, the hunting cry of a hawk and nights of owl sounds and their own voices joined in one ecstatic shout.

Rom.

Another world.

It was Farah who said at last they should go, that Filigrano's staff would be robbing her blind if she didn't get back.

"When will I see you again," he said, his lips tracing the dancer's curve of her thigh, the sculptured plane of her small brown stomach as she reached to scrape together all her jewelry, gather it into the velvet cloth and lock it in the safe.

"When I get a chance. I told you what my mother's like. I'll call you." She looked into his eyes. "Want to do it with me one more time before we go?" she said softly.

"I want to do it with you and never stop."

"In the sand where it's warm..."

Slow now, tender, as if it must last them forever, storing up memories of skin, of texture, of heat and cool; they lay unmoving for a long time, body on body, mouth on mouth. The end was gradual, no fireworks, no explosions of madness, just a long slow release that was the most exquisite agony he could imagine. When it was done their faces were wet with tears and no way to know who had shed them.

He was appalled at the stack of messages on his desk. Many from Pete Preston, many more from Felix. Nothing from Ellie.

He called her. "I'll be leaving first plane out tomorrow, I'm about done here," although he'd done nothing at all about the Sacramento property and probably would not. He saw it now for what it was. An expedient, an excuse to come.

Her voice was cool, normal, no sharp edges. "There's not much point now," she said, "we're all due to fly there in ten days. Anna too, by the way—they've found Jenny a teacher in L.A. that's supposed to be top-notch, so naturally..."

"And Anna wants to check him out, yes..."

"You did tell me we had the L.A. staff party scheduled for July second?"

Did he? He couldn't remember, but he must have. Ellie was never wrong. "Yes. Can I do anything ahead of time?"

"Just have your secretary send me the list, I'll plan from here when she sends me the numbers."

"The children are okay?"

"Fine." A subtle change in her voice now that he tried to identify. It was caution. "Simon heard you talking to Felix about the Sacramento property. He wanted to go and you should know that Felix has promised to take him. Promised."

"Goddammit! What's he thinking about—"

"This is his reasoning and it *is* reasonable. Jenny is going to be very busy with her dancing... We can't expect a little boy to spend *every* day at the beach even if I were always free to take him and there *is* some entertaining—"

"What will Mary Beth be doing while you're playing hostess?"

"She's coming for a vacation, remember? She's entitled."

"Mmmm—we may have to get extra help—"

"I don't want strangers taking care of the children, you know that, Michael."

Exhaustion and indecision seemed to settle on him like a film of dust. "Let's wait... see what happens... I'll be up in the Bay Area a lot anyway."

"'Bye then—I'll let you know when to pick us up in L.A.—I gather you've not made our reservations?"

Damn! He *always* made their reservations, never missed. "Of course I have," he said quickly, "but the agency hasn't confirmed yet and now I'll have to get Anna on it too, I didn't know for sure. I'll be in touch, okay?"

When he hung up, the receiver slipped out of his hand, wet with sweat. Maybe Ellie hadn't noticed but he had, too late to correct it; in all the years of their marriage he'd never before talked to her on the phone without saying he loved and missed her. And he'd always meant it.

THIRTY-FIVE

*E*LLIE HAD ALWAYS ENJOYED SUMMERS at the Southern California-
nia place, looked forward to easy days of sun and sand, the
pervasive smell of tanning lotion that seemed to saturate the scarred old
floorboards, an occasional trip into Malibu or Santa Monica for essentials
but mainly staying close to home, shopping by phone—a chore Americans in this area had cultivated to a fine art.

Unlike Greenlings this house was not grand, just an average old frame
farmhouse in indifferent repair, perfect for casual summers at the beach.
As Michael told them repeatedly, particularly Felix, it was not Que Vista
itself but its location that had shot its value into the stratosphere in the
three short years they'd owned it. Winter rentals had long since returned
his outlay; seclusion made it a gold mine; inflation made it the most
rock-solid investment they had or were likely to have.

"In fifteen years," he used to say when they first bought it, "it'll be
worth two million at least."

"In fifteen years it will have collapsed!" Anna retorted.

"The land it stands on will not."

"It stands on sand, which the sea will one day take."

But Michael's expectations had been surpassed. Already it was worth more than he'd predicted, and offers arrived regularly from oil-rich Arabs who were buying up Beverly Hills and now turning aquiline noses north.

"Greedy foreigners! They'd build a bomb shelter and paint it purple," Anna warned.

The others smiled. How typical that Anna, quintessential foreigner everywhere, including the new Russia she loathed and daily mourned, was so ready to lump others into a category she denied, absolutely, to be her own.

Her attitude amused everyone but Ellie, who hid her irritation behind private monologues and a brisk facade. Oh, this shallow, this stupid Anna whose life had a hundred tragedies and only three passions—none of them Felix, despite what he and the others might think! Anna cared deeply for Anna, Mischa, and Jenny, in more or less that order. What a blessing after all that Ellie was not of their exclusive company and what a burden the love of this woman could be, the load of guilt, of obligation it seemed to carry. Not that Jenny had felt its sting. Yet.

"We plan on keeping this house for some years," Ellie said firmly, soothing them all and silencing Anna, not exactly a snap. "We're fond of it."

Technically inside L.A. county, the property sat squat and ugly and comfortable in that enviable locale north of Malibu but south of Sequit Point—in spittin' distance of Ventura County, claimed Chita, the live-in help. Fenced and covered with pink ice plant, it was close enough to L.A. when necessary, but far enough to escape the press, making it a temporary haven to visiting actors, screenwriters, directors, rock groups, anyone in the business needing a home and not a hotel in which to house family and pets for the months spent working in Hollywood.

Here were no fancy draperies, no deep carpets to hold the sand, just braided colorful rugs which Chita shook over the railings each morning and which were gritty with sand by noon.

Michael and Felix worked mostly out of the San Francisco office and came down weekends, leaving Ellie with the children and Mary Beth, but this year, with Mary Beth and Anna sweeping Jenny off to a Santa Monica studio at first light, Ellie spent mornings alone with Simon. They took long walks down the beach, poked about in tide pools, threw sticks for Chita's dog.

This time alone with Simon brought them only marginally closer. He

was a loner, no happier with her than if he went alone—though he always
made a point of taking the dog along. Hardly flattering to Ellie, but
Simon never had been. She tried to recall his ever kissing her or Michael
without prompting; no instance came to mind. Mary Beth was again
giving him daily lessons, but that was no permanent answer; eventually
he must go to *some* school—and little hints he dropped now and then
made it very obvious how unhappy he'd been at Brimley, whose reputation, among private schools, was excellent.

"I hated it," he said one day, his lashes even darker now his hair was so
sun-bleached. "I hated the school and the masters and the rotten toffee-
nosed boys!"

"But they were kind!" she protested.

"I don't *want* kind, I want—"

"Yes? You want—?"

But he followed the dog into a sand dune, shrieking like a banshee at
nothing at all, emerging with an old Coke bottle and sand in his eyes. He
never did tell her just what it was he wanted; it remained a mystery, one
among many hanging now in Ellie's mental closet.

Michael.

Don't think about it. Don't think what you're thinking about Michael.
Pretend you don't know what everyone else is thinking. Pretend you
don't see how they're looking at you. With concern. Pity. If something's
wrong it will pass, and if you don't think about it it may go away before
you find out what it is. Above all *say* nothing, keep the closet bolted, for
it's something to do with *them* again and you cannot fight them because
he will not let you into their arena.

She'd half-suggested he bring Rose down for some sun and air. "We
could pitch a tent on the beach for her," she said, not really joking but
not wanting her either. Rose might solve the mystery and she wasn't sure
she was ready for the solution.

She needn't have worried. Michael frowned, rubbed the back of her
hand with that sorrowing air he had lately. "Rose doesn't want to be with
us any more than we want her—and I don't want her that close to
Simon."

"Has he asked any more about Sacramento?"

"Every time he sees us."

"Well? There's not a lot of time left—we'll have to take him to the Bay
Area in a couple of weeks for the company picnic, after that there's only a
week before we leave for Greenlings."

"I know all that. D'you think I can't read a calendar? When we have time to look at the property we'll take him. Maybe. Until then I'm tired of hearing about it."

That note in his voice. Private. Keep out. Off limits. Wait.

Which was exactly what she was doing. Was she the wise owl? Or the ostrich? She didn't know and perhaps never would, but instinct whispered that under this warm and friendly sun lay powerful traps—for Michael, Simon, perhaps for her marriage—and that she must guard her steps, her tongue, and even her thoughts.

Her days passed smoothly because she organized them so, just as she organized her sunbathing and her visits to the gym. When she went home in a month she would be tanned, slim, firm, and rested. Whether she would be happy was another matter.

This year had been no different from the others. Michael met them at the airport, perfect husband, father, and host during the first chaotic week of settling in—yet each member of the party saw subtle changes they had not noticed when he'd left Greenlings several weeks before.

The changes had been obvious first to Pete Preston, who'd arrived at the Bay Area branch a week early and could hardly miss Michael's extended absences from the office, his distracted air when he did show up, that feeling that he constantly waited for phone calls that never came; worst of all was his apparent lack of interest in day-to-day workings of the business.

Felix had noticed things too. Mischa worn? Worried? Could he not be sleeping well? Was it business? Surely not that hasty promise of his to take Simon to Sacramento?—a mistake, he knew, but the boy needed something... He sighed. Mischa. Simon. His own hips worse, the verdict he'd told no one. How had the doctor put it? "No more the pussyfoot? Next year stainless joints and you run like a baby." Who wanted to run like baby and start life over? That was his answer. God knew, if he wanted to worry he need look no further than Anna, still her dizzy moments, forgetful about the pills... stubborn too. And Ellie... so guarded, careful. More than the usual reserve.

Anna had seen changes in Mischa also; her conclusions were sharper, more worrisome than the rest.

"Are you sick?" she asked him bluntly, but she knew he was not—except in the soul, where no amount of fruit could reach.

"Fine—I wish people would stop asking," he said.

"How long you didn't take barre?"

"A few weeks."

"Tssk! No wonder you look like the stray cat! You will make barre! It clears the mind, makes it to think."

"Tomorrow," he promised. He kept this kind of promise.

But it will not help you, she had mourned.

He looked (any man *but* Mischa and she'd have been sure) like a man obsessed. Not with love, which makes the lips smile and the eyes dance —but a deep insatiable need, a pain for which there was no cure. She knew, had seen the same hunger on the face of Hans von Reiker. It was sickness, tragedy. Mischa was not a von Reiker, would not rape; if he killed it would be himself.

With the thought came a glimpse of Ellie anointing herself in the sun, smoothing oil on shoulders and neck and long elegant legs. Anna shook with rage, the pounding in her head so loud she must run in fear for the pills the doctor said would quiet the hammers. This Ellie von Reiker! Did she not know, could she not see, was she so dumb, so insensitive, so Teutonic, that she could not see her husband slipping away, away, that she could lose him? And because of her blindness they could all lose him?

They could all lose him?

No, not Mischa, pray God not Mischa. Stop to worry. She would fix. She would make him dance a class with her and Jenny, then she would know. The face, even the eyes lie, but a dancer's body does not. If joy is there it shows; misery, it shows; passion, jealousy, hopelessness, love, they show. If she was right, if Mischa was in love, something must be done. What good to lie in the sun pouring oil in the navel while the husband is slipping away? Such a perfect family Mischa had made, it must not be threatened, he must not be hurt, the little Jenny must not be diverted by private sorrows, she was too good, too perfect, too much like the young Anna.

Mary Beth Warren, who liked them all and loved none—except perhaps Ellie—saw most of the game and knew beyond question that there was another woman. She sensed that Ellie knew also, but subconsciously —and did not want to face the knowledge.

It was so obvious. Every weekend the three men came down for sun, fun, and relaxation. And to be with the family.

Pete Preston walked the hills around Decker Road with her in the evenings; daytimes, he swam and sunbathed with Ellie.

Felix, in Panama hat and knee-length shorts over thin white legs, painfully hobbled the water's edge with the children, collected shells with Jenny or searched for sea snails with Simon; evenings he drank sherry on the deck while Anna read Russian at him in her rolling sonorous voice.

Michael Abramsky, host, father, boss, and husband, went to bed.

On one pretext or another, headache, fatigue, stomach upset, eye strain, sometimes not bothering to come up with an excuse at all, Michael Abramsky lay on his bed. Mary Beth knew he did not sleep. Her reading spot on the patio looked slantwise into the master bedroom. Glancing up from her book she'd find herself looking straight into the dressing table mirror which reflected the bed and Michael Abramsky staring at the ceiling, brown and grave and so utterly still he could have been meditating or dead. And if she, who was only a houseguest-cum-governess, knew this, then Michael's wife knew it too.

Once she tackled Ellie.

"You're not worried about Michael?"

"Why?"

"He's so quiet—"

"What do you expect? He's been working all week."

"You know what I mean."

"No." Her voice even, flat, almost warning Mary Beth not to go too far. "Perhaps you'll tell me what you mean."

"Oh Ellie—look, this is your buddy speaking, all the way back from good old Grossmutter days—"

"And Michael's my husband. He has worries, businessmen do."

"It doesn't seem to you that when he's here he's killing time until he can go back?"

Ellie looked at her across a hastily erected barrier of employer and employee, gave her the same cool smile she gave tradesmen delivering fish at the back door. "What a colorful imagination you're developing, Mary Beth. It must be the sun or those novels you read. Maybe you should be writing them instead of teaching children their ABC's."

She swept out, every inch the mistress of the house. A second later she was back, a suspicion of tears in her eyes and an apology on her lips.

"I'm sorry. That was unforgivable. You don't deserve—it's just that—I *really* can't talk about it, Mary Beth, if I could you'd be the one I'd talk to but—*don't you see?*"

Mary Beth saw. Conflicting loyalties. In Ellie's code of conduct one did not criticize one's husband, not even to a best friend. Once that kind of girl-to-girl bitching began there was no end to it. Ellie would hold it all in, button it down—but oh the turmoil that must be simmering underneath!

"Okay. Just an idea, then I'll shut up. When they get in tonight, why don't you suggest going up there with him on Monday? It'll only be a week early—we're all going the week after anyway for the company wingding—why not have a week together on your own, the two of you, sort of a second honeymoon?"

Her friend turned crimson, patted her face with a damp cloth and murmured something about too much sun. "With Felix and Pete in the apartment too? You really do have that imagination I was talking about! But we'll see."

"It would be fun, Michael, you know I love Chinatown and—"

"You'll be there in a week anyway," he said, ducking into the shower and staying rather longer than usual.

When he came out she steeled herself, went on as if there'd been no interruption. "Mmm, but there'll be the picnic thing to arrange, so we'll have no time on our own then—I could spend a bit of time with Rose, sort of watch that Simon didn't make any . . . unwelcome contacts while you're not around to see him. He's had a dull sort of summer . . ."

"My God, eight weeks in California dull! At his age! He should be glad he's not stooping, picking tomatoes all day!"

"But still—"

"Look, you can come if you want, but Simon would be wasting his time. There aren't any contacts to make, even suppose we get time to see the Sacramento property—still not definite anyway. The whole *kumpania* left Sacramento a couple of weeks ago, heaven knows where to."

"They didn't tell you?"

He shook his head, and in his eyes she caught a glimpse, quickly hooded, of despair, of utter desolation. She had the sudden urge to hold him the way she would hold Jenny or Simon if they'd had a crushing disappointment.

"They'll be back of course?"

"Eventually. They go on the road in the summers, I'd almost forgotten that . . . Remember Appleby?"

"Yes." Remembering that first June, the year they married, the look on his face when he walked into Greenlings, smoke in his hair, confusion in his eyes, and hearing now the sob of the sea as the tide turned and began to ebb, she did draw him to her.

Each weekend they'd had sex, but Ellie would not have said they made love. Tonight was different. They made love, different love, Ellie tender and giving, Michael desperate and driven. When it was over he buried his face in her hair and whispered so low that the sea-moan outside the window almost drowned his words. "What would I do without you, Ellie... Ellie... Ellie, what am I going to do?"

"About what?" she whispered back, concealing her fears in a shower of kisses. What would he do without her? *Without her?* Could he be thinking of it? No, no, no, not Michael. She was his whole world and she knew it—except for the children and except for... oh hell, admit it, except for the Rom. Would he ever be free of them? But as he said, what was he to do? "About what?" she whispered again.

He didn't answer, and after a time he slept. She pulled the sheet over his naked shoulder and knew she wouldn't go back with him on Monday. It was the way he'd said: "Come if you want, but—" With so little enthusiasm from him, how could she want to? He hurt, somewhere he hurt terribly, and it might be a long time before he could tell her where, before they were ready for that second honeymoon Mary Beth talked about.

Whatever hurt, she knew it went far deeper than her friend imagined. Another woman? Maybe, and if that were all... Ellie believed, believed absolutely, that marriage vows did not entitle one to eternal ownership of another's body. Caring, yes, that was an absolute—they each must *care,* they must want each other's happiness more than their own, they must stand together against anything life could deliver. But acts of the flesh? His body was his and hers was hers. To lack dominion over one's own flesh was to be utterly and abjectly destitute, a point on which even she and Anna would have agreed, supposing they could have discussed so intimate a subject.

Mary Beth didn't know his background the way she did, had no concept of the thread that stretched in him between Rom and *gaje,* a thread so taut, so acutely tuned that the flick of a fingernail reverberated through every nerve in his body. At first she'd thought him armored, invulnerable. Over the years she'd come gradually to see that he was naked and always had been, that the struggle to pile up wealth was nothing more than an instinct to cover young Micah. The thicker the fur, the warmer the winter.

And still she knew she loved him, could wait for the tide to turn, to begin to flow again.

* * *

At Sunday breakfast Anna had Jenny and herself all dressed to go out, as usual serving opinions with her superb coffee.

"All summer you did not see the child dance, Mischa! The new teacher has done miracles—at first I think, My God! Al Watson, a name like that, how could he even teach hopscotch, but then I see, this country have some . . . smart cookies?"

"Anna, my dove, please pass the toast—"

Without a glance she pushed toaster, bread knife, and a French loaf at Felix. "Anyway, Al is excellent, superb! The small Jenny is now polished like a diamond . . . the *pointe* work still needs a little . . . such a pity we can't stay, but Al thinks maybe he comes to London at Christmas and if— anyway, is of no consequence now. Today, Mischa, you shall see!"

"Anna, it's Sunday . . ."

"Does the dancer have a forty-hour week?"

"Anna."

"Time you took a barre also—"

"I took one every day last week, a studio near the office—"

"Good! You need! Pretty soon the muscles will not stretch, will crack like old leather."

"Anna, *I am very tired.*" His voice had a finality that would have stopped a tank.

Not Anna.

"Then who is to drive us?" She paused, giving Mischa time to glance over the table, notice that Mary Beth and Pete Preston were gone, that Ellie—behind the Sunday paper—was not offering.

In the end only Felix and Simon stayed home. Michael drove with Ellie beside him, Jenny and Anna in back listening to tapes of Al's last class, an innovation Anna would have ridiculed last year. Jenny's class went first, Intermediates among whom Jenny was almost, but not quite, the small-est. It was years since Ellie had seen her in a class situation rather than working alone with Anna in the Greenlings studio.

The comparison left her breathless.

Even with her limited knowledge she'd spent enough years now around the studios to separate the true talent from the yearners. At this level most yearners had left the ranks, but even a total stranger to ballet could have pointed straight at Jenny and said:

"There is talent."

At the barre she was an acolyte, devout, frighteningly serious, alert to the high priest's most minute instructions, earning every word of the praise he heaped upon her. When they went to center Ellie held her breath. The child was a sprite, a wisp, a puff of breeze, a cloud—but then she spun *en pointe* and so precise was the strength of her toe that she seemed to be drilling a hole straight through the boards. Her neck had the requisite length, the angle of a natural ballerina, her back deceptively fragile—but her arms, oh her arms were pure magic . . .

Impulsively Ellie turned to Anna, who stood beside her but never for a moment took her eyes from her student. "Oh thank you, Anna, thank you, I can't believe it . . . what you've done, she's—"

"Brilliant. The instinctive dancer. Very rare—and when you find one, easy to teach. But hard to control, very hard. Always they need more than the teacher can give."

"But she's so . . . it must come from Michael, I saw him once—"

Anna gave her scornful what-a-fool-you-are laugh. "No-no-no! Mischa dances from the heart, he's the odd one, the—how are they saying in this country, the maverick! Yes! But Jenny, her talent comes from tradition. It comes from me."

How modest of you, Ellie thought.

"Through you, of course," Anna acknowledged.

Michael watched without expression from the other side of the room. Anna wondered if he even saw—but yes, when the class was over he crossed to Al, chatted briefly and quietly, shook his hand, kissed Jenny, then turned to embrace Anna, whispered to her in his terrible, fractured, wonderful Russian.

"My mother, I thank you."

She caught her breath, with difficulty stopped herself touching his arresting, grieving face. Instead she made a fist, pressed it to his chin, and pushed upward.

"Now is for you," she said quietly. "Now *you* will work, iron out the pains, no?" She intended her words to mean only what they said, but he flushed a dark dark red when he took his place at the mirrors with the senior class.

At barre he was efficient, correct, concentrated. Wooden. For him an exercise, nothing more. And no more had she expected. The Gypsy could be as stubborn as the Russian, hadn't she always told Felix—but now Al closed exercises at the barre and prepared to move to center, divide the students, begin class.

She hurried over, whispered, hinted that since Al would be teaching the talented little Jenny next season maybe a favor? Al nodded, whispered in turn to his wife, who played the records. Class continued, the first moves routine, still a workout. Jump here, spin there, *jeté* there, *cabriole*...

"And now!"

Today's workout began to Debussy, sweet and appealing, then to passionate (but still sweet) Chopin, then a new plaintive note, haunting, sobbing, insistent, edging in...

Gypsy music.

Guitars, violins, smoke, and campfires, in the notes a whirl of skirts and czardas and dark eyes and endless journeys, joy and sadness so entwined now that who knew where one began and the other ended?

And her Mischa, oh her Mischa... again he danced with his heart, at first setting the other dancers on fire, then pulling them aside so he and only he had the boards, his eyes a torture, his body a sweating, agonizing, panting crucifix that danced on and on and on, could not seem to stop, a body that loved and wept and laughed and loved again, a body that hurt, oh how it hurt...

But she had to know and now she knew.

She knew him and she loved him. Was he not her son as much as, perhaps more than, the baby Sasha had ever been? She knew where his beads of sweat ended and his tears began—and at the end it was her own tears that sent her to Al's private office, where she locked the door and sobbed to herself until someone rattled the knob and she must get up, compose her face, and go back to him.

She had wanted to know.

Now she knew.

She wished, yes she *wished* she did not. If she just felt well, could cope... dear God, the tyranny of growing old, when you see what must be done and are too feeble to do it.

THIRTY-SIX

*S*UMMER WAS OVER.

Summer was over and he was still here, watching the plane shudder on its San Francisco runway with all his family in it; due to a last-minute emergency at the office his own seat next to Ellie remained empty.

It was not entirely a fiction—yesterday out of the blue the assistant manager had announced he'd accepted an offer from the competition. The manager wanted to match the other company's offer and Michael had in any case been planning to reward the man with a bonus and a better commission ratio but, as he explained to Felix, the rest of the staff must be considered. They see one member get away with this kind of overt blackmail and what happens? They all jump on the bandwagon and where are you? Held to ransom every time the sales figures show an increase.

The minute Michael had a chance to talk to the man, reason with him, he'd be back at his desk and Michael would be on the next plane to Greenlings. By mid-September without fail.

The truth was, if the man hadn't turned in his resignation Michael would have seized on some other excuse to delay his departure, to wait just a little longer, at least to see her, to ask what he'd done wrong.

She'd said she'd be in touch and had not been. The Sacramento compound had been cleared for the summer and no place to inquire but the Filigrano, which was still open but she wasn't in it. And with Farah he was afraid to threaten whatever fragile link had been forged. Farah called the tune and could silence the band whenever she wanted.

He had to see her again before he left. Just once, he promised himself. Even if she told him to get lost, to get back to his lady-wife, get back to the *gaje*, jump off the Golden Gate Bridge—still he had to see her once more, touch her, assure himself she had been real, that their flesh had joined.

Three months. How could she? Three months and not a word.

Last week in desperation he'd rented a nondescript car and driven to Sacramento, slunk by the compound and seen the trailers of the *kumpania*, hers included, all in their places. She was back. So, unfortunately, were Dui and Rose, whom he certainly didn't want to see.

Her trailer phone was unlisted and he'd no idea what name she went under anyway. He called the Filigrano. No, La Rubi was not appearing for a week or so. But she was there? But of course, it was her establishment. Then could he please speak to her? A pitying silence. If, said the speaker, La Rubi answered every call she got . . . The phone thumped back on its cradle and he was left listening to the dial tone.

The plane gave a last convulsive roar, trembled like a roped stallion, and thundered past him, the small hand of—was it Jenny?—waving until the last possible moment, then it was off and up, shrinking rapidly as it headed north.

At last.

He was alone. No need to pretend to read the paper, to watch rubbish on television, to come out of the shower whistling, no need to smile, no—

"*Micaaah!*"

He whipped around and she was there, waving a yellow chiffon scarf as she swung through the crowd, an early sun winking off facets of the great hoop earrings and the white dazzle of small teeth in a dark little cat-face. She walked easily but fast, full skirt swinging, summer blouse gathered low on the shoulders, peasant style, black hair blowing, streaming. Oh God . . .

"Why—where—you said you'd call!" He reached to take her shoulders, to kiss her, but all he got was a wisp of honeysuckle and she'd stepped away, out of his reach, laughing.

"Hey, we're in public, remember?"

"But why didn't you call? I waited, I went crazy—"

She turned to walk back and he had no choice but to fall in beside her, keep pace as she headed straight down the terminal. "First we set off for Vancouver, I told you, right? No? Well anyway, after Vancouver we had to stop off in Eugene, Uncle Vashti's sister had died so there was a *pomana*, then when we got back I did a bit of checking and found you still had the wife and family up here with you so naturally—"

"But if you'd called me at the office I could have gotten away for an afternoon—"

"*An afternoon?*" For a moment she stopped, stared at him as if he'd gone mad. "You think I'm a girl for an afternoon? And when the afternoon's over off you trot to the wife's bed?"

"But what did you expect? Farah, I've a business to see to, my family was here, what else could I *do,* just tell me what you want for God's sake, Farah, you can't just—"

She tossed back the hair and walked on. "Don't tell me what I can't do. I can do what I like. I'm not married, you are. I said I'd be in touch." She stopped again, looked straight into his eyes for the first time, challenging him, oblivious to crowds that were forced to separate around them. "So now I'm in touch, tell me what you want."

"I want—"

But she was off again, hurrying, almost running for the bank of elevators. They stepped into one and she pressed the button quickly, shutting off the mob behind them, wrapping her arms around him as they descended. "What do you want, Micah?" she whispered into his mouth, covering his lips, forcing her hummingbird's tongue under his. "Tell me what you want."

"Oh God, you know what! I want you—you—you—you—you—"

A lightning reconnoiter of his face with her open, seeking mouth. "I can't get away until the weekend."

"Lord, I have to get back to England, I've a business to—"

"—run and a family to tend, yes, I know, I heard you first time. Like I said, I can't get away before the weekend. We can go to Big Sur... Yosemite... Shasta—see, I'm even letting you pick—"

The elevator slowed to a stop. With one small brown hand she held the door shut and pressed the button to go back up as the other hand moved over his lips, his neck, down the sleek silk shirt, unfastened a button so she could touch his chest with the tip of her tongue. "So tell me, Micah, where shall we go next week, huh?"

* * *

"He did not call?" Anna asked of Felix.

"Yes. He called the office, did not ask for me or Pete, left word with the secretary, said to tell us he'd been delayed a little longer, to expect him in a few days."

"He's gone mad."

Felix sighed. "He's . . . treating Ellie very badly. I don't know what can be the matter with him—"

"I've told you. He's obsessed. You are the man of the family, Felix, you must speak to him, reason with him, he has the beautiful home, the children, the business—"

"He is a grown man, old enough to handle his own affairs—"

"Affairs! Exactly! That is the trouble—"

"My treasure, he is not a child now. I should be the last one to talk to him—why, even in the business, even when he is away, it goes on and on making money."

"But his family, will they go on and on? Simon mopes about like a lost lamb, the angel Jenny waits for her papa, wants—"

"Ellie is a sensible woman, she will know when it is time to speak to Mischa—"

"You think I worry about *her?*" Her fist thumped the dining table and a jar of marmalade jumped three inches. "If she had sense she would not have left him alone in San Francisco! It is for the children I worry."

"Mary Beth is here to help."

"Aha! And you think *she* doesn't know what is going on also? Everyone seems to know but his wife, because she does not *want* to know."

"Calm, my darling, only be calm, look, I bring your pills—tsk! Again you did not take last night—there were eleven in the bottle, still there are eleven. How you can be such a naughty girl when the little Jenny depends on you to teach her?"

"How can I think, how can I do, how can I prepare her for a career on the stage with all this trouble around us. She needs also a father, security, and tomorrow she may not have a home."

"Always you exaggerate. Think of something happy, see how well the chrysanthemums look in the corner beds, so clever of the gardener to mix bronze and white."

"If you do not call him I shall."

Felix was very still. "Please, Anna. I beg you don't interfere. Wait. So yes, something is happening and no, we don't know what, but above all

Mischa is wise. One day soon—please, tell me you will not interfere." To his amazement, she promised.

Bareheaded, wishing he'd left his jacket in his car, sweat streaming down his face, Michael stuck with the road that ran by the sea and tried not to look like a bum begging a ride.

"If you're *that* short of time I'll come into *your* neck of the woods," she'd conceded. "Take Seventeen to Santa Cruz, head north on One, park your car at the entry to Bonny Doon, and start walking up towards Half-moon Bay, you can't miss the signs, I'll pick you up about eleven, we'll have lunch on the beach—and don't call me, okay?"

His neck of the woods! He was a hundred miles from "his neck of the woods," his office, and it was a full week since she'd surprised him at the airport, a week of little sleep and fevered blood, pounding temples and erotic dreams that turned to nightmares from which he woke more exhausted than if he hadn't slept. He even took class every day to work off the tension, but it didn't, nothing did. There was only one way to spend this kind of tension and she knew just what it was.

She was playing with him, a cat with a mouse, and he knew it, he knew it, but dear God he'd see her again any minute, her car would stop beside him and he'd climb in, hold her, feel her breath on his face, that small warm hand on him, but when? when? when? and why was she punishing him? what had he done except leave the Rom and marry Ellie? Farah had married too—ah! but her marriage had been a hell, his a heaven, perhaps *that's* what she couldn't forgive—and what was he saying, his marriage had been a heaven. *Had been?* As if it were already over . . . if he didn't get back soon perhaps it would be, and what could he do without Ellie, the cool of her, the comfort, the calm, above all the calm. Order in his life again. Plans made and kept. Certainty. Now he had none, now he waited like a lovesick kid for a woman's husky voice on the phone to lead him on wild goose chases.

Surely she wasn't coming, never intended to, it was after one already, no breakfast and no lunch, that two-hour workout at some run-down anonymous studio, a shower he wouldn't have washed a dog in, what depths was she bringing him to, what . . . the sun was getting to him, distorting the road, waving it, no sidewalks, he trudged through dust on the shoulder, here was a possum flat as a wafer, too slow off the highway, over there a hole in which some small animal burrowed to escape the sun, to his left the sea, again the sea, like last time, oh let it be like last time, once more in his life like the last time . . . last time he was in his car with cool champagne and caviar and roses for her all on ice. This time another gold chain that weighed a ton, tribute, taxes, maybe he should have got something else, it was too heavy, showy, suppose she didn't come, half an hour and he hadn't seen a gas station let alone a restaurant, ahead of him nothing but empty road and the occasional car whizzing by at seventy-five and the hell with all the signs saying 55, ahead of him a turnoff, a sign saying Beach Access and a car parked, a rented car and oh Christ she was in it, laughing at him from the driver's window as she bit into a hamburger wrapped in yellow paper, sipped Coke through a straw from a gigantic paper cup—

"Want a bite?"

He took in a ragged breath. "You said eleven o'clock!"

"Look at him, the perfect *gajo,* lives all his life by the clock, whatever shall I do with him?"—knowing damn well what she'd do with him, jumping out of the car, tossing him a picnic basket, towels, rush mats, oranges, and a bottle of red wine.

"Farah..."

And again they were running down to the sea, no people here, she fed him hamburger and kisses as they ran, and it wasn't five minutes before she had their clothes off, hung the new gold chain between her breasts and pulled him down to kiss it, then drew him again into the surf to roll and laugh and love in the cool white water.

Afterwards, talking again, resting, pushing orange slices into his mouth and following them with long deep kisses, she said, "Oh Micah, I do like doing it with you, I missed it, too bad you didn't come to 'Couver with us, a dozen *kumpanias* there, all asking after you—and our people, you know how they are, they had their little meeting, we mentioned you, they said maybe like for goodwill you should make a present of Grandmam's ruby to the families, put it in kind of a trust, another way of saying you were one of us, but I told them 'No way! it belongs to Micah's wife and that's that—'" She leaned over him, touched the tip of her tongue to his mouth, his ear, his thighs, and his groans mixed with her laugh as she assured him yet again, "Oh God, Micah, if only your da hadn't done what he did, if we could just be like this all the time..."

Each day he was away Mary Beth couldn't leave it alone, crossing far-ther and farther over that barrier between friend and employee. She seemed unable to stop herself because, as she said, Ellie walked through the days like a wraith. An exaggeration, Ellie thought, but hadn't the heart to stop Mary Beth's well-intentioned efforts at cheerleading.

"I've no patience with you! If you know there's something, if you still want him no matter what, then why not get over there and fight for him!"

"Because he's a man, not a lump of meat. I'm not a dog to fight over him in an alley."

"But you hold all the cards, the children, the home—"

"Are we playing bridge or fighting in back alleys?"

"Your goddam dignity's going to lose him for you."

"I don't think so, and if it does...I can only be myself. When he's ready...if he want me he knows where I am."

"At home! Where *he* should be!"

"I think we'll change the subject. You're having trouble with Simon again, you said?"

"Yes, he's not learning a damn thing. Jenny's working two years ahead of him now and no way can I hide it from him—not that he cares. I've tried every approach I know, motivation, explanation, conceptualization—hell, I've even come down to bribery. All that's left's a damned good licking."

"Licking...?"

"I believe the locals call it 'pasting,' a 'good hiding,' as in a visit to the woodshed with Papa—who is not here! I believe it's called corporal punishment!"

"No."

"He's nine. The hour grows late."

"Then it will have to be a military school."

"When?"

"As soon as Michael comes back we'll decide on one."

Somehow she got rid of her, lay down on her bed and tried not to count off the days. How was she to keep it up? Object of everyone's pity. Before it had been veiled, but the veils were wearing thin. He would come home, oh she knew he'd come home, wasn't Greenlings here? Wasn't Greenlings the main thing in his life—and when he came what was she to say to him? Impossible any longer to pretend. That time was well past.

She looked around this bedroom, remembered them planning it. That chair, that dresser, those lamps. How much they'd loved then, to pick out furniture that would last them a lifetime. His words. Last them a lifetime. Let's get this bedspread, it matches your eyes...when we're old and gray your eyes will still be blue, this bed will still be here...

Yes.

But would they be in it?

*   *   *

She'd been back almost two weeks before he came. The same look on him as before. Drained. Haunted. Unhappy. Perhaps in future it would always be there when he came back, and if so, how could he bear it? How could she?

She asked about the trip, what a pity there was only rain to welcome him back from the sun. She followed him upstairs, helped him unpack, shook out his suits, separated those for hanging, those for cleaning, sorted shirts for the laundry—

No.

Oh no.

Oh no no no no no . . .

Her hands shook as she swept them aside, pushed away blue cotton and cream silk and yellow linen and tried to concentrate on what he was saying.

He'd brought presents for the children, did she think Jenny would like this doll? She nodded in dumb silence. He had a present for her too, always when he'd been on a trip . . . this time pearl earrings to go with the string he'd given her before, which she was now wearing. He bent to place the box in her lap, to kiss her cheek, and she watched her hands as if they were not her own, pushing him away, pushing, pushing, pearls spilling to the rug.

"Michael . . . I'm sorry . . . I thought I could go on as if nothing were happening but it is, it is . . ."

Dimly she felt him move away, knew the room was darker because he stood at the window. When she lifted her head he was looking at her, his face in shadow, the subdued gray light of a rainy day shining on him.

On his tears.

No sound, just the glitter of them on his cheeks, in the stubble of his chin. She put out a hand and he took it, pressed it to his burning face.

"Cool, always so cool," he murmured.

"It's all right, Michael. You don't have to tell me anything. I know."

"How much?"

"I thought it was something else, something you couldn't escape, to do with the Rom—"

"It is."

"—that you'd come back just the way you have before."

"I *am* the same, I *am* back," he pleaded.

She shook her head. "This time you're carrying her spoor." The toe of her black shoe touched his shirts, disturbing again the faint scent of honeysuckle. "I can smell her, Michael."

"Oh God..."

"When it's finished maybe we can start over, but until we can I'd rather we...that you used the dressing room."

He swallowed hard. "You don't want...I thought you'd ask for a divorce, for—oh hell I don't know what—"

"I thought so too, but I've invested too many years in us. Too much effort in the studios. I could take the children away from you but the loss would be theirs also, and why punish them for what you're doing? Something I think you cannot help?"

"You know I love you?"

"Yes. If I were not sure of that I'd leave."

"I don't deserve you."

"No, you don't." Her legs shook but she stood, touched his hand and his wet cheek. "You'll move your things?"

"Yes."

"The shirts. Please take away the shirts..."

In the next months they found a school for Simon; he was happy enough to go, announcing, on his last night at home, that when he came back he'd be so far ahead of Jenny she'd think she was in kindergarten. He also said it was time he got a real allowance. Michael told him it was already taken care of, that he was a big boy and needed money of his own, that it was sent to the school and included in the fees and would be paid out to him once a week by the principal, Major Black.

Also in the next months Michael made two unexpected trips to California, business of course. Once he asked Ellie to go with him and she refused. He did not press.

Also in the next months Jenny performed a small exhibition in Manchester which was "seen" (as backstage gossip had it) by a top scout from *the* London company; it was therefore now only a matter of time, of being old enough, before she auditioned and received her invitation to join the school, which would lead automatically to a place in the company—in Anna's opinion the most prestigious in the world. Anna was ecstatic, could scarcely contain herself, had to stop herself from singing— what a tragedy to be tone-deaf!—but to have produced a student of Jenny's caliber! When the child was thirty years old and a *ballerina assoluta*—how could she be anything else?—it would be remembered that this miracle had been trained by Anna Abramsky, and when Jenny was old and teaching and also produced a miracle student, then people would say, "Well, she was trained by Jenny Abramsky, who was trained by Anna Abramsky, so what can you expect?" Like racehorses, she thought. The line is passed on, from that one to the next one, to the next, it could go on and on, their names forever echoing down the centuries.

"Maybe two more years only," Anna warned Ellie as they waited in the sitting room for Mischa, sipping the predinner cocktail which had become an institution since his first visit to the U.S. Outside it was again raining, but the fire burned brightly, smells of roast veal *suprème* and stuffed mushrooms filtered in from the kitchen accompanied by "Blaydon Races," sung at the top of Lily Finn's lungs. "Yes, two, perhaps three years—then off Jenny goes to London, to live, to study—"

"Nothing is sure, two years is a long time," Ellie said.

Oh, this maddening woman, this Ellie, why could she not rejoice, take pleasure in the spun-sugar castles, what harm when they were certain to come true?

"Rubbish," Anna insisted. "Two years is nothing."

"Be calm, my darling," soothed Felix, "you are proud of the young Jenny, you are right to be proud, you see the fruit of your work—"

"Also I see you limp worse each day—oh, when *will* that Finn woman shut *up!* How long before you see the doctor again?" She had the look of a hawk on the pounce, long nose almost dipping into her gin as she sniffed it suspiciously.

"A few months."

"Better you go now—"

The ring of the phone cut the fractious air and Anna broke off to answer in her usual shrill soprano. "House of Abramsky here! Who you want?"

She listened, her predatory look giving way to the flush of anger, of outrage. "On his way from office. Yes. What message? You give me message, lady, you give *me* message!"

The click of another receiver clearly audible, then the dial tone. Anna slammed the phone.

"Who was it?" Ellie said coolly.

"A joker, am I supposed to know voice of every joker?"

Ellie got up, disappeared to the kitchen, murmuring about dinner, the roast to look at, as if Lily Finn were not this minute opening and shutting the oven door. Constantly!

"Who was it?" Felix asked.

"Her. From California. The Gypsy."

"Rose?"

"Rose! Rose is nossink! No, it is the girl who came to my kitchen at

Ryder Street! That woman at the grandmother's funeral! I told you, did I not tell you, her eyes were all over Mischa, all over him!"

"What message—"

"None! No message! I ask! She laugh! She will 'call later thank you very much'!"

A coal shifted in the fire. Ice clinked in Anna's drink. Felix shifted his hip. "How long has he been home this time?"

"Four weeks. A little less."

"So soon..."

"This time you must talk to him, Felix, you must..."

But already Mischa was in the room, his eyes hooded, no expression on the face, but lonely, oh how lonely, fixing himself a drink. He'd barely taken the first sip when the phone again rang and he was quick to pick it up, to turn away at the sound of the voice.

"Yes?" Oh, he was careful.

"Oh, what a pity..."

"I see." Now he nods.

"Yes." Nods again.

"You mean now?" The tone rising, perhaps in panic?

"I understand, yes. Yes of course."

Then something fast, very... impromptu? in Romani, and he hung up, turned around, speaking mainly to Ellie, who'd just walked in, had heard everything.

"I'm sorry, darling, I'll have to leave tonight. If I can I'll go from Manchester, if not I'll have to drive to Heathrow—"

Anna gave her daughter credit. She trembled for a second, but that was all. Then she picked up her drink and her cue like a pro. "Oh, *not* Rose again, that poor girl..."

"...proud to present farewell performance of *La Rubi!*"

Waiting for the music to start she flashed him a smile, struck the traditional pose and waited.

Tonight there was silence. They all waited. For weeks banners had flapped across Sacramento streets, full-page ads appeared in the paper. The entire *kumpania* was out in force. SRO, the doorman said, letting Michael in through a side door anyway in exchange for a word in Romani and a quick rustle of money under the table.

He'd found a table at the back in the dark, wondered what was so urgent this time that he should again come flying to see her, but he didn't

care, once he was here he didn't care, that was the devil of it. The knowledge that she was in this building, in some room, dressing that body that
he would later undress, touch with his own—it was enough.

But she slipped in for a word before the show.

"You came," she said, taking his hand in both of hers. "I knew you
would."

"You shouldn't call me at home..."

But the candle flickered, shone on her moist lips and the pointed
tongue as she licked them, and it wouldn't have mattered if she'd called
him every night and every day.

"I had to, you'd left the office, I knew you'd want to see the last show,
tonight I'm going to do it, the real thing. One last time before I quit
altogether, you wouldn't want to miss that, would you? I'm doing it just
for you and I'm good, Micah, I am good, I wouldn't want to stop until
you'd seen me, I'll be great, you're never going to forget it."

"Farah—" His mouth was dry, his palms wet, and already he wanted
her. "I want you, God knows it's all I think about, all I—but I live at the
other side of the world—"

"So move! Move here!"

"It's not that easy. Besides, I've got a house, an apartment here, you
won't even come to them."

"I will if she's not in them."

"That's not what you said before. You said you wanted me in your
place—"

"I can't have you in the trailer, there's Feya and my—"

"I know, I know, so where—"

"Maybe later this week—"

"No! Tonight! You called me all the way over here, it better be for
more than flamenco because I'm leaving tomorrow!"

"Oh Micaaah," she whispered, pulling his hand toward her, pressing it
inside her blouse where there was no bra, just smooth brown breasts
ending in nipples tight as rosebuds, dark, hot to the touch. "You like that,
Micah, you do—"

"I mean it, Farah. You're killing my marriage, you're a goddamned
addiction—"

"You didn't have to come, I don't twist your arm—"

"I've booked a hotel tonight." He gave her the name. "If you don't
come there I'm gone in the morning. I won't be back."

Abruptly she flicked his hand away from her breast. "Are you threatening me?"

"No." He sighed. "I'm at the end of my rope."

"Wait till you see my flamenco."

She did not use castanets, a signal this was to be a "pure" performance, faithful to tradition. Her dress was white, ruffled with silver and gold. She looked like a bride.

She was a wonder.

A sinuous, sensuous, explosive miracle, working to such a crescendo she must surely fall, the human body could not sustain such lightning *zapateado*. And through it all her eyes remained fixed on Micah's, never let him go, held him like two black hooks—God, she had Da's eyes.

He shuddered, tried to look away, longing for her and hating her but still she held him, caressed him, kissed him, worshiped him with her hips, her eyes, her open lips. It was a bravura performance, classic and orgasmic, and the audience was on its feet long before she finished.

She was at the hotel almost as soon as he, locking the door, again spreading her gold chains, wanting the ritual, pressing him for praise.

"Was I good, Micah? Was it the best flamenco you ever saw?"

"I haven't seen many but it was wonderful. You don't need me to tell you."

Oh but she did, she did. "D'you like the *filigrano,* where I put my arms up like this, turn like this—"

Oh yes, even more now she was naked, moving in front of the huge mirror, draping herself with gold as she danced, turning down the lights so they touched her here and there, flashed off sweat beads as she moved, glittered on facets of gold. She was in love with her own image but deliberately inciting him, watching him through the mirror as she danced, swayed, yearned, ached—and as before, it was just for him.

"Come and dance with me, Micah," she whispered, "dance with me in the mirror . . ."

He stood behind her, clasped her upraised hands, arched his body into hers and began to move with her, warm himself with her, knowing again that he was under a spell as deliberate as an infantry campaign and not caring, not caring—

"Oh, Farah—"

She turned, pressed her open mouth on him. "Want to do it with me in the mirror, Micah—"

The phone jangled, shattering the moment, her plan, her carefully built scenario. She grabbed it off the hook. "What?" She was a cat hissing its fury, frustration. "What you want?"

A dim polite voice, hotel operator perhaps, then Michael was taking the phone from her.

"Mr. Abramsky? A moment, I have an overseas call—"

Michael felt the blood leave his face. Greenlings, it had to be...but who knew where he was, who—

"Mischa, oh thank God, Mischa..." It was Felix weeping seven thousand miles away, trying to speak, mixing Russian and English.

"Slow, Felix. Tell me slowly."

"So many hotels we call and no Mischa Abramsky. It is my Anna, when I wake her this morning she cannot talk, not walk, her mouth it hangs down at the side, the ambulance took her away—"

A stroke. "Where's Ellie?"

"I'm here."

"Thank God...look, get a doctor to Felix quick."

"I did already. Anna's in Intensive Care, Felix just had a sedative. In half an hour he'll sleep."

Naturally. Calm capable Ellie. "I'll be on the next plane."

"I thought you might," she said, her voice bitter.

He told Farah as he dressed, threw his things into a case, called for a plane reservation. She was aghast, affronted.

"That old Russian? You'd leave me for her? She's not even your flesh and blood."

He pushed her out of the way and hurried to the hall. In the lobby he noticed one of her rich gold chains on his neck and handed it to the desk clerk. "This belongs to the lady in my room. Make sure she gets it, okay?"

THIRTY-SEVEN

*T*HEY'D PUT HER IN ROOM 22, a quiet cubicle overlooking a parking lot and a brick wall. Screens surrounded her bed; a luncheon tray lay untouched on a trolley; high on the wall a television flickered unwatched; crimson and white carnations Michael had telegraphed while waiting for his flight from San Francisco stood on a hall table for visitors to enjoy, out of sight and scent of the patient.

He stepped inside and stood a long time listening. There was a sound, not quite snoring, more the wheeze of disused bellows, slow and labored, so that when one exhalation finished he held his own breath, waiting for her next one and afraid it would not come—afraid also to open the screen, to see what lay behind it. At last he nerved himself, silently opened the curtain.

Exhausted, jet-lagged, guilty, grieving, he felt himself encased in a numbing emotional vacuum as he looked down at her.

She was asleep, no doubt sedated, a long thin sword in the exact center of the bed, her bird's nest of gray hair smoother than he'd ever seen it, her face waxen and tranquil except that the right side seemed to have caved in as if the wax had slipped, melted a little in the sun. Her right eyelid drooped, her cheek below it sagged in creases, her mouth hung open and a trickle of drool ran down her chin. Oh how mortified she'd be, Anna who couldn't stand so much as a crumb on the tablecloth and must constantly reach for a butler's brush and a small silver tray. He took a tissue and gently dried off her chin.

Her eye flew open.

Just one, bright and piercingly blue. The other remained flaccidly closed; in combination with the loose mouth there was a momentary impression, shocking in the circumstances, that she'd given him a particularly lewd wink, the impression strengthened when she, who had lost the power of speech, actually spoke, her enunciation perfect.

"Fuck!"

Her mouth tried to stretch. In surprise? shock? unable to believe what she'd said? Given to strong opinions, her language had always been circumspect, born perhaps of years instructing the very young.

Her open eye blazed with anger. Her mouth tried again. "Fa—falth-th-th—*Se faire faire . . . kava!*" For a moment she brightened. She'd said words. French and Russian and out of any reasonable context, but they were words—then the eye brimmed with furious tears. The words, like "fuck," were not what she was looking for.

He moved to the foot of the bed where she could see him without turning her head, an effort which seemed beyond her at the moment. Her left hand came up, pointed vaguely and shakily at her feet, which Michael now noticed were uncovered, had somehow shed the blankets, were blue with cold.

His insulated envelope, his emotional vacuum, cracked; the cocoon of fatigue in which he'd hidden for twenty traveling hours ripped open and a sob forced itself up from somewhere in his belly.

Her feet, the abused and ugly instruments of which she was so irrationally sensitive. They broke him, brought him to his knees, made him take the insteps in his hands, rub them until his own warmth brought color back into long misshapen toes, wrap his soft wool jacket around them, pulling the sleeve over a high arch, folding the cuffs securely over her toes . . . God, her feet, the thousands on thousands of miles they'd traveled—*en pointe* yet!—but seldom leaving the bare boards of stage or studio; the nightly soaks; powderings; tendonitis; broken blisters; the agony of forcing a footlight smile after two shows on an ingrown nail; the uninjured pads of the toes so brutally and constantly pounded that it was nothing at all for minuscule drops of blood to ooze through the skin; the daily plea from Wardrobe *not* to stain the costume again, please...

Dancer's feet. Caught without shoes, she'd sit quickly and hide them under her skirt. In satin slippers they were elegant, pointed extensions of the leg. Uncovered, they were shameful deformities, poor crabbed creatures with twisted toes, ridged nails and bunions, lumps and dents nature had never intended.

When he was ten and a stranger to this woman, when she taught class from morning till night six days a week—then she'd worn so many tufts of lamb's wool between her toes he'd wondered how she ever got her feet into street shoes.

A few years later his own feet looked no better and by then he was used to them, never gave them a thought, was certainly not ashamed. They were the same as the castanet calluses on Farah's small thumbs, Lily Finn's reddened dishpan hands.

Marks of one's trade.

But Anna, quintessential dancer, had never accepted these monstrosities, had kept them hidden, skeletons in her personal closet. Now aged and with this sudden, cruel infirmity, to be at the mercy of strangers—

A grunt from the pillow, another shaky gesture with the left arm, this time passing it over her chin and pointing to Michael.

He nodded. "Yes, I need a shave. Trust you to tell me."

Half her face tried to laugh but a dreadful gurgling came out which scared up a nurse, a starched uniform crackling behind the screen. She bustled in, adjusted her cap, looked with outrage at her patient's feet wrapped in a man's gray jacket. Shaking her head, she reached for a blanket, motioning Michael outside as she prepared to whip away the jacket. A commotion from the bed, a sudden babble, a gray head frantically shaking, the spastic lurch of a shoulder that would not of itself move.

"Leave the coat where it is!" Michael said.

"Oh, I couldn't do that, sir, against the rules it is—"

"Fuck the rules."

He winked at Anna, whose good eye shone with sardonic glee. Imagine the Abramskys! Not a swearing family, yet twice in five minutes—and in front of strangers, yet!

The nurse put a finger to her lips and he followed her out. "Oh, you should never have left your coat, sir, when Sister sees it on rounds she'll have my hide—"

"I'll take care of Sister. Since when has my mother used words like 'fuck'?"

"Since they brought her in, sir, a lot of 'em do it at first. Seems like they're the only words that come out right so they keep on saying 'em. I had a minister's wife once, oh my, it were blue up here then, I'll tell you!"

"My mother's feet were blue. With cold. Who do I see about private nurses?"

"Your wife already fixed it up, sir, the shifts start up this afternoon. A neurologist's coming in then and—"

"Until then put her flowers where she can see them, turn off the television—she can't stand it—leave my jacket where it is, and bloody well keep her warm. Is that too much to ask?"

Trust Ellie. All done with mirrors and a minimum of hassle. How would she take care of the next problem? he wondered. Or was the problem his? He'd left them, gone kiting off to the States without leaving so much as an address where he could be reached, heaven knew how many Sacramento hotels they'd called before they found him—thank God he'd registered in his own name or he'd still be begging at Farah's altar, burying himself in her flesh, playing hypnotized mouse to her acquisitive little cat.

But oh God, her warmth when it suited her! A single image—small white teeth, pointed face, eyes so quick and black she'd read a man's past and his future before he even knew she was there—already he felt himself stir, quiver, want his mouth on that smooth hard belly, the reluctantly parting thighs.

The hall at Greenlings was warm with deep red carpets and bowls of giant yellow mums, Ellie waiting for him, the light from wall sconces golden on her hair. Ellie waiting for him.

His sudden rush of relief almost overwhelmed him, almost made him babble his love, his gratitude, beg her forgiveness—but she was not Farah, would not welcome a supplicant.

"The hospital called, mentioned you'd stopped in." She did not offer her cheek. "Is she speaking yet?—she was trying this morning."

"'Fuck' was about all she could manage."

She sighed. "The same yesterday and this morning, poor Felix is so shocked . . . first by the stroke, now her language—I don't think he even realizes yet that she could stay aphasic."

"Where is he?"

"Seeing his own doctor, Mary Beth just drove him into town. He's . . . upset with you."

Here it came. "Because you didn't know where to find me?"

She shook her head. "No, just that...he'll tell you. *I* was upset about that, as if you'd abandoned every shred of decency, of normal living. Suppose it had been Simon or Jenny seriously ill? Or me? And you'd been needed for a decision? And we couldn't find you because you were..."

"Playing around?"

"Playing? From the beginning there's never been anything playful about this, has there?" She crossed to the mirror, and he saw that her fists were clenched at her sides. "Do you know how mortifying it is to call one hotel after another humbly asking receptionists if your husband is registered there? To know exactly what they're thinking, that here's another suspicious wife checking on her husband, trying to trap him? And when we did get the right hotel, if only *she* hadn't answered I think I could have..."

"Yes?"

She spun around and for the first time in their marriage he saw a blaze of anger in her that more than matched her mother's memorable flare-ups. Ellie the imperturbable. Ellie, who always said jealousy was the most primitive of emotions, not worthy of civilized people, that human beings didn't own one another, that a sexual liaison was just that. "Maybe I could have pretended to myself that it wasn't happening."

"It won't, not again."

"You'll forgive me if I'm doubtful? If she crooks her little finger tomorrow, off you'll go again to...find Rose, check on a piece of property, attend some urgent thing at the office that could just as well be done by phone? I'm sure there's no limit to the excuses..."

"You said you'd never be jealous of a casual—"

"Oh, stop playing word games! This wasn't casual and I'm *not* jealous another woman has touched your precious body. I *am* furious that you've humiliated me, forced me to call around the world asking strangers if they knew where my husband might be. You've made me an object of pity. I played that role already, Michael, in Grossmutter's house, in her village. I will not—"

"But these hotel people are all strangers."

"Mary Beth, Felix, Pete Preston are not. Even Anna, much as she despises her darling daughter, was sorry for me."

"But I've told you, it'll never happen—"

"Michael, can you tell me honestly—" Her voice had dropped to a whisper and her eyes were two daggers of a terrible burning blue; he tried to look away and found he could not. "If she were to call this minute, could you stop yourself?"

If.

"Micah, let's take a houseboat on Shasta, go to the middle where it's dark dark blue like my velvet, nobody knows how deep—want to do it with me there Micah and never never stop?" Be Rom, submerge yourself in them as you do in Farah, for now Granddad's voice joined with hers across the fire of an old kris and nobody knew how deep that fire burned either, not even Micah.

"And you, Micah, what do you choose?"

Could he stop himself? Easy to say yes with Ellie here, everything she represented in her eyes, her steadfastness, their children, Greenlings, and the pyramid of businesses that supported them all, not least the Abs, without whom he wouldn't have her, wouldn't have anything.

The way her eyes looked now, Ellie could have been young Anna in the wings waiting for a conductor's cue, not sure she'd pick it up when it came—and now there was no time. Mary Beth was helping Felix through the front door, Felix who'd aged twenty years in a week, who aged even more when he looked at his adopted son across this familiar center of their home.

Mary Beth exchanged a quick glance with Ellie, shook her head ever so slightly.

"You were a long time," Ellie said. "Did the doctor keep you, Felix?"

He answered her but did not take his eyes off Michael. "I stop by hospital, still she speaks nonsense, cannot move one side." He turned to the ladies and almost bowed, his distress throwing him back to manners and speech patterns of forty years ago. "If you would be so kind? If we could be left alone? I wish words with my son. In the study, Mischa, if you please."

"Felix..." But Felix was hobbling on his canes, was halfway there, and what could Michael do but follow him, make a pretense of trying to seat him in the wing chair when Felix shook him off, refused to be seated at all, preferring to lean on his canes.

"Felix... I'm sorry, how could I know what had happened—"

"What do you think happened?"

"Anna had a stroke."

"But first *you* happened! You! The Gypsy she took to her heart, you are why my Anna have stroke, why she cannot move, why she speaks from the gutter. *You!*"

"I wasn't even here—"

"No, you were warming yourself at your Gypsy flame across the other side of the world, you were doing what men do with such women—and here my Anna is frantic, has been frantic for months, ever since this thing started."

"Felix . . . oh hell, look, I'm not a hero over there right now either—I'm on everybody's list." He was pleading for sympathy. He knew it, was ashamed of it—in any case Felix was deaf to it.

"Why do you think she has the blood pressure?"

"She's *always* been excitable—"

"But she has never been desperate, not since . . . but of that I do not speak. Has she not been a mother to you? cared for you? worried for you? made her plans and schemes for you? And then what you do? What? You think it's easy to be quiet while your son makes the most stupid mistake of his life, risks everything—"

Afternoon light from the window caught his halo, more transparent every year, turned the man into the avenging angel, and for the first time ever Michael felt stripped before this aging, defenseless man. He struggled to cover himself, to preserve the dignity that Felix, by example, had shown him to be man's most enviable quality.

"It may seem stupid, frivolous to you, to risk my marriage, but that's between Ellie and me—"

"Oh yes! Risk the marriage! And then what? This Ellie whom you do not deserve, if she goes away, then—"

"You're telling me *that* would break Anna's heart? that the very idea gave her a stroke? She *hates* Ellie." And oh how I hate speaking like this to you, to your kind, self-deluding, gullible, suffering face that never hurt anyone and now hurts me with charges that are not fair, not true! "She's always hated her. Anna would be happy if Ellie left."

"Oh Mischa, Mischa, how can you not see? You love my Anna, how can you not see?" His voice dropped to a shaking, fearful whisper. "If Ellie leaves she takes the children. Without the little Jenny what would become of my Anna, Mischa! Tell me!"

"I still don't—"

But Felix would not be diverted. "Ever since Sasha, my wife looks for some safe place to put her love, then you come to us and everything is better, better, but you bring Ellie and again there is doubt. But then Jenny! Mischa, Anna's whole life is this child. She could lose me and survive. She could even lose you. *She could not lose Jenny.* In this life are many kinds of debt. Hamish owed us and we got his house, his business, his life, but what of other debts? We accept affection because we must, we are weak, human, we have need—but each time we accept we owe more and more and more until our debt it is a mountain! If we are a man, a decent man, the day comes when it must be repaid."

The old man leaned forward, now no angel at all but a bird of prey, and in the warm room Michael felt a chill, a loss, a trust he'd betrayed without a thought—because with Farah no thought was possible, only sensations.

"This is why I blame you, Mischa. It was time to repay the loan, to see what you did to Anna, to read her fears, to give up that cousin-who-is-also-lover, to be our own Mischa like before. You did not. You kept on. And now my Anna is a cripple."

Felix, the mildest, kindest man Michael had ever known, had discharged the stored anger of a lifetime in five wrenching minutes. Now it was spent he reached for the chair. In his agitation he missed it.

Michael sprang forward too late. Felix was a heap of bones on the floor, humiliated because his steel canes were just out of reach and without them he was helpless as a turtle on its back. As he'd done many times before, Michael gathered him up, propped him against the desk, reached for the canes and slotted frail, liver-spotted hands firmly in the grips, steadying him, making sure there was no rug to trip him. Again, as he'd done many times before, he asked:

"Okay? Can you make it, Felix?"

Their faces were not five inches apart when Felix blinked and tried to wipe his eyes, but he had no hand free, not even to save his dignity. It was Michael who fished out a handkerchief, who pushed him down into a chair, who kneeled on the floor and leaned his young man's head against an old man's knee, felt fragile, palsied fingers touch his hair, stroke his cheek. It was many minutes later when Felix said quietly:

"And you, son? Can you make it?"

He nodded, the scratch of Felix's gray flannel pants unimaginably comforting. "Yeah."

"You need the shave, Mischa—soon my Anna will complain."

Mischa wanted to tell him she'd complained already but, just like Anna, when he tried the words would not come.

THIRTY-EIGHT

*A*FTER THE INITIAL WEEKS OF RECOVERY it was uncertain which, if any, of Anna's lost functions could be regained by further therapy. When she returned to Greenlings her right side was no longer a flaccid bundle of bone and muscle; fingers began to spasm, then to fumble imperfectly but purposefully at buttons and belts; her right leg did not, as yet, show any such progress, but a cane and powerful muscles in her left leg propelled her along.

"Imagine," Felix complained, "how wealthy! Together we have four canes and four legs. The canes all work, but only one leg. It is terrible, humiliating, to be old!"

Anna's words were badly slurred, complicated by a scramble of three languages stored perfectly in the brain but dependent on a half-paralyzed delivery system. Some consonants were so far out of reach that after weeks of frustrated effort even Anna gave up, sharply rapping the knuckles of a well-meaning nurse with her cane for suggesting she learn to write messages with the left hand. Dammit, she could *do* that—and scrawled "I can!" across a progress chart.

"Then why *don't* you?" the woman said.

But anger had broken Anna's pencil and her self-control; tears, also a legacy of the stroke, were her answer of last resort.

Something more was needed, but the entire household seemed locked into a lethargy no less paralyzing than Anna's condition. Their lives had changed irreversibly, yet no adjustments beyond structural necessities had been made.

One winter morning the family gathered to watch anxiously from behind the drawing-room curtain as Felix and Anna, after a laborious hour of dressing themselves (remarking that they were at last a perfectly matched couple), embarked on their first small stroll since the stroke. Mellow bricks had given way to smoothly concreted walks more suitable for walking canes; not two minutes ago a gardener had finished clearing the walks of snow, washing them with heavily salted water so they could not freeze under the tap of four thin canes.

Into this land of snow-mounded shrubs and three-pronged bird prints on a white lawn, Anna and Felix Abramsky tottered alone, as they had demanded—for they must be again self-sufficient, Mischa, no? Yes, sure. So out they came in mufflers and gloves, overcoats and snow boots, leaning one on another, walking ever so slowly, stopping now and then, sniffing the crisp air. For a moment or two all was harmony, they could have been a Norman Rockwell painting, a couple edging cautiously but symbolically into the winter of their lives—until Anna's cane skidded. Felix reacted (Anna said later) like a hen with one chick, grabbing her useless arm and almost toppling her into a snowbank soon to be an iris bed again.

The tableau moved everyone, even Lily Finn, almost to tears—then characteristically to laughter, as Anna caught her balance but not her temper, jabbed her cane firmly at Felix's slight paunch, and pushed him into soft snow piled under the oak, leaving him for Michael and Ellie to gather up.

The incident was funny, its implications less so. There were conferences, many phone calls; decisions were at last taken.

As a result, the village was once again agog.

Would you believe the Abs were shutting up Greenlings and leaving for California? The United States! Yes! God strike Lily Finn dead if she told a lie!

"At least a year, perhaps indefinitely." The butcher's wife mimicked Ellie's slightly accented English to a tee. "Who'd have thought it," the postmistress said behind a sweet sherry in the bar of the Tip and Tater, "all that work done on Greenlings, all them stables and greenhouses, gardeners for this and grooms for that—now they's dropping the whole kit and caboodle, leaving a daft old twit like Lily Finn in charge!—begging your pardon, Lily!"

Ellie, who neither heard nor contributed to village gossip, saw no reason to mention that the move was prompted by several considerations, only one of which was a top-notch stroke therapy team which Abramo's network of sources located in seconds after Pete Preston asked his computer the right question. Inga, a young specialist, had already been assigned to work with Anna.

Abramo's Investment Division was booming, especially in the U.S., which now generated ten times as much business as the U.K. operation; Electronics, under Pete Preston's management, produced much of its merchandise offshore, which seemed to require a Tokyo office, followed naturally by a Tokyo apartment; it made sense, then, to set the main operation in California, from where they could and did travel east or west easily and often.

Another reason for the move was Jenny, who now urgently needed a regular ballet teacher. Almost the first comprehensible words from Anna after the stroke were "Al Watson," followed next day by "Auntie Monica" —a version of Santa Monica that utterly charmed Jenny, who threw her arms around Anna's neck and said it was the loveliest, funniest name she'd ever heard. She promptly called Al Watson. He agreed absolutely with everything, and set up lesson schedules with Ellie.

"That way," Jenny explained to Anna with the gravity of a nine-year-old sage, "you'll watch me work with Al and I'll watch you with Inga— so at home we'll help each other practice, right?"

"R...r...r...ess!"

"Y! Y! Y! Yes! Yes! Do try, Anna, I know you can—"

"Y...y...y...yes!"

"Oh how—Mummy! Daddy! Felix! Do come listen to Anna, soon she'll be the grumpy old slave driver she always was."

Anna gave them her new one-sided smile and immediately began to weep, a phase of her condition which distressed Felix and Michael even more than Anna herself, for whom weeping in public betrayed the weakest of characters.

Either from luck, innate wisdom, or what was developing into her own quirky sense of humor, Jenny was the only one who handled these apparently involuntary tears well. She'd had a doll once which could either weep or wet her knickers depending on which one of her plastic arms you raised.

"I do wonder," she said to Anna one day as she dried the ever flowing tears, "what's going to happen when we get to Auntie Monica and Inga teaches you to lift your right arm."

"Jenny!" Ellie said. "That is not nice!"

Maybe not, but Anna was laughing instead of crying, even pulling the child closer and pressing trembling lips to her firm young cheek.

Taking Simon to California was no problem either. Major Black at the military school was no less reluctant to see the back of Simon Abramsky than Mr. Brimley had been. Michael told Mary Beth he was sure the more relaxed atmosphere of American schools would be just what the boy needed; Mary Beth lifted one neatly plucked eyebrow and said nothing.

But for Ellie the main, the overriding reason was private. Since Anna's stroke Michael had not been back to California; when his presence seemed required he found reasons to hedge, postpone; California calls to the house, of which there were many, he refused to accept. At the office he ducked even legitimate business calls and correspondence from California, delegating them through Pete, who took them as a matter of course, because without being told, Pete somehow knew and tried to protect her—but she did not *want* to be protected. She wanted to know exactly where Michael's loyalties lay and she would never find out from here.

So easy to dodge the phone—but in moving to California they moved into *her* territory. Not so easy then for him to hide behind business, behind the family. One way or another the woman who smelled of honeysuckle would force a meeting and when she did Ellie would know, because now she knew what to look for; he'd be no more able to hide his feelings than the *gaje*—of which he'd spoken so often with contempt.

One way or another California would solve problems or bring them to a head. And she wanted that, was tired of sleeping alone, lying awake knowing that he too lay wakeful at the other side of the dressing-room door, tired of wanting him and denying him. Not that he asked. He kissed her good night with his hands on her shoulders, and it would have taken only the slightest inclination of her body towards him for his arms to hold her—then they'd be back where they were, neither of them knowing what would happen if his troublesome relative walked back into their lives.

In California, at some point, she would.

Que Vista bowed Ellie into its wide drive with tossing palms, a trellis heavy with purple trumpet vine, and the gentle lapping of a calm shore. Out past the white ruffle of breakers a migratory whale slapped at the water with an enormous fluke while another rolled lazily and waved a fin on its way south. Only February, yet there was no ice on which to slip, no cold days and colder nights when the old and infirm simply could not venture out—and to everyone's relief no Lily Finn caterwauling as she swept and polished and ironed.

Chita, wide, strong, stolidly silent, took one look at Anna, crossed herself, and had to be restrained from carrying her bodily into the house by a tall blond woman who was also part of the welcoming committee.

Inga. She made no effort to help her patient up the porch steps and even when it seemed she might stumble, Inga's large hand motioned everyone back like a policeman directing traffic; she would not be moved, she was a statue watching Anna's lone struggle to negotiate the stairs.

Michael muttered that she needed help, Felix wrung his hands, and Jenny stamped her foot. Ellie watched: it had seemed to her at Greenlings that Anna's frustration sprang from too much help, but on the subject of Anna, Ellie's opinions were invariably suspect and she was careful to keep them to herself. Since Anna's stroke the tension between them had changed subtly. Where always an emotional tightrope had stretched between revulsion on Anna's part and contempt on Ellie's, there was now a tacit peace: hostilities, for the length of Anna's disability, were suspended.

Anna reached the top stair, clutched the banister for support, and turned round to direct the glaring searchlight of her one open eye on this new tormentor.

"You see!" Felix said to Inga. "Now all is spoiled, already she does not like you."

"But she will learn to walk. And talk."

To everyone's surprise but Ellie's, that's exactly what happened. It seemed that Anna *forced* herself to learn to speak if only to tell Inga what she thought of her. Due to her meager vocabulary she began modestly. One day Inga was "tat ooma," the next she was "t 'at ooman," which in no time at all became "that woman," and then "that Nazi."

"I'm Swedish," Inga said, placidly massaging Anna's wasted leg. "Straighten your knee."

"I can not," Anna said carefully, truthfully, looking to Ellie to bear her out; Inga had chosen Ellie to help with the sessions because, as she confided when they were alone, "the others treat her like a baby."

"Try."

"I can not."

Inga got up, unfastened her apron, and reached for her purse. "Very well, if you want to hop on one leg forever."

Slowly, painfully, Anna straightened her knee.

"Good. Now again. Good. You see, is it so hard?"

"Yes."

When she left Anna pointed to the closing door and nodded. "Is Nazi. I know."

"She's helping you, you've improved a lot."

She nodded. "I know." She also cared—more than she would have admitted, even if her tongue could have formed the complex structure of ideas into words. Helplessness. She hated it even more than she'd hated von Reiker. This well-tuned body had turned on her. Had she not kept it in tune? deprived it of sweets, fats, and all but the most natural of carbohydrates? And in the end it too had betrayed her. Yes, she hated the Swede, a bossy woman, she could never *stand* bossy women, but if she had the knowledge to make the legs work, the arm...

After the first traumatic weeks Inga returned to her institute and Mary Beth began the daily routine of driving to Auntie Monica, dropping off Anna with Inga, Jenny with Al, and Simon at Malibu Elementary School, picking them all up at the end of the day, just, she complained happily, like UPS. Mary Beth was delighted to be home, had been away much too long; but her relatives, during the several years of her exile, had either died off or drifted away, and so by now, even here on home ground, she felt more an Abramsky than a Warren.

Michael ran the new L.A. office on Wilshire, to which Felix went doggedly every day although it was increasingly obvious that even climbing into the car was a burden. "In the new year I shall have the surgery, Mischa."

"Why wait?"

"Because it may take some time to recover, and I should like to get better at Greenlings—oh, don't mistake me! Is beautiful, this place you bring us, but the happiest days I remember are at Greenlings when we first moved. Then I could walk not too bad, remember? And you brought home your wife and your children and we were all happy."

"I guess," Michael said to Ellie when they were alone, "he's forgotten the bad times, when we wondered how to meet the payroll and the mortgage, when we robbed Peter to pay Paul...when every day was war between you and Anna, when Dui hung around—"

"I agree with Felix," she said quietly. "The early days were good for me too."

He turned away. They both knew that she was not speaking of Greenlings or Santa Monica or Dui, but *their* early days.

"Why," she said, "do you never go to the San Francisco office?"

"Why?" He shrugged. "I have capable people in charge, I talk to them every day—and in any case *you* don't want to come."

"Michael, I love it there, the wharf, the shops, the people—what I don't like is knowing you want me along for a keeper, as if you can't be trusted alone in her vicinity."

"You know it's not like that," he said.

But they both knew it was just like that. In June Ellie flew to England on studio business and Michael came with her—just to check on Greenlings. The resident nightingale kept everything in perfect order, including the gardener and his son, and the family could, she said graciously, come back whenever they liked.

"Kind of you," Michael said dryly.

"It's June," Ellie reminded him. "Think you'd like a trip to Appleby for the fair?"

"No."

No, she thought. The *kumpania* wouldn't be there but the associations would.

The calls, which came in on Michael's private unlisted number at the office, began at the end of summer.

The first was Dui. When was he going to see his brother, eh? From what he'd heard Micah had been in the States months and months, not a hop-skip-and-jump from Sacramento, right? Not that he had a reason for asking, but how was business?

Fine.

"...only I'm in a spot o' trouble, a few too many beers and this fella punches me, calls the coppers—"

"Tell your Rom Baro. Let her bail you out."

"Who d'you think gave me your number, Micah?"

Just Dui's heavy breathing on the line. Was she standing there? he wondered. Listening? Her head tilted just so, pointed little tongue licking her lips? Warm little fingers worrying her ropes of gold? Planning her next move? If she had this number she had the home number too, also unlisted. He hung up, called Ma Bell and canceled them both, extracted promises of new numbers by tomorrow. And then he had to tell them all. Felix, Mary Beth, Anna, Jenny, Al Watson, Inga, Simon's school.

And of course Ellie. He told her when they were alone on the beach after sunset, the sea a metallic raft with its single passenger, the silver moon, riding its undulating surface.

"Dui again," he said. "Any calls to the house?"

"No."

"I've had the numbers changed anyway."

"I don't think it will help," she said softly. "If she knew the phone numbers she knows where we are."

"*She?* What d'you mean, *she? Dui* called me!"

"Yes."

How intense he looked, how lean and sharp and *listening*—a threatened animal—and how suddenly she *must* speak, must shatter this emotional silence that was tearing at them both. "Michael, what *is* she that she can do this to you, frighten you...I don't want to be jealous, a keeper, a shrew, I don't want to wonder every time you come home if...*I don't want to go on like this!*"

"What is she?" His voice was a flat echo of her own.

He picked up a hunk of driftwood and hurled it savagely out to sea, seemed surprised when it came back—but of course it came back and back and back, what could they expect, it would always come back because the tide said it must, pushed it—

"What is she, Michael?"

"It sounds...childish to say we were promised to each other, but we were, Ellie, we were. I was almost five, she no more than four, and we talked of furnishings and bride-price and—"

"But you were *small children!*"

He shook his head. "The Rom are never small children. Until they can speak they are babies. When they can speak they are little people learning how to make their way, manipulate, by that time they *understand!* They know they are of the families, they *know* they are different, privileged—"

"*Privileged?*"

"They think so," he said, bitter, hard. "They live off us, therefore they're better than us. That's how they see it."

Better than *us. Us.* Did he at last feel *gajo?* Maybe. "But you still haven't answered. What is *she?*"

He faced the sea; the moonlight turned his face into a steel hatchet. "She is a small dark woman with calluses on her hands and on her soul and she'll never forgive me for leaving her, for rejecting her and the *kumpania.*"

The next call came to the house about a month later. They were all at their daily pursuits and Ellie was home alone.

She'd expected a light voice, feminine, perhaps dainty. This was husky, confident, demanding.

"Get me Micah."

"I'm sorry, my husband's not at home."

"Where is he?"

"If I could take a message? He's not at home—"

"I heard you first time. You didn't answer my question."

"May I tell him who called?"

"Forget it, lady, I'll tell him myself!"

Slam.

Ellie tried to swallow her anger but it wouldn't go down. Then Michael came home early, looked haggard again, hunted, vaguely guilty but not sure about what.

"She called here too?" he asked.

"Right."

"So you finally talked to her." He turned, stared out at the small breakers and a few surfers waiting for something fit to ride. "How was she?"

"Her health or her manners?"

"That bad, huh?"

She shrugged. "Of course, I'm only Micah's wife—"

"You think she's jealous of *you?*" He shook his head. "Oh no. If she was rude it's not because you're my wife, it's because you're a *gaja,* of no consequence in her scheme of things."

"Flattering."

"I'm sorry..."

"What did she want?"

"Dui's in jail. Would you believe Hawaii? I guess the whole bunch of them spent the summer there and came back, now they took Dui back again, all expenses paid."

"What's he done?"

"I don't want to know—but if they extradited him it's more than drunk and disorderly."

"And what did *she* want?"

"Money for a lawyer, support for his family."

"And?"

"I said no."

A year ago Ellie might have protested; ten years ago certainly. "Good," she said now. "Good."

Good yes, but his hand shook as he poured himself a straight Scotch and swallowed it down.

Inga said (not in Anna's hearing) that her patient's progress was nothing short of phenomenal. She now spoke slowly and carefully but with piercing clarity; if she forgot herself and reverted to the old excitements and waving of arms her words were unintelligible. Much of the paralysis had been exercised, massaged, or just plain sweated away. Her right foot dragged ever so slightly and her right arm raised slower and lower than the left—but twice a week now she took a special dance class for the disabled and Inga reported that she played the part of star with great aplomb. Since most of the others had never danced in their lives she must surely have known she had an unfair advantage, just *why* she was so admired, but the boost came right when her confidence needed it, and so . . .

And so she accepted it—but she did wish the family wouldn't *whisper* about her in corners. She'd always had hearing like a lynx and her illness hadn't diminished it one jot. Of course she'd made a good recovery—of course she had to work to make her shoulder move when she told it to. They thought this was hard? Let them try *grands jetés* with cramp in the instep, a full house, and the performance director in the front row with his clipboard, then they'd know *hard!* No, the worst of the illness was not physical, she'd spent her life mastering the body and could do it again, it was the damned *crying*—how she hated to weep in front of Jenny! Such a bad example, dancers don't weep, dancers work, and the child was to be a dancer, a great dancer. A nuisance that Al's studio was four flights up and no elevator, but soon she'd be ready to climb four flights, then they'd see. She'd promised herself. *She would see Jenny's class.* The day after Christmas she would get up those four flights of stairs if she had to go on her knees. This was Anna's Christmas present to Anna and no one would stop her, no one. Certainly not that slab-faced Inga who whispered in corners with Ellie.

Oh, this Ellie, when would she get back to being married to Mischa? So provincial, all this time holding a grudge! So what if he'd had a woman on the side? He hadn't lost the children, that's what mattered—but such a foolish risk he took, and for what? A Russian saying of Papa's that Maman frowned on: All cows are black at night, all women are beautiful in bed. Marriage is for better or worse—and a sensible woman shuts her eyes and waits for the worst to pass. Oh, but if Mischa had lost the children!

As Thanksgiving turkey ads disappeared from the paper and Christmas tree lots sprouted along Pacific Coast Highway her plans and self-imposed workouts accelerated, spurred on perhaps by that seasonal air of subdued excitement in the house, packages arriving and disappearing in a blink of an eye, locked closets, Jenny and Mary Beth making too many mysterious trips to Santa Monica, shopping no doubt, but why did they never take Simon with them—if they could find him! That boy! Twice lately he'd ducked school to "bum around" (what vulgarities he used!)

and the truant officer began calling the house. What a shame, two children, one an angel, the other a sullen young lout, poor Mischa! But he bore the disappointments with dignity, as he did the situation with his wife. And always so thoughtful to *her*...

A day or so before Christmas he arrived home early with theater tickets for them all, even Inga, some sort of Christmas treat and dinner first at a new French restaurant on Wilshire in which Abramo had some investment. So smart he was always.

She disliked restaurant meals, the gargantuan portions they served, but he meant well, so she dressed as she was told and let herself be shepherded along, but oh dear, sitting in the car for another trip to L.A., not her favorite city, traffic a nightmare, people so busy, so rushing...

The Chicken Kiev in her honor was, she had to admit, not bad—too rich, but now and then... and the melon was superb. Jenny seemed too excited to eat, bright pink spots in her cheeks—of course Ellie should have been checking her temperature, perhaps taking her home instead of to the theater, but such an unobservant mother, what could one expect?

A mob at the theater, but somehow they arrived just at curtain time and two young ushers helped her tap along the dark aisles, oh this *shameful* cane, seating her between Mischa and Felix just as the overture struck up, programs rustled, hisses and hushes and the sudden scent of fir trees.

The *Nutcracker*—so near to Christmas, what else? Of course Jenny and Mary Beth disappeared before they were even seated—to get ice cream they said—but they did not come back. Probably the child was sick as she'd predicted, unless... she didn't even want to think... no, not yet, it never happened, they wouldn't, not yet, not even in *Nutcracker*.

Whatever the nebulous hope, it did not materialize. Anna couldn't find her. She searched the face of every little girl in the corps. Jenny's pink and gold innocence was not there; she searched the feet, Jenny's crisp technique was not there. She searched necks and spines and above all arms, but nowhere was Jenny's certainty, her presence... but how foolish to expect... and how intense her disappointment, the treacherous tears gathering again in her throat, thank God the lights were down.

The tempo changed, house lights flickered, and now the "Dance of the Flowers," the stage a pastel bouquet of delicacy, of lightness, of young life that would never be so fragile, so precious again, could disappear with a breath... and a yellow flower, the color with the prettiest steps, was... of course it was Jenny, who else could they have chosen, the poise of her, ten years old and already the ease of a pro, steps so precise you could have etched a choreographic diagram from them. Her arms spread, fragile as a songbird's wings but tensile steel in the shoulder. She turned and there was joy, she crossed the stage, ephemeral as mist, and there was magic. Head up, neck at that special angle, looking straight out at the audience, at her, smiling *directly at her,* dancing for *her.*

Her granddaughter.

Anna Abramsky's blood, her talent, her technique all poured into this small perfect vessel.

Never had she been so proud nor would be again. Months, years of "Pretty hands, my darling—hold it straight the spine—nice, ah, nice *alongée*—pick-pick-pick at the boards, my love, your toes like little pinpricks fast, now faster, faster—" years on the rack for an hour in the spotlight, but oh how warm the light, even its reflection.

She glanced to either side, Mischa and Felix watching her, reaching for her hands, sharing her pride. Thirty years a woman bitter over a war that robbed her of many things, this career among them, this joy of giving and receiving from an audience. The rancor of all that pain and effort spilled in vain—and now none of it mattered. The skill was not wasted, only passed on, and to her own blood.

So good, not a mistake, not one, her little role ending, the music fading, and now the bows, the pretty curtsy of a yellow dress and that shared triumph aimed directly at Anna Abramsky.

Now Anna smelled roses, somebody pressed a florist's box on her—Ellie perhaps?—pointed to the stage, whispered that she should walk that long dimly lighted aisle and present them—she, Anna, who dragged her foot and was uncertain even in daylight, she should have the privilege of giving roses to this flower of her heart, this granddaughter. Dimly, at the edge of awareness, a small something begged to be acknowledged, the ghost perhaps of a grandfather, Hans von Reiker, but there was no time, no time ...

It was the most hard won, the most perfect performance of Anna Abramsky's life. She refused to look down at the carpet, trusted to God and providence to leave no programs, candy wrappers, cigarette boxes in her path; she did not drag her foot; when she reached the footlights and handed the box to the conductor to pass up to Jenny she blew her a perfect stage kiss *with her right hand,* and who cared if she was crying because she was, and this time it had nothing to do with shame, with weakness.

Oh, but she was proud.

THIRTY-NINE

"*I* THINK, MISCHA, IT IS TIME." The year was already in its second week and Felix had not made it into the office since the staff Christmas party. Even as a passenger, with the backseat to accommodate him, the daily drive into L.A. had finally become too much. "I must make plans."

"I agree—you should have had it done years ago. But this is routine surgery now, they have superb facilities here, wonderful doctors. Why go all the way back to England at the coldest time of the year?"

"I told you. When it comes time for me to walk 'like a baby' as they keep saying, I want it should be at Greenlings . . ."

"You're forgetting how the wind blows through the larches this time of year, what the gardeners have to do just to keep the ornamentals *alive*. Here there's no problem. Look outside, there's sun and warmth and—"

"I am an old man. Humor me, yes? Sit and I tell you—this Que Vista is heaven—but I don't want to go there yet or even to run on the earth like a baby. *I want only to walk without pain*. This is a nice house—but we bought it with money. Greenlings was bought with dreams, maybe even with love, for we had no money then, remember? So for me—and I think also for you—Greenlings is home."

"Yes, but we can all go in summer—"

"We came for one year, remember? It has been one year. Anna and I go next week or the week after. I have the surgery next month, then maybe a month in the house to recuperate. By the time I am ready to walk the grounds, the early tulips will be up, the Japanese cherry will be in bud... such a shame to miss it all."

"If you go we all go."

Ellie, when Michael told her, agreed. Out of the question for Anna and Felix to go alone. Suppose Anna had another... not that she would. "But she could. Under stress, Felix in danger." In the end it was decided to leave Jenny here in Mary Beth's care for a while longer, they both loved it so, and her training wouldn't be disrupted—but they'd take Simon home with them. "He's not doing much here," she said with a sigh.

She knew they couldn't leave Felix to face his surgery alone, but oh how she hated to leave now, just when it seemed Farah might make her move; she had the excuse, Dui out of action and his family a financial drain on the *kumpania*. And Ellie herself had begun to long for the confrontation, to think of little else. To get it over. If Michael, when the time came, went to that woman again, then it was all over. She'd get a divorce and move permanently to Que Vista with the children. She'd reached the decision the night of Jenny's debut as a professional performer. After the show they'd had some friends over to the house, among them Pete Preston, en route from Japan to London. When the others were drinking on the porch Ellie took a walk on the firm wet sand of an ebbing tide. Pete followed her.

Just out of sight of the house he caught up with her, took her in his arm and kissed her. "Why not?" His urgent whisper just made it over the low surge-back of surf, over a scatter of shells and pebbles that rolled like dice under a full moon, were left shining, neglected, waiting for the next great pull of the sea. "Why not? You've no marriage left, Ellie. A fool could see it. You act like strangers to each other. Polite strangers."

Again he kissed her, and against her will she found herself responding, wanting his mouth on her, his hands, sensations she'd almost forgotten beginning to stir in her, her arms reaching for him, guiding his hands to her waist, then higher, to her breasts—

She pushed him away, remembering another Peter, a young doctor she'd used because she needed *somebody* to want her and he happened to be there. There should be more to it than wanting, there should be a desire to *give*. With Pete there wasn't. She liked him, always had, but in all these years she'd never given him so much as a single romantic or emotional thought. She wanted him now, yes, because she was hungry and he'd satisfy that hunger—maybe anyone could right now. But tomorrow? How would she face him tomorrow? What would she say? Sorry about last night, Pete, but you happened to be there? He deserved better.

"No. I'm sorry."

"But why? You wanted it, I know you did! Please, Ellie, it would mean everything to me, everything—"

"I know. That's why."

She walked on alone and Pete returned to the party, disappearing later with a pretty little redhead who clung to him and whispered to Ellie, "He's just so *darling,* I could listen to him talk forever. That accent!"

Pete, no better for the several martinis he'd gulped down one after another, hiccuped as he steered her to his car. "Talking wasn't quite what I had in mind."

"Me neither," the girl giggled, and off they shot down the driveway dragging a cloud of moonlit sand behind them.

Hot morning, cool water, nothing to do but wait, wait, wait. Simon paddled out on his board, waited at the spot the rollers began to show their form, waited for a wave worth catching. Too calm. Today he could be here all day. Nothing to do but watch the house. Watch them get stuff ready.

He could see Chita shaking rugs off the deck; Mom carrying another paper sack over to the trash; Dad helping Felix settle down on the lounger, then stacking books into wooden crates for the shippers due to come pack this afternoon; Anna in a floppy purple hat that looked like pickled cabbage walking barefoot on wet sand because Inga told her it strengthened the insteps. Mary Beth and Jenny in Santa Monica because *they* were staying. Naturally. Whatever Jenny wanted.

Beyond the house, hills and more hills; if you went back far enough there were lonely roads where you could walk for maybe an hour without seeing a house. If you walked far enough and no cops picked you up he bet you could get all the way to Sacramento, no sweat. If.

Like Dad said all the time. Yes, I'll take you to Sacramento if we go; I'll take you to one of their horse fairs if we get the time; yes, I'll tell you about the Rom sometime if...; yes, I'll show you wild honey if I see the right bushes.

A year in California and he hadn't gotten to see Tomo and Uncle Dui once, not one time. And now they were leaving, back to that Greenlings. He hated it, hated it. Even here—and he liked it here because he was free, could do what he wanted—he had nightmares sometimes about Greenlings. In his dreams the walls were even higher than they really were, the gates like prison bars, the house itself old, closed in, stifling. He shivered, tried not to think about being there in three days, about them putting him back in another school. He hated school too, all that time learning stuff he didn't want to know. If you didn't learn it they thought you were dumb. Didn't they ever think you just might not want to know?

Now Chita's dog barked at him from the water's edge, telling him to come in. Poor Poco, to live at the beach and be scared of the water! Maybe he'd head in himself pretty soon, walk the dog. Poco was going to miss him, he bet. Come Friday Poco'd be running up and down, looking out to sea for Simon's bright green board. He scrubbed at his eyes. He wasn't crying, he wasn't. It was salt water did that. He'd wait a bit longer for the salt to quit stinging his eyes. He paddled in place, went neither farther in nor out, just hung there in the water, almost let his eyes go blank. He could have dropped off to sleep in the gentle rocking of sea and sun. After a while he thought maybe he had, and rubbed his eyes again, checking out Que Vista.

It was noon now, hard to see anything in the heat shimmer that came off the land. Some sort of commotion at the entrance, arms waving, gates opening, something driving in, the mover's truck maybe—not big enough. It was a trailer, shiny cream and all its windows open, driving fast for the house, whipping round that circular drive as if whoever drove it was hopping *mad*. Then it stopped and he could see nothing for whole minutes until the dust settled. He squinted, wished he'd brought the field glasses Dad gave him for Christmas—he would have, except he hated for Dad to see him use stuff he gave him.

A woman was getting out. She looked small, from here anybody would, but her red skirt flew like a flag. People were out of the house, he could see Dad's blue shirt and the pale knot of Mom's hair the way she twisted it on top of her head when she was busy. They talked—it seemed like forever—then the little woman turned and beckoned inside the trailer and people poured out of it, two tiny kids, a fat woman, then—

Oh, wow, it was *him*, it was *him!*

"Wait up! Wait up!"

He shouted himself hoarse, paddling like mad for shore.

Ellie saw her first, no question who she was, no question now why Michael had been so besotted. Had been? Or still was? Now he saw her—and a stack of books cascaded to the deck.

Not a pretty woman, too bold, the feline features more those of a bobcat than a kitten. But just walking down the trailer steps she moved the way other women danced. Liquid, all of a piece, small and neatly shaped, a swinging red skirt and white blouse, neck and arms smothered in gold. Barefoot. Exciting. Sultry. Animal. Impossible to look at her and not think of sex. Earthy sex, wild sex, uninhibited sex. *Different*.

Now Michael moved forward, to the casual eye a reluctant and puzzled host, to Ellie's an angry, bemused man facing a situation he's dreaded and longed for.

As had she.

"Micah!" The woman swept past Ellie and flowed to Michael, took his hands, looked up into his eyes. "Micaaah!" She breathed on the name, loving it, caressing it, drawing it out.

Looking at them together, dark, vital, there could be no question, even in the mind of Chita if she was watching from the kitchen window, that these two had been together in the most intimate of ways, knew each other's body totally, its needs, its responses, its secret pleasures. And had reveled in the knowledge.

Impossible to tell from Michael's face whether he still yearned for it, but yet she felt some thread connected them, the same thread as when Michael had talked with Dui, with Grandmam and Rose. Instinctively she knew now the name of that thread. *Kumpania*. This is what it was. Not members of a club, not fraternal at all. Paternal maybe; eternal certainly —and Ellie wished now she could be anywhere but within its electric orbit.

Ellie the *gaja*.

The intruder.

In her own home.

Now Michael loosed his hands, was introducing her very clearly. "Farah, this is my wife, Gabriella. Ellie, this is—" But Farah's glance merely flicked over her like a whip, left its sting, and returned to Michael. Who was still Micah.

"You're not asking me in?" she said to him, mocking him.

"I don't think you heard. I introduced you to my wife."

"I came to see you!"

"This is our home, Farah." His tone was frighteningly quiet, but as confident now as hers. *"And here is my wife!"*

But Farah would look only at Michael; she laughed at him, lifted a pointed chin, showed off a long shapely throat as if for his inspection, and her eyes glittered with a dark hard shine. "What d'you expect me to say? 'Pleased to meet your highness'?"

Ellie forced herself to be calm, called up from the past an old woman brusquely disposing of a local matron attempting to scale the social heights of Trier on Grossmutter's shoulders, watching the pushy woman leave, then turning to Ellie: "Outflank them with manners, Gabriella, it's the only weapon they'll never have." Perhaps that's why Michael introduced her as Gabriella, something he never did. A subconscious reminder of who she was? She found her tongue, her hostess's wits.

"How do you do," she murmured, "so sorry we're not...we're indisposed, as you see..." Her single weapon was brushed completely aside as Farah took Michael by the shoulders, forced him to turn toward the sea, crooning at him.

"Oh that lovely surf, Micah. All cool...makes you think, doesn't it make you think though?"

He shook off her hands as if they were sand crabs, turned back to Ellie, and slipped an arm around her shoulder. "Yes. It makes me think I was out of my mind. You come here, where my children are, my wife, no thought for their feelings, no—"

"So?" She shrugged smooth brown shoulders, the sun flashing off facets of gold. *"They're* not family, don't mean nothin' to me."

"They're *my* family."

"The *kumpania*'s your family, our Micah! The *kumpania!*"

Ellie heard it, the harsh thrust of it, and knew that her own poor word weapons were teaspoons hurled at a steamroller. In case she'd missed its significance, Farah said it again.

"Our kumpania—*they're your family!"*

He'd break. The intensity of the associations, the woman, the word, all too much, too much, how could she even blame him—

But he was shaking his head, gripping Ellie's shoulder as his right arm made a gesture as natural, as dignified as Grandmam presenting the ruby at the wedding. The sweep of it included them all, Ellie pulled close beside him, Felix in his chair, Anna walking with her careful new gait at water's edge, Simon paddling frantically for shore, even Jenny's leg warmers airing on the deck.

"This is my family."

The finality was unmistakable, even to Farah.

She turned a dull olive green, the whites of her eyes muddy, sick. Her only shine now was the gold at throat and wrists.

"In that case"—she tried to grin and again Ellie saw the snarl of a bobcat—"you missed a few members."

She turned to the trailer, whistled, beckoned, watching with obvious relish as two children came tumbling down the steps to roll and laugh in the sand, a girl of maybe nine and a baby barely toddling. Following them, again huge with child, Dui's wife. Behind her, lounging in the trailer door, smoke curling from his thin nostrils, slim young fingers clutching a can of beer, stood Tomo. He'd be all of thirteen or fourteen.

Farah laughed again, her color and her spirits returned. "Well! Now you've *really* got a family, huh?"

Michael stiffened. "What's all this about? Why are they here? We're leaving in a couple of days."

She rolled her hips, very confident. "That's what we heard, that you were leaving. I figured I'd give you one last chance but you blew it—and there's this little problem with Dui not cleared up. I called you about it, remember?"

"And I told you. It's nothing to do with me."

"Oh, I know you didn't commit manslaughter, not you, but—"

"Manslaughter?"

Her eyes opened wide. "I didn't tell you? Oh, pity. Anyway, I got a lawyer in Honolulu that's used to our people, our ways, but we're a working *kumpania*, Micah, and Dui's little clan just don't earn its keep, see what I mean? I know you wouldn't want to see *family* go without . . ."

"Whatever happened to Welfare? Aid to this and that? I thought you were all experts at it."

"And I thought I told *you* we were through with it."

"Since when?"

"Since I'm Rom Baro." She brushed her palms together, and in the silence around them Ellie distinctly heard a rasp—the calluses Michael had told her about. These were on her thumbs, but she was sure, now, that this woman grew them bigger and harder on her soul. "So!" she said now, whirling around with a swing of red skirts, waved them a final jingle of gold as she climbed into the trailer. "They're your business now. See ya!"

At the top she paused, turned to Michael and made a slow, deliberate gesture, stroked small brown hands smoothly over the pointed swell of her breasts. She said something very quiet and intense in Romani, and it was as if she were spitting on him. Then she swung her hair like a black scarf, switched on the motor, and roared off into the dazzle of a Que Vista noon.

"What was it, what did she say, Michael?" Ellie whispered.

"Her *armaya*. Curse. 'May the wild dogs spill her blood if she ever forgets this day.' It means nothing, just for effect."

Then why was he shaking, why could he not seem to let go her hand as they discussed what to do with Dui's family?

Already Tomo foraged in the fridge on the deck, throwing out Cokes for his sister and mother, grabbing a couple of beers for himself, sprawling in a lounger as he tossed a spent cigarette over the rail. The toddler dropped its empty feeding bottle in the sand, picked it up and began to suck on it, sand and all. The older girl fingered Jenny's leg warmers with some speculation in her touch. Dui's wife waddled up the steps, her pudgy hands trying unsuccessfully to bear some of the burden of her all-too-productive belly.

"They can't stay, even for an hour," he said to Ellie.

"Oh, Michael . . ."

"No 'oh Michael'—they're going."

He drew her by the hand to their small study, shut the door, lifted her chin and kissed her slowly, lingeringly, on the lips as if he would drink her in, drop by slow drop. He still clung to her hand as he tapped numbers into the phone, called a secretary, told her exactly what he wanted.

"Furnished. Nothing fancy, but respectable, not a dump, understand? Lease it for . . . oh, six months. Yes, in advance."

A pause while she scribbled notes, thought up questions, while Michael touched his mouth to his wife's cheek.

"Right! Downey, Burbank, Lakewood, anywhere but here. But it has to be *now*. Send a car the minute you firm it up—I'd like them out of here and settled in a couple of hours."

"Wow," Ellie said when he'd hung up and was stroking her hair, "you really expect service."

He nodded. "One of the benefits of money . . . Ellie?"

"Yes?"

But he had nothing to say. He kissed her instead, ran his hand down the long length of her, held her against him, sighed and buried his head in the hollow of her neck, took the pins from her hair and kissed her through the clean fresh veil of it. After a while she locked the door and drew the curtains.

"And just think," she sighed a little later, "in a couple of days we'll be home again, too."

"We're home now. We're together."

They were. Travelers on the same passionate sea as before, its tides, swells, hollows, tastes, its sudden urgent thrusts sweeter now, more intense as they explored half-remembered caves, one moment breathless with newfound wonder, the next tossed helplessly on rediscovered tides of pulsating warmth. Tides that swept them all the way home.

While they all, in their different ways, waited for the company car to arrive and whisk Dui's family off to its rented home in Wherever, Simon spent spellbound hours listening at the feet of his cousin Tomo, who greeted him casually, warmly, happily, as if he'd lived only for this moment, as if they'd seen each other just last week.

"Hey! Kid! How've ya been?" He tossed a pack of cigarettes at Simon. "Want one?"

"No," Simon lied. "My throat's sore. Tell me what you told me on the phone when I was little, Tomo."

"What did I tell you, kid?"

"About the fairs, the traveling . . . you know, stuff."

"I'm working now, didja know that?"

"Jeez, you're only fourteen—what do you do?"

"Roofin', sometimes I strip cars."

"Wow!"

FORTY

THE ACTUAL SURGERY, they said, had been a success, perfect except for the small chip of bone that wasn't there and the frag-
ment of shrapnel that was. But no matter. It was done. Rest, later
exercise...a pity the patient insisted on recuperating at home. A major
medical facility was invariably the best choice, just in case.

Felix was adamant and Anna supported him absolutely. "We have nurse
for him. We have Gabriella who watches. We have me. We have the Finn
woman if she does not burst Felix's eardrums—"

"I like to hear her," he said, his voice weak, perhaps petulant. "A little
loud, but..."

The doctors had refused absolutely to allow him to sleep in the great
marshmallow bed that was also his marriage bed. Much too soft. Instead
a contraption they called a hospital recliner was wheeled in, complete
with pulleys and levers and cranks which gave off strange noises when its
bank of controls was touched.

It petrified Anna, Lily Finn approached it with caution, but when it was time each morning to make what they referred to as his barre—a spastic stagger from bed to hall and back, supported on every side—the device tilted him vertical at the beginning and laid him down, exhausted and pale, at the end. Anna's therapy rendered her infallible, and she informed family, nurses, even the doctors, just what should and should not be done for Felix.

"For once," she said, in her slow, deliberate new voice, "we are a matched set. Not since we first married—now again we are equal."

No, Felix thought, she had her own bones in her own body; he had this miraculous new metal which did not feel right, never mind that they stood in the hall applauding his every step as if he were indeed a baby.

"One step, only one, just try, Felix."

Come to Anna... come to Ellie... come to Lily. Such cries of wonder at each halting shuffle toward them! And how each step exhausted him! It was better with Mischa, who talked to him like a man but who could pick him up and carry him back to bed when Felix whispered, "Enough, Mischa, I have enough."

He had thought to find peace away from the busy corridors of a great hospital, but at Greenlings it was in short supply too. He loved their voices, their visits, the small talk of the house, what will be for dinner, Lily Finn's cheerful arias, should the gazebo be painted white or cream this year, a few tiles off the roof and wasn't it too bad another oak branch would have to go but of course the roof came first...

He loved it all, but their anxiety distressed him, why must he be the source of so much worry? They thought he did not see, that their cheerful voices and pasted-on smiles fooled him. They thought he could not *feel* the tension after the doctor left him each morning and one family member after another would find an excuse to help the doctor drink his tea down in the study.

Then the murmur of their concern drifting up the stairs, the rumble of the doctor's measured tones. Once he thought he heard a single cry of anguish, but Simon was at school, Jenny still in California, so why? and who? He thought it was not Anna; in each marriage one must love more than the other, and of his own role he had never been in doubt. Ellie? No, and for the same reason—her love for Mischa went beyond even what she felt for the children. Mischa? How to tell with such a tangle of wants and needs—yes, he loved Felix, he loved Anna, he loved Ellie and his children, he loved this house—but if Mischa had to choose just one? Felix thought maybe the businesses, the money—because money protected him from the past.

* * *

"I don't believe you," Michael said. "You said it was a success."

"The nuts-and-bolts part yes, that's routine these days, but he wasn't robust to start with, *any* surgery carries risk—"

"But he's walking . . . well, he's taking steps."

"The first time on his feet he took two and fell into the nurse's arms. That was over a month ago. Yesterday was his best day yet. Five steps. Then he passed out. He's running a fever, infection at the—"

"Surely antibiotics—"

"Michael, he's never been *off* them since a week before surgery! I'm sorry, but we'll have to go in again. The X-rays look—well, to be frank, not promising."

"Then why not leave him alone, let him live in peace in a wheelchair?"

The doctor shook his head. It might come to that, but they still had to go back in, get at the infection, clear the source, close him up. Maybe after a month or so they could try the main surgery again if things seemed . . .

"But better not get too optimistic, old chap, always wise to be prepared . . ."

"*No!*" Michael cried, suddenly realizing what the man was telling him, that Felix had a lot of fighting to do and nothing to fight with. "When . . ."

"Soon."

"Can it wait a week?"

The doctor shrugged. "I don't see why not."

That's when he knew, quite definitely. Far back in his head a silent keening began, a voice shouting no, no, it wasn't fair! Just when they had everything, everything! The doctor didn't see why not because it made no damned difference, from here on it was all just going through the motions. He started to babble and couldn't seem to stop, images bombarding him from every side, Felix at the zoo making some cockeyed remark about elephants and ears; Felix with ice-cream cones in his hand; Felix anguished not only that Hamish Froggatt would lose but that they would gain.

". . . and there's this tree in the arbor—you did know he laid out all that south side of the house, didn't you? Well, there's this tree, a Japanese flowering cherry, pretty thing he planted ten years ago, waits eleven months a year for it to bloom, a mass of these little flowers, you'd swear they were paper, he sets a lot of store by it, kept talking about it in

California, and it's just coming into bud now, I know when he sees it bloom he'll be stronger, have more . . . be more . . ."

"Positive?" The doctor drained his cup and stood to leave. "Make it a week then—but his problems aren't psychological, don't get too set up about it, okay?"

Michael and the gardener rigged up a screen to keep the coldest winds off it, and when the buds still refused to open they set up reflector plates, moved them every hour to the sun.

"You'll burn it," Anna warned, and it seemed once as if they had; a few pink tips had discolored slightly, but they backed off the reflectors a few feet and the gardener's boy stood guard duty all day. Then toward the end of March, a few weeks before it normally bloomed and a couple of days before Felix was to be taken back to hospital, the boy ran in to get Ellie first thing in the morning when she was still in her robe. She hurried into the breakfast room all smiles.

"It's opening! Come and see, Michael, Anna—"

Michael saw. A few buds from the topmost mass had burst in the night, a few scraps of tissue-thin petals showed their fluted edges. He snapped one off and raced upstairs to show Felix, who was noticeably paler and weaker each day, who ate less and less, whose fever stayed stubbornly up.

"Look here, Felix! One more day and the whole thing's going to be a blasted fireworks display! You'll never believe the bloom this year, every branch drooping down with the weight! This time tomorrow—"

Felix set the small blossom on his tray with fingers no less papery than the flower. Slowly he rubbed each petal between thumb and forefinger and just as slowly shook his head.

"That poor boy out in this cold to watch a tree . . . how hard you all worked—" He lifted pale bruised petals to his mouth and rubbed them on paler lips.

"One more day, Felix!"

He closed his eyes, the lids almost transparent, every vein a thin blue line, rivers on a worn old map.

"But Mischa, I have no more days."

He died that evening and the house, so determinedly busy and cheerful for weeks, settled into quiet. They could all be quiet. No more need to pretend to themselves, to one another, to *him*—who'd known all the time.

"Simon will come home from school for the funeral . . ."

Ellie spoke vaguely, for once unsure of anything. She was by the window, alone with Anna in that room with the feather bed and the hospital contraption from which they'd just taken Felix, and neither woman knew quite what to do with this new thing between them, a shared loss in which neither could give or take comfort from the other. The gates to compassion had been locked far too long, were rusted shut. She tried to tell herself that Felix had never come first with Anna, but she knew otherwise. Once he *must* have been first but, as she'd found out for herself, each child stole a little from its father. The same couple, they made the same love, but the moment there were children some part of a woman, a part impossible to ignore, listened. For that cough in the night, that cry, that nightmare only *she* could chase away, the ego of the mother constantly at war with the ego of the wife.

Suppose it had been Michael they'd just taken away, oh how she'd have wanted arms around her, human warmth touching her, giving her something back for what was gone. How must she feel, this embattled woman who'd just won her own great war only to see her husband lose his? In this room that was theirs, that held their good moments and their bad, that great feather bed large enough for six and now only her own bony frame to fill it? A spirit that could neither forgive nor weep nor *give*.

She avoided Ellie's eyes, wandering from yellowed pictures to a hideous pink lampshade, stroking old carved boxes, china dolls, chanting to herself in—what? Russian? Sometimes English. "In the end, in the end, it always comes to this in the end...everything, love and hate and it all ends the same way...waste, such waste." She was quiet for a long time then, and Ellie never did discover what was wasted, but what could she do but say something herself? The silence was unbearable.

"I don't know if we should have Mary Beth bring Jenny over or not, it seems a long trip for one day but she adored..."

Anna put down an old fur piece she'd been fingering and turned to her, the winter light merciless on her face.

"Bring her," Anna whispered. "Bring Jenny. For me."

Anna Abramsky pleading with her. Was this the time to drag out an old portrait, hold it in front of her, advance, make her back up and up and up? Make her admit that she, in her implacable righteousness, had treated her own child like rubbish?

No. The time for that, if there'd ever been one, was past. It would be the most hollow of victories now.

"Will you call Mary Beth or shall I?" she said.

She watched her mother's face dissolve, awash with grief and relief and—oh God—gratitude, remorse, pride, every emotion on that great suffering spectrum. "Gabriella . . ."

"Yes?"

A pause, Anna turning to a window as thin and narrow as she; outside, the last of the icicles melted, drip, drip, drip, off the eaves. "You call. You are good with such things . . ." A sigh, not her usual theatrical inhalation. This was natural. Beaten. Heartbroken and heartbreaking. "You are good with so many things, I suppose I never told you . . ."

As if it had just now come to mind.

"Oh Anna—" Ellie held on to her through the storm of tears which she realized were shed for Felix and not for her, but did it matter?

"The Gypsy in you should be proud," Ellie whispered to him through the service, around them the village church in which not a single seat was vacant.

So yes, he was proud, and it had nothing to do with Gypsies. Where had Felix found them, all these people who'd come to say good-bye to him? The family and the Abramo people, of course, but the household staff showed up full strength too—not just the gardener and son but a wife and four daughters, and surely that lanky, hung-over, hangdog chap in back was Lily Finn's wandering here-today-gone-tomorrow husband? But who were these others? That woman with gnawed fingernails and chapped knuckles—didn't she keep their cars topped up with gas? The man in Donegal tweed and Argyle socks, wasn't he their butcher? The kid in red leather pants, white silk cravat, and pink pimples, wasn't he the paperboy, Anna's token nossink? Naturally the doctors showed up, the least—the bloody least!—they could do! But that sniffly girl in the corner, hadn't she been one of Felix's surgical nurses? Yes. They'd all made time, they'd come here for Felix Ab, the despised foreigner in the big house. So it wasn't Felix, with his halo and his smile, they'd despised. It was he—Michael Abramsky, Gypsy upstart, pariah. The local yokels had come to pay respects to Felix, who'd lived his life in many places of the world without making a single enemy.

Could he say the same?

Would these people have come for Michael?

But he knew the answer and shut out the rest of the service, watched

Anna, sad but composed, on one side, Ellie the same on the other, beyond them Jenny fighting tears and Simon sulky and defensive, afraid to feel and waiting for it to be over.

The graveyard was at the very top of aptly named Bleakhill, and the minister had winter burials down to a fine swift art for which not a mourner blamed him. Up here the wind blew cruelly sharp, and even now, the season almost past, every mossy headstone glittered with rime. The paths were treacherous and he kept tight hold of Anna, who had refused to use a cane on this day.

They began the short walk home, Michael and Ellie on either side of Anna, who staunchly refused to use the cars which crept beside them. Just in case.

"In case of what?" she demanded.

"You are a stubborn woman and it's very cold." And they'd just buried Felix who died, after all, of pneumonia.

"You think maybe I fall? weep like *bébé*? have hysterics such as the people at your grandmother's funeral? Never! You forget the children, they watch, must learn strength." She exhaled, her breath a thin white plume preceding her. "In church I am thinking many things. It is better that Felix die before me, no? I am strong, can live without Felix—but Felix without Anna?" Her long hands spread wide at the very idea. "He would be lost, my Felix would be lost without me..."

Her voice quavered, its deliberate cadence lost, then she was whispering so only Ellie and Michael could hear.

"Gabriella...make me favor, yes? Say you are too cold, that you wish to ride? That I come with you to keep company?"

It was a signal that only Michael did not welcome. The twins and Mary Beth jumped in one car, Anna and Ellie in the other.

The warmth of the car, the heavy lap rugs, the enforced intimacy of two women alone, one of whom had lost a husband, the other a beloved friend, seemed to erode Anna's iron control.

"I lie, you know I lie," she whispered. "I lie now and it is wicked, wicked. Without Felix it is I who am lost. I am! Everything he did for me! He bring my tea, make me to sleep, to wake, to take my pills, to eat when I forget. Now Mischa, such a busy man already, my poor son (am I not lucky to have him?) he will have to think of everything..."

Even through Anna's tears, certainly genuine, Ellie thought she detected the small blue gleam of calculation and knew that to hesitate now would be to lose for many years to come.

She took Anna's hand, looked her firmly in the eye. "Yes, you *are* a lucky woman, Anna. You have me, the children, Mary Beth—and Michael, but he works, has a wife and children too. If you need permanent help we'll find someone, but I think you'll be happier to join in with the family. It's not as if you're a dependent sort of person."

Anna shot her a shrewd glance and dabbed at the corner of her eye. "Of course you are right. I have too much pride for that . . ."

After a meager, silent dinner—the empty place at table was all too new, too raw—the family dispersed, and Michael walked restlessly through the grounds of this house in which Felix, he saw now, had so obviously intended to die. But the grounds were stiff with winter, as bleak as the cemetery on the hill. On impulse he took the car down the hill to town, warmer there, frost melting to a dirty, sleety rain. The car seemed to nose its own way into Ryder Street, to park itself at a well-remembered curb.

Now there was an Abramo store downstairs, above it a studio. Neither did much business, but they'd kept them open from one year to the next out of sentiment—Felix's sentiment. "Remember, Mischa, the day you came to us, your poor arm and your terrible lies?" Being Felix, he did not mention the lice and the barnyard stink the urchin had brought into their clean home.

He peered through the window, beyond television sets and radios and washing machines, a newer counter for electronic components, beyond all that to a cheap lace curtain, had it been pink? and a man who'd seemed old then, thumping away on a piano, his cane swinging like a metronome on the chair, the strident voice of the woman in the foreground but always the man's halo behind her.

Felix Abramsky had given him his first bath in a real tub, showed him his first view of the world, gave him the first—perhaps the only—compliment that had ever meant anything to him at all. It was when spring came to Ryder Street and Michael hid in a broom closet, sure they would send him away and where, then, could he go? Who in the world would want that hopeless, thieving, devious child but Felix Abramsky, for whom nothing human was hopeless?

Downstairs Anna yelling at her Advanced Girls to pick up the chin and present themselves; with him in the closet the smell of furniture polish and carbolic soap, then the door opening and the heathery smell of Felix's wool sweater, an audible creak as hip and knee adjusted to the tiny closet. The tactfully worded invitation. Then:

"You have given us pleasure."

He crossed the street and looked up at the roof, the tiles he'd set that first winter still in place but again in need of repair. And there was the grocer's shop where Felix made him return a stolen pound of butter; the window with the pink lamp, the Friday soirees, Felix's prewar suit and squeaky shoes; years later Felix determined to do the duty of a gentleman and a father by warning a precocious young liar that friendship was better than sex. Gentleman.

A gentle man.

He drove home through crisp moonlight and hard bright stars and it wasn't until he parked and switched off the motor that he heard the racket, a furious clanging of hammer on metal.

What the hell . . .

He followed the din—nothing could have been easier—and there under the flowering cherry was Simon in flannel dressing gown and Robin Hood pajamas pounding ineffectually at a reflector screen, his thin young body so concentrated on each feeble blow he didn't even see Michael behind him, hardly paused when his father's arms went around him, clasped brown hands over pink on the hammer's shaft, added his man's strength to that of the boy as they beat minuscule dimples into a sheet of metal.

They were sweating when they gave up and hurled a reflector plate aside, when Simon squirmed away, flailing at the trunk with his bare hands, shaking it, shaking it, not stopping until a few pale petals fluttered down on him like confetti and he allowed himself to weep, to be gathered, for once, into his father's arms.

"How come?" he said fiercely. "How come they all go?"

Wanting to weep with him, Michael held him, brushed dust and bark and cherry blossoms from his shoulders.

"I don't know." He sighed. "Do you believe this tree? All that work and its season's almost done?"

FORTY-ONE

*T*HE GREEN AND GOLD AFTERNOON dozed in the sun, an idyll of playing fields and leafy shade, of faculty wives presiding over picnic hampers and, when they remembered, scattering applause like confetti over home team and opponents alike. In the hedges wrens chirruped and scolded, in the pavilion bumble bees swarmed over a rose-covered trellis, and from the field itself a stready crack of bat on ball as young men in cricket whites, their teammates voicing well-bred encouragement, earnestly played the game.

"Go on, man, hit it for six!"

"Oh, well played, well played!"

Eventually a perfunctory cheer went up for a new player who showed markedly less enthusiasm than the rest.

"Good luck, Abramsky..."

Seconds later: "Do get after it, man...no, oh no!"

A rattle of wickets falling.

A concerted, agonized groan.

"Missed it, he missed it on purpose! Lord, what a *wet!*"

Scowling, Simon strode off the field without waiting for the umpire's cry of "Out!" Damn them all anyway. Who cared about a stupid game? They raved about it as if it really *mattered*—not who won or lost but who blindly, earnestly, bloody well played the game.

The games master waited off the field, concerned disapproval on his beefy, outdoorsy face.

"You didn't even try."

"I told you I didn't want to play. It's a waste of time—"

"Time? You're almost sixteen, chappie, about *time* you found a sense of responsibility! You're letting down the side. Me, your family, the team, the school . . . a dozen boys begging for a place on that team and like a fool I gave it to you."

"I didn't ask for it."

"Oh wake *up,* you're a smart lad with a good eye, you hit a true ball and run like blazes. A born athlete if ever I saw one. You could beat the best we've got if you'd just try."

"I keep telling you. I don't want to beat anybody."

"But we have our orders, your father wants you whipped into shape and I can't say I blame him—he specifically told us to involve you in sports—"

"It's not his business—"

"You know it is. He's giving you every advantage. He wants you *prepared,* ready to look life in the eye and lick it, man!"

Simon tried not to laugh. He liked the games master, but his mind ran on one track guided by a single precept: Team sports built character, whacking a ball about and running like hell produced mysterious qualities of use to the team, the class, the school. Ultimately to Abramo. To try was to succeed and success was what mattered. The games master now confirmed it.

"A successful man like your father, d'you think he'd be proud of your performance on the field just now?"

Now Simon did laugh, couldn't stop it. It gushed up from his throat in a tide of genuine incredulity. "My father wouldn't know a cricket bat from a hockey stick if you knocked him senseless with it."

Not that you'd get the chance, he thought. Michael Abramsky was way too quick for clods like the games master. With the knowledge came a grudging pride in his father, followed as usual by searing, inexplicable anger. He'd been given every advantage? He was a prisoner condemned to one school after another after another, and for what? So he'd be welcome in the right circles, the acceptable clubs, become the jolly good chap—which a Gypsy like Dad couldn't be and his son didn't want to be. He wanted to be left alone. Dad never understood that, crabby old Anna either. Mother knew it, even Mary Beth and Jenny, but Dad had the last word and it never varied:

"If you don't want to learn, what *do* you want?"

He didn't know, but he knew it wasn't *this,* to be shut up in a high-class establishment for boys who hadn't quite made it in conventional schools, who had a few rough edges to be sanded down before they fit the neat round slots of the business world. That would be blasphemy to his father, against everything he believed in, had faith in. If Dad had a religion it was to be a *somebody.* Whatever was Gypsy in them had to be smashed, stomped on, crushed out of existence because something in it was deeply shameful.

"Abramsky!"

Now it was Headmaster frowning down on him from an impressive six feet six. Resigned, Simon followed him to the office, his hands already clenched defensively in his pockets against the all too familiar cane. Six of the best. That's what they still called it here. If Headmaster had a reputation for discipline to uphold, then surely Michael Abramsky's son was a heaven-sent opportunity to reaffirm it.

"One thing I despise," he said now, "is a lad who won't try. Hold out your hand."

As usual, Simon refused to look at the teacher's face. He focused on that first vindictive whistle of the descending cane, waiting for its welt to rise on his palm and the stinging pain to follow it. He almost welcomed the pain, one more grievance to describe in his next letter home—yet another aspect of the school's spartan regimen. Mondays after prayers every boy must write a two-page letter home. Two pages exactly. Not one, not three. Just two. But first, six of the best.

Wham.

Wham.

Wham.

Simon stopped counting and closed his eyes.

Before setting out for the studios, Mary Beth sorted the morning's mail, firmly closing her ears to the undiminished power of Lily Finn's voice.

She felt, shuffling letters and parcels and sundry household accounts,

that she sat at the very hub of an ever-moving wheel that was the
Abramsky family. For didn't they depend on her, still permanently at
Greenlings, to hold tight to the reins, keep them all in touch? Wasn't she
the only one who knew, from day to day, exactly where each was located
and could be reached at a moment's notice?

As always she started with Ellie and Michael, in Tokyo this month for
an elaborate round of entertaining that should hold the Asian sector of
Abramo well into the next year. In the courier's envelope went a letter
with *Mischa* scrawled in Anna's angular hand; with it a note from Jenny
addressed to Mummy and Daddy and sealed with a hundred X's; both
letters were written backstage in the London theater where Jenny was
now a regular soloist poised to become, next season, a prima ballerina on
loan to New York for the opening of a new ballet some meteoric young
choreographer had "made on her"—as they said in the States. As they
said in the States! Odd how she herself no longer seemed to have any
country but Abramo—it was young Jenny now who buzzed over the
Atlantic every few weeks, speaking more and more in that distinctive
mid-Atlantic accent, a patois exclusive to entertainers and multinational
businessmen. In Jenny, it was sprinkled with ballet terms known only to
insiders like Anna and herself. Imagine, not sixteen and already the child
was familiar with backstages in every city civilized enough to support a
ballet company. Of course Anna traveled with her; at Jenny's age someone must, and Anna guarded the privilege as fiercely as a dog with a
bone.

Also into the Tokyo envelope went a memo of household doings from
yesterday, of no importance except to reassure Ellie that everything on
this side of the water was fine, that she needn't feel guilty for leaving
house and family to go swanning off to the Orient with Michael.

Pete Preston, in Osaka for the week, got a postcard from his mother;
his baby son merited a blue hand-knitted cap and bootees; for Pete's
Japanese wife (who'd been a severe shock to Pete's mother) there was a
recipe for Yorkshire pudding.

Into the London package were letters from Ellie, who wrote both children each day, a length of lavender silk Michael had sent Anna, and a
sharp reminder limiting the hours Jenny could work and practice. It was
hardly worth including it, since neither Jenny nor Anna would pay the
slightest attention, but...

For Simon there was his allowance, his mother's letter, and a photo of
the samurai sword Michael had promised for his birthday *if* he brought
home good marks. From Jenny a bag of chocolate mints for his sweet

tooth, and from Mary Beth herself a new book on herbal medicines to add to his growing collection.

The packages done and sealed, she wrote Lily Finn's paycheck and propped it on the mantel, giving silent thanks that in fifteen minutes she would be in the comparative calm of the studios, out of reach of Lily's voice which, over the years, had improved only in volume. She was just visible now through the open kitchen door, wringing a dishcloth in chapped paws as she sang, with unbridled passion, of *pale hands she loved beside the Shalimar-ar, where are you now-ow-ow, where are you*—

Mary Beth slammed the door on the final ululating note and left, remembering at the last moment that in all the mail she had prepared there was no word from Simon. His compulsory letter from school should have arrived yesterday. So it was a day late. Perhaps the post was delayed. The school, tucked into a sleepy corner of the north, had been chosen for just that reason—it was so far from anywhere that the boy would *have* to buckle down to work. There was certainly nothing else for him to do.

She fancied, turning on the ignition, that she heard the faint ring of a phone, but then Lily swung into her best Ethel Merman style with a rousing chorus of "Alexander's Ragtime Band," and Mary Beth was left humming it all the way to the new studio in Leeds.

Come on along, come on along . . .

Suddenly, for the first time in years, an unbearable tide of homesickness engulfed her. Greenlings and its owners took a backseat to childhood summers at Martha's Vineyard, to fall in New England, winters on Fifth Avenue, the shops lit for Christmas.

Perhaps if Jenny succeeded in New York, Michael might buy a flat there . . . he'd said he might, that it could be a good investment. Pleasant, to dream of going home—but what was she thinking about? They all still vacationed in California, and if she wanted her own home on the East Coast there was nothing to stop her going. Permanently if she wanted. A little house on the Cape, maybe . . . she wasn't tied to the Abramskys . . . but then she imagined life without them and knew it would be no life at all. By now they were her family. Who else would she care for if not her old pupil Ellie von Reiker and the family she'd collected around her? And who would care for her, treat her like the loved, surrogate aunt she felt herself to be?

Back at the house Lily sang on, deliberately pitching her voice over the hum of the vacuum cleaner and the persistent ring of the hall phone. If there was one thing she liked it was having the house to herself, could almost believe it belonged to her, could even, with her spot of lunch, sample the cellar. A bottle of wine was never missed. Rubbing Mansion Polish into the top of a Louis Seize table she pondered, not for the first time, on life's injustice. This beautiful house damn near empty, and them that owned it scattered all over the globe.

Well, their loss was her gain. And better make the most of it. It wouldn't last. A couple of weeks and they'd all be back for the twins' birthday shindig—and a nice how-de-do it was to be, too. Marquee over by the pool, a stage for that rock band Miss Jenny wanted (no punks, young Mrs. Ab put her foot down there), caterers coming up from London, the lot. Close on a hundred guests due, Jenny's friends most like, skinny lasses and airy-fairy lads from the show—young ladies and gents, though, none of the trailer riffraff that used to show up when the twins were little. Them days were over, thank God. The only Gypsy in these parts now was Mr. Michael, and he didn't seem like one, never had.

Picking her paycheck off the mantel she trudged into the kitchen for lunch, putting her feet up as her lips puckered over the first taste of Mouton Cadet. By the second glass she figured she could get to like it. The third she sipped slowly, already the connoisseur. When the phone jangled on the kitchen wall she blinked, hiccuped, and absentmindedly picked up the receiver.

Ellie woke on and off many times in the night, uneasy, as if somewhere she'd left a small task undone. She got out of bed once, careful not to wake Michael, and pulled aside the bamboo blind. The moon hung behind tatters of cloud, a great pearl pendant in a foreign sky. Beautiful, this Japan, intriguing, more distant than California had ever been. Greenlings cushioned them in privacy, Que Vista welcomed them with pitchers of sunshine and sprawling platters of sea and sky, but here was only order and well-used space, muted footfalls in the hall. Tranquillity had a different weight and color, dawn gray, light as gauze, soft as the smiles of shopgirls on the Ginza, delicate as their hands, deft ivory gestures that could mean volumes or perhaps nothing at all. It would be hard to make a friend here, she thought, to push formality aside and know another woman as she'd come to know Mary Beth.

In the street below a shadowy figure prepared his giozo stand for the morning rush; on the corner Mr. Matsamura unlocked his curio shop, dusting cheap bamboo vases no less carefully than the quality enamels in back. In two hours the Ginza, closed to traffic on weekends, would be a moving thoroughfare of glossy black heads. If he was back in town Pete Preston would be among them, heading for his favorite noodle shop, too tall, too fair, too lanky, as wildly incongruous as a birch sapling in a grove of bonsai. Extraordinary that Pete, quintessential Englishman, should so avidly have embraced not only an Oriental wife but her country's customs, cuisine, every nuance of her language. Michael teased him, called him a modern-day Blackthorne, but between Pete and the hero mariner of *Shogun* was one important difference. Pete did not dream of going home. He dreaded it, visiting England only when he must and hurrying back at the first opportunity. Unspoken among them all was the knowledge that if Abramo should ever pull its manufacturing capability out of Japan it would have to find a new chief engineer. Pete's priorities had shifted.

As had Michael's. Despite his love for Greenlings he seemed always on the move, jetting from country to country, making new deals and expanding old ones. He professed to be, and was, a family man—but he was not fatherly. Proud of Jenny's success, exasperated at Simon's lack of it, he still had no more idea what made his children tick than when they were two pink scraps toddling the Greenlings lawn. Nurturing was her job—yet he liked to have her with him when she could make it, oblivious of the daily balancing act she and Mary Beth must perform to maintain stability in a home which saw so many arrivals and departures.

Back in bed she checked the clock—only six—and tucked herself spoon-fashion behind Michael, grateful for his old habit, even in sleep, of touching his mouth to her fingertips before resting them under his chin. But he'd changed over the years, in so many subtle ways he didn't even notice. The *kumpania* was never mentioned; she suspected he no longer thought of it at all. No worries now about Farah. How long had it been? Five, six years and never once had she had cause to doubt or even wonder. If there were other women on his travels (and there could well be, his appetites were undiminished) they'd be casual women, of no more significance than business appointments. Emotionally the Rom were out of their lives. Rose would always be a burden but her needs were handled by accountants now, the same faceless men who took Dui's demands in stride, turning them down without once bothering Michael with them.

Even Anna did not wield the power she once had—perhaps she didn't need him so much now she had Jenny to croon over. Michael, wiry and abstemious as ever, jogged compulsively but no longer took barre and Anna had ceased to nag him about it.

Ellie was asleep when coffee arrived. By the time she bathed and dressed for breakfast Michael was already back from his morning run, shaved and showered, rattling crinkly airmail editions of the London and New York papers, throwing her an absentminded kiss over the head of a houseboy who served him half a grapefruit as elegantly as if it were the Koh-i-noor diamond. Here a polished lemon leaf, there the single perfect strawberry, the tiny cup of green tea. Michael's eyes registered each small garnish before he picked up his spoon.

"Pete's right, you know," he said. "They do have something."

"Exquisite taste." She opened the Abramo courier bag and scanned its contents, immediately aware something was missing. "What day is it, Michael?" counting on her fingers. Monday he wrote, Tuesday it went to Greenlings, and today was—

"Wednesday."

Damn the time lag, she never could work out whose side it came down on and why it changed when they were in the States. But now the unease which had kept her awake had a name. "It's Simon, there's no letter from him."

Last week's note hadn't been exactly reassuring either, describing punishments Michael assured her were exaggerated. If they still hit naughty boys, he said, it wasn't hard enough to make a dent, judging from the results.

"He probably didn't write," Michael said now.

"He has to. They make them."

"The mail's not infallible."

Ellie upended the courier bag. A paper clip, two buttons, and a pencil. No envelope with Simon's large fill-the-space-somehow handwriting. "I think I'll call Mary Beth," she said, panic rising. "Better yet, the school—"

She didn't have to; the houseboy was bowing, pointing out to Michael the flashing light on the communications console, its bell turned off for the night and not yet switched on.

She saw Michael pick up the phone, nod, shoot a glance at her in the living room, and close the door between them.

Her mind spun circles, spirals, curlicues of worry. Jenny, Simon, Anna, Mary Beth—

Now Michael was in the door, his face a sallow, waxy yellow. "It was Mary Beth. Seems Simon's run away from school. I've left word for the headmaster to call me."

Her first reaction was relief. Was that all? Children often ran away and came back. It was summer, he wasn't hurt, dead, he wasn't—"D'you think somebody could have—"

"Kidnapped him? No."

"No." Abstracted, as if he'd already faced that possibility and rejected it.

But kidnap. She thought of it often, feared it more than anything. It wasn't impossible or even improbable. The name Abramsky popped up regularly in the financial columns, Michael routinely described as Acquisitive Ab, with wildly exaggerated estimates of his real estate holdings. "If I were as rich as they say, I could hang the moon around your neck," he'd told her once. Stung by his routine absences to survey, buy, and subdivide land, she'd said, "Not you, you'd cut it up and sell it." But in fact, in terms of liquid assets, they were not that wealthy. At least once a month Michael said money in the bank was money lying idle, to be turned into bricks and mortar as soon as possible.

"But in case," she whispered, "we could get our hands on some quickly if... you know... before—" Before they did things to him. Such horrendous things you read in the papers and he was so young, how could he stand it, just a baby—

Michael nodded. "Of course we could, but it's not that. We'd have been contacted straightaway. No, it's just Simon being his usual inconsiderate self, worrying us for nothing."

She wanted to believe that, she tried, but— "Maybe he was unhappy at school and decided to fly here?" To me, his mother. Not Michael, he didn't like him, perhaps never would.

"Where would he get the kind of money to fly to Japan?"

She sighed. The twins had neither credit cards nor bank accounts, just nominal weekly allowances. Even Jenny's small earnings were in trust. Michael had insisted, saying children shouldn't have money until they were mature enough to handle it. And Ellie had agreed with him, she'd agreed! Oh, how stupid, if Simon had had money, enough money, he could have taken a plane, would be here now, shamefaced but safe across the table from them.

"We'll have to call the police—"

Michael's face hardened, lips tight, eyes on fire with sudden fury. "Not the coppers. We're not having them."

"But we have to do *something,* we can't just... your own son, you couldn't be so hard, if you won't call them I—" She stopped herself before saying what could not be called back, but inside she wept, she wept and wanted her little boy, her unhappy little boy...Who knew where he was? what was happening to him? The police could find him, those reliable British bobbies Michael despised so much.

"We'll handle it ourselves, cancel the Trade Association thing we were giving tomorrow, and we go home, look for him. He'll be skulking around at a friend's house—"

A friend? As far as Ellie knew, Simon didn't have one.

The phone again. A sick feeling numbed her brain, stopped her breath. The headmaster. Michael grabbed up the receiver.

"Well?" he barked, as if it were the headmaster who'd shoved a difficult boy into a school he hated.

Watching him, Ellie saw the strain in his face turn to pure anger, the nostrils pinched and white, his brown hands beating a tattoo on the table. "All of it? You're sure?"

She heard a man's distant "Yes" as Michael quietly hung up.

"Well, you can stop worrying."

"They've found him?"

"No, but he's not been kidnapped. He took his things, a load of food from the school kitchen, and all the small change he could find in the other boys' lockers. Still want to call in the police so they can arrest him? We'll be lucky if the school doesn't do it for us."

She tried to think, to shift blame. "Maybe another boy took the money, you know, making it look like—"

"And maybe Simon's a poor misunderstood kid with no idea of the trouble he's causing."

"But Michael, we have to find him—"

"I'll find him. When I do he'll wish to God I hadn't."

FORTY-TWO

*A*T FIRST HE WAS RELIEVED; the only first-class passengers on board, they were alone, a breathing space, he thought, time to talk things over, reach some sort of unity before the inevitable decisions to be taken. They tried but, perhaps because she was too worried to think straight, perhaps because he was angry, disappointed in Simon, they were farther apart waiting for their connection in San Francisco than when they'd boarded in Tokyo. They had a problem to face together, but nowhere did their points of concern converge.

She only wanted Simon home. He wanted him transformed, made over. She was looking for excuses, he for permanent change.

"If you were home more instead of always off chasing money," she accused him, "it would never have come to this."

"He gets as much of my time as Jenny—more. She's a credit to both of us."

"She does as she's told, that's what you want, right? Mary Beth says 'Learn!' she learns. Anna says 'Dance!' she dances."

"She has a purpose. Is there something wrong with that?"

"Maybe Simon hasn't found his yet—"

"He won't damned well look! If he showed any ambition I'd back him all the way. That's what I work for, to give him—them—every possible chance, but he's not interested. I thought once he'd want the business. He doesn't. I have to accept that—but there's got to be something he wants out of life. I wouldn't care what. A plumber? He could go to trade school, then get into his own place. Chef? An apprenticeship in Paris, later a restaurant, any place he wanted. Pilot? I'd buy him lessons, a plane—"

"Buy. With money. You don't think he needs something else?"

"Like?"

"Like a father who lives at home."

"How would I run a business from Greenlings?"

"You did once."

"It's a bigger business now," he said dryly.

"Because all you think about is build, build, build."

A steward hovered between them in the departure lounge and they both realized their voices had been tense, urgent, less than subdued. Ellie, soul of discretion, murmured: "Why don't you call home? See if he's there?"

"I did. And the school. They've heard nothing."

She bit her lip and he saw she was fighting for control. "It *is* a school for problem boys, Michael. Suppose another boy took the money and Simon . . . you know . . . ran away rather than be blamed."

"Does that sound like the Simon we both know and love?" In spite of himself sarcasm crept into his voice. "Darling, you have to stop looking for scapegoats and see Simon as he is. Reasons may vary, but he's been *invited to leave* five schools in seven years. 'Difficult to manage, disobedient, lazy, insolent.' You don't imagine for a minute they'll take him back at this last place, do you?"

"I wouldn't let him back there."

"They don't want him. I'm wondering where we can send him next. His reputation will have preceeded him. That was about the only school left with a claim to recognized academic standards."

Two pink spots flared in her cheeks. "Recognized by whom?"

"Anybody who knows the difference."

She drew as far away as possible on the long seat of the departure lounge and he saw her expression change, her profile sharpen. She desperately needed sympathy, reassurance, and he wasn't offering any—how could he? Sooner or later she had to face facts, but right now she must weep or lash out at someone, and he was available.

"Odd," she said, "how a man who never went to school knows all about them."

"Ellie, we're in enough trouble without hurting each other. We have to figure out his plans, if any, why he took the money—it was only small change, so why steal..."

"Now *there's* a subject you're an expert on."

"Stop it. I stole to eat." Not always true, he admitted to himself. Often he'd stolen to punish *gaje* for being what they were, to teach them they were not superior, never had been. So what was Simon's excuse?

The London plane was called. This time it was fully booked, with no privacy at all in which to comfort her or fight her. She pretended to sleep. He hid behind a newspaper and thought about Simon, tried to reconstruct his actions. After some prodding the principal had admitted punishing him the day before he ran away, so yes, he'd left because he was unhappy. Had he stolen just to buy food, intending to lie low? If so, until when? Or had he thought that far ahead? Michael sighed. He was naive, this boy. England was a small country, difficult to hide in. Young Micah had known what he was doing, yet one encounter with a lethal dog had flushed him out. For such as Simon, spoiled by civilization, accustomed to round-the-clock maid service, hot baths, and regular meals... Michael gave him three days on the road before he came limping home with blisters on his feet. The experience wouldn't hurt him. It was the scum he'd meet on the road that terrified Michael, that kept him awake through endless airborne hours. Ellie worried about something as unlikely as kidnap. He feared a worse outcome, one far more common. Hardly a day went by but the front page of every newspaper was splashed with such cases. A boy like Simon, pink and gold, innocent, vulnerable, *alone*... such boys were prime meat on the hoof. Lone wolves waited in alleys, by roadside cafés, cruised motorways in innocuous little vans that concealed a multitude of aberrations. For the unimaginative hunter there were videos to jab the adrenaline, set vicious juices spurting—chain-saw games, rivers of blood, flick knives, and malled fists—and always, always, an overt sex symbol and a young victim. Moronic stuff, but to the sick mind, pure TNT.

Yes, he must be found. *But where would he go?*

Beside him Ellie stirred, her eyes awash with tears.

"Michael, I'm sorry, I didn't mean that, but I keep thinking what could happen..."

"Me too." But she had meant that. Some of it, anyway.

"We'll call the police... they know what to do."

"No. Think about it. They'll question the school, persuade them to press charges. When Simon comes home, and he will, he'll be charged with petty theft. So he'll have a permanent police record. That's a damned slippery slope."

"The school punished him, it's their fault he ran away. They won't press charges—"

"Maybe not. In which case Simon will be just another name on the police runaways list. *Low on the list.* From where they sit he's sixteen in two weeks, legally old enough to work. He wasn't abducted, he left of his own choice. They'll assume he's taken to the streets, with everything that implies."

"Michael!"

"I'm telling you why they won't break any records looking for him. Maybe a private agency..." Anybody but the coppers.

"A private agency!" She shook her head, refusing a steward's offer of a drink. "They wouldn't know where to start!"

He stared at the unread newspaper in front of him, open now at the green pages of yesterday's racing results and tomorrow's hot tips. Deep in his subconscious a long-abandoned notion began to stir. "Maybe not," he said, "but I think I do."

Following his hunch, he began with the racecourse:

"Programs, get your race programs here."

"Place your bets, only five minutes to the first."

Stableboys scurried in the backfield; tipsters shouted offers of a sure thing in the first; ticktack men signaled their bookmakers; at the starting gate a rainbow of owners' silks and the gloss of prime horseflesh; beneath the stands hawkers offered everything from candy apples to kebabs; last-minute bettors waved wads of money at harried girls in the ticket windows. A rumble from the p.a. system, then:

"They're off!"

Michael stood still and let the excitement of the race meet wash around him. He watched neither horses nor punters. Under the screams for the first race, he slipped to the back of the crowd and made for the fields behind the racecourse, for the cluster of trailers that gathered at every important meeting on the racing calendar. Gypsies, tinkers, travelers of every stripe and ethic did business at the races. They sold fruit, cheap radios, cassette tapes pirated in the Orient, towels that were "perfick, sir, perfick," despite SECONDS rubber-stamped in the corners. Women read palms and crystal balls and, less often, the tarot cards.

The class system, evident in the rigid grouping of trailers, flourished as strongly among the travelers as in the country at large. Tinkers, many fresh from the bogs of Ireland, were here; a second group, misfits, people who simply took to the road and never left it, were there. The third group camped well away from the rest, pure-blood Rom superior to all because they still kept bloodlines as unpolluted as was humanly possible.

Michael wasted no time looking for Farah's *kumpania*. It was still in Sacramento. Through the years he'd kept careful track. None had been back to England and these days were involved in enterprises only a hair short of legit; at last report they'd formed a company and bought a trailer park; its members traveled as and when they liked, but the park was their place. Even Dui, when out of jail, was a semisolvent horse dealer. Probably more through Tomo's efforts than Dui's—but at least they were off Michael's back and out of Simon's orbit.

He nevertheless approached the Rom with care, leaving himself open to scrutiny before introducing himself. In Romani. Smiles, yes. But caution, random groups of men casually closing in on him, questions beginning. Clearly he was not of their *kumpania*. So. Was he perhaps related to any of its members?

He shook his head. His people were Romanichals who took up life in California eleven years ago.

Lovely place, California, why wasn't he with them?

Well, he'd married a *gaja*, they knew how that went?

They knew. Too many Rom did that now, more's the pity.

Michael felt the cool chill of their disapproval but did not respond.

Who was Rom Baro of his group?

"It used to be Dui, my brother, but now—" His throat felt as if it were stuffed with feathers.

"But now?"

They could have been asking for his ID. They *were* asking for his ID. He breathed deep, afraid to bring her name to his lips.

"Farah."

Ah-ha! Smiles again, wider than before. The women were gathering, nodding, remembering Farah. Live wire. Flamenco. Powerful Rom Baro, they heard. A beautiful daughter, yes, held tight with the People, Micah would know how it was, right?

Right. They meant she was chaste, kept to the ways of the Rom, was an obedient daughter. So.

"What did you say your name was again?"

"Micah." He said it with reluctance, knowing full well that details of this visit would be in Sacramento within the month.

Formalities were over. If they'd been shopkeepers they'd have rubbed their hands now. As it was they asked him to sit, poured him a small glass of wine, and settled down to cases.

So what could they do for him?

"A boy... blond, blue eyes, slim, nearly sixteen, at a school he didn't like, you understand?"

Of course! What idiot would like school?

"So he's on his own somewhere. No money—well, not much."

"So?" They looked mystified. At that age a boy could take care of himself. "He'll be home when he's done his wanderin', we all have to wander sometimes, that's natural, isn't it?"

"The boy's *gajo*. *Us, our* people, we know—" How strange to be saying "our people" again, not meaning it now, not meaning it at all. He felt as different from these strangers as he would from Martians. "The Rom, they know how to be careful. But this boy's been protected."

Behind high walls and NO TRESPASSING signs carefully erected by his father. With love.

The oldest man among them frowned. "A boy should learn. How can he learn under shelter?"

"I wondered if you'd heard anything," Michael said meekly, a pulse of rage beating in his throat. That they should presume to lecture him, *him,* on the raising of children. "Before she died he was fond of his grandmam. It's possible he tried to meet up with some of our people..."

A muttering at the back of the crowd. "Who wants to know?"

"I do," he said softly. "He's my son."

Their eyes accused him much as Ellie's had, but for other crimes. Ellie blamed him for not giving Simon his time, for following the upper-class tradition of sending him away to school. The Rom blamed him for not teaching Simon, brutally if need be, what lurked on the streets for stupid innocents like the *gaje*. So maybe he was guilty as charged, but he thought not.

A woman stepped forward, whispered to the spokesman, who nodded. She turned to Michael.

"We're down here from Appleby Fair, but one of the Heron men got kicked by a horse. His leg gangrened up so they had to wait, see... we heard somethin' about a kid hanging around 'em like you said, light hair an' that."

Michael breathed—for the first time, it seemed, since they'd surrounded him. "Thank you," he said in Romani, meaning it. They could just as easily have sent him off with a threat.

The road towards Appleby was much as he remembered it. High, bleak, and narrow, with the modern hazard of endless trucks speeding to Scotland and back.

So his hunch had been right. Simon had run to the Rom. They'd always fascinated him, Michael had known that since Grandmam's funeral; that first marathon phone call to Tomo only confirmed it; later there was the annual pilgrimage to Grandmam's grave, Simon's blue eyes wistful as the family car sped past clusters of trailers at the roadsides. More recently, bunches of herbs hung in the potting shed, carefully dried, then packed in jars and, as far as Michael knew, thrown away.

As far as Michael knew. Remarkable how little he *did* know about his son. Perhaps Ellie was right. Maybe he'd take the rest of the summer off, they'd all go somewhere together the way they used to. Que Vista...damn, he'd forgotten. Jenny was to be in New York. A busy family, his, everyone in it had a different schedule. Except Simon. Always except Simon, whose life had no discernible focus. Okay then, why not New York, he'd half-promised Mary Beth anyway. Ellie would enjoy being with Jenny—and while they were there it wouldn't hurt to look around, check out the real estate picture, show Simon the ropes. God, just let him be there...

The car swallowed up the miles, every crack in the road chanting the Simon song. Si-mon. Si-mon. Si-mon. Si-mon. Si-mon. How could he face Ellie until he found him? God, don't let this be a wild goose chase. The world was full of light-haired boys. Was it really Simon who'd been seen with the Heron band? And was he still there? Maybe. The Rom were amazingly tolerant of other people's kids if they gave no trouble and helped around the camp.

Michael parked and began to walk under white clouds moving fast. High above them the deep, heavenly blue he remembered, the shifting green shadows and the voice of the river.

And here she was, the Eden. On her hospitable bank a trailer discreetly hidden behind a thicket of blackberry canes. A man with a bandaged leg smoked a cigarette on the trailer steps, a woman brooded over an open fire.

Behind them two dogs, inevitably lurchers, fought over a bone. With them a boy, waist deep in canes, picked blackberries, tossed some into a yellow basin and the others nonchalantly into his mouth. His hair was unkempt, oil-streaked and matted with hay; berry juice stained his lips and old ketchup decorated his shirt, the tail of which had been ripped off for a bandanna. Berry thorns had scratched his bare arms and as Michael watched, the boy paused to examine a single drop of blood, ruby-bright in the sun, before licking it up and returning to his task. Picking fruit, he could have been young Micah or Dui or Tomo.

Picking fruit.

Simon Abramsky, heir to Greenlings and Abramo. Gabriella's son. Grandson to proud Anna and patrician Hans. *And Da.*

Weak with relief, half blind with anger, Michael forced himself to stand still, torn between the need to hug the breath out of this boy and to thrash the daylights out of him. Or both.

"Son?"

Simon looked up, startled. A veil slipped over his face. One minute relaxed and natural, the next guilty, defensive, furious. Ashamed. Under dirt and blackberry stains and the sun-warmed bloom on his cheeks he turned pale, then flushed the helpless red of a kettled lobster. He swallowed, his neck pathetically vulnerable in the dirty kerchief.

If he'd shown remorse then, even a hint of it, Michael might have kissed him, hugged him, forgiven him, started over with no questions or recriminations, but with a swift glance at his audience of two Gypsies and their dogs, Simon decided to play it cool. He grinned.

"Hey! How come? I thought you guys were in Japan."

A pulse beat behind Michael's eyes. "We were. Some little matter brought us back early." The lash in his voice jerked Simon's head, opened his eyes wide, spilled a blue-black stream of berries unheeded into the canes.

"I'm not going back to that school."

"What makes you think they'd have you?"

"I'm staying here—"

"Who with?" he snapped. "These people will be moving soon, joining up with their *kumpania.*"

Too late Michael realized he'd used the wrong word, the magic word. Simon saw the opening he'd been looking for, perhaps subconsciously, all of his life. He jumped straight into it.

"So how come we can't join up with *ours?*" Under the bravado, the defiance, was a softness, a wistfulness, the hint of a plea Michael chose to ignore.

Ours.

The frustrations of a lifetime, internal battles fought and won, yes won, dammit!—boiled up, exploded in a sudden rage which made him reach for this bright, enigmatic boy, shake him by the collar of his soiled and tattered shirt, shake him until his even, expensively tended teeth chattered like little white jackhammers. The years of running from factory to factory, shop to shop, estate agent to developer to contractor to building site, all to ensure that this cocky young pup could never revert to a Micah, Micah who must never, ever, be resurrected in this one. Years a man works, years. He turns his back, takes a quick, dammit *essential,* business trip, and what happens? The Rom sneaks back in, wanting what he hasn't earned.

"Ours?" he thundered. "If we have a *kumpania* it's based at Greenlings and it's called Abramsky. It's given you everything you've ever wanted, you idle, ungrateful young lout."

Roused by the passion in Michael's voice, the dogs advanced uncertainly, muzzles drawn back, ruff hairs twitching, willing to growl but awaiting a command from the couple.

"You...you can't touch me," Simon said uncertainly. "They'd kill you."

Michael's hands fell to his sides. He sighed. "I was handling dogs like them before I could talk. You're embarrassing me. For God's sake get in the car. I'll pay these people for your keep."

He turned to the couple, thanked them for taking care of his son, and asked in Romani what he owed them. When they shook their heads he thanked them again and followed Simon.

Michael made sure the car was well and truly rolling, all its doors locked from the driver's console, before he spoke. Simon looked trapped, desperate enough to jump.

"Do you know the anguish you've caused your mother? Can you imagine what we've been afraid of? You read the papers, watch TV, you know what can happen to kids on the loose."

"I can look after myself."

Don't answer that, don't humiliate him any more. "You're damned lucky I found you and not the police. The school could have called them in."

"It was the Head. He shouldn't have hit me."

"Did *I* hit you? Mary Beth? Your mother? We're the ones who've been worried sick. Do you care about anybody but you?"

No answer. He slumped in his seat, picked threads from the ragged edge of his shirt, and tried to whistle. Michael stomped on the gas pedal to stop himself slapping at his son's dirty hand.

"I suppose you do intend to apologize? Sometime?"

A shrug. A theatrical sigh worthy of Jenny or Anna. "Jenny never went to school, did she? Oh no, but *she* lives in London, her own apartment and everything, she can ring anybody she wants anytime, she eats in restaurants, and now she's off to New York. *You* never had to go to school, even Mom didn't. So what do *I* get? Shoved in a rotten school to play stupid cricket. When I don't want to play they bash me around—"

"They gave you a taste of the cane and you deserved it, for stealing if nothing else—"

"I didn't steal!"

"Sure. You don't lie either. Maybe you deserve another taste of the cane. From me. What d'you think? You worry your mother to death, can't even say you're sorry—"

He risked a glance at Simon's face, but it was turned blindly away, staring out the car window, registering nothing. From the tight angle of the jaw Michael guessed tears were dammed up—but he wouldn't cry here, wouldn't hand his father a weapon he didn't already have. Scowling, swallowing hard, he fell back to the teenager's universal defense, a nonchalant shrug that never quite came off because the shoulders were rigid with tension.

"So okay, when we get home...yeah, so maybe I made a bit of trouble—"

Maybe?

A rift between himself and Ellie, a lasting scar on the marriage because words had been spoken that couldn't be taken back; now bridges must be built over the rift, detours negotiated around the scars.

A calendar of business appointments months in the making all postponed —with regrets of course. A meticulously planned dinner for a hundred canceled at the last moment, so sorry. The Japanese were sensitive about such slights, would remember when contract time came around.

An exhausting, frantic dash around the world—hold the plane, commandeer a cab, bring a car, have it gassed up and waiting in London, a dozen travel agents hitting every button on their terminals—so Abramsky and Son could hold emergency session in a blackberry patch.

Because Simon Abramsky didn't care for cricket.

And one way or another they must yet find this boy another hidey-hole in which to mark time until he was mature enough to be out on his own.

"Yeah, maybe you made a bit of trouble, son."

FORTY-THREE

*T*HEY WEREN'T FAIR, NEVER. They didn't listen.

Tomo had. Even Uncle Dui, when he wasn't squiffed. Felix had listened, and before him Grandmam. Now nobody at all.

So okay. Jenny, between her liniments and exercises and stupid arabesques, a goddamned "career" and her pansy-schmansy friends, she listened when she had time. She and Mary Beth. He thought maybe they even heard. And did nothing. But hell, what could they do, or anybody else? Might as well expect Screaming-meemie Lily to run the family.

Yeah, okay, there was Mom. He felt bad about that, making her rush back, but he didn't know she'd get all hysterical and come running. She'd listen and she'd believe him about the money. It was true he didn't take it. Dad must think he was dumb. The minute anybody lit out from *that* school the rest cleaned up the loose change. What did they expect from a school for bad lads? Farewell notes? Just because they had the right accent didn't mean they were knights in shining armor, for God's sake!

Mom was okay if Dad wasn't around, but she was like that Alsatian puppy they got one Christmas that Dad said was for the family—Penny her name was, on account of a silver patch under her chin—but by the time Dad got done teaching her to sit and heel and walk and stay, heck, the only voice Penny listened to was Dad's. And then he went off to San Diego or some place and Penny wouldn't eat, wouldn't do anything but pine away, then she bit the postman and a man from the animal shelter came for her.

Dad spoiled everything. Whose fault was it he got sent away to school in the first place, anyway? He'd been doing okay with Mary Beth. She was boring, but bearable. And what was wrong with the village school, where everybody left at sixteen? But no, that wasn't good enough for the Abramskys, they had to wear a clean shirt every day and learn Latin and Greek.

He knew what Grandmam would have said about that. He knew what she would have said about everything, but he worried sometimes because lately he couldn't remember her face until he checked with Mom and Dad's wedding pictures—and they didn't count because he'd not been born then and besides, Grandmam was dressed different for a wedding. He'd looked all over the house, even through musty old boxes in the attic, and never once found a photo of Grandmam with her pipe and her herb bag. Tomo had one, he bet. Tomo knew all there was to know about the Rom. Maybe he'd know why everything was such a great big secret.

That was all he wanted to learn about and nowhere to learn it. The couple at Appleby told him a few new words, after he'd shown the woman Grandmam's gravestone at the cemetery, but he wanted more than that, all the secrets, the rules and ceremonies, what foods they ate and how they lived when they were on the road...Dad knew, he could tell Simon everything he wanted to know, but Dad tried to pretend he'd never been Rom. Not Simon, he'd rather be Rom than anything, he'd rather be what Grandmam had told him to be, what Dad should have been if he hadn't left the Rom. Grandmam's face might have got lost someplace but not her words: *Blood calls to blood*, chala, *blood knows its own*.

Last summer he collected some of the herbs she'd shown him. He dried them, put them up in jars, and hid them at the back of his closet. Times like now, when his door was closed and everybody downstairs, he'd take off the lids and bury his nose in pungent leaves, powder them in his fingers, chant their names the way she used to do so they almost made a song. Ripple grass and pennyroyal, Solomon's seal and dittany, Pickpurse and Tormentil, traveler's-joy and hop. The names seemed to call her back;

he could almost see her rocking in his bedroom chair, puffing on her pipe and laughing at him for getting into another crossaxe with Dad.

"Simon? Are you in your room?"

It was Mom calling from the foot of the stairs. They were talking him over, he knew that. Another family conference on the problem child. He stood in front of the mirror and set his lips firm. They could talk until they were blue in the face. He wasn't going back to school.

"Simon!" Dad's voice now. Reinforcements. Te-dum, te-dum, te-dum-dum-dum. The Lone Ranger comes to save the day. *"Simon!"*

"Yeah."

"Didn't you hear your mother calling you?"

"Nope."

A muttering, and now Mom's voice again. "Dinner in half an hour, darling—Lily's made a jam roll for dessert."

In his mind he could see her standing under the chandelier, her head tipped a bit to the side, the light giving her hair that color nobody else's had, like honey Grandmam used to take off the moors and put up in bottles for wintertime. Looking at Mom made him hurt sometimes, as if he'd done something bad but wasn't quite sure what. She didn't call him again, but he could feel her listening, waiting. He opened his door. "I'll be there in a bit, okay, Mom?"

"Okay." She smiled at him, and he wished she'd come up so he could throw his arms round her neck and let her rock him like she used to when he was little, but he wasn't little anymore and Dad was there anyway, so maybe he'd come too and no *way* did he want Dad's arms around him. It made him want to cry. It had always been like that and he never knew why.

Down in the drawing room the conversational ball, bouncing from speaker to speaker, had no more direction than its subject:

Jenny, in a shell-pink jump suit and shocking-purple sash, swung an elegantly pointed toe from her perch on the arm of Anna's chair; under the reading lamp her head rode serenely atop the long curve of her dancer's neck. "I don't see the problem," she said. "When we go to New York, *if* they still want me, he can come with us. I'll bet he'd love a public high school—Anna can be mother hen to both of us, can't you, darling?" No one pointed out that it was now Jenny who played mother hen to Anna.

Michael couldn't help comparing his children. Simon, still pouting upstairs, seemed always pressed down under sullen clouds, his smile rare and

fleeting in a face still tender, untried, its beautiful features too balanced.
Jenny hummed like fine-drawn wire. Forged under years of dance and
diet, she'd grown angular, her features sharply defined, eyes and smile
wider—too wide for the small face—but she carried sunlight with her
like a lamp. Strangers began by admiring Simon's perfection, ended by
gazing at Jenny, warming themselves in her spirit. She lit up every room
she entered. The difference hadn't always been so apparent, and Michael
tried to pinpoint just when it began to show. Was it—yes, it was when
she began to be a *good* dancer rather than just a dancer. What was it, that
odd little maxim Felix used to trot out? It had seemed so snobbish at the
time: "Each person should do something very well, something the riffraff
cannot do." So when, Michael wondered, would Simon ever find it,
something to give him real confidence instead of the pathetic bravado of
the teenager.

"An American public school?" he said now, with some doubt. "We
tried that years ago in Santa Monica, remember?"

"He didn't run away," Jenny pointed out. "And he seemed happy."

"He did not learn." Anna spoke slowly and clearly. *She* should suffer for
a boy too immature to confer with the family, who showed every sign of
pending delinquency? No! Imperative Jenny's triumph be supervised, that
she be exposed to useful contacts, steered clear of sharks—with which
their world was all too infested. So young a girl, so busy, someone must
make the appointments, advise her which critic to cultivate, which to
avoid, how to manage injuries, weight, company gossip, which roles were
for her, which were not. Who but Anna—never, never, had she been so
busy! A boy like Simon she did not need! If he went to New York he
must be Mary Beth's responsibility, not hers.

Mary Beth was thinking on the same lines. Simon in New York City
schools would suit her very well. It was obvious Anna would give him no
time, so she herself would be sent—but in all honesty she'd have to
advise against it. "A kid like Simon could find a lot of trouble in New
York public schools," she murmured. Find it, hell. It would find him.
He'd only have to walk down the street. It was like he wore a sandwich
board: Rich. Unhappy. Rebellious. Misunderstood. He wasn't misunderstood. Standing on the outside, she saw him more clearly than parents,
sister, or grandmother ever could. She understood him. They thought he
was a failure, that he lacked ambition. Couldn't they see the boy crawled
with ambition, burned with it, and if it was not soon satisfied he would
turn sour with it? She didn't know what he wanted, only that he'd better

get it. *Place* was no solution. Yes, there was education to be found in New York, but at his age nobody would force-feed him, he'd have to help himself, the danger being that in the city there were easier ways of helping oneself over a bad patch—and a thousand kindred spirits to point the way. With a needle. "I don't have to tell you there's a drug problem there...from what I read it looks like any schoolkid who wants to buy..." She didn't have to finish. So far Simon had not demonstrated the strongest of wills.

"Risky." Michael chewed his lip. "About the only thing we haven't tried is one of these modern places, no rules, they learn what and when they want, make their own pace. If we knew Simon *had* a pace...I suppose we could give it a try."

"No."

It was Ellie. She'd been quiet, one ear cocked for sounds from upstairs, the other hearing the talk swirl around her. Surely she was listening to a group of actors trying out lines for the first time? When the reading was done they'd go their separate ways, Simon wiped clean from their minds. They didn't care, they really didn't care—except maybe Jenny, who was too young and too preoccupied with her own career to form a clear picture. The rest thought they loved him, but what they really loved was *their* image of what he ought to be. Nobody had ever asked him what *he* needed. She hadn't either. But she knew, she suddenly knew very clearly, and it was the last thing she would have wanted for him. But above all she wanted to see him happy, and without a champion in this family he'd never find any kind of content. His father was too strong. Until now he'd made every decision for and about the children and she'd gone along because she'd agreed with him. He really did want the best for them, but the best as he saw it.

"No," she said again, her voice firm. They all looked taken aback, especially Michael. Of course, wasn't she the perfect European wife, used to airing personal opinions in the privacy of their room?

"Wherever we are next year," she said evenly, "Simon will be with me if he chooses to be. For too long he's been pushed around like some package nobody wants. *I* want him. He can please himself about school, make his own choice. Imagine, nearly sixteen and he's never made a single important decision! They've all been made for him."

"A couple of days ago you thought sixteen was only one step removed from the cradle," Michael said.

She didn't argue. It had seemed that way then, but while Michael was

away looking for Simon she'd had time to think, to examine past patterns. Yes, he still seemed like her baby, but when had she or any of them
let him be anything else?

Anna pulled herself very tall in her chair. "Personally I should not permit even Jenny to make her own decisions. Capable as she is, she is
simply too young—"

And suddenly Ellie was ready for Anna too. "You are not her mother.
You have no right to permit or deny her anything." This was farther than
she had intended to go, but caution had somehow run away with Simon
and had not yet come back.

Michael's frown deepened and Anna puffed out her lips and rapped
fingernails on the arm of her chair. "I merely say a child should be protected. By whom if not by its parents?" She threw out her arms to extract
maximum drama from her words and implored the room at large: "Tell
Anna by whom!"

Normally Ellie would have let it go, unwilling to anger Michael over a
situation she'd come to regard with amusement, but this time she refused
to let Anna warm herself in the spotlight, this time she said exactly what
was on her mind.

"That depends on whose doorstep the child is abandoned."

Michael frowned, Mary Beth gasped, and both of them stole apprehen-
sive glances at Anna. It was Jenny, who looked from her mother to her
grandmother several times, who patted Anna's hand. "It's time Anna took
me through a barre," she said quietly. "Come on, Anna—okay?"

As Ellie expected, Michael saved his questions, his outrage, until they
closed their bedroom door. "Keep him with you? tied to Momma's apron
strings? You think that will make a man of him?"

"No," she said coolly, "but it might stop him going off the deep end."

"Which means?"

"He's desperately unhappy, Michael."

"And of course I'm to blame—"

"It's too late for blame, maybe it's too late for Simon. Do you know
how many unhappy kids commit suicide?"

"Oh come on, he's hardly unique, this world's full of spoiled brats who
can't get what they want."

"You don't even *know* what he wants!"

"Do you?"

"Not another school. And he *is* unique, a bundle of tension within a
hair of a nervous breakdown. At least."

"And I'm doing that to him."

"Did I say it? You mean well, Michael, but you've even less idea of his needs than you have of mine. You live in boardrooms, dart out for a crisis and can't wait to duck back in."

This couldn't be Ellie talking. But it was, it was. And she wasn't finished. "When he was tiny you treated him like a naughty boy. Now he seems to have graduated to the family 'problem,' a time-consuming matter that gets in the way of business."

"Back up. What you just said, that I've no idea of your needs. You have a beautiful home, several in fact. It's been years since I had . . . other interests. You know I love you, that there's nothing in this world I wouldn't give you, within reason."

"Except your time—but that is not within reason."

He ran exasperated fingers through his hair. "When you were even younger than Simon you had the running of a large house, a business, *and* an invalid. Surely you, of all people, know that what we have requires constant attention—"

"—and thanks to your efforts we have more of it every day, needing more and more attention in the future. Am I right?"

What could he say? Across the room, in her dressing-table mirror, rhythmic strokes of her hairbrush punctuated the entire exchange. In the dry summer air, sparks of static electricity shot like tiny stars from honey-colored hair only just beginning to have a silvery sheen at the temples.

"Am I right?" she said again. Insistent now.

He took a deep breath. "I suppose you are. Simon may be your baby, Greenlings and Abramo are mine. I built them for us."

He looked with speculation at the set of her shoulders. He'd hoped, now the tension of Simon's disappearance was over, that they could clear the air between them, make up, forget all the words spoken in anger and get back to where they'd been when they were in Tokyo. He took a tentative step towards her.

He could not have been more surprised than she when the hairbrush flew from her hand and spun across the space between them.

He stepped aside just in time and they both watched, frozen, as it whipped into the velvet padding of the bed's headboard and dropped face down onto the satin pillow.

Without a word he crossed the room to stand behind her in the mirror, run his hands softly across the smooth whiteness of her shoulders. It was as if he'd touched a spring. Tears brimmed her blue eyes and slid, uncontrolled, down her cheeks.

"Oh Michael," she whispered, "what *are* we to do with him?"

FORTY-FOUR

*J*ENNY ABRAMSKY, ballet's latest darling.

Company promo (assisted by Anna's stage-whispered campaign among the cognoscenti) made enough advance waves to guarantee full houses before Jenny so much as set foot on a New York stage. The city's knowledgeable audiences did the rest.

Ellie, spectator to the hoopla, felt a small part of herself cringe. Simon's path so pitted with traps, many of which he dug himself—yet Jenny's way strewn with roses as dewy and perfect as she herself. Was there anything she did not have? According to her p.r., not a thing. Her youth (crossing the Atlantic she'd somehow shed two years and was now fourteen); excellent classical training; a technique strong yet lyrical. Even the light of Michael's business acumen was made to reflect favorably upon his daughter. Her future was as perfectly prepared as money and self-discipline could make it. So who could be surprised when she spun onto the New York scene like a pink and gold comet?

She'd earned her accolades.

Yet Ellie, in the house seat kept for her, faintly smiling at Simon and Michael by her side as a wave of applause and reflected glory washed over them, had to wonder what the audience saw in her thin intense daughter, all bone and line and unswerving resolve. The same thing Hans von Reiker had seen in Anna? This diamond-hard brilliance that supposedly caused him to lose his head?

It was many years since Jenny had acknowledged any unmet needs, wrapped her insecure, Momma-I'm-so-sorry arms around Ellie's neck in the night and begged forgiveness for some imagined sin. Eager to please as ever, Jenny now sought that same approval from her audience. And Anna.

Anna. My mother, my enemy, my rival in everything, including the love of my daughter. Yet how that ruthless, preposterous woman had succeeded! She'd taken the timid clay that was young Jenny and sculpted it into a dancer of glittering promise. Better, she'd fired the finished product with an impenetrable glaze of absolute assurance. Could Ellie have done the same? No. God knew she'd failed with Simon—but then, she hadn't tried to shape him into anything but Simon. And even as a tot he'd never cared whether he pleased or offended. Ellie recalled a birthday party, their young guests agog, Felix wringing pale hands over the cake as Jenny pleaded with Simon to let them blow out the flickering candles *now*.

Simon, exactly four, said a firm "Later!"

"But they're all *waiting*," Jenny whimpered.

"So?"

So twenty guests had been made to bide their time until Simon was ready.

A rustle of programs and applause pulled Ellie back to the stage where a spotlight sought out Jenny's innocence, bathed it in lights of soft pink and a hard, bright white.

Watching Jenny dance, Ellie never quite understood her own reactions. Yes, she loved her, but not in the way she loved Simon, who daily filled her with anxiety. Jenny was to admire, to take pride in—but seeing her dance, Ellie was reminded of that first ballet, Germany, and the company of a young doctor. Jenny's slender arms, a great asset in her world, called back other arms, skinny and bruised, the arms of an aging dancer; in Jenny's soft, pink-curving lips was it possible there lurked the taut beginnings of that bitter, livid slash of the other dancer's mouth? And where, really, was the comparison? Jenny was all freshness and floating air . . . but seeds floated too, flourished and rooted. Success or failure, the theater took a savage toll. What would it steal from this child of sharp edges and liquid arms, this sprite of the swift and sliding glance, the cool professional shell? Under its surface the compassion of a small child still lingered, but could it survive alongside the rampant growth of ego?

Perhaps. Jenny was that rare and lucky creature, a success in the field she had chosen.

And if by some miracle Simon were to get what *he* chose, would he be happy? Ellie thought not. His needs went far deeper than the approval of a vast and impersonal audience.

Cal Ricci, Abramo's new area manager, leaned across Simon to whisper to Ellie and Michael. He knew nothing of ballet, but the praise he poured over them was as open and lavish as his country.

"She's . . . wonderful . . . beautiful! You've got to be proud, you have to be proud of a little kid like that, huh?"

Little kid! "She's sixteen," Ellie said tartly. Sixteen, and just about old enough to date this impressionable young man with whom Michael was so highly impressed.

And did Ricci, by omission, mean they should be ashamed of Simon? Did the implication hang in the air, or was she imagining it? Stop it. Ricci was too innocent, too stricken with Jenny to mean any such thing. Stop analyzing every word. Enjoy Jenny's triumph *and* Simon's astonishing content.

Simon liked New York.

Even as she allowed herself to think the words, she held her breath. But it was true, he seemed happy. From the first day he'd walked easier, hands in pockets, sneakers padding, shoulders loose, whistling, slouching down Fifth Avenue humming, turning up his Walkman, snapping his fingers on the corners of Eighth and 42nd. He even loved the small penthouse Michael bought on 34th; nights were still warm and he could take a sleeping bag up to the roof garden rather than bed down in his suite, which his father had designed pretty much on the order of his own bachelor quarters when he'd been the same age.

How could he? Simon wondered. What could have made Dad think he'd *want* cork-brown walls and all that cream stuff? Quilt, rug, drapes, blinds, phone; brown tub, shower, coffeepot, cups and trays; futuristic divans done up in brown fake fur and even, heaven help him, a brown-tinted mirror wall from which cream cranes spread their enameled wings. Brown and cream, brown and cream. Brown and cream. They felt like burial colors pressing in on him, and he stayed outdoors when he could; when he couldn't, he watched TV or videos long into the night—another thing Dad had never allowed at Greenlings, even though Abramo's ads showed kids lying in bed happily guzzling hot chocolate as they watched movie after movie. But now Mom said he could watch whatever he wanted, and Dad didn't say a word; when Mom asked, he even brought home earphones so Simon could watch without anybody's knowing. He even had his own room key now, and Mom said he could lock up whenever he felt like it. It was as if Mom and Dad had switched places. Dad still gave the orders, except that where Simon was concerned he seemed to kind of look at Mom before he said anything. And he didn't say much, not anymore. He didn't even bitch about fresh donuts Simon ordered up from the restaurant on the first floor—though Anna said he'd get pimples and seemed to hope he would. He didn't.

The roof, wow, that was the most. He felt free as a starling up there, no doors to lock, no walls hemming him in, no ceilings, just that great night sky that took up every color of the neons down there in the street. Life went on day and night here, night and day. No school bell sent him to bed at ten and jangled him awake at six.

Man, he really did go for this town. Especially with no school. Mom said maybe he ought to be thinking about it, just thinking, she wasn't *pressing,* he understood that, right?

Right. Sure. So okay, if all he had to do was think about it, no sweat, but he didn't ever intend to see inside a classroom as long as he lived.

The big library downtown, now *that* was different, rows and rows of phone books from every state in the union, other stuff he (and for sure not Mom or Dad) had never dreamed of. He also found, to his chagrin, that he could have gotten the same stuff from London any old time, that there was a Lore Society with its own special journal, copies neatly bound and sent to New York. So the years of searching, of dialing random Sacramento numbers in hopes of a strike had all been so much wasted effort. It was all here. Language, names, sociological studies, approximate locations of various *kumpanias,* even the ways in which each group made a living.

From now on it would be easy. All he had to do was keep on looking.

Michael saw the improvement in Simon and was gratified. He even congratulated Ellie on her good sense in not forcing him into school. "I thought I might take him down to the office with me, sit in on a meeting or so. But just imagine—" he said, already half out the door for a downtown meeting with the new sales manager, "Simon spending all that time in a library! You're *sure* that's where he goes?"

"Positive. He's there when I pick him up—and he seems to be on first-name terms with one of the reference librarians."

Michael grinned. "Aha! How old is she?"

"Pushing sixty."

"Oh. So it's not that. Has he said what he's studying?"

"If I ask it could come to a sudden stop. You know how secretive he can be."

"Mmm . . . maybe if you had a quiet word with his librarian?"

"*Michael!* Look, he's entitled to the same privacy you give Jenny. You don't ask which studio she's using today, what steps they worked on, you don't expect Anna to spy on her for you—"

He sighed. "Jenny is not Simon." He caught Ellie's sudden flush of anger. "Okay, okay—I'm off."

He allowed the mystery to puzzle him only briefly. By the time he reached the office there was a smile on his face as he paid the cabbie, a spring to his step as he crossed the sidewalk to the office. Common sense told him to keep a careful eye on Abramo's new young executive, but it was admiration and genuine liking which brought him down here almost daily to counsel and confer with this promising young American who'd walked into the L.A. office less than two years ago as a prospective sales trainee. No résumé, no previous experience in the field, just a smile as wide and open as America itself.

"No college?" Michael had probed. *All* ambitious Americans went to college. Practically written into their bill of rights.

"No." No apology in the square white smile. "Law, medicine, architecture, music, engineering, yes, but selling, it's more like juggling or farming or writing poems. Either you can sell or you can't—and if you can't a fistful of Ph.D.'s won't make a lick of difference."

"And you think you can sell my computer?"

"I know I can, but it's not my choice. The field's way too crowded since the Japanese jumped in. I figure a lot of companies gotta go belly-up the next couple of years. Abramo's new model's just a rehash of last year's and so is everybody else's. By now most homes that are going to have one have got one, and it's way too soon for them to start trading in. *All* the offices have 'em. I figure giants like IBM and Xerox, maybe a few others, they'll be fighting it out on their own pretty soon. The rest will be dead in the water. It's just not a good field now. I'd a lot sooner be selling your real estate, one of these new developments . . ."

He'd leaned forward to hover over the mock-up of Michael's latest baby, a small, exclusive little development in what used to be the sticks. Ten years he'd held onto that piece of cheap land that everyone said was expensive at the time. It had been. But it was paying off big now. Watching this young man, Michael saw a blaze of enthusiasm in his blue eyes.

"Who doesn't want a new home? People are trading in houses like they used to trade in cars. Every two years. Same with offices. Prestige. It's what everybody's looking for. Every year a tad more space, more glass, thicker rugs for the boss's office, bigger elevators, a reception desk that's a cross between the Ritz Carlton and a high-priced girlie house."

He didn't blush and Michael liked that too. The last thing he wanted representing Abramsky was a twenty-two-year-old virgin. As for the computer industry, the boy was right; six months from now half the new companies would be dead in the water, their young wizards standing dazed in unemployment lines.

"Okay," Michael had said then. "I'll make a deal. Store manager to start. One month's training, six months' trial in a poor store, what you make depends on merchandise moved. And I might as well tell you now, people in that neighborhood are more into drugs than electronics. It barely breaks even, but this is a bad time to unload. If you do okay maybe I'll give you a shot at a development." He waved his hand at the mock-up of neat plastic houses, plastic lawns, suburban streets. "Not this one, it's a sellout now, but I'll have something coming up soon."

They shook hands on it, but not before young Calvin Ricci had picked up one of the plastic houses, grinned, and set it down again. "Yes sir, I'll sure sell 'em to fools who want to buy—but I'm damned if I'd ever live in one."

A few months later he had indeed brought up the sales curve of the store he managed, and Michael took him onto his personal staff, helping coordinate the newest development. Ricci proved as skillful playing watchdog to hard-nosed contractors as he had been at selling small appliances. Michael used the time to watch, to ask questions; when Calvin was twenty-four Michael went to the trouble of seeing Cal in his own setting.

Calvin Ricci came by his oddly assorted name through an Italian father who ran a small-town dry cleaner's and a mother of staunch New England values. The family home, small, sad, and very old, stood alone at the end of a lane. Its roof was furred green with moss, its chimney tilted east, and it appeared to have grown up out of the ground. So, when Michael met them, did Cal's parents. A hunched, beaten man of sixty and a thin gray woman, dour, uncompromising, who could have been her husband's age except Calvin said she was ten years his junior. Michael dismissed them with a glance. Except for the begetting of young Calvin they were not exceptional. But the boy . . . just watching him run young hands over the worn ridged grain of the oaken front door made Michael glad he'd invented this excuse to stop by.

He's the way I was! Michael thought, wondering at the reverence in

Calvin's touch. How was it possible that a young man such as this, raised in a young country, a man of unquestionably middle-class upbringing and far, so very far removed from the thieving, conniving, forever hungry Micah, could be so . . . caring about certain things, so cavalier about others?

The new five-bedroomers Calvin was selling for Abramsky Developments, two sunken tubs, an atrium in every conceivable space, open staircase spiraling down (white-painted wrought iron naturally, nothing so depressing as black, these were *young* families, right? right!) to a multilevel family room looking out on a square front lawn, every last house with precisely seventeen hundred square feet of living space, hot tubs standard, fake-stone fireplaces optional . . . these were simply merchandise. To Michael and now to Calvin, expensive goods to be sold and then forgotten.

They were houses.

Yet this tilting, run-down little place moved Calvin.

"It's falling apart," he told Michael. "When I was little Dad got in the market a tad deep. Since then they've had nothing left over for repairs . . . fixing old places like this costs more than starting over."

"I know."

Michael remembered. They'd said that about Greenlings and they'd been so *right*—but every last brick was worth the sacrifices made . . . they'd all made. All? No, not Felix and Anna, who, but for him, would have lived out their lives in Ryder Street and counted themselves content. Relatively. Ellie yes, Greenlings had been a sacrifice for her. Without that expensive millstone they'd have more investments now, stocks in companies more . . . secure than Abramo. All their eggs would not be in one basket. But for them Greenlings was home.

Home.

As this old New England place was for Calvin.

"You want to keep it."

"Why d'you think I'm selling your houses? No offense, Mr. Abramsky, I'm sure they're fine for some, but well . . . money? Yeah okay, so it's gonna come in handy to get stonework fixed, the roof shored up, paint jobs, double glazing—"

"And this place is yours," Michael said quietly.

"Well . . ."

"It will be?"

"It belongs to my folks."

"And when they're gone it's yours."

"I guess."

"It's what you want?"

"Yeah..."

"I see."

Michael sighed heavily and thought of Greenlings, of his plans. When he was away, like now, it should have been Simon watching out for excess seepage in the damp course, dry rot in the foundation. Instead it was the inept Lily Finn and the very ept firm of caretakers paid to care for property they did not care for.

What choice was there?

He knew, without even consulting Simon, that woodworm could munch Hamish's old paneling to a million heaps of sawdust right before Simon's eyes and he wouldn't even notice, much less care.

Oh, Simon.

FORTY-FIVE

*T*HEIR EIGHTEENTH SUMMER was the last Jenny and Simon were
to spend together before their lives took paths too widely diver-
gent for them ever to join forces again on quite the same footing. For all
practical purposes both were still under the family roof—in this case the
New York penthouse, with Simon still more often *on* it than under it.

The previous Christmas Anna had suffered a series of small strokes,
none causing major damage but cumulatively taking their toll; sight and
hearing had dimmed; her neck no longer had the swanlike curve on
which Felix had lavished so much pride. She spent the winter at Que
Vista under the benevolent eye of Chita; she summered at Greenlings
under the pervasive blast from Lily Finn's larynx. As she often said to
Lily—with not a trace of hesitation—"Each night in my prayers I thank
the good God he steals my hearing faster than my sanity."

Lily beamed, carried on regardless, and would not for the world have
admitted that she missed the acerbic old woman when Mr. Michael sometimes appeared to sweep Anna off to first nights in New York, London,

and Los Angeles—if Jenny was billed to take center stage. For Anna, the Western world had no other dancer worth watching.

Mary Beth, her dream cottage at the Cape as far off as ever, now accompanied Jenny, whose star continued to ascend as she flitted from coast to coast like a radiant, pampered butterfly. The public never saw beyond the smile and the hard white glitter of her diamond; never saw her feet with the bandages off, the bunions, deformed joints, the bleeding toes of her trade.

Calvin Ricci, to whom she'd been engaged for a year, saw and adored and agonized over every blister. He would have taken Jenny on any terms; that her name was Abramsky was so fortuitous as to be an embarrassment.

When Anna (who admired Calvin because Michael did) wrote that it was a partnership made in heaven, Mary Beth muttered to Ellie that if such was the case the articles of settlement had surely been drawn up in the boardroom.

The shaft was typical now of Mary Beth, her two predinner cocktails no excuse; as the twins reached near-adulthood she was more and more aware she'd missed the boat, that her chances of any life of her own were fading. Jenny's impending wedding, not two weeks away, only underscored the bleakness of what Mary Beth's life would be without this family. Which she felt now to be her own, hers to praise and criticize as freely as any of its bona fide members.

"They *love* each other!" Ellie protested. "You're implying Cal's marrying Jenny only because she's Michael's daughter."

"I'm implying the opposite. That she's marrying him because it suits Michael. That if Michael told her to hold her breath for ten minutes she'd die trying. That if Simon can't be knocked into shape—and let's face it, wise family that we are, we've not seen his star rise in the east yet, right? —then Jenny's husband is the new heir apparent, a son-in-law to . . . keep it in the family, so to speak."

"Keep *what* in the—"

"Oh, come on! What makes Michael, in his own eyes, better than the Gypsies? *Superior* to them? What's his bulwark against them? His suit of armor?" Mary Beth paced the room's fluffy white carpet with short, almost angry strides, her arms folded tightly across her chest. Far below them the traffic barely whispered. They could have been fighting on a cloud.

Mary Beth was thickening about the middle, Ellie noticed, unconsciously smoothing her own still-slender thighs under a shantung dress from Hong Kong. Turquoise rings from Colorado perfectly complimented hands that were still long and creamy—unlike Mary Beth's, which were becoming heavily veined. Well, how old would she be? Mid-fifties at least. If only she were not so . . . combative lately, especially where Michael was concerned. At the moment Jenny was resting a pulled tendon, which left Mary Beth with nothing to do now the studios had been franchised out. Idle for once, perhaps she felt obliged to speak as one of the family, to stake her claim to the position in order to justify an enforced rest she had in any case earned.

But she had not finished, was raging on:

"If Michael listed his assets in order of importance *to him personally,* business wouldn't top the list, Ellie, though I know you think it would. It wouldn't be Simon either, nor Jenny, although she's much closer to the top—success has drawn her up to your level and out of *their* orbit. But even you wouldn't head the list, Ellie. No. Sorry. You're all window dressing for the *real* asset, the Great Wall of Greenlings."

"What a rotten thing to say!"

"It keeps out the Rom."

"Why, you cynical—"

"We're talking about Michael. A cynical man."

"He's a romantic! Look what happened over that woman! When he realized what it was doing to us, to me, the children, Anna—"

"And to Michael. She was pulling him back to them, wasn't she? Into their orbit? That was the real factor."

Ellie sighed, tried not to hear. Did it matter what Mary Beth thought? She and Michael loved each other. Surely that's what counted. Yes, it was a different marriage now, pulled from one side and another, battered by the Rom and by Anna—but it had held, settled into early, comfortable middle age. No doubt Farah gave it the first push, then Felix's death, and perhaps the ever-present shadow of Simon's future. Yes. But she and Michael were a pair, happy. They made love. Not so often perhaps, they were older now, but when they did it was as good. More important, they *cared about each other* in ways Mary Beth couldn't understand because she'd never cared for anyone in that way. And no one had cared for her. Understandably she'd grown bitter; like wine, a tart tongue sharpened with time, eventually turned acidic. Forgive. She's a good friend, she cares.

"Mary Beth, we're talking about Jenny. She's making a good marriage. They'll be happy." Ellie had no doubts. Jenny did love Cal and if one was to love, how much better it be a *good* man, which Cal unquestionably was. "Jenny *loves* Cal."

Livid splotches appeared on Mary Beth's neck. "Of course. Isn't he exactly like her father? Dominating? Ambitious?"

Ellie turned away. This was too much, even from a friend. "Michael's ambition has kept you comfortably employed for many years. A governess, you could have been shuttled from family to family, one group of children to another. Instead you live exactly as we do, the same life, the same accommodations—"

"Yes, the best that money can buy. I know. But I say again. Jenny would marry Idi Amin if Michael smiled upon the union."

It was no use. In this mood... even friendship as old as theirs had limits. "If you're not careful you could become a bitter, crabbed old spinster."

What was she saying? Mary Beth *could* become? She was halfway there.

Simon had not been idle. He had a driver's license now, the convertible Dad gave him for his birthday, and a triple-A map he worked over as hard as the original cartographer. He was done browsing phone books. Now he quizzed social workers, noted down this gathering place and that. Dates. Festivals. At Greenlings last summer he picked a lock, rummaged through Dad's private file, unearthed Grandmam's death certificate and discovered that she really did have a last name, not just one but six; four of the six were names that cropped up over and over in *kumpanias* of the Los Angeles basin, the Sacramento delta, the San Francisco Bay Area, all the way up to Portland, Oregon.

He thought he had it made then.

He didn't. Gypsies had phones but not phone numbers. Social workers he called turned out to be links in a long string of contacts. In most cases the names he asked for were "in France for the summer" or "up Montreal way." Or Vancouver, Guadalajara, Miami. More often they were "traveling," nobody knew where or when they'd be back, evasions that would have infuriated him had he not admired them so much.

Okay.

He could live with it, work round it.

It was easy now he was older, easier still when he took a job in a repair shop for a month or so—not without raised eyebrows from Dad and veiled promises of his own body shop if he felt so inclined—but he saved every dollar, nickel, dime, and quarter that came his way, including those the family tossed into ashtrays and candy dishes when they cleared out pockets and purses. Ever since they'd arrived in New York there'd been a heady new freedom in his days, Mom and Dad careful not to ask, to pry, and now, as a direct result, a handy stash of crisp bills were folded into the herb bag under the brown fake-fur bed cover.

Planning, he was happy.

He wasn't just marking time.

Now, with Jenny's wedding coming up, it was going to be easy after all. Everybody preoccupied, busy, all the razzmatazz of fittings and rehearsals and shopping, nobody really watching Simon.

He picked the weekend before the wedding when the others, even Mary Beth, were staying over with Cal's folks to make last-minute arrangements. Simon said he didn't feel like going and under the new freedom nobody argued with him.

They left for Cal's place around dusk on Friday.

Simon slipped out of the underground parking lot a half hour after them. Earlier in the day he'd gassed up the little silver-blue BMW, had it tuned, the trunk packed with canned stuff so he wouldn't have to eat at truck stops where Dad could trace him—but in any case he'd be across the country long before anybody knew he was gone.

Mile upon mile of open road disappearing under the car, exhilarating dashes on the downslopes, flooring it on the ups to pass trucks whose drivers gave a friendly wave to his rearview mirror. When fatigue made the road weave in front of the hood he pulled off, found a tree to park under, locked himself in and slept for an hour, two at most, but always the main road thundered close, a magnet drawing him on. For the first time in his life he traveled with no fixed destination, only that vast coast drawing him ever westerly, the car a little blue dart zooming through endless yellow flatlands of Kansas in September, Colorado's towering green peaks and great swooping valleys, little towns in Utah tidier-than-thou, the broiling hell of Las Vegas, over 100 degrees at midnight and climbing.

Once through the Mojave he fancied he could smell the sea and drove faster and faster towards the L.A. basin, not because he expected to find what he was looking for but because he had a need to see Que Vista again in passing, remind himself of that last scene, the woman in the red skirt and Tomo on the deck with a can of beer. Right now it was rented to a rock star and his retinue, but in the dark who'd know he'd been around?

Trapped in the unfamiliar snake nest of L.A.'s downtown freeways, he maneuvered into a lane he was sure would take him west to Santa Monica. Minutes later, when every green and white marker bore street names he'd never seen and only vaguely heard of, he took the off-ramp, looking for a gas station to fill up, check out the map, get his bearings.

It was three in the morning and hot, the Santana adding a still malevolence to the prevailing pollution. With half the streetlights burned out or shot out, the few remaining cast their dim glow on mashed Colonel Sanders cartons, Juicy Fruit wrappers, bent Coors cans. In a littered doorway he caught the flutter of a skirt followed by a beckoning finger. Boy, this was some neighborhood! A glance at the gas gauge told him he'd better find some fast, but where in this run-down back street of an L.A. slum would he find a station open at this hour?

Two blocks over he found a one-pumper selling an off brand. When Simon's wheels tripped the alarm an attendant ambled out. He didn't wash the dead desert bugs off the windshield but he did smile, running a black hand over the pretty little convertible's hood. He smiled wider as Simon handed him a hundred, shuffling off, head wagging, muttering to himself. He was a long time making change, and when he finally handed it over he gave Simon a yes-suh-I-done-mah-duty salute which seemed oddly out of place.

"You come back now, you heah?" He laughed softly as he locked himself back into his cubicle.

Simon had driven maybe two blocks very slow, the heat pressing him back into the seat, before a shadow seemed to fall across the hood with a thump and he had no choice but to stop, wishing as he stepped on the brake that he'd put the top up, locked the doors. Wishing even harder as separate shadows appeared on both sides of the car and at the rear, formed up into a circle, very white smiles murmuring "honky dude" as fingers slipped covetously along the car's gleaming sides. Brown velvet voices whispering out of the dark. Quiet voices, almost murmurs in the hot deserted night.

"You just a punk kid, where you get off driving a heap like this, white boy?"

"Yeah, oh yeah, sure is a pretty thing."

"Us now, we don't got money for pretty little things."

"We don't got no hun'-dollah bills for to buy gas—"

Almost before he realized it one hand was reaching in his shirt for his wallet, and in the other a knife gleamed blue in the streetlamp. Dazzling blue. Simon felt the wallet leave his pocket a split second before the knife pricked his throat, before another hand grabbed a handful of his hair.

"Lookee heah this pretty white-boy hair, what you *say*—"

And all the time the knife point pricking deeper.

Panic slammed Simon's foot on the gas, threw heavy bodies off the windshield, dragged the one with a knife in its hand over fifty yards before the weight suddenly let go and he was free, wallet miraculously in his lap but his heart in his mouth, racing, racing, right foot jammed solid on the gas, afraid to brake even at red lights until a cop appeared beside him, flagged him down . . .

Oh God, a ticket, now Dad would know where...the car—

"What's the rush, kid?"

"Nothin'."

"License?"

Simon's hands shook so hard he could barely fumble his wallet as he searched in the steady beam of the cop's flashlight, finally produced the precious document for scrutiny.

The cop nodded. "Not from around here, huh?"

"No sir, I got lost on the freeway."

"Where you headed?"

Simon hesitated. "Malibu."

Now it was cop's eyes examining the pretty little silver-blue toy. "It figures."

"Yes sir."

"That blood on your neck?"

"Uh-uh." Oh shit, he was going to cry, he was going to fucking well cry in front of a cop—

"Meet up with a gang?"

"Y-yes sir."

He nodded. "Plenty around. Did they have firearms?"

"W-what..."

The cop snapped his fingers. "Guns. Weapons."

Simon shook his head. "A...knife, kinda like a paring knife the cook does potatoes with at home—"

The cop sighed, muttered something about God and strength. "Kids then, be a while before they graduate to high octane. Did they get anything?"

"No, I floored the acc—"

Suddenly the patrol car's radio squawked. Fast, urgent, verging on hysteria. The cop threw the license at him and left on the run.

Simon watched him go, for once in his life happy to be Simon Abramsky and not an L.A. cop patrolling a run-down slum. The next minute not so happy, a warm splash of blood hitting the back of his hand.

His neck, they'd nicked his neck.

Maybe not much or the cop would have stuck around, but enough, better find someplace safe, pull over, get the Band-Aids from the trunk, find Que Vista, maybe the rock group had kept Chita on like they were supposed to, she liked him, Chita did...

The complex of freeway systems welcomed him back like a brother. Up and down their lanes he drove, across and over and under, figure eights and interchanges, seven lanes to three and back again to seven, Carson next right, east to Fountain Valley, right lane for Paramount, left lane for... where... now Downey, now Pasadena, then Culver City, Burbank, Glendale, Simon at sea but afraid to leave the relative safety of the roller coaster for the darker uncertainties of downtown streets. Bewildered, exhausted, he gave up on names, concentrated hard on direction, took every ramp that waved a promise of *west*.

At last.

It wasn't even daylight when he shot under a familiar underpass and the morning beaches of Santa Monica lay deserted on his left. Almost. This early there was always the dedicated jogger, his less dedicated dog sniffing at tide pools and small dead rays washed in on last night's tide. Simon remembered when once after a storm he'd found hundreds of dead squid, another time Chita's dog... what was its name? he couldn't remember... yes he could! he could!—it was Poco and he was scared of the water, barked himself hoarse when he found a seal's bloated corpse tangled in great ropes of seaweed.

Storefronts in Santa Monica still had that tacky look, sun-bleached but not matured as Mary Beth used to say; just up the dried-out canyons, odd little specialty shops run by odd little refugees from the more stable canyons of New York.

The morning was hazy or maybe he was faint, he couldn't be sure which... deeper canyons on the right now, scorched brown this time of year, but stores got classier the farther north he went. Pretty soon there were the expensive narrow beach houses of the current stars, their Alfas and Rollses parked out front, status symbols everybody had to have because tomorrow a series might be axed, then somebody came and took all the toys back. But for now, while they'd got 'em, even their tiny garages were worth more, in investable dollars and cents, than a mansion back east. So Dad said.

Pretty soon even the beach houses thinned out; now he passed the hidden entry to Paradise Cove, the Sandcastle Restaurant where they used to eat Sunday breakfast as they watched skin divers get into their gear and go flapping down the beach like seals out of water. He knew now he was getting close, Dume Point coming up soon, a few hundred yards more and he could park, eat something maybe, wash his neck in the ocean—salt always cleaned everything, Grandmam used to say that—find that Band-Aid, spy out the setup at Que Vista.

Boy, he sure could go for some of Chita's eggs ranchero and she'd make 'em for him too . . . but while he was eating she'd call Mom for sure. They were all in it together. What he'd do was, he'd creep up behind the dunes, approach Que Vista on its blind side where the only window was Chita's kitchen.

Even if she was there she wouldn't be up yet.

Remembering to lock the car, he parked by the road, taking the familiar path that threaded through the dunes. After the searing heat of the Santanas, scrub and ice plant were all that were left, but come the first drops of dew everything'd be back—if a canyon fire didn't get 'em first.

Lugging bottles of Pepsi and a bag of barbecue potato chips, he made his way barefoot over shining untrodden sand to the clean sea, soaked a cloth in salt water and let it run over the wound in his neck. Washed, it wasn't that bad, wide but not deep. He cut a Band-Aid butterfly fashion and, using the inside of the Johnson & Johnson can lid for a mirror, pulled the edges of the wound together. Like Grandmam showed him— only she hadn't used any Band-Aids or mirrors. She used a plantain poultice tied on with iron grass and her mirror was the nearest pond. She'd have liked it here, he thought. Everything natural, no people—

"Out kinda early, aren't you? Don't you know this is a private beach?"

He looked up, straight into eyes of the Western world's biggest, newest sensation, a rock star who, in videos, looked more like a very pretty woman than a handsome man. But now he was in swim trunks and no makeup, and he was all man.

"Gosh . . . I mean . . ."

"What you up to?"

If Simon said this was his father's house, that he was just stopping by, he knew the kid would have asked him in, fed him, invited him to stay. But maybe there was Chita. Who'd call home.

"I'm leaving," he said. "Soon as I get cleaned up."

The star picked up a Pepsi, knocked the top off, and ripped into the bag of potato chips. "Hey man, I'm starving. There's a woman up at the house, all she knows is fucking eggs—"

"Yeah." Saliva surged over Simon's tongue.

The star suddenly leapt up, guzzled the Pepsi, and sent the bottle spinning into the waves, cramming his mouth with the last of the chips before sending the bag after it. "Hey kid, bet I took your breakfast, huh? And me about ready to hit the sack. Tell ya what, let's have a toke and then you'll shove off, huh?"

"Yeah," said Simon weakly, not sure what he meant.

The star rolled and lit a joint, took a puff and passed it to Simon, who'd never smoked anything before, never mind pot. "Suck it right down into your stomach like this, see?"

"Yeah," Simon said, trying.

"That's the way, go on, have another drag, another."

Feeling vaguely pressured, Simon obeyed, and between them they finished it, then the star pointed to the road. "Okay, playtime's over, the star's gotta catch some sleepy-bye. You go thataways, stranger! I thought I told you, you're on private beach here, now off it!"

Simon trudged back to his car, drove a little ways north until nobody could see him at all, then he got out of the car and threw up.

Curled under a sand hill he passed out, images coming and going, whooooing and shooooshing to the drum of the surf, and always he was crying a name, a name...each time he came to, there were tears on his face and still he cried the name, puzzled because it wasn't Dad or Jenny or Grandmam, it wasn't even Mom, it was Tomo, Tomo, Tomo...

When he woke up he felt better, bought oranges off a roadside stand, and headed straight north, foot all the way down now, no more messing around, no stopping to look at Big Sur, no hankering after any Golden Gate Bridge, no passing go, no going to jail, no nothing, just north, then directly east to Sacramento.

Once there he just drove around. Around and around and around, looking for the place. He had no doubt at all that when he found it he'd know it.

He was half right. In a semirun-down neighborhood he stopped in a Taco Bell, chatted up a Mexican boy behind the counter who'd complained bitterly about blacks moving in the area. Next minute it was Viets, spoilin' everything, no sooner got here than they had houses, cars—

"Bet you get Gypsies too, huh?"

The boy smiled. "Yeah, sure, three-four blocks over, down by Wreck Alley there's plenty, but they don't bother me none, they stick where they belong."

Wreck Alley turned out to be where the body shops were. The rest was easy. Simon drove around it slow, real slow, showing his pretty little car, watching the faces, feeling his blood quicken as he saw the cast of cheekbones, a certain flat angle, noses long, mouths thin and wary. But the eyes confirmed it. Soft and black, almost lazy until you saw they missed nothing at all.

When he stopped they circled, as he knew they would, touched his car much as the gang in L.A. had touched it, but this time he wasn't afraid. He asked for Tomo and they said Tomo Who?

He smiled. "Tomo my cousin. Romanitchal. His dad's name's Dui."

Tomo would be a coupla minutes, okay? They had to go get him from another body shop. What was *his* name again?

"Simon. He knows me."

They backed off then, all of them, put off perhaps by the too perfect car or by Simon's coloring—though there were plenty there with lightish hair and a few had blue eyes. Simon was left in isolation, but not for a second unwatched.

Behind him there was a sudden commotion, voices shouting in Romani, some in English, "Hey Tomo, somebody to see ya!"

Then a warm brown hand clapped Simon's shoulder, a brown and white smile got between him and the steering wheel. A smell of tobacco and garlic and sweat and somehow of Grandmam, a dirty red kerchief and a torn checked shirt.

Tomo.

A man.

"Simon! So what the hell kept ya? We'd about give up on you, man!"

FORTY-SIX

*T*HAT NIGHT the families opened their arms to him.

It was a welcome it seemed he'd waited for all of his life. Tomo's hand never left Simon's shoulder as he was led from group to group, introduced not as Simon, son of Michael Abramsky, head of Abramo—not even as Simon, brother of Jenny Abramsky, prima ballerina.

Here he was Simon of the families, Tomo's cousin, Uncle Dui's nephew, and Grandmam's—they all remembered Grandmam, right?— yes, well Simon had been Grandmam's favorite.

At some point they took him to Uncle Dui's trailer, Uncle Dui who was now fat in the pale, doughy fashion of the kidney sufferer; his wife was unexpectedly thin and had little to say beyond making sure Simon had a bed made up in Tomo's trailer, which was shared with younger brother Amos.

Later Tomo produced three sisters, but this first night it was impossible to sort out one from another. All were dark, giggly, and shy. Aunt Rose came by for a second and stayed three hours, drinking wine and smoking, by Simon's count, an entire pack of cigarettes.

Outdoors were many small cooking fires and one large communal blaze lit, it turned out, in Simon's honor. Though the night was murderously hot they served the usual peppery stew that again brought Grandmam back, even the smell of her pipe when some of the women lit up after the meal, tamping down the baccy with hardwood plugs.

One by one, other families joined at the fire until all the *kumpanias* must surely be represented.

"You'll stay tonight," Tomo whispered, "and I guess after that you'll likely be here for good, huh?"

"I don't know, I haven't thought, I'll have to work—"

"Work with me any day. Car bodies, motors, anything in the auto line I can do . . . if you don't fancy that you can help my dad, he's into horses, lotsa *gaje* out in the country around here, they buys horses, don't know what the hell they're doin' but they stick their kids up top, put a whip in their hands, dress 'em up in riding pants and velvet coats and caps and bingo, they're gentry. Bleedin' magic, innit, Dad? You could do that, easy. . ."

A great lump rose in Simon's throat so he could barely speak. He'd just arrived and they were taking him in as if he'd every right to live with them, join in their work. "I like horses," he said. "I'll bet I could sell them."

"I know you could—catch! here's a beer—'course, it'll depend on the Rom Baro." Tomo's voice dipped. He seemed to lose a little of his confidence and looked towards his father, who glanced around him with caution but didn't answer. "The rule of the *kumpania,* see, Rom Baro's gotta give the okay when somebody new comes in—no problem with you, a matter of form, you're real family, full blood and everything."

"Not quite," Rose said, coughing. "He's *didicoit*. And don't forget he's our Micah's lad—you know what Rom Baro's gonna say about *that!* No way she's gonna forget what happened."

Didicoit. Half and half. Simon didn't want to look at her, he'd never liked Aunt Rose and neither had Grandmam, but she was right now, she was *right*.

Uncle Dui, well oiled with wine, spoke up. "My nephew, my brother's only boy, if he wants to work horses with me then he's gonna work horses with me. Teach him all I know, I will, there's no better man in the delta when it comes to doctoring horses. I've cured horses after the best vets in the county's thrown up their hands on 'em. Give 'em up for dead before they calls in Dui. And I got 'em up on their feet."

His wife whispered something behind her hand and Dui spun round, but there was nothing behind him but a shadow, maybe a leaf moved in the jacaranda trees lining the trailer park, maybe a dog snuffling after a bit of paprika beef Tomo had tossed aside. The men all lit cigarettes and offered one to Simon, who lit up because it was obviously expected of him. Every male in sight smoked constantly, lit one cigarette from another; every male drank beer or wine, also without letup.

As the meal was cleared away and the younger children sent to bed, more and more women came to the great fire, their small cooking fires dying fireflies now around the great blaze of the main fire. Simon wasn't really aware of how many women came, but one minute there were maybe half a dozen, the next there were twenty–thirty, all in the ordinary clothes of the working-class wife, but not a woman among them lacked gold hoops in her ears and chains at her neck.

Toward midnight sometime, Simon's head felt slightly foggy after two cans of beer, and he steadfastly refused a third—he never drank, Grandmam had always told him drink was the downfall of the Gypsy man and he believed her, he'd believed everything she ever told him, so for sure he wasn't going to let her down here among her own. She had to be watching him. He felt eyes on him, had since the first beer, the first cigarette. Somewhere somebody watched every move he made, but when he looked around he saw nobody. That's when he realized.

It must be Grandmam.

She'd led him here, was watching, smiling.

Pretty soon Uncle Dui fell asleep sitting in a lawn chair, and his wife led him up the trailer steps to bed.

It was about then that the woman appeared.

She was neither young nor old, maybe Mom's age, and when she walked into the circle of light he felt the skin on his scalp tingle, as though every hair had lifted up. Suddenly his throat seemed full of sand and he gulped the last drops of beer from the can but they didn't help.

Memory nudged, poked, eluded, and all the time she stood still at the other side of the fire, looking down at where he sat with the empty beer can at his feet and an unsmoked cig in his hand.

She moved. It was slow, a small movement, nothing more than hips swaying, maybe a step or two, or maybe it was just that she turned her head, but he suddenly knew he'd seen her someplace a long time before, a red skirt she'd had on and a way of carrying herself, flowing like a river, and like a river she didn't care for nobody, like she was *it*, man, followed her own barefoot course, a gold chain thin as filament around one ankle, heavy chains at her neck, brown fingers quicker than fish as she made some sudden gesture and sparks shot from fire to gold rings to diamonds and back again to the fire.

Then he knew who she was.

Just standing still she shot sparks.

Like a woman who came to Que Vista one summer afternoon out of no place, a day Mom was packing to go back to Greenlings and he was out on his board waiting for a wave. Maybe she came in a cream trailer, he wasn't sure, but one thing he knew. It was the same woman. He didn't remember her face, her hair, her figure, he wasn't even sure of the red skirt—but one thing he couldn't forget.

Even in the hot sun of a Que Vista noon the woman had made her own light, just like she made it here. And now she was talking to him and it was the same voice.

Husky.

Quiet.

If music could be said to have a threat in it, then her voice was music.

Everybody shut up, even the dogs, and it seemed to Simon the *kumpania* held its breath.

"You'll be Micah's boy."

"Yes. Simon."

"You've been asking people about us."

"Yes . . . to find out—"

"Who told you to? Him?"

"Him?"

"Micah." Now it was the woman who held her breath. Simon could tell. She hadn't blinked, not once. "Did Micah send you?"

Simon shook his head, almost laughed. "No way. If he knew I was here he'd kill me."

The woman breathed then. He saw her chest rise and fall, saw gold chains again spark light off the fire.

"This is my *kumpania*. I'm Rom Baro. Come see me before you bed down, okay?"

Simon knew for sure it wasn't an invitation, was double sure when Tomo whispered, "You'd better get in there fast."

Her trailer was darkened, a small Tiffany lamp shed yellow light on tawny rugs and gold velvet cushions, on velour curtains the color of garnets, on cups and saucers thin as eggshells, glazed a fine peacock blue edged with gold. Somewhere in another room a kettle hissed and spat, and everywhere there was a smell of some vine they'd had at Greenlings . . . honeysuckle maybe, it grew up the trellis by the back paddock.

She sat with the lamp at her back so her face was in shadow, only her hands in the light, her quick brown hands that glittered with metal and precious stones and taut-drawn nerves.

"You want to stay with the families? That's why you've come?"

"Yeah. If I can. Tomo and Uncle Dui said I could work with them, I know horses—"

"You better know something. We're a working group, the richest this side of New York City—and they're a mixed lot, not like us. We don't want no welfare crap, no do-gooders poking their noses in, been too many o' them already, asking questions, writing books. Studies, they call 'em! Anybody asks questions send 'em here, understand? You tell nobody nothin'. It's nobody's business how we live, what we do, where we go, see? *Gaje* blab their guts out to everybody and his mother. That's not our way. If there's trouble it stops within the families. Problems you bring to me, I'll handle 'em. That's my job. You never tell nothing to the cops."

"Yes ma'am."

"Say it."

"Never tell nothin' to the cops."

"Good. See you remember it. Your father don't know you're here?"

"No."

"You going to tell him?"

"He'd try to bring me back but—"

"But?"

"But this is what I've always wanted. Not to be tied to rooms, walls . . . I want to be Rom like my Grandmam."

"We're mostly pure blood in this compound." She spoke with pride, as if it set them apart. "Your mother's a *gaja*. What would *she* say to you joining up with our people?"

Simon thought for a minute. "I guess she'd miss me, but she'd understand. Dad wouldn't."

Absently she shuffled and reshuffled a pack of cards; her rings shot fire in his eyes. "Micah's doin' pretty good, huh?"

"I guess . . ."

Her voice sharpened. "Businesswise? You don't *know?*"

"Well, okay, sure he's doing good, he's always doing good."

"That's better. Remember, the *gaje* is on one side, Rom on the other, like war, always war between us and them. We gotta know all about them, they don't need to know nothin' about us."

"Yes." Grandmam had said the same, more or less.

"One thing. As far as this *kumpania*'s concerned, your father's *gajo*. That's how he wants it so it puts you in the middle, you'll have to make up your own mind. It's us or them."

Simon swallowed. "Yeah."

"Okay then."

She stood up, stretched her arms above her head as if she were about to dance, but then she clapped her hands lightly, and her lips curved in a secret little smile of triumph.

"You'll have a cup of tea with me before you go off to your bed. While we're waiting you'll take some advice from your new Rom Baro. Yes. Our men smoke and drink too much. The smart ones know it, have stopped it—not like your uncle Dui. Watch out for him, he's bone idle. Sorry."

Simon was about to nod, bemused at the sudden change in his fortunes. He'd found them, they liked him, they were letting him be Rom, they'd taken him in, even the Rom Baro herself—

Thought stopped then, his mind blanked completely as a door opened somewhere. A tea tray and a silver service appeared, again catching the yellow light from the Tiffany, turning it to gold for a moment, almost as gold and shining as the face floating above it in the dark, a young face, younger than his own maybe, tender, pointed, sharp as a kitten's, calm as a madonna's, her eyes two soft black lamps shining down on him, a smile at the corners of her mouth exactly like the Rom Baro's.

He felt something infinitely sweet and pleasurable squeeze inside his chest and he couldn't seem to stop his mouth from smiling, smiling, smiling into her eyes.

"Feya," the Rom Baro said. "This is my daughter Feya."

FORTY-SEVEN

*W*HAT OTHER COURSE could Michael have taken? Didn't any decent man do his best for his kids, the best as he saw it? And hadn't he done that for Simon? Would a court convict him of neglect because he'd tried to raise him like a *something*—and when that failed, turned him over to his wife, unquestionably a lady, to see if she could do better?

Anxiety was short and sharp. A baby-face boy like Simon, dangerously innocent of the world's scabrous underbelly, traveling three thousand miles alone, no money to speak of, in a car with "spoiled rich kid" splashed all over it. Christ. Of course he knew where Simon had *gone*, the question was could he *get* there without first swimming through the scum of every big city from one coast to the other?

Then Dui's drunken, truimphant, benevolent call the West Coast accountant had, at Michael's request, switched through. "Didn't want my brother worrying, did I, I'll look after Simon as if he was me own..."

Thus the rage, now nearly blinded with it, yet here was Ellie begging him, wringing her hands when half of it was her fault anyway, the other half Mary Beth's, he should never have listened, never—

"Please don't go, Michael, it won't change anything."

"Of course it bloody well won't! The only way to change anything was years ago, to give him a damned good thrashing but no, *I* didn't understand him! It was you, you and Mary Beth with all your psychology books and your insights, *you* understood him, *you* could solve everything, keep him out of school, in New York with you, make something of him, *you* could work miracles."

"I never said that. I said he was unhappy, that the schools weren't helping him, just making him miserable. And they were!"

"So congratulations! He's happy, you've made something of him. *You've turned my son into a goddam Gypsy!*"

"If that's what he wants to be . . ." She spoke softly, gently, and he knew, knew, knew he wasn't being fair, that at heart Simon had always been a Gypsy, that it was too late for any of this, years too late, and what could she have done anyway, what could any of them have done, but after all his work, after—

"Nothing's going to help, darling, he's gone and he's safe, if we let him go we'll keep part of him, he'll stay in touch, might even come back when he's had enough. If you force the issue we'll never hear from him . . . and in law he's old enough anyway, he can do what he likes."

Michael tried to push back the red haze behind his eyes, tried to think. "Jenny's wedding's in three days. How's it going to look if he's not there, eight hundred guests, every blasted gossip columnist in New York and no eldest son, *only* son, to show his face!"

"If it's just pride—"

"Of course it's pride, dammit! I am proud of Jenny, I'm proud of Cal, I don't want people whispering in corners about 'poor Simon who always seems to be left out' because that's just what they *do* say! How are *they* to know he chooses to be left out because he's got some stupid notion that the Rom have it easy? He's an idle dreamer, he thinks he's opted for the perfect life, nothing to do, moseying along—dear God, if only he knew!"

"Now he'll have a chance to find out."

No. "He'll find out *after* the wedding when Jenny and Cal are gone." Even shaken by rage, he was filled with tenderness that Jenny, who could honeymoon in any glamorous watering hole the world had to offer, should choose to begin her married life at Greenlings, where he and Ellie had begun theirs . . . or maybe it was so she could be with Anna, who weakened steadily . . . either way, Michael approved the sentiment. Had

Simon ever given cause for approval? No. So he'd be damned if he'd let him spoil his sister's wedding. That blasted Dui, all his life sponging off Abramo and for once he's asked to do something, send Simon back, and he wouldn't even listen—they even had the nerve to set dogs on Michael's man up there when he tried to reason with them.

"Maybe if you hadn't sent a detective, darling—"

"Yeah. If you want something done right, do it yourself."

The trip out was nothing, a few hours direct with the charter pilot told to wait up, there'd be another passenger on the return flight. The cab found the *kumpania* district, no problem, no problem finding Dui's trailer either, it was the tackiest in the compound—he refused to look at the biggest trailer, spanking new, cream as usual, plastic flowers and a little fence around it, a different dog tethered out front.

Dui's wife appeared, frightened, wringing her hands, giving a little yelp when Michael pushed past her to get inside.

"So where is he?"

"Dui's up Paso Robles way buying horses for down here—"

"Simon! Where's Simon!" Michael didn't know how he kept his hands off her, except one shriek from her and a dozen Rom would materialize.

She shrugged. "With Dui, where else? A breeder, Limpy Lol somebody, he's going bankrupt, ain't he, so Dui's taking stock off his hands—"

The pilot knew Paso Robles, a cabdriver knew Limpy Lol somebody's place. It lay in hiding, folded away in burnt yellow hills sparsely dotted with thin brown cows, the gnarled dark green of live oaks and the black balm of their shade; all under a bowl of piercing, relentless blue in which red-tailed hawks circled and swooped, hovered and watched.

Michael watched too. He'd approached on the ranch's blind side to stand just inside the swinging, broken-hinged door of the stable. He watched, closer to Simon than to the other men, waiting his chance.

They were a trio. A whippy little man with a sniffle, Limpy Lol no doubt, his checkered shirt tattered and filthy besides. Dui, mustachioed and sleepy-looking, legs spread to balance the width of his great belly, dickered with the man, alternately pleading and demanding, his arms in the air one minute, pressed to his heart in supplication the next. Michael, well out of earshot, could have recited the script by heart.

And Simon.

Simon. Designer jeans filthy; his face already that apricot tan of the very blond that made his eyes—the blue of Ellie's and Jenny's and Anna's

—all the bluer behind a thick gold fringe of lashes; a yellow kerchief that was now bright orange with sweat; surprisingly deft hands that ran quickly over a group of animals herded into a makeshift pen. Horses—if such they could be called.

His son's tanned hands running over scruffy coats and ridged backs, examining the glazed eye of the patently unhealthy animal, probing fingers revealing a parrot mouth...

For a moment Michael had to turn away.

When he thought of the horses at Greenlings, fine bloodstock acquired with Simon in mind, animals with proud patrician heads, muscles to gather for that higher fence, that country wall, that clear stream... horses with the class and temperament to gallop Greenlings' beautiful extended acres tirelessly, horses bought for Simon, Simon's children, horses to sire more horses for his children's children... when he thought of the future his blood boiled. And now here was this boy happily lavishing what little skill he had gleaned on these swaybacked, spavined nags that symbolized everything Michael had been running from for thirty years. Like the Rom, these creatures were played out, played out, played out...

And Simon fondled them, happy, his eyes bright with intention, his mouth smiling, proud, confident.

Confident.

"Simon." Michael spoke quietly, well under the hearing of the two men.

The boy looked up, flushed deep scarlet, then all color fled, leaving him white to the lips. But his back was straight, his hand steady as he stroked the bowed and dusty neck of the nearest horse.

"Hi, Dad."

"That's it? 'Hi, Dad'? You pull the usual trick, sneak off without telling a soul, this time clear across country on your own? Jenny's wedding nearly here? And all you can say is 'Hi, Dad'?"

"I'm not coming back, I'm not, I'm going to do the horse thing with Uncle Dui—"

"Horses? Is that what you call them? Do you honest-to-God think you can make a living off played-out nags like that—"

Simon's color rushed back. "Played out? A bit of TLC, groomed a bit, fattened up, docile enough for kids to ride—"

"Docile! They're damn near dead!"

"—some *gajo's* gonna pay plenty..."

Already a gleam in the boy's blue eye, the same gleam he remembered in Da's, not the push for profits so much as the need to best the enemy, to prove the Rom were better, smarter, quicker.

"You're a *gajo* yourself," Michael retorted.

His son corrected him. *"Didicoit!* Half and half."

For a second Michael couldn't see, blinded not by the sun but by Simon's bitterness and his own numbing fury. This kid, this grandson of a murdering lush like Da, was actually blaming *him,* Michael, for giving him a mother such as Ellie? the single drop of class in the boy's blood-stream? Ellie, who loved her son—even loved a Gypsy husband— "Why, you little sod, you're so flaming proud you're half Gypsy, let me tell you where your precious half came from—if you can stand the shock. My father, my da, your wonderful link with Rom—"

"I know what he did. Grandmam told me, about the *kris* and every-thing. She told me about your ma too, showed me her picture. You never told me about her—"

"Because I hardly remember her, and what I do remember I want to forget. The last time I saw her she was in a coffin. The time before that she was on the floor with her head bashed in!"

Now Michael was shouting, and Dui finally turned around. His eyes widened but he did not seem surprised. "Micah-Micah-Micah! You've finally made it—Farah said you'd come running now we got something you want, right?"

"You've got my son," Michael whispered. "You're trying to steal my son—"

Dui laughed his rich fat laugh that shook his belly, his mottled cheeks, his stubbled black jowls, then sobered on the instant as he invited his mark, Limpy Lol, then his nephew, to witness his betrayal.

"My brother, my little brother, we all know you're more *gajo* than the *gaje* themselves, but even you don't believe that old wives' tale? The Rom don't steal children—God knows we have enough of our own."

True enough.

But children with legacies, children who would one day have endless wealth? If Dui was stupid there were those in the *kumpania* who were not, Farah was just one, who would know the riches this one young member could someday bring to the families.

Dui now pointed to Simon. "Tell me, Micah, does he look mistreated, my nephew? Does he look unloved?"

Simon's eyes begged with Michael, holding him by nothing more than the intense happiness blazing in them, the desperation in his voice.

"Please, Dad. I don't want to go back. I'm Rom and that's all I ever want to be, okay Dad? Okay?"

He held out a tentative hand, but Michael didn't see it. He stumbled away, down a hill pitted with gopher holes and cart tracks, falling and picking himself up, brushing at his cheeks to clear moisture that could have been sweat or tears. At the bottom of the hill he climbed into the cab, nodding to the driver to get him back to the little airfield. Later, under the roar of the chartered plane and the pilot's ground-to-air chatter, he wept his way back to the New York night and Ellie, whose son he'd let slip through his fingers.

What to tell Jenny, whose wedding would be shunned by her beloved brother? What to tell Anna, who was tart enough already about Simon?

And Ellie? What, what, what to tell Ellie?

She knew. Perhaps she'd known before he left. When he walked into their room she opened her arms to him and for the first time in many months they were joined in a storm that was more than just a passionate meeting of the flesh. It was a grief shared, consolation, commiseration, loss, the bitter knowledge that children were not private property and no fence yet invented would hold them against their will.

Afterwards, his voice was calm.

"I've done with him. It's over."

He heard the muffled sob in her throat. "Oh, Michael—"

"I don't want to hear. I don't want to know. You'll keep contact with him, okay, but don't tell me. Please?"

He felt her swallow. "I *must*, I *want* to keep contact if he'll let me, if it's what he chooses. There's nothing more we can do."

In the darkness, Ellie's sweet flesh beside him, Michael nodded. He knew all about choices. A boy of five made a choice, it altered his whole life.

Now a boy of eighteen had made his.

Without knowing exactly why, his father was afraid.

FORTY-EIGHT

*D*ESPITE MICHAEL'S FEAR—Mary Beth called it paranoia—no one outside the family remarked on Simon's absence from the wedding, which went off as most meticulously planned weddings do: very well indeed.

The bride radiated happiness, confidence in the future, and inevitable grace; the groom patently adored her every breath; both sets of parents nodded amicably throughout the ceremony and sighed with mutual relief that they would be unlikely to meet again until the first christening.

After a blissful honeymoon in which Cal fell totally under the spell of Greenlings, the two returned to New York, Cal to watch and to learn as Abramo, after due consideration by Michael, prepared to go public. Michael would keep just enough shares between himself, Ellie, Jenny, and Cal to retain a controlling interest. Over Ellie's protests no shares were to be issued in Simon's name.

"If he comes back he can have some of ours," Michael said. "I'm not holding my breath."

But he was, he was. He'd given Simon up, left him to the Rom, but something in him leapt eagerly at the doorbell, phones ringing at unorthodox times, letters bearing unfamiliar postmarks addressed in a childish hand—but he kept forgetting, Simon was no child now. He knew Ellie kept in touch with him, but by mutual consent the contact was ephemeral, guarded and never discussed. But when he looked at the hard-won holdings about to be opened up to the public he mourned—it was as if he'd built a temple for a prince who'd died just as the roof went on, and now it was to be thrown open to a faceless, anonymous public who'd never met Simon or Felix or Anna Abramsky. And if they had met them they'd have sniggered behind their hands and called them eccentrics.

Watching the flow of paper that was to accomplish all this divestiture, Michael felt like a man walking a desert, shedding garment after garment as the sun rose higher in the sky. Barring idiotic management, a communist takeover, or nuclear cataclysm, when every financial knot was tied each individual member of his family, and all their descendants until kingdom come, would be assured steady, unassailable incomes. Safe. Except for Simon—but he'd made his choice.

Michael's income from Abramo would now be no greater than that of the others. Also, he'd determined to shoulder the entire maintenance of Greenlings. It was his pride and perhaps his folly, certainly a monumental drain guaranteed to keep him the least affluent member of the family.

Already he began to feel lighter. Letting go of Abramo was a major step made reluctantly, but with Simon gone there was little pleasure in decisions which had once seemed vital.

Everything he'd done had been for Simon, for his future—which the Rom had now taken out of his hands.

The Rom the Rom the Rom the Rom ... words that beat a pulse in his veins. They'd envied everything he had and now they'd got the best of it. His son. Now Jenny belonged to Cal. Anna didn't have too much longer, according to the doctors.

Anna knew, they all did. Except for Michael, they seemed to accept it, but his every thought wanted to deny reality. If he never thought of her death it wouldn't happen. When the subject came up he left the room, knowing that a part of himself still shivered in a broom closet on Ryder Street, waiting for the ax to fall, for summer to come, for Felix and Anna to send a young boy on his way. Now it was the other way about, Felix gone and Anna soon to follow, but the feeling was the same. Dread. Fear of loss. A void that would never be filled. Which left him with Greenlings and Ellie.

Ellie, who'd always been in a different category, love and passion mixed, therefore not the same as ownership. Now that he would soon no longer own Abramo, he confided to her that the routine of business had begun to pall. Pretty soon he'd be one of these old geezers who took up golf just to escape the office. Making money was too easy now. The zest was gone.

The studio franchises were a separate deal. Except for a block of stock to Mary Beth, enough to ensure her independence, the rest was to go totally to Anna, who had already arranged to sign it over to Jenny.

After the legal ends were tied up, he and Ellie returned to Greenlings to wait for what they'd begun to call the Big Kiss-off—the day stock was available to investors. A massive shareholders' ball would officially open the new head office block in Los Angeles, a tower of black glass and chromium that Michael would not for the world have lived in, but was more than happy to invest in.

Ellie was having the last fitting for her ball gown when Jenny called from backstage in New York, her joy rushing, spilling, tumbling over three thousand miles of ocean.

She was pregnant.

"Seven months and I'll be a mother! Imagine, Mummy, a baby! Maybe it'll have red hair like Cal, he is just *so* happy he can't see straight, but oh Mummy, the company's not pleased with me *at all*—but then, Anna said they wouldn't be, they never are, ballerinas aren't supposed to get—oh my goodness, you'd better put me through to her, she'll be simply livid that I didn't tell her first!"

Ellie smiled and let it pass, happy for Jenny, glad there would be something left for her when the dancing days were done. After so many years around studios and ballet theaters Ellie'd come to think the saddest things in the world were aging performers whose whole life was the theater. At one swoop age took it all, art, adoration, applause—all seen as love until it faded to fame and then to a brief mention, a what-was-his-name squib at the end of some column.

Better to live for children even if, like Simon, loving them hurt. But he'd hurt his father more than her. She'd never harbored Michael's expectations, so the disappointment had less of a sting, more of an ache. She knew he loved her. He wrote cryptic little notes now and then, and very occasionally he called—always at times Michael was sure to be away from home.

Unknown to Michael she'd met with him once. He'd called when Michael was in Japan with Pete, knowing it was time for Chita's annual trip to her family in Guadalajara. Ellie was surprised he suggested they meet at Que Vista, surprised and delighted—but she tried not to count on too much. She knew he was happy with the Rom, that he wouldn't ask to come home. But he wanted to see her and for the moment it was enough. For the starving, a crumb is a banquet.

He arrived silently and on foot as she was fixing their dinner of salad and shrimp, his favorite. Sinewy from work, he was leaner but not thinner. He was also older, much older. And uneasy.

She wanted to hold him, tell him it didn't matter, but he touched her hand briefly and backed off, clinging to the weathered rail of Que Vista's porch as if it were a life raft.

It was night, the sea a solid dish of pewter with a moon rocking in it. Somewhere out to the horizon a yacht lay at anchor, and now and then snatches of music came from her decks.

"I've missed you," she said gently.

"Yes. Me too."

"But you're here..."

Take my hand! she wanted to cry, take your mother's hand because she is afraid to touch you, the distance now so great she's afraid you'll push her away, again run off, leave before—

"Yeah," he said, staring out to sea. "Sure is pretty, huh?"

"You always liked this place the best."

"It's open...that's what Dad could never see. I *hated* Greenlings—when I came home it was like coming through prison gates—and the schools were worse...like a transfer, from one prison to another. I couldn't seem to like the things Dad wanted me to. You had to be a joiner, get in the club, and I never wanted to. They were dumb. And Dad thought it was me that was dumb—"

"No, he thought you weren't trying—"

"I wasn't. They didn't do anything I wanted to try *at!*"

They ate on the deck from paper plates, sat in silence until the moon seemed to pull them, pull them to water's edge, the wet and silver sand that would all be changed by morning, the yacht's prow a silhouette black on silver, too beautiful to last.

"I love this walk best of all," she said. "It reminds me...the sea's always here, will be here for ever and ever—"

"And we won't, right?"

She shrugged. "Grandmam, Felix, now Anna not well—"

"Look, I'm sorry, I know she's your mom and everything, I know, I know, but I don't like her and I never did."

Ellie laughed softly. She'd never told him the whole story and didn't intend to, only that she'd been raised by paternal grandparents in Germany. She'd been tempted often to tell him, but already too many skeletons rattled in his ancestral closet. "I'll be honest, Simon. I admire my mother, sometimes very much, but *I* have never liked her either."

He turned to her, his face washed in moonlight. "It's not like that with you. I felt kinda stupid if you kissed me and somebody was around, but you're okay, I mean, *really* okay."

"I understood. Boys are like that."

"Only if somebody's watching. But I did like it."

"Yes." She knew too that he was trying to say he liked her, loved her, but was too self-conscious to form the words.

They walked on in silence. At the rocks they turned, and Simon took her hand as a wave larger than the rest lapped at their ankles. When it receded he kept on holding her hand as he'd done when he was little, companionably swinging her arm with his. His hand was wide now, a man's hand, but still it felt like him, squirmy and restless . . . but so very good in hers.

His talk came easier, first about his uncle, whom he both despised and liked.

". . . he's a glutton and he's killing himself with drink and cigs, but he's . . . easy, you know? When I dicker for a horse, or if I'm selling one, he's not expecting miracles, see? I make a profit and he's happy, a bigger profit he's happier still. Tomo now, he's different. He's my friend. We pal around together."

There was a question she desperately wanted to ask but was afraid. In the end he answered it for her.

"Tomo's a terror with the women . . . only *gajas* . . . the Rom girls aren't like that . . . well, you know. The kids at the fires don't go on about it like the boys at school did, even the littlest kids at school! In the dorms after lights-out that was all they talked about, rugger and sex and how many girls they'd . . . you know . . . They were lying, they didn't even know any girls and even if they did most of 'em were too young to . . ."

"A lot of boys lie about that."

"*Gaje* maybe. They're rotten liars, it's dumb to lie when everybody knows. I lie but I'm good at it and I lie to swing a deal . . . and only when I'm sure they can't find out."

Should she deliver some homily on the virtues of truth? It would be pointless. The Rom lived by lying, prized the ability to do it well.

"I told you Jenny's marriage is very happy, that she's expecting a baby?" It was a clumsy lead-in, but she had to know. Perhaps there was something he—they—would need. "How about you, is there a girl you're serious about?"

The wind shifted, bringing threads of music with it.

"Maybe—" But he suddenly turned away and dropped her hand as if he'd said too much. "Did *he* tell you to ask me that?"

"Of course not, he doesn't know we're—"

"It's not his business! He'd better not expect me to come crawling back when I get married—"

She sighed. "You're not being fair to him at all, you know. He just wanted what he thought was best for *you*—"

"*And* the business, right? He wanted me to go into it. Felix knew I'd hate it, Grandmam knew. She knew just about everything."

"But she loved your father very much," Ellie said quietly.

"So you think I should, right?"

"No, but I wish you did. He loves you, in his way."

"Oh no. I'm Rom and he hates us all. He's ashamed of us, too *good* for us with his silk suits and fancy shoes. They know it, everybody in the *kumpania* knows, they talk about it at the fires. It hurts them. Gypsies got feelings."

"So has your father."

He laughed, short and sharp. "For his house and business."

And Simon hated them both. He hated their owner even more.

The lights of Que Vista came up too soon. "Look," he said suddenly, slipping a scrap of paper into her pocket. "If you need to, you can leave word..."

So he was going already. "You could stay over," she said, knowing he wouldn't. "Sleep on the porch like you used to."

She saw, just for a moment, a wistful, hurting look in his eyes, or perhaps it was a trick of the light.

"No, I have to go. I've got business tomorrow in Sac."

Business. Bargaining for a broken-down old horse. How young you are, she thought, how raw. No armor, no shell. Oh, but the suffering you have brought us...

Impulsively, as if he must do it now or not at all, he leaned forward and put his arms around her, held her tight so she could smell the sea on him and horses. His warm young cheek touched hers for an instant, no more.

"Bye Mom, see ya," he said, his voice husky.

He'd left then, trudging through the sand to the dented remains of his pretty little kiddy car.

Its tail lights had seemed to wink at her round the bend just as a final thread of music had drifted off the yacht.

Yes, she thought now. It *was* better to live for children, even when sometimes the living hurt. She was glad about Jenny's pregnancy, very glad.

FORTY-NINE

*M*EETING OVER, the families of the *kumpania* left. Routine business had been routinely dispatched. A member's son injured in Ohio, his parents broke, the question of the day being whether to fly them back. The Rom Baro nodded agreement, the rest concurred, a hat circulated, donations presented, prayers incanted for the son's recovery. Done, they drifted back to their own trailers to sit on the steps and smoke, drink, hash over the pros and cons.

Farah stayed by the *kumpania*'s fire and signaled Simon to join her, an order that came his way more and more often.

"If everything were that easy," she said, sighing. She sighed a lot now. In the dying light of the flames her eyes were deep black holes that reflected nothing. She rubbed at her back, rested it against the telephone pole.

"It's great the way they chip in to help each other," Simon said, meaning every word.

"Aye, but it's not all whipping the hat round, is it? Next week we'll have trouble. Bilbo's offered for Dui's girl, but that damned Dui wants bride-price too—asking two thousand and the girl not worth five cents! Wants to follow the old ways, he says. God knows I'm for tradition all the way, but it's a miracle a man's daft enough to want her. She can neither sell nor *dukker*—what good's a wife that can't turn a dollar telling fortunes, eh? *And* they say she's been . . . used."

Farah whispered the last word; an unmarried girl's virginity was assumed beyond question, even the subject almost a taboo. She poked at the fire, sparks flew, and she threw on more wood, although Sacramento summer nights were hot.

"I got work for Dui's girl once, a day cleaning house for a rich old girl they'd shoved in the loony bin. Her family wanted the place tidied before they 'took stock.' Chance of a lifetime, right? You'd think she'd bring *something* out in her apron, eh? A watch or two, rings, gold, silver, crystal? Not Dui's little treasure. She brings minimum wage and a jar of wrinkle cream! It smelled nice! Aye, bein' Rom Baro's no plum, believe me."

He felt her eyes like knives on him, but he was waiting for Feya to appear, a glance, a word—but Farah kept her under wraps. Often all the kids worked in a bunch, badgering lucky punters as they left the track with pockets full of winnings; dropping in on classy one-woman shops they'd cased beforehand. By the time cops appeared they were well away, every pocket and apron full. Those were about the only times he'd been with Feya.

But Farah knew how he felt, he could tell.

All this time with the *kumpania* and he'd been alone with Feya only once. An unexpected moment at a relative's wedding, magic, sudden darkness when a candle burned down, its replacement not yet lit.

Feya close then, so close then, she brushed against him and he'd pulled her to him, touched his mouth to her bare shoulder before he kissed her mouth, smelled the gardenia in her hair, the honey and rosewater cream on her neck, that odd mix of milk and wine on her lips.

After that nothing but swift glimpses, her downcast eyes, a dusky blush, sometimes a flashing smile—but in his mind the yielding silk of her mouth had warmed his every day since.

He took *gajas* out, all the boys did, but among the girls of the Rom things were different and he was still finding his way. Casual affairs were out, even serious intentions were recognized slowly, their implications weighed, decisions arrived at only after bargains were struck. With virtue the ultimate marketable commodity, mothers kept watch like duennas of old, and Farah was not even your ordinary Gypsy woman. She was a tiger. And she'd singled him out a lot lately, probing, hinting—or like now, hashing over *kumpania* affairs. Why?

"Look at 'em," she said now with scorn, waving a small brown hand at the trailers, each with its fire, its huddle of Gypsies. "They have to be *led* all the time like sheep. God alone knows who'll take over when I'm done. I don't see one of 'em looks like he'd make Rom Baro. What d'you think?"

A Rom Baro was not chosen, he knew that. Anybody could say "I'm Rom Baro"—but unless he had manipulative clout to back it up the others only laughed, did what they liked, fought among themselves, got in bad troubles from what he'd heard.

"Gosh, I don't know. Tomo maybe?" He suggested it mainly out of loyalty because he knew Tomo wanted it, talked about it often. They were still friends, still shared a trailer, but there'd been this atmosphere lately, not hostile, not even cool, but . . . casual, yes, that was it, casual.

Farah grinned. "Tomo. 'As the twig's bent.' No, I think not. In the end he'll run to fat and idleness like Dui. A leader's got to *lead,* give *gajo* a lesson now and then, remind him *we're* still top dog. It needs a man with . . . nerve." She looked sideways at him through a sweep of midnight hair. "'Course, it can be a woman, but men got more . . . force, know what I mean? There's naturals like Micah, Grandmam always said your father was best o' the lot. Oh well, maybe Feya'll marry somebody capable. God knows there's plenty of young chaps asking to talk terms. Tomo, for one . . ."

She let the name hang in the air.

Tomo, for one.

And how many others "asking to talk terms"?

"Still," she said, standing up, "I reckon it'll have to be a *rich* man to meet Feya's bride-price. What do *you* think?"

If Abramo's black and chrome tower for the Big Kiss-off was austere, the evening's decor was anything but. The theme colors were pink and white and the great reception hall was a mass of flowers.

Pink and white carnations in great silver buckets lined the staircase; Camelot and Queen Elizabeth roses in their thousands covered white-painted trellises that formed an avenue to central columns where white bowers of Matterhorns and Pascalis intertwined with First Love and Portrait and Tiffany.

When the decorously dancing guests circled the orchestra the scent of pink lilies flown in from the Orient became so sweetly overpowering that as the evening wore on the great doors of the balcony were flung open to the lights of Los Angeles, to Wilshire Boulevard thundering far below.

At small tables couples, chosen with great care, sipped pink champagne served by white-gloved waiters as the gracious Mrs. Michael Abramsky, in burgundy velvet, and her lovely ballerina daughter, in petal pink, made their rounds, smiling here, shaking hands there, murmuring pleasantries, always murmuring, committing themselves to nothing, conferring often with a Miss Warren who also seemed to be mistress of the polite evasion.

Marvelous hostesses, all three of them, Michael thought. Couldn't do better if they'd been trained for it. He said as much to Calvin by his side.

"Yes, every company should be so lucky... but I wonder now if we needed to go the whole hog at all. The latest squib from the exchange was that we'd likely be oversubscribed by morning."

"We'll see."

Several cases of champagne later, the guests were mingling more, dancing on the terrace, gathering in animated clusters on the stairs.

These were people with all the financial status they could handle. Now they were looking for Culture and felt somehow that the Abramskys could point the way, a notion that made Ellie long to lend them Lily Finn for a week or hand out copies of Lotte's leaden potato dumpling recipe.

But these people were not the least interested in food—there wasn't a bulging middle or a double chin in sight; the buffet table, its offerings all nouvelle cuisine, was visited seldom. They hadn't come to eat. This was a gathering sure to be reported heavily in the social columns, therefore while one might not have yearned to attend one certainly couldn't afford not to be there.

Besides, the family was something of an enigma.

The senior Abramskys tended to keep to themselves on the West Coast and had been largely written off as impossible to get at, but the radiant younger pair were *the* couple to have at one's dinner party this season. She, already brushed with the magic of stardom in what was considered art rather than entertainment, was simply adorable, and he—well, they did say Michael Ab would never have turned over the reins to anybody else. Even his son... though you never heard much about him, did you? He always seemed to be away at school. Amazing how many perpetual students were sons of successful men, wasn't it? Charlotte's shrink told her it's harder for a successful man's son to get into the kingdom of commerce than—oh look, Marvin, how cute! Would you *look* what they're bringing on stage...

A bouquet of six junior dancers borrowed from the ballet school were performing a simple dance in frilly, flouncy Nell Gwyn costumes; each child carried a basket filled not with oranges but with party favors for the ladies, miniature Cartier pins with the Abramo logo picked out in tiny diamonds.

Under the aahs of the ladies opening pink and white boxes Ellie smiled prettily at Michael and murmured "ridiculously ostentatious!" under her breath only a second before Mary Beth said the same to Ellie under the same gracious smile.

Michael laughed. "You thought the advance publicity was big?" Michael said quietly. "Now wait for tomorrow's coverage!"

But then Cal was at his elbow, whispering what sounded like: "Good God, what's wrong with the waiters? Oh-oh, I think we're being invaded, hang on—I'll see if something—"

But it was now all too obvious something *was* wrong. Michael was the first to realize just what.

At the door all was commotion, tousle-haired groups pushing in, rowdy and laughing, calling to one another between the tables, picking champagne from laden trays, tossing it off and throwing the empties over their shoulders, laughing at the tinkle of breaking crystal.

The kerchiefed young men then surveyed the table, grabbing handfuls of wafer-thin smoked salmon and prosciutto as if they were paper, wrapping up mushroom vol-au-vents, entire wheels of fine cheese, the most delicate of pâtés.

Some mingled with the guests admiring ties, fingering Yves St. Laurent suits, Gucci shoes, the snakeskin purses of the women—most of whom still sat frozen as dark fingers reached out to touch diamond earrings, pearl necklaces. Was it possible these newcomers were another phase of the entertainment?

Still uncertain, many of the women allowed their elegant palms to be grabbed, examined, read at breakneck speed, only to be set back into helpless laps as they were bombarded with a barrage of demands for payment. Outrageous demands, but like sheep they reached for their purses and obediently paid up.

Braver guests were getting up, moving in urgent little flurries to other seats in futile efforts to escape young girls who advanced on them, gesturing, begging, placating, in the end brazenly intimidating.

Michael watched, stupefied as the rest.

The Rom. Out in force to deliberately create embarrassment. Deliberate because this was not their pattern, to move into such gatherings as these, not their pattern to send only the young, to risk mass arrest. Normally they preyed on the ignorant, two or three moving on a single individual, badgering until that person gave in and bought something or gave something. This caper was not their game, not their game at all. Much too risky for such slim pickings. Michael grabbed the nearest young man, swarthy, in need of a shave. He smelled of sweat and the Bollinger champagne he was guzzling from a bottle.

"Get out! Get out this minute, the lot of you!"

"Says who?"

"Me. My building, my party. You're trespassing."

The young man smiled; there was something teasingly familiar in him that Michael could not, at the moment, place.

"And if we don't go?" This in Romani, and no question now who this was. Tomo.

"Then I send for the cops."

Tomo sauntered off to report, and a group seemed to form around another young man with his back to Michael, a man in a black leather jacket and cap to match, a girl hanging on his arm, looking adoringly up into his face. This girl too was familiar . . . but not very, and from a long time ago, something to do with—

"Shall I call the cops, Michael?" It was Cal, concerned at the party's unorthodox turn, more concerned that these were Gypsies. He knew the family history. Michael was about to say no, give them a chance to go quietly, when Leather Jacket picked up the crystal punch ladle and struck the matching bowl a resounding blow, its scattered shards flying like prisms under the light.

"Yeah, call the cops. Fast."

In this neighborhood, for this kind of party, patrol cars arrived almost before Cal put the phone down. The Gypsies shut up then, gathered together and turned almost as one to face Michael.

"What's the charge?" Leather Jacket asked the cop.

"Trespassing on private property, vandalism—"

Behind him Michael heard Ellie gasp. Black Jacket's cap was off now. Under it, his blond hair hung long and unkempt.

Simon.

Defiant.

Staring him down.

Beside him, gazing up adoringly, the pointed little face of a hauntingly beautiful girl. A moonpenny girl. *Farah's girl.*

Feya.

Now he knew what pulled Simon to the Rom. Not just the memory of Grandmam, not just contempt for his father. A girl, the most powerful magnet of all. If she was half the temptress her mother was . . .

"Shall I book 'em?" asked the cop.

"No. Book nobody. Just *get them out of my sight.*"

Then Simon was looking straight at him, laughing at him. "What? You're not prosecuting? And us on *private property?*"

Michael confronted the instigator next day. He knew who'd set it up, but not why. He drove all night and was banging on the door of the cream trailer by six next morning.

He was shocked when she opened the door. Her face was gaunt, her eyes deep and black and full of hate when she saw who it was.

"Come in."

"I thought women didn't invite men to their trailers."

"I'm not a woman now. I'm Rom Baro. In case you've forgot your Romani it means Big Man. That's how I'm treated."

"You know why I'm here."

A fleeting smile touched with malice. "Yes. How did it go, Micah, your little soiree? Didn't know the ignorant Rom knew words like that, did you?"

"I knew. I've never thought you stupid. Or ignorant."

"Just disposable." The blaze of hatred in her eyes made him step back.

"You knew I was married."

"To a *gaja,* that's nothin', don't mean nothin'."

"Get back to last night. Why?"

She shrugged. "Your boy. He needed a taste of leadership." Across the immaculate trailer she laughed at him, even fingered the gold chains at her throat in a gesture that brought back surf and kisses and a madness that had seemed, then, to have no end.

"Why, Farah?" he insisted.

"Ask Simon. It was in the papers about your big shindig, he thought it'd be a good lesson for our people. Reminds them we still got some power over the *gaje* even if it's only to mess up their snobby little games."

"You didn't mess up anything except a nice party for nice people. I know it wasn't his idea so again I ask you. Why did you send them? I think you owe me an answer."

"All I owe you, Micah, is trouble, every bit of grief I can bring you, that's what I owe you."

"You've got my son, isn't that enough?"

She laughed, was still laughing when he closed the door and drove off.

After meals and drinks in an all-night tavern, the young Gypsies drove back to Sac in a truck and four cars. Simon still drove the little silver-blue dart which could carry only two, himself and Feya. Deliberately he missed the turn for the freeway in the dark but had no trouble at all finding the lane leading to Paradise Cove.

"D'you want to walk, Feya?"

Her eyes were huge, scared, tempted, her hair fragrant against his face, her hand small and warm in his.

"Okay," she breathed, "but only for a minute, only a minute, Simon—"

"Yeah."

They walked hand in hand at water's edge, great sandstone cliffs to their right, to their left the teeming silver sea that surged and pounded and roared in concert with his blood.

"Feya—"

He turned to her but she was ahead of him, her mouth open under his, breathing, moaning into his mouth, running her tongue over his lips, his chin.

"Simon, Simon, oh but I want you Simon, oh God I do want you, please don't let me—don't let me—don't let me, my mother will kill me, kill us, aah, oh, touch me, touch me here, I want your mouth on me, Simon"—pulling his face to her throat, her bare breast. "Oh yes . . . again Simon, again, oh the nights I've thought about you, all night till morning, all the time I think about you, on fire with it and her in the other bed watching me, watching, never taking her eyes off me—she's always there and she knows, she knows I want it, want it, want it with you—oh God, Simon—"

"We could run off—"

"You *know* I can't, it's not our way—"

"Then let me, please let me . . . Feya, I can't stand it—"

"No-no-no-no, you promised, don't make me let you, just kiss me here, yes, oh yes, kiss me, kiss me there, yes! yes! *yes!* ah, don't stop, never stop, never . . . stop . . . never never stop . . ."

She came to a shuddering silence, a long trembling sigh, pushing him away as she buttoned her blouse.

"Look Feya, I can't stand it, I tell you, I—"

"You can! You can stand it, Simon. You can wait, when we're married it'll be all the time, all . . . the . . . time." A kiss with every word, a promise, pulling at his hand, back to the car, because Farah was waiting in Sac "—and she'll be timing, Simon, timing us all. We can't be the last car back. You'll have to drive like hell all the way."

FIFTY

*M*ONTHS RUNNING TO YEARS of it now and he dared wait no longer, every day Feya saying, "Have you asked her, Simon? Have you asked yet?" Her lips parted, a tempting red pod lined with small even pearls.

"Not yet," he had to say, aching.

He hadn't asked because he'd been saving his money. Farah's earlier hint about bride-price had been broad enough, God knew, so he'd worked himself to a standstill month after back-breaking month. Not just horse dealing with Dui but asphalting driveways and tiling roofs with Tomo—whose fever to pile up money seemed as urgent as his own. For a predictable reason. Even now Simon didn't think he had enough saved but, Tomo's hot breath behind him, he dared wait no longer.

He asked to talk to Farah in private, a procedure almost as formalized as the mating dance of the peacock.

"Except this isn't quite the way it's supposed to be," she reminded him. "By rights it should be your father speaking for you but . . ." Reaching up to a cupboard, she brought down two cut-crystal glasses elegant enough to grace the tables of a palace and a matching decanter half filled with amber drink. "Even the Queen of England can't get Scotch like this no more, so sip careful. When it's gone it's gone."

"Thanks, Farah."

She poured, her hands small, brown, and deft, all the time delivering what passed for social preliminaries. "Maybe I forgot to tell you—I'm real pleased the way you're shaping up, Simon. You'll be a credit to us. You started out right well when you broke up your da's little party. And last spring, that *pomana* what you took the youngsters to up through Oregon, it were smart to lift a few shops on the way, keeps the youngsters' hands in, reminds 'em what their real trade is, don't it? Roofing and like that, well, it's okay in its way, but we shouldn't have to depend on *that*—nearly as bad as welfare when you gotta make wages off the *gaje*, eh? Enterprise is what I like to see, and that's what you've got. A man's reach should be longer than his grasp."

He'd been waiting for an opening, perhaps she was giving him one. "I'm not sure... my reach, well, that's for Feya—"

Her lips twitched and she sipped her Scotch. "I'd noticed you were interested but like I told you before, there's more than you fancies their chance. Not many like Feya around these days. Some of our girls are as cheap and lax as *gajas!* Might work out nice though, eh? You could even get to be Rom Baro."

A tide of pleasure swept over him. Farah never praised, never. She must be on his side. "I hadn't thought that far, I didn't think I was... well... worthy."

The old word felt awkward, melodramatic on his tongue, but it was what he meant so he let it stand. If Grandmam knew she'd be proud —maybe she *did* know, maybe pushing up daisies on that bleak hill across the sea she heard what Farah said and chuckled, figuring she'd soon be able to sleep easy, her beloved *kumpania* in the hands of Micah's son.

"Hey, ease up there!" Farah laughed to herself as she refreshed her glass. Not his. "We're a long way from that stage yet, Simon. There's other things to think about—"

"Feya's agreeable." He leaned forward, eager to get it over, set a date.

"Maybe so, but it's not only up to her. There's other matters to talk about." As she closed in on the business to hand her voice developed a keener edge, and Simon realized she was enjoying herself. "We haven't come to the bride-price yet—"

"I've been working, saving for over a year and a half, damn near every cent I make!"

Again that laugh.

For the first time he felt a chill, began to wonder if this would really be the formal civilized minuet he'd envisioned not a moment ago.

"I'll tell you how I do it, Simon. We don't talk money, we're not savages, right? But in my pocket's a bit of paper with a figure written on it." She licked her lips and leaned toward him, and two little flames seemed to leap into her eyes. *"Do you, son of Micah, great-grandson of Grandmam, ask to read what's on this paper?"*

Nothing moved in the trailer. Outside in the street traffic roared and honked and braked and squealed, but in here nothing moved except light flickering off gold chains at Farah's neck.

Surely his Adam's apple would choke him, surely he'd never swallow it down.

"Yes," he whispered through bone-dry lips.

The paper crackled as it passed from her small brown hand to lie on the table between them, crackled again as he reached for it, unfolded it.

No.

He'd misread it.

He looked up, saw Farah's smile, and knew he had not misread anything. They were there, that single number and all the zeros after it. He felt the color leave his face. When it surged back anger came with it.

"But Feya *loves* me, *wants* to marry me! This...this *paper*, it's just a matter of form, nothing else, an archaic—"

Farah sat back in mock surprise. "But it's tradition, the way of our people, what you say you want. To be Rom. One of us."

"But—"

"What you're looking at is the price of my virgin daughter, a full-blooded Romany bride—and *your* right to sit at our fires for life."

"Farah, I could work all my life, two lifetimes, three!—and never get my hands on that kind of money *and you know it!*"

"But that's where you're luckier than most. Sometimes it comes in handy to have a rich daddy, huh?"

"She'll marry me anyway, with or without your blood money!"

She smiled. "You know she won't." Implacable. She knew her daughter, was sure of her. And she was right. He forced himself to speak evenly, to hold his temper.

"Tell me, Farah. Would the price have been the same for Tomo or somebody, *anybody* else? Would they have to wait years?"

She stood up very slowly, placed the glasses in the sink, set the decanter back in the cupboard, and faced him.

"You're *not* anybody else," she said softly. "You're our Micah's boy."

He was half out the door when she called him back, poking the scrap of paper in his palm with fingers like screwdrivers.

"You're forgetting the price-tag. If you ask Mommy nicely maybe she'll ask Daddy to buy you a Feya. Like I said, you're enterprisin'. I've got confidence in you, Simon."

FIFTY-ONE

*I*T HAD BEEN A LONG TIME since the evening at Que Vista when Simon walked with his mother, touched her hand in moonlight and the music from a stranger's yacht. A long, lonely time.

Worse since the ultimate betrayal in Los Angeles, the fact that could not be wished away. He'd been their leader, *he'd* stabbed his father in the back. In public, before family, friends, press, and a few business enemies for extra flavor.

Now she faced yet another Christmas without him. Jenny and Cal were coming. Jenny had just had her second child and hoped eventually for a third, not knowing when if ever she would go back to the ballet.

Anna, still lingering against all odds, was almost too far gone to care but—as she'd told Ellie many times—not far gone enough. Her life had become an intolerable burden. Almost totally bedridden but still continent, she died a little each time she must ask the nurse for the bedpan, then ask her again to please leave the room and close the door for a moment.

"What are you thinking, girl, that I am some animal to do its duty in front of the public? I danced for an audience. I prefer to pee alone."

When Cal brought Jenny and the babies from New York to see her she made a monumental effort, but with each visit the performances were more ragged, so now there was little left but tattered flags of the old pride in what had been her passion.

"Sloppy techniques they have today, never would we have been permitted it, never . . . what a Giselle I was, Jenny, perhaps even better than you, my angel? but no, pretend I did not say that, may the good God saw off my tongue to say such lies, a foolish old woman to talk too much, my Felix always says I am talking too much."

She talked to Jenny and Felix even when they were not there, even when she knew they were not there. She talked to Michael, who was almost always there:

"Ah Mischa, how proud you made my Felix, do you imagine how he feels when our son brings us to this fine house . . . then to that other house, also very fine, by the warm sea . . ."

Mischa. Our son. In her ramblings Anna no longer mentioned Sasha. Ellie suspected his memory to be as fossilized now as the old war wound which had given Felix so much trouble and in the end killed him. No, Anna talked to and of Jenny and Felix. To Mischa she spoke of long-ago students so bad as to be beyond forgetting. She even spoke daily to Ellie, but never of Hans.

And never of Simon.

Except in Ellie's own thoughts, which touched him a dozen times a day, he could have been dead. No little notes now, no calls, not even when Michael was likely to be away. Just silence. Perhaps he knew Michael seldom left Greenlings anymore, that they were all, including Anna, waiting for her to die?

But it had been so long. She *wanted* to see him.

One cold December afternoon Anna called her upstairs.

The nurse was home in Dundee through the holiday period, Michael was shopping for his grandsons in London, Lily Finn was at her daughter's house delivering another baby. "Just think," Anna had said when she heard. "If the first sound it hears should be that voice! That poor little creature."

But today Anna was out of bed, shakily clinging to the rails of the great marshmallow bed in which she'd loved and mourned her Felix.

"Anna, what *are* you doing up?"

"Don't start, Gabriella. You are not my nurse. Today I ask a favor from you. Did I ask before? No."

Oh God, what did she want? Don't ask that I call you Mother, don't ask that I hold you, don't—

"I wish to sit in my studio. You will help me there."

"You forget—"

"I forget nothing!"

"—it's the nurse's room now, we had to put her close so she could hear you at night. It's her bed-sitter, hotel room if you like, for her clothes, supplies, books, all her personal—"

"Yes, her personal television which she plays day and night, night and day, so how is she to hear me? I *know* my studio is her room. I was not asked for permission but it is her room. And now *I* wish to sit in it, to touch my barre, look in my mirrors..." Her eyes seemed to film over. "Maybe I see Jenny in them, maybe some young Anna, who know what I can see?"

So Ellie helped her on with her robe, gave her a supporting arm to the chaise by the great revealing mirror without which the dancer cannot function and into which Anna did not, after all, look. Perhaps she had no need.

"Now bring tea."

When Ellie brought it, something in the room had changed. Anna seemed not to have moved, but her robe was mussed, the cover on the chaise crumpled, and thin gray hair hung in wisps about her face. Which wore a smile almost of triumph.

Her fist was clenched tightly in her lap.

"Now we take tea. Sit."

Anna spoke. Ellie listened. It seemed she listened for a very long time, about pride and growing old, about infirmity, about all the indignities lingering in the wings. Waiting.

"Soon they come to me. To *me!* Some people have the luck, one moment alive, the next, poof! But for me there would first be all the childish, shameful things..."

Which she could not bring herself to name, describe, think about.

Instead she opened her hand. Lying in the center of the long wrinkled palm lay her bottle of sleeping pills. The nurse served her one each night on a silver salver. The nurse had delusions of grandeur that Anna swore she had caught, like whooping cough, from "Dynasty" reruns.

Very deliberately she now allowed the bottle to roll off her palm and under the nurse's bed.

"So. Already I talk with the doctor who cannot be frank because he takes some oath so he is forever hypocrite, poor thing, but no matter, he is a wise hypocrite, he understood my questions and why I ask. He tells me. One pill makes me sleep the night, two and I sleep the clock around. Four, five, I don't wake for a very...long...time. I am old. The old make many mistakes."

"Anna!" Ellie leapt up, teacup clattering on saucer. "Oh you haven't, you haven't, tell me you haven't—"

Anna's smile was now unmistakably sly. Triumphant.

"But I have."

Ellie sprang up. Oh God, now the hospital, the stomach pump—

"Never! One favor you promised, one! *Mother to daughter!* So go. Permit your mother to die with dignity. You are pale, too long in the house. Take your coat and walk. Perhaps on the hill you can find some wisdom."

Mother to daughter. Acknowledged at last—so she could kill herself in peace. And even then this monstrous woman must attach a sting to the tail. *Perhaps on the hill you can find some wisdom.*

She was speaking again, her words beginning to slur as pills melted, joined the bloodstream...bloodstream...bloodstream...

"This trouble between Mischa and the boy...it hurts Mischa, hurts him very bad—"

"*The boy* has a name! Simon. And he hurts very bad too!"

"So phone to him. Tell him to come."

"You know Michael. He has forbidden him the house, he'd be furious, he's finished with him, has said so a dozen times—"

"Pooh! Men! What do they know? Say it's for me, that I wanted to see him. You will not get a better excuse. Mischa refuses me nothing."

She was doing it again, crowing, but Ellie barely noticed. For the first time in many years their eyes met, conspired, sparked a sudden clandestine knowledge, too secret to name.

Anna sighed. "Gabriella, I am tired, soon I shall die. I hear some women get foolish notions at such times." She laughed her scorn on such women. "So maybe she asks for Simon, this foolish old woman? Who knows? Who cares? Not the old woman, her troubles will be over long before he comes. But the boy's mother sees him, is happy, no? Again I say—do you have a better excuse to call your son home? To comfort you on the death of your beloved mother?"

You old bitch.

You never, never give up, even now.

Of course she couldn't call, how could she? Not fair to Michael, whom Simon had hurt deeply, deeply. *But what about me?* It was too much, too much. This woman who'd given her life and nothing else was now offering a gift as bizarre and improbable as she herself.

"I don't know," she murmured, "I just..."

Anna sighed. "Woman, you labor under a terrible handicap. Unlike Mischa and I you have a conscience. Felix also. They are a great nuisance, waste so much time. Now put me in my bed, put your conscience to sleep, and go—but first use the telephone."

In a dream Ellie helped Anna across the hall, plumped up fat downy pillows, settled her into bed, smoothed the great feather quilt.

Leaving, she risked a single brief touch to a withered cheek that even now was unnaturally cool in the overheated room. Anna, peaceful now, did not object. Perhaps she was too far gone—or perhaps at the last the touch of a human hand was welcome. But as Ellie's hand reached for the door the blue eyes flew open.

"Call!" she said clearly, closing her eyes.

...if you need to, you can leave word...

Yes.

Ellie left the message with an anonymous voice and climbed the small hill behind Greenlings, forcing herself not to look back, not to stare at the house where a woman drifted into self-willed death.

Such courage and cowardice in one package. Brave enough to accept a lonely death, too craven to face a half-life of baby foods and diapers, breathing tubes and catheters. And who was to say she was wrong? Those she envied, the others, one moment alive, the next dead, they were the lucky ones. Like Hans...how odd that she hadn't thought of her father or his handsome picture for years...where was it? Misplaced somewhere in the great house. Rotting behind a wardrobe? Yet once she'd been his defender, had refused to believe he had done what they said he did. She knew better now.

To be alive, to love another person, lover, parent, husband, son, was to be capable of anything. The foolish pride of killing oneself to avoid pity. The guilt of being party to the sin—for hadn't she agreed when she put on her coat and walked out, leaving a woman to die? When she was younger and had ideals, she might have consoled herself that this collusion was a last small kindness.

Maybe it was—but without the chance of Simon's coming home, would she have been so kind? She doubted it.

And conscience...did she have one? Where and what was it? A river? one bank in the sun, the other in merciful, kindly shade, dark water in which traits less than admirable could hide?

Conscience.

When it squawks do a good deed quickly. Throw it a sprat to keep it silent.

FIFTY-TWO

*A*s THE NEWSPAPERS dutifully reported, Anna Abramsky died quietly in her sleep of natural causes.

Arriving from London laden with Christmas presents for his baby grandsons, Michael was a couple of hours too late to witness Anna's stubborn spirit let go of life, but Ellie didn't have to tell him. He knew Anna was gone the instant he walked through the door, although everything in the house was as usual.

Huge crimson and gold chrysanthemums from the greenhouse filled vases throughout the house; softly shaded lamps glowed; coffee and dinner smells from the kitchen joined with furniture polish and pine boughs from the hall, their welcome drifting through every room—always warm rooms at Greenlings, for everywhere thermostats clicked incessantly as central heating supplemented wood fires blazing in every grate.

But there was an unfamiliar emptiness, the air too soft, particularly on the stairs, as if something sharply astringent had been taken from the atmosphere. Something else was missing also, but he couldn't place that at all, not yet.

Just Anna.

Dazed, he walked from room to room, not sure where he was going or what to do... he wanted the nurse's obscene rubbish packed and taken out of Anna's studio, but the woman was in Leith or Dundee or some damn place... just look what she'd tacked over Anna's faded old friends from the Paris days, the Piotrs and Olgas and Tamaras. A giant poster of Elvis Presley lying in state, for God's sake, sequins all aglitter! He looked around for Lily Finn to get rid of it, but even she was off somewhere.

"If I just hadn't stopped to put chains on the car, but the snow... Ellie, you're *sure* it was peaceful, she didn't hurt?"

"No. She was ready, Michael."

It wasn't that he was surprised. No. He'd been expecting it for weeks, months. There'd been times, weary of constant anxiety, he'd wished for it and felt guilt for the wishing. Get it over, get back to living. But for him Anna *was* life. Without her and Felix there would have been only Micah, no Michael Abramsky.

What would he have been? A con man of some sort, that's where his talents seemed to lie. If the Rom had found him first he'd be married to Farah, by now he'd be the fat Rom Baro of some tacky little *kumpania,* regularly waddling down to the station to bail out this miscreant or that, sitting in judgment on family quarrels: who hit who first, who's gotta pay the damage, the doctor, maybe the undertaker.

Instead Glinka, Tolstoy, Prokofiev, Dostoevski, Friday sherry and almond cakes because one must not be a nossink, no, anything but that. The incomparable riches of their world! They, who'd thought themselves poor because they lacked money. Poor! And now their riches had spilled over him, his wife and children, his grandchildren.

He looked at the cup of coffee Ellie handed him as if he'd never seen one before.

"You called Jenny." It wasn't a question.

"They'll be here by morning with Mary Beth." Her voice sounded ragged, nervous. "And Michael—"

"Yes?"

"I called Simon, too. Wired him a ticket."

For a moment he honestly thought he'd heard her wrong. "You *what?* After everything I said?"

"I called, left word for him to come."

There had to be an explanation. "Did Anna ask for him, was that it?"

Ellie's eyes were level, dry, much too cold meeting his under the drawing-room lamp. "No. I did."

"What right had you, after—"

"Every right. I need him."

His thoughts engaged briefly. "Sorry, I wasn't thinking. She was your mother. I suppose you need Simon, someone, anyone for comfort." Knowing that for the moment he could offer her none at all, was in desperate need himself. Without quite registering it, he heard her fingertips beating out a tattoo on the edge of the coffee table.

"The entire world did not spin on Anna's axis, Michael. I need Simon because he's my son, because I love him."

Anger then, a volcano years in the forming, ready to erupt. Caution, speak soft. "In spite of what he's done to us?"

"To you, maybe." Her shoulders stirred under turquoise silk; he thought she might be weeping, but no, she was shrugging, as if what she said was of no more moment than one lump or two in his coffee. "You don't like each other, I know. Neither did Anna and I—we merely exchanged courtesies when it suited us. We none of us choose our relatives but we can try to treat them equally. You have always said this was our home. Yours. Mine. The children's."

"It is. Well, Jenny and Cal's anyway, Simon's when he comes to his senses."

"His senses. So Mary Beth was exactly right, always was, this place is *it!* It belongs to those of us who meet your terms, who measure up to your concept of what it is, not a family home but a Private Residence. A *desirable property,* a fortress against the Gypsies. Have you perhaps considered a moat?"

"Ellie, Anna has just died, is this the time for Mary Beth's half-baked *Psychology Today* claptrap? Must I hear—"

"No. If you want to wear blinders that's your problem. It doesn't have to be mine or Simon's. You want to run from the Rom, run. But why should he run with you? This is his home too."

"He's never wanted to live in it—"

"Because it's home only under *your* conditions."

He shook his head, baffled, bleeding from some unexpected blow, but now he knew what the other mssing item was.

"Look," he said, knowing he must sound weak, pathetic—but he was beyond caring. "Anna was . . . hell, you *know* what she was to me. She's gone. In all the years of marriage you've been there no matter what. Now I need you, you're suddenly my enemy, you who've always been *on my side!* Since I walked in the door all you've offered is coffee. No sympathy, no love. Why is that? What have I suddenly done that's changed everything?"

"Nothing. It's not just you, us . . ."

Either she wasn't making sense or he was going crazy.

"I don't know why you're choosing a time like this when . . . I don't know what you want!"

"You said I'd always been on your side. Maybe it's time you realized I've got a side too, and it's not always the same as yours. Maybe I really learned something from Anna after all. Her death taught me what Grossmutter's didn't. Felix's either. Life's just a big exchange of favors—you do this for me, I do that for you—and you've always done less than I, Michael. Something else too. Life's a damned short ride, even a long haul such as Anna had. There's room in it, yes, but is there *time?* For hate? Must you hate the Rom? *Must* I, just because I love you? *Must* Simon? To keep your love *must* we think as you think?"

She left him sitting in the half dark. He felt bruised, as if he'd fought ten rounds with a boxer instead of a short exchange with Ellie, and no closer to her now than when he'd walked in. So tired, yet somewhere in him energy pounded, must be discharged before . . . she'd come around . . . or he'd understand her . . .

The poster. Get the damn thing off Anna's wall. Now, so she can rest. Clean up her studio so you can face her before they take her away. When had Ellie said? Or maybe she hadn't . . . but she organized *everything, everything,* always had, breathing in, breathing out, paying bills, lining up doctors and dentists and piano tuners and window cleaners, fill-in typists and scrub women, plumbers and catering services, last-minute everything . . . *before* the last minute so the world should spin smoothly. Surely then she'd had the phone number of a mortician ready?

Two hours he worked in the studio and the bedroom, the room Anna and Felix had shared since the day they left Ryder Street. He did not look at Anna on the bed, could not face her until things were as she had wanted them.

Such and such will be kept, Mischa, for Jenny's babies.

Such and such will go, they are finished, finished.

Ellie looked in the door once, murmured that it could all be done later, but he shook his head and she tiptoed away.

The great dressing table they'd brought from Ryder Street took longest, its drawers stuffed with the clutter of a lifetime, all the things that may one day come in handy and never do until the day after they're thrown away. Incomprehensible things from an era more forgiving than this: a beribboned corset of whalebone and lace and faded rosebuds; Felix's flannel underdrawers worn thin at the knee. Full-length, calico-wrapped, reeking of camphor, there was a mangy fur coat from God alone knew what period; an ivory fan with a broken slat; dead toe shoes that had danced from Paris to León to Madrid to London—*en pointe* yet! Drawer after drawer, humdrum things from the lives of two Russians, an obscure dancer nobody had heard of and a small-town electrician who was not even very good at his trade. White Russians who never saw Russia. Never saw their son, their real son, grow to a man.

When he'd finished there were two stacks. On top of the discards, according to Anna's instructions, a bundle of once-pink leg warmers, pilled and unlovely, long since turned gray—woolen tubes that could never have been pretty, even when new. They were merely insulation, acolytes to the muscles, keeping them warm and limber so they could dance and dance and dance and dance until at last the muscles died. But not the leg warmers, bizarre life-support systems that seemed to live forever.

They lay on Anna's new lavender carpet, a gray snake's nest; after two lonely hours, they were Mischa Abramsky's undoing. He remembered that first night at Ryder Street, a wash rack of them drying at the top of the stairs, smelling so like wet sheep that a delirious young Gypsy thought he was still walking the moors...thought briefly of stealing them against the winter to come and would have if they'd been dry and he'd been well. Now he picked up one, then another, held them against the light, saw how they were lumpy with much mending, that even their darns had darns, saw the inside knees where Anna's brave bones had rubbed them threadbare.

He remembered a girl's voice many years later, a student in class who'd picked them up, snickering as she showed them around.

"God, doesn't she ever buy *new* ones?"

He'd laughed with the rest, but now he wept, his face buried in tubes of gray.

Farah delivered the message to Simon. They were all filtered through her anyway, it paid to keep tabs, but she normally left deliveries to whoever took the calls. This time she called Simon to the trailer as he came in off the roofing truck, tired, hopeless, despairing of ever making the money he needed, had to have if he was ever to meet Feya's bride-price.

"Simon! Your lady mommy called, wants you back in England on the double. Ticket waiting for you at the airport and everything. Limo service at the other end, I shouldn't wonder. Must be nice to be filthy rich."

"What... is she okay, is Mom okay?" Oh, why hadn't he called, he should have but he'd never dared after the L.A. thing, Dad had been livid, suppose he'd answered the phone? Besides, calls to England cost and he had to save, to save—

"The old Russian's cockin' her clogs by the sound of it."

"Anna doesn't care about me. She wouldn't want me there."

"Sure sounds like Mommy does."

"I don't know. It seems kind of rotten to go for Anna when I don't like her." He wanted to go for Mom, for Jenny, even for Lily, for the horses in the stable, he missed them all.

But how could he face Dad?

Farah was smiling, reading his face as if she knew every thought as it went through. "Your father's pretty taken with that old girl, isn't he?"

"I guess. She kinda rescued him or somethin'."

Farah laughed softly. "Yeah, from a fate worse than death. Life among the Gypsies."

"No, he wasn't with the *kumpania* then." She *knew* he wasn't, why did she have to act like Dad ran off and left 'em all high and dry or something? And why'd she have to make that crack about limo service? The family took trains like everybody else.

"Still, Micah'll be feeling pretty low, I reckon. This could be a good time to smooth things over with him. A nasty thing, bad blood in a family, Simon."

"Sure." Some hope of smoothing things over with Dad!

She leaned forward. "You still have it, right?"

"Have what?"

"You know, the paper with the bride-price on it."

He laughed bitterly. The numbers were engraved on his brain, his heart, some nights he thought they were branded into his testicles. "Farah, I told you. I'll never have that kind of money, so what's the point?"

She shrugged and turned away. "I wouldn't know. It's not me going home to see the rich family, is it?"

Interview over.

* * *

Anna Abramsky's funeral was very different from Felix's. Unlike her husband, she had not been well liked in the village and had never taken the trouble to be civil with Michael's business associates. The least hypocritical of women, she was pleasant only to those she loved or liked, which made for a very small turnout at the cemetery on the hill.

Jenny was there, puffy-eyed and newly pregnant, supported by Cal's adoring arm. On her other side Al Watson, who'd flown in from Stockholm and must be back for that evening's curtain.

Ellie was there because Anna, in ways the old woman could never have imagined, had taught her much; also because they both loved Michael; last and definitely least, she'd been her mother.

Mary Beth was there because the two women had respected each other; Lily Finn because she'd lost the other half of a zestful and continuing animosity; Pete Preston, who happened to be home because his own mother was ill, showed up to pay last respects to a woman who, until he'd met his wife, had been the most exotic creature he'd ever known.

Simon arrived at the cemetery just as the service began and as yet had spoken to no one. Blushing furiously, he'd nodded to Ellie and Jenny, but Michael steadfastly refused to look at him, concentrating instead on a hole in the ground into which the remains of Anna Abramsky were lowered, to lie next to Felix.

When it was over and the first clods of earth thudded on the box Michael nodded to them, indicated that they go to the house without him. The last car disappeared down the hill but still Michael waited in silence until the gravediggers had filled the hole, mounded the earth, and left him on this barren hillside, a new wind from the north picking out the smallest gaps between the stitches of his gloves, his suit, his winter coat.

Alone, he knelt in the snow between Anna and Felix, filled suddenly with the futile desire somehow to warm this patch of earth, this bleakest of resting places. Felix's marker was white with hoarfrost; by morning the flowers in Anna's wreaths and crosses would be black with it.

Before the ground could freeze harder he took a small trowel and a box of bulbs from his car. The diggers had told him her grave would sink and in a few days be covered with snow. No matter. Come spring these fat onionlike bulbs and wrinkled brown corms would burst into bloom.

He'd chosen Anna's spring wardrobe with great care. Not for her the pretty colors, the gay, the lighthearted tones; she'd had no time for royal blues and emerald greens, vivid oranges and cherry red. Her colors were purple, violet, plum, aubergine, brooding colors, *sad* colors—for Anna, under the cutting edge of her tongue and the severity of her judgments, had been the saddest of women.

How was he to live without them? He felt now as he'd felt when he came to them. Hurt. Poor. Alone.

Yes, there was his family, the good and lovely wife and the children and grandchildren who loved him—excepting possibly his problem boy, his Simon.

But Felix.

Now Anna.

What to do without them?

If he were Rom again he'd rend his clothes and tear his hair, perhaps relief lay in excess—but he'd traveled much too far from them for that, but not far enough to bow his head, swallow hard, and hold it all in like the *gaje*. They'd been so wise, these two, but they'd never told him how it would be. Neither had Da. Perhaps none of them knew. No road maps anywhere, for anyone.

But, in this cold and quiet place, in the rub and rattle of bare tree limbs, in frost glittering on granite stones, in his hands brown against a white marble urn filled with blood-red roses that would shrivel by morning—in this place their echoes were everywhere, Anna's voice astringent, sharp to the end, the other mild, precisely worded, filled with reason.

Pas de bourrée en avant! *Your arms, Mischa, make them soft, they are sticks poking the air! Better... better.* Relevé, relevé, *ah, nice, nice* allongée *—head UP! boy, head UP! Shoulders down, back straight, show us your throat!*

Felix's quiet whisper: *Present yourself, Mischa, so others may know who you are*...

Bulbs safely in, he tamped down the soil and stood.

Under fast-moving clouds bringing winter closer every minute, he stretched his back and his memory. Finding in it some music they had all loved, he spread his arms and made a few barely remembered steps for their bones. Overhead, a bitter wind beat through sycamore branches. Mischa, son of Anna and Felix, looked up, finding it in himself to smile.

Applause from the balcony, no less.

FIFTY-THREE

*M*ICHAEL, anxious to scrub the heavy clay of the cemetery from his hands, hurried to the house, but once in it, for the first time ever, he couldn't wait to escape its walls. Better to wash in the icy taps of the stable, away from the scent of flowers, which suddenly all seemed redolent of death.

Grief hung like crepe in every room, Jenny's quivering loss so raw it was impossible even to speak of Anna, Cal forever holding her, murmuring, for Jenny's loss was greatest of all, her grandmother-almost-mother, mentor, teacher, inspiration, eternal laudatory audience. Mary Beth for some reason walked on tiptoe as if she might inadvertently waken Anna on the hill; Ellie in the kitchen sent him glances that were by turns tender, resolute, sympathetic, determined, all as she busied herself helping Lily set the dinner table; Lily who, out of deference to the dead, did not sing today. She hummed "Nearer My God to Thee" instead, lubricating her sorrow with very many nips from the martini pitcher.

He threw them off, a relief to escape the women and the anxious young husband, to crunch through crisp snow under the beeches into the clean smell of a well-run stable, to lather his hands in carbolic soap and freezing water, dry them on hard, scrubby towels as four mildly curious heads appeared over stall doors, snorting plumes of warm sweet breath at him that drifted to the rafters in scarves of vapor.

His hunter whickered, lifted its lips, and Michael obliged with a windfall apple from the barrel by the door. Sighing, he rubbed the nose pushing at him now in hopes of another treat. Poor beggars weren't ridden nearly enough anymore, the twins' horses to exercise as well as his own, and who but himself and a stable lad to keep all that power and muscle in condition?

Nestor, the Welsh pony, more or less took care of himself; they'd had him since the twins and Nestor were all four years old together, and happy. Nestor was game enough still, but his riding days were long done even if there'd been a mount light enough for him. By the time Jenny's bunch were big enough there'd be no Nestor. How much longer could he have? One, two years at most, the dear old devil—and in his prime he'd been just that.

Everywhere this feeling of things drawing away from him, out of his grasp. Jenny and Cal permanently in the States, she more American even than Mary Beth—who was now nurse, nanny, soon to be governess to *that* brood, between whiles nipping off to the clapboard cottage she'd finally bought on the Cape. Pete Preston so Oriental it was something of a shock when he spoke English at all. And Simon . . . he'd drawn farther away than any of them.

Pretty soon there'd be just Ellie and himself rattling around Greenlings like two dried peas in a very large pod. He settled into the stable boy's beat-up captain's chair in the corner, its scarred wood a relief. How many hours since he'd sat? Just sat. How many *years*? From nowhere a line from Grandmam, or maybe Da, who knew? It was so long since either of them had spoken to him . . .

Chala, *with one behind you cannot sit two horses.*

Simple. Earthy. Grandmam then. Crude, Anna would have said. So, oddly enough, would her daughter.

Alone, just the breathing of the horses and an icicle on the downspout melting drip-drip-drip into snow that would grasp it, freeze it again tonight, he felt suddenly isolated, adrift from something Micah-Mischa-Michael always had. Frowning, he hunted for it, found it almost immediately.

Ambition.

All his life, even in the trailer with Da, he'd made plans, striven for this-that-and-the-other, every this-'n'-that a brick in the great wall of security.

Now it was built, and what the hell was he to do with it? What was left to aim at?

In the steamed window he saw the day was fading. Soon they'd call him to dinner from the house and he didn't want to go. He was hungry but he *didn't want to go,* to face the grief, the fortitude, the *leaning.* On him. For wasn't he head of the family? A concept he'd fostered since the day he wrapped his arms around the oak and wept into its bark?

Under him the chair rocked gently in time to his breathing.

To his right the stable door creaked open. The last of the daylight admitted Simon, stealthy, hunched, looking neither right nor left but somehow hungering as he moved toward the horses, running his hand over the polished back of Michael's bay hunter, then opening Nestor's box, making the identical whinny he'd always made to Nestor, wrapping his arms around the pony's neck, burying his face in the shaggy black mane. Watching him, feeling through him, Michael felt the roughness of the pony's mane on his own chin. Abrasive, familiar, welcome.

But now Simon's shoulders moved, his head burrowed deeper into Nestor's accommodating neck.

He was weeping.

This troublesome boy whose grandmother had just died could weep for an old nag kept on for no other reason but charity.

An ache began in Michael's chest, a deep knowledge of belonging, being part of everything around him, at one with ice melting off the eaves, patient Nestor dimly feeling the beginning of the end, of Simon coming home to uncertainty—hostility from his father, love from his mother, the poor beggar pulled from two sides like a Christmas cracker, except the prize in this one was no paper hat or penny whistle. It was a kid's future.

But where was the girl, Farah's moonpenny girl? Why wasn't she with him now?

"I guess we're alone." He said it quietly out of half-dark as he flicked a light switch, waiting until Simon spun around blushing, guilty as charged though he'd done nothing yet. Said nothing. "So you're not married yet? I thought you might be."

Simon turned away again to Nestor. "No I'm not." He reached for a brush and began to groom the mane, one stroke, two, on and on until Michael thought he wouldn't speak again. Then: "It's the bride-price, a damn stupid thing, archaic—"

"You'll marry Farah," Da said. *"When the time comes, and if we can meet her bride-price."*

So Farah had hamstrung Simon. He'd left home, risked everything on a single throw, to live the simple life, join the Rom, marry one of their girls, *become* Rom—only to find Farah in the wings with a winning hand and spare aces up her sleeve besides. And now he didn't know where to turn, what to do with the rest of his life. Yes, death was rotten, about the lousiest trick in the book, but aimless life was worse. You had to *live* through that.

Michael sighed. All these centuries, and still the blasted bride-price. Would they never change? No, and maybe that was the key to their magnetism for such as Simon. The other world changed every minute. But the Rom . . . even their faults were eternal.

"And naturally Farah wants an arm and a leg, right?"

"How did you know?"

"Call it an educated guess. How much?"

Simon blanched as he whispered the figure. "It's . . . God, I still don't believe it, how do any of them ever get married—"

"You're not 'any of them.'"

"That's just what *she* said or something damn close, and I don't see why not. So okay, I guess she thinks because you're rich she can really rake it in." His shoulders slumped and he began to fill the hay nets for morning, automatically remembering Nestor's special anti-asthma mixture.

Michael hesitated and hesitated again, but he was so tired of mysteries, of hiding himself from this boy who'd need all the ammo he could get against an old mercenary like Farah.

"It's not all avarice, Simon. Maybe none of it is. You'd better sit. It seems you've made your choice, so you'll be dealing with Farah's kind for a long time to come. Yes, she's charging you a thousand times the norm, and no, it doesn't surprise me. There's past history you don't know . . ."

For the first time he told Simon all about his childhood, not just with Da but before, when he'd been more or less promised to Farah "if they could meet her bride-price." Sparing himself nothing, he told what happened later, after they met again at Grandmam's funeral, the old relationship renewed—

"But you were married to Mom then, you had us—"

Nevertheless. He told how he'd been with Farah when Anna was first taken ill, how Felix and Ellie had to hunt Sac for him by transatlantic phone. "Anyway, it stopped then, I made it stop, but she's never forgiven me and never will. D'you understand? She can't get at *me* directly but she'll punish me through you as long as she can get away with it. It's nothing you did. You just got caught in the middle. I'm sorry."

Simon was quiet a long time, staring at his fingernails, at Michael, at Nestor's coat, the walls, the skittish eye of Jenny's horse, again at Michael.

With outrage, incredulity, maybe even wonderment. Finally, *"You? With Farah? I can't believe it!"* he burst out. "You had Mom and you did all that? You had us and Anna and Felix—"

"Yeah. At your age it may be hard to take in, but there's a fever every man runs one time in his life. Having kids, wife, a good home—they don't give immunity, offer choices."

"Okay okay, it happened, it's done—but me, I'm free, all we've got to do is go to Vegas one weekend, I shouldn't *have* to pay that money, Feya *wants* to marry me."

"But without Farah's say-so she won't, right?"

"How did you know?"

Over Nestor's grizzled black head Michael looked directly into his son's eyes.

"Farah raised her."

Ellie had waited for this moment, longed to see him alone, to talk to him, make sure he was well, content, that he wasn't in need. Clearly he was well, lean but well. Clearly he wasn't in need. If he didn't seem quite content (surely he'd been weeping a little?), then it probably wasn't terminal, so she should have been happy to see him, happier still that Michael had sent him.

Instead, within ten minutes of having him to herself in her little sitting room she was very close to screaming at him. First, he'd said he had to leave "real fast, Mom, I gotta go tonight." Swallowing her disappointment and finding a smile, she'd asked the same questions, heard much the same answers he'd given Michael. But unlike Michael she was deeply and bitterly shocked at his mention of bride-price; she'd have been just as shocked had the girl's mother been anyone but Farah.

"This girl, this Feya—"

"She's so beautiful, Mom—"

"I'm sure she is, I remember her from L.A., but that's not the point. The point is, her mother holds a gun to your head and this girl who says she loves you does *nothing*?"

"Look, Gypsies grow up different, they do as their parents tell them." He blushed, smiling ruefully. "Not like us, huh?"

"And after you're married, *if* you can get that idiotic bride-price canceled, waived, postponed or whatever they do, suppose Momma tells her to poison your coffee? push you under a bus? divorce you? refuse to let you see your children?"

"You've got it wrong, it's a way of looking at things. Right now Feya's her mom's. When we're married she'll be mine. Their *tradition*, things like that, it makes 'em special, see?"

"No I don't. One person buying another, that's not special, that's despicable! When you've made this ... purchase, what have you got? Wife? Lover? Housekeeper? Doormat? Breadwinner? Don't *you* see? You're buying private property! Yours! The very thing you accuse Dad of—but at least he deals in land, bricks and mortar. You'll be buying a person."

He turned away and she wanted to apologize, knowing she was being unfair. He was in love and couldn't help himself, would go along with anything they said as far as he was financially able. Could she have done any different when Michael showed up that first time at Grossmutter's auction? No. To be young and in love was to have no choice. But how could she apologize? She'd said what she felt. Why make a hypocrite of herself?

"I didn't mean to yell," she said. "And I'm *so* glad you came even if you won't stay. I promise to be nicer next time, okay? But *please* come again, I've missed you so—and when you don't write or call or anything and I see train crashes, earthquakes, buildings blown up on TV, well, if it's California I'm *positive* you were in it and—"

"Yeah, it's kinda like that for me. I guess I just ... gosh, I knew I'd made a mess of things with Dad, I was scared—then today he seemed different, like he kind of knew what I meant, and he didn't blame me or anything, he just ..."

She knew he was going to cry again, and couldn't bear it for him. Not twice. First in front of his father, then her. Just when he was trying so hard to be a *man,* to take a wife. Buy one. Oh, the damned Gypsies.

"You'll say hello to Mary Beth and Jenny? And at least look in here before you go, okay? You're *not* to walk to the station in this cold when it's so easy to drive you to the airport."

"I told you, Mom. I like getting places myself."

"Look in anyway, I have something for you."

"I don't *want*—"

"It's not for you, so look in."

Michael searched for answers in the dark stables and found nothing but the company of good dumb beasts who asked only that their physical needs be met. He sought out Ellie in her little room.

"Tell me what to do with him, Ellie. I can't seem to think straight anymore. I thought I'd tried hard and yet I don't seem to have pleased anybody at all—"

"You've pleased me. I was kind of...upset the day Anna died, and it really wasn't you or her, you were handy, that's all."

He put his arms around her, leaned his chin on the top of her fragrant head. "Tell me what to do..."

"Seems to me you did pretty well. He more or less said you were kind to him. You didn't blame him was how he put it."

"Yes...poor little bugger, I felt so damn sorry for him. He's being manipulated by a champion."

"If the girl's the same—"

"As yet she's just doing as she's told. She *may* be in love with him, it looked that way to me. She might even make a fine wife, who knows. But when I think of the punishing price that bitch hung on her I—"

"How much?"

"Don't ask."

"Can we afford it?"

He sighed. "Of course. That's not the point." Ellie didn't understand either, or maybe she understood too well. Farah knew exactly what she was doing. She'd maneuvered him into a corner, forced him to make a choice.

And you, Micah, what do you choose?

What *did* he choose?

Give Simon the money to buy Feya and thus lose him forever to the Rom?

Or withhold it and merit his son's deepest contempt. For withholding money out of spite, not reason.

Farah was asking as much and no more than Simon's inheritance would have been. She'd calculated it so close she could almost have had access to his will. Always, even at four, Farah knew her numbers, could buy a penny candle and have the shopkeeper so fuddled she'd come home with candle, penny, a smile for the pretty little girl, and maybe the end off a boiled ham because it wasn't really big enough to sell, now was it? and Farah could put on a starving face quicker than blink her eye.

"Ellie," he said again. "Help. Tell me what to do." Another departure. Michael made the financial decisions. But this was more than money. "I keep thinking, Felix and Anna...she'd have said: 'Unthinkable!' and he'd have said, 'Give, if it makes happy...'"

"In principle," Ellie said carefully, "I'm against. But I'm *for* Simon, I want to see him happy. It's your choice, Michael."

Then, very quietly, she whispered something that astounded him, something that a few weeks ago she wouldn't have dreamed of, not without asking him first. But maybe he'd misheard.

"You're going to do *that*?"

She nodded. "Yes. It's right that I should."

So they each made their own decision.

Michael opened a drawer, reached blindly for a pen, and under the lamp in Ellie's little private sitting room wrote a very large check. He wrote it with regret, but the feeling that somehow he was giving back what Da took away.

Now the ghosts were all laid.

Granddad. Grandmam. Farah. Rose. *Micah*.

When Simon stood shuffling one foot on another at the door, anxious to leave and unsure how to do it, Michael tucked the folded check into the boy's pocket. Blindly, he placed his hand on his son's shoulders, felt their young thinness through a too light coat, a shabby coat, and kissed him on both cheeks, folding him in his arms in a brief, fierce embrace.

"Good health and happiness. Our love you have already."

Simon flushed scarlet. "Gosh, Dad...thanks, I'm just sorry it's so much, but you know the way they are."

The way they are. *They. Not we.* Not yet. So he still felt alien to the Rom; maybe there was hope. "It's only money, son. It's not a wedding present. It's *yours*. Not Farah's or Feya's. Do exactly what you want with it."

How badly he wanted to warn him to watch for the Rom, who smiled in your eyes as their hands reached in your pocket. But it was only money. He'd once thought it was God, could buy anything, now all it was good for was to set his son free.

Ellie handed over her gift. "This is really your property. Grandmam gave it to me, she'd want you to have it. It's been set but you can have it reset, a ring for yourself, your wife...."

Watching, Michael made no move to stop her. They had more than twenty shared years holding them together, any day of them worth more than a chip of red rock that happened to surface from the center of the earth. Oh, but something in him still wanted that ruby, all they had left of the Rom.

"I don't know what to say," Simon stammered.

"That you'll come home sometimes, okay? With..." But Michael knew Feya would never come here. Her mother wouldn't let her.

Again he refused their offer of a ride to the airport. He'd hitch, he said, so together they walked with him down the long path to the gates, stood watching as he swung them open and walked through, looking back not at Michael and Ellie but at the small floodlit sign:

PRIVATE PROPERTY—NO ADMITTANCE

Quite deliberately, it seemed, he left the gate open. They watched him down the road and out of the glow of streetlamps before Ellie reached out to close the great gates of Greenlings. Behind her Michael's arms wrapped her around, warming her.

"No," he whispered. "We'll leave them open."

"Maybe he'll be back," she said, "and Michael, you really had no choice."

He turned away and let the golden windows of the house lure him back. She was wrong. There was always a choice, a fork in the road. But with no road map how could a man know?

MARGARET P. KIRK, born and educated in Yorkshire, England, emigrated to the United States in 1957. After publishing short stories in major women's magazines on both sides of the Atlantic, Kirk made her debut as a novelist with the international best seller *Always a Stranger*, published in the United States in 1985. Ms. Kirk has recently returned to England, where she currently resides with her husband.